'... epic fantasy's finest'
Tor.com* on *Mage's Blood

'For anyone looking for a new sprawling fantasy epic to stick
their teeth into, *Empress of the Fall* is an ultimately satisfying
journey into a fascinating and chaotic landscape'
SciFiNow* on *Empress of the Fall

'Modern epic fantasy at its best'
Fantasy Book Critic* on *Scarlet Tides

'Hair is adept at building characters as well as worlds,
and his attention to his female players is welcome in
a genre that too often excludes them'
Kirkus

'Adult fantasy lovers who enjoy historical fiction and
intricate political plots will love this book . . . Epic'
Boho Mind* on *Empress of the Fall

'Vivid, dynamic characters and terrific worldbuilding . . . Readers
of epic fantasy should definitely check out this series'
***Bibliosanctum* on The Moontide Quartet**

'Truly epic'
***Fantasy Review Barn* on The Moontide Quartet**

'It has everything a fan could want'
A Bitter Draft

Also by David Hair

THE MOONTIDE QUARTET

Mage's Blood
Scarlet Tides
Unholy War
Ascendant's Rite

THE SUNSURGE QUARTET

Empress of the Fall
Prince of the Spear
Hearts of Ice

THE RETURN OF RAVANA

The Pyre
The Adversaries
The Exile
The King

THE TETHERED CITADEL

Map's Edge

MOTHER OF DAEMONS

THE SUNSURGE QUARTET BOOK IV

DAVID HAIR

Jo Fletcher

BOOKS

First published in Great Britain in 2020
This edition published in 2020 by

Jo Fletcher Books
an imprint of Quercus Editions Ltd
Carmelite House
50 Victoria Embankment
London EC4Y 0DZ

An Hachette UK company

A CIP catalogue record for this book is available
from the British Library

PB ISBN 978 1 78429 056 6
EBOOK ISBN 978 1 78429 089 4

10 9 8 7 6 5 4 3 2 1

Printe .A.

This book is dedicated to Eric Greig, my father-in-law, a witty, clever and thoroughly decent man whose life in provincial New Zealand is like a chronicle of our country, from a time of gravel roads linking our countryside to the information highways of the present. He's now in his ninetieth year. Very best wishes to you, Eric: it's a privilege to know you and be a part of your family.

TABLE OF CONTENTS

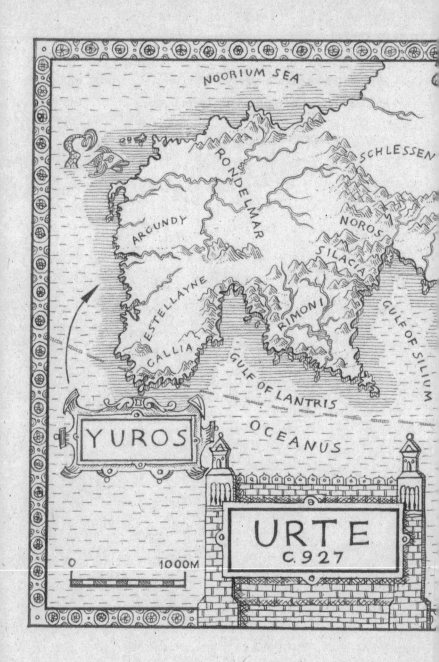

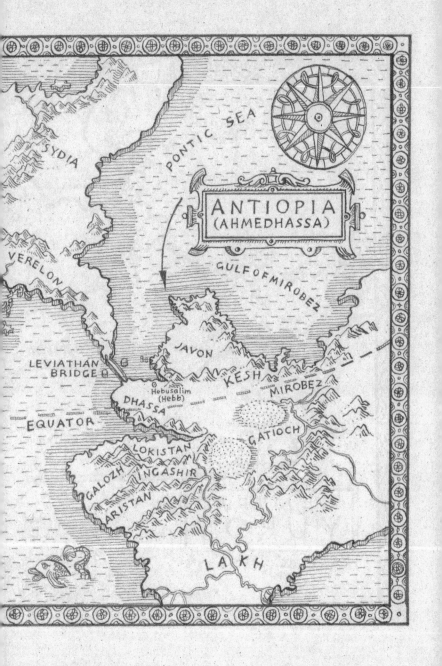

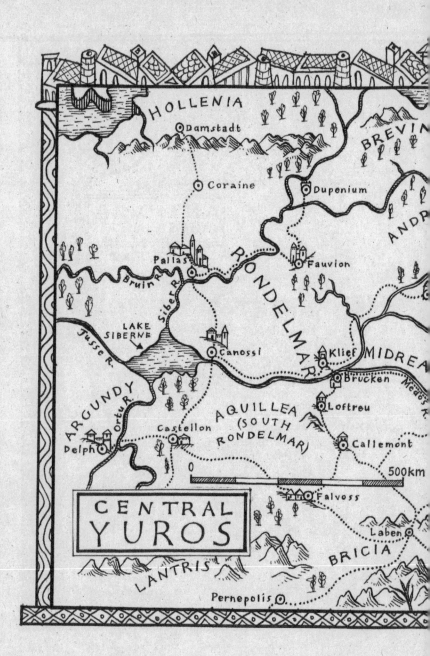

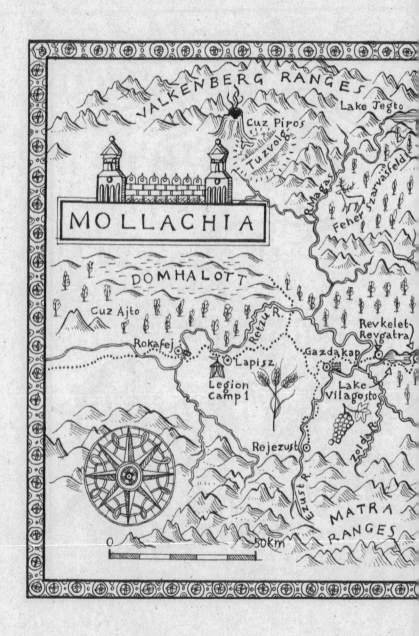

WHAT HAS GONE BEFORE

The Events of 930–935, as related in
Empress of the Fall

In Junesse 930, a newly formed mage order, the Merozain Bhaicara, save the Leviathan Bridge and use its gnostic energy to destroy the Imperial Windfleet above, killing Emperor Constant and Mater-Imperia Lucia.

These deaths create a power vacuum at the heart of the Rondian Empire. The first to react is the Church of Kore – Grand Prelate Dominius Wurther, guardian of the emperor's children, Prince Cordan and Princess Coramore, prepares to form a Regency Council in Cordan's name to continue the Sacrecour dynasty. But Wurther's confidante, Ostevan Jandreux, tips off his kinswoman, Duchess Radine Jandreux, in the northern city of Coraine. Radine sends Corani mage-knights led by Solon Takwyth and the Volsai spy-master Dirklan Setallius to capture Cordan and Coramore from under the Church's nose. More importantly, they free the hitherto unknown Lyra Vereinen, the daughter of the late Princess Natia, a claimant for the throne.

The Corani take Lyra, Cordan and Coramore to their fortress in Coraine and plan a return to power. With their rivals paralysed by the disasters of the Third Crusade, they persuade Grand Prelate Wurther and Treasurer Calan Dubrayle to abandon the Sacrecours and aid the Corani (an agreement that includes the banishment of Ostevan, in revenge for his betrayal of Wurther). Duchess Radine marches her soldiers into Pallas, where the populace, fearing a civil war (and beguiled by the fairy-tale circumstances of Lyra's rescue) greet them with great rejoicing.

However Lyra is no compliant tool of Corani ambitions, but a complex young woman with secrets. Her full parentage is uncertain and despite being born a pure-blood mage, she was never trained in the gnosis. When she does awaken to magic, it's not the gnosis, but the heretical power of dwymancy. And worse, she's fallen in love with her rescuer, Corani knight Ril Endarion, an unsuitable relationship for the figure-head of the Corani cause.

On the eve of Lyra's coronation, with Radine demanding that she accept the formidable Solon Takwyth as her husband, Lyra blindsides the duchess and persuades Ostevan (facing exile and acting out of spite) to marry her to Ril. After Lyra is crowned the next day, she declares her marriage before the world; Radine, Takwyth and Setallius are forced to accept her actions – and Takwyth is exiled for striking Ril, the new Crown Prince.

Despite this shaky start, the Corani are able to face down their rivals and the succession crisis appears to have been resolved. In relief, Pallas and the empire settles into dealing with a new world and a new ruler.

For five years the Rondian Empire struggles on. The Treasury is forced to impose heavy taxes to rebuild Imperial finances, vassal states like Argundy, Estellayne and Noros are clamouring for greater autonomy and warlords and mercenaries are warring in the far south. Duchess Radine dies, embittered by what she considers to be Lyra's betrayal, but Ril and Lyra continue to reign in Pallas, although Lyra has two miscarriages and has no heir of her blood. Cordan and Coramore, her *de facto* heirs, remain her prisoners in Pallas.

In Ahmedhassa, Sultan Salim Kabarakhi I of Kesh is trying to rebuild his realm, with the aid of Rashid Mubarak, the mighty Eastern mage. His efforts are undermined by corruption – and by the Shihadi faction who are demanding revenge against the West, even though the Leviathan Bridge, the only link to Yuros, will be submerged until 940.

In 935, new crises are developing in the East and West. A secret cabal whose identities are concealed even from each other by the Lantric theatre masks they wear is formed by Ervyn Naxius, a genius unconstrained by anything even remotely resembling morality. He offers the cabal members powers to match the Merozain Bhaicara through a link to an ancient super-daemon named Abraxas: Ascendant strength and use of all sixteen facets of the gnosis, as well as the ability to enslave others using the daemon's ichor. The 'Masks' join him in his quest to rule the new era.

In the West, the cabal plans to supplant Empress Lyra with the pliant Prince Cordan, starting with snatching Cordan and his sister from Corani custody. They strike during a jousting tournament staged to bolster Lyra and Ril's faltering rule. The exiled, bitter Ostevan, now 'Jest' of the Masks cabal, having engineered a return to court as Lyra's confessor, begins to infect courtiers and the general populace with the daemon's ichor, masking the effects behind the seasonal outbreak of the riverreek illness, in readiness for seizing the royal children.

The climax of the tourney sees Ril, a fine warrior for all his faults, against an 'Incognito Knight' – who on his victory reveals himself to be Solon Takwyth, returned from exile. He begs a boon before the adoring crowd, that he be forgiven and permitted to return to Corani service. Lyra cannot refuse his manipulative request – then she learns that Cordan and Coramore have been abducted and orders Dirklan Setallius, her spymaster, to find them before they can be used against her.

Meanwhile in the East, the Masks have struck a savage blow: at the height of the Convocation, a religious and political event to shape future policy, Sultan Salim is assassinated by masked assassins. The only survivor of his household is Latif, his chief impersonator, who immediately goes into hiding. Rashid Mubarak seizes control; his sons, the brutal Attam and the cunning Xoredh, advance his stated plan for Shihad, a holy war against the vast and hostile nation of Lakh, their old enemy.

Prince Waqar, Rashid's nephew, investigates Salim's murder and the related poisoning of his own mother Sakita. With the help of Tarita Alhani, a Javon spy, he learns that he and his sister Jehana may be heirs to a mysterious power, but before they can dig deeper, Waqar is sent south on a secret mission for Rashid to Lokistan, leaving Tarita to continue on her own.

In Dhassa, the mage-brothers Kyrik Sarkany and Valdyr Sarkany, princes of the tiny Yurosi kingdom of Mollachia, who have been captives in the dehumanising breeding-houses of the Eastern magi, are reunited. The meeting is not amicable: after the war, Kyrik was released into the care of Godspeaker Paruq, a priest of Ahm, but Valdyr, remaining true to Kore, has been a slave-labourer for five years. He has never gained the gnosis, having been under a gnosis-suppressing Rune of the Chain since his capture as a child. Paruq, having secured the release of the Sarkany brothers, takes them to Yuros, to a tribe of Sydian nomads he's been working with as a missionary; there, they discover the Sydians might be distant racial kin to their people. The brothers journey alone to Mollachia, where they are captured by tax-farmers, an unfortunate by-product of Empress Lyra's efforts to fund her reign. The tax-farmers have draconian laws on their side to extract the fortune owed by the Sarkanys' dead father. There are two Rondian legions stripping the land and people of their wealth, one led by Robear and Sacrista Delestre, the other by Rondian Governor Ansel Inoxion.

The brothers are locked up and left to die, but they are freed by the legendary Vitezai Sarkanum, local freedom fighters, and a resistance movement begins. Kyrik returns to the Sydian steppes to recruit aid; the price is marriage to the fiery Sydian witch Hajya. Valdyr distinguishes himself against the Rondian occupiers, but is still unable to gain the gnosis, despite having his Chain-rune removed.

In Pallas, Naxius and his Masks are readying their coup, using ordinary citizens apparently suffering from a virulent outbreak of the riverreek illness but in reality, possessed minions of the daemon Abraxas. They are used as shock troops in coordinated assaults on the Imperial Bastion and the Church of Kore's holiest site, the Celestium. Using secret underground tunnels, the attack penetrates all defences; it's coordinated with a planned unveiling of Prince Cordan as the new emperor and the arrival of a Sacrecour army at the gates.

Meanwhile in the East, the new sultan's careful long-term planning reaches fulfilment. Rashid has assembled a vast windfleet: now he reveals that his real target isn't Lakh, but Yuros. The only thing preventing invasion of the West is the Leviathan Bridge itself: if the Ordo

Costruo or the Merozain Bhaicara unleash the powers of the Bridge's towers, as they did against Emperor Constant's fleet in 930, Rashid's fleet will be destroyed.

At this stage, a new variable enters play: dwyma, or pandaemancy, a heretical form of magic believed extinct. Now Fate or coincidence has placed four people with the power to use it in the midst of these world-changing events – although two of them don't even suspect they have the power.

In Pallas, the attacks on the Bastion and Celestium appear to be succeeding and the Masks are on the brink of seizing power. But Empress Lyra uses dwyma to slay one of the apparently indestructible Masks, while in the Celestium, a burst of light from a shrine associated with Saint Eloy, a dwymancer who supposedly abjured his powers, destroys another Mask.

In Mollachia, on a wild night on the sacred Watcher's Peak, Valdyr Sarkany wields the dwyma to freeze a legion of Rondian solders just as they're about to defeat Kyrik and his Sydian riders. Robear Delestre perishes, but his sister Sacrista survives.

In the East, the dark side of dwyma is revealed. Sakita Mubarak is also a dwymancer, part of an attempt by the Ordo Costruo to resurrect the long-extinct form of magic. Now a servant of the Masks and kept alive by necromancy, she uses her devastating powers to destroy Midpoint Tower, though it costs her 'life'. Arriving too late, Waqar and Tarita recover artefacts from the tower and find clues concerning the Masks – then the sultan's windfleet appears on the southern horizon, heading for Yuros, and Waqar realises that Uncle Rashid, his idol, may have been working with the masked assassins – and was probably behind Sakita's death.

It is Julsep 935, and for the first time in recorded history, the East is invading the West. The Ordo Costruo and Merozain Bhaicara cannot prevent the invasion; all their energies must go into repairing the Bridge before it's washed away. And for the first time in five centuries, dwymancers are walking the lands, with unpredictable and devastating powers.

The Events of Autumn (Julsep–Octen 935)
as related in Prince of the Spear

After barely surviving the Masked Cabal's attempts to unseat Empress Lyra Vereinen and Grand Prelate Dominius Wurther on Reeker Night, the Rondian Empire reels in shock at the tidings of an Eastern invasion.

The Masked Cabal are still at large: Jest, Tear and Angelstar hatch a new plot to bring Pallas under their power; while the Eastern conspirators, Ironhelm, Heartface and Beak, prepare for the next phase of their own campaign, to take control of the Shihad.

Crown Prince Ril Endarion is appointed to command the Imperial Army. He is grateful for the job, not just to help safeguard the realm, but also to escape the steady breakdown of his relationship with Lyra. A fateful kiss on Reeker Night with Lyra's Volsai bodyguard, his best friend Basia de Sirou, has burgeoned into a passionate affair. Leaving his tangled personal life behind, he throws himself into the impossible task of pulling five rival factions into one Imperial Army. As the Rondian soldiers trek south, they are increasingly divided and uncoordinated. In exasperation, Ril escapes the responsibilities of command by taking on aerial reconnaissance, where he comes into violent contact with a new enemy: Keshi magi riding rocs, giant eagle-constructs. The roc-riders are led by Waqar Mubarak, who has been given responsibility for protecting the air above the Eastern advance.

Left behind in Pallas, Lyra, now heavily pregnant, researches the dwyma, the heretical magic that saved her on Reeker Night. She's helped by Dirklan Setallius, Solon Takwyth and Basia de Sirou, but her progress is hampered by her blind spot: Ostevan Jandreux, her comfateri, or confessor, and closest confidante. Ostevan, Jest of the Masked Cabal, uses drugs and religion to bend Lyra to his will.

A new conspiracy forms to unseat Lyra. The beautiful Medelie Aventour seduces Solon Takwyth and lures him into the group, then reveals herself to be Radine Jandreux, the former Duchess of Coraine, supposedly dead but in fact very much alive, with her youth restored and bent upon Lyra's destruction. The conspirators believe they have the numbers to succeed where the Reekers failed. Popular movements are also growing, including support for 'suffragium', an ancient democratic system, propounded by a radical named Ari Frankel, while in the far south the empire has lost control of Rimoni to the mysterious Lord of Rym.

Ostevan, using Lyra's insecurities over Ril's relationship with Basia, almost succeeds in his attempts to seduce her, but just in time his perfidy is exposed and in her fury Lyra unleashes the dwyma. Ostevan barely escapes and Naxius, worried that his plans may be uncovered, accelerates his plans to seize both Bastion and Celestium. Initiating mystical contact with Lyra, he lures her to the Shrine of Saint Eloy, where he intends to capture her himself.

In Mollachia, the people are not happy about their new Sydian allies, but Valdyr Sarkany is concentrating on learning more of his new power, which means returning to Watcher's Peak. Along the way he rescues an injured wolf; he names it Gricoama. Unknown to Valdyr, his nemesis, the mage Asiv Fariddan of Gatioch (Beak of the Masked Cabal), has arrived to trace the outpouring of dwyma energy his master Naxius has sensed. Asiv infects Governor Inoxion with daemon ichor, but the governor is slain by Sacrista Delestre when he attacks and infects her. Sacrista in turn is captured and slain by Dragan, head of the Vitezai Sarkanum, in a barbaric Mollach custom called the Witch's Grave.

Meanwhile, Valdyr's brother Kyrik, guiding the rest of Clan Vlpa into Mollachia, is joined by a group of Schlessen and Mantauri, minotaur-like constructs, led by Fridryk 'Kip' Kippenegger. Kyrik learns that he is sterile, but knowing the revelation that he and Hajya cannot produce heirs to the Mollach throne will destroy the vital alliance, he doesn't tell anyone.

Waqar is so busy leading the Eastern roc-riders, he is forced to relinquish the hunt for his sister Jehana to Tarita Alhani, the Merozain mage from Javon. Alyssa Dulayne – Heartface of the Masked Cabal – is also hunting Jehana. The trail leads to Sunset Tower, part of the damaged Leviathan Bridge. Alyssa lays siege, but Tarita gets inside to protect the Tower and Jehana.

Meanwhile, the Shihad is advancing across southeastern Yuros, capturing cities in the sparsely populated region of Verelon, while Sydian tribes flock to their banner. Latif, the former sultan's impersonator, is part of an elephant unit enduring the horrors of the march.

Ari Frankel has made contact with men willing to advance the cause of suffragium and in so doing, break up the empire – but before this relationship bears fruit, he is captured by the Inquisition, to be shipped north to stand trial.

As autumn advances towards winter, matters come to a head. At Sunset Tower, Alyssa is aided by a traitor, her nephew Kestrel Tovar, and breaks in – but Jehana escapes, thanks to Tarita and an intelligent construct known as Ogre, who once served Naxius.

In Mollachia, Valdyr is ambushed by Asiv Fariddan, who has infected Dragan and his daughter Sezkia, with daemon ichor. Asiv kills the White Stag, the guardian spirit of Watcher's Peak, and wounds the ghostly dwymancer Luhti, trapping Valdyr on the mountain with Gricoama, who assumes the mantle of guardian spirit. Asiv then turns his attention to Kyrik's coronation, unleashing a horde of Reekers and capturing or killing Hajya, but Kyrik manages to escape.

In Pallas, while Lyra is visiting the shrine of Saint Eloy in the Holy City, the Masked Cabal strike, with Medelie (Tear) moving against the Bastion and Ostevan (Jest) and Dravis Ryburn, Knight Princeps of the Inquisition (Angelstar), seizing the Celestium. But Solon Takwyth has actually been spying for Lyra, and with Dirklan Setallius, they kill Medelie/Tear. However, the renegade Keeper Edetta escapes with the children and takes them to their uncle, Garod Sacrecour.

In the Celestium, Lyra and Wurther escape Naxius and the Masks, thanks to the dwyma and to Wurther's new bodyguard Exilium Excelsior, a master swordsman. But the Winter Tree is badly burned, weakening Lyra's grip on the dwyma, and she goes into labour.

Despite everything, Lyra safely delivers a son, Rildan, heir to the empire.

At Collistein Junction, the Imperial Army finally meets the Shihad in open battle. Ril's disjointed, feuding and badly outnumbered army is defeated when Waqar's roc-riders win the air battle; only the experienced hero of the Third Crusade, General Seth Korion, now Earl of Bres, prevents a total rout. Ril is slain by Waqar in a desperate mid-air duel.

It is now Noveleve 935, and winter is almost upon Yuros. Valdyr, although fearing for Kyrik's life and dreading Asiv's return, tends the dying Luhti on Watcher's Peak. Jehana, Tarita and Ogre are on the ocean, seeking to escape Alyssa. Rashid celebrates victory, knowing his army must find shelter before winter or a million men will likely freeze to death. And in Pallas, the widowed Lyra's only consolation in defeat is that her enemies are finally unmasked – and staring at her from across the Bruin River, which is now the front line of a new civil war.

The Events of Winter (Noveleve 935–Janune 936), as related in Hearts of Ice

As the Sunsurge winter brings heavy snowfalls to Yuros, Ostevan takes the title 'Pontifex', signalling his desire to rule both Church and State, and with Dravis Ryburn he launches attacks across the Bruin River, burning the Pallas docklands. Garod Sacrecour prepares to support Ostevan with his army. Lyra fights back by sanctioning Treasurer Dubrayle's imposition of tax on the Church. She faces down the Pallas mob and gains the funds to prevent the imminent collapse of the government, while Solon Takwyth drives Ostevan's Reekers from the North Bank.

Rashid's victorious army marches on Jastenberg, seeking a winter base, but the Imperial generals burn the city and retreat north, leaving Noros unprotected. General Seth Korion, defying orders, diverts his army south to Norostein, meaning to deny Rashid his winter base. Waqar helps Rashid's advance, but he is worried for his missing sister Jehana and his friend Baneet, who is now wielding the gnostic spear that killed their friend Lukadin at Collistein Junction. Waqar doesn't know Jehana is trying to awaken her dwymancy in the village of Epineo in Verelon or that she's being hunted by Alyssa Dulayne (Heartface of the Masked Cabal).

In Mollachia, the death of his mentor Luhti breaks Valdyr's connection to the dwyma; to restore it he must go to the volcano known as Cuz

Sarkan. But Asiv Fariddan and his infected minions, now led by Dragan Zhagy, are hunting him. Valdyr believes his brother Kyrik, the rightful king, is dead – but Kyrik is alive and has escaped Hegikaro.

He and Kip travel to Freihaafen, the hidden valley where Kip's people have taken refuge, to share the news that silver is deadly to the daemon-possessed; Valdyr finds him there.

Lyra, in desperate need, contacts Valdyr through the dwyma: Duke Garod's men are marching on Pallas and Lyra's army is too small to defeat them. Valdyr helps, despite not knowing her true identity, and with his guidance Lyra hurls blizzards at the Sacrecour armies, wreaking havoc on Garod's forces. The rivers freeze and Lyra's men are able to cross and take the Holy City by storm. Dravis Ryburn is slain, but Ostevan escapes. Amid the tumultuous celebrations, Lyra allows herself to be seduced by Solon, another ill-advised liaison.

Ari Frankel, identified as a rebellion-preaching traitor, has been sent to Pallas to face execution.

In the south, Seth's retreat is cut off by Prince Attam, Rashid's elder son and heir, but Seth is saved by mercenaries led by his old Third Crusade comrade, Ramon Sensini. The pair retreat to Norostein.

When Baneet dies in the battle, despite Waqar's pleas, the gnostic spear is taken by Fatima, Baneet's lover and Waqar's friend. Heartbroken, Waqar leaves the Shihad to seek his missing sister Jehana.

Jehana and Tarita are in trouble: Alyssa has captured them and forced Jehana to accompany her to Epineo, believing she can gain the dwyma herself by consuming Jehana's essence once the girl becomes a dwymancer. Ogre then rescues Tarita, but Alyssa has miscalculated: the daemon-ichor in her body and the dwyma are inimical and as she tries to take in the dwyma, it destroys her. Unfortunately for Jehana, the guardian spirit which had come to awaken her also perishes, so she's still unable to awaken her power.

It's now early Janune, midwinter, and Rashid had reached Norostein, knowing he has only weeks to get inside the city and shelter his forces. He launches an all-out assault, but Seth, helped by Ramon, holds on. Latif and his elephant crew, at the forefront of the attacks, barely avoid death. But inside Norostein, Governor Rhys Myron is not just refusing to relinquish authority to Seth, but is hoarding supplies, undermining the defence. The siege hangs in the balance.

In Pallas, Lyra has won a victory, and a respite. Intrigued by Ari Frankel's ideas, she pardons him, but he promptly launches a new campaign of disobedience. Scared and lonely, Lyra continues her relationship with Solon, although she is troubled both by his ambition and his domineering manner, ending it only when he turns violently abusive – which means losing her most able commander. She faces many enemies: Ostevan has allied with Duke Garod; Father Germane, his agent in Pallas, is poisoning the mind of Domara, the royal midwife; and Lef Yarle, Ryburn's former lieutenant, tries to murder her and Wurther. They are saved by Basia and Exilium, and by use of the dwyma.

Meanwhile in Mollachia, Kyrik, Valdyr and their allies are trapped in a silver mine by Dragan's possessed daughter, Sezkia. Valdyr reaches out through the dwyma: he finds Jehana, who has been reunited with Waqar, and the siblings, accompanied by Tarita and Ogre, fly to Mollachia. They capture Sezkia and rescue Kyrik and Valdyr – but Ogre is captured by Asiv and taken to Hegikaro. Naxius sends agents to collect his former servant: ogre-constructs masked as figures from the *Book of Kore*: the Angels of Plague and Famine. Famine is Cadearvo, a superior version of Ogre, while Plague is Semakha, a former friend Ogre had dreamed of being reunited with, but she is no longer the innocent he knew but daemon-possessed and evil.

Asiv proposes a hostage exchange: Ogre and Hajya for Sezkia, Valdyr and Jehana. The proposal is accepted, although both sides intend to renege. Tarita will disguise Kyrik and the Sydian mage Korznici as Valdyr and Jehana; Asiv plans his own daemonic surprise.

Using the hostage exchange drama as a distraction, Valdyr, Jehana and Waqar head for Cuz Sarkan, hoping to become full dwymancers – but Asiv is swiftly in pursuit with Cadearvo, leaving Semakha and Dragan to deal with the hostage exchange.

In the last days of Janune, carnage unfolds. At Norostein, Rashid's desperate assault breaks through, but at the height of the battle, Sultan Rashid and his son Attam are slain. Xoredh takes command and captures Lowertown, but the mandatory period of mourning leaves him unable to press the attack. Unknown to Xoredh, the dying Rashid, believing Latif is the ghost of Sultan Salim, reveals that he commanded Xoredh to join the Masks, in return for the throne and the Shihad.

Meanwhile, in Mollachia, the hostage exchange has turned bloody: Ogre kills his first love Semakha and Kyrik slays Dragan, who was closer to him than his own father. Thinking he's dying, the wounded Ogre confesses his love for Tarita, only to awake next day, alive – and acutely embarrassed. At Cuz Sarkan, Valdyr, Jehana and Waqar find a path into the dwyma, revealing the Elétfa, a vast Tree of Life – but Asiv and Cadearvo attack, capturing Jehana. Valdyr is already inside the Elétfa, but Waqar, who chooses to step back, although he's too late to rescue his sister, is forced to return to Freihaafen empty-handed. Inside the Elétfa, where minutes take hours, Valdyr starts climbing, with only Gricoama for company.

The distraught Waqar enlists Tarita's help to find Jehana, tracing her to Norostein. En route to confront his cousin Xoredh, Waqar is warned by Latif of their new sultan's true nature.

Back in Mollachia, Kyrik is in despair, for Hajya is still possessed by Abraxas. Ogre buries the ache of losing Tarita by trying to translate Naxius' *Daemonicon*, hoping to discover Naxius' plans.

In Pallas, Lyra's counsellors, fearing the empire's collapse without Solon in charge, try to force her to marry him and make him emperor. Lyra, seeing no other choice, is about to concede defeat when the balance of power inside the council is altered on two counts: Dubrayle was being blackmailed to support the motion, but that hold is broken by his bastard son, Ramon Sensini – then spymaster Dirklan Setallius reveals himself as Lyra's father; his vote tips the balance in Lyra's favour. Now a pariah, Solon flees to Coraine to raise rebellion. Sister Domara, in Germane's thrall, attempts to murder the infant Prince Rildan, but is killed by Exilium.

And the ambassadors of five of the vassal states arrive at court demanding the empire be disbanded.

Febreux, the coldest month of a bitter Sunsurge year, is about to begin. Xoredh prepares to unite his Shihad with the daemon-possessed armies of Naxius' minion, the Lord of Rym. In Dupenium, Garod marshalls his forces for war and in Coraine, Solon does likewise. And in his secret lair, Ervyn Naxius gloats over his prize: Jehana, a semi-awakened dwymancer who can't reach those powers is the perfect clay for him to shape. He places a mask over her face: that of Glamortha, the Angel of Death. In the Last Days, the *Book of Kore* foretells, Glamortha will lay with Lucian, Lord of Hel, and become the Mother of Daemons, beginning the eternal rule of daemons on Urte . . .

PART ONE

PROLOGUE

The Masquerade (Macharo)

The Last Days

... and the righteous shall abandon Urte, ascending unto Paradise to take their place before the throne of Corineus, their Saviour. The last days of Urte shall be filled with wailing and lamentation as the sinners left behind are beset by daemons, who shalt make of Urte their lair. Lucian, the lord of Hel, shall reign, with Glamortha the Angel of Death his queen.

BOOK OF KORE

Coraine, Northern Rondelmar
Febreux 936

Two squires hefted a breastplate embossed with the badger crest of Coraine and strapped it to the heavily built man standing with spread arms in the middle of the room. Another pair knelt at his feet, strapping on the greaves. The seneschal frowned over the helm, handing it to a servant with a glare and pointing out an almost invisible blemish in the polishing. The servant blanched and reached for a cloth, casting an anxious glance at his lord.

Solon Takwyth was barely aware of their silent angst for the daily ritual had set his mind adrift. The familiar burden of forty pounds of metal and leather settled onto his shoulders while he dreamed of glory.

Today, my redemption begins. No woman refuses me and walks away, not even a queen. The imperial throne is mine by right: I've earned it. I will show Lyra that I command the Corani legions, not her. She should have married me when she had

3

the chance. An image filled his mind, of himself on the throne, Lyra kneeling before him with frightened but adoring eyes, scared of her own passions. *She loves me; it's the others who have poisoned her against me. Setallius, Wurther and the rest. I'll behead the lot of them, then she'll have no one but me.*

The seneschal, breaking into his reverie, handed him his helm, a ceremonial affair with winged flanges finished in silver and gold. 'Milord, the Duke awaits.'

'Thank you, Bailey,' Solon replied, and the servants scuttled away.

When he was alone, Solon turned to the mirror. He'd never considered himself a vain man – for several years his face had been horrifically scarred after bandits had applied a red-hot brand to his cheeks. He'd considered every wound a trophy, and he knew the scars intimidated some. But over the past days he'd let the best healer-magi in Coraine work their magic on him because he needed to exude a different kind of energy now. Those healers had – at considerable expense, thanks to a lot of exotic ingredients – done a remarkable job. He looked nearer thirty years old than fifty and the scars were barely visible any more. The face in the mirror was experienced, dignified, decisive-looking. *Regal.*

Then the air in the corner of the room shimmered and from the gloom stepped a shadowy, translucent figure clad in scarlet, his long dark brown hair oiled and his fashionable goatee shaped into a spike.

'Hail, Lord Takwyth,' Ostevan Jandreux said in his greasy, mocking voice. The ghostly figure extended his right hand, offering the Pontifical Ring for Takwyth to kiss.

'You can kiss my puckered arse ring, "Pontifex",' Solon told him. The title stuck in his throat: it denoted Ostevan's lust to be both temporal and spiritual ruler of Yuros, which would never happen if he could stop it.

'Manners, dear Solon,' Ostevan chided nonchalantly. 'We've worked together before and we need each other now. Between you and Garod, there are enough men to guarantee Lyra's demise – but divided, we leave our fates subject to the whims of chance. We need to join forces.'

'You don't know my resources and I'll not make common cause with Garod bloody Sacrecour.'

'Don't be so hasty,' Ostevan reproved. 'I'm still Corani. We've had our differences, I grant you, but I want a Corani emperor, even if it's you. Ally with Garod, but keep your hand on your sword hilt.'

'Garod Sacrecour and his cronies murdered half my brothers-in-arms back in 909. I've vowed to see him and everyone with him hanged, drawn and quartered for that.'

'Keep a perspective,' Ostevan chided. 'You need the Church on your side and Wurther's not going to give you the throne now.'

'No,' Solon said flatly, conjuring gnostic energy. 'I know what runs through your veins, Ostevan and it's not good Corani blood any more, but daemonic ichor.' Light flared menacingly in Solon's hands.

Instead of recoiling, Ostevan's gnostic image drifted closer. 'So what if it does? My Master has struck a bargain with these daemons. It's a symbiotic relationship, a mutual enhancement – and it's not too late for you to share in it, Solon. The Master offered you a position once and you turned him down. He's authorised me to offer you another.' He produced a mask from beneath his robes, a skull visage wrought in copper and bone, spattered in blood that looked fresh. 'The endgame has begun, Solon. Join us, or perish.'

Solon eyed the mask uneasily. Unlike the previous set, this wasn't a Lantric theatre mask, but taken from the *Book of Kore*: the face of Macharo, the Angel of War, one of Kore's four agents of destruction in the Last Days.

When he thought about Lyra's perfidy, he involuntarily reached out–

–and stopped. 'I refuse, and you can tell your Master to go and rukk himself.' He sent a blast of spiritualist gnosis that ripped through Ostevan's projected image and blew it away, then checked the wards to ensure it couldn't return.

Unfortunately, Ostevan was right about one thing: he still had too little support. The loyalty of a few men, however devoted, would not be enough.

It's time to rally my people.

He clipped his heels together, saluted himself in the mirror, then marched from the room.

Sir Roland de Farenbrette was waiting outside, with young Nestor Sulpeter. The former, a grizzled, hollow-eyed man with a strong, spare frame, rose stiffly, while Nestor bounced up like an eager puppy. Roland made a show of looking over Solon's newly enhanced face. 'Never thought you one to value prettiness, Sôl.'

'With this good-looking young fellow with us? They'll be wanting to crown him instead,' Solon replied, slapping Nestor on the back, making the young man, whose father commanded the imperial army in the south, blush.

'Come on, let's do this,' Solon told them, striding on towards the throne hall of the Sett, as the Corani stronghold was known. Green-and-white clad soldiers snapped to attention and a gaggle of minor nobles and hangers-on bowed or curtseyed as they marched into Duke Torun's throne room.

Trumpets blared.

'Lord Solon Takwyth, Knight-Commander of Coraine and the Rondian Empire!' the herald boomed and the hall, packed with men and women in sumptuous velvets and furs, burst into applause, welcoming their 'finest son'.

Here we go . . .

He took his time, making sure to grip the out-stretched hands of the most prominent men who'd positioned themselves carefully in his path: the biggest landowners, the wealthiest merchants, the most renowned of the mage-nobles. Behind him, Roland and Nestor were doing the same, establishing themselves as his right-hand men. It took a good five minutes to reach the front of the room, where Torun Jandreux, Duke of Coraine, waited, sweating.

If I proclaimed myself Duke right now, no one would protest.

But Solon needed Torun, at least for a while, and when he was emperor, he'd need a loyal man in Coraine, one with the right lineage. So he made a show of going down on one knee and kissing the ducal ring, as befitted a loyal Corani returning home. There were grown men weeping as they watched, older families who felt that Lyra had forgotten both Coraine and the need for revenge on the Sacrecours.

'It's I who should bow to you,' murmured Torun, a distinctly unimpressive bald man tending towards portliness, a pale shadow of his illustrious forebears, not least his formidable mother Radine.

Solon shivered at the memory of *her*, then quickly regained his poise. It appeared only women could unman him.

'No, you *are* Coraine,' he told Torun loudly. 'I am but a loyal Corani.' He rose, turned and faced the room, effortlessly upstaging the Duke, giving voice to the speech already ringing in his mind. 'Lords and Ladies of my beloved Coraine, thank you for this welcome. My heart swells and my eyes mist to see you all. I have travelled far and wide, but this is ever my home. I will never forget: *I am Corani . . .*'

They loved that, of course: praise for them and the land that united them. But the next message was not so easy to frame: that last sentence was no throwaway platitude but the bridge into his next passage.

'. . . so it grieves me that so many of our people have forgotten who they are,' he told them.

That brought an intake of breath among the packed throne hall, although most of them must surely have been aware that he'd broken with Lyra. Hearing it from him made it real.

'Five years ago,' he went on, 'House Corani marched south to *take* Pallas. We did so, but at a cost we had not expected: because in the case of certain individuals, Pallas *took* them. You know who I mean: people we thought loyal, have been corrupted by wealth and power and opportunity.'

The murmurs started, some of anger, some of consternation. He raised his hand for silence and got it.

'I do not blame our queen,' he told them: because she was *legitimacy*, the piece you took to win the tabula game. 'She was seduced, my friends: by Ril Endarion, that son of an Estellan whore, who seized his chance to elevate himself and to Hel with us!'

Blame the dead – they can't answer back. His fellow Northerners had never taken to Ril, the only bronze-skinned, black-haired man in a sea of pallor, and no one looked offended hearing him defamed.

'Even so, they were babes in a dark wood, he and Lyra: caught up in the coils of snakes like Dominius Wurther and Calan Dubrayle. They've been blinded to the truth. Kore knows I tried to be the strong arm and true heart our queen could rely upon.' He touched his heart, bowing his head as if caught up in sorrow. Most of them had heard the rumours, that for a time he'd been Lyra's lover, but he needed them to see that as the only *true* love she'd ever experienced. 'I know she longs for reconciliation – but they tore us apart, those heartless bastards: Wurther, Dubrayle, Relantine – and worst of all, one of *us* – yes, Dirklan *rukking* Setallius. Dear Kore, I could tell you all some things –' he shouted, then he silenced himself as if fighting his emotions.

The room simmered with his anger – and all it had taken was to feed them some ill-liked names and feign a broken heart.

'And now, Lyra is a virtual prisoner in the Bastion,' he raged, his voice hoarse with raw emotion. 'Fearing for her life, she parrots the words they feed her. Those who should know better – like Oryn Levis and the knights who remain loyal to her – aren't allowed close. They've been duped, my friends, as have the good lads in the legions we sent south. They don't know what's being done to the woman they were sent to protect – they don't see the danger. But I see – *I* know – and I must act!'

'Aye –' a few shouted.

'What will you do, Lord Takky?' someone shouted.

'What will I do? What I've always done: my duty to Coraine. Our queen is a prisoner in her own keep and I will tear down the walls if I must, to free her.'

'And marry her?' a young woman blurted, her eyes shining like swollen stars.

'Aye,' others chorused, 'become our emperor, Lord Takky.'

He feigned modesty, although inside he was roaring in agreement. 'I don't think so far ahead,' he told them. 'Such thoughts are for gentler times, when this crisis is over. For now, all I know is that our queen needs me and I must go to her aid.' He looked up in appeal, the humble knight who wouldn't presume to lead such an august gathering. 'I only hope I'll not go alone.'

The room erupted, chanting support, while Duke Torun, also overcome with emotion, rose and embraced him.

'We'll win her back,' Torun sobbed. 'It's our Kore-given duty.'

Dupenium, Northern Rondelmar

Brylion Fasterius was knocking back a very fine Brevian whiskey after an evening spent with his cousin Duke Garod Sacrecour and their legion commanders, plotting their reclamation of Pallas. Scions of pure-blood families who'd ruled the empire for centuries, they hated their diminished status with a savage vengeance. The meeting had simmered with fury against the queen and those traitors who were siding with her, but still they'd failed to reach consensus.

That was down to fear: the same dread that kept Brylion up at all hours, drinking hard liquor like it was water, rooted in a wild night only a few months past, when that *bitch* Lyra had destroyed five of his legions and almost taken his own life as well. She'd sent blizzards into the face of his exposed men as they'd marched north – no wonder some of their most loyal supporters still baulked at open war.

It was mass murder. She slaughtered my boys from the safety of some tower in Pallas. I'll never rest until she pays for that. I'll make her scream for the rest of eternity.

Outside, it was raining – natural rain. But the queen could turn that to howling gales and ice with a click of her fingers, Brylion knew, and so did all Garod's people. Fear overrode hatred, paralysing them.

We need a dwymancer of our own, or some other power that overmatches it.

He pushed the whiskey aside as his sour gut clenched. *This stuff is no cure for despair,* he reflected, uncharacteristically thoughtful as the weight of night settled on him. *But what is?*

Then the door opened to admit a cowled priest – through doors that were warded, a subtle, chilling display of mastery. Brylion's eyes narrowed and his customary belligerence rose to mask a flare of fear. 'Who the fuck are you?' he growled.

The newcomer merely sat and said calmly, 'Good evening – or rather, good morning, Sir Brylion.' Then he flicked back his cowl, revealing his face.

Brylion scowled at the smooth, impeccably groomed clergyman – the holiest man in Koredom, in theory, but a slimy, backsliding, womanising snake for all that. 'Ostevan,' he barked, 'You can—'

'Brylion,' the Pontifex interrupted, reclining in the opposite chair and gesturing towards the whiskey jar, which rose and tipped amber fluid into a clean tumbler that floated to the clergyman's hand. 'Thanks, don't mind if I do.'

'You've got a bloody nerve—'

'You need one in my line,' Ostevan drawled. 'Fear not, I mean you no harm. But really, you need to look to your security. Do you think Dirklan Setallius' Volsai will have any trouble if a mere priest can get in?'

'You're more than a priest.'

'True,' Ostevan agreed, 'much more. And that's what brings me here . . .' He pulled a musing face. 'I'm here on behalf of a powerful man who is always seeking like-minded individuals.'

'Who?'

'In good time,' Ostevan said. 'Suffice it to say that even I, Pontifex, rightful ruler of the Church of Kore, call him "Master". He's sworn to end the dwymancer-queen through a secret power, one which allows a way to wield every facet of the gnosis, tirelessly and at will.'

Brylion stared suspiciously, while his mind made connections. It was true that someone had been seeking to bring down Lyra Vereinen for the past year: a Masked Cabal whose powers were said to be extraordinary – and Ostevan had been accused of being one of them. Publicly, the Pontifex had laughed them off, but this sounded suspiciously like an admission.

He leaned forward. 'Was this Master of yours behind Reeker Night and all those mad fuckers, rampaging round killing whomever they encountered?' The rumours of that night had grown in the telling and the reality had never been adequately explained here in Dupenium.

Ostevan's face twisted into a smirk. 'The Pallas mob are mindless animals to begin with. Does it matter how they're controlled, as long as they serve one's needs?'

'People say they were possessed?'

'So? Lyra controls the mob by smiling winsomely and giving alms; Solon Takwyth by promising them victory. Even common street-speakers can start a riot by ranting about freedom. They're a herd, Brylion, shitting in their own pastures. Tell me you think any different.'

Brylion's nostrils flared, not at the words, but the arrogant tone. Ostevan had always set his teeth on edge, but he did have a knack of getting what he wanted, most of the time. 'Lyra still cast you from the Celestium, "Pontifex". That tells me that this secret Master of yours isn't as powerful as you pretend.'

It was Ostevan's turn to snarl. 'There are many kinds of power, including this!' He snapped his fingers and with blinding speed, a kinesis-binding flared, slamming into Brylion from all sides – even as a pure-blood mage, he found himself utterly helpless against it. His clothing flattened to his skin, his hair and beard pushed flat, and he could feel cold unseen fingers around his throat as the Pontifex rose and stalked towards him.

'My Master's servants are the greatest magi in Yuros,' Ostevan told him. 'There is no individual man or woman alive who can match us – but we are few, because who the fuck wants to *share* power? Not I – and not you, Brylion Fasterius.' He leaned over the paralysed knight. 'Don't pretend you care about "common people" and don't pretend you've got a conscience. There's a new age coming and my Master will rule it. Join us, serve him and be a part of it.'

For all Brylion strained, sweat streaming down his face, soaking his underarms and crotch, he couldn't move so much as a muscle.

If I don't accept, he's going to murder me . . . but if I accept, then I can kill the bastard. 'Very well,' he managed through clenched teeth. 'Now release me.'

Ostevan gave him a knowing look, clearly anticipating Brylion's duplicity, but he still reached inside his robes and brought out a mask of copper and bone: a skull, drenched in lacquered blood so real and fresh-looking it almost dripped. Brylion knew the image from the only part of the *Book of Kore* he'd ever found interesting: 'The Prophecies of the Last Days'.

'Macharo?' he said, as the kinesis spell faded; but Brylion made no move against Ostevan. Revenge could wait: he was intrigued.

'Aye, Brylion,' the Pontifex purred. 'The Master wants you to be his

Angel of War. He's been waiting for the right moment and the right man. That's *now*, and *you*, Brylion. Take it, and gain all you desire – or refuse, and fade into obscurity.'

Brylion didn't hesitate, sweeping up the mask and feeling the power of it tingling through his fingers. 'The queen's heralds say the Masked Cabal are all daemon-possessed,' he noted, daring to look up at Ostevan.

The Pontifex's eyes turned black. 'So we are – but *we* control the power. I am still me – but I am so much more.'

The enormity of what he was agreeing to struck Brylion's whiskey-blurred mind. 'If I take it, I'll be eternally damned,' he breathed, wavering.

'What does that even mean?' Ostevan said, with a chuckle. 'There's no Kore, no Halls of Paradise, you know that. Just the long damnation of darkness when we die. Why not embrace a daemon? You gain far more than you lose, I can assure you.'

Brylion stared at the mask and it stared back. 'What else is involved?'

'Well, there is also this,' Ostevan said. He made a choking sound, something writhed in his throat and a giant white millipede coated in viscous black, bloody ichor crawled out of his mouth. He held it on the palm of his hand. 'It will rest beside your heart, allowing the daemon into your soul and opening up the infinite.'

I will truly be damned, Brylion thought, but still he stretched out his hand. *I'll take it – I'll take the power . . . and then I will kill him for the snake he is.*

But by the time he'd swallowed that hideous thing and the ichor had worked its magic upon him, he no longer wished to take back control. Instead, his eyes gleaming black, he fell to his knees and kissed Ostevan's hand.

'How may I serve?' he asked, without a trace of rebellion. Nothing the daemon had screamed into his skull wasn't already there.

The Pontifex smiled down at him. 'By killing whomsoever I charge you to slay.' He handed him a list of names. 'Let's start with the dissenters in your own ranks. Garod must march, so any who gainsay him have to die.'

At War With Ourselves

The Heroic Lie

Ancient tales of deposed princes trampling over mountains of corpses on their 'heroic' quests to claim thrones that are 'rightfully theirs' are the worst lies of all. Such stories sanction violence in the name of personal gain, perpetuating the lie that certain ranks are divinely allotted and only a true-born king can rule. One day, instead of taking sides in these contests, the people will take power for themselves.

THE BLACK HISTORIES, ANONYMOUS, 776

Pallas, Rondelmar
Febreux 936

Empress Lyra Vereinen, ruler of the Rondian Empire, sat in her garden and frowned over the words of Vico Makelli, a three-hundred-years-dead Rimoni philosopher both revered and reviled for a pragmatic realism bordering on cynicism.

The gathering, maintenance and exercise of power – the ability to exert one's will over one's subjects and rivals – is the Ruler's only concern. Without his authority there is no kingdom and his lands and people will be swallowed by rivals amid the chaos of war and all the suffering that brings. A Ruler must be untroubled by scruples or conscience, for his rule will never be so ruinous as the conflagration that will be unleashed if he loses control of his territories. The military, the church, the bureaucracy, the mythology of kingship: these are his greatest weapons, and he must use them all. There can be no dissent. Weakness is evil; strength is virtue.

'Is that so?' she whispered, thinking of the streets in Pallas that even now were barricaded against her soldiers by common people fighting to be free of both her and the dukes who wanted to crush her and drive the Corani back to the north. Perceiving her very real weakness, they demanded autonomy, recognising that even her own councillors had conspired against her, to force her into marriage to a man she'd made the mistake of favouring.

Not of favouring – of bedding, she corrected herself, wincing at the thought. She couldn't think of Solon Takwyth, even now marshalling his forces in Coraine, without remembering the weight of his body on hers, the smell and feel and taste and sound of him. The memories made her cringe. *I fell so low, and so stupidly.*

She pushed the Makelli text aside – *What heartless, self-serving bile!* – and looked up as a shrill cry somewhere between a bird's shriek and a horse's whinny echoed above her long, narrow garden. White wings gleaming like snow glinted in the winter sunlight, a shadow flashed overhead, then a winged creature swooped in and landed at a run: a brilliant white pegasus with eagle-wings twelve feet from shoulder to pinion tip. Hooves thudded into the turf as she snorted in exhilaration, her breath turning to clouds of steam as she trotted up.

'There, Pearl,' Lyra said, rising and pulling back her hood to reveal severely tied-back blonde hair and a tired face. She was only in her late twenties, but her brow was increasingly lined with worry and dark rings bruised her eyes. The stresses of the crown weighed heavily. She smiled though, as she rested her face against the winged horse's soft muzzle. 'Did you have a good fly, Pooty-girl? Did you have fun?'

Even as she spoke, she flinched inside: 'Pooty-girl' had been Ril's nickname for the pegasus he'd raised from a nestling. His blood had been on Pearl's back when she'd arrived home from the battle at Collistein Junction, four months ago. For a moment the familiar, choking feeling of grief threatened to undo Lyra all over again. She'd thought she'd cried herself out over Ril when she buried him, but it appeared not. They'd not been truly happy together, but sometimes his absence made her whole existence stall.

Her eyes went up to the window of her apartments, where their son Rildan was sleeping: her last link to her dead husband. She suddenly ached to hold the child against her chest, as a wave of loneliness struck her.

Loneliness can destroy you.

Solon Takwyth had told her that. She'd thought to hold that isolation at bay by letting him bed her, pretending that having the wrong someone was better than having no one at all.

Another disastrous mistake . . .

Now Takwyth was in Coraine, raising an army against her; and he wasn't her only foe. Garod Sacrecour, the Duke of Dupenium, wanted the previous regime returned to power; the Duke of Argundy, Kurt Borodium, and the other secessionists wanted the empire dissolved; Sultan Xoredh Mubarak of Kesh and his Shihadi wanted to destroy all of Yurosi civilisation in his so-called 'holy war' – and the Pallas Mob were demanding the downfall of *all* of them.

She clung to the neck of the pegasus, her cheek against the silky mane, letting the beast's unconditional love ground her.

Eventually, she raised her head and looked around her garden, which filled the narrow space between the inner walls of the Bastion and the fortress atop Roidan Heights. The city, caught in the toils of late winter, was coated in ice that slowly melted in afternoon sun that did little to warm the air, then hardened in the twilight until by midnight, everything was frozen again. The bushes were still encrusted in snow, except for one sapling: the cutting from the Winter Tree, her link to the immense powers of the dwyma, had both blossom and scarlet berries clinging to its spindly branches. All afternoon she'd been seeking her fellow dwymancer, Valdyr of Mollachia. Although she had never met him in person, speaking to him had become a lifeline – but she'd not heard from him for days. She worried that he was dead as well.

'I don't know what to do,' she confessed to Pearl. 'I can't even find Valdyr's presence any more.'

She'd lost so many people this past year; he would be one loss too many. The only other dwymancer she knew of was a Keshi girl called Jehana, but her voice was also absent from the dwyma now.

Am I the only one of us left?

Despair stirred inside her; that same miasma had dragged her into Solon's clutches. So much had been packed into this terrible winter and she'd been at the heart of it all: battles, assassinations, mob violence, court cases, love and lust and loss. It barely felt real, and she could scarcely believe she'd survived.

Only I did make it through, thanks to Dirklan and Basia and Exilium, Valdyr and the dwyma; and so many people whose name I don't even know, who fought and died for me.

But it still hasn't been enough.

Despite all that courage and sacrifice, the sixth year of her reign looked like it would be the last. The temptation to just run away and hide was almost overwhelming.

'One day, Pooty-girl, we'll fly away,' she murmured. 'You, me and Rildan.'

But that wouldn't be today. She left the pegasus to graze and ascended the stairs to her apartments on the highest floor of the Bastion, where her maid Nita was readying today's outfit: a plain white dress, now she had cast off her mourning robes.

By the time she'd dressed, her bodyguards were awaiting her in the antechamber. Basia de Sirou and Exilium Excelsior, newly returned to duty after recovering from injuries sustained in an assassination attempt, were talking intently. As usual, Basia was pricking at Exilium's black-and-white view of the world. Lyra empathised with the young Estellan: the pillars he clung to were those she'd grown up with: faith in Kore and the Church. They hadn't served her well.

Then Dirklan Setallius appeared, clad in his usual grey, his long silver hair shrouding his eyepatch and the scarred side of his face. She rose, hurried to him and hugged him briefly: her father, finally identified, the new pillar of her life. It was a balm to be held, but his parentage was still a secret, so they stepped apart and fell into their more regular relationship of queen and spymaster.

'What news, Lord Setallius?' she asked, as they headed for the door, Basia and Exilium following.

'Some good, most bad, I'm afraid,' Dirklan replied as they descended to the public areas of the palace. 'Duke Torun of Coraine has declared for Takwyth, and both he and Garod Sacrecour are seeking mercenaries in Hollenia to bolster their forces.'

'Can we prevent that?'

'The Mercenary guilds are a law unto themselves. The most important Hollenian captain is Endus Rykjard: he lost legions in the Third Crusade but returned from the East with enough money to rebuild. He's shifty, ruthless and competent enough to pull the other mercenaries in behind him. They'll follow his lead.'

'He sounds like a perfect match for Garod Sacrecour,' Lyra sighed. 'Can we buy him off?'

'I doubt it,' Dirklan replied. 'The Treasury reports aren't good: our plundering of the churches has run its course. We're almost broke again.'

'What about our men down south? Lord Sulpeter has six legions, doesn't he?'

'He's asked permission to return north, but he is likely to support Takwyth,' Dirklan admitted. 'In fact, the Argundians are also looking to pull out if the secession goes ahead, and the Aquilleans may follow suit. Worst case, our entire Southern Army may desert, allowing the Shihad into Midrea unopposed.'

'You mentioned some good news?' Lyra asked plaintively.

Dirklan's single eye met her gaze. 'Norostein is holding, and Sultan Rashid has been slain in battle.'

'He's *dead*? *The* Sultan *is dead*?' Lyra put a hand to her breast. 'It's wrong to pray for a man to die, but I confess I've wished for such a thing. How did it happen?'

'During an all-out assault: according to reports, the sultan's son Attam joined the fray and died; Rashid went to his aid and also perished. An Argundian battle-mage slew both, at the cost of her own life. But the Shihad has still managed to take half the city, which means that unless Seth Korion can drive them out again, they now have their winter shelter.'

'Seth Korion,' Lyra breathed. 'Do we know where he stands on the secession?'

Dirklan shook his head. 'Bricia and Noros have remained silent. Phyllios, King of Noros, died in the siege, so Governor Myron of Noros should now be in full control, but he claims to be walled into the inner bailey in Norostein, surrounded by what he describes as a "homicidal mob incited by Seth Korion". Between the Shihad and Korion, we've lost control of Noros for now.'

'Even your good news is half-bad! This Korion worries me.' She thought a moment, then asked, 'So who's the new sultan?'

'Xoredh, the second son. He was Rashid's spymaster.'

'So he's mysterious and clever then, like all such men?' Lyra asked archly.

Dirklan flashed his ghostly smile. 'He's no Rashid, who was universally revered. Xoredh's got a reputation for cruelty. The Shihad is made up from many nations, so perhaps they'll fragment without a unifying leader.'

'Let us pray so.' She returned her thoughts to Coraine. 'You really think Rolven Sulpeter will side with Takwyth?'

'His son Nestor is Solon's aide and hero-worships Takwyth. Rolven is a fence-sitter by nature, but his son's presence might force him into Takwyth's camp.'

'Should we keep Rolven in the south, then?'

Dirklan shook his head. 'If you forbid him to come north when he feels compelled to do so, you'll force him to break with you. Invite him here and he may remain loyal and persuade his son to re-join us.'

It sounded unlikely to Lyra, but she agreed. 'All right. Let's see what he does.'

He spent a few minutes briefing her on local issues: more rioting overnight in Tockburn and Kenside, more pamphlets denouncing her distributed by the rebellious citizenry. It was dispiriting, but she straightened her shoulders as they entered, for her counsellors were waiting. She took her seat at the head of the table, her more ornate chair the only sign of rank, while Dirklan, Chancellor by merit of being Lyra's parent, went to the foot of the table.

Beside Dirklan sat big, stolid Oryn Levis. A born subordinate, he looked ill-at-ease at the high table. 'Good morning, Majesty,' he called, his words echoed by the others.

'Good morning all,' she said briskly. 'What's first?'

To her left, the dapper, grey-haired Treasurer, Calan Dubrayle, looked up. To her surprise, he'd emerged as a staunch supporter in the recent crises. 'Milady, could we start with the—?' he began.

'If we start with money, we'll never get off the damned subject,' Grand Prelate Dominius Wurther interrupted. 'Let's talk about these riots, Milady – surely that's more pressing?'

Wurther's long-standing feud with Dubrayle had been exacerbated when Lyra allowed her Treasurer to tax the Church; in retaliation, Wurther had backed Takwyth's attempts to force her into marriage. The Grand Prelate's usually genial confidence was subdued and he was clearly unsure of her attitude to him now.

As you should be, Lyra thought, her anger rising again. *You tried to sanction rape.*

It especially hurt because she'd liked and mostly trusted Wurther. But he was Church and she was State; it wasn't legally possible for her to depose or exclude him and in any case, she needed Church support more than ever.

'You've often told me that money lies at the root of evil,' she told Wurther, 'so let's get to the root of our problems. Lord Dubrayle, pray continue.'

Dubrayle brightened at this small sign of favour, his eyes trailing from Wurther to the empty seat where the Imperocrator, the head of the bureaucracy, would normally sit. The last Imperocrator, Rael Relantine, had lasted only a month before his overt support for Takwyth had seen him ousted. Unlike Wurther, Relantine's fate was in Lyra's hands. Right now, he was incarcerated in a not-too-unpleasant cell, awaiting her pleasure. She felt little inclination towards clemency.

'What I was *trying* to say is, might we start with the Imperocracy?' Dubrayle asked drily.

'Give me a list of candidates,' Lyra told him. 'Right now I want to know about the Treasury.'

Dubrayle summarised the Crown finances. As usual, the figures were mostly red. 'In short, the money raised by back-taxing the Church is almost gone and the threat of secession has paralysed our spring tax intake. The ambassadors of Argundy, Hollenia, Brevis, Andressea and Estellayne have formally declared that they will secede, suspecting the empire is too weak to oppose them. The vassal-states are already closing their borders,' he went on, 'which includes the movement of goods and money and imperial messengers into and out of Rondelmar. Our governors fear for their personal safety, and for their staff and legions.'

'How many legions do those who have signed the Secession account for?' Lyra asked anxiously, looking at her new Knight-Commander.

'More than forty,' Oryn Levis answered, 'but most are local men. If there is open conflict, no legion will wholly side with us.' He looked around the table miserably. 'Not even in Coraine or here in Pallas.'

Lyra wondered yet again if Oryn was up to the trials ahead. But there was no other credible candidate to lead their army and his assessment rang true. 'How long do we have before we run out of money?' she asked.

'A month at most,' Dubrayle replied. 'Then we'll be unable to pay our soldiers and staff and all will be lost.' He glanced at Wurther. 'The Grand Prelate insists his coffers are empty, but the Celestium has collections—'

'Sacrilege!' Wurther barked. 'We have nothing left but purely religious artefacts.'

'But—'

'Who does have money?' Dirklan interjected.

Dubrayle hesitated, then said, 'The Merchants' Guild. The bankers. Ordinary people, although not enough, not the way prices are escalating during this crisis. I don't—'

'The *banks* have money?' Dirklan repeated.

'Of course – it's what they do. But it's not their money – it belongs to other people. Most have shifted their bullion out of Pallas, now that the Merchants' Guild has left the capital.'

They took that in gloomily. 'Who are the main banks?' Lyra asked.

'Jusst & Holsen are the biggest,' Dubrayle replied. 'Then there's

Ankargild, and Gravenhurst Stronghold and Petra-Belk. Those four between them control the market. They have branches in every ducal capital.'

'Do they support us?'

'They're ostensibly neutral, but the word is out that our credit is bad and with Jean Benoit's Merchants' Guild actively backing Garod, we can't get credit any more.'

'Do you have any more magic wands, Treasurer?' Lyra asked, as calmly as she could.

Dubrayle's eyes flickered from Wurther, who looked ready to pounce on him physically if he suggested more Church raids, then shook his head. 'I have a few ideas, but nothing developed, Milady,' he said meekly.

Lyra felt her fragile hopes crumble a little more. 'Be sure to explore every possibility,' she urged him, before looking around the table. 'What do we do about the secession threat, gentlemen?'

'It's more than a threat,' Wurther grumbled. 'Come the first of Martrois, they're going to evict your embassies and seize all the imperial holdings in their territories. Anyone who tries to fight them will be slain – there will likely be a purging of Rondians living in their lands. The Rondian Empire will no longer exist.'

The 'Empress of the Fall' people called me when I was crowned. Here comes that fall . . .

Lyra had to fight to keep her voice from cracking. 'Can we do anything about it?'

'Militarily, not much,' the spymaster said. 'The Third Crusade weakened Rondelmar more than any other region. You shouldn't blame yourself: the Sacrecours would also be facing this moment had they retained power.'

'That's of no consolation,' Lyra replied. 'I need a plan to deal with it.'

The four men around the table shared worried looks, then all began to speak at once. Characteristically, Levis immediately deferred, Dirklan shut his mouth to listen and Dubrayle and Wurther began again, but the Grand Prelate was loudest and spoke over the top of his adversary.

'Majesty, the Church and the Crown are two sides of the same coin.

21

The first emperor, Sertain, knew he had to win the hearts and souls of the people when the magi established their rule or he would face incessant warfare. He did this by uniting his reign with the Word of Kore. We have had our differences, Lyra, and I have made mistakes, but to weather this you and I must stand together. I pray you forgive my role in, *ahem*, recent events, and allow me to help you.'

She met the obese old clergyman's eyes and read considerable fear in them.

He's facing Ostevan as a rival for his position as Head of the Church and if the empire fragments, the Church may also break up. His world is falling apart, just as mine is. He means what he's saying. I'm still angry with him, but he's right. I have to repair our rift.

'Dominius,' she said, as calmly as she could, 'we've been friends too long to abandon each other. You underestimated me, but I'm sure you won't again. I uphold your status as Grand Prelate of the Church of Kore and you uphold my right to the throne.'

Wurther smiled gratefully and she was surprised to feel a slight lightening in the weight on her shoulders. 'My priests will speak from the pulpit of the virtues of unity and condemn the secession,' he promised.

'How strong is your control?' Dirklan asked. 'My people tell me the local prelates can be laws unto themselves, especially in the south.'

'Your people are correct,' Wurther conceded grudgingly. 'I'm struggling to find reliable prelates as it is: I don't have a quorum and must rule by emergency decree. The most influential clergy of the vassal-states see this as a chance to screw me royally – erm –'

'Manners, Grand Prelate,' Lyra said mildly.

'Apologies, Milady. The point is, secession hurts me as well as you: the Church is likely to break up when the empire does.'

'Secession isn't guaranteed,' Dirklan put in. 'The thing is, being a big fish in a small pond is nice, but being the biggest fish in a big pond is nicer. I'm told the Duke of Argundy still harbours imperial ambitions: he'd happily make himself King of an independent Argundy if that's the best deal he can get, but what he'd *really* like is to be Emperor of Yuros. He'd rather seize the empire than break it up – and he's not the only one.'

Lyra frowned. 'So is the secession ultimatum a bluff?'

'No, but it's not what they *really* crave. The Borodium family have always been ambitious – but the rest of the vassal-states fear them, just as much as they fear the Sacrecours. Estellayne doesn't want an Argundian Emperor, nor do Brevis and Andressea. And not all Argundians like the Borodiums. We can divide our enemies.'

'I suppose the obvious way to do that is for me to court a Borodium?' Lyra suggested, squirming at the thought. 'Or a powerful rival of his?'

'That's an option to investigate,' the Treasurer agreed. 'It could split the secessionists, and make Garod hesitate too.'

Dear Kore, Lyra thought, *after the Takwyth affair, the last thing I want is another man in my life.* But there didn't appear to be much choice. 'Dirklan, speak to the ambassador from Argundy in secret. Explore the possibilities – and do it swiftly. This must be resolved before the first of Martrois. We have twenty-four days.'

'Your son will be a sticking point,' Oryn Levis said hesitantly.

Lyra felt her hackles rise. 'My son is my heir. That's not negotiable.'

'Oryn's right,' Dirklan said gently. 'Whoever you marry will want their own progeny to be first in line to the throne after himself. Rildan will be a target for conspiracy if you insist on his primogeniture. Would you condemn him to such an existence?'

She felt her eyes sting, but she clenched her fists. 'I'm not doing this just for him – I'm trying to prevent a bloodbath. You've all told me time and again that civil war will destroy us.'

'Indeed, Majesty,' Dominius agreed. 'You're doing it to prevent the fragmentation of both Crown and Church, and a bloodbath as Rondians stationed in foreign states are massacred out of greed and vengeance. To prevent wars of retribution for the centuries in which Rondelmar has lorded it over the rest, and to quell civil war here in the north. You're doing it to preserve the rule of law and civilisation itself. You're doing it for the soul of Yuros.'

His words reminded Lyra forcibly of passages from the *Book of Kore* telling of the end of mankind, the ascension of the Blessed and of the daemons inheriting Urte. 'The Masked Cabal have loosed daemons upon us. War is here, bringing famine and plague: are these the Last Days, Grand Prelate?'

Dominius gave her a haunted look. 'That's the fear I can't deny.'

Oryn made the Blessing of Corineus sign over his heart, but Calan Dubrayle snorted. 'Pah! Don't you fall for that rot, Majesty. The Last Days are a myth, like Kore and Seraphs and Paradise itself. Nothing is preordained, as any diviner will tell you. We determine our own futures.'

His words warred in Lyra's heart with twenty years of convent life, all those hours of rote prayer and catechisms. *Dear Kore, is it so? Is Your judgement at hand?* Her eyes went to her father's face, seeking hope.

'Majesty, it's not for us to know the hour,' Dirklan said. 'History is studded with men and women who became convinced the end was at hand and whose name is now a laughing-stock, or the stuff of tragedy. We must trust that life goes on. To do less is to fail all those who place their hopes in us. If you behave as if the world is ending, you will fall into despair. We must fight on.'

'Dirklan's right, for once,' Dominius put in. 'There have been too many false prophets and tragedies – suicide pacts and such abominations. If these are the Last Days, Kore expects us to bear up nobly, fighting for what is right. And if these are not the Last Days, we must do likewise. Pray for guidance, Majesty, but don't despair.'

She took a deep breath. *He's right. Last Days or not, we can't give in to our fears.* 'What are Garod and Ostevan going to do? And Takwyth?' she added reluctantly.

'If they want to come out of this ruling an empire, they must act fast,' Dirklan replied. 'The secession ultimatum will force their hand – they'll have to march immediately, no matter the conditions . . . and even knowing what you're capable of, Majesty,' he added meaningfully.

They expect me to destroy another army with dwyma-storms . . . She swallowed, remembering the death and destruction she'd wrought that awful night. *But if that's what I must do . . .*

She nodded firmly, and all four men exhaled.

'Then organise our defences, Lord Levis,' she told Oryn. 'Rally your men, make them understand that brother does not fight brother at our will, but Takwyth's. Our men are the true Corani, not those traitors.'

Oryn's face was miserable as he said, 'The men are confused, Majesty, and scared. To them, Solon Takwyth is the name of Victory itself.'

'Then clear their minds,' she snapped. 'You must appear *certain*.' She swept her gaze around the room, then moved on. 'And now, let's talk about Pallas. How can we defend a city we do not wholly control? We've lost control of the docklands, the river trade has collapsed and wheat prices are now ridiculous. We have to regain control – but I won't make war on my own people. Find me a solution.'

This was the hardest matter of them all, and one that hours of wrangling couldn't resolve. At last she threw up her hands and said, 'Enough! Dirklan, I want to talk to that man Ari Frankel. You remember him, surely? Find him, and convince him to meet with me. No tricks, no traps. I just want to talk with him.'

The men frowned. 'But why?' Dominius asked, in an exasperated voice. 'The man's a traitor.'

Lyra remembered Frankel as someone so passionate in his convictions that he'd risk torture and execution. She'd pardoned him of sedition but he'd gone straight back to his rabble-rousing ways. 'He's the key. If he and I can find common ground, these problems may go away.'

Oryn shook his head, his usually mild features angry. 'I've seen the pamphlets – the filth and lies this man spreads. The only way to make his sort of problem go away is with a noose.'

'I don't share that view,' Lyra said firmly. 'Find him.'

Tockburn, the docklands area east of Roidan Heights, benefited from the calmer waters where the Aerflus discharged into the lower reaches of the Bruin River and commenced its epic journey through Ventia and on to the sea. The docklands had for centuries been the least governable, most incendiary part of Pallas, and while Kenside, Fisheart and Oldtown were more dangerous, Tockburn – 'Tockers' – was the most rebellious. Tockers was where thwarted ambition met loose morals: a maze of vice, seething beneath a veneer of exuberant pleasure. The most exotic lusts, from opium to drink to carnality, could be satisfied there, and it was a hotbed of radical ideas.

For a month now, Tockburn had been closed to Lyra's people. Barricades blocked the main streets; they might be more symbolic than anything, but they were still slowing the City Guard when they tried to react to fires and riots. Warehouses filled with food had been raided, then burned to the ground. The vigilantes patrolling the streets had been using rocks and other crude weapons to batter those few City Guard who tried to enter, but more recently, patrols had also been facing an unseen group of gnosis-wielders, the mage-criminals known as the Kaden Rats.

Ari Frankel was heading for a meeting with the Rats now, escorted by fellow rebels. Armed lurkers kept watch, furtively signalling when it was safe to move. No one was fooling themselves that the Imperial Volsai weren't watching.

This meeting was in a burnt-out manor belonging to a merchant who'd conveniently fled to Dupenium months back. A man brandishing a crossbow opened the door, then a bald mage flaunting his gemstone periapt checked Ari over before ushering him upstairs to the sitting room above, where five men and women awaited him. Two of them were rakishly dressed magi, wearing wide leather hats and tooled leather armour, silk shirts and flamboyant pantaloons: Tad Kaden, sporting a goatee and ponytail, and his square-jawed, septic-tongued sister Braeda, who was lounging on a chair, slurping red wine.

Opposite them at the long table were the chilling renegade centurion Lazar of Midrea and his brutish henchman Gorn; these men had been behind the worst of the thuggery since the movement turned violent. They nodded respectfully when Ari entered, though, for it was his words that had sparked this insurrection.

The only man Ari didn't know, a priest with an unctuous face, pale brown tonsured hair and spotlessly clean robes, rose. 'My name is Germane,' he introduced himself. 'I bring the greetings of Ostevan Pontifex.'

I've seen posters and heard the town criers declare him a wanted man, Ari thought suspiciously, but all he said was, 'You were the Royal Comfateri, yes?'

'I was, until the queen spread lies about me,' Germane replied smoothly. 'But my loyalties are as they have always been: to Kore and his rightful voice on Urte, Ostevan Pontifex.'

Ari looked at Tad Kaden. 'Are we now taking sides in the succession battle?' he demanded. 'That's not what my movement is about.'

'*Your* movement?' Tad replied sharply. 'My family has been in the insurrection business for generations, boy.'

'You've been a criminal for decades, certainly,' Ari retorted. 'But this is about suffragium.' After so many brushes with death, he'd lost most of his fear of magi. 'I've lost my friends, my family, my employment, my home, all for this one thing. My words are on the lips of the people. Your name is still a curse.'

Braeda conjured fire in her fingers, but Ari didn't flinch.

Then Father Germane stepped between them. 'Please – we're here to discuss common ground, not fight over that which might divide us. We all want Lyra Vereinen gone.'

'True,' Ari said sharply; he hadn't meant to create a scene that this damned priest could use to show his peace-making skills. 'But we don't want a Sacrecour restoration. Nor do we want a Pontifex ruling us.'

'Ostevan represents your greatest chance of achieving your goals,' Germane declared, pulling a rolled-up parchment from an inner pocket and displaying it: it was one of Ari's pamphlets. ' "Suffragium: the power to vote for one's rulers. Equality before the law applying to all. Freedom of expression, without censure. An end to dynasties and nepotism. Equal distribution of wealth".' He shrugged. 'My master has no quarrel with any of this, but power rests with magi and legions and you have none. Lyra Vereinen may at this stage scruple to attack her own citizenry, but Garod Sacrecour won't.'

'Garod, who is Ostevan's ally,' Ari reminded them all.

'Ostevan was once Corani and he remembers that,' Germane countered. 'He doesn't want to see Garod enthroned, or Garod's nephew Cordan. My master is a visionary, Frankel, and some of his visions align with your own. He doesn't deny his mores – he's always thought chastity among the clergy to be a nonsense, for example. Did Kore make him male for no reason? But he believes in equality strongly: the *Book of Kore* itself proclaims all men equal in Kore's eyes. Ostevan has no love of the Great Houses either. Imagine a world in which his benevolent guidance permits every community autonomy. Imagine the magi working *for* the people, building bridges and roads, not squabbling over riches. Imagine freedom, upheld by love of Kore. That's my master's vision.'

Ari had already dismissed most of the man's words the moment they left his mouth. Rumour had it that Ostevan was a seducer of women – including the queen herself – and the force behind the Reeker Night attacks of last year: a murderer and conspirator who couldn't be trusted.

But his suffragium movement did need powerful allies. *Can we accept this one without losing control?* He looked around the room, saw the Kaden siblings in wordless communion, while Lazar rubbed his stubbled chin and Gorn nodded absently, his mouth hanging open.

'Imperialism is still tyranny, even if it comes in clerical garb,' he told Germane.

But the very fact the man was here told him that the Kadens, and probably Lazar too, were in favour.

'It's not just your decision, Frankel,' Tad retorted. 'Germane offers us the resources we need: weapons, supplies, real soldiers. If we provide Ostevan's men passage into the city, we can end this stand-off swiftly, in our favour.'

Lazar was nodding now and Ari realised that this would be decided without him if he didn't respond persuasively. 'Last time we spoke, you said you could supply the weapons and manpower we needed *without* taking sides in the succession,' he complained to Tad.

'We're criminals, not mercenaries,' Braeda sniffed. 'We can steal guarded treasures and assassinate enemies, but we can't fill the streets with soldiers.'

'We can't just trade one tyrant for another!'

'Only Ostevan sympathises with your position,' Germane put in. 'Takwyth wishes to be emperor, just like Garod. Ostevan will leave secular governance to your movement. He's only interested in peace.'

'The word "Pontifex" denotes a greater tyranny than either Emperor or Grand Prelate,' Ari retorted.

'It's just a word, denoting a clean break from the current regime,' Germane answered. 'Ostevan is content to let secular men rule the secular, while he reforms the clergy. Believe me, he's your only chance. The empress will move against you soon – she must deal with internal resistance before Garod and Takwyth arrive.'

That sounded uncomfortably true. 'But what men does Ostevan

have?' Ari asked, still convinced they were being duped. 'He lost everything when the empress drove him from Pallas.'

'You will see,' Germane replied. 'My master is a man of great resource.'

That's true, Ari thought, *but everyone says he's too dangerous to work with.*

'How do we know we won't be forgotten the moment your master has what he wants?'

'Produce a manifesto and he'll sign it and bind himself to it,' Germane replied glibly. 'He will become your champion, Frankel. I advise you not to put aside so generous an offer: you'll get none better.'

It was the smoothness of the response that made up Ari's mind – no man who cared about something would so smoothly dismiss the detail. 'No,' he said sharply, 'the moment he doesn't need us, we'll be discarded. Ostevan has been Wurther's right-hand man, a disgraced exile, the queen's confessor and lover, a self-crowned Pontifex and Garod Sacrecour's ally. He's betrayed everyone he's ever served. Why should we believe him now?'

Germane's expression didn't change, but Ari saw the man's pupils narrow, then the priest turned to Tad Kaden. 'I presume as believers in suffragium, you'll be taking a vote,' he said archly. 'Shall I wait outside?'

'That won't be necessary,' Tad drawled, his eyes trailing from Germane to Ari. 'I'm persuaded, Master Frankel. We need an ally. Draw up your manifesto and we'll place it before the Pontifex.'

Ari was angry, but he was afraid that if the Kadens discarded him, he'd have no one. Lazar and Gorn clearly wanted this alliance too. His own standing was clear. *I'm just a figurehead.*

Germane's smug expression said that he understood that too.

'Fine,' Ari snapped. *Let's see what Ostevan will and won't sign.* 'I'll draft something.'

He really wanted to storm out, but unfortunately, they had actual business to discuss. As soon as Germane had departed, they moved – because even the Kaden siblings weren't so sure of the priest that they'd linger. They reunited an hour later in the upper room of a closed store on a square in Tockburn East.

For a time the five of them watched a thousand or more ragged Tockers hurling themselves at a thin line of legionaries protecting wagons full of wheat meant for the Bastion. The air throbbed with chants and shouting and the barked orders of the soldiers, the clash of wood on shield bosses and the screams of the injured. Ari winced at the din, but Lazar and the Kadens watched with satisfied smirks on their lips.

'This road is the frontline,' Tad remarked. 'Every day they land supplies at the docks and every day we fight to take them away. But right now it's sticks and stones against blades.'

'If the empress wasn't a squeam, it'd be a slaughterhouse,' Braeda added, trimming her fingernails with a dagger. 'We're asking ordinary people to confront legionaries. Can your conscience handle that, Frankel?'

'Those legionaries are also people,' Ari reminded them. 'Families are being pulled apart and the queen knows that. She's got her soldiers under orders not to draw their blades – look at them, they're using spear-butts and shields.'

'Tell that to the hundreds injured and the dozens who die each day from broken skulls,' Lazar rasped. 'We need soldiers on our side, Wordsmith. The fact is, we're not making inroads any more. It's been days since we stopped a wagon-train getting through and we're bleeding men. The Guard have dragged off more'n three hundred of our hardest lads – the Bastion dungeons are full. People are spending their savings on food, but the price of bread has trebled in a month. Folks are desperate.'

'If we could drive the Imperials out of the Tockburn docks, the empress would be rukked,' Gorn added, the first coherent sentence Ari had heard the man say. 'But they's got a legion encamped down there.'

'Another legion that can't defend the walls,' Tad smirked. 'They've got another in Kenside and another patrolling Fisheart and Oldtown. That's almost half the men Lyra's got, stuck inside the city. This is the tipping point: let Ostevan arm us and she's going to break. She'll have to run. If she doesn't control the whole city by the time Garod arrives, she's finished. And when she runs, *we'll* seize control and defy Garod.'

'With us in control of the Bastion, and the city behind us, Garod Sacrecour won't be able to take the city back,' Braeda added. 'When Lyra runs, the Corani go. The secession will do the rest: with no empire to defend, the Pallacian legions will join us to defend the city from the Sacrecours. I tell you, this is a unique moment in time: the empire is disintegrating and we're in exactly the right place to capitalise. We'll be kings – and queens – all of us.'

'We'll be *citizens*,' Ari replied sharply. 'The people don't want kings, they want power.'

Tad glanced at his sister, then shrugged genially. 'Of course. I speak figuratively only: as the engineers of this coup, we'll be the heroes of the new era. Your suffragium will deliver us control.'

'And then we'll take the rukkin' head of anyone who's kept us down,' Lazar snarled, his eyes shining as he peered through the shutters at the unfolding chaos below.

And there it is, Ari thought. *I'm fighting for an ideal, but the Kadens want riches and Lazar wants blood.*

Dupenium, Northern Rondelmar

'I'm telling you, the time to march is now,' Ostevan Pontifex said from his throne.

It wasn't his *real* throne: that was in the Celestium, from where he'd been driven at the end of last year, almost two months ago. This was his residence-in-exile, a cold, draughty manor with guttering fires in Dupenium. But tonight he hosted the duke, his closest counsellors and a handful of Keepers, the self-styled Guardians of the Gnosis.

It was a dark, dismal setting, but a convenient place for Garod Sacrecour to hold a council of war, away from the eyes of his less-trusted courtiers. The dozen men and women sat around a long table, the aides standing attendance on their masters lining the tapestried walls. The doors were guarded and locked, with gnostic wards to protect against scrying.

Duke Garod's throne, on Ostevan's right, was of the same height. The duke's lank grey hair looked greasy and his lips were wine-red. 'You know what happened last time we marched on Pallas,' he said sullenly.

His kinsman Brylion Fasterius made a snarling noise. 'The bloody-handed queen slaughtered my lads, the filthy witch. I'm going to burn her alive.'

That's the spirit, Brylion, Ostevan thought wryly. It hadn't taken long for the daemon-spawn to conquer Brylion, who'd always been a ravening beast. No one had really noticed the snuffing-out of his humanity.

But uncertainty still haunted Brylion's eyes: that dwymancy could destroy them again. That dread was shared by most of the mage-nobles gathered here: old, great names of the Blessed Three Hundred who'd clung to Sacrecour coattails for centuries. House Fasterius, House Lovarius, House Bramachius and all the others who had fled Pallas for their provincial holdings six years ago when the Corani took power. Now they haunted Dupenium, whining about the tyranny of the empress, when they weren't deriding her ineffectuality. But the dwyma storm had added a new factor: fear of what a heretical dwymancer could do. They'd begun to wonder if they'd lost Pallas for ever.

And I must convince them to gamble all on another march, Ostevan fumed silently.

It wasn't going well. For almost an hour the discussion had been all about how they couldn't afford another disaster. The mage-nobles were frightened and the much-vaunted Keepers had been silent throughout – but then, they'd mostly been reduced by age and attrition to dotards drooling into their laps.

'We don't need to march,' quavered old Lady Violetta Molt, dowager of a Fauvion line that owned half of western Brevis. 'The secession will break her: she'll flee any day now.'

There were too many nodding heads whenever 'do nothing' was suggested.

'No,' Ostevan snapped, ignoring the daemon wrapped around his heart suggesting a number of violent punishments for the old biddy and her timid cronies. 'If we don't force Lyra's hand, she'll find someone to prop her up. My spies say her ambassador is meeting privately with the Duke of Argundy. We're going to end up with an Argundian emperor if we don't act now!'

This was in fact true: Lyra appeared to be playing on her Argundian kinship, whoring herself to the Borodiums, in a desperate ploy for survival.

'If she marries an Argundian swine, her own people will desert her,' Lady Violetta sneered.

'By then there'll be Argundian legions in Pallas,' Ostevan retorted. 'You have until the first of Martrois: twenty days. There's barely time to reach Pallas as it is, unless you march – or rather, sail down the Bruin – right now. Duke Garod, you *must* seize this moment: Pallas will never be weaker than it is right now. The Corani are divided, half the city is in revolt and even if Lyra agrees a royal wedding to secure allies, they'll be too far away to intervene.'

Garod shifted uncomfortably on his bony behind. 'But last time, she buried the best part of eight legions with heretical magic – but has anyone put the bitch on trial? You issued your Pontifical Ban, so there should be a Holy Crusade against her, but no one heeds you. And *no one* wants to march into the teeth of another dwyma storm.'

She's says you're the daemon-possessed murderer behind Reeker Night, Garod's eyes added.

Ostevan leaned forward. 'What if I can guarantee you'll face no such thing?'

The duke's eye narrowed. 'Guarantee? How can you?'

In response, Ostevan turned to the last Keeper who truly looked the part. 'Margentius, your views?'

Standing erect, shaven-skulled to conceal the grey, he peered around with a reptilian stare, his hooded eyes alert. 'When the heretic queen's dwyma storm broke last year, we could do nothing: we were unaware her power was even being exerted, much less able to counter it with Air-gnosis. However, thanks to the Pontifex, we have discovered an answer. A dwymancer's *blood* can be used as a bridge to attune our gnosis and counter their magic.'

The room fell silent as everyone contemplated that. Everyone here was a mage, most of them pure-bloods, though few were as skilled as Margentius Keeper. And none of them had direct experience of a dwymancer. 'How came you by this knowledge?' Arn Regor, Earl of Brevis, asked sharply.

The truth was that Naxius had made the discovery, but Ostevan wasn't about the share that. 'Old Church records I saved from the sacking of the Celestium,' he lied.

'But there've been no dwymancers for five centuries,' Lady Violetta protested. 'There's only Lyra . . . isn't there?'

'I know of one,' Ostevan announced, 'and I have men ready to seize them.'

'Who?' Garod demanded.

'The name doesn't matter,' Ostevan replied. 'Indeed, it's best not to know.'

'If there's another of these murdering heretics in reach, I want to know who the Hel he is,' Brylion spat. 'I'll rip their accursed heart out!' That was the knight, not the daemon speaking.

'I will identify them in due course,' Ostevan replied. Right now it was only an educated guess; he might still be wrong.

Garod drummed his fingers on the armrest of his throne, his expression sour, but he capitulated. 'Very well. But you will bring them to me. I want to look the evil bastard in the eye.'

Ostevan smiled inwardly, then sent a signal, mind to mind, to one of his possessed men half a mile away. <*Take her.*> Then he turned back to Garod. 'So, Milord, you will sanction the march?'

The duke considered. The risks were horrible, putting his men out in the elements again, gambling that the Keepers were right and they could counter a power that had so recently devastated his forces. It was conceivable that the Sacrecour dynasty might not survive another such disaster.

For all Garod was cautious, he was also willing to sacrifice everyone – except himself – for wealth and power. It wasn't in his nature to slowly rebuild: he wanted the glory of restoration to be his alone.

'I will not be remembered as the man who let opportunity slip him by,' Garod announced decisively. 'We march.'

Driven by vanity, he gambles all, Ostevan mused, as the others praised Garod's boldness while exchanging fearful glances. *Including the lives of everyone here. Anyone would think I'd infected him . . .*

The matter resolved, Ostevan departed, letting the duke and his cronies get on with drinking and boasting. His suspected dwymancer was close by and he wanted to secure her swiftly. As he left, he glanced at young Prince Cordan, who was looking anxiously around, also eager to be gone.

To be with his sister – the potential dwymancer in question.

Cordan also suspects what she is, Ostevan mused, *and yet he says nothing – he's no more to be trusted than she is. A traitor to his own cause. Interesting.* But he put that aside for another time and hurried on, eager for his prey.

The wind howling in the eaves and over the toothy battlements reminded twelve year-old Princess Coramore of daemon voices, making her shiver. She had announced she was sick, but that was just a ruse to keep the unwanted from her rooms. She had three maidens with her, girls her own age from noble families, playing a boring childish dice game, but any company at all was better than being alone, waiting in dread for Ostevan to make his move.

'Three sixes,' Lydia Molt shrieked. 'I win again! I win!'

Coramore suspected Lydia, the only one of them with the gnosis so far, was using kinesis to nudge the dice. Pietrice Banner and Gela Solston's faces crumpled in disappointment, but Coramore didn't care. She clapped her hands gracefully and called for more juice and honey-cakes, then went to the tiny garderobe, shivering at the thought of having to endure the cold air blasting up the hole, freezing her behind as she peed.

Tap, tap, tap. Someone or something struck the small shutter behind her head. It wasn't the wind.

She rose, dropped her skirts and peered down the foetid hole to see the distant glow of daylight shining from below. Cautiously, she pulled the little lever on the shutters, cracking a layer of ice, and let in a little light – and a lot of frigid air – into the confined room.

The black outline of a raven was silhouetted against the pallid light of the winter sky, its eye pressed to one of the cracks. It cawed harshly and while Coramore had no gnosis and knew nothing of birds, she understood instantly.

The raven came from Aradea, the Fey Queen, and it was telling her to run.

Now.

2

His Master's Voice

A Tree of Life

The early dwymancers spoke of a Tree of Life, termed 'Elétfa', a word of Sydian
extraction. The tree signified the cyclical nature of life. The curious thing is that it is
exactly the same motif as that used by the pagan Sollan drui, who predated the
dwymancers by centuries. Did the dwymancers adopt that symbol consciously, or
more intriguingly, is this heresy older than we suspect?

YROL DAISH, ORDO COSTRUO ARCANUM, PONTUS 653

Freihaafen, Upper Osiapa Valley, Mollachia
Febreux 936

Kyrik Sarkany paused outside the cave, looked up at the morning sky,
pale and cloudy through the ice-crusted pines, then called, 'Ogre? Are
you here?'

The cavern, a natural formation, was half a mile from the main settle-
ment in the hidden valley of Freihaafen, alongside a stream that ran
from the enclosing mountains and drained into the lake. Kip's settlers
called the place 'Nebbelwasser', which translated as 'Foggy Falls', because
of the way boiling hot springs caused the stream to run through the pine
trees like a trail of smoke. The cave had a warm, ripe smell to it.

A deep mournful voice answered from within, 'Ogre is here.'

Kyrik followed a slushy trail of mud into the poorly lit cavern.
Brighter light ahead led to a second cavern illuminated by four gnosis
orbs hanging like small suns from the stalactites.

Inside was a massive figure, over seven foot tall. His limbs were thick as two men's, his chest and belly heavy, his skin a dirty khaki colour, his long black hair thin and straggling. He looked like a monster from a child's tale, but he was a construct, made by a mage from human and animal elements. He wore just a loincloth and a crudely made leather jerkin. A massive sledgehammer was propped against the wall.

Ogre was no simple brute, though, and the task he was engaged in underlined that. He had a big leather-bound book in his left hand and in his right, a stick glowing with gnostic energy that he was using to patiently etch letters and runes onto a smoothed section of wall. All the cavern walls were covered in such markings.

'How do you fare?' Kyrik asked.

Ogre frowned, studying his handiwork, his heavy brows lowered over bright, alert eyes, barely acknowledging his guest. As king, Kyrik was entitled to greater respect, but he seldom stood on protocol and instead, patiently awaited a response.

Finally Ogre grunted, leaned forward and tentatively etched a letter 'r' beside a runic symbol. 'Maybe,' he muttered. 'But only maybe.' Only then did he remember to bow his head. 'Ogre welcomes Kirol Kyrik.'

For a few moments they took the measure of one another. Ogre's red-rimmed eyes had dark bags beneath. He'd probably been up all night again, immersed in his arcane task.

'I've brought you breakfast,' Kyrik said, placing a basket containing bread, cheese and relish onto a rock.

'Is it morning?' The construct yawned apologetically. 'Ogre thanks you.' The construct was generally polite, when he wasn't distracted.

Kyrik studied the wall blankly. 'Have you made progress?'

'Ogre believes so, but it is slow. This is written in no known language.' He brandished the book: the *Daemonicon di Naxius*. Ervyn Naxius was a rogue mage, a former member of the peaceful Ordo Costruo who'd become what Kyrik could only think of as *evil*. He'd infected certain magi with daemonic ichor, allowing malevolent spirits to possess them, to further his obscure ambitions. All the evidence suggested it was he who was behind the troubles besetting Kyrik's kingdom too.

But Naxius was also Ogre's maker. In most places just being an intelligent construct would have been enough to see Ogre condemned to death, but Kyrik had always believed in taking a person as they came – even if Ogre challenged the notion that *person* meant *human*.

A *daemonicon* was a wizard's record of their dealings with the spirit world, but Naxius' book was filled with unintelligible gibberish in a script Kyrik had never seen before. But Ogre had been Naxius' servant . . .

'So did Naxius invent his own language?' Kyrik asked.

'He invented several, and taught them to me when I served him,' Ogre rumbled, staring at the branched lines of symbols etched on the walls. 'But he never anticipated losing me, nor that I'd ever get to see this book.'

Every time Kyrik spoke to Ogre, the construct revealed a fierce intellect caught in an outsized, outlandish frame. And tellingly, he was starting to use 'I' and 'me' more frequently, as if growing into his own identity.

'So you can read it?' Kyrik asked, intrigued. *What might the mind of this man Naxius reveal?*

'Eventually. But the script isn't one he showed me, which means I must first solve the encryption.'

'So these symbols could mean anything?'

'Yes and no. Ogre believes the Master would want to read such a thing freely, without recourse to other documents and deciphering, so these must be real words. I'm trying to match symbols to sounds; only then will Ogre be able to decipher the words and seek their meaning.' Ogre yawned heavily, his lugubrious face shifting from concentration to his more habitual expression of residual sadness. 'Is there news?'

'A little. Our scouts report that Asiv Fariddan has been seen with the Rondian legion in Lapisz – they were deferring to him, so I assume he's infected them with this daemon ichor too.' Kyrik tapped his sword hilt. 'At least our blades are now either argenstael or silver-dipped. We have a fighting chance.'

'Does your wife improve?' Ogre asked, breaking off some bread and dipping it in the relish.

'No,' Kyrik replied sadly. 'Hajya is still possessed by the ichor. She spouts gibberish, she can't eat anything but raw meat, she flinches from silver and sunlight and suffers nightmares and waking horrors.'

He hung his head. 'All I can do is keep her in the dark and give her what she needs.'

Ogre's big ugly face turned anxious. 'No, Kirol Kyrik, that is the *wrong* thing to do. Darkness, bloody meat – these are things the daemon *wants*. You must deprive it, to weaken it and drive it out.'

'I'm trying – I've used wizardry-gnosis but nothing can drive the daemon out. It's tied to her blood, somehow. And I can't starve her – it'll kill her.'

'You must purify her blood,' Ogre insisted. 'I saw such things in my Master's service – you must starve the daemon. Make her sit in sunlight, give her only water and vegetables. Weaken the daemon so that her body can fight it.'

Kyrik shuddered at the thought. 'She's my *wife*, Ogre: when she screams, my soul is lacerated. The whole of Freihaafen suffers when they hear her cries. They already think me cruel for not simply putting an end to her.'

'No, you must not do that: that would give her to the daemon for eternity.' Ogre's big hand gripped Kyrik's arm. 'You must endure it, as she does. Take her away from your people so they are not distressed and do what must be done, for her sake. That is my counsel.'

'I'll consider it,' Kyrik said finally, looking up at his strange companion. It was unsettling, to feel so small when he himself was a big man, but Kyrik liked Ogre; he'd been visiting him regularly since his arrival here in Freihaafen. 'You shouldn't isolate yourself, Ogre. You're welcome in the village, you know that.' He grinned. 'Hel, you're not even our strangest construct.'

Ogre smiled, then his face reverted to sadness. 'Ogre must be here, to concentrate. At your village, he is a stranger. Your men and Mantauri try to learn him, but Ogre must solve this riddle.' He tapped the book. 'The Master lies behind all this.'

'What does Naxius want?'

'Immortality, omnipotence, dominion: these are the dreams he spoke of to me. And revenge on the Ordo Costruo, for casting him out. He once said that only in vast experiments can the keys to true knowledge be unlocked. A dozen subjects, a hundred, even a thousand were not enough. He wants to make all of Creation his laboratory.'

Kyrik simply couldn't comprehend such a desire. 'But people are more than just . . . subjects for experimentation.'

'Not to the Master.'

Dear Kore, is that who we truly fight? He must *be stopped.*

They sat in silence for a time while Kyrik studied the marks on the walls without comprehension and Ogre munched on the food.

Finally the construct asked, 'Is there news of your brother?'

Kyrik's brother Valdyr hadn't been seen since he'd vanished inside Cuz Sarkan, the volcano in the mountains east of Mollachia. Waqar Mubarak had said something about Valdyr ascending a Tree of Light, that he was 'inside the dwyma', whatever that meant. To Kyrik it made as little sense as the marks on the cave wall. 'No news yet. He's been gone almost two weeks now, so unless wherever he is has water, he's dead.'

More likely he simply fell into the lava pit . . .

'Have faith. He will return,' Ogre said. They fell silent again, then he added, 'And the war?'

News of Waqar and Tarita, in other words. Ogre never used the young Merozain woman's name, Kyrik noticed, but he clearly pined for her; he might be surprisingly intelligent, but he couldn't hide his emotions. *He's in love with her, but she's gone away with a prince of Kesh. The world's opening up for her, but his is closing in.*

'Nothing. I'm sorry.' Abruptly Kyrik rose, because time was passing, and he had much to do. 'I must return to the village – we're holding a meeting this afternoon. We must decide whether to remain here in hiding, or emerge to protect Hegikaro and provide a rallying point for my people.'

Ogre nodded distractedly, his mind already returning to the puzzle of the book.

'I'd like you to attend, Ogre. Your voice should be heard.'

The big construct shook his head. 'Ogre is not used to people.' He stroked the leather cover of the *Daemonicon* dourly. 'Ogre was made to be alone.'

Ogre wasn't really alone, though.

The Master never lets me be.

Naxius was with him, even here – not in any tangible sense, but reading the *Daemonicon* took Ogre back to his old life. Every passage resonated with Naxius' dry rattle of scorn.

Ogre had first woken to a fully formed body with residual knowledge of certain things, like the nature of stone, fire and water. He'd understood words in a language he later found to be Dhassan, but had swiftly been taught to speak Rondian by the only other being he knew: the Master, Ervyn Naxius, a small, bald, wizened man with a faint lisp and an arch, knowing cruelty. Naxius mocked, Naxius chided, Naxius was bitter, but he was the *Master*, and although dwarfed by his creation, he could flatten Ogre with a hand-gesture.

The Master was a harsh, impatient teacher, as Ogre quickly learned. Pain sharpened the mind, but Ogre had a burning need to prove himself worthy anyway, so he endured the savage punishments, the marathon trials of memory and the vicious tests of logic. Naxius was fond of setting him deadly tests, like learning to brew the remedy to a poison he'd already been infected with. Ogre survived, and learned voraciously.

At night, his master's voice rattled through his dreams, and when he unlocked a word in the *Daemonicon*, it was Naxius' voice he heard in his head, praising and mocking in the same breath. *Well done, Brute, but you're barely scratching the surface.*

So when he heard his Master's voice in the aether, he barely knew if he was awake or asleep on his feet.

Ogre? Ogre . . . I know you can hear me, my child . . .

It was some hours after Kyrik had departed. The food was gone and Ogre's stomach was rumbling – so surely he was awake. He looked up fearfully at the stone ceiling. Could scrying penetrate stone so deep?

My wayward, homeless child, the voice went on, *lost in the great world. Adrift. Unloved . . . I sent Semakha back to you, Ogre, as I promised I would – but what did you do to her? Did you know I was there, watching from inside her skull as she choked and drowned? You ungrateful animal . . .*

'You sent me back a monster,' Ogre retorted, his voice booming in the dimly lit cave. But even in his distress he wasn't so foolish as to reply with the gnosis and give Naxius a thread to follow back to his refuge.

Were you jealous, Ogre, that I made Semakha better than you? Is that what it was? Or are you so faithless that you abandoned her in your heart? The dark voice chuckled. *Do you really think the Merozain would have you? A great ugly lumpen beast like you?*

Ogre groaned. 'No, Master. I know she's not for me . . .'

Ogre's head had been telling his heart so for weeks, although his heart wouldn't listen.

Naxius' voice rasped inside his brain, in the declamatory tones of his lectures. *You have a choice in life, Ogre. Accept your station and what you are: an animated piece of offal and offcuts from better creatures – or you can use all you are to rise up. Is that not what I taught you?*

Ogre closed his eyes, closed his mind, but the voice went on, *I was just a drifter when I fell in with Corin and his devotees. And now look at me: deathless, all-powerful, because I forsook all emotion except ambition. Morality is an illusion, Ogre: one must take from others to rise above them. Predators feast on prey – that is the lesson of nature: I learned and I prevailed.*

Ogre refused to respond. Only a fool tried to outwit the Master. Even so he had to clench his whole body up to ignore those all-knowing, malevolent tones, his every muscle twitching at the edge of response.

But Naxius wasn't done yet. *These are the Last Days, Ogre,* he went on. *When they're done, it is I who shall inherit Urte. Reach out to me, my creature, and I may still let you share in my ascension to godhood.*

'No, Master,' Ogre whispered, for his own sake, still careful not to speak with his mind into the aether.

Are you going to accept life's beatings, Ogre, or are you going to rise up and take whatever you want? I made you strong, my child: I gave you a brain and I moulded it. I made you what you are, and your place is by my side. You slew Semakha – now return to me and take her place. I'll even give you the little Merozain as a reward.

'Do not speak of her,' Ogre roared, his sudden outburst resounding through the cavern.

A sudden burst of laughter filled the air. *So you are listening, Ogre. Listen, my child, I—*

In utter dread, Ogre threw up the most wards he could and the voice was cut off.

But he knew that the Master was hunting him and the walls of the cave no longer felt like stone but as thin as the parchment in the book he laboured over.

'My love?' Kyrik called tentatively.

The bowed figure wrapped in blankets hunched deeper into her covers, her greasy grey-black curls shrouding her face. She was shaking with the sobs coming from deep within her chest. The small hut stank of human waste and vomit and the walls were covered with drying splatters of fluids and food.

Unthinkingly, he reached to comfort her.

In a flash, she erupted from the blankets, her mouth widening as her teeth sought his arm, her black eyes gleaming. But the chains around her neck, wrists and ankles wrenched her backwards. She yowled in frustrated hate and spat black gobbets of fluid at him. He had discovered they were harmless unless they were ingested, or got in a wound or an eye, but he was careful to quickly wipe them away. They stank of clotted blood and decay.

His heart thudding, Kyrik castigated himself for the stupid lapse. 'Hajya,' he breathed, staring helplessly at his wife.

She shuddered, then her eyes cleared, and she seemed to see him. 'Kyrik? Kyrik?' She burst into tears.

He ached to gather her into his arms, but instead he reached out with mysticism into the turmoil that was her crowded mind and snuffed the candle of awareness. She fell into an unconscious trance.

Then he gagged her, because the daemon was sometimes strong enough to break his control and rouse her, before unlocking the chains from the hooks and carrying her out into the light. She was lighter than ever, just skin and bone, and covered in sores. It was all he could do to keep his gorge down at the reek of her clothes and body.

The small group waiting outside sucked in their breath when they saw her. The big Schlessen Fridryk Kippenegger hugged his wife Sabina, while the hunter Rothgar Baredge and the Sydian mage Korznici stared silently. Behind them, the tower of horned hide and muscle that was Maegogh, chieftain of the Mantauri, watched with guarded eyes.

'Pater Sol, she's wasting away,' Rothgar breathed.

'That's why I have to try something else,' Kyrik replied. 'Locking her up in the dark isn't working.'

They all looked doubtful, for they had all seen what Hajya was like when exposed to light. Even now, unconscious, she was twitching at the thin sunlight penetrating the clouds.

'It could kill her,' Korznici said; the young woman could be unthinkingly blunt at times.

'She can't go on as she is,' Kyrik replied. 'I can't bear it.' He'd decided that Ogre might be right. At least, it was worth a try. 'I'm going to try sunlight and wholesome, living foods.'

'Then let me help,' Korznici said decisively.

'Thank you,' he said. He carried Hajya to a small handcart and loaded her onto it, then wheeled it around the shore of the lake. The ground was covered in several inches of snow, which softened the journey. The day was cold, the skies grey; the sunlight would be fleeting, even without the ramparts of mountains surrounding Freihaafen, which would cast them into shadow within an hour or two.

Kyrik led his little group into the pines where Valdyr had built a small lean-to to use when communing with the dwyma. They settled Hajya on the ground, then Kyrik built up a fire, while Korznici removed the gag and managed to get some water down the sleeping woman, before gagging her again.

'I hate to see her this way,' she said. 'She raised me like a mother among the Sfera.'

'Then let's do what we can.'

They steeled themselves and started removing Hajya's clothes. Her veins were as mottled as ever, thick with daemonic ichor, and even the weak sunlight barely penetrating the clouds began to raise welts on her skin. Hajya moaned in her gnostic sleep.

Kyrik and Korznici undressed too, then he scooped up his wife and carried her down to the water, the Sydian girl following with a cake of soap and a cleaning cloth. There was a hot water vent near the bank which allowed the heated gases to bubble up through the bottom of the lake. The wonderfully warm water was soothing to his tense muscles, but Kyrik barely noticed, so anxious was he for his wife.

Together, they washed Hajya, hanging unmoving but pliant in Kyrik's arms, first cleaning her skin, then lathering her hair – until suddenly the daemon broke through Kyrik's spell and her eyes flashed open, revealing jet-black orbs. She thrashed about in his grip, trying to bite his throat through the gag. Her arms flailed, her nails raking as she sought to free herself, but with kinesis and muscle, he thwarted her until after a few minutes of heartrending struggle, she subsided. Her eyes cleared to brown, tears streaming from them.

Through his own blurred vision Kyrik sent soothing emotion into her mind. The daemon had once again receded, but of his wife there was also little, for she'd retreated deep inside herself, but at least she was pliant again.

Kyrik and Korznici finished washing her, then took her back to the bank where they dried her and laid her on the blankets, naked to the skies, next to the fire. Then they dressed themselves, suddenly shy of each other, and began preparing the meal. Afternoon was waning and they'd lose the sun soon.

'She needs as much direct sunlight as possible,' he remarked, 'and no meat.'

'So the opposite of what we've been doing,' Korznici noted.

'It's Ogre's idea,' Kyrik admitted.

'Ah. He is wise, this Ogre?'

'I think so.'

Korznici frowned thoughtfully. 'He has the gnosis, yes? And he is partly man?'

Ogre was still something of an enigma in Freihaafen: he'd been rescued from Asiv two weeks ago, but had immediately retreated to the cave. He'd met very few people and rumours were clearly running rampant.

'More than the Mantauri, certainly,' Kyrik replied. 'But I'm no animage.'

Korznici had been there when Ogre and Hajya had been recovered. 'What's his connection to the ogress we fought beside the lake?'

'Her name was Semakha and she was made by the same man who made Ogre, a renegade Ordo Costruo mage named Ervyn Naxius. Ogre believes Naxius is the master of Asiv Fariddan and all our enemies.'

Korznici looked startled. 'But this Ogre can be trusted?'

It was a good question, but Tarita had believed so, and Kyrik had been impressed by the Merozain. Waqar and Jehana Mubarak had also appeared – cautiously – to regard Ogre as true. 'I've spoken to Ogre about his former master: I believe he fears him, but I see no sign of any residual allegiance.'

Korznici said slowly, 'Then I hope that you're a good judge.'

Just then Hajya made a snarling noise behind the gag and they both turned, startled, to see her eyes were once again jet-black and her face a rictus of mockery and malice.

Kyrik shuddered, shared a look with Korznici, then reached out cautiously and holding Hajya's skull in a kinesis grip so she couldn't lunge at him, pulled down the gag.

'Kirol Kyrik,' someone drawled in Rondian. 'Asiv and Dragan have told us all about you.' Her eyes trailed to Korznici. 'Lined up a replacement for your wife already, have you?'

'Who are you?' Kyrik demanded.

'The one who will eat your soul,' the daemon snickered. 'You'd do better to murder that construct creature, Kirol. The Master owns Ogre and will reclaim him in time.'

Daemons lie, Kyrik thought: it was the first thing every young wizard was told. *But he knows that Ogre is here* . . . 'We know your weaknesses, daemon. Best you tell Asiv to run.'

The daemon spat black ichor at him, which he swatted aside with kinesis. 'Asiv is hunting you right now, fool.' Then Hajya's eyes lifted and she scanned the darkening valley. 'Where are we? What place is this?'

Kyrik immediately slammed a hand over Hajya's eyes and pulsed darkness into her, blinding her. The daemon shrieked and snapped her teeth, but Kyrik was already conjuring mystic-gnosis, sending her back into oblivion.

He took a deep breath. *Dear Kore, dear Ahm, how will I endure this?*

Tentatively, Korznici laid a hand on his shoulder, but he brushed it away angrily. 'She's *my wife*, damn it!'

The young Sydian flinched. 'Nothing was offered but comfort.'

He winced, immediately despising himself. 'I'm sorry,' he told her. 'I just . . . I'm sorry.' He looked away across the lake, not wanting to see what his Hajya had become, nor to see the calm, self-possessed young woman beside him who had told him so many times that he should be doing his best to beget children on her and the other Sydian women, to strengthen the mage-blood of the Sfera, the clan's magi.

She doesn't know I can't father children anyway . . .

'I must soon return to my people in the Tuzvolg,' Korznici said, after a few minutes. 'They have culled the herd to survive, but the pastures are now thin and they must soon move. Unless you know of more highland pasture, that means entering the lower valley, risking Asiv Fariddan's possessed men.'

'Rothgar knows Mollachia well. He can guide your people to pasture to see them through until spring.'

'You're determined to throw us together,' Korznici observed drily.

'It's not such a bad match,' he observed.

Her face wrinkled into a pout. 'I have let him know that he is desirable to me, but my womb is for begetting magi – and as a Sfera mage, I am forbidden to wed. He has let me know that he finds me desirable also, but will not sleep with a woman who is not his wife, nor share my womb with another man. So no, it is not a "match".'

'You're not in the plains any more,' Kyrik told her. 'This is Mollachia, where people may marry for love.'

'A foolish tradition,' Korznici – all of nineteen – said gravely. 'This place is more dangerous than all the plains, so Clan Vlpa must rebuild her strength in war and the gnosis.'

He couldn't really argue with that. 'I just want to see someone I like happy.'

She sniffed in amusement. 'Kip and Sabina are happy, like frolicking otters in mating season.'

He laughed. 'Maybe not quite how I think of them, but yes.'

'Happiness comes in many forms, and not always through mating,'

Korznici went on severely. 'For you, happiness will come when your wife is restored and your brother returns. I pray to the Great Stallion that these things will come to pass.'

Kyrik had been trying not to think about Valdyr.

Where are you, brother? Are you lost in this 'dwyma', in this Tree of Light? Or are you burned to ash?

Where am I? Valdyr Sarkany wondered as he climbed. *Is this even my own body?* Perhaps his physical form was still inside the volcano's peak, or maybe it had fallen and been consumed by the lava pit and he was now a ghost in the Elétfa. He'd seen Gricoama fall and yet the wolf was beside him on this strange journey. Perhaps the same had happened to him?

But some things were becoming clear. The distant cold ball of light that arced overhead on a regular course was the Sun, but it was travelling much faster than normal – or he was travelling much more slowly. And the volcano was gone. There was just this immense stairway, which sometimes resembled stone and other times wood or even dark ice, winding up an equally immense cylinder of rock or wood or water or fire. At times, branches led away into the void, but so far, he'd shunned these. They'd encountered no perils, and as yet, hunger and thirst had not troubled them, but he sensed they soon would. Time might be passing oddly, but it was still passing and it had been some time since they had finished the last of the water and rations. The Tree spread above him, climbing on upwards into eternity, always subtly in motion, ever changing, like the light. Far above hung golden orbs like fruit, glowing distantly, calling him on.

Mostly, the Elétfa appeared to be a vast tree with heavily entwined branches and roots, but at other times it was a heart and arteries, or clouds above an ocean, exchanging droplets of rain and rising vapours in gravity-defying rivers, but always it was a closed system, spinning in the void: an embodiment of the dwyma, the cycle of life. It sang, a chiming note that reverberated through him and filled his nostrils with rich, wholesome air. Despite the strangeness, he felt safe.

'Come, Brother Wolf,' he said. 'Another hour.'

Gricoama grumbled, but bounded on at his side, bright-eyed as a young dog.

Gradually, though, the lack of sustenance overtook him and he stumbled dizzily on a step, his aching muscles suddenly too weak to lift him. He might have slipped off the edge, had not Gricoama seized his arm in his jaws and pulled him back. That shocked him, because he hadn't realised his peril. For a time he just knelt and hugged the great wolf.

'That was a near thing,' he confessed shakily. 'Thank you, my friend.'

The wolf made a rumbling sound that struck Valdyr as both reassurance and warning.

'I know,' he agreed, 'I have to be careful. But I'm hungry, and we've seen nothing to eat or drink.'

The wolf whined unhappily. Valdyr stroked his back, trying to decide whether the respite of sleep – and the further hours without sustenance that would entail – would weaken or strengthen him. But when he tried to get up, he couldn't. Exhaustion had crept up on him, ambushing him, though he'd thought himself well enough to go on a bit further.

'Whoever drops first, the other has to eat them and go on,' he told Gricoama, then he chuckled uneasily. 'That was a joke: I don't taste good.'

I'll be the judge of that, the wolf's expression seemed to say – he at least looked to be in the fullness of health and not the slightest bit hungry. That reassured Valdyr – not that he'd been seriously afraid of his companion. And clearly he couldn't go on, so he just rolled onto his side on the stair and closed his eyes . . .

'Wake up,' a woman's voice called insistently. 'Wake up, Valdyr. You must get up.'

Blearily, he opened his eyes, or thought he did, but what he saw wasn't the tree: instead, he was on a well-remembered mountaintop: the camp on Watcher's Peak where he'd kept vigil with Luhti and learned of the dwyma. And here he was, sitting beside the fire-pit on his usual log beside the old woman, her grey hair blowing in the chill breeze and the flames guttering. But he could feel neither heat nor cold.

And Luhti was dead.

'I'm dreaming,' he said flatly.

'Are you?' Luhti asked. Her features smoothed and she became the younger woman he'd glimpsed before she died: golden hair, pale skin, a small nose and freckled face. North Rondian, perhaps, or Hollenian. Lanthea, her birth-name had been, he recalled, and she was one of the first great dwymancers.

'I must be,' he answered, looking round. The peak was clear, the skies studded with stars. Somewhere in the distance he heard a wolf howl and knew it was Gricoama, hunting. 'I'm in the Elétfa.'

'So you are,' she agreed, as he supposed a dream person would, seeing as his own mind had conjured her. 'Perhaps we're all a dream of the Elétfa?' she suggested.

'Then why did you wake me?' he asked.

I'm talking to my subconscious, he thought. *She's not really here.*

'You need to wake,' she replied. 'You're in danger. You need to eat and drink.'

Valdyr looked down at himself, seeing only his normal frame. 'It's only been a few days.'

'A body can't go without water for long,' Luhti replied sternly.

'But there's nothing here!'

'Does fruit grow on the trunk of a tree?'

He went to reply, then said, 'I suppose not.'

'The branches,' she said sternly.

He blinked and twisted and his eyes flew open. He was still lying on the stair where he'd fallen asleep.

Gricoama at the edge, staring out at the distant canopy of leaves and branches and the starry void beyond. He turned his head when Valdyr roused.

'The branches,' he breathed. 'We must take the next branch.'

He carefully got to his feet, feeling a little recovered but still perilously weak. He laid a hand on Gricoama's shoulder and they ascended slowly and carefully, each stair threatening to trip him, but within a few turns they were suddenly at the base of a branching path that twisted out into the darkness. The main stair still climbed upwards and he eyed it, wondering how far it would take to get wherever they were going, but this diversion was necessary, so they turned and took the unlit branch.

At first it was like walking on a stone bridge, or crossing a fallen log over a river, but then they were groping through mist until, abruptly, they were on a stony path. He stopped, clutched at Gricoama and turned. The way back was clearly visible, a hole in air that led to the stars. He stared at it fearfully, wondering whether, if he took another step, it might vanish, but moments passed and it didn't waver.

The path, now some kind of goat track, led down into a cutting. After building a small cairn marker, he warily took that path, wondering if all of this was part of the same dream, but the ground felt solid, the stones could be picked up and the vegetation was of a scrawny, desiccated type. A smoky smell of dung-fires and spiced gravy hung in the air, vaguely familiar, making Valdyr's stomach churn, and he realised how desperately hungry he was. Drawn inexorably by the rich aromas, he descended a long narrow cleft between two ridges to a flat piece of dry red dirt in front of a tiny mud-brick hut, a cylinder with a straw roof and a chimney, from which smoke rose, hanging thick and meaty in the air.

A goat and a cow roamed listlessly, both of them so skinny their ribs showed. Gricoama growled hungrily and both looked up. The goat bleated and backed up to the edge of the tether, while the cow lowed a warning.

'Don't come any closer!' a boyish voice called out in Keshi. 'I have a bow!'

Dear Kore, Valdyr thought, astounded, *I'm in Ahmedhassa.*

3

The Copperleaf Walls

A Just War

The concept of a 'just war' has troubled ethical philosophers since the first scholars of Lantris tried to interpret the will of their wayward, amoral gods. War by its nature is grisly, brings out the worst in most men and leaves generations of damage. It is argued that some people are so evil that if war is required to stop them, then that war is just. But one philosopher's tyrant is another scholar's strong and virtuous ruler.

ADONNA MYST, KEEPER, PALLAS 749

Norostein, Noros
Febreux 936

Drums boomed out, a rolling, hastening beat that filled the air until it throbbed. The richly turbaned caliph who entered the royal pavilion had to shout to make himself heard. 'Great Sultan, it is time.'

The warning was unnecessary: Xoredh Mubarak knew the hour. He was examining himself in a mirror that was propped amid a massive pile of captured coin, silk, jewellery and trinkets. *Perfect,* he decided: a true vision of majesty, fitting for a moment he'd been preparing for all his life, though it had been thrust on him sooner than he'd dreamed.

Who knew my father and elder brother would die in battle, within seconds of each other? Attam had made a habit of risking himself, but Rashid knew better. Soldiers fought, commanders directed and rulers simply observed, for they were too valuable to be risked.

The two great obstacles to my ascent removed and I didn't even have to do it myself.

As the drums subsided, Xoredh turned to the caliph. 'Do you believe in divine favour, Japheel?'

'I believe it shines upon you, Great Sultan,' the man replied, like a good courtier should.

I suppose I'll never hear another honest word, only praise and flattery, Xoredh mused. But it didn't trouble him: he liked flattery, and anyway, if he needed truth, he had the eyes of the daemon Abraxas, whose spawn was wrapped around his heart. That didn't overly trouble him either: only one thing mildly concerned him just now.

'Japheel,' he asked coolly, 'what of that matter I referred to last night?'

The caliph dropped to his knees. 'Forgive me, Great Sultan, but your cousin Prince Waqar is unable to be found.'

'Unable to be found'. Xoredh smiled at the expression, but not with pleasure. He'd been fasting and praying – or at least pretending to – when his cousin had returned from his hunt for his sister Jehana. Xoredh had despatched men to apprehend Waqar, but their quarry had vanished.

Did someone tip him off that his welcome would not be amiable? Though surely he could work that out himself? And where's Jehana? Do either of them now have this mysterious power, the dwyma?

'Find him, Japheel,' he growled, as the daemon snarled in displeasure.

The caliph flinched as if he'd heard some hint of that malevolent presence and planted his forehead on the carpeted ground. 'He shall be found, Great Sultan, I swear it.'

'You swear?' Xoredh enquired. *Why do so many men do that?*

Japheel immediately coloured. 'Er . . . ah . . . if he is to be found . . . if he's near here . . . if–'

'So you don't really *swear* at all?'

'But he . . . I–' The caliph buried his head again, now shaking, for Xoredh had a reputation. 'I will find him or die trying, Great Sultan!'

It's his own doing.

'I accept your sacrifice. Now, shall we get on with my coronation?'

He left the man grovelling and strode from the pavilion to the open ground outside. They were a mile from the walls of Norostein, for fear the Rondians might interfere in this holy moment. The date and time had been kept deliberately obscure and only the most senior of his nobles, commanders and clergy were permitted to attend. Those men – only males were allowed, of course – fell to their knees and touched their foreheads to the muddy ground in supplication as he appeared. Incense burned in censers swung by clergy, who softly hummed.

The ceremony was simple, for the Amteh was an austere religion at heart. As custom decreed, he came unarmed and unarmoured to kneel before the most senior of the Godspeakers, Ali Beyrami, an avid Shihadi. Beyrami recited from the *Kalistham* while anointing his hair with oil, before commencing the crowning.

'Are you Xoredh, offspring of the body and blood of Rashid Mubarak, Sultan of Kesh?'

'Ai.'

'Are you a devout son of Ahm, dedicated to his mission on Urte?'

'Ai.'

'What is a sultan?'

'The first servant of the people.'

'Do you pledge your life to that earthly role, confident in the heavenly reward of Ahm should you remain true?'

'I do.'

'Who is your Enemy?'

'Shaitan, and his spawn on Urte, cursed be their existence.'

'Do you pledge their destruction?'

'I do.'

Though a daemon is lodged against my heart and I serve a Rondian monster. The Last Days are upon us, Beyrami, but you are too blind to see it. Only the daemonic shall inherit the world.

'Then I crown you, Xoredh Mubarak, first of that name, second of the line of Mubarak, as Sultan of Kesh and paramount ruler of all Ahmedhassa. Take this crown, Great Sultan, and wear it to victory over Evil.'

Xoredh knelt a moment longer, savouring the moment.

Master, are you watching? I am now ruler of half the world.

Beyrami led Xoredh to his throne, where his father Rashid had sat, and he accepted the worship and oaths of his emirs, caliphs and senapatis. Finally he could really begin to rule.

He rose to his feet, took up the sacred royal scimitar and extended his right arm towards the walls of Norostein. 'There are our enemies. Tomorrow will be a day of celebration and rejoicing, so that the men may give thanks for my ascension to the throne. But the day after, let the assault recommence. The holy Shihad must be fulfilled.'

'Well, this's all very matey, innit?' Serjant Bowe remarked, dangling his feet over the Copperleaf walls and peering into the Lowertown tier, some fifty feet below. 'Look't all them Noories, just kinda noorying about, like.'

'Ain't right, seein' 'em in Yuros,' Harmon yawned, one foot on the wall, his forearm resting on his thigh. 'I reckon they should rukk off home, an' let us do the same. Apparently it's all kickin' off in Tockers right now.'

Vidran, the third of Pilus Lukaz's serjants, scratched his nose, a sure sign of mischief-making. 'Hey, Bowe, how come, of all the cohort what went over on the Third Crusade, you're the only one what din' come back with a wife?'

'Yeah, you one o' them race-hater pricks what won't marry a Noorie?' enquired Harmon slyly – his wife was a hard-faced Khotri woman who wore knives in her sash and had duelling scars.

'Nah, nuffink like that,' the ferret-faced Bowe said defensively. 'Jus' din' meet one I fancied.'

'Couldn't meet one he could catch in a foot-race, more like,' Vidran chuckled. 'He ain't run a woman down back 'ome either, fun'ly enough.'

'I'm savin' meself for the lady o' me dreams,' Bowe declared, hand on heart.

'Who's that, then?' Harmon sniffed. 'Lyra Vereinen? She's single again. Better be in quick.'

'Nay, I 'eard she only fancies priests,' Vidran chuckled.

'Leave the empress out of it,' Lukaz put in tersely, and the men fell silent again.

Seth Korion, listening nearby, smiled to himself. The banter of his cohort was one of life's few pleasures right now. He'd joined them on the wall to watch the city below, to try to read what was about to unfold.

The herald from Sultan-elect Xoredh Mubarak had requested a two-week truce, due to the loss of both Sultan Rashid and his first heir, his elder son Attam. Seth had been only too happy to grant the request, although he suspected the enemy needed it just as badly as they did. But the two weeks were almost up.

He'd had to settle refugees three families per house in Copperleaf and find them food, while buttressing the Copperleaf walls and blocking the aqueducts that fed Lowertown. After that he'd had to bed down new routines and get alongside the Imperial legionaries to remind them that loyalty to the empress was no longer their first rule. He'd also established an emergency ruling council and dealt with communications from Lord Sulpeter and from Pallas. It hadn't been dull, and sleep had been rare and precious, despite the lull in the fighting.

Interestingly, the contacts with Pallas had been contradictory: he had a congratulatory message from the empress urging him to fight on, while Sulpeter was still demanding that he present himself before a courts-martial. He'd kept the former and burned the latter.

Ramon Sensini had wanted to violate the truce and raid the Shihad – of course – but Seth had convinced him not to. The time they spent fortifying would repay them many times over, compared to the minimal gains of raiding and precipitating reprisals. And the men badly needed the respite, even if it was granting the enemy the same.

Abruptly, Vidran stiffened and peered below. They all followed his gaze and Seth saw a robed and head-scarfed woman scuttle to the well halfway down the alley below, a lock of blonde hair visible on her shoulder. 'Hey, lass,' Vidran called, 'come on up. We have magi here: we can 'elp ye climb.'

The woman paused, looking over her shoulder, and they saw that she was pregnant. 'You lot Northerners?' she called. 'You talk funny.'

'Says the rukkin' Southern yokel,' Bowe snorted.

'We're from Pallas, lass: Tockburn-on-Water,' Harmon called. 'Come on up.'

The girl laughed as a tall Keshi came round the corner and caught her around the waist from behind. He stroked her belly as she twisted her head and kissed him.

'See, I've got me a mage-born too, right 'ere,' the woman called back, patting her stomach and resting against the Easterner's chest. 'An' a palace in Noorieland waitin'. So thanks, lads, but I'm all right, jus' where I am.' She gave a cheeky wave and left, hand in hand with her man.

'Aw, that's jus' wrong,' Bowe complained.

'Yeah, Ahmedhassans comin' over 'ere, takin' our women,' drawled Harmon, fondling the wedding bracelet his Khotri wife had given him. 'What sorta fella does that?'

'Boot's on t'other foot, Bowe,' Vidran remarked. 'Jus' the way it is.' Vidran's wife was a small, plump Dhassan woman whose cooking was renowned.

Seth took pride in the fact that none of his veterans had abandoned their wives after the Crusade. Not all the marriages had turned out well, but he'd protected those women, even sending some home on traders' windships.

It's a big, ugly-lovely place, this mongrel world. so why do we fight all the time?

Scarcity was one reason. *There's plenty for all, but most of it's hoarded by the few. There's only enough food in this city for us or them, and we've likely got about half each.* The race-hate Vidran had spoken of was another reason. His veterans might be tolerant, but most Yurosi had never left their homelands and feared anything foreign – different skin colour, different features, languages, customs, religions. For every person prepared to live and let live, there were many more ready to lash out at the unknown.

Either way, Rashid's mourning will soon be over and we'll begin killing each other again.

A bird's cry carried on the breeze and he saw four of the giant Keshi eagles swooping towards Lowertown from the north. He admired the graceful descent, wishing he had a few such creatures himself to contest the skies in the days to come. Or even just to fly. They'd come in from due east, the coastal road up from Silacia. He hoped it was just a Keshi patrol, but worried that it presaged the end of this uneasy truce.

Norostein was a fortress-city, built beneath the alps in three semi-circular tiers. Below him was Lowertown, a mile-wide arc of packed housing and a lake fed by aqueducts, currently frozen solid, which he'd been forced to abandon after a month-long siege. The Shihad was now housed there and a haze of smoke rose from the countless cooking fires as the Eastern soldiers finally enjoyed proper shelter from the elements. How many had died in the cold, Seth couldn't guess, but they estimated three or four hundred thousand men were down there.

But what's their morale like now? They've lost Rashid, the genius who got them here. What's Xoredh like? Is he a general or a courtier-prince? Do his men revere him as they did his father? What's his mettle?

He turned his attention to the tier his own forces held. Unlike the homely sprawl of Lowertown, Copperleaf was narrow and maze-like, noted for its craftsmen and artisan traders, especially the metal-workers who'd given the place its name. The Copperleaf walls were higher than the outer walls, but only a third as long, and they were tightly packed with refugees from Lowertown and the rest of the kingdom. Two-thirds of the city were now sleeping cheek by jowl on the floors of warehouses and churches and living on rationed supplies. Sickness was sweeping in, although his healer-magi were labouring hard to prevent it spreading. The people were trapped and frightened and they were beginning to suspect what Seth already knew: that food supplies would last only a few more weeks.

During this truce, mass protests had been held outside the gates of Ringwald, the inner tier where Governor Rhys Myron still clung on, hoarding supplies and refusing to help the defence in any way – worse, he'd openly supported attempts to have Seth arrested, as well as undermining the defence by trying to blackmail Ramon. Not that the governor supported the Shihad: he just wanted the defence to fail so he could abandon his post and leave with his gold-laden windship fleet.

The moment the Shihad breach Copperleaf, Myron will be off.

Trying to storm Ringwald while defending Copperleaf was an impossibility, and declaring war on his own governor would be an act of high treason, so Seth had been forced to walk a fine line, allowing civilian protests beneath the walls of Ringwald, but unable to openly support them. The fact that his own family in Bricia was vulnerable if the empire moved against him was also making him anxious.

Just then there was a thunderous roll of drums from somewhere beyond the city walls. They all pricked up their ears, a few of the men making religious signs.

Pilus Lukaz looked at Seth enquiringly. 'What's that mean, sir?'

'It means this truce is just about done,' Seth guessed. 'I heard something similar when they crowned the new calipha in Khotri.' He turned to his aides. 'We're at war again – spread the word.'

He turned away, thinking, *This makes what Ramon's trying to do all the more vital.*

<Are you ready?> Vania di Aelno whispered into Ramon Sensini's mind. Something of her surroundings came with the sending: she was clad in nun's garb, sitting on someone's shoulders in the midst of a heaving throng of burghers punching the air in unison and chanting 'MYRON OUT, MYRON OUT' at the top of their voices.

<We're about to go in,> Ramon sent back. <Get yourself into Ringwald, Vee.>

<But this is such fun,> Vania protested. <I swear, when I'm done killing folk for money, I'm going to travel Yuros protesting against shitty governors for a living.>

Ramon laughed – he could well imagine Vania doing just that – but reiterated his order. Then he put the relay-stave aside and waved his people in. He'd assembled almost half his battle-magi for this task, a dozen experienced men and women, each carrying leather satchels as long as their bodies. Their mission: to get inside Ringwald unseen.

Ringwald had gnostically reinforced walls, wards on every battlement to detect even veiled magi and aerial wards as well. After several days studying the defences, he'd been forced to concede that *just possibly* this was a place he couldn't get his men into undetected.

Then he'd seen the obvious.

He straightened. 'Right, lads, ladies, it's time to go. Me first.'

'Are you sure?' cautious Tabia asked. 'You being the boss-man and valuable an' all?'

'Allegedly valuable,' the lanky Melicho grinned. The rest of the group smirked.

'I wouldn't trust any of you incompetents not to get lost halfway,' Ramon replied evenly.

'It's a tunnel,' Postyn noted. 'You can't get lost in a tunnel.'

'You lot could,' Ramon chuckled, 'and that's why I'm leading.'

'Why en't we going in at night?' bald Moxy wanted to know.

'Because what we're doing is noisy and nights are quiet. Remember, it's going to be cold, but you *must not* use the gnosis for heat: one, anyone nearby with magical senses may realise; two: you might melt the passage. Once we're in, make for the barracks – you know where it is. We're *infiltrating*, so be discreet, and take your time.'

With that, he turned and climbed up the ladder to where Melicho, an Earth-mage, had opened a hole in the side of one of the frozen aqueducts. Tabia, a Water-mage, had carved a tunnel into the frozen ice in the race.

Norostein lay on the slopes of Mount Fettelorn, built on either side of the Krystevoss River. It fell from the high alps in a torrential rush in spring and summer, but froze in the depths of winter. The river had been captured and tamed by a series of lochs and races that controlled the flow and supplied the city's drinking water. It also irrigated the surrounding countryside and fed the manmade Lowertown Lake, the canals and the moat. The aqueduct was normally highly dangerous; even a Water-mage attempting to wade up it would be immediately swept away – but now it was frozen solid and as far as Ramon could tell, Governor Myron hadn't bothered to place detection wards in the ice. For the last week he'd sent in Water-magi with labourers to slowly, carefully chip a tunnel through that ice, just large enough that men could crawl up and into Ringwald.

'Boss,' Melicho said, as he was about to enter, 'good luck.'

Ramon winked back. 'No farting in the tunnel, *amici* – we don't want a collapse.'

Always leave them laughing, he thought as he pushed his head into the hole and slithered inside.

The tunnel was narrow, but none of his men would be armoured in more than a leather jerkin and the surface was slick. They'd sanded the floor smooth and he was able to move comfortably, even pulling the leather satchel along with him. The first section was easy. They were still hundreds of yards and a full loch from the Ringwald walls. Although anyone on those walls could see down into the race, the ice was cloudy enough that the guards shouldn't see them below the surface – and hopefully, all the activity at the main gates was distracting them.

Ramon hauled himself up the gentle slope, unaffected by claustrophobia but shivering from the cold. Behind him he heard the next in line, Postyn, his best Water-mage, humming as he wriggled along.

<*Hush*,> he sent, <*we're nearly at the loch below the walls.*>

Postyn went quiet and Ramon gave himself over to the next task. The governor's guards were now only a dozen yards away and the ice was just a few feet thick here. He was in the lee of the loch gates, which weren't one solid barrier but had smaller sluice-gates built in below the waterline for controlled release of water during droughts. Ramon's magi had tampered with the cables controlling one portal, enabling it to be worked from the other side, and he slipped silently through, right under the walls, and paused, ready to enter the next race, which had only about six feet of ice in it. That would ordinarily have been too shallow to conceal them, but they'd contrived to spread a particular winter moss over the past few nights which had streaked the ice with green in a way that looked entirely natural – and made the ice fully opaque.

Let's see if the guards up there have been paying attention . . .

The slope made it harder, but he forced himself upwards towards the top, where the ice was thinner still, just a few inches thick. He could hear the protesting crowds again, dimly reverberating from a quarter of a mile away.

A voice just a few feet above suddenly made him freeze.

'All quiet here?' it asked.

'Yes, sir,' someone answered. Ramon heard a few more muttered words, complaints about the 'blasted mob' at the gates that made him grin, and then boots clip-clopped away. Someone sighed in relief, followed by the pop of a cork being removed from a flask.

With the smile still on his lips, Ramon slithered up and into the next section, a fifteen-foot-deep loch through which their tunnel continued, and into the race that led to the heart of Ringwald, away from the manned walls. He crawled on swiftly until he came to a public garden, their chosen exit point, although the watercourse continued through Ringwald to the mountains. They'd left the digging unfinished here, just a foot from the surface.

Now for the gamble . . .

With Ringwald under siege, there was no reason for anyone to be in this garden, but water and ice, like stone, inhibited scrying, so he'd just have to poke his head through and trust to luck. He was a Fire- and theurgy-mage, not a lot of use with elemental magic, except for burning things, so he called Postyn forward. He'd used his Water-gnosis to create a small burrow here, where two or three could work. Postyn was a stolid, surprisingly whimsical Midrean, his sunny face belying a dark history. He was also a careful man. He patiently shaved away the ice, layer after layer, as the next few magi arrived and waited silently in the tunnel. Moon-faced Tabia gave Ramon a small, anxious wave and he held up five fingers, his estimate of how many minutes before they went into action.

Those minutes took an eternity, but at last Postyn edged backwards. 'I left an inch to hide the digging, boss,' he whispered. 'Thought you might like to go first . . . an' get your head knocked off 'stead o' me.' He ran a hand over his tousled brown hair.

'Mercenaries,' Ramon sniffed. 'Most risk-averse people you'll meet.'

'The living ones are,' Postyn agreed.

Ramon eased past Postyn, then after listening hard, gently pushed, first poking a finger through, then his head. The ice cracked into shards that slipped down his neck.

'Hello,' said a voice, and he almost leaped ten feet in the air.

Then he realised it was a child's voice and he spun around, automatically fixing his most winsome smile to his face. 'Hello to you too,' he said brightly, his eyes fixing on a cherubic face. The little boy was maybe eight years old, with blond hair and cheeks flushed from the cold, framed by a rich fur cowl. He had mittens on, beautifully made, and he was leaning over the edge of the wall that separated the race from the gardens. Bare-branched trees hung overhead, but no other faces were peering into the iced-over channel.

'I thought you might be an otter,' the boy said. 'Sometimes they swim in the race. Otters are my favourite thing.' He peered at Ramon worriedly. 'Are you hunting otters?'

He's not going to be alone . . . And he's a local, a Noros boy . . .

'Not otters,' Ramon replied, improvising. 'I'm hunting the foxes that hunt otters.' He rose slowly to his feet, half out of the hole.

'Foxes!' the boy exclaimed. 'I *love* foxes. They're my favourite thing.'

Make up your mind, kid: foxes or otters?

'We don't hurt them,' Ramon reassured him, climbing out of the hole and staying low so that he was still below the race wall. 'We just trap them, then release them into the wild.' He showed the boy his tabard – one of the false uniforms he'd had some of his legion's camp-followers whip up. 'I'm with the Imperial Guard.'

'My father says the Imperial Guard are a bunch of lug-tuggers,' the boy said conspiratorially. 'Is that good?'

'It's very high praise,' Ramon replied, slithering across the frozen surface towards the boy, fixing him with a little mesmeric-gnosis to keep him from running, though the boy was showing no inclination to do so. 'You're brave to be out on your own on a cold day like this,' he remarked.

'Oh, I'm not alone,' the boy said. 'My nanny is with me.'

Just a nanny, Ramon thought, relieved.

'And my bodyguard. I think they're sweet on each other,' the boy said, in mystified tones.

Okay, not so good. But if I can't fool them, no one's going to be able to fool anyone today. Ramon stood, vaulted the wall and sat on it beside the boy. 'What's your name, young man?'

'Bestie. Well, Bestyr Dainsen, but everyone calls me Bestie.'

'I'm Rai,' Ramon said, shaking his hand solemnly while surveying the gardens. They were empty, but inside a small brick pavilion he could make out the silhouette of a person; or perhaps it was two, in a clinch. Surrounding the garden were brick walls studded with closed shutters. The noise of Vania's riots at the main gates echoed distantly.

<Postyn, move in one minute, but stay in the canal until I've resolved this,>

Ramon sent silently, while offering his hand to the boy. 'Let's go and see your nanny and guard, Bestie,' he suggested.

Bestie took his hand unhesitatingly and they walked to the pavilion along the icy path. They were almost there when two people came to the entrance, peering at him anxiously – a young man in a livery of blue and white quarters and a badge Ramon might have known if he'd bothered to learn heraldry, and a young woman with a cheery face, wearing a bonnet over somewhat mussed-up hair.

The young guard stepped forward, eyeing Ramon and opting for bravado. 'Here, what are you doing, Imperial?' He was wearing a periapt, which meant that Bestie's family was important.

'Bestie?' the young girl added anxiously.

'This is Rai,' Bestie said. 'He's my best friend in the whole world.'

Ramon squeezed his hand then let go. 'Go to your nanny, lad,' he told him, while he met the eyes of the guard. They all had Noros accents, and a light scan of their minds revealed no great love of the empire or Governor Myron, and therefore no liking for the uniform Ramon wore. 'You shouldn't let him near the canal unsupervised,' he told them. 'The ice will begin to break up again at some stage and the water will flow. The lad could be swept away.'

The observation immediately made the pair defensive, as he'd intended, making them forget their concerns about him. 'We were just about to collect him,' the young guard said, then his eyes focused more closely on Ramon and his uniform and his face turned puzzled. 'I thought I knew all the captains in the Governor's Guard,' he said. Then his eyes widened. 'You were presented at court, but you're not–'

His hand moved and Ramon reacted, gripping the man's wrist where Bestie and the nanny couldn't see. Gnostic energies flared, but Ramon was an Ascendant and his grip, physical and mental, locked the other man's body and mind instantly. 'Sorry,' he said. 'Are you one of Myron's friends?'

The young man's face was fearful, but to his credit he defiantly spat, 'Noros voor de vrei.'

Ramon knew enough of the local dialect to understand: *Noros for the free*, not something a wise man would say to an imperial captain. 'I share your sentiments,' he murmured, conscious of Bestie and the nanny watching anxiously, sensing the confrontation but not understanding it. 'What's your name?'

'Laryn Sturi. And you're Ramon Sens—'

'No, I'm Rai, an Imperial Guardsman,' Ramon told Laryn firmly. 'My advice is this: take Bestie and the young lady home. There's rumours of mutiny, and violence may break out.'

Laryn's eyes lit up. 'I'll get them home,' he promised, then he asked, 'Is there any way I can help?'

'No – just keep my new best friend in all the world safe,' Ramon told him.

They left, Ramon and Bestie exchanging energetic military salutes, then he returned to the canal to find a dozen of his battle-magi now pressed against the wall. 'About rukkin' time,' Melicho grumbled. 'It's freezing in here.'

'Then let's warm things up.' Ramon looked at Tabia, who was clearly the most nervous. 'Tabs, you're with me. The rest of you, in pairs, one minute apart. You know the route – don't improvise. I'll meet you at the back of the old barracks.' He settled his own satchel onto his shoulder, then gave Tabia a hand over the wall and the two of them set off as if they owned the streets. They met one patrol who saluted them and complained about the weather. The streets were all but empty and no one challenged them.

Everyone's at the gates, Ramon thought, relieved.

Their route took them past the broad plaza in front of the Governor's Mansion, where eight windships were moored, with crewmen swarming around them. The governor's wealth was already loaded, ready for immediate evacuation if Copperleaf's walls were breached.

The mansion itself was a multi-storeyed rectangular edifice that doubled as an administrative block and residence, much more luxurious than the Royal Palace, a dour old castle on a low rise overlooking Ringwald. Black flags still hung over the old fortress, mourning the death in battle of King Phyllios III of Noros two weeks ago. He'd died with no successor so what little powers were left to the Crown had legally devolved to Governor Myron.

Ramon nudged Tabia's shoulder. 'Only a dozen or so guards . . . the protests are working.'

'But we'll never get inside that mansion,' Tabia breathed. 'It's crawling with people.'

'Actually, I broke into it when I was a student mage here,' Ramon replied, smiling at the memory. 'But that governor wasn't at home at the time. Anyway, we don't have to get inside there today. Come on.'

They took to the backstreets again, making their way down silent snow-clogged streets winding between the high walls of rich men's houses, scrawling arrows in the snow every few turns, in case any of his people got lost. Inside five minutes they were loitering near the old Royal Palace, where a few sentries huddling in blankets were staring into space in a semi-doze.

'Are you sure the people you want are inside?' Tabia whispered.

'I'm sure. Relax, Tabs, it'll all be fine.'

Over the next few minutes, the rest of his team arrived, led by Postyn and Melicho. 'Some prick tried to order me to the main gate,' Melicho reported. 'He was only a bloody serjant. I flashed my periapt and he backed right off.'

Governor Myron had cultivated a regime of secrecy and favouritism, but that didn't always help security: left hands often didn't know what right hands were doing and people feared to ask questions. Ironically for someone who often dealt in secrets, Ramon found openness paid off.

Once his full group had arrived, he quickly reminded them of their roles, then turned to his smallest battle-mage, Jeno Commarys. The skinny, sour-faced woman unpacked a powerful shortbow from her satchel, strung it and tested the pull as the rest of them studied the building before them. The old Royal Palace had been converted to a barracks for the Royal Guard, which Myron had disbanded when King Phyllios died. Ramon had discovered that when the Royal Guards had refused to be stood down, they'd been stripped of arms and armour and locked up in their own barracks, pending trial on whatever trumped-up charges Myron was in the mood to level at them. Most were ordinary men, but the few magi among them had had their powers Chained.

'Right, lads,' Ramon told them, 'we can't get enough of our own men inside the walls to take on Myron, but in there are men enough for the job. Our task is to break them out on the quiet. Everyone ready?'

They growled assent. Ramon looked up at the sky: the clouds were heavy, but for now there was no rain or snow and the sun was glowing behind the dark shroud, low to the south and soon to be lost in the alpine peaks.

He was about to give the order to move when there came a massive rumble of drums: not from the main gates but further afield, down in Lowertown, where the Shihad were encamped.

'What's that?' Postyn wondered aloud, voicing the question on all their lips.

'That's the Noories up to something,' Ramon told them. 'I don't know what, but I take it as a sign that the truce is soon to end. So let's get on with this.' He patted Jeno on the shoulder. '*Amica*, we're in your hands.'

The drums were just a dim murmur inside the stone building where Waqar Mubarak was concealed in a cellar with the hatch covered in straw and an elephant sitting on top of that. But he heard them and pulled the flask of water from his lips.

'Hear that?' he said softly. 'They're crowning Xoredh right now.'

'Salim was anointed before all the people,' his companion replied bitterly. 'Even Rashid did so openly.'

'That's not Xoredh's way: he is treacherous, so he fears treachery.'

Waqar scratched at his beard: he'd always gone clean-shaven, but keeping up courtly appearance wasn't easy when hiding in a hole. He was clad in a boiled leather breastplate and greaves designed for flying. He didn't know the whereabouts of his roc, but he'd sent Ajniha a mental impulse to fly away and he hoped she'd obeyed. Since then he'd hidden here, because if Xoredh had the power of the daemon-possessed magi, he was truly to be feared.

'The drums signal the end of the mourning,' Waqar noted. 'The fighting will resume soon.'

His companion, Latif, nodded grimly. He'd once been a court impersonator of the late Sultan Salim Kabarakhi, whose murder had led to the ascension of the Mubaraks. Since then, Latif, his past unknown, had been living as an enslaved archer in an elephant crew. Right now, Waqar's life was in Latif's hands; it was he who'd warned him what Xoredh was.

Rashid allowed his second son to be possessed by a daemon, in exchange for the help of Ervyn Naxius to gain the throne and launch a Shihad against the West. I can still scarcely believe it.

'Will you be joining the assault?' Waqar asked.

'We've been told the elephants will be used for labouring tasks, not for the assault on the walls,' Latif replied. 'The inner walls guarding this "Copper Leaf" are too thick and high for elephants to make a difference. The army is building siege-towers and catapults; we're to be put to work moving those into position.'

'I hope you can stay safe,' Waqar said, his mind moving to his erstwhile companion. He'd left Tarita Alhani in the wilds outside the Shihad camp – was she safe? And he was still fretting over his sister, Jehana, abducted by one of Naxius' servants. He and Tarita had come south from Mollachia to find her; following their scried trail. If Latif was right about Xoredh, it stood to reason that his cousin now had Jehana. *I have to find her . . .*

Perhaps the resumption of warfare might present an opportunity. 'I need to get out of the city,' he told Latif. 'I have an accomplice waiting in the wild. We have a mission to perform.'

Latif surprised him by saying, 'You must be careful – if Xoredh has done this, he is an affront to Ahm. You must kill him and take the throne yourself.'

'But Teileman is the heir: he's Rashid's younger brother,' Waqar objected.

'No one believes in Teileman – not even Teileman.'

That's true enough.

'But for now, you must be invisible,' Latif went on. 'Xoredh will purge the leadership and he is already hunting you: one of his magi came through last night, asking if you'd been seen and offering a reward. He couched it as seeking a missing person, but it wasn't hard to see through.'

'Is the reward substantial?'

'Ai, but Ashmak swore he'd say nothing.'

'How well do you know Ashmak?'

'I've spoken to him. He knows better than to trust Xoredh.'

'I pray you're right, but it makes it even more urgent that I get out of the city.'

'Tomorrow there'll be a celebration for the crowning of the new sultan,' Latif predicted. 'Discipline will be lax: you can move then.'

Waqar bowed his head. 'Then let that be our plan.'

Rym, Rimoni

Jehana Mubarak drifted through memories, disconnected tableaus of past days, *remembering* . . .

. . . laughing with other girls over some silly game . . . hugging her mother the day she gained the gnosis . . . in the audience at a lecture by a senior mage at the Ordo Costruo Collegiate in Hebusalim, trying not to giggle at his lisp . . . With her brother Waqar in Halli'kut Palace, comforting him after a beating from Attam and Xoredh when they were all still children . . . *I remember* . . .

Her mother's waxen face, dead on a stone byre in Domus Costruo, awaiting interment in the Mausoleum. The eye of a giant water beast pressed to the glass at Sunset Tower. The pool at Epineo where the dwyma had opened up to her, only to be snatched away in a fountain of ripped flesh and blood. A masked ogre ripping her from the Elétfa inside the volcano Cuz Sarkan.

Where have I been? Where am I now?

It was those thoughts, and the sudden awareness of a body that was yearning for sustenance, that dragged her out of dreaming and back into life. She felt a cold hard surface pressing against her buttocks and back through thin cloth and dimly heard a distinct sound in the silence: the click of a door.

Her eyes flicked open and she could see, although her field of vision was restricted by eyeholes. She was wearing a mask, she realised with a start, and her hands flew to her face to feel a cold metal shape, smooth and shaped in some unguessed expression, covering her upper face. Tugging at it couldn't remove it, which was alarming enough for her to draw a sharp breath, roll onto her side and sit up.

She was in a hexagonal room without windows or natural light, just braziers that flickered with a gnostic light akin to fire, though this flame was bluish-purple. The walls were marble and the ceiling had a mosaic of a fish-tailed woman with pale skin.

She looked down at herself. She was barefoot, clad only in a light shift, and her body had a scented dampness that suggested that someone had bathed her whilst she was unconscious. That left her with a queasy feeling of violation, though she felt no evidence that she'd been abused. Then she noticed a mirror on the wall, went to it, stared – and stifled a sob.

Her long, thick cloud of black hair had turned from ebony to ivory. Her hands snatched at a tress and she jerked it to her eyes, in case the mirror lied, but it didn't – her hair had gone completely white. But her coppery skin was still taut, dewy and youthful, and the white hair didn't extend anywhere else, she discovered when she shyly lifted her shift. What it meant, she had no idea.

Her attention shifted to the mask, a skull the colour of old bone. The fierce bronze teeth had jagged canines. It left only her chin uncovered. Its deathly gaze chilled her.

She put her hands to her face again, trying to find the string or catch for the mask, but there was nothing; it fitted seamlessly to her skin and she couldn't find a way to release it. When she pulled harder, it hurt so badly that she felt she might rip the skin from her face. That frightened her enough that tears stung her eyes.

No, I won't cry.

She went to the ornately arched door made of lacquered wood and bolted with a bronze latch. It was locked and when she tried to exert her gnosis, she got nothing. She sought the dwyma instead, but it remained out of reach. She raised a fist and went to strike the surface when it suddenly swung open and, gasping, she recoiled in fright.

A man stood there, her own height, a Rondian with a clever face and a mane of red-gold hair. He was clad in a white silk robe with a square-patterned black border at the collar, sleeves and hem. He was handsome in a bland way, reminding Jehana of magi who'd used morphic-gnosis to beautify themselves and lost their own facial character in doing so.

Her heart thudding at the sudden confrontation, she stumbled backwards, fearing violence. But all the man said was, 'Ah, the princess awakes.' His voice was older than his features.

'Who are you?' she squeaked.

The stranger gave her a wry look. 'I'm your host. My name, about which I am sure you have heard many untruths, is Ervyn Naxius.'

Cold fear gripped Jehana's heart. Naxius: the renegade cast out of the Ordo Costruo for violating the Gnostic Codes. His name was a byword for immoral research. And he was the man behind the Masked Cabal, who had murdered her mother and sought to capture her. She backed from him until her back struck the stone slab.

'Keep away from me,' she warned, though without the gnosis, she had no idea how to protect herself.

Naxius chuckled sadly. 'My dear, you've been in my power for the best part of two weeks and I've not laid a finger on you. My servants – all female, I should add – have massaged your body to keep it supple while you reposed. We've fed you, washed you and tended to your ablutions. I mean you no harm – indeed, I want to help you fully come into your power.'

Jehana felt a trembling sense of helplessness, but she refused to show it. 'Alyssa Dulayne wanted the same thing,' she snarled. 'Do you know what happened to her?'

Naxius smiled mildly. 'I do indeed. She overreached and her greed got the better of her.'

Jehana remembered she was a Mubarak and drew herself up. 'What do you want with me?'

His smile never reached his eyes. 'My dear, we're going to do great things together. These are the Last Days, when the Blessed ascend to Paradise – and the damned are enslaved by the daemons that seize control of Urte. Thus it is written, and it falls upon me to make it so.'

She'd never heard that Naxius was a religious fanatic. 'You think to

71

bring on the Last Days to ascend to Paradise?' she said incredulously. It was the sort of deluded dream that had got madmen stoned in Halli'kut and Hebusalim. 'You can't believe that Ahm or Kore or whoever you believe in would welcome you?'

'Oh no, my child, I suffer no such delusion. I am most certainly on the side of the daemons.'

4

How Far Will You Go?

The Kaden Rats

The most celebrated criminal magi are the 'Kaden Rats', who rose to notoriety in the ninth century by using the gnosis to rob from wealthy targets, which gives them some cachet among the poor. They prospered until they made the mistake of preying upon an Imperial Treasurer, sparking a six-month manhunt that ended with the capture and public execution of their founder. But the Rats persist, generation after generation.

ENIK TAMBLYN, THE BRICIAN CHRONICLES, BRES 913

Coraine, Rondelmar
Febreux 936

Solon Takwyth climbed from an unmarked carriage wearing a plain grey cloak and with his cowl up. His destination was an elegant house with a walled garden in the richest part of Coraine city. Despite being a private residence – at least officially – it had fearsome gnostic wards and many guards.

The door was opened for him by a masked, anonymous man. Then a woman wearing a Heartface mask – a sight that sent a shiver down his spine – curtseyed and said, 'Welcome to the House of Lantris, Milord. Your assignation awaits in the Blue Room.' She indicated the stairs. 'Third floor, and to the right.'

Solon nodded brusquely and hurried up the stairs, found the required door and walked into a small cloakroom, where he shed his outer garments. When he regarded himself in the mirror, he saw a dour-looking man, powerfully built with close-cropped, fading brown

73

hair, full-bearded and filled with grim purpose. His face retained its gnostic youth, but tonight his eyes were feverish, when usually they radiated calm.

That's the nerves, he told himself.

There was a decanter of Brevian whiskey on a sideboard, and two crystal glasses. He poured a full measure into one then downed it, feeling his heartbeat quicken unevenly.

He undressed, paused to peer at the muscular bulk of himself, worrying at the signs of age and decay – he was reaching the far end of his fighting age: a scarred pack-leader with younger wolves snapping at his heels. Turning away gloomily, he pulled on a knee-length nightshirt, took a deep breath and opened the inner door. Beyond was a sitting room where two armchairs faced a roaring wood-fire. A big bearskin rug lay before the hearth and there was a sideboard set with a choice of wine and other liquor. A double bed in the corner was turned down and ready. Through the door to a bathroom beyond, he glimpsed a claw-footed bath.

Empress Lyra was sitting in one of the armchairs, her velvet dress unlaced at the front and her full breasts, swollen with milk, protruding ripe and heavy. Her blonde curls were immaculately styled. Her pale face looked up at him with apprehension and wanting.

'My Queen,' he said in a raw voice, falling to his right knee before her, unable to take his eyes from her. She made no effort to cover herself, just gazed back at him, breathing in shallow bursts.

'Dear Solon,' she said, her voice tense. 'I've been waiting for you.'

He couldn't take his eyes from her breasts. His heart was in his throat. Scarcely breathing, he shuffled forward, until he could reach out and touch her knees. 'Lyra,' he whispered, 'I've wanted this so much . . .'

'I too,' she replied urgently. 'Come to me,' she said, putting her hands under her breasts and offering them. 'These are for you, Solon. To give you the strength to go on.'

His mother had breastfed him until he was three; he had always credited his prowess to that. He could still recall what it had felt like, and the smell of a woman's milk always transported him. It hit him now as he drew near and Lyra parted her legs, pulling him between her thighs and taking his head in her hands, drawing his mouth to her swollen right aureole. His lips touched her engorged teat, drinking in the smell, intending only to kiss it: but a powerful impulse took him and he latched on, his arms gripping her shoulders and pinning her where she sat, as he sucked hard. Milk flooded his mouth and he moaned, remembering the taste.

'*Drink, my little man, it'll make you strong, the strongest knight in Koredom,*' his mother used to whisper to him as he fed. *Dear Kore, I need that strength now*.

Lyra groaned, clutching him to her, sighing and quivering with each powerful drawing on her, widening her thighs and drawing her knees upwards, the smell of her loins blending with that of her milk. The sheer eroticism of the moment was overpowering, driving blood to his member and making it hard, swollen, aching. He moved to the left nipple, suckling feverishly, the cream of her filling his senses, his hands pulling her down as she scooted her hips to meet his, on the edge of the seat.

'Rukk me, Milord,' Lyra moaned. 'Shove it in and take me.'

He stopped, the spell broken, pulling his mouth from the woman's breasts and glaring furiously. 'You stupid girl, that's not in the script!'

The prostitute – whose only real resemblance to Lyra was her blonde hair and pale complexion – stammered in fright, 'I'm so sorry–'

'The real Lyra would *never* speak like that,' he growled, gripping her chin, wanting to silence her. 'She is naïve but willing, succumbing to desire with innocence. She's not a *slut* like you!'

'I'm sorry – I'm sorry–'

The milk in his mouth curdled, but his cock was still stiff, so he channelled his anger, grabbing the whore's waist and pulling her off the armchair entirely. Her feet flailed, then she found the floor and slid to her knees as he speared her from behind, her oiled vagina taking him easily as he thrust in hard and fast, wanting to punish her transgression. He rukked her powerfully, until their panting ran together into one continuous moan. He didn't know or care if she came, but he did, in a hot rush that left him shuddering, but did little to dampen his disappointed anger.

What did you expect? his inner voice taunted him. *She's not the queen and you knew that before you started.*

He groaned heavily, pulled out and stood, letting the whore flop to the floor, spent in the messy aftermath of passion. For a moment they stared at each other, then both looked away, the awkwardness of intimacy with a stranger reminding him why he'd seldom had women after his wife died, despite years of loneliness.

It also reminded him of how much better his lovemaking had been with the real Lyra, before she rejected him and life became a torment. He backed away, slumped into the other armchair and pulling his nightshirt down, told the girl, 'Clean up. Pour me a whiskey and go.'

The girl burst into tears. He felt somewhat sorry for her, but he couldn't bring himself to give her a comforting word. This had been foolish, and he was the fool. It was a relief when she exited, still sobbing.

He was almost done with the whiskey when someone knocked and the woman in the Heartface mask peered in. 'Milord? May I join you?' When he nodded, she curtseyed, then took the other chair. 'I apologise, Milord. Your encounter was not up to House of Lantris standards. I shall have her punished – and of course, there'll be no charge.'

He waved a hand dismissively, because he despised sulking. 'Don't be overly harsh on her; just see that she learns. If I'd not been given licence to err, I would never have become the person I am.'

Whoever that is, these days.

Speaking to anyone in a Lantric Mask made him feel queasy at the moment, but this establishment had used them for decades. It catered to one particular fetish: those – apparently women as well as men – who lusted after a certain unobtainable person. He'd been given a menu that included various singers, courtesans and notable women – even the Estellan nun Valetta, who'd recently begun the Sisters' Crusade. But for the past five years, he understood, their main trade had been in prostitutes impersonating Lyra herself.

'Is there anything further we can do to make this right, Milord?' the masked woman asked. 'We value our clientele at the House of Lantris.'

He closed his eyes, trying to think past that moment when the scene fell apart, to when the illusion had still been intact. But now that the heat of the moment was gone, all he felt was self-disgust. The insult 'milksop' was the derisory term for what he'd done – he hadn't intended to feed, just to smell and kiss – but if anyone got wind of what he'd done, he'd be a laughing-stock.

And how will I ever face the real Lyra again?

Some part of him had been soothed when he drank from the girl, though . . . and he craved more. As long as the girl had learned her lesson, she might suffice. 'I'll consider,' he told Heartface. He indicated the door. 'Now if you will excuse me, I believe I have this room for the remainder of the hour, and this is a very fine whiskey.'

The woman rose, bowed like a man and left. Solon sat back, sipping the smoky fluid and wondering where Lyra was and what she was doing.

Are you thinking of me, my Queen?

Pallas, Rondelmar

Tap, tap, tap . . .

Lyra looked up sharply, her reverie broken. Rildan, cradled in her arms as she fed him from a bottle, sensed her disquiet and began to grizzle. The sound came from her balcony, where the setting sun cast shadows across the city. She saw a silhouette, a large bird-shape, outside the window, which meant Aradea wanted her.

She called to the next room, 'Nita, can you take Rildan, please?'

Nita, a diligent worker – and a brave girl, considering her predecessor had died horribly during an attack on Lyra a few months ago – bustled in, swept up Rildan and the bottle and began coddling him back to calmness, casting a curious look at Lyra as she wrapped a shawl about herself and went to the curtains. When she opened them, a raven shrieked from the balcony ledge, then swooped away and out of sight.

'That bird gives me the creeps,' Nita said. 'Shall I have the guards shoot it?'

'It's got as much right to come and go as us,' Lyra replied. She unlatched the door, feeling a tingling as the wards recognised her hand and came undone. 'I won't be long,' she said.

The balcony steps took her to the back of Greengate, the main entrance to her private garden. The two guards stationed outside the gates touched fists to chests as she passed them and went through the Rose Bower to the pond. It was a cold, damp evening and already frost crunched under her slippers. Careless of her nightdress and gown, she knelt and broke the ice on the pool, scooped up frigid water and drank. An eel rose and nibbled at the surface before swirling away. She wondered how it survived the cold, yet another of the small mysteries of this place. Then she closed her eyes and opened herself to the dwyma.

As the mesh of light ignited behind her eyes, she listened for some sign that Valdyr Sarkany had returned, but instead, she sensed something else: a scurrying, furtive feeling, dark passages and loamy earth, and a palpable sense of fear. 'Hello?' she murmured into the web of light. 'Who's there?'

There was no response, just a dimly heard sob, such as a girl might make.

'Hello—'

She waited, hoping . . . but no one answered.

Then boots crunched on the frosted grass and she turned to find Dirklan approaching. Surprise sharpened her voice. 'Father? What is it?'

'I'm sorry to disturb you here,' Dirklan replied, studying the Winter Tree sapling, its green leaves and red berries the only colour in the garden. 'The Treasurer wants to see you in private, and he asked for me to be present.'

'What does Calan want?'

'He has a proposal for raising funds, but he wants to sound you out outside of the Council.'

Lyra hugged herself against the cold. 'Well, I suppose we should hear him out.' She glanced about, troubled by this inconclusive foray into the dwyma. Was it another dwymancer, one she didn't know, in trouble somewhere? But if so, how could she help?

Help her, she sent to the genilocus, hoping that was sufficient, but doubting it would be enough . . .

Dupenium

It was the most disgusting, scariest, bravest thing Coramore had ever done. When she heard the hammering on her doors and the tapping of the raven on her shutters, she *knew* that Ostevan had finally decided he could do what he liked with her and Uncle Garod wouldn't stop him.

She was twelve, but she'd always been small, a thin girl with limbs like twigs who could slip through any gap. The only other way out of the garderobe was down the chute, but she could hear her companions going to open the doors, where fists hammered and voice called.

The brick chute was sloped, which would help slow her descent. It was about eighteen inches square, opening onto a concrete lip and the open air. That it was coated in dried faeces and recent piss made her stomach churn, but so did falling into Ostevan's grasp.

And back into Abraxas' clutches . . . Memories of her months as a possessed soul made her stomach knot. *I can't ever go back to that.*

Ensuring the bolt in the door was firmly in place, she lifted the lid and with a shudder of disgust, sat on the rim and lowered her feet, then her hips, holding on until she could be sure her hands could support her, then she lowered herself, her back to the door and the sloped wall of the chute, seeking purchase as her feet scooted down, still unsure she'd fit – what if she was trapped halfway? Then she heard male voices on the other side of the door.

She'd have to take the gamble. She shifted her grip and slithered downwards, her head entering the stinking shaft and her arms extending to full length, holding on . . .

. . . until she lost her grip and plummeted, first barking her buttocks and back against the stone as she slid, then suppressing a shriek as she lost skin on her ankles and knees, until she struck the lip and slammed the back of her head as she dropped, flailing and dazed, into the mound of snow-covered grass and manure below.

It was a soft but putrid landing. She rolled and unexpectedly fell again, ending up in the bottom of the empty, frost-rimed moat, her head ringing and seeing double, but there was no time for that. She staggered upright, frantically crawling hand over hand up the far side of the ditch. She had to get underground where she couldn't be scryed and she had only moments. She pounded down the path to the graveyard, her footprints spotted with blood. Though it was only mid-afternoon, the light was failing, which gave her some hope that she could find refuge in time.

There was no hue and cry raised yet, but when she peered around a grave monument, she saw a soldier on the balcony of her suite, so she stayed low, half-crawling to the old grave marked by her special brackenberry bush. She plucked the four berries on the branches and swallowed them. As the tart juices filled her mouth, she felt a strange sense of dislocation, as if she were watching herself move from all sides, but she suppressed her alarm.

Glancing back at the castle, she saw another man on the balcony now, a priest – but even from here she could see it wasn't Ostevan, the man she dreaded most. She pushed on, making for her family crypt, trying to ignore the battering she'd taken from the drop and hoping the increasing darkness would hide her trail. Her head throbbed, her fingers were turning blue from the cold and her heart was thumping so hard it might break her ribs.

Help me, she whispered to the wind, to the dark, to the flurries of snow as the weather closed in again. *Help me . . .*

Then she saw an opening in the ground, one she'd never seen before – but she didn't question, just darted in head-first. It was barely the size of the garderobe shaft, but she could squeeze down it and that was all that mattered. Putting aside the horrors of being enclosed, the dread of ghosts and old bones, she wriggled her way along the tight tunnel into the dark. The air was stale, but breathable. At last the tunnel opened into a space floored with stone slabs. There was even a faint glow and when she peered cautiously around she saw someone had left enchanted candles in the grave, a traditional offering for a dead mage. She was trying to identify the crypt when she heard a frightening rush of crumbling earth: the earth *shifted* and the tunnel she'd just left collapsed upon itself, sealing her into the near-darkness.

Coramore was petrified. Everyone knew mages' crypts were often haunted: spirits bound to their resting place could even become dangerous revenants who required a fully trained necromancer to deal with them. But she could now see that she was actually in a warren of crypts, one of the many interlinked mausoleums of the Sacrecour clan. These were her ancestors' bones around her. Oddly, that thought calmed her a little.

They'll protect me. I'm one of them.

But she didn't want to be a ghost or a bag of bones just yet. She groped around, wishing her gnosis had come to her so she could make magical light and fire for heat, and other useful things. Although it wasn't so long since she'd eaten, she was already parched and ravenous – how would she find food or water down here? She couldn't leave, not yet, for Ostevan would be hunting for her.

But he's not found me yet, despite the trail I must have left – and he's not scryed me out either. Earth can shield me. I'm still free . . .

She moved carefully, examining everything, recognising old names on the brass panels screwed into the stone sarcophagi. Coming to a wall where condensation ran down the bricks, she licked it, too thirsty for shame, then sat down and cried it all out, because she was only twelve and she was terrified.

Help me, she wailed tearfully at the dark. *Please, help me!*

Then she almost choked, because the darkness spoke back: a distant female voice she knew: the empress, her cousin Lyra, calling: *Hello? Who's there? Hello*—

Coramore didn't know how to respond – but then she heard a grating sound, scraping metal, and from somewhere in the distance, a bright light suddenly shone out.

The damned girl has vanished. Ostevan Pontifex strode through the cemetery, glowering at the snowflakes filling the air; huge flecks that glittered in the light of the lamps and torches of the searchers – and hid any footprints the fugitive might have left.

'Princess Coramore?' servants and soldiers shouted. 'Princess!'

He'd lied, telling Garod he had the dwymancer in custody

somewhere outside of Fauvion, that his men would bring him to Dupenium in due course. Margentius Keeper and his fellows were anxious, but understood why they had to remain silent – Garod wouldn't march if he even suspected they had no captive dwymancer.

Meantime, the princess' disappearance was being treated as nothing more serious than a confused young girl running away. Perhaps she'd come into her gnosis and was frightened, someone had suggested, which was, Ostevan had to admit, a good cover for the truth.

But where is the little bitch?

He'd soon worked out that she'd escaped through the garderobe shaft, but her trail had quickly vanished under a sudden snowstorm. Presumably she was now underground – but where? Was she still in this Kore-bedamned cemetery, or had she leaped the fences and run into the town?

What worried him more was how she had even known to run.

Is the dwyma somehow involved? he wondered.

It wasn't just an academic question. Apart from beheading, virtually the only thing that could kill him now was the dwyma. He'd been inside Lef Yarle's mind when the assassin had been about to slay Lyra: somehow the queen had blazed light and the daemon-possessed Yarle had died instantly, the ichor in his veins blasted to ash. No mere mage could do such a thing.

The tales say that dwymancy is slow, unsuited to combat, but Lyra's beam of light was sudden and deadly . . .

Finding Coramore was of paramount urgency if he was to avoid Yarle's fate. Worse, Naxius had already captured his own dwymancer, the new sultan's kinswoman.

'Jehana Mubarak is the key to unlocking my true purpose,' Naxius had gloated. 'She can reach the dwyma but not use it, which makes her a powerful weapon that cannot turn in my hand. With her in my thrall, I shall have the means to destroy Urte and usher in the Age of Daemons.'

The way Naxius had spoken made it clear that this was no idle boast but *exactly* what he intended to do. That terrified Ostevan.

I didn't join the Master's cabal to destroy the world, but to rule it.

82

If Naxius needed a tame dwymancer, so did he. He'd let that damned girl flit about thinking she was fooling him – and now she was gone. Had Cordan warned her, mind to mind? He had men watching the young prince and his frantic fear for his missing sister certainly looked genuine – and guileless Cordan had always been an easily read book. The boy might have doubts about the military campaign, but every now and then his father's greed shone out as he contemplated life as emperor.

No, he doesn't know where she is either. Someone else warned her.

'Master,' a priest called, holding up a lantern that partly illuminated the crypt entrance: a fanciful edifice of marble adorned with seraph statues, 'we've opened up the girl's family crypt. Do you wish to enter first?'

Ostevan pictured Lef Yarle's final moments again. *Why take a chance?* 'Go ahead,' he told the man, 'hunt in pairs, check every tomb and sarcophagus – and take your time. I would bet my soul she's down there.'

Coramore snuffed her candle, for all the good it would do, and slithered into a gap between the tombs just as lamplight filled the aisles. Then something moved beside her and she had to shove her hand in her mouth to stifle her scream ... until a furry body stroked against her arm and a soft *meow* caught her ear. She understood instantly: *Aradea is watching me.* She squeezed deeper into the gap, following the cat, which led her on a zigzag route into deep pools of shadow, while men in heavy boots stomped past, calling her name but oblivious to her presence. The cat guided her to a rotting door into a long-forgotten tomb and sat beside it, looking at her expectantly. Coramore smiled at it and murmured thanks before slipping through the hole, an instant before light swept by, revealing the cat, calm as you like, sweeping away her footprints with its tail. Then she groped into the dark, found an open wall-slot and slipped in among a pile of old bones.

The searchers never even opened the broken door, for someone remarked on the cat and someone else must have thrown something at it, for Coramore heard something clatter on the stone flags. For some reason, they all forgot about the door in their annoyance at the animal.

After half an hour, as both the shouting and the dimly flickering lights began to die away, Coramore was almost beginning to breathe when she felt a trembling in the air and Ostevan's hated voice whispered into her mind.

<*I know you're in here, Princess,*> he murmured darkly, and the thousand voices of Abraxas, an echo behind his voice, made her shudder. <*There's nothing to eat or drink, so if you don't die of the cold you'll come out soon enough – and don't you worry, for we'll be waiting.*>

But he didn't come in himself and within a few minutes, his loathsome voice was gone.

She felt the eerie presence of Aradea inside the cat when it returned and curled up next to her, purring, and that soothed her fear.

She couldn't say how she knew the Fey Queen was here, only that she was, and that she'd been looking out for her for weeks, ever since Coramore had first eaten the fruit from the brackenberry tree. *She'll protect me*, Coramore decided, closing her eyes, shivering on the cold stone slab, but warmed by the cat. *She won't let Abraxas have me again.*

Despite her fear, the pain and the cold, that thought was enough to carry her down into sleep.

Pallas

Lyra sent Nita and Rildan to the nursery and ordered tea. She changed hurriedly into a simple day gown that might not be the height of fashion, but was warm and easy to put on unaided, then she summoned Dirklan and Calan. She buttered some freshly baked bread and bit into the steaming morsel, then pushed the tray across the table as her two counsellors arrived.

'Help yourselves,' she said, then looked at the Treasurer. 'Lord Dubrayle, what is this about?'

'Milady,' Calan replied, putting his tea aside after a single sip, 'you asked yesterday if I had a plan for rebalancing the Treasury accounts. I do: but it isn't one I wished to voice before the rest of the council.'

'Why is that? You know I like all business to be done openly through the Council.'

'Not this.' He leaned forward, intent. 'At our last meeting, you asked who has money, the answer being the banks. Legally, we can't seize that money, obviously: it doesn't belong to us, or indeed, to the banks themselves – it belongs to their investors. But we can seek a loan.'

'I thought you said no one would lend to us,' Lyra replied, wishing she could gauge whether her father knew where this was going, and if he approved.

'That's true, Milady,' Calan said, 'or at least, no one in their right mind would lend to us. But if we had a controlling interest in a bank, then we could *make* them lend to us.'

Dirklan frowned. 'That's illegal. The Treasury cannot act as a bank, for one thing – and as for forcing them to use their investors' funds to make a loan that would likely never be repaid . . .'

'Excuse my ignorance,' Lyra put in, wishing yet again that she was not so ill-educated when it came to matters of high finance, 'but how exactly does a bank work?'

Calan frowned impatiently, but he explained, 'Broadly speaking, Majesty, they look after the wealth of those who wish to safeguard their own gold and to increase their fortunes. That money is lent to other people at a rate of interest – in its simplest form, if one borrows one hundred gilden at an interest rate of ten per cent, one must repay one hundred and ten gilden. When the loan is repaid, the bank will divide that interest between the investor – the person whose money it is – and the bank itself, which covers the bank's costs of storage, security and administration; the rest is the bank's profit.'

'Is it lucrative?'

'Oh, indeed: successful bankers are the richest men in Koredom,' Calan drawled. Then he laughed. 'Other than clergymen, of course.'

Lyra stared into space for a moment, then asked, 'Isn't our Treasury a bank?'

'Ah, that's a common misconception. The Treasury is actually a public fund holding the taxes accumulated to run government. It's not the same thing.'

'I suppose it's obvious, but not to me: why don't *we* have a bank?'

Calan smiled wryly. 'Religion.'

Is that why Dominius wasn't invited today?

'Why does religion prevent us from having a Crown Bank?'

Dirklan tapped the table. 'The *Book of Kore* forbids "usury", which is the old term for earning money from interest, but the real issue is historical. Several centuries ago, Emperor Celestian set up a Crown Bank, which failed. He bankrupted the empire within ten years of taking the throne.'

'*Failed . . .*' Lyra echoed meaningfully.

Calan smiled wryly. 'He used it as his private purse and just about destroyed the Rondian Empire. Few people know because it was so diligently . . . um . . . *covered up*. That's why we have a Crown Treasury which is distinct from your personal wealth, Milady. As a result of Celestian Sacrecour's proclivities, it was written into law that neither Crown nor Church – just to keep things even – could operate a bank, which opened the way for the wealthier Houses like the Jussts and the Belks to set up themselves. It's true that some have failed, but they've not dragged down the Treasury or the Rondian Empire.'

All the same, it smelled like an opportunity to Lyra. 'Setting aside the legalities for a moment,' she began, then paused before finishing, 'could you set up a bank for us?'

The Treasurer shook his head. 'We don't have the manpower, the expertise or the time, Majesty. We need money *now*, not in a year or two, which is how long it would take, even if the law was changed.'

'Plus, we have no gold to back it,' Dirklan added.

'Sorry,' Lyra said, feeling stupid again and hating it. 'I don't follow.'

Calan couldn't quite hide his urge to roll his eyes. 'Every gilden the Treasury issues must be backed by bullion. Each region has its own Treasury office, responsible for collecting taxes and maintaining the reserves – and by the way, let's not forget we'll lose those if the vassal-states do secede.'

'The reality is that there's roughly five times more coin out there than we could back anyway,' Dirklan concluded. 'It's another area where we're critically vulnerable.'

'If there's already five times more coin than reserves, why not raise that to ten times, or twenty times?' Lyra asked plaintively. Her head was spinning.

'Because that would just lower the value of it,' Calan explained. 'The market assesses the value of a coin by the estimated reserves. Just adding coins lowers the purchasing power of what's out there, to no gain – and it means those who do have coin are suddenly poorer, while sellers just raise their prices. It's called "inflation". We'd have major food riots in days.'

'We're having food riots anyway,' Dirklan put in. 'The churches are dealing with hundreds of people begging alms every day. Where we've lost control, gangs are looting and using the stolen goods to purchase supplies, which they sell on the black market. They're becoming rich while everyone else starves, or uses the last of their savings to subsist.'

'For us, there's no magic spell to conjure up money,' Calan told Lyra, 'but we could at least redistribute lots of it back to us, if we were, um, *legally flexible*.'

He fell silent, while Lyra was wondering if flying away and hiding out in the countryside to escape this unholy mess was actually an option.

Except they've already told me that secession and flight would result in the massacre of loyal Corani and imperial families all over the empire. I'd be responsible for a bloodbath.

'But I thought you said opening our own bank wouldn't work?'

'Ah ... but there is another way,' the Treasurer said. 'It's illegal, at present at least, but if it were not, what I would do is – secretly, of course – forcibly purchase a moderately large bank – say, Gravenhurst Stronghold, who operate only in this region. We would give them a royal warrant to produce coin, which would fund the loan that we make right back to ourselves. It's fraudulent, but it would get us through to spring, maybe even summer. Our soldiers and staff would be paid and other loans kept solvent.'

Lyra sat back, processing this. 'So we'd forcibly take over a bank to make them lend to us?'

'Exactly. We'd need to pass the law in secret – if it became known, every bank would close its Pallas operations in a flash, for fear that we'd seize their assets. We'd purchase Gravenhurst in utter secrecy, buying the loyalty of their key people, inject our reserves into their books, issue the warrant and lend ourselves the money we need.'

'And if you succeed?'

'As long as people believe the bank is solvent and their loan to us valid, we're saved. If not, our currency will collapse, our bank will be destroyed, and that will drag us down with it. We'll be forced to stand trial – or run.'

'Kore on high, are you serious?' Lyra blurted.

'Deadly serious,' Calan replied evenly.

'And obviously,' Dirklan added, 'if anyone were to tell the bankers or any of the guilds what we were doing, the game would be up and no one would ever extend us credit again, which would trigger the fall of your regime and leave thousands of good people destitute – and that's without even mentioning the carnage of the following rebellion.'

Kore on High . . . it's against everything I thought I stood for – but the alternatives . . . She forced herself to think through the possibilities. *Makelli would say we must do what is necessary, regardless of morality . . . and I thought him heartless.*

'So either I accept that we're being ousted and do nothing, or I dirty my hands in a way that could destroy us later, even if we survive the immediate danger.'

'You could put in that way,' Calan responded. 'I don't suggest this lightly, Majesty, truly. It goes against *everything* I've been taught to value – and even then, it will only work if we hold our own in the battlefield – in other words, if we can defend Pallas. But if they are to put up a fight, our soldiers must be fed, armed and paid.'

It felt utterly wrong, but then she imagined her enemies sweeping in and making the Pallas streets run with blood. 'Do you support this, Father?' she asked at last.

Dirklan rubbed the eye socket under his eyepatch. 'My people can keep it secret. If we spend the loan well, we stay in the game. If we do nothing, we're going to lose. So I'm for.'

She looked at Calan, who licked his lips, then said, 'It's my only idea, Milady – the only one with a ghost of a chance. I'm willing to try it, even though I wrote many of the laws we're talking about breaking. The question is, are you? How far will you go to survive this crisis?'

He's that desperate, Lyra thought, *that he'd break his own system.*

'Should we not involve Grand Prelate Wurther and Knight Commander Levis?'

Calan shook his head emphatically. 'Wurther would instantly move his not inconsiderable wealth and that would alert the market. And frankly, Lumpy wouldn't understand what we're doing anyway, so why ask him?'

That's harsh, Lyra thought, *but probably fair*. She turned over the pros and cons in her mind until it was spinning. *Dear Kore, I think we have to do this . . .*

'Then let it be set in motion swiftly,' she said decisively. 'Only those who absolutely must be involved can know. We'll publically deny all knowledge if anyone raises any suspicions.' The words tasted bad in her mouth, but Garod and Solon were marching. This was what desperation tasted like.

I'm becoming as bad as my enemies, she worried. *But what else can I do?*

'What about Frankel?' she asked Dirklan. 'Have you made contact with him?'

His expression was doubtful. 'I have. I'm awaiting a response, but they've not yet refused.'

'Can we trust it not to be a trap?' Calan asked. 'This feels like an unnecessary risk to me.'

'I have to talk to Frankel,' Lyra replied firmly.

'They're criminals, rabble-rousers and fools,' the Treasurer sniffed. 'The Empress should not be talking to such people – it gives them a legitimacy they don't warrant and encourages further upheavals. I'm with Levis on this: send in the legions and cut down anyone who gets in our way.'

'No,' Lyra replied firmly. 'That might be how the Sacrecours worked, but not me. They have genuine grievances and if I can hear them out, perhaps we can defuse the whole situation.'

Even to her own ears, it sounded naïve, but she refused to change her mind.

'It's a trap, isn't it?' Braeda Kaden said into the silence that followed her brother Tad's announcement. 'She wants to *talk* to us? *Rukka mia*, does the convent girl think we're imbeciles?'

'It's clear that she is, at any rate,' Lazar drawled. 'But perhaps it can be turned to our favour?'

'Aye,' Gorn growled. 'Tell her to come see us, then we'll string up the silly bitch.'

'She named you specifically, Wordsmith,' Tad said, turning to Ari. 'Why would she do that?'

'Because she thinks he's in charge,' Braeda tittered, before Ari could open his mouth. 'If it's even her idea at all. Setallius is behind this, trust me.'

'Probably,' Tad mused. 'You've spoken to her before, haven't you, Frankel? She pardoned you, yes? And then you betrayed that pardon. What on Urte would she have to say to you?'

Outside the inn where they were meeting, their followers were busy barricading more streets and ransacking the houses of those who'd fled. The movement was swallowing up more of the city every night. The Imperial legions just watched, emasculated by Lyra's unwillingness to unleash them.

She understood me, he thought. *I expected her to be a sheltered, stupid noble brat, but she* understood *me*.

'I want to speak to her,' he said.

The others rolled their eyes at each other.

'That's our decision to make,' Tad said. 'Braeda's likely right: this'll be a ploy conceived by Setallius. He'll flood the meeting place with Volsai, close off the retreats and try to take us all.'

The room fell silent.

Then Lazar said, 'So, knowing that, is there a way to sweep the queen from the tabula board and win the game?'

5

A Journey of the Soul

Our Greatest Enemy

We all have the potential to be the very best version of ourselves that is possible. But few of us realise that potential, because we expend our energies on that which does not allow us to grow. In this sense, we are ourselves our own worst foe.

MASTER SHRAMA, ZAIN GURU (ATTRIBUTED), C.592

The Elétfa
Febreux 936

'Be off,' the reedy voice repeated in Keshi. Valdyr couldn't tell if it was a girl or a young boy whose voice hadn't broken. Beside him, a growling Gricoama began to slink forward.

Valdyr gestured for the wolf to halt and called out in Keshi, 'Sal' Ahm – I won't hurt you.' The foreign words rising in his memory came with many unwanted images of Kesh and the breeding-houses. 'I just need water.'

'There's a stream a thousand paces further on,' the young person called back.

A thousand paces . . . Valdyr groaned. He looked back, but the rift in the air he'd stepped through was out of sight. He wondered how long it would stay open – or was he already stranded here?

'I need it now,' he called. 'I can pay.'

He scanned the landscape: he was at the mouth of a defile, a stiff climb into the rocky heights behind him. Before him was this tiny, run-down wilderness farm. He could see no animals except for a trio of bleating goats in the pens, two full grown and one a yearling. And there were two fresh mounds of earth at the rear, man-sized, marked with funerary stones.

Recent deaths . . . and only a youngster calling out . . .

Slowly, he raised his arms above his head and standing, called, 'I'm coming down.'

'No—' the voice squeaked and he caught a glimpse of movement behind the corner of the hut, a thin figure with a bow. An arrow flashed and buried in the ground at his feet. He walked past it. 'Stop,' the youth shouted, an octave higher, 'or I'll kill you—'

Valdyr walked on, fixing his unwavering gaze on the shadowy figure. He knew he must be a fearsome sight to a child, clad for the wilds with his long-bladed sword strapped to his back and standing more than six feet tall, lean but strong, with his long black hair and bushy mous-taches. His grim, haunted face was too pale to pass for an Ahmedhassan; he'd be seen as a *ferang*, one of the hated foreign devils.

'I have coin,' he called, grateful that he'd automatically stuffed a few in his pockets, in case he needed to buy food from a hunter. 'Rondian money.'

'I don't want your *ferang* money,' the boy – Valdyr was pretty certain – shouted back shrilly. 'Go away.'

Daring him, Valdyr walked to the trough, scooped up the goats' water and drank. It tasted like nectar and wine, for all that it was stale and dirty.

The boy – with short, raggedly cut hair as black as his, a narrow face and hawkish nose – was glaring furiously at him. The bow in his hand was trembling so badly he couldn't aim.

Valdyr gave him a sympathetic look, then sniffed hungrily. The smell of baking hung in the air. 'I'll not harm you,' he said. Slowly he drew out his coin pouch and placed two silver coins on the rim of the trough. 'This, for some goat's milk and bread – and the young goat.'

He has a mated pair; I'm paying more than the value of the yearling at market.

He turned and whistled and Gricoama trotted into the opening. The goats bleated and pressed against the bars of their pen. The boy yelped and cowered against the wall of his hut, on the brink of fleeing.

'Run, and he'll chase,' Valdyr warned. 'Show no fear.'

The young Keshi made a strangled noise, but didn't move as the great wolf trotted to the edge of the small farm and paused. The boy was shaking so hard he'd dropped his arrow, but still he stood his ground.

Gricoama wouldn't attack without permission, but the boy didn't know that. Valdyr felt for him. 'I won't come near you,' he called. 'Please, just give us what we need to sustain us and we'll be on our way.'

This was the only dwelling in the gully. Looking at the graves and the hacked-off hair, an Eastern mourning custom, he was certain the boy was alone.

He's probably pretending his parents are still alive, likely going to market in their stead, making excuses for them. But pretty soon, someone's going to realise . . .

The boy was destined for slavery.

With a soft whimper, the boy vanished into the hut and quickly re-emerged with a platter of blackened flatbread, a mash of roots and spices and a pot of goat's milk. He warily placed them at the edge of the building, then scampered over to the far side of the goats' pen.

'*Shukran*,' Valdyr called in thanks, then the smell of food overcame him and he snatched up the mash, spread half on a chunk of the flatbread and ate furiously, while Gricoama watched hungrily. Feeling stronger already, Valdyr packed away what was left before walking to the pen. He clambered in, gathered the yearling in his arms and clambered out again, then moved some way away before swiftly cutting its throat and butchering it carefully to waste nothing. He scraped the hide clean and stretched it out to dry, then packed away most of the meat before taking the carcase over to Gricoama, who ate as voraciously as he had.

Then Valdyr approached the hut, carrying several of the larger chunks of meat.

'No,' the boy called, lifting his bow again. '*Don't* come in – I *will* shoot–'

His voice cracked and Valdyr, wondering what he was so desperate to hide, opened his senses to the dwyma. He could feel the dryness of the air in his skin, the parched hills and the presence of the stream somewhere in the distance. He tasted the hunger of the vultures above . . . and sensed an even younger presence inside: frightened – and female.

He stopped, carefully placed the meat on the ground, then backed away, his eyes stinging for the predicament of the two children, but there was nothing he could do to help them except to honour his promise and go.

He returned to the trough, filled his waterskin, drank again, then washed. Gricoama finished tearing at the goat, ripped off the largest haunch and holding it between his powerful jaws, walked away. Together, they climbed back into the heights.

At the ridgeline, he turned: the young bowman was beside the hut, staring up at him. There was a smaller presence with him, a stick-figure with the same ragged tufts of hair. As they watched, the boy ran to the remains of the dead goat to salvage what he could; the bones would make a hearty stew, maybe enough to sustain them for a week or two.

Prayers were useless, but Valdyr felt the urge to help in other ways: he opened himself up to the dwyma, raised a hand and drew down the clouds clinging to the heights above, forcing them into directions they wouldn't naturally flow. That done, he released the power, raised a hand in farewell and trudged back the way they'd come, Gricoama at his side.

In a few minutes, cloud engulfed them and it began to rain: the only gift he could leave his helpless benefactors. It wouldn't protect them from rapacious villagers, but perhaps it might give them something they desperately needed to survive. He blessed them both in his mind, wishing that whatever powers there were might protect them. 'Be with them,' he asked, unsure if such a wish could ever come true.

In half an hour, they reached the small cleft where the rift had torn open – and to his enormous relief, it was still there, a tear in the fabric of existence only visible from right in front. Through the ragged black hole, Valdyr could see the surface of the giant branch of the Tree he'd been walking along. He bowed his head, clambered through and in moments the eternal night of the Elétfa had enclosed them, daylight and Kesh gone as the spatial rip repaired. The vastness of the giant tree spread above and below him once more, the stars dotting the darkness lending a ghostly light to the tree. The branch was at least thirty paces wide, descending towards the immense trunk and the stairway that spiralled upwards out of sight.

Would another branch take me back to Mollachia? He wondered what was happening there. *Is Kyrik safe? What happened to Jehana and Waqar – and is Asiv still hunting me?*

Just more unknowable questions.

'Well, we've got a few days' food,' he remarked to Gricoama. 'Will it be enough, do you think? Or can we do this again at need? It's been three days now and the top of the tree is no closer.'

The wolf gave him a measured look full of comprehension and his shoulders hunched, then lowered in a very human gesture of ambivalence.

'Ysh, I don't know either.' Valdyr sighed. 'Let's go and find out.'

Freihaafen, Mollachia

Where are you, Valdyr? It's been three weeks . . .

Kyrik grimaced, then firmly pushed his brother from his thoughts and concentrated on the task at hand, which was spooning a vegetable broth into Hajya's mouth while Korznici held her down. The way Hajya fought against them, teeth snapping madly, berserk with rage, was heartrending, but she was keeping food down now and both he and Korznici were certain it was making a difference.

The sun shone through high clouds on the warmest day in months; snow still covered the peaks that surrounded the hidden valley but spring was coming.

At his signal, Korznici leaped clear, leaving Hajya choking on the final mouthful, retching but then swallowing before collapsing onto the grass, weeping. He longed to hold her but still didn't dare, not as long as the ichor was still pulsing in her veins and blackening her spittle.

'The Ogre creature was right,' Korznici observed. 'Sunlight and green food *is* helping her.'

Kyrik sat on his haunches, his eyes stinging; he hated forcing her like this. 'Her eyes don't go dark so often,' he agreed, 'and she's more manageable.'

But that isn't her either. Hajya's tough, hard-headed, earthy and passionate, never weak or pliant. Will she ever be restored to her true self?

'She will recover, Kirol,' Korznici told him, as if reading his mind. 'We will prevail.'

'Dear Kore, Great Ahm, I hope so,' Kyrik breathed.

Korznici gave him a sideways look. 'Why do you pray to two gods who hate each other?'

Kyrik grimaced. 'Godspeaker Paruq, my mentor, told me that all gods are one. The unifying life energy of the world is the only real god: all the different names are for the one being.'

Korznici sniffed. 'Paruq was a strange man.' She'd met him while he was doing missionary work with the Vlpa tribe.

'I've been wondering if perhaps that unified energy is what Valdyr calls the dwyma,' Kyrik went on, trying to ignore his beloved wife's misery – then his skin prickled as Hajya's sobs suddenly turned to harsh chuckling. She swiped her tangled black curls to one side as her face, contorting with pain at the sunlight, turned to him. Her squinting black eyes were filled with malice.

'Kyrik,' she drawled in the Gatti accent of Asiv Fariddan. 'I wonder: does buggery hold the same appeal for you as it did for your brother?'

'Get out, daemon,' Kyrik snapped, conjuring wizardry-gnosis.

'No, wait,' Asiv said, 'I'm here to parley.'

'What have we to talk about?' He raised his hands.

'Because neither of us has what we need, Mollach,' Asiv replied. 'I don't care about this wretched, frozen country of yours, or your woman, but I need your brother and the Ogre creature. Give them to me and I'll give you back your woman.' Hajya's full mouth twisted into a sneer. 'She *loves* you, to her own surprise. You wouldn't want to throw that away, would you? Not when love is so elusive in this hard, evil world.'

She loves me, Kyrik thought. He knew that, or thought he did, but to hear it from another, even such a one as Asiv, still quickened his pulse. *But I also love Valdyr.*

'You know I'd never give my brother to you, so why waste our time asking?'

Korznici nodded in approval. Gnostic energies were glowing at her fingertips too.

Hajya leaned forward, glaring at him, her daemon-eyes full of hate. 'Then let me put it this way, Sarkany. I possess the Imperial Legion in Lapisz, and most of the citizens. The rest of your people I'm driving out – to Hegikaro, in case you were wondering, your own city you've not had the guts to return to.'

'I'll retake Hegikaro in my own time,' Kyrik retorted.

'Then best you do it soon,' Asiv-Hajya leered, 'for once all those help-less peasants are safe within its walls, I'll march. I can barely restrain myself, with so many delectable women and children waiting for my hungry men to harvest. But I am a generous man. You have a week to come to their aid.'

'You don't set the terms –'

'Of course I do,' the daemon snarled. 'How do you not understand that? Bring your idiot brother and the Ogre-beast to Hegikaro, or sit here safe in your sylvan hidey-hole and watch your entire kingdom be massacred, Sarkany. *One week.*'

Kyrik went to retort, but Asiv had left and it was just Hajya staring up at him, quivering in fear, her drool running black.

'It's a trap,' Korznici stated.

'Of course it's a rukking trap,' he snapped back, 'but what choice do I have?'

Kyrik convened his leaders after the evening's communal meal. Leaving the rest of his disparate people – Mollachs, Schlessen and the construct-Mantauri – to relax after a hard day's labour constructing new longhouses, he joined Kip, Maegogh, Rothgar and Korznici to discuss the daemon's ultimatum.

'He's herding every uninfected person, anyone left in the valley with an independent thought, towards Hegikaro.'

'Can we shelter them here?' Maegogh rumbled.

'It could be as many as twenty thousand people,' Rothgar told him. 'We couldn't fit them all into this valley, let alone feed them – and if we did try, the valley would no longer be secret.'

'Yar,' Kip agreed, 'that's clearly why he's doing this: he can't find us, so he's luring us out.'

'And I have no choice but to be lured,' Kyrik said. 'If he slaughters all my people, I'll have no kingdom.'

'They are not all your people,' Korznici put in. 'There is also the Vlpa clan, my kindred, sheltering in the Tuzvolg.' There were some twenty thousand Sydian men, women and children in the tundra, preserved from the full blast of a Mollachian winter by the volcanic basin beneath Cuz Piros, the fire mountain. 'You are also their king.'

'I've not forgotten that,' Kyrik said. He looked around the room, most especially at Kip and Korznici, whose assent he needed. He'd brought the Vlpa clan to Mollachia, and Kip's people too. His sovereignty was meant to offer protection, but so far it had brought them only danger. 'I have no choice: I must return to Hegikaro and rally my people. Only if they're armed and organised will they stand any chance against Asiv.'

'Obviously,' Maegogh rumbled.

'I do *not* command this,' Kyrik went on, 'I *ask*. I believe it is better to fight together than hide separately, so I hope you will all come with me. We must fortify the town – only by holding together will we have any chance of defeating Asiv. Remaining here might be safer in the short term, but it guarantees ultimate failure.'

Kip shared a look with Maegogh, then said, 'You need not ask – we are the Bullheads of Minaus. Where the fight is deadliest, the blood flowing swiftest, there we stand.'

He must sing the old lays in his sleep, Kyrik thought, breathing a huge sigh of relief, for he hadn't dared take anything as a given. He clasped the giant Schlessen's big right hand.

Korznici was a little more grudging. 'My people followed you halfway across Yuros and now we have nowhere else to go. We have committed to more than we ever expected, lost more than we ever feared.' She raised her head as she went on, 'But we will see this through, for the sakes of the fallen and those who still live. I say this as head of the Sfera; I am only one voice on the tribe's leadership council, but in this, my voice will prevail.'

She's more and more queenly every day, Kyrik thought, then, wondering when his own true queen would be restored to him, *Will that ever happen?*

'Then I'll send you and Rothgar to bring them to Hegikaro,' he replied. 'Thank you all. We are in a terrible predicament, but your support gives me hope. Pass the word. In three days' time all who are willing will leave this haven and go to Hegikaro.'

Ogre glared morosely at the coal scratchings on the wall of the cave and tried to ignore Naxius' voice as it echoed in the aether, sometimes commanding, sometimes conversational and sometimes even wheedling, as it was tonight.

I know you can hear me, Ogre. Let's talk, as we used to.

Ogre blanked his Master's voice and concentrated hard on the symbols. They were from the alphabets of three languages, mixed in with made-up runes. He needed to find the patterns these incomprehensible formations made. He was certain the *Daemonicon di Naxius* was an encryption of a tongue he knew, one he'd learned at his Master's feet, but every word was like a fragment of some whole, as if every fourth letter was missing. It was driving him mad.

There is no thought in your head that I did not place there, Naxius murmured at the edge of aetheric hearing. *All your urges and desires stem from me.*

Ogre was careful not to respond, but in any case, the puzzle was engrossing. He was studying the way some patterns recurred, others almost never, trying over and over, using words in every language, real and made-up, the Master had used in the old days. 'He must have kept one to himself, one I never knew,' Ogre murmured, and realised his voice was rusty from lack of use.

In which case your task is impossible, the Master whispered smugly.

It was becoming impossible to tell which of his Master's words were imagined and which an actual sending through the aether. The itch to *ask* him, to be the focus of that ferocious intellect's attention again, was almost irresistible –

Ogre suddenly broke off and stomped through a low arch at the back of the cave into a new chamber, one he'd not yet showed to Kyrik. It was to here he retreated when it all became too much and he had to escape the walls of arcane symbols he'd drawn.

He lit a gnosis-light, sat in the centre and stared about him.

He'd smoothed the wall with Earth-gnosis before drawing Tarita, her wonderfully expressive, mobile, exciting face, in every possible mood: laughing, smiling, making a point, determined, angry and impatient. Here she was tired, there exasperated, or sad, asleep, alert, focused, vague, bored, teasing . . .

You're nothing to her, the Master told him. *She's with Waqar right now. I see all – I penetrate every veil – and I can tell you that right now his cock is in her and she's grunting like the animal she is –*

'*Shut up –*' Ogre suddenly roared . . . and that was all it took.

<*There you are, Ogre –* there!>

Ogre felt the reaching coils and slammed up a wall, shutting out the Master completely, at the cost of a splitting headache that immediately began to hammer the inside of his skull. Not sure he'd closed the connection in time to prevent being located, he just sat shaking, tears streaming down his rough-hewn face.

Kyrik breathed in, then exhaled, watching his breath plume in the cold evening air. He repeated it, and again, knowing he was procrastinating, gathering courage for the next bout of force-feeding his wife.

'Are you ready?' Sabina asked in Dhassan, then she apologised. 'Sorry; I forget to whom I speak sometimes.'

'I understood you,' Kyrik told her, in her own tongue. 'I lived a long time in the East, remember?'

'Of course,' she said, smiling shyly, then admitted, 'It is good to speak my own tongue sometimes. Rondian is a struggle.' Now that Korznici had departed for the Tuzvolg, she'd appointed herself Hajya's chief caregiver. Their patient was visibly improving, but it remained a harrowing process. 'Ready?' she repeated, and when he nodded, 'Then let's do it.'

She bent to pick up a steaming pot of vegetable stew, fresh from the kitchens.

He took up his water ewer and together they walked to the small hut where Hajya was kept chained up during the night. She woke up as they entered, cowering away from the torch. Kyrik held her secure while Sabina forced water down her throat, but to their surprise, she didn't struggle this time and her eyes didn't darken. Instead, she gave a weak shudder, then swallowed the pure spring water placidly.

When she was done, she looked up at Kyrik and murmured, 'My love . . .'

His heart thudded: these were the first words he'd heard her utter since the aborted coronation that he was sure were wholly her own.

'Hajya?' he started, but his throat choked up. He was about to throw himself at her, but Sabina caught his arm, checking him. He stared at Hajya, reading her aura and finding only *her*. 'It's truly you . . .' His eyes began to stream.

'Fetch Faleesa and Pani, please,' he told Sabina, and when they arrived, he allowed himself to be bustled aside while the women came and went with hot water and sweet-smelling soap, blankets, even perfumes. Each time they passed him, they flashed a hopeful smile.

Kip joined him. 'This is good, yar? We can delay the march to Hegikaro if you want?' His voice sounded like he didn't think that was a good idea, and in truth, Kyrik didn't either.

'No, we'll still go . . .' His mind churned, then he added, 'I'm going to bring Hajya with me.'

'Yar? Is that wise?'

Kyrik sighed. 'Probably not, but I can't let her out of my sight again. Not after all this.'

6

The Governor

The Fall of Women

A common thread runs through both the Kalistham and the Book of Kore, that a weak-willed woman cost man-kind a perfect world. Through the centuries women have been forced to endure the condescending sneers of supercilious clergymen telling us that the very gender we are born into is being punished for the crimes of the first woman. It makes me angry – to which my confessor says, 'Anger is a symptom of your fall.'

ODESSA D'ARK, ORDO COSTRUO, 933

Norostein, Noros
Febreux 936

Ramon Sensini slid into an alcove on the covered walkway that led to the Royal Guardsmen's barracks. All round the snowy compound, shadowy figures were moving in, but the guards remained oblivious. He glanced up at the rock-face where Jeno Commarys was now perched, wreathed in illusory shadows as she readied her shortbow and picked her target.

A taut-faced Tabia slipped into the small space behind him and a moment later Melicho squeezed his tall, angular form into the alcove opposite and raised a thumb, letting Ramon know they were ready.

The barracks were now a prison for the 'mutinying' Royal Guards: two hundred prime fighting men were facing a death sentence because Governor Myron feared their allegiance to the Noros Crown – this despite the fact that King Phyllios was dead and there was no heir apparent.

Ramon conjured a light illusory veil, just enough that someone would have to concentrate hard to see him, and leading Tabia and Melicho forward, pulsed out a signal. All round the barracks, others began to move with him. He was just sixty yards shy of the main doors when a guardsman above the gatehouse stopped his pacing and stared. He was reaching for the warning bell beside him when a glowing shaft took him in the chest, bursting through chainmail and impaling his heart. He slid to the ground and the alarm went unraised.

<*Nice, Jeno,*> Ramon sent, then, <*Move, everyone: now.*>

Running, they burst into the open for the final thirty yards. Ramon saw the slit in the doors open and instantly lanced a mage-bolt through it. He heard a soft cry and a thud as they dashed towards those gates. Tabia used kinesis to reach in and lift the bar on the inside while Melicho was pulsing Earth-gnosis into the stonework around the hinges and floor bolts. Only then did Ramon, using his full Ascendant strength, weave Air-gnosis and kinesis into a smashing blow that ripped the huge gates off their hinges and sent them hurtling down the passage beyond, bowling over a pair of the governor's men.

All around the compound, Ramon's battle-magi were hitting the walls, flying or leaping to the top of the thirty-foot barriers and flashing mage-bolts into the defenders, who were mostly ordinary men. Ramon gathered his strength – Ascendant or not, the exercise of great power came at a cost – and slipping in behind Melicho and Tabia, took the passage through the gatehouse. A soldier appeared from the right, but Melicho quickly cut him down. An arrow slashed past Tabia's ear, glancing off her shielding, and she blazed back with gnostic-fire.

Ramon broke past the pair as the doors opposite opened and a battle-mage emerged, wreathed in the pale blue web of shields and streaming a volley of mage-bolts while roaring out orders. Ramon closed in with a blinding, kinesis-propelled leap, the mage-bolts dispersing on his stronger shields, and thrust his shortsword at the man's chest. The Imperial magé managed to interpose the wrought-iron rod he was brandishing, wielding it like a quarterstaff, and Ramon was momentarily driven back – until he blazed a massive burst of energy along his blade which cleaved the mage's stave in half before the sword impaled the man's chest.

The mage was still trying to choke out a final call of encouragement to his men as he died.

Waste of a brave man, Ramon thought sourly, yanking out his weapon. Ducking to avoid a purple-wreathed crossbow bolt, he darted to the door. He sent a massive ball of fire rolling through the doorway, laced with additional illusions to attack the senses of anyone caught in the blast, and followed immediately after, wreathed in shields to protect himself from the flames now roaring up the plastered timber walls. A young woman in mage-robes was writhing on the floor, screaming that she was on fire, although she was barely singed: his illusions had completely taken her in. *At least I can stop her caterwauling*, he told himself as he hammered the hilt of his blade into her temple, laying her out, then he moved on. Kicking open the next door, he found a crossbow-wielding battle-mage, loading a bolt wreathed in purple light.

Necromancer . . .

Ramon blurred across the room, slashed down and shattered the crossbow, then hacked into the man's shoulder blade. The sword crunched through muscle and bone and into something vital and a moment later the necromancer was down, choking on blood and swiftly losing consciousness.

Ramon only noticed Tabia and Melicho had pushed in behind him when Melicho's boot came stomping down on the small scarab that emerged from the mouth of the fallen battle-mage, reducing the insect – and the necromancer's intellect – to a smear before it could dart to safety.

'I rukkin' *despise* necromancers,' the tall mercenary grumbled, coughing from the smoke.

'Um . . . you're one yourself,' Ramon noted.

'*Other* necromancers,' Melicho clarified.

'That was a human being,' Tabia noted, always the most compassionate of his magi.

'Nah, it was a rukkin' bug.'

She gave the two men a reproving look, then closed her eyes and listened to the aether. 'We're all in, boss,' she reported. 'No one down, and most of the defenders surrendered pretty quick once they realised it was us. Looks like we're the only ones who ran into magi.'

Ramon grunted in satisfaction. 'Tell them "good work",' he said, pulling the key-chain from the massive hook on the wall and flicking it to Melicho. 'Get the cells unlocked, put Myron's people inside, re-arm the Royal Guards and bring the captain to me. His name's Era Hyson. Tell the lads to man the walls in case someone's managed to warn the governor that we've come outside visiting hours.'

In a few minutes they had the Royal Guards freed and the surviving Imperial guardsmen locked up in their place. Ramon watched from the window, listening to the aether, as reports from the men on watch streamed into his mind.

No alarm sounding, Boss, was the message. *All clear*.

I doubt that, Ramon thought. *I bet Myron knows. We need to move quickly.*

Melicho brought in Era Hyson, a sober-looking young man with short blond hair and an uncharacteristically scruffy beard, the legacy of his interment. He immediately offered Ramon his hand. 'Thank you, Capitano. My men and I are obliged.' He glanced at the fallen imperial necromancer and his eyes narrowed. 'I'm not sorry to see that one's body, I must confess. He was a Questioner. Did you—?'

Melicho indicated the crushed smear of insect of the floor with an air of vindication.

Hyson smiled grimly, then told Ramon, 'My men are at your disposal, Capitano.'

'Call me Ramon. We're going after Myron. Will you aid us?'

'Ah.' Hyson looked out the window at the parade ground, where his men were slowly emerging, blinking at the brightness of the sun and snow. Ramon's men were bringing out their gear from an armoury. 'Governor Myron has certainly not done well by Norostein during his reign as governor.'

Despite the urgency of the situation – even now Myron could be boarding his treasure-laden windships – Ramon gave the Guard Captain time, for this was no small decision. Rhys Myron was, after all, the imperially appointed governor of Noros, which gave him full legal authority to act as he pleased. Even though he was failing to defend his province and undermining those who were, acting against him was an act of treason that could bring down brutal reprisals from Pallas.

'We are the Royal Guard,' Hyson mused aloud, 'but our king is dead and there is no heir. The governor had the legal right to disband us.'

'But not to lock you up and accuse you of treason,' Ramon noted.

'No, not that.' Hyson flexed his fists thoughtfully. 'We're not soldiers, Ramon, we're burghers of Norostein sworn to serve and protect our fellows. Or we were. Now we're just . . . I don't know. Citizens?'

'Justiciar Detabrey's counsel is that Governor Myron is failing his province and endangering the people in his charge. We – Justiciar Detabrey, Lord Korion and I – have lodged Terms of impeachment with Empress Lyra. Regardless, this is a war zone and the ranking general has the right to assume command. I'm here with General Korion's approval.'

'Does the empress know or care?' Hyson wondered, then he sighed. 'Regardless, this isn't about her, is it? It's about Noros: the enemy is at *our* gate, not hers. I'm with you.'

'Good,' said Ramon. 'Let's get started.'

The moment the signal came from the dying mage stationed at the barracks-prison, Governor Rhys Myron knew it was time to run. Fortunately, he was fully prepared for such an exigency.

'We should've beheaded the whole rukking Royal Guard,' he snarled at Freimark, his aide. 'It's time to leave – grab your things.' He shouldered past the dithering assistant. '*Now*, Freimark,' he snapped, realising the young man had barely moved. 'Sound the bells, man!'

Freimark composed himself and pulsed a signal through the aether. In seconds bells were tolling through the Governor's Mansion. Myron abandoned his office and burst in on servants hefting cases of clothes and jewellery from his personal chambers: the last few bits of plunder from this dank, grey Kore-forsaken ice box.

'*Move!*' he bawled, flinging open the bedroom door to reveal the luscious Lady Whatshername naked on his bed, tangled in sheets. '*Out, out,*' he roared. '*Get out, whore!*' He ran for the bed, dropped to his knees and hauled out his strong-box, backhanding her furiously when she tried to take his arm. 'Get out of the way, slut–'

'Rhys,' she wailed, 'you said you'd take me with you—'

'You? Rukk off!' He hit her again, sending her sprawling. She pulled herself shakily to her feet, grabbed the sheet and fled, screaming.

Stupid cow. She'd been an enthusiastic fuck for sure, but there'd be another just like her in the next city. *What matters is leaving here with my fortune intact.*

He shouted for Neimanson, his bloodman. The pure-blood battle-mage was Hollenian, a mercenary at heart, battle-scarred and vengeful of the merest slight. In truth, Myron feared him, but he felt better having the man at his back.

'Get us to the windship,' he ordered, and Neimanson's men formed up around Myron as he bustled down the stairs, powering through the exploding chaos of imperocrats realising their own games of wealth and power were over too. If they'd had the forethought to secure their own passage on one of the windships, he'd doubtless see them in Bricia.

If not, I'll read about their hangings in a few weeks.

Someone tried to accost him, but Neimanson hurled the man over the railing; a woman screamed as the body plummeted three flights and *splatted* on the tiled floor of the entrance hall. Freimark sprinted to catch up just as the governor's group burst from the main doors. Even through the wildly pealing bells, Myron heard a giant crash from the Ringwald Gatehouse and the cries of the mob, baying for his blood.

Farewell, bumpkins. I hope the Shihad slaughters you all.

The giant square before the Governor's Mansion was lined with a dozen windships. The crews were frantically hauling up sails and trying to board those who'd purchased passage, at the same time attempting to keep out the hundreds who hadn't, slamming pike-hafts into the faces of the besieging interlopers. All the while, soldiers were clattering on the double to the perimeters.

Myron's group headed for the largest ship, with Neimanson's men cutting brutally through the swarming crowds. Then he felt the sudden concussion of gnostic power nearby and the shouting reached a crescendo. A blast of fire exploded among a detachment of imperial legionaries as men sporting Royal Guard tabards, flanked by a score of maroon-robed magi, burst into the southern end of the plaza.

Sensini's rukking battle-magi, he thought. The aether throbbed with gnostic blasts, but his most loyal magi had purchased passage out, so no one of merit was fighting to hold the perimeter. Sensini's men were carving through the flimsy defences at an alarming rate.

'Get us aboard!' he roared, and his escort redoubled their efforts to reach his flagship, smashing aside hapless servants and panic-stricken functionaries. Neimanson, a force of nature, continued hacking a bloody path through the press, sweeping Myron along in his wake, and thirty seconds later he was being bundled onto his vessel. Anxious hands started tugging him this way and that, while the windship captain dithered over who else to haul up from the throng below.

'*Rukk them, Captain,*' Myron roared, '*just get us out of here!*'

The captain complied with alacrity. His pilot kindled the Air-gnosis pent up in the keel and without warning the ship shot upwards to the full extent of the mooring ropes. Those left below shrieked in dismay – and then horror as one man in the process of clambering aboard lost his balance and fell, crushing someone below. The crew began cutting the windship free of the ropes, dislodging frantic men and women as the ship wrenched free and shot into the air.

Myron's fears subsided. There was no way Sensini's blackguards could reach them now.

'Those pricks below have already paid me for passage,' he smirked at Freimark, 'but it's not my fault if they miss the flight.'

At the edge of the plaza, Sensini's mages and the Royal Guards were driving through the imperial soldiers, who bereft of gnostic support, were turning tail as they realised the person they were supposed to be defending was already gone. Other windships were now trying to leave, but most were ensnared, the despairing crowds pulling on the anchor ropes, trying to haul the vessels back down. The sheer weight of bodies was causing most of them to founder – only one other had got airborne . . . *No, there's a third*, he thought, watching as the ship rose from the throng at the southern end. It wallowed, then caught the wind and started climbing into the skies in their wake. The rest had been swamped – and two had been set alight.

Not my problem, Myron thought smugly.

'Get us up above ballista range, then make for Bres,' he told the captain, before turning back to Freimark. 'We've got to get our report in first, make sure Korion wears the blame. Start drafting and I'll join you presently.'

Freimark bobbed his head dutifully and scurried off towards the stern cabins, which had already been laid out with a view to Governor Myron's pleasure. As the aide left, Neimanson stalked to Myron's side. 'The main gates to the upper tier of the city have fallen to the mob,' he reported, glaring down at the receding city, before adding, 'I'd hoped to cross blades with Sensini. Last night I cast the cards. They told me that I am fated to meet him in battle and take his head.'

'I'd have liked to have seen that very much,' Myron replied, 'but with the Shihad already inside the walls, I expect he's destined for a Noorie's axe.'

'The cards never lie,' Neimanson said dismissively. 'It is fated that I shall be his death.'

'Kore will it so,' Myron said tolerantly. He could overlook a man's superstitions when he was as competent a bloodman as Neimanson.

The vessel swung on the breeze, the bow turning towards the northwest. Below, Myron could see the dirty stain of the mob spilling into the upper tier of the city, then he cast his vision wider to take in Copperleaf, the second tier still held by Korion's men; and then to the burned-out expanse of Lowertown, where the unholy Noories swarmed like an infestation of rats in the charred wreckage and snows.

They'll take decades to rebuild this pigsty, he thought dismissively. *I'm glad to be out of it.*

Neimanson looked behind at the two vessels in their wake and frowned. Myron followed his gaze and saw immediately what had perturbed his bloodman. The third vessel, a swift sloop, was drawing up alongside the second windship. It was flying too close, fouling their air.

'What're they—' Neimanson began, but stopped when gnostic energy blazed and without warning, fire and lightning slammed into the stern. The pilot-mage must've been killed or at least injured, because the merchantman immediately veered aside, then foundered and started drifting downwards – but the sloop was now trimming its sails and surging in Myron's wake.

Neimanson grunted in satisfaction. 'Looks like I'll get that chance at Sensini after all.'

Myron felt the colour drain from his face. He strode to the captain, shouting, 'Get this damned ship moving—' Spraying spittle, he added, 'You've got the better craft – outrun them!'

'It's the bigger ship, but not the faster,' the captain replied, wiping his face. 'Run out the stern ballista,' he bellowed at his crew. 'Shield the pilot – archers to stations!'

'Get us out of this, captain, and you'll be a peer of the realm,' Myron told him, not meaning a word of it. 'Send them crashing down and I'll marry your fucking daughter.'

The captain threw him a doubtful look, but self-preservation was evidently all the motivation he needed, for he strode off bawling orders, while Neimanson, licking his lips in anticipation, loosed his sword in his scabbard and conjured shields.

This is the bigger ship, Myron reminded himself. *They might catch us, but they can't best us.*

With the crewmen dispersed to action stations, the ship lost some of its momentum and the sloop gained swiftly. It was filled with maroon-clad battle-magi and blue-clad Royal Guard. Myron recognised Era Hyson and cursed himself for not having throttled the wretch in his cell. Then he saw a lean, dark-haired mage: Ramon Sensini himself.

'You've stuck your neck out too far this time,' Myron told the distant figure.

The half-breed mercenary capitano didn't worry him, but there were a lot of magi on that sloop, and on this vessel too. *That much power in one place could bring us all down.* With that in mind, Myron scuttled to the cabin doors, unwilling to be a target for Sensini's marksmen.

Perhaps there's a safe place below?

Norostein was a mile astern and fast receding. The air was frigid and the winds bitter, the terrain below nothing but rocks and ice: the foothills of the Alps. The initial exhilaration of the chase had given way to grim pursuit.

Ramon watched Era Hyson array his guardsmen for battle as the sloop came into range. Their captain had quickly changed sides, the sort of moral agility Ramon appreciated; when he'd told the panicked crew that they were going to drag Myron back in chains, they'd cheered and set their backs willingly to help them get underway. But words were easier than deeds and now the cold reality was setting in.

None of my lads are used to airborne warfare, Ramon admitted, *and that's an Imperial warbird we're chasing – plus, we're thousands of feet above jagged rocks. This could end very, very badly.*

He'd more than half a mind to let the governor be: he'd long ago given up on concepts like divine justice balancing things out, having seen too many bad men reap the rewards of crime unscathed.

So what if Myron gets away? He's gone, that's the important thing. But the thought rankled, so he kept promising himself, *Just a few minutes more, and we'll see how it goes . . .*

The air below-decks stank, Myron found as he clambered down the ladder and strode to his cabin. Some bastard had clearly been dreading the approaching fight, because they'd already shat themselves. He wrinkled his nose and hurried on past Freimark's little bunkroom, from whence the stench was emanating.

Cowardly prick, Myron thought, pushing open his own cabin and slipping inside, turning and locking it . . .

. . . as the tip of a blade touched his throat, right above the jugular.

'Shush, Governor,' a woman's accented voice whispered gleefully.

A Rimoni . . . one of Sensini's . . . Myron froze as the steel edge stung his skin. His captor used another blade in her free hand to slice his belt and his trousers and sword-belt fell to the floor. She kicked them under the bed, then shoved him face-first onto the mattress. He groaned as his knees hit the floor painfully hard, but a second later something jabbed his right buttock. His captor behind him had her own knees pressed to his back, one blade still against his neck.

'You're a bad man, Governor,' she tittered. 'Should I spank you?'

'I . . . uh–'

He wondered if he could get a spell away before she had time to react, but she pricked his neck again, almost as if she'd read his thoughts. 'Just keep it quiet, si?'

He managed to twist his head enough to get a glimpse of her: a narrow-faced woman with coppery skin and black ringlets, bizarrely clad in a nun's habit.

'You're on the wrong side,' he told her. 'I could make it worth your while to let me go.'

She pulled a faux vexed face. 'No, you couldn't, sorry. Wouldn't dream of pissing the boss off.'

'So gold means nothing to you?' Myron asked slyly.

''course it does,' she sing-songed. 'I'm as corruptible as all Hel. Just not around the boss.'

'Then why are we even talking?' Myron reasoned aloud. 'If you meant to kill me, you'd have done it by now.'

The Rimoni woman chuckled darkly in his ear. 'Who says I haven't?'

At first Myron didn't understand, then he was suddenly stricken with a debilitating, numbing sensation, like acid and opium running in his veins, spreading from his right buttock, up his spine and down his legs. He tried to scream for Freimark – then he realised that Freimark must be dead already – and in any case, his throat wouldn't work any more, for his tongue had seized up and his bowels were turning to liquid, gushing out to ruin his under-breeches as his muscles went flaccid.

'Pooh,' the woman sniffed. 'Wish they'd give me a poison that didn't give folk the runs.' Then she shoved his face into the mattress again and said, 'Goodbye, Governor.'

He tried to plead, but darkness rushed in as his vision collapsed . . .

Ramon pushed through to the captain's side. 'Captain Arkham, right? Can you get us close without that damned ballista wrecking our day?'

The magnificently whiskered windshipman shook his head. 'Not unless they're the worst shots in Koredom.'

Ramon *tsked*. 'Right then, this has gone far enough. The mission's done, close enough, and who cares if–'

He broke off as a hatch in the stern of the governor's vessel opened and flames licked around a figure in black and white clambering out. Whoever it was waved at Ramon's sloop, then launched into the air, arms spread like a giant magpie, and swooped towards him.

He caught Arkham's arm. 'Cancel all that, Captain. Get that nun aboard, will you? She's just saved us a lot of trouble.'

Ramon hurried to the prow as Vania di Aelno landed, striking an artistic pose just as smoke and red tongues billowed from the portals of the governor's warbird. They heard cries of alarm and saw the crewmen dropping their weapons and go racing for axes, buckets and blankets.

Her fellow battle-magi engulfed Vania, backslapping and crowing, but Ramon was still watching the stricken warbird as it dipped and wallowed. He saw a rugged-looking mage stalk to the stern and give him a hard stare, the only calm man amid chaos.

<*I am Arnulf Neimanson and I am fated to be your death, Sensini,*> the man sent.

Ramon sent him back a quizzical, <*Really? There's no such thing as Fate, Neimanson.*>

Behind Neimanson, the warbird's crew were rushing hither and thither as the pilot hurled negation spells into the keel, desperately trying to de-power it before the flames reached it and it exploded. The captain was on his knees, pleading to Kore.

<*It is written in the cards,*> Neimanson roared.

<*Good luck with that,*> Ramon sent, giving the man an ironic salute and turning away. 'How's the Governor?' he called to the beaming Vania.

'Shitting himself, in a posthumous kind of way,' she replied merrily. 'What a glorious day! Does anyone wanna get drunk with me?' She laughed at the chorus of offers and blew a kiss at Ramon. 'What about it, boss-man?'

Ramon pulled a face. 'It'd just undermine my authority, such as it is,' he told her.

He turned to the captain, about to tell him to shadow the warbird down, as there was likely plunder to be had – but a blinding flash erupted from its hull and the whole craft came apart in a burst of fire and jagged splinters that ripped passengers and crew to shreds.

Neimanson fell amid the wreckage, already in pieces.

Cards, eh? What next – tea leaves?

Seth Korion strode into the governor's suite, followed by Vann Mercer. After his magi had checked the place for gnostic traps, the soldiers had been through seeking fugitives. All clear on both counts, he'd been told.

He was leafing through the governor's papers when Era Hyson and Vorn Detabrey entered, followed swiftly by Ramon Sensini, whose stolen windship had landed minutes ago in the main square to great applause. The other ships had all been grounded and those who'd been trying to escape were currently being detained in one of the ballrooms. The more senior, including some of Norostein's wealthiest pure-blood magi, were under arrest; they'd mostly eschewed keeping their gnosis up to martial standards in favour of a life of luxury and ease, so there'd been little resistance. They were probably safer here anyway: the city was filled with people who wanted them all hung.

'How're we doing?' he asked Mercer.

'We're distributing food,' Vann reported, 'and that's taking the edge off the riot. Impounding the windcraft and everything on them has pissed everyone off, but we've got control, for now at least.'

Seth looked at Ramon. 'Governor Myron?'

'I had someone aboard his ship when it went up,' Ramon smirked. 'They set fire to it and leaped before it exploded. There were no survivors.'

Seth met his friend's eye. 'Give your agent my commendation.'

'It'd only go to her head,' Ramon replied. 'So, we can feed the lads a while longer. How many of Myron's people are prepared to defend the walls?'

'All of them claim to be,' Detabrey noted, 'but whether that's honest I can't say.'

'We'll give them the chance,' Seth said. 'We're cornered here – even the rats should be motivated to fight.' He looked north, towards

Lowertown. 'The Shihad have been making the change in sultan for the past week, but they'll attack any day now. We need to look to our defences again.'

Ramon raised a hand. 'Regarding that,' he said gravely, 'when we overflew them on our return, there was a large formation of men approaching the Shihad camp from the east.'

Hyson and Detabrey groaned, and inwardly Seth did too, but he was also puzzled. 'From the *east*? Are you sure? The only way the Shihad reinforcements *should* approach is from the north, down the King's Road from Jastenberg. That's where the rest of their forces are. Even if new men were coming in from Verelon through Trachen Pass, they'd still come that way.'

Ramon agreed. 'The only road leading here from the east is the coastal track that winds around the alps from the south up from Silacia and Rimoni.'

'Then is this a Rimoni army, come to our aid?' Era Hyson asked hopefully.

Ramon was shaking his head and looking worried. 'I wish. I'm afraid that I recognised the banners. For the past five years, my legion has been fighting alongside the Becchio Mercenary Guild against a Rimoni army full of men who fight like savages. Long story short, we've been driven from the south. They're led by someone known only as "the Lord of Rym".'

Seth looked at Ramon and saw his eyes were burning with an unusual intensity. *This Lord of Rym means something personal to him*, Seth guessed, but he left that for now.

'Then our enemy has been reinforced,' he said aloud. 'It's a damned good thing we've dealt with Myron.'

'It is,' Ramon agreed, 'but if the Lord of Rym is here to aid our enemies, we're in worse trouble than ever.'

When Waqar Mubarak crawled through the cellar hatch and out into the mud, the frigid air hit him like a slap to the face. He rose and found himself eyeball to eyeball with the elephant Rani, who was sitting under a canvas sending plumes of white steam into the starry firmament. She made a grumbling noise, blinking at him as he stroked her trunk.

Latif followed him up the ladder. The impersonator looked tired but sounded feverishly alert as he whispered, 'My Prince, I wish you didn't have to leave us.'

'What choice do I have?' Waqar asked. 'I can hardly stand up and denounce Xoredh, and every moment I'm here just endangers us more.'

'But the task you've set yourself ... I wish we could aid you somehow.'

The task': killing the sultan, my cousin Xoredh, a daemon in human guise. He sighed. 'I'll do it, this I swear,' he said. 'You should leave too.'

'We can't: this is Yuros,' Latif replied. 'There's nowhere we can go that's safer than here.'

Waqar disagreed, but of course, he was a mage, better able to fend for himself in the wild. There was no way these men could, especially not with an elephant they couldn't bear to part with. He patted Rani's trunk fondly – even he'd grown to appreciate the beast's patience, intelligence and loyalty. He also respected the courage of Latif and his friends: elephants always attracted the enemy's fire in battle. They'd faced Rondian archers, magi and ballistae and somehow, through a mix of courage, luck and knowing when to run, come through alive.

All attributes I'm going to need.

'Then keep your heads down,' he exhorted, taking Latif's hand and pressing a signet ring into it; he had only one left now. 'If you're discovered, this might buy you a sympathetic ear with some of the court.'

Then he crept out into the night, past the slumbering elephant teams and into a muddy garbage-filled alley. The air was bitter, the moon shrouded and the light poor, but with gnostic night-sight he was able to ghost through Lowertown, a maze-like sea of broken stone houses covered in snow and ice. The upper tiers of Copperleaf and Ringwald, still unconquered, loomed above, dimly lit by the cloud-shrouded moon.

He made his way down the slope towards the outer walls, passing few patrols, for he was still well inside the vast Shihadi camp. Anyone he saw was completely anonymous, enveloped in scarves and blankets, anything to keep the bitter chill at bay.

He reached Lowertown Lake unchallenged, but as he neared the damaged outer walls, he took more care, for only foraging parties were allowed outside the walls. Moving cautiously, he wended his way forward, crouching behind the charred remains of a fallen brick wall, as a patrol of Shihadi soldiers swaggered past. They didn't look his way, too engrossed with boasting about the drink and women they'd had during the celebrations. By Waqar's calculations, the army had devoured a month's supplies in one week; there couldn't be much food left.

'Ahm bless Sultan Xoredh,' one laughed, 'a more generous lord than Rashid ever was.'

The officer cuffed the man's ear and growled, 'Don't speak ill of the dead, you fool, even in jest. Rashid was beloved of Ahm. He is seated even now in Paradise, watching us all.'

Are you in Paradise, Rashid? Waqar wondered, *or deep in Shaitan's Pit? I could make a case either way.*

Once they'd moved on, he hurried through the moonlit night. Deserters were executed without trial – not that he feared the soldiers, just the magi who'd come after them – but no one stopped him. He reached the mass of buildings behind a section of breached walls, half-wrecked Rondian taverns and whorehouses, and judging by the racket, functioning largely as they always had. There were women of all races and ages, catering to all tastes, and no shortage of alcohol – that might be a sin in Ahm's eyes but soldiers still drowned themselves in it, along with the opium that bedevilled the army.

Two men emerged from an alley to accost him, footpads from Dhassa, he guessed by their accents, but kinesis-enhanced fists quickly saw to them. Easily bypassing a cordon of guards huddled around braziers, their gazes turned inwards, he reached the breach. Discipline had grown lax under Xoredh.

What game is he playing now he's the ruler? Waqar wondered. *Does he still care about this war? Did he ever?*

He climbed a broken section of wall, used kinesis to leap the moat and stole into the flat expanse of the killing zone. It had been cleared of bodies, but there were still pyres burning here and there, and mounds of charred bones taller than houses.

Beyond that was the forest, where Xoredh had set wide patrols to guard against the mounted Rondians who still plagued the supply lines, but Waqar was lucky: only minutes later he was under cover and undetected. He was wondering where to seek Tarita when he saw a line of horses emerge from the shattered main gates of the city. The horses were white and therefore from the sultan's court, and both they and the riders were encased in a nimbus of gnostic shielding, haloed like the saints of Koredom.

It's Xoredh, he realised. *Where's he going tonight?* His interest deepened when the sultan's party didn't take the north road but went east. *There's nothing there but a back road to the coast, then it turns south into Silacia*, he remembered. *Is he going to meet someone? Is this my opportunity already?*

Impulsively he followed, using the gnosis to avoid blundering into men or trees and to bolster his speed. He kept the riders in sight as they wound through farmlands for some three miles until they reached a burnt-out manor where the paddocks were filled with rows of huddled shapes, dark mounds dotting the snow. He was wondering what they were – *Haystacks, perhaps?* – when they all rose soundlessly.

He stared, horrified, as his night sight showed him hundreds of emaciated living corpses, their eyes a luminous black, like the men Asiv Fariddan had enslaved in Mollachia. But these wore some strange Yurosi mail, a style he'd not encountered before.

Possessed men, like we fought in Mollachia – but from where?

Waqar crept forward through the undergrowth until he was close enough to see that his cousin's guards were as black-eyed as the dead-alive men they'd encountered. Xoredh had evidently been spreading his blessing.

He preys even on his friends . . . A wave of nausea washed over him. *This is just like Mollachia and Asiv Fariddan all over again.*

Equally horrified and intrigued, he moved closer, regretting his lack of clairvoyance and feeling dangerously exposed, but everyone's attention was on the sultan.

From the wrecked manor house emerged a great hulking masked being, a construct type he was familiar with – and then he went rigid, for he recognised the very ogre who had captured Jehana. He was taller, straighter and more lordly than Tarita's friend, and clad in ornate crested armour, but he wore the mask Waqar had seen in Guz Sarkan:, that of a green scaled skull with a scarlet snake-tongue. His shining eyes were not black, but tarnished gold, and as he approached, Xoredh *knelt* – an obeisance no sultan should ever have to make.

'My Lord of Rym,' Xoredh started, with none of his usual superiority. The title puzzled Waqar, for surely the ancient capital of Rimoni was empty, a vast ruin left deserted by imperial decree. There was no 'Lord of Rym'.

'Rise, Sultan of Kesh,' the huge construct boomed. 'Call me Cadearvo. Are you ready for us?'

Waqar frowned. *Cadearvo is from the heathen* Book of Kore. *He's the Angel of Famine . . .*

'We're more than ready,' Xoredh replied, still sounding subservient, but adding, 'We needed you last month.'

'The previous sultan refused our Master's aid and even this army takes time to move,' Cadearvo growled. 'Be grateful we're here now. How swiftly can we integrate our forces?'

Integrate? What does that mean? Waqar wondered, straining his senses – then he blanched. *Do they mean to infect the entire Shihad with daemon ichor?* The thought almost stopped his heart.

In matter-of-fact tones, Xoredh replied, 'I suggest we march them one hazarabam at a time, unarmed, into your camp – we'll pretend it's a celebration for their valour, or some such nonsense.'

No, Waqar thought in horror, *that cannot be permitted –*

But Xoredh was still speaking. 'And you have how many men?'

'I bring you fifty thousand possessed beings,' the Lord of Rym said grandly. 'They do not need to sleep or rest, and they fight like savages. How many do you have?'

Fifty thousand? Dear Ahm . . .

'I have three hundred thousand men here,' Xoredh replied, 'and another two hundred thousand at the southern end of the Augenheim Pass; we can integrate them in due course.'

'Enough to conquer the whole of Yuros,' the Lord of Rym said lightly, 'should we need to.' He dropped his voice, and so did Xoredh.

No longer able to hear, Waqar cursed and looked around until he spotted a narrow ditch that might get him nearer. He slipped from his hiding place—

Crack!

The sound of the stick breaking under his heel filled the night.

Every head turned his way, every black eye lancing through the frozen air to skewer him. He felt each stabbing glance like a blow, from the unmoving, lordly, inhuman visage of Cadearvo to the ferocity on the ruined faces of the dead men to Xoredh's surprise and anger – but attacking him was impossible: he had to *run*—

Waqar spun around. Streaming energy into his limbs, he propelled himself into the darkness, concentrating his shielding behind him. Mage-bolts were already slashing past him and battering his shields when he heard a bloodcurdling yowl from a thousand throats and the ground suddenly shook as every man in the fields behind launched into pursuit. Even worse, he heard Xoredh's horses whinnying and the thud of heavy hooves – and *something* shrieked like Shaitan in the night sky above.

Seeking the cover of the trees, he ran, leaping yards at a time thanks to kinesis – but many of those hunting him could do the same and energy blasts constantly sniped at his heels.

Hooves pounding on the road were drawing near; he'd soon be overtaken – then a beast snarled, far too close, and he whipped round just in time to see a pair of black-eyed drooling dogs closing in, jaws agape. He planted his feet and blasted energy from either hand: their skulls igniting, revealing the outline of bone inside the lit-up flesh – but there was a third hound he'd not seen, already airborne and arcing towards him—

– as another blast of light burned incandescent, ripping down from above to tear the third hound apart, and Tarita's voice called urgently, '*Up here!*'

Looking up at a flurry of feathers and light and guessing her intent, he put all his energy into a kinesis-fuelled jump. Tarita helped, pulling him towards her, until his flailing hand found her bony shoulders and he was able to grab her.

The golden-winged roc bearing them both rose and tore through the raking branches of the pines and into the sky – and with a great *whoop!* of joy, Waqar suddenly realised it was *his* roc – his own Ajniha, who'd flown away weeks ago. Tarita enveloped them in illusory veils and kept the bird low, skimming the tree-tops.

Despite the freezing air stinging his cheeks and fingers, Waqar held tight, marvelling at his rescue and trembling at what he'd learned, but eventually he leaned forward, pressed his mouth to her ear and called, 'Where are we going?'

Tarita jerked her head in acknowledgement and shouted, 'We're nearly there –' and seconds later they were landing beside a damaged building, another manor house. Waqar jolted from Ajniha's back and hit the ground, but was immediately on his feet and hugging his beloved bird, stroking her giant beaked head and crying, 'Shukran, you wonderful lady, shukran!'

Tarita slid from the saddle with an ironic, 'You're welcome.'

'And as for you –' He strode to the Merozain, picked her up and bearhugged her hard enough to push the air from her lungs. 'You're a *miracle* – truly you are. How did you know to find me there?'

'I didn't,' she replied, blushing at his fervour. 'I was watching the city. When I saw the sultan leave, I followed – when you blundered into it all, I couldn't have been more surprised.'

At last he released her and looked around, surveying his surroundings. 'Where are we? How did you find Ajniha?'

Tarita curtseyed like a dancer acknowledging her audience. 'I needed to find out what was going on so I pretended I was a Keshi mage and infiltrated the Shihad camp. I discovered the traitor prince – that's you – had a price on his head. They hoped you'd come back for your roc, so they locked her away to bait a trap. So I stole her,' she added nonchalantly.

'And you managed it without getting caught? You got clean away?'

'Of course.' She handed him Ajniha's reins and led the way into tumbledown stables off the courtyard, stopping to point out a heraldic emblem carved on the doors. 'As for this place, it's Anborn Manor.' She said this grandly, as if Waqar should know what that meant.

'Um . . . which is?'

She rolled her eyes. 'This is the family home of my mistress, the great Lady Elena Anborn, and her nephew Alaron Mercer – I presume you've heard of *him*?'

The Merozain leader, Waqar thought, startled. 'But the Shihad know of it?'

'Of course,' Tarita said, and even in the darkness he could see her eyes turning stony. 'They ransacked it, they pissed and shat everywhere, and then they set it alight, because they're that sort of stupid. But I guess there must have been someone with half a brain who recognised its use as a winter shelter for wide patrols because they did at least get the fires put out and made some effort at cleaning up.'

'How did you find it?'

'My mistress told me about her childhood many times, so I knew where to look. I've got wards set on the approaches now and I keep my cooking fire hidden. It's been my base for the last few weeks. Now, how about you?'

Waqar gave her a brief outline – after all, hiding in a cellar with an elephant crew didn't require a lot of narrative – and in any case, what he'd just witnessed was much more important. 'So, my cousin – sorry, I mean our exalted Sultan Xoredh, may he live for ever – is working with this Cadearvo, the Lord of Rym, and they're going to infect *everyone* – the *entire* Shihad,' he concluded, 'and somehow, I have to stop them.'

'I thought you needed to save your sister?'

'I can do both.'

Tarita grimaced. 'Can you?'

'The whole Shihad are going to be enslaved to our enemy – that's half a million men!'

'We still don't know what Ervyn Naxius wants your sister for,' she retorted. 'Do you think that's going to be any less dangerous to us all?'

Waqar went to reply, then hesitated. Naxius wielded both power and creativity: he was capable of *anything*. And honour demanded he find his sister.

But half a million men enslaved . . . ?

He suddenly felt completely overwhelmed. Tomorrow Xoredh was going to start sending his men to Cadearvo, but he might already be too late to find Jehana.

Deal with what's in front of you, he decided. 'We have to warn the Shihad.'

He half-expected a fight, but Tarita sighed and said, 'I think that's the right choice too – but how?'

'I'm not sure yet, but I do know a few people who might listen. Some of Rashid's commanders like Admiral Valphath, who's been brought south in readiness for the next assault. And my own roc-riders, of course . . . and the men who've been sheltering me these last few days.' It sounded a paltry group for a prince. 'In any case, I have to try. But are we safe here for tonight?'

'Safe as anywhere. I have blankets, cooking gear and a little food and there's a fire set in the kitchen.' She gave a sudden grin. 'There's no servants here, my Prince. We have to cook our own meals.'

'Just set me to work,' he told her.

'What, and let you cook? I don't think so! We'll do it together. You'll find a bucket by the door there and there's a stream right outside.'

While they worked companionably together, lighting the fire, fetching water, soaking lentils and dried meat, almost the last of Tarita's rations, he filled in the gaps in his story, pleased to be able to bring a smile to Tarita's eyes when she heard that Latif was still alive; in turn, she told Waqar how she'd helped Latif escape the slaughter of Sultan Salim's household in Sagostabad.

They shared a welcome meal, but conversation petered out as the night loomed before them. Waqar couldn't stop himself wondering what happened next. *I've kissed her. She offered herself before and I turned her down . . .* But that had been at the fortress at Trachen Pass, when he'd not long lost Bashara, his most recent lover, and it had felt all wrong that night.

But life goes on . . .

If she sensed the change in mood, she didn't show it, and she'd laid out the blankets with the fireplace between them. In any case, he still wasn't sure he wanted her. He'd been popular with the gold-digging ladies of the courts but had found only infatuations, never love.

But when he stripped down to his smallclothes and turned, he saw she'd gone further. Standing on the far side of the fire, the flames basted her skin red-gold. She had a voluptuous bosom, shapely and high, and she knew how to hold herself for maximum effect. Desire rose despite his misgivings and goaded by her eyes, he walked around the fire to her, only then noticing a mass of scars running down her spine.

'I haven't been laid in a year,' Tarita said calmly, 'so whatever you've got, I can take. Whatever you want, I can give.' She sank to her haunches.

He peeled his clothing off silently and sat beside her. For a moment or two they didn't move, then Tarita reached out to explore his face with her fingers. He bent down and kissed her, tasting her, and as the embrace deepened, their hands explored each other until impatience took over and he lay down and pulled her onto him. She settled herself, planting a hand on his chest, and then lowering herself onto him, groaning as she was pierced then grinding her hips onto him, one hand planted on his chest and the other stroking her own breasts, a sight which enflamed him, until he rolled her onto her back and rode her, both panting wildly. Finally he expended himself and they subsided into soft gasps of appreciation. Their sweaty bodies still locked together, they shuddered into stillness.

Almost as an afterthought, they kissed again, then disentangled wordlessly and rolled onto their sides, facing each other.

'Shukran,' she murmured. 'It'd been too long.'

'Am I going to find you knocking on my door carrying a child in a year?' he blurted, as it suddenly occurred to him that she might just be that calculating.

She pulled a sour face. 'I'm barren, my Prince, so you've nothing to worry about.' Then she added sadly, 'I'd hoped you had a higher opinion of me than that.'

'I'm sorry,' he muttered, ashamed. 'It's just . . . well, friends of mine have been entrapped so.' He stroked her shoulder until she seemed to accept his apology, then said, 'You once told me you'd never make love to a friend or befriend a lover. So what was this?'

'I don't know yet. Staying warm? What's it to you? You're the Keshi prince here – I'm just dirt-caste. Isn't it my duty to give you whatever you want?'

'It's not like that. You're a mage. Though that doesn't matter . . .'

. . . if you're barren . . .

She heard his unthinking meaning and her face turned sullen, then she shrugged. 'Well, perhaps as an outcast prince you're not such a catch either. But maybe we might end up friends.'

Her summation of his status rankled, but he couldn't fault it. 'If we can't bring Xoredh down then yes, I'm an outcast.' He wondered if her pricklish words were meant to re-establish distance between them again. 'Anyway . . .'

'Ai,' she murmured, yawning, 'I don't want to talk about it now.' She patted his cheek. 'Thanks for the fuck.' She rolled over and wriggled backwards into the crook of his body. 'Hold me while we sleep – it's damned cold on this frigid continent.'

Conversation over. Is that making friends, in her world? Mind you, after what I said to her, can I blame her?

Whatever the reason, she clearly didn't want to talk. Her breathing slowed and he too found himself fading into slumber.

Tarita woke and knew instantly that Waqar was awake as well. The air was frigid around her face and exposed shoulders but the fragments of sky she could see through the broken windows were beginning to lighten. She squirmed backwards, pushing against Waqar's body, felt his arousal, then grunted in discomfort until he worked through her dry outer lips and found the slickness inside. His arms enfolded her and pulled her even closer as he filled her and for a few minutes they moved as one, his breath hot on her neck and his fingers pinching at her nipples. She was building nicely toward release, but all too soon he gasped, thrusting harder and faster, and came.

Feeling somewhat unfulfilled, she murmured, 'Good morning.'

He slid his hand down her belly to her mound, still speared, and teased her nub, making an enquiring, 'Mmm?'

'Shush,' she said, putting a hand over his, 'we've got all day – we can't move during the daylight.'

He returned his hand to her breast, while his cock slipped out wetly. 'Did you . . . climax?'

'Ai,' she lied, snuggling back into the blanket. 'Let's get some more sleep.'

He was awake, though. 'About our . . . um, arrangement,' he said tentatively. 'I couldn't offer you a title, but if you wished, I could make you a concubine. You'd live in luxury.'

'I'm a known Jhafi spy,' she reminded him. 'Not to mention a dirt-caste girl with no manners.' She rolled over to face him – it was definitely lighter outside now and she could dimly make out his face. 'I'd be an embarrassment at court.'

'Manners can be learned, and you're smart – renounce Javon and pledge to me. I can offer you palaces, silks and jewels. Comfort, safety . . .' He flashed his teeth. 'Regular bedding.'

She found herself teetering on the edge of saying 'yes', then wondered why she wasn't feeling grateful for his offer. What more could she hope for? This was a chance to swap a life of danger for pleasure with a decent man whose future was glittering.

But royal households were large and he'd marry, several times. There'd be other concubines as well, all vying for supremacy, and she'd be outranked and despised by the rest, who would inevitably be high-born and beautiful. And despite the problems, there was a lot she loved about her current life – the travel, the moments of triumph, the stolen pleasures . . . and yes, even the danger . . .

It was strange to examine a dream and find it so empty.

'I'd be just another harem girl,' she mused aloud. 'A caged bird.'

'No, I'd not waste your talents,' he promised her, stroking her thigh. You're a warrior-mage – you'd be your own mistress, answering only to me.' He looked at her seriously. 'Such an alliance offers us both something.'

He sounded in earnest and perhaps it was possible, even if their liaison felt tenuous right now; he was still more stranger than lover. She wasn't feeling any leap of joy, though, for the riddle that had plagued her so long – could she have both friendship and love? – remained unanswered.

But an alliance? People spoke of dynastic marriages as 'alliances', so perhaps that might work? 'I will think about it,' she told him, and pressed her lips to his.

The day passed in a languid blur of sleeping and screwing, which was exactly what she needed after the hardships she'd endured.

I could get used to him, she decided much later, watching him sleep. *And my mistress will welcome having a spy in a Keshi prince's bed – if he lives long enough to be useful.*

No one came near and at dusk they rose, washed and dressed, then sent Ajniha out with instructions to hunt and find shelter, before setting out on foot towards Norostein.

Rym, Rimoni

Jehana stared along the starkly furnished table, feeling utterly wretched. Tears welled again from her eyes and spilled through the eye-holes of her mask to splatter on the wood.

Through the barred window, cold sunlight revealed the ruined expanse of Rym, reflecting off slabs of pale stone to make the shadows deepen. There was no warmth in the sterile air – she felt perpetually cold. For days on end she had been drifting from room to room like a wraith, unable to reach either gnosis or dwyma and unable to leave her suite. There were no books or musical instruments, nothing to distract her from her plight, and no company but despair – and Ervyn Naxius.

Black-eyed men and women came and went silently, bringing hot water and drink, making her eat, taking away her waste. She was paralysed in their presence, dreading them, though none had harmed her.

Mostly she paced her cage, pausing only at the mirror to stare at herself. They'd left her no clothes, not even smallclothes, except for a silken shift, the flimsy white fabric displaying her body in ways she didn't like, revealing her shape by the way the silk clung to her curves. But it was the skull mask and the shimmering white hair that frightened her most. She hadn't been able to get it off and her skin still bled around the copper edges where she'd tried to rip it away.

The door swung silently open to admit Ervyn Naxius, in his favoured guise of a slim, sharp-faced redhead. Immediately Jehana's pulse quickened, fear and tension making her throat tighten. She stood petrified as he glided towards her, all smooth confidence.

'Lady Jehana,' he greeted her, running his eyes over her. 'Are you in good heart this morning?'

She didn't dignify that with a response but stared straight ahead as he circled her, murmuring appreciatively, 'Eternity will be a far finer thing with such as you beside me.'

Such as you . . . *as if I'm nothing but an object.*

'You'll be spending eternity in the Pit,' she retorted, mustering a brief spurt of defiance.

He smiled as if she'd made a witty remark. 'Of course, once we've broken down the walls of the world, Urte will effectively become Shaitan's Pit. But I will be Shaitan.'

'You already are.'

'Not yet,' he said lightly. 'Have you ever read the *Book of Kore*? No, of course not, a Keshi princess has far better things to do, eh? But you should: it's a masterpiece in social conditioning, training every generation of Yurosi in how to be good compliant Kore worshippers. I wrote some of it myself, did you know that?'

She stared, caught off-guard by the boast. 'You helped *write* the Yurosi holy book?'

'Indeed. It wasn't dictated by Kore or Corineus, as the text proclaims, just by priests, and for a time I was one. It gave me something to do while hiding from my enemies. Emperor Sertain wished to anoint his dynasty as demigods, effectively, so we produced a "holy book" designed specifically to turn subjects into worshippers.' He made an elegant gesture and added, 'His line rules still, after all – even little Lyra is of Sertain's blood, for all she is a disgrace to it.'

'We Keshi have always known it to be lies.'

'Oh, the *Kalistham* is no less a work of fiction, I assure you,' Naxius countered, then changed the subject back. 'But we digress, Princess. My point is that you are part of the *Book of Kore*. Your fate is foretold there.'

Jehana had no idea what he was talking about, but she did know that prophecy using the gnosis was impossible. Only gods could see through time, and only the *Kalistham* foretold truly.

Naxius' voice changed to one of recital as he started, 'Glamortha, Skull-faced Queen of Death, she of the lustrous white hair and untouched body, shall lie with Lucian, the Lord of Hel, and in so doing, shall end time. The Kingdom of Daemons shall arise on Urte, and eternity will begin.'

Jehana swallowed. 'You think you are this Lucian?'

'I shall be, for the name simply means "Prince of Daemons".'

'I will never lie with you.'

'Ah, but my dear, nowhere does it say that it must be consensual.' He smiled cruelly, stopped circling her and reaching out a cold hand, fondled her breast through the silk. She tried to slap him away, but he caught her wrist. His eyes gleamed golden and she *knew* that rape was coming.

Then he laughed and dropped his hand. 'The thing is, there *is* a need for consent: not in acts of copulation, but in what I want of you: to destroy this world and enable daemonic rule – *my* rule – to begin.'

That he expected the impossible gave her the courage to say, 'I would never do a single thing you wanted of me.'

But he just laughed. 'Perhaps. It's easy to say so now. And indeed, it is a conundrum.' He wandered to the window. 'Did you see the great tree – the Elétfa, the manifestation of the dwyma – when you went to the volcano? It is the embodiment of all the energies of life, self-sustaining and infinite, for it is a circle: pure life, rooted in the earth, the water, even the air. It's both a by-product of Urte and the pillar that sustains our world. When we die, our bodies become part of the Elétfa while our spirits are cast out into the void. Some say we journey on to some god's realm; others *know* that our souls are fed on, swallowed and absorbed, by the beings floating outside the Tree – the daemons.'

'That's heresy,' Jehana retorted.

'But no less a fact for that. Heresies, like laws, are just points of view.' He chuckled to himself as if he'd just won some great debate. 'The problem I face with you, my dear, is that I need you to decide, of your own free will, to use the dwyma to destroy the Elétfa, because once you're a fully-fledged dwymancer I can't make you do it. But the Elétfa sustains the dwyma, so why would you?'

'I'm not a dwymancer,' she said dismissively.

'No, but you have the potential – that's why you're here. I can arrange the rest.'

Jehana found her gaze drawn to the mirror, where a skull-faced woman with albino hair was conversing with a charismatic red-headed man. Just speaking with Naxius felt dangerous, but every time she did, she learned something important. 'I'm not the only one.'

'No, but you're the one I *need*. It's really all about timing, my dear. When I realised there were dwymancers among the Ordo Costruo – your mother and her three pupils – I was still finalising my plans and my ambitions were limited to ruling Urte as it is. I didn't then understand that the daemonic and the dwyma – death and life – were inimical energies, so I infected all four dwymancers and used them to destroy the Midpoint Tower, to test their powers as well as to permit the Shihad to begin. But that massive drawing on the dwyma caused the ichor in their blood to combust. They were destroyed in their own act of destruction.'

'That's my *mother* you forced to destroy herself,' she snarled.

'Regrettably, yes,' he admitted, not sounding in the least bit sorry. 'Especially as at that moment the pieces of the puzzle fell into place. Part of my intention in unleashing the ichor was to create a threat that the dwyma must *react* to – and it did: Lyra Vereinen was revealed, as was Valdyr Sarkany – and you, my darling. I needed just one of you to bend to my will.'

Jehana was almost speechless. '*Lyra Vereinen?* The Rondian Empress?'

'Even so. I was as stunned as you.'

Valdyr spoke of someone called 'Nara' – is that really Lyra, or is it someone else? But she also remembered what her mother had told her. 'The dwyma chooses us. None of us would betray it.'

'Indeed,' Naxius agreed. 'What I found I needed was someone with unfulfilled potential and Lyra and Valdyr had already gained their power before I knew what I was dealing with. They're no use to me now. But you . . .' He sauntered languidly back to her. 'You're *exactly* what I need. The question is how to persuade you of the same.'

She lifted her chin. 'You're wasting your time.'

'Am I? So seduction is out of the question?' He cocked an eyebrow at her suggestively.

'I'd rather die,' she vowed.

He smiled wryly. 'Oh, I'm not that hideous, am I? And I come with quite a grand throne: you could be Queen of Hel alongside my King, no?'

'Go there and burn.'

'Dear, dear. A shame. Perhaps torture? Suffering is a great persuader.'

She swallowed, took a step away and repeated, 'I will die before doing your will.'

'I doubt that,' he said laconically, then admitted, 'but giving you to the Elétfa when you hate me isn't going to make you do as I want. You'll be doubly my enemy. No, it needs to be of your own volition – a conundrum, you see, as I said.'

'You'll never solve it,' she told him. 'Now leave me alone.'

'And then it came to me,' Naxius went on, as if she hadn't spoken, '"Life is suffering", a poet once wrote. You strike me as a creature of empathy, girl: the suffering of others upsets you – and Alyssa reported that too. And if there is one thing this world is full of, it's suffering: especially now that I've unleashed war, starvation and a master daemon on it. Every living soul in this world is suffering, Jehana, and I can show it all to you through the shared intellect of Abraxas. We're going torture, maim, starve, rape, mutilate and burn every unpolluted human in Yuros – and then we'll start on Ahmedhassa.'

His blithe, uncaring tones were worse than any ravings might have been. Jehana shrank in on herself, understanding just how certain he was. 'I . . . I won't break . . .' she stammered.

'When all humanity begs you to?' He stepped towards her and this time when she tried to move away he gripped her in unseen kinesis bonds and held her, stroking her collarbone, throat and chin before resting his fingers on the copper mask that covered the rest of her face. 'This mask is a special artefact I've constructed just for you. Through a combination of mystic-gnosis and illusion, I can link you to the mind of Abraxas without recourse to ichor – and Abraxas can sense everything his victims are going through.'

Jehana felt herself go white under the copper mask. 'No–'

'Ah, but yes,' Naxius purred. 'Forced empathy is the way forward, my dear. You are going to share every sickening crime Abraxas and his possessed brood inflict on the helpless until you are begging me for mercy – and still it will go on. I'm going to break you until you're ready to tear down the entire world just to get out of it.'

She tried to run, but he held her in place as effortlessly as if she were a child, then sent a cold stab of energy between her eyes.

She fell, fell and kept falling . . .

. . . into a web of mouths and claws that covered her sky and pulled her into a vortex of eyes, a forest of raking limbs that reached for her. She was naked and tenebrous, a wraith on a howling wind, but every sensation felt real, from the blasts of sulphurous heat that burst from the open mouths of the vast body to the pain when fingernails raked her back. Then a giant claw seized her, closed on her waist and pulled her into a massive maw that swallowed her and she fell screaming–

–*into the body of an old man, moments before two giggling possessed men plunged hands into his open belly and began to pull his intestines out–*

–*and then into a young girl as a heavy, stinking body lowered its weight onto her back and an awful ripping sensation tore her nethers apart–*

–*and into a young man chained to a stake on a heap of coals and timber as a snarling daemon lit the pyre–*

–*into a woman lying in the dirt, watching black threads of fluid crawling up her arm from a bite wound and hearing the foul voice of the daemon crawl into her skull, until she sat up and studied the slumbering frames of her husband and children, huddled in the snowbound hut, with fresh eyes–*

132

On and on, so many ways to suffer, so many ways to inflict hurt, to be defiled and destroyed, so many ways to die – and the worst thing was that all of it was happening *right now*. This was Yuros, this was the plague unleashed by Naxius and it was going to ruin all of Creation . . .

Make it stop, her mind shrieked. *Make it stop.*

7

The Cats of Dupenium

Secession

It is impossible to conceive of the fall of any empire not plunging the world into devastation. For this reason, the stability and integrity of the empire must be paramount and any threat of secession must be stamped out swiftly.

MYKLOS TORMAND, IMPERIAL VOLSAI, PALLAS 820

Dupenium, Northern Rondelmar
Febreux 936

Coramore Sacrecour woke to find three more cats wedged around her in the crypt, all purring softly and snoring. The air was frigid and it stank, but thanks to her companions it was warmer than when she'd closed her eyes. The darkness was almost total, but there was a strange, pale, unmoving light shining through the broken door.

She nudged aside the cats and the bones of whichever forgotten Sacrecour adherent had been buried here; an extinct line, she presumed, to be so neglected. She crawled off of the burial shelf, clambered to the floor and stood on aching legs, feeling curiously lightheaded as she crept to the door, wrinkling her nose at her own stench of sweat and the plunge down the garderobe chute. Tentatively, she put her eye to the hole in the door, then stared.

She'd thought someone had left a lamp in the mausoleum, perhaps to lure her out, but instead what she saw was a line of white light running along the floor. She had no idea what it was, but it certainly hadn't been there before. Puzzlingly, it illuminated nothing: it was simply a line of light in the black.

The cats joined her, rubbing against her as they stalked past and out into the darkness. In a moment she was alone, with a gnawing dryness in the throat. 'Dear Kore, I'm starving,' she whispered to no one. She crawled through the broken door and stood, reeling dizzily.

I'm a princess – I deserve better than this ... Then her mind went to Cordan. *What if they've harmed him?* The urge to go to him was almost overpowering, but Ostevan was out there somewhere. Was he waiting in the dark to pin her down and force the daemon back into her body?

She crawled up to the puzzling line of light, which ran dead straight along the narrow pathway between the tombs and sarcophagi. She raised a finger, meaning to touch it, when one of the cats hissed.

She froze as another wave of dizziness struck her and for an instant she was looking so closely at the line of light that she could see that it was made up of tiny linked filaments of energy – then she had a vision of a man bent over it, drawing it with his fingers, making branches of light shoot out along the walkway. A moment later, she had the name too: Brother Quintus, a mage-priest in Ostevan's retinue.

It's a gnostic trap, she suddenly realised. *Quintus put it here to find me.* She carefully withdrew her finger, wondering why she should suddenly be able to see such things. *Is this my magical awakening?* she wondered, quivering in excitement at the thought, then she paused. *Or is it something to do with the dwyma? Is this a gift from Aradea?*

Either way, Brother Quintus' ward had her fenced in and she had no idea how she'd get out of the mausoleum now. She backed away in despair until one of the cats rubbed against her leg and then jumped up, caught her robe in its claws and *pulled*. Hope rising, she let it lead her along the wall behind the sarcophagi into a maze of stone and statuary, deeper into the tombs. Finally she felt a cold draught and spun, sniffing the air like an animal. The cat, meowing at her, walked serenely to a place against the wall where a little heap of loose soil suggested there might be a hole, and sure enough, some of the bricks had crumbled away. Coramore had to work to widen it enough to squeeze through, but soon she was scrambling over roots and loose stones.

When she saw light, she had to stop herself wailing in relief. She had emerged from some animal's abandoned den at the far edge of the cemetery, shrouded by a leafless tangle of blackberry thorns right against the wall. She scooped up the snow covering the bushes, fighting to restrain herself from wolfing it down, but cupped in her hands, it melted quickly enough and soon she was gratefully slurping down the cold, clean fluid.

Smoke hung in the air, wafting from chimneys just visible in the pre-dawn light. Was Cordan awake, she wondered, and more importantly, was he safe? What could she even do?

Scrying is blocked by stone and water, so I have to find shelter – but first, I need food. She might look skinny but she'd never gone without in her life.

But that was the girl she'd been before Abraxas had invaded her soul. The daemon had revelled in faults and frailties, weakness and vice; it preyed on diseases of body and mind. It had shredded her innocence in passing, leaving a more calculating being behind.

I have to remain underground – but perhaps I can come out at times like this? Surely even Ostevan must sleep?

She clambered through a gap in the wall and found a muddy alley full of snow-covered detritus. The cat followed, mewing softly. At the end was another alley, and now the wondrous smell of baking bread was mingling with the smoke. Her mouth filled with liquid and her stomach growled.

Then a yawning middle-aged woman emerged and placed a bucket beneath a cloth-wrapped tap. She watched the woman pump water into the bucket, then take it inside.

The instant she was gone, Coramore rushed to the tap and drank her fill, fighting not to break down in tears as she knelt there in the mud. The cat rubbed against her, licking the drops she spilled. Through the door she could hear laughing banter: a clutch of baker-women complaining of the cold and their husbands and their work, guileless chatter that made her ache for company, anyone, even for the stupid bints she'd shared her childhood with.

She pressed an eye to the keyhole and saw that the back door opened directly into the baking chamber. It would be impossible to enter unseen. The smell of fresh bread was a torment, so near but out of reach, but the cat was making it clear they should move on. Together, they crept through the mud, her slippers sticking in the slush.

Peering round the corner of the building, she saw a man with a heavy stick standing in front of the bakery's front door, stamping his feet while lifting a steaming mug to his mouth. The smells of broth and bread mingled on the air. When he turned away, Coramore peeked through the window to see a stout old couple placing freshly baked loaves into the racks behind a low counter.

She realised with a start that she wasn't the only one watching: across the street a gaggle of children gathered beneath a verandah were watching hungrily. Nothing but torn layers of cloth protected them against the cold. Their yearning eyes were huge as they watched the bakery.

Then the door opened and the children – there were at least two dozen – came flooding forward as the old man appeared with a basket in his hands, beaming about.

'G'mornin', lads 'n' lasses,' he wheezed, and gestured them into an orderly line. The children's faces shone with more reverence than Coramore had ever seen on the faces of Uncle Garod's courtiers, and sorted themselves into a queue with the smallest at the front, biggest at the back. The old man gave each of them a bun – they weren't steaming, so she guessed they were the previous day's leavings – and when he ran out, he called inside and the old woman, surely his wife, brought more, this time fresh-baked.

'Now get along, afore we get some real customers – this is a business, not a bloody charity!' the baker scolded, laughing, and the children scampered off, cheeks now pink and eyes bright. 'Best part o' me day,' he chuckled to his wife when they'd vanished.

Then the woman caught sight of Coramore. Her heart thudded in terror. *Does she know who I am? Has Uncle Garod told people to look out for me?*

But the woman called out, 'Here, lovie, did ye miss out? Jus' ye wait there,' she cooed, producing a large, fresh-backed bun. 'Here, lass, it's yours, if ye want it.'

Timidly, Coramore reached out for it, wary of any sudden movements, and the moment her fingers closed round the bread, she snatched it and ran, terrified that any clear glimpse of her face could lead to ruin. She shot down the alley, vaulted the rubbish, slipping and skidding on the icy muck, the loaf cradled against her chest. At the end she paused for just an instant to look back and saw the man with the stick peering down the narrow alley, but he didn't call out or follow.

Once out of sight, she ate her prize, again forcing herself to eat slowly, then the cats closed in and guided her through the unfamiliar back streets to the docklands, which were slowly coming to life. She wasn't the only one sleeping rough, she realised as she crept past a young man with wrists as skinny as hers who was so still she couldn't tell if he was even breathing.

The cats took her to a culvert that flowed into the River Beck, a subsidiary of the Bruin. There she found a narrow shelf on one side that was clear of the water and just big enough for her to perch on. She huddled there, frightened and shivering, as the city woke, trying to ignore the stench from the sewage flowing from the well-to-do homes around Dupenium Castle, shuddering whenever one of the boats constantly passing the end of the drain just a few feet away scraped the stonework, until she fell into an uneasy sleep.

She remained unfound throughout the day, waking at sunset chilled to the bone and starving and too scared to move, hearing the laughter and ribald jollity of dockworkers and sailors drinking only a few yards away.

They'd turn me in for a copper – or do worse . . .

Her stomach was empty and burning with acid, her throat dry as parchment and her thin limbs felt hollowed out. '*Help me*,' she whispered – to Kore, to Aradea, to anyone who might care about a girl alone in a frightening world. '*Please help me*.' Her eyes stung and she felt herself trembling uncontrollably, her courage ebbing away . . .

Coramore?

The voice – Queen Lyra's voice – rang inside her head like a clarion call and it felt like someone had laid a hand on her shoulder and jerked her back from the edge. She went rigid, strangling a cry as all her senses quivered.

Lyra? Coramore whispered, straining to hear, waiting with bated breath, but nothing else reached her, just the night noises of the docks. Hours passed and despair seeped back in while the night fell silent.

And then a dark shape jumped onto the end of the culvert and yipped – but not in a threatening way, more like an urgent greeting. It was a fox. They stared at each other, then the fox made a soft coughing sound, turned and vanished.

The cats had handed her over.

She crawled to the end of the culvert and peered out, but what little she could see of the docks was empty. Under a rare starry night, the moon was basting the river in pale light. It took her a few moments to spot the fox again, but when she did, her heart leaped.

The fox, silvery in the moonlight, was sitting on a small coracle tethered to a post, the sort a child might use to go fishing.

Shivering in excitement, Coramore crept out and crept along the shore to the coracle. The fox was gone, but that didn't matter: the message was clear. There were no paddles, but she found a pole. It took but a moment to untie the mooring rope and clamber aboard, and then she was spinning out into the current.

She was four hundred miles from Pallas and her uncle's army was ahead of her on the river. She supposed she should be frightened, but she wasn't: she was in Aradea's hands, and Lyra had heard her call.

At the confluence of the Beck and Bruin was the town of Beckford, where Garod Sacrecour's remaining barges awaited the morning, when another legion would take to the river and float down towards destiny. All evening Dupeni soldiers filled the taverns and brothels lining the docklands, doing what soldiers the world over did: eating, drinking, rukking and fighting.

By midnight, though, the streets were quiet except for the Night Watch, ambling down the cobbled streets, collecting drunks and hauling them off to cool their heels overnight in the gaol.

No one saw the coracle with the small figure huddled in the stern as it drifted by. The little craft bobbed along as the currents of the confluence threatened to trap it, then sent it spinning away into the vast, sluggish flow of the Bruin.

By the middle of the night it was miles downstream.

Ostevan was watching Garod Sacrecour and Brylion Fasterius beat the Hel out of an old man when a message was handed to him. It was written in Germane's handwriting; he would have only just written it, into a colleague's mind, from Pallas, four hundred miles away.

The rebellion leadership have reached out. G.

Ostevan smiled quietly to himself and discreetly burned the scrap of paper while the two men in front of him continued to smash up the face of their prey. They were still full of fire, but Ostevan was bored now.

'Enough, gentlemen, please,' he said. 'We do need him mostly alive.'

With Coramore still eluding him, he'd been forced to take a risk and present a false dwymancer, some rustic greybeard chosen for his craggy, weather-beaten looks and well-lived-in furs. He'd scrambled the man's brain so badly he now actually believed he *was* a dwymancer; he'd been cackling about 'blasting your souls with the power of the Elétfa' through broken teeth.

Reluctantly, Brylion Fasterius unballed his bloody fist and released his grip on the old codger's collar. Ostevan's greatest fear had been that in the bloodlust of violence, Brylion would reveal his own daemonic possession, but somehow he'd managed to keep just the right side of going completely berserk.

The battered man slumped to the ground, barely conscious. Garod kicked him one last time, then turned to Ostevan. 'You're sure his blood is enough to keep Lyra from striking us?'

'Fear not. She won't be able to touch you,' Ostevan drawled, devoutly hoping he'd find the missing princess before it became critical. 'But he does need to be alive for his blood to be efficacious.' He shared a glance with Margentius Keeper; he was one of the few people in on the ruse, but he knew to keep his mouth shut. 'If you will give us leave, gentlemen, we'll take this from here.'

Garod rubbed his knuckles, sending healing gnosis to seal the broken skin and remove the pain, while Brylion panted his way back to relative calmness. 'You'd better be right about this,' the Duke muttered. 'Half the army's already loaded on the barges.'

'We're watching the skies, your Grace,' Margentius responded smoothly. 'Our best weather magi are scanning the clouds from here to Pallas. The moment a storm forms, we'll know.'

'And you'll be able to counter it?' Garod insisted.

'We shall,' Ostevan lied firmly.

The duke and his cousin looked satisfied with that. Giving the broken man on the floor a vengeful look, Garod stalked out, leaving Brylion glaring hotly at Ostevan. He knew as well as Ostevan that the real dwymancer was still at large.

'Kore's Balls, you're a fine gambler with the lives of others, Ostevan,' Margentius breathed, pushing the door closed. The only one without a daemon-spawn, he had no idea how close he stood to such predators.

'Never stake that which you can't afford to lose,' Ostevan quipped.

'It's the ruling dynasty of Yuros you're gambling, my Lord Pontifex,' Margentius reminded him. 'We can't protect the column unless we find that damned girl. We've left drugged food in the cemetery in case she's still hiding in that underground warren, although so far it's only yielded a mass of vermin and a few orphaned children. We've posted rewards and we're scrying relentlessly, but there's no trace of her. Perhaps she's dead?'

'She'd better not be,' Ostevan replied, 'because if we don't find her in the next few days, Lyra's going to destroy Garod's armies and there won't be a Sacrecour cause to rally to. Now, please give Brylion and me a moment alone.'

Once Margentius was gone, Brylion's eyes turned black. 'Why don't we just mass-infect the rukking army? They'll be impervious to the weather.'

Ostevan shook his head. 'The moment we begin, someone will see what's happening and the people will rally against us. It might work in a sparsely populated region like Rimoni, where communities are small and widespread, but up here it'd be noticed instantly. The army is only a tenth of the populace at best and infected men are vulnerable now everyone knows about the silver and the sunlight weaknesses. Reeker Night only worked because it was a surprise.' He shook his head firmly. 'No, the ichor works best as a means of power, infiltration and control. We do this secretly and use our hidden edge to ensure victory.'

Brylion glared at the broken old man on the floor, but he nodded grudgingly. 'Aye, I can see that. You just make sure you catch that chit, because I tell you this: I might have a spawn in my chest, but I'm still a Sacrecour and I will not see us fail again.'

Coraine, Northern Rondelmar

Solon Takwyth took his place beside Duke Torun's throne in the ducal hall. The court was almost empty, only a few of the Corani mage-nobles present. The duke was nervous, his bland features flushed, his brow sweaty.

He's lucky he's got me to think for him, Solon mused. He shifted his gaze to the supplicant before him and scowled. *Because there's no way Torun could find this capitano's price.*

The capitano in question swaggered up the carpet, a small entourage at his back: two older knights, if knights they were, four guards and an eye-catching copper-skinned woman with a horse-like face and a mane of black hair – an Ahmedhassan, incredibly.

He dares bring Noories to a Rondian ducal court during a Shihad invasion? That's confidence.

'Capitano Endus Rykjard of the Hollenian Freeblades,' the herald boomed.

Rykjard had the characteristic square, snub-nosed Hollenian face, though he was deeply tanned and his sandy hair had been bleached by the sun. He was rated the most able mercenary commander in Hollenia, having served in Javon during the Third Crusade, escaping that disaster with a handful of aides and a war-chest of gold, enough to re-establish himself in Damstadt on his return. He brought with him five legions, all battle-hardened – but he came with a hefty price tag.

Rykjard knelt nimbly, the two commanders at his back doing likewise, while the Ahmedhassan woman made a graceful Eastern curtsey, her frank eyes flashing around the room. She wore a periapt, Solon noticed, though he doubted she was high-blooded, given her Eastern heritage.

'Your Grace Duke Torun, Lord Takwyth; may I introduce my senior legates, Laada and Vanyorin, and this is my chief wife, Atafee.'

'Your ch–um . . . *chief* wife?' Duke Torun stammered.

'I have four,' Rykjard said easily.

Takwyth supressed a smile.

'But . . . the Church . . .'

'I married them under Amteh law,' the Hollenian drawled, without a hint of repentance.

Solon already knew all this; apparently the man had become obsessed with Eastern cunni during the Crusade and had since indulged his addiction to the hilt. A weakness, perhaps, but no one questioned the man's ability in the field. His fidelity was the real issue: the Damstadt mercenary guilds were notorious for duplicity.

'But the Shihad–' Torun began.

'A stupid, secular invasion by a greedy sultan, who's paid with his life,' Rykjard sniffed. 'Who the Hel did Rashid think he was, invading Yuros? But inconvenient for you, because it took Sulpeter's legions off the table,' he added. 'Or conveniently, I don't know. Whose side is Lord Sulpeter actually on?'

'My father supports us, of course,' young Nestor Sulpeter blurted from among Solon's retinue.

'Then it's a shame for you he's a thousand miles or more away,' Rykjard noted amiably. 'But good for me, because it'll add to my price, I feel.'

'You *will* sign then?' Torun asked anxiously, when he should have shut up. Solon grimaced; his mother had sheltered him, taking too much on herself and leaving her son as an empty glove.

Rykjard's eyes lit up as the price went up yet again. 'I've yet to assess your chances, Milord. I try to sign only to *winning* causes.'

'There's no doubt as to this outcome,' Solon said firmly.

'That's what I was told in Javon during the Crusade,' the Hollenian replied in a noncommittal voice. 'The cleverest man I ever knew told me that, but we still got right royally rukked over. So if you'll forgive me, I'll make up my own mind.'

At Solon's gesture, the duke rose and led the delegation to the next room, where tables had been set with wine. For the next hour, while dinner was readied, Solon explained the military capacity of his Corani – inflating it, in case Rykjard was talking to his rivals – and making derogatory assessments of both the Imperial and Sacrecour forces.

'Garod's forces are crippled and rumours of the queen's heresy are spreading,' he concluded. 'The people don't want a dwymancer on the throne. Rebellion already stalks the Pallas streets.'

'Damn their souls,' Torun blurted. 'That blasted Pallas Mob – I'll deal with them as they should be dealt with!'

'Mmm,' Rykjard said, as if puzzled. 'I heard they want to vote in their rulers, abolish tithing and taxes, enjoy equality of justice . . . that sort of thing. Ridiculous, obviously, but shouldn't you be courting them if you want the gates opened for you without a fight?'

'We don't deal with rebels,' Roland de Farenbrette grunted. 'Once we're in control, we'll smash them.'

'No doubt.' Rykjard gave a wry smile. 'Back to this "heresy": is it true that the queen can summon devastating storms which weather-magi can neither detect nor counter? Didn't she destroy half the Sacrecour forces in a blizzard?'

The room fell silent until Solon replied, 'That's true: but we know the queen. She refuses to wage real war upon the rebels in her own city because she thinks of them as "her people". We, the Corani, are also "her people". Even if she could do such a feat again – and her grip on that power is uncertain – she won't do so. We'll be on her doorstep before she gathers the nerve.'

'So if you march with us, you'll be safe,' Roland added. 'The Sacre-cours can't offer that.'

'So you say, but a cornered vixen is unpredictable,' Rykjard pointed out. 'And afterwards, what then? This is a three-way fight – and Argundy may also invade. That makes for a messy battlefield – the worst sort of fight.'

'Are you saying you *won't* sign?' Torun blurted, making Solon wince.

Every time Torun opens his rukking mouth, the price goes up.

'I'm just saying that the terms will have to cover the additional risk,' Rykjard said.

'Milord Torun,' Solon put in, 'I think perhaps we should enjoy dinner and reconvene in the morning to discuss business. That will give us all time to collect our thoughts.'

Torun went to object, then saw the look in Solon's eyes and stammered, 'R-right, yes, of course . . .'

Solon took care to have Rykjard seated beside him for the meal, with his exotic wife on the Hollenian's other side. She picked at her food – no doubt it was too bland for her taste – but listened attentively. Solon struggled with seeing her angular, copper-dark features at a civilised dinner table, especially as her silks were finer than any Rondian woman could afford, and she sported more jewellery than he'd ever seen, even on the queen.

'Your wife is a mage?' Solon asked, as the platters were removed.

'Through pregnancy manifestation, whilst bearing our first child,' the mercenary responded. 'Atafee is therefore a quarter-blood – not strong, but she is skilled and diligent.'

'Did you convert to the Amteh, to be permitted to marry four times?' Solon asked, still a little troubled at allying their cause with a Noorie-lover when the empire was at war with the East.

'I went through the motions, but my motives weren't religious, I can assure you,' Rykjard smirked. 'Once you've had an Eastern woman, you don't go back. My wives are trained in arts of the bedroom that Yurosi women could never imagine – anyway, Kore is a dull sort of fellow. I wasn't sorry to let him go. Like any real man, the only god I acknowledge hangs between my legs.' He winked at Solon. 'Women are made for pleasure, mm? Even queens.'

Solon coloured slightly. Even so gentle a reminder of Lyra's faithlessness rankled. 'Lyra gave me her heart – it was the bastards whispering in her ear who tore us apart.'

'Of course,' Rykjard said lightly. 'What woman could voluntarily set aside the great Solon Takwyth, eh?'

I could take a serious dislike to you, Hollenian, Solon thought sourly. 'Have the Sacrecours approached you?' he asked, knowing they must have. Mercenary armies of Rykjard's strength had to factor in to Garod's equations.

'Of course, with a heavy purse. But I've heard Garod call Hollenia a "worm-infested marsh of godless turncoats",' Rykjard replied, mimicking the Duke of Dupenium's voice. 'So I'm not in any rush to sign with him.'

Solon wasn't sure if he trusted that, but it was increasingly clear that he had to have the Hollenian Freeblades in their column, if only so that he knew precisely where they were.

Solon entered the House of Lantris some hours later, surprised at a surge of renewed vigour. 'Good evening, Milord,' the woman in the Heartface mask greeted him. 'I'm so glad to see you again. The Blue Room awaits, just as you asked. The girl won't let you down this time.'

She didn't either, the lesson well learned, and when he lowered her to the rug and penetrated her, she breathed, 'Oh my Lord, yes –' in just the right tones and he could almost believe it was real. He took her hard, twice in succession, crying out '*Lyra* –' as he came, and she moaned his name with what sounded like genuine release.

As they lay on the rug afterwards, he rolled onto his side and pulled the blonde wig from her head, curious to see her natural colouring. She flinched, and so did he when he saw that her head had been completely shaved to permit the wig to sit properly.

'Now it's you who's spoiled the illusion, Milord,' she scolded.

He caught her chin in his hand and studied her face – she had pleasing looks, with full lips and high cheekbones. *Strange how changing the hair changes the woman*, Solon thought, stroking her smooth scalp. It felt alien, and oddly attractive, as if the naked skull revealed inner layers of beauty.

'You have borne a child,' he stated – that much was clear from her body. 'Who's the father of your child?'

'I don't know. The barrenroot failed. That happens sometimes.' Her eyes went wet. 'I wanted to keep her, but I couldn't . . . She was taken away and I don't even know what happened to her.'

Suddenly she was sobbing, leaving him utterly at a loss.

This isn't what I paid for . . .

But that aspect of chivalry concerning the protection of women had always spoken loudly to him, so he cradled her wordlessly. The lives of ordinary people felt strange to him – he'd only ever known the life of a mage-noble: courts and legions, practise-yards and jousting lists – and this story of ill luck and bad choices felt repugnant. But he could hear genuine affection for her lost child and that moved him.

'Find a good man and get out of this life,' he advised her. 'For your daughter's sake.'

She looked up at him and blurted, 'You're a good man.'

Am I? I no longer know . . .

He knew she wouldn't take his advice – she probably couldn't. Brothels, even high-class salons, owned their girls and he doubted she had anywhere else to go.

Don't get involved, he reminded himself. *She's just a whore.*

He sat up. 'We're done,' he said abruptly. 'Pour me a whiskey before you leave.'

'Did I displease you, Milord?' she asked meekly.

He remembered the consequences for her and tempered his reply. 'No, you did well. I'll return.'

She's not Lyra . . . but she'll do for now.

Pallas

'Good evening, Majesty,' Dirklan called to Lyra as she returned from her garden, where she'd been listening to the dwyma's silence. There had been nothing from Valdyr, but another fleeting brush with the girl who might be Coramore left her wringing her hands, wondering what to do.

'Good evening, Father,' she said, putting the matter aside as she joined him. It was only late afternoon, but the clouds darkening the sky promised rain, though not snow. The temperatures were a little milder this week, hinting that winter would not last for ever. 'Is there news?'

'Lots,' the spymaster said grimly, flicking the silver curtain of hair from his left side and scratching under his eyepatch. 'Duke Torun – or perhaps we should say Solon Takwyth – has just hired the Hollenian Freeblades. They'll be riding south by the end of tomorrow. We expect to be invaded from the north by early Martrois.'

'So two weeks. Well, we knew that was coming.'

'Aye, and the first Sacrecour legions are being loaded onto barges at Beckford on the Bruin. They'll be joined by four more from Fauvion so we'll be facing the entire Sacrecour army, twelve legions in all.'

Lyra clasped both hands to her chest. 'Then it's begun,' she said, reeling a little. Discussing civil war was one thing; seeing it become reality was another. 'I suppose our only consolation is that they're not allied.'

'True, but either one of them still outnumbers our own forces.' Dirklan hesitated, then added, 'Lyra, I don't think you should go to this rendezvous tonight. I'm smelling treachery.'

He'd progressed her request to meet Ari Frankel swiftly, though not fast enough to prevent more destruction in the city, with dissent now spreading through the poorer areas. Across the river in Pallas-Sud, emboldened by Dominius Wurther's own depleted manpower, Fenreach and Southside were also in a state of revolt. At Lyra's last public appearance, a traditional alms-giving in the Place d'Accord, right before the Bastion gates, there had been abuse and cat-calls.

When someone shouted vindictively, *'Takky's coming for you!'* the words had struck her to the core.

'I must meet Frankel,' Lyra insisted. She'd felt a connection with the man and admired his passion for a better world. *If I can persuade him that his cause is better served by peaceful means, perhaps he'll support us?* It was a naïve hope, maybe, but she clung to it.

'Then you'd better get ready,' Dirklan said. 'It's almost time to go.'

Basia de Sirou finished strapping on her shin-greaves – wooden limbs still needed armour – and stood, teetering a little before muscle memory took hold. She made her way to a shadowy room at the back of the Bastion. From a window overlooking the courtyard, she could see an unmarked carriage waiting. The air was freezing, but the clouds had thinned, allowing the full moon to flood the place. The brisk wind was unpleasant and Basia huddled into her cloak, but Exilium Excelsior didn't keep her waiting. His helm was tucked under his arm, revealing his perfectly coiffed jet-black hair. His mechanical gait was becoming familiar to her, as was the way his head moved as he took in his surroundings, constantly readjusting. She approved of that – a good trait in a bodyguard – although he never let it lapse, even off-duty.

'Is the queen ready?' Exilium asked.

'She's just getting a last-minute briefing from Dirk,' Basia replied.

Exilium peered at the carriage. 'Wouldn't anyone wanting to follow us simply presume any unmarked carriage is the queen's?' he asked.

'We've despatched six in the last half-hour,' Basia replied. 'This is the last – and we'll not be in this one either.'

'Then how are we travelling?'

'We're walking.'

Exilium's perfectly sculpted eyebrows shot up. 'Queens don't walk.'

'Tell that to Lyra. Anyway, no one will expect it, and it's not far: there's another carriage waiting below the Heights. Another of Dirk's little tricks.'

The door opened in the Bastion wall again and a trio of figures emerged: Dirklan and the queen were followed by the hulking shape of Mort Singolo, axes slung over his shoulders.

'Disguising our approach is irrelevant if they know the rendezvous point,' Exilium muttered.

'True, but we've other plans for that,' Basia answered, as they walked over to Lyra. 'Are you sure you want to do this, Milady?' she asked. She too thought this meeting foolish.

'My mind's made up,' Lyra snapped, exhaling a steamy gust of air. She turned back to Dirklan. 'I know you fear treachery, but my honour is at stake. We, at least, will deal fairly.'

'We'll deal honestly if they do,' he replied, before turning to Basia and Exilium. 'You know what to do.'

'We protect the queen,' Basia replied.

'With our lives,' Exilium added fervently.

'At the first sign of trouble, we're getting you out, Milady,' Basia finished.

'I believe Master Frankel will keep his word,' Lyra said irritably.

'And I believe Tad Kaden *won't*,' Dirklan answered. 'The Kaden Rats have decades of crime under their belts and in all those years, we've only ever hanged eight of them. We must be vigilant, take nothing on trust.'

Once the last carriage containing decoy queen and pretend body-guards had rumbled away, Dirklan took them through a postern gate. Basia knew the street; she and Ril had used it on Reeker Night. They followed a series of narrow switchbacks down the south side of the Heights to a tavern where another unmarked carriage was waiting. Exilium checked the driver was the man they were expecting, then settled the queen and off they went, rattling along unmade roads in a circuitous approach to the rendezvous.

Basia, seeing the anxiety on Lyra's face, reminded her, 'We can back out any time.'

Lyra shook her head firmly, while muttering to herself – marshalling her arguments, Basia guessed, although why she would give this rabble-rouser the time of day was beyond her. *It's beneath the dignity of her office.* But Lyra had been raised as a nun, not a queen, and she didn't always do as queens should.

It's not worth the risk. A single arrow or well-placed spell and her reign is over . . .

It was thoughts like that that kept her on edge as the carriage drew up outside Sancta Esmera Church, a chapel once used by the imperial legions, at the edge of Esdale. Using a church as neutral ground was an old custom and as the nearby buildings had been gutted during the recent troubles, this one could now be approached openly on all sides, making it ideal. It stood alone, surrounded by well-watered lawns and its cemetery and warded by old protection spells, its enduring solidity a miracle of architecture and gnosis rather than divine favour.

The carriage lurched to a stop a hundred yards across open ground from Sancta Esmera as a gash in the clouds allowed Luna to illuminate the scene. The driver raised his lamp and swung it, and an answering light appeared on the far side, from the ruined warehouses where those they were to meet were waiting.

'They're here,' Basia murmured, her throat going dry. It always did when Lyra went into danger. She scanned the area with gnostic sight, then stepped out, shielding hard. Dirklan had soldiers and Volsai in the buildings behind them: if anything happened, the area would be flooded with some of the best fighting men and magi they had.

But in the church it would just be Exilium and Lyra and her.

Exilium was helping Lyra dismount with reverence on his face. Basia thought it hilarious that he regarded the queen as a living saint, but then, Exilium lived in a world of absolutes.

No doubt in his eyes I'm a Fallen Woman. She smiled at the notion, then put all mirth aside as the immediacy of the dangers they risked took over.

Flanking the queen, gnostic shields up, they crossed the wasteland towards the front of the church. Four cowled figures – Frankel, presumably, plus three magi – had emerged on the other side and were heading for the rear of the building. The Kadens didn't know that Lyra had no gnostic power – everyone assumed a heretic dwymancer was pretty much the same as a mage – so Frankel's group had a numeric advantage that could be fatal.

'Kore protect us,' Exilium breathed piously. 'Thy will be done tonight.'

How about my will be done, Basia thought, *which is that we all get out alive . . .*

Ari Frankel hadn't prayed for a while. His time within the Church, seeing all the corruption and lies and cynical manipulation of people's beliefs, had destroyed any real faith, but on nights like this, when he had no control over events, the habits of his youth reasserted themselves.

Kore, if you truly be and can speak to a man's heart, tell all here not to betray the sanctity of this place. Tell them to respect the oaths of peace. All I want to do is talk.

Even now, advancing through the rubble of a building lost to the fires, the church a silhouette before them, he had no idea what Tad and Braeda Kaden meant to do. They'd told him they'd talked it over and decided that attacking the queen was too risky, so they'd let the parley go ahead, but he wasn't sure he believed that.

He was also horribly conscious that everyone else in the church was a mage: if someone took offence to something, he, Master No-Magic, would been the first to die.

Before him stalked three lions, as he thought of the guards the

Kadens had assigned to him: Braeda herself, a fearsome fighter, and two burly golden-maned men with bulging muscles, Schlessen brothers named Kys and Morn.

The church had been fully lit to allow both sides to check for gnostic traps earlier, although that didn't mean there weren't any. *Between the Kaden Rats and the Imperial Volsai there's more than enough skill*, Ari worried. Walking into the building felt like putting his head in the jaws of a beast.

Braeda led the way to the back of the church with Ari, flanked by the Schlessen brothers, traversing a small vestry and emerging beside the altar at the top of the central aisle. The queen and her entourage were at the other end, at the main doors.

Ari swallowed as he saw Lyra. He'd expected her to be an idiot, but instead she was intelligent and more, possessed of moral courage. *She freed me because she approved of my words. I rewarded her by inciting warfare on the streets.*

The queen, her lips thinned and her eyes narrowed, met his gaze coolly.

Beside the queen were those they'd been told to expect: Basia de Sirou, the bodyguard with wooden legs, and an almost pretty Estellan knight named Exilium Excelsior, of all things. Both had hands on their sword-hilts, but the queen looked unarmed.

Braeda lifted her hand and burned some kind of scarlet rune in the air. As the Schlessens did the same, the queen's bodyguards looked at each other doubtfully.

'Come, don't you recognise the old magi greeting?' Braeda drawled. 'The Rune of Becoming, "Angay", to proclaim and confirm one's possession of the gnosis.'

'A discontinued practice,' the female guard, Basia de Sirou, responded.

'But then, perhaps your queen can't actually form the rune?' Braeda teased. 'Not in fact being a mage?'

'I am mage-born,' Lyra retorted. 'I'm not here to perform tricks, but to speak to Master Frankel.'

'And I too am here to converse,' Ari said, moving forward. *Dear Kore, we both need this.* 'I'll take this from here.'

He took another step towards Lyra, gambling his life – then Braeda laid a hand on his shoulder and dropping her voice, murmured for his ear only, 'I don't give a rukking toss what *you're* here to do, Frankel. *We're* here to kill the queen.'

As Ari drew breath to protest, she hurled him aside and a bolt of brilliant energy flashed from her hand, just as the two Schlessen magi also unleashed, blasting balls of fire down the aisle at Lyra Vereinen.

The queen didn't even have time to scream—

8

Hegikaro

The Nature of Daemons

The word 'daemon' derives from the Lantric word for ghost or spirit and was never meant to imply any inherent evil, but the Book of Kore 'demonised' the word. However, while most daemons are quite harmless, and useful servants for a skilled wizard, a powerful daemon is dangerous and must be treated with utmost caution.

ERVYN NAXIUS, ORDO COSTRUO, PONTUS 722

Hegikaro, Mollachia
Febreux 936

Kyrik remembered another day like this one just a few months ago, when he'd led a contingent of Vlpa riders through the gates of Hegikaro. The streets had been lined with citizens straining for a glimpse of their new king and his strange allies, their cheering muted by uncertainty, but there had been a tangible feeling of relief in the air, because the hated Rondian tax-farmers had fled and the town was free.

Nacelnik Thraan was with me, and his eldest sons . . . They're all dead now.

The great and good of Mollachia, led by Pater Kostyn and Dragan Zhagy, had been waiting on the steps to greet him.

They're dead and gone as well.

Valdyr had been there too, released after so many years of abuse and captivity.

Where are you, brother?

Hajya was still with him, though: weak, shaky, often lost inside her own head, a legacy of the horrors of having Abraxas stealing her mind

154

MOTHER OF DAEMONS

and body. Though clearly distressed, recognising Hegikaro as a place of torment, she was visibly battling those memories as she sat her horse, and her courage gave him hope. She was still appallingly weak, her body unhealthily thin, and her hair was now more grey than black. *But she's coming back to me, a little more each day.*

The shadows of the coronation bloodbath hung heavy over the scene as he led Kip's Schlessen and Rothgar's hunters, who'd joined them a few miles previously, into the town. Rothgar himself had already left with Korznici to rally the Vlpa, so all the watching burghers saw were ragged hunters and Schlessen barbarians leading some big-horned cattle. Maegogh himself had suggested that the Mantauri not yet reveal their true nature, for fear of panicking the populace.

The faces that met them were blank with distress and horror. There was no cheering. Kyrik shuddered at the thought of the hardships his people were enduring; many had fled into the countryside, but those few who had clung on in the city had been hiding in root cellars and subsisting on what remained of winter stores, sometimes for weeks on end, while daemons prowled above.

A few called hoarse greetings, but most just stared as Kip's Schlessen warriors swaggered by, counting heads and shaking their own.

Yes, there're fewer than a hundred of us, and we face a legion . . .

Inside the town walls were burnt-out houses and other signs of depredation. Returning burghers were trawling through the remains, piling up what couldn't be salvaged for firewood. A street preacher was bawling out phrases from the *Book of Kore*, all concerning the Last Days.

'*The daemons shall inherit Urte,*' the man was shouting. '*It's too late to repent!*'

'Someone shut him up,' Fridryk Kippenegger growled. One of his men did just that, with a sharp right hook that laid the man out. No one went to his aid.

But when Kyrik and his party reached the town square, it was packed, hundreds of men and not a few women bearing weapons ranging from woodsmen's bows and axes to old family swords to crudely made spears. There were few familiar faces, so many had died, but Kyrik did recognise the man atop the steps, Milosh Nirabhy. He'd been fat, florid and

155

stubborn; now he was a skinny man with a silver Kore dagger icon about his neck. He still looked stubborn, though.

Kyrik kissed Hajya's hand, then advanced to face the 'welcoming' committee.

'Kirol Kyrik,' Nirabhy called warily, as the crowd hushed itself, staring. 'Why do you come here?' His followers moved together, barring Kyrik from the steps. Fear and mistrust were tangible.

Kyrik took out a silver coin and pressed it to his own forehead, in proof that he wasn't possessed. He wasn't sure that Nirabhy would recognise the gesture, but Rothgar's hunters had been passing the word and that message must have been heard here, because everyone present did the same.

'We've come to protect you all,' Kyrik called. 'A king doesn't hide. He stands with his people.'

Few of the harrowed faces looked greatly cheered at his words.

'That thought has taken a long time to occur to you, Kirol,' Nirabhy noted bitterly.

'No, the thought has been with me every waking moment,' Kyrik countered. 'But I escaped the bloodbath at the cathedral alone. It has taken time to find fellow refugees and allies, to build our strength and learn our enemy's weaknesses, before I could return.'

Some of the crowd began to nod at that, but Nirabhy didn't look appeased. He gazed over the Schlessen with distaste: Mollachs had always viewed Schlessen as barbarian animals. 'Are these . . . *men* . . . all you have?'

Kip and his men glowered, but didn't react; they'd known not to expect any welcome.

Kyrik strode right to the foot of the castle steps and looked up at Nirabhy and his men. 'Milosh Nirabhy, I have heard good things of you: that you had the courage to upbraid Dragan in the throne hall. Mollachia needs your fearlessness. But I am not the enemy.'

'Are you not? You returned from exile and daemons followed you. Perhaps if you were to just leave, the daemons would follow you and plague us no more?'

That sounds like exactly the sort of whisper Asiv might circulate to undermine us.

Kyrik let that pass. 'Here is what I know: Asiv Fariddan contacted me a week ago. He told me he'd drive all those who remain free here, to Hegikaro, so that all his enemies were in the same place. He told me that in two weeks he would slaughter any who still stood against him. He did this to draw me out, obviously – but if I did not love my people, I would not have emerged.'

'Leave and he will leave too,' someone shouted.

'Ysh, and take your stinking Schlessens and Sydians with you,' someone else shouted from the safety of the rear, rousing murmurs of agreement.

'I could do that, certainly – but that won't stop Asiv from killing or enslaving you all,' Kyrik retorted. 'He's coming here whether I'm present or not – *and predators have to feed.* The high passes are still ice-bound, so there is nowhere to run, my people. Here we fight, where we have walls to defend and stores to feed us. Here is where Mollachia stands or falls.'

That silenced them all, even the hecklers at the back, leaving only the whistle of the cold winds over the jagged battlements and broken roofs.

'Would you rather fight alongside Schlessen warriors, born to war, and Sydian archers, the deadliest in the world – or are you too proud to ask for help?' he challenged them.

Now Nirabhy was hanging his head and his comrades were looking at each other sheepishly.

They are just sheep, herded here by rabid dogs and penned for the slaughter.

Kyrik gestured Kip forward. 'Some of you saw this man at my wedding and coronation: this is Fridryk Kippenegger, former battle-mage of Pallacios XIII. Many of his men marched with him on the Third Crusade and returned with him across the Leviathan Bridge. He has offered his aid – will you scorn it?'

The towering Schlessen looked like a God of War as his muscles flexed and his blade rose towards the skies, and even the doubters began to nod.

Every head slowly turned to Milosh Nirabhy, who was studying the ground as if deep in thought. Finally he looked up and met Kyrik's gaze.

'My Kirol,' he said hoarsely, and with stiff pride, he dropped to one knee, and all around him followed suit. The gesture swept through the square like a ripple on water. 'We are yours to command.'

This time when Kyrik placed a foot on the steps, those before him parted. He went first to Milosh, pulled him to his feet and said, 'Join my council and bring all of your courage and realism.'

Milosh had clearly feared censure, for his rough features were suddenly suffused with gratitude. Kyrik still marvelled that he'd dared take on Dragan – and that he'd come away unharmed.

'My Kirol,' Milosh said again, in a husky voice, 'I'm with you.'

It didn't take long for Kyrik to realise what a monumental task he faced. All upkeep had fallen by the wayside once the castle had fallen to Asiv and Dragan. Every scrap of meat had been devoured by the possessed, but the granaries had been emptied too, by vermin. The daemons had unleashed their savagery on the fleeing citizens and those they'd caught had been slain and eaten, or bitten and infected. Some of the town had been destroyed by fire, including the southern section of the outer walls. Right now, fixing that was their highest priority, along with scavenging supplies from the surrounding farms.

'We've got four thousand people sheltering here, with more arriving every day,' Milosh told Kyrik and Kip at the first council meeting. There was just the three of them present; Kyrik had no time for larger, longer meetings, not when there was so much to do. 'Most are women, children or the elderly,' he went on. 'We're sending those who can't fight into the southern heights to seek shelter.'

'I thought there'd be many more,' Kyrik admitted. 'Once Mollachia numbered more than fifty thousand.'

'Many thousands fled west down the river into Midrea after the Bloody Crowning,' Milosh replied. 'There are many refugees in the hills who haven't returned, and won't if Hegikaro falls.'

The Bloody Crowning, thought Kyrik. *How apt.* 'How many fighting men do we have?'

'Maybe six hundred, mostly hunters and farmers. Few have any real military training.'

'That's barely enough to man the walls,' Kip rumbled.

'And too many to feed,' Kyrik added. 'How are the foragers faring?'

'The farms have already been well picked over,' Milosh reported. 'We can't endure a siege.'

'There won't be a siege,' Kip opined. 'Asiv's daemons will attack and attack, until we break.'

'Five thousand possessed legionaries,' Milosh groaned, 'including whomsoever of our own people they've possessed.'

We're doomed, Kyrik thought bleakly. *Asiv himself is as strong as an Ascendant Mage. He and his possessed legion battle-magi could probably destroy us on their own.* He wondered if Milosh had been right. *If I fled, perhaps Asiv would pursue me and let my people be?*

But he truly doubted that: Asiv's predators had to feed. There would be a bloodbath here, no matter what he did. But it did raise the question of what Asiv actually wanted.

He says he'll leave if he's given Valdyr and Ogre, so they must be his immediate goals. Valdyr destroyed the tax-farmers' legion, so they must consider him a threat. And Ogre once knew Naxius, Asiv's master – perhaps he fears what Ogre knows about him?

He wouldn't hand either of them over, even if they'd been here: that was out of the question. He glanced up at the painted ceiling which depicted his forebears slaying the draken of Cuz Sarkan: it was inside that same volcano that Valdyr had vanished.

Where are you now, brother? Why won't you return? We need you!

The ceiling and the gods didn't answer, so he returned his eyes to his counsellors. 'Then we must prepare a defence that our ancestors will sing of for years to come. All our skills and cunning must go into making every step costly. Silver and sunlight are our allies, so we must use them. We must arm every soul, from eldest to youngest, because this battle is for survival.'

Milosh asked frankly, 'Is there any hope we can cling to, Kirol Kyrik?'

Kyrik didn't wish to speak of his brother, but could offer some hope. 'Rothgar Baredge has gone to the Tuzvolg to lead the Vlpa riders here. If they can arrive at our enemy's rear, in sunlight and well-armed, they could yet save us.'

Milosh had likely been one of those who had decried Kyrik for bring-ing the Vlpa into Mollachia. 'The Tuzvolg is several days' ride away,' he muttered, but he was visibly heartened.

We all need a hope to cling to, Kyrik thought.

'How does Queen Hajya fare?' Milosh asked. His voice was kind but hesitant, as if unsure he had the right to ask. 'They say Asiv tormented her personally.'

'Thank you – she is improving,' Kyrik replied. She'd not left the royal suite, but she was calm. 'She's been deeply unwell, but she's coming right.'

Kip belched thoughtfully, rose and stretched. 'Best we get doing,' he said grimly.

'Do you think we have a chance?' Milosh asked him outright.

'Yar, of course, there is always a chance,' the Schlessen replied non-chalantly. 'But Minaus doesn't count the odds, only the heads as they roll. We're all bound for the grave eventually, so who cares where or when? It's *how* you die that matters.' He made the horned-hand gesture for luck and swaggered away.

But I do care, Kyrik thought. *This is my land, my people. I don't want to face Kore knowing I led them to ruin.*

Freihaafen

Ogre was drowsing in his secret chamber when he was awakened by the sound of a woman's voice, shouting in Dhassan. It was Sabina, Fridryk Kippenegger's Eastern wife, calling, 'Sal'Ahm, Masakh? Ogre? I've brought you breakfast.'

The women had taken to bringing him food since Kyrik had led the fighting men to Hegikaro, for he'd been so wrapped up in his task he'd been forgetting to eat. But he'd never allowed himself to be caught asleep before. He stumbled to his feet, managed a ragged conjuration of gnostic light and shouted, 'I'm coming–' but to his chagrin, Sabina was already making her way into his hidden chamber, wrinkling her nose at the stale air.

Even in the shadows, Sabina shone, tawny eyes full of empathy, her narrow oval face framed by gleaming dark hair falling to her waist.

Ogre immediately felt ugly and unworthy. *She is very beautiful . . . but she pales before my Tarita.*

He tried to block her view, but her eyes were already widening. 'Oh my,' she breathed, taking in Tarita's face etched on every surface, half a hundred portraits. 'You are an artist, friend Ogre.'

'No, I'm not,' he mumbled. 'These are nothing.'

Her small hand gripped his bulging forearm, freezing him in place. 'Poor Ogre.'

He didn't know if Tarita had said anything before leaving, but Sabina clearly knew.

Yes, I love her, he admitted to himself. *She befriended me, fought alongside me, shared jokes and laughter instead of treating me like a freak, and trusted me enough that she slept against my side knowing I would never threaten her. She saw things in me I never did. And now she's gone.*

Sabina let go of his arm and examined his work, lifting her candle to illuminate the coal-etched walls. Pausing before one picture of Tarita looking pensive, she murmured, 'Three years ago, my love and I argued. To prove his adoration, he spent three days carving a lightning-struck tree into a giant image of me.' She giggled, adding, 'Me with nothing on and six months pregnant!'

'Did it work?' Ogre found himself asking.

Sabina snorted. 'I already knew he loved me. I just disagreed with something he'd done. I didn't need him to carve a giant wooden statue, but to come home and do what I wanted.' She straightened and put her hands on hips. 'Which he finally did.'

'But he knew you loved him.'

'Not right then he didn't: not when he'd agreed that we Bullheads would sell ourselves into the service of a tribe even other Schlessen believed barbaric.' She scowled at the memory. 'I was furious with him.'

Ogre couldn't quite grasp what she was trying to tell him. 'Um . . . what became of the wooden carving?'

'People began to leave offerings. In a few years I'll be a goddess.' She laughed, then fixed him with a purposeful eye. 'Ogre, men will make stupid grand gestures to win a woman, when all they need to do is love us. That carving was a stupid waste of energy – but at least while he was brooding he was thinking, and he did come to his senses, so perhaps it had some value.'

He hung his head. 'I did tell her, when I thought I was dying. She made a joke of it, then told me it was impossible. A few days later she went south with Waqar.'

'Well, I think it is for you to decide if she's right. Is she? Is it impossible?'

He looked at his feet, feeling profoundly uncomfortable, but he answered, 'I'm a construct, not even a proper person. I'm probably mostly some kind of animal. Normal people are repulsed by me. I can't offer her anything but a life in hiding, when she was born to shine. I'm ugly where she is lovely. I'm almost twice her height and thrice her bulk – we could not even . . . um . . . embrace . . . even should she be so insane as to want me. She's right: it *is* impossible.'

But my heart won't listen.

He turned his head so she wouldn't see the tears welling in his eyes.

'Well, it certainly is if you're just going to sulk about it,' Sabina sniffed. 'But I don't think of you as an animal, and neither does anyone else. Especially Tarita. My husband is not handsome – he's a big, broken-nosed brute covered with scars and warts – but he is my steadfast rock. He's easily twice my size, but he's gentle and he has put two babies in me. Ogre, do not forget a woman's body is built to push out children – an ordinary woman could lie with you if you were gentle, as I know you would be. The real question is whether she is big-hearted enough to look past your imperfections.' She stared at him. 'And whether you are.'

'She left with Waqar,' Ogre groaned.

'She left because of the war,' Sabina corrected him, and now she was sounding exasperated.

'She said *impossible*,' he growled.

'Ogre, she likely doesn't know her heart any better than you do. Look past what she says to what she doesn't say. I've seen you two together. She is always touching you, which tells me she trusts you, utterly. She laughs and is serious with you, talks about shallow and deep things.

That tells me that your souls have a connection. She's only twenty, don't forget, so be her true friend, don't pressure or condemn her, just give her time to make up her mind. And don't waste your time on grand gestures. Get out and breathe the air.'

For a long while after Sabina was gone, Ogre sat and pondered her words and decided that she was right: he needed to breathe cleaner air and remind himself of what he was fighting for.

So he left the cave and squinting into the sunlight, walked out into a cold, crisp morning. He could hear the lowing of the female Mantauri as they laboured, building their new homes, and nearer at hand were children's voices, shrieking and laughing. It was all music. He hesitated, then trudged out of the trees to the lake's edge.

Ignoring the wide eyes of the staring children, he stripped off his leather tunic and waded out through the freezing water to where the steam rose from the thermal vents. Immersing himself fully in the blissful warmth, he slowly stretched, getting all the kinks out of his muscles, before rolling onto his back and floating there.

Give her time. Think of what she doesn't say.

It felt like it would be a long, lonely wait. *But I'll endure . . .*

He closed his eyes to shut out the splash and clamour of the children – until he suddenly realised that it was all around him and he sat up just as someone launched themselves onto his shoulders with a shrill yell – then a dozen more crashed into him and there was triumphant shouting as he went under in a flurry of limbs, before rising with a bellow, sending boys and girls flying in all directions.

Everyone stopped to see his reaction – and at his great roar of laughter, the children hurled themselves at him again, shouting battle-cries and vowing to '*Kill the Masakh!*' There was no malice, just hilarity, and he threw himself wholeheartedly into the game, hooting and calling, trying to make sure he didn't hurt anyone and that everyone got a turn to ride on his shoulders.

Finally a couple of the women summoned the children to lunch and Ogre looked around, blinking. He hadn't realised how long he'd been playing, and then he realised that he'd never actually *played* before . . .

It occurred to him that he was happy.

He waded ashore, shivering through the colder water, feeling cleansed, not just physically but emotionally too.

Sabina's words echoed in his mind as he dried himself and returned to his cave: *Listen to what she doesn't say aloud* . . .

'How do I listen to something unsaid?' he asked himself. 'How do I see what's not there?' Then, peering at the wall covered in meaningless symbols from the code he couldn't break, 'By the *shape* of that absence . . .' He took a deep breath and looked at all his abortive working anew as his jumbled thoughts became clearer.

The Master had sometimes used shortened scripts to take swift notes: *brk* could mean *bark*, *break* or *broke*; it was the context that provided the omitted letters. 'How could I have forgotten that?' he wondered aloud. 'Is *this* what this is? Such systems can only work for alphabets that use symbols for sounds – and the language might not even be Rondian . . . ah! But *Lantric* is the Master's birth-tongue!'

Suddenly invigorated, Ogre rubbed out a previous attempt and began hurriedly scrawling, eliminating all the vowel sounds . . .

By midnight, after hours of trial and error, he'd broken the code. It had been a quick enough job to prove he'd been right: the Master had written the *Daemonicon* in a shortened script using made-up symbols to replace Rondian letters. It took another hour to determine that the tongue wasn't Lantric but Rimoni. Then the letters had to be deciphered, each word sounded out and placed into context, although it became a little easier as he became familiar with the symbols and more used to groping through the tones until they formed actual words . . .

It took another three hours to read the first page, which turned out to be, by way of an introduction, a self-congratulatory love-letter written by Naxius to himself, crowing about what he'd learned.

That page chilled Ogre's soul.

The *Daemonicon di Naxius* wasn't a diary of daemonic contacts but a thesis, the distillation of thousands of experiments towards one stupefying goal. From anyone else, it would have been laughable – but Ervyn Naxius had written it, and that made it credible.

Ogre returned to the final paragraph and read it aloud.

'*The daemonic world is not chaotic, but ruthlessly unified. It is a more efficient world than our own, yet these immortal, eternal super-beings made of thought, who devour lesser intellects and become stronger with each feast, desire the one thing we have that they do not: our physical world – because once, they were us. I now know enough to bring about the ascent of the daemons, which will mean the fall of humanity. I know how to open the gate from their world to ours – and I know enough to become the Master Daemon who will rule this new world and all its inhabitants, mortal and immortal, for the rest of eternity.*

'*That is now my goal.*'

Ogre found himself sorely tormented by the Master's *Daemonicon*. That Naxius held humanity in contempt was no great revelation, nor was the suggestion that he was prepared to turn people's lives into a living Hel in the service of knowledge. It was the scope of his plan – the sheer *audacity* – that appalled him. *Daemons*, Naxius wrote, and Ogre could almost taste the admiration, *are pure: pure refined* hunger. He was preparing to overthrow Nature, to cast down mankind and replace them with pitiless, depraved spirits, because he thought he could control them more completely.

He hadn't thought he could hate the Master any more than he already did, but it turned out he could. *Much* more. His skin crawled when he read about *himself*: how he'd been bred, and why, and what Naxius had learned. 'There are faults to be eradicated, so I have destroyed his siblings, but Ogre has residual value,' Ogre read aloud, his voice shaking, 'so I let him live. The next batch, however, will be superior.'

I had siblings. He never told me . . .

But so far all Ogre had deciphered was *intent*. How this 'grand reconstitution of Urte' was to be achieved, he had yet to discover. There was still much work to be done.

The Elétfa

There was neither sunrise nor sunset to measure time as Valdyr and Gricoama climbed through the dimly lit world of the great tree, but as they spiralled ever higher, Valdyr began to notice changes. Squirrels chased each other along the branches while birds were flitting among the leaves of the distant canopy. There were more branches, too, some bearing edible fruit.

How long have I been gone? he wondered, the thought goading him onwards, but doubts crept in: should he have gone *down*? Should he try another branch? Was this a puzzle, not an endurance test? He started skipping sleep, pushing himself harder – but for all that, he felt a profound *oneness* with this place. The dwyma was effortless here, pulsing through the veins of the leaves, beating through the wings of the insects and birds, flowing in the sap of the tree itself, ever-changing, ever-constant, eternity in motion. Whether he was doing the right thing or not, it felt like a gift, just being here.

Then, abruptly, things changed. They rounded the next bend and found the path bisected: one branch continued the spiralling climb around the trunk, but a second passed into the tree itself through an arch beautifully carved with old Frandian knotwork. The gap exuded cold, clammy air ripe with decay and a strange sense of malice. As he got closer, he saw the carving was worm-eaten and the stink of rotting bark filled his mouth and nostrils: the foetid stench of death.

He felt his pulse quicken as a pale shape formed in the opening: Luhti, young and golden-haired, as she'd been when she died on Watcher's Peak. 'Valdyr,' she called, 'welcome.'

He thought her a ghost, but she embraced him and then Gricoama, her body solid and warm, and smelling of wholesome herbs.

'You're not dead,' he said redundantly.

'There's no death for the likes of you and me.' She gestured at the carved opening where Zlateyr, the great Mollach founder, now reclined against the carven frame. The hero gave Valdyr an ironic wave. 'But there are different paths we can take,' Luhti said. 'Sometimes the darkest paths are those which help us grow.'

'But shouldn't I just continue on?' Valdyr asked, pointing at the stairs, which continued to wind up the outside of the trunk.

'Ysh, but you'll learn nothing new,' Zlateyr replied. 'If you don't learn, you won't prevail.'

Valdyr faced the passage, flinching as Asiv's distinctive scent of stale sweat and musk wafted from it. He remembered how he'd frozen in terror at Cuz Sarkan when confronted with his abuser. *That's why they test me: they know I failed at Cuz Sarkan.*

'This . . . this won't be real . . . will it?' he stammered.

'What would be the point of a false test?' Luhti asked. 'What would you learn?'

He had no answer to that. 'And what happens afterwards?'

Luhti patted his arm. 'You go on climbing, until you find the place you need to be, if you are to save us all.'

He stared at her. '*To save us all?* From what? And why me –?'

'A darkness is gathering, a storm that even this great tree cannot withstand,' Zlateyr said. 'Just as a genilocus is weak without a dwymancer to articulate and shape its will, so this tree is impaired without a living dwymancer to bond with it. Right now, there's only you.'

'But Nara of Misencourt–'

'She has still to find the Elétfa, so it is up to you to become what we need.' Luhti pointed to the dark doorway again. 'This is part of that journey.'

Valdyr took a deep breath. Gricoama came to stand beside him, hackles rising against the stench gusting through the hole like the exhalations of a dying man, a toxic mix of vomit, smoke and opium. The wolf growled, then barked out a challenge.

Valdyr wished he felt as brave, but when Zlateyr and Luhti moved either side of him and laid hands on his shoulders, he felt renewed strength. 'What can I expect?' he asked.

'The worst,' Luhti replied in a tight voice. 'It would not be a true test if it were not the worst.'

That's what I was afraid of.

He turned his head and took a gulp of clean air, and another, trying to slow his heartbeat, but it kept accelerating, even as his skin went cold.

He walked away from his dead mentors, first one step, then another, and with Gricoama pacing at his side, they entered the notch, stepping into darkness. The floor was squishy and damp, like rotten timber, and the air was now so foul with shit and perfume that he staggered, retching. He reached for the wall, but it felt as unsteady as the floor, noisomely warm and unpleasant to the touch.

With a great *c-r-r-r-r-rack!* the opening behind him snapped shut.

'Hey!' he shouted, turning to hammer on the wood, shouting for Luhti as darkness engulfed him. He turned back blindly, calling, 'Gricoama? Boy? Where are you?'

There was no response. There was no sound at all but for the weird breathy tones of the passage itself.

He was utterly alone.

9

East and West

Hospitality

Many cultures pride themselves on their hospitality, holding that strangers are welcome, but any cursory examination of history quickly disproves this myth. I'm loath to abandon the ideal, however, for strangers should be welcome. The world is great enough to share. This is an ideal worth striving for.

ANTONIN MEIROS, ORDO COSTRUO COLLEGIUM, HEBUSALIM 811

Norostein, Noros
Febreux 936

Latif and Ashmak stood waiting outside Senapati Onfali's pavilion, heads bowed and eyes averted, as officers and magi came and went. If anything, Ashmak was even more uncomfortable than Latif, even though he was a mage.

I was an imposter in Court circles, but I was taught how to belong. This is another world for Ashmak. 'Keep your eyes down,' he reminded his friend.

'The commander won't listen,' Ashmak hissed. 'We're wasting our time.'

He was probably right, but they had to try. Yesterday five hazarabam, each unit a thousand-strong, had been marched out of Lowertown and down the road to the east, 'to be rewarded for their valour.' They'd returned the next evening. Now their camps were lifeless by day, without even cooking fires, and outsiders were being turned away. Latif's mind was churning at the implications.

Prince Waqar said the sultan is daemon-possessed. He spoke of a Yurosi kingdom of black-eyed savages who shun sunlight. And another five thousand are to march down Eastern Road tomorrow – including us. We must *make the senapati believe us . . .*

The camp was rife with rumours, but it wasn't easy to ask questions in a place like this. Whatever happened though, there was no way he was going to take that road tomorrow.

A shaven-skulled young kalfas bustled up to them and addressed Ashmak. 'Honoured magus, the senapati will see you now.'

The other men waiting, human officers without the mage-blood that opened all doors, looked at them resentfully.

Ashmak clearly wanted to back out, but Latif replied firmly, 'We are grateful.'

The pavilion was cluttered, parchments strewn over a desk beside an officer's cot and a wooden cruciform bearing the general's armour. Senapati Haseem Onfali, overall commander of the division, looked exhausted. He glanced up from the scroll unrolled on the desk and scowled.

'You are of Piru-Satabam III, ai?' he grumbled, continuing to write while they sank into the required prostrations. 'Why can't you see your own commander about this matter, whatever it is?'

Latif and Ashmak sat up on their knees and Latif responded, 'Great General, there is a rumour going around the camp of a Yurosi disease. The men are afraid that those men going down Eastern Road are returning infected.' He dropped his head and stared at the mat under his knees.

They knew their story, the best they could come up with, wouldn't be enough on its own and sure enough, the senapati shook his head impatiently. 'If I listened to every rumour that swept through this camp, nothing would get done. So unless you have proof . . . ?'

Latif raised his head again. 'I bear the token of a great prince, one who will vouch for me on his return to camp.'

Onfali looked at his scribe and flicked a finger in dismissal. There was only one prince absent from camp and Xoredh had condemned Waqar Mubarak as a traitor.

And they're saying Waqar's eagle-construct broke free and flew away . . .

'Tell me more,' Onfali said, his voice hushed, as soon as they were alone.

Latif pulled out the signet ring Waqar had left with him and placed it at Onfali's feet. With a troubled glance at the tent-flap, the general took it. 'How came you by this?'

Latif took a deep breath. 'It was given to me by Prince Waqar himself. He told me that you can be trusted.'

Waqar had said no such thing, but Onfali was a Ja'arathi, one of the moderate Amteh, and he had a reputation for fairness. More importantly, he'd been Sultan Rashid's man, one of a fast-shrinking circle of men who owed their position to the former sultan.

Onfali pursed his lips, then returned the signet. 'Tell me what you know,' he ordered.

My story is ludicrous, but if he doesn't believe me, we're doomed, Latif thought, then he started, 'Prince Waqar found evidence of a disease, one that drives men out of their minds. Initially it enhances ferocity, but ultimately, it is fatal. He believes those close to the new sultan are deliberately infecting our men ahead of the next assault.'

'Men close to the sultan?' Onfali repeated. It was forbidden to slander the sultan, but advisors could be criticised, if one was careful. 'What kind of disease?'

'It's spread by blood – by bites, or through infected food and drink.' Latif described what Waqar had seen in Mollachia, whole communities decimated by hordes of ravenous killers.

'Are you saying this infection is being spread by someone somewhere down Eastern Road?' Onfali asked, then he mused, 'We've been ordered to march down there tomorrow.'

'I know. Please, Senapati, we must not go –'

Onfali's face was an agony of indecision: without proof, this was all just hearsay and rumour. Predictably, the senapati took refuge in delegation. 'This is too big a matter,' he muttered. 'Admiral Valphath must be briefed – it must be his decision . . .'

Latif winced. That meant more delays and more chances that Xoredh would get wind of what was happening. But in Onfali's position, he'd have done the same. 'Great Senapati,' he said humbly, 'I beg you, be *very* careful whom you summon. Powerful men are behind this, men who will not wish to be thwarted.'

Onfali peered at him. 'You seem a perceptive fellow – have you served at court? You look familiar?'

Latif kept his head bowed, his expression subservient, thankful that with his hair hacked short and his beard grown full against the cold, not to mention his weathered skin and hands, he looked little like the urbane Salim. 'No, Great Senapati.'

Onfali didn't look satisfied, but he bade them wait outside and summoned his kalfas. Runners went out and returned, first bringing in a grey-robed Ja'arathi Godspeaker named Zaar, a confidante of Jhiram Henayon, the highest-ranking Ja'arathi in Ahmedhassa. He was followed by Admiral Valphath, the windfleet commander who also saw to the army's supplies, who bustled in looking anxious.

At last Latif and Ashmak were summoned back to repeat their allegations.

Onfali looked at Valphath, who looked at Godspeaker Zaar.

'I would dismiss it, were it not that I have corroborating evidence,' the Godspeaker said. 'With the ascension of Sultan Xoredh, my Ja'arathi clergy have been barred from certain camps – but one of my more . . . um . . . *determined* colleagues tried to enter the camp of a hazarabam newly returned from Eastern Road. He was menaced by savage men and he swears he saw bite wounds, as well as signs of . . . um . . . reduced civility.'

Latif's heart thumped. 'That is exactly as Prince Waqar reported, Lords.'

The three men looked at him. 'Where is Waqar now?' Valphath demanded.

'I wish I knew,' Latif replied. 'I met the prince by accident – I witnessed his arrival and warned him when I saw he was being stalked by assassins. This was before he was declared outlaw, so I had no idea other than to prevent a grievous crime against our royal family. After he used his gnosis to escape' – Latif paused to make the sign against evil, as a suspicious and ignorant archer ought – 'he thanked me. He told me the attackers suffered from this disease.'

The trio exchanged glances, then Valphath asked, 'Were you once a scribe, archer? You speak well for one of your station.'

'Prior to being enslaved and conscripted, I was taught my letters by a trader,' Latif lied.

'He taught you well,' Godspeaker Zaar commented. 'What was your name again?'

'Latif, Great Lord,' he replied, wishing he'd chosen another alias, but none of them showed any recognition.

Onfali exhaled heavily. Looking around, he admitted, 'I'm not convinced we have enough to act on, but could we contrive some excuse that the sultan would accept while we investigate?'

They put their heads together, murmuring, until Valphath said, 'Ai, let us speak of an epidemic—'

He broke off as a shrouded figure pushed his way unannounced into the pavilion and instantly dropped his hood.

'Prince Waqar!' the three men exclaimed as one, while Ashmak and Latif shared a fraught, relieved look.

Waqar looked tired, dark circles heavy under his eyes, and his clothing was dishevelled, but there was a quality in his face that Latif recognised: the implacable Mubarak streak that had propelled Rashid to the summit of the world.

'Please, don't kneel,' Waqar told them. 'As an outlaw, I cannot claim royal rights. We have much to discuss.' He looked at Latif. 'My friends, it is better for you if you leave now.'

Latif went to protest, but Ashmak laid a hand on his shoulder. 'My Prince, we obey.' The battle-mage hauled him up and murmured, 'He's protecting your secret. The longer you talk to those men, the more likely they are to recognise you.'

'You're right,' Latif conceded, following Ashmak from the pavilion. It was now dark outside, and they took a lane running between the tents lit with torches where more supplicants were still hovering, although the kalfas was calling, 'The senapati will see no one else. Audiences for the day are closed—'

Suddenly cloaked men appeared from all sides, drawing weapons and shoving men aside. The scribe tried to shout a warning but a blue blaze flashed through the night and he clutched his face, crumpling to the ground.

'Ahm on high!' Latif exclaimed, opening his mouth to shout a warning, but Ashmak's rough hand slapped over his mouth and he was slammed to the ground. He struggled, but Ashmak's grip was unbreakable.

A man in black Hadishah robes called, 'Is that one of the traitors?'

'I've got him,' Ashmak snarled, shoving Latif's face into the mud. A nimbus of mage-light flared around his free hand and he pointed towards Onfali's tent. 'The rest are inside.'

The mage-assassin grunted, 'Good work,' and ran on.

Ashmak grabbed Latif's collar, hauled him to his knees and hissed, 'Sorry about the muck. Let's get the Hel out of here.'

They moved like prisoner and captor while more Hadishah flooded past and the clamour around the pavilion reached a crescendo. When flashes of energy lit up the night Ashmak snapped, '*Run!*'

Xoredh Mubarak, clad in a grey robe and wearing his Beak mask to hide his identity, sat astride his horse, overlooking the field where more of his army was being fed to the Lord of Rym's possessed monsters. Five thousand newly infected men were screaming and writhing madly on the ground.

It hadn't been difficult. The Shihadi soldiers, told their unit was being rewarded for their valour, were marched off to a clearing a mile out of camp and plied with alcohol and opium. As intoxication set in, Cadearvo sent in possessed whores and the infection quickly spread, the prostitutes biting the men, who then started biting each other.

The screams were changing now: the progression was almost musical to one who appreciated such things. Inside a few minutes, the resistance of all but the most devout had collapsed and those still struggling were simply butchered. Abraxas didn't like to be denied the pleasure of breaking such men, but time was short.

Xoredh turned to Cadearvo, the tower of flesh soon to be known the world over as the Lord of Rym. 'This process must be accelerated,' he urged.

The huge ogre looked Xoredh in the eye despite being on foot. 'Haste risks exposure. If word spreads, panic will set in and your men will desert in droves. We are powerful, but we need every one of them.'

'But if—'

The masked ogre planted a thick finger on Xoredh's chest. His golden eyes blazing, he growled, 'Too many of your masked brethren betrayed us, Beak. Do your duty – follow your orders – or the Master will create a special Hel just for you.'

Xoredh was sick of the bullying and longed to lash out – but he wasn't stupid. 'Ai.'

'Do not test my patience again.' Cadearvo turned away and gazed at the carnage with a satisfied growl. 'Go. Organise the next batch of specimens.'

Xoredh seethed, but had no choice but to leave, cantering off to join his escort, a dozen possessed mage-knights, once his closest friends and now just another set of eyes for Naxius to watch him.

I should have kept you free, my friends.

He didn't know why he suddenly felt sentimental – in truth, he'd had little but contempt for those "friends": they were just people he'd collected to protect him and do his bidding. But now he found himself remembering the good times – the drunken parties, the girls they'd shared, the weaklings they'd broken.

We cut a swathe through the court, he recalled. *We were feared. Now there's just me.*

He spurred his horse to escape them, wanting to ride alone, but they thundered inexorably in his wake down the dark wooded road – until an unspoken ripple of warning brought them all to a halt and he whipped off his mask, seconds before a clutch of torches appeared. A group of men were walking down this road, but he'd forbidden it to anyone unless invited. At once his hackles rose, especially when he recognised Ali Beyrami, the fanatical Amteh imam. He was escorted by more than fifty men, mostly former Hadishah.

Beyrami was about the only person in the army Xoredh couldn't swat with impunity, so he rode forward, silently ordering his minions to keep their distance so the clergyman wouldn't get a good look at them. There were too many signs of their true nature now and Beyrami wasn't blind.

'Greetings, Imam Beyrami,' he called.

The holy man prostrated himself in the pine needles and mud, as did his escort. 'Great Sultan,' he called, rising. If he found it strange that Xoredh and his men could ride at the gallop in the darkness, he said nothing of it. 'Your kalfas said to seek you here. I have news, but—'

'My kalfas was forbidden to divulge my whereabouts,' Xoredh interrupted. 'Shall I have his ears lopped for his failure to listen?'

Despite Beyrami's reputation as a zealot who'd put whole villages to the sword for alleged Unbelief, he didn't waste the lives of fellow Believers as blithely. 'I'm sure your verbal chastisement will suffice, Great Sultan,' he replied deferentially 'Rumours are rife in the camp that there is something amiss down this road – disease, people are saying. A Yurosi plague.'

'Rumours? Lies, more like.' Xoredh leaned forward. 'Who is spreading such falsehoods?'

Beyrami's eyes flickered to the men massed behind Xoredh, but he didn't appear to see anything untoward. 'Who knows how such tales start, Great Sultan? But I imagine you have matters in hand?'

'Of course,' Xoredh responded, wondering, *Is this the time to harvest his soul? With his clergy spreading the ichor, the process could be speeded up vastly.* But Beyrami had magi in his escort, which meant there would be losses on both sides, not to mention the risk of exposure. *The Master has counselled patience.*

Passing up the urge to kill him, Xoredh made a gesture of dismissal and went to ride on – then he paused and asked, 'What was your news, Imam?' *A pretext to explore this road, I don't doubt.*

Beyrami hesitated, then said, 'The governor's flag no longer flies in Norostein. He has either fled or fallen, but either way, it doesn't look likely that the empire will relieve the siege.'

'Interesting,' Xoredh conceded, thinking, *Something Beyrami has seen or heard in this conversation changed his mind about what he intended to tell me . . .* He studied the imam's hard face carefully for apprehension or conflict, but found only his normal impassively devout expression. When he probed with the gnosis, he found nothing but a schooled mind.

I'll infect him, but not tonight, he decided. *I will need to make preparations before I take such a prominent man.*

'Goodnight, old friend,' he said aloud. 'I have checked the supply dump – the only thing down this road – myself, and I can assure you there is nothing to worry us there.'

Beyrami prostrated himself again, then Xoredh slammed spurs into his horse's flanks and burst into motion, his men hard on his heels. In moments the old Godspeaker and his retinue were far behind.

Tomorrow night, he thought as he rode. *I'll bite him myself.*

Waqar woke, spluttering, as icy water on his face shocked though his senses. 'Waghh–' he groaned, already chiding himself.

I should have kept Tarita close, but of course I thought I could handle anything. Idiot!

Men had burst into the pavilion, sending spells hammering into his mental defences. He'd tried to defend the non-magi, but Valphath, Onfali and Zaar had gone down instantly and the gnostic strikes from all sides had overwhelmed him, until light exploded inside his temple and his awareness winked out.

He strained against his bonds, but the knots were immoveable and his gnosis was Chained. Someone loomed over him and he tried to kick out with his bound feet, but unseen hands gripped him and slammed him onto his back.

Faces formed in his dazed vision.

'Please, do not struggle,' a woman said in Keshi.

That was unusual enough to make him pause and focus on a pudgy Dhassan girl in full bekira-shroud kneeling over him, only her moon-shaped face visible. A periapt dangled from her neck. Two heavily bearded, muscular men with scarred faces loomed behind her.

'What is the meaning of this?' he demanded of the female mage, going for bluster. But she made a harbadab gesture that essentially meant, *For the love of Ahm, shut up.*

'He's awake, Master,' she called over her shoulder.

She stood aside for just about the last person on Urte he wanted to see.

The Copperleaf tavern currently serving as Ramon Sensini's mess hall rang with song as those with the greatest staying power dug in for a long night. Ramon peered down from the balcony overlooking the taproom and decided it wasn't doing any harm: the tavern was out of beer and those carousing had just come off duty. He knew when to crack the whip; tonight it wasn't necessary.

'Come on, Vania, let's do the rounds before bed.'

Vania di Aelno, back in uniform, had been complaining that her nun's habit had been warmer. 'Whose bed?' she asked perkily. 'I could do with some shared body-heat.'

Ramon laughed. 'Each to their own.'

'Dullard. I thought you had more spunk when I signed up.'

'And I thought you'd be quiet and demure. Life's full of disappointments.'

They took the back door and sloshed their way down the south alley towards their section of the walls. Men saluted as they passed and a cluster of diminutive street-sellers, none older than ten, scattered at the sight of officers' insignia.

Vania was prattling about whether she fancied becoming a nun for real after the war. 'I reckon I've a better chance of getting laid in a habit, frankly. I got propositioned more times during those riots than most nights in a packed tavern.'

'So not exactly a calling from Kore, then?'

'Of course it is: Kore knows I deserve more sex after what I've been through. If vows of chastity mean I get nailed more regularly, then it just proves that Kore works in mysterious—'

She shut up as Ramon suddenly raised a hand: shouting had broken out and torches were flaring along the outer walls. Now he could hear the clomping of boots on stone – and then more shouting, this time in Keshi.

'Come on,' he told Vania, already running towards the serrated tower that was the keystone of his section of the wall. Calling into the aether, he summoned Melicho. They arrived to find him waiting in the cupola with a squad of archers.

'What is it, Mel?' he called as they emerged from the stairwell.

'Some guy tried to rush the wall,' the lanky battle-mage replied in a perplexed voice. 'He was yelling something – in Rondian – about "plague" – so we shot him.'

Ramon blanched 'Plague?' Disease in any walled city was a horror; whatever infected the besiegers didn't spare those within. 'Holy Hel, that's the last thing we need.'

'It's inevitable, boss,' Vania pointed out. 'Come spring, if we've not lifted this siege, the vermin'll outnumber us ten to one – you know what it's like.'

Ramon did: three years of fighting the Lord of Rym down south had shown him the full topography of Hel.

'Good work, Mel. Maybe they were attempting to spread the sickness by using an infected deserter. Don't let any others in.'

10

Sancta Esmera

The Dark Confessor

Brother Ulcan was an Argundian priest of the seventh century who preyed upon his flock, using the secrets of the confessional against his own congregation. He was eventually found to have instigated four murders and dozens of other crimes, despite never having involved himself directly. At his trial he famously declared, 'Once I have heard a man or woman's confession, I own their soul. I have the divinely given right to pass judgement.'

ANNALS OF PALLAS, 756

Pallas, Rondelmar
Febreux 936

The first mage-bolts nearly ended everything.

Moments before the fires of Hel were unleashed, Lyra was peering down the dimly lit aisle of the church at Ari Frankel. Unlike when she'd freed him two months ago, he looked oddly uncertain. He exchanged a few words with the hard-faced brunette and it was clear to Lyra that whatever she'd said had appalled him.

That was the only warning she got before the woman spun to face her as the two leonine men with her raised their hands, periapts blazed and the three of them tore the air apart. A beam of azure light flashed towards her, flanked by two balls of billowing flame.

She didn't stand a chance as death flashed towards her.

The Kaden Rats were fast – but preparation was what mattered and Basia de Sirou hadn't trusted them from the start. Working in unison, she and Exilium hurled themselves between Lyra and the deadly hail of gnosis-fire sweeping towards them. Her shields flashed scarlet but caught the mage-bolt, while Exilium's wards took the brunt of the fire-balls. Intense heat washed over them, the air became flame and Basia's mortal eyes were dazzled.

But her inner eye sensed further strikes and she poured more energy into her shields, blocking another mage-bolt aimed at Lyra. The queen had frozen for an instant, but now she was ducking behind the pews.

<*Basia!*> Dirklan called, but he and safety were a hundred yards away right now.

Then the brunette Rat – Braeda herself, if the posters were accurate – shot up into the rafters, while her bulky flankmen rushed forward with drawn blades. Gnostic sight made sense of their silhouettes and the lines of force, and with kinesis strengthening her arm against the first pulverising blow, Basia threw herself into fighting for her life.

'No –' Ari shrieked, as the treacherous attack was launched. '*Nooo – I came to talk!*' he howled down the length of the building as Braeda shot into the shadowy rafters above and the Schlessen brothers stampeded towards the queen and her guards. 'I swear this isn't my doing–'

No one was listening – no one cared. Braeda, aiming into the pews, snapped off another burst of mage-bolts and Ari heard a woman cry out in sudden agony.

They've turned me into a backstabbing liar – they've made me complicit in regicide!

His fury made him want to storm down the aisle, but that would be certain death, so all he could do was back away from the blazing violence unfolding in this holy place.

Then the door behind him opened –

<*Move!*> Dirklan roared into the aether and light flooded the wasteland around the church. Mage-knights on venators came flashing down, while thirty or more Volsai erupted from the nearest buildings, leading armoured legionaries. *We can reach Lyra's side in half a minute, but that's an eternity in a mage-fight . . .*

And the instant they moved, crossbows started cracking from the far side, their bolts hammering into shields, and even worse, dark shapes wreathed in pale violet light erupted from the graveyard between Dirklan's men and the church. The oncoming Volsai pounded them with mage-bolts, but to Dirklan's alarm, the shambling figures didn't fall.

Walking dead! Hidden from scrying by the soil . . . Sylvan gnosis to hide the disturbed ground . . . reanimated, so no nervous system to feel pain . . . Necromancy – with something more . . .

He turned to Mort Singolo. 'Come on – we need every man.' He whipped out his longsword and with the Axeman bounding at his side, flew into the fray. The first of his Volsai had struck the dead men and the furious fight would have been over in seconds had their foes been mortal. Some Volsai used kinesis to leap, but Dirklan heard the crack of ballistae and three eight-foot shafts ripped through the night, spitting two of his people and bearing them to the ground.

'Holy Hel,' Mort swore, 'I hate it when the other guys prepare better than we do.'

But Dirklan's venators were over the field now: one had already landed on the church roof and the rider had leaped into the bell-tower. Three others soared towards the buildings from whence the ballista shafts had come, unleashing glowing balls of flame.

Dirklan and Mort vaulted a low fence, only to be confronted by a trio of dead men – they might have been little more than rotting flesh clinging to bones, but they stood up to the kinesis and mage-bolts with preternatural resilience, like thorn-bushes weathering a storm, bending but not breaking, until one of Mort's massive axes crunched through the first and the dead man fell apart in two pieces. But more were rising from the graves and the ballistae shafts were still flying and inside the church all Dirklan could sense was Basia's rising panic . . . and one dreadful thought: *The queen is down.*

The mage-bolt from the rafters that pierced the edges of her body-guards' wards and struck home left Lyra howling in pain and clutching her shoulder, the fabric seared away and her flesh blackened. The stench of roasted meat rose as the queen huddled there, her face contorted in agony.

That glimpse was all Basia could spare, because the two man-mountains were battering her and Exilium like madmen, their blows almost too fast to counter. Her grip became numb from the impacts of previous blows – then her blade shattered into steel splinters as her opponent's broadsword tore through her leather jerkin and chainmail, carving open her side. The man, a Schlessen, she thought, grunted in satisfaction and swept his blade back again.

This time, she thought, *I really am dead . . .*

Then Exilium moved as only he could: somehow gliding aside from a vicious blow and launching a sidewise kick that battered his own foe's sword aside – but instead of slashing at his suddenly unprotected enemy, he tossed his blade upwards, caught it halfway down the blade in a spear-grip and *threw* it – at the man about to cleave Basia's skull.

His aim was straight and true, taking her man in the right eye and transfixing the brain.

The sight of the dead man unhinged his colleague; he gaped in horror, screamed and then swung wildly at the unarmed Exilium, who swayed to one side – but then the man caught himself and with Basia still stunned, her side torn and bleeding, he went for the queen. His blade crashed down at Lyra, just as she twisted aside in desperation, the sword crunching into the floorboards beside Lyra's head and catching in the timber. The queen, still grimacing in pain, rolled away – just as a mage-bolt from the rafters struck the pew she'd darted behind, leaving it charred.

Exilium blasted back at the unseen mage while Basia launched herself at the enemy. Before he could wrench his blade free, she'd slashed at the man's wrist with her sword-stump – it might have been shortened, but it was still razor-sharp – and severed his hand. The fingers were still twitching as it dropped to the floor, but the man went rigid, gaping first at the blood fountaining from his wrist – and then at the hilt of Basia's broken sword, which she slammed into his chest, pumping raw energy into it until his ribcage exploded and he crashed to the floor.

Basia threw herself over Lyra to shield her before looking up to see Braeda Kaden's frustrated snarl turn to fright, for Exilium had leaped at her using kinesis, his sword flying back to his hand. He grasped a rafter with one hand, then struck again, driving Braeda to drop to the ground then following as she sprinted towards the door where Frankel was cowering, his face aghast, surrounded by dead men, lurching corpses that were more bone than flesh.

Basia twisted to send a bolt at Frankel, but instead it struck the head of one of the corpses, blasting the skull apart. It dropped, but more dead kept entering from the rear of the church.

'Exilium!' she shouted, coming to her feet and reaching down to help Lyra up.

But the Estellan was gone, caught up in the pursuit of Braeda Kaden, so Basia turned her attention back to Lyra. There was a great crater, several inches wide and half an inch or more deep, burned into the livid red flesh of her shoulder. The charred tissue was oozing blood and pus and she was shaking like a leaf, but her jaw was set and her eyes blazing.

If the bolt had caught her a foot higher or eight inches over, she'd be dead.

'Majesty, let's go,' Basia said urgently, but to her horror, the queen staggered forward, towards the living dead men.

Her shoulder was agonisingly painful, her vision swimming and she was utterly terrified, but Lyra knew what she had to do.

The dwyma is life and they are death . . .

Braeda Kaden was seeking to flee by a side door, but a Corani mage-knight had appeared from the bell-tower right over her head. He leaped down, trapping her, while Exilium was closing in, but the walking dead were filling the central aisle, all of them coming for her, and there were now a dozen or more of them.

Aradea is with me. Lyra had preserved a link all the way from the Bastion, readying herself for this moment ever since she'd left.

Because I'm not as trusting and naïve as they all think.

A few weeks ago she'd channelled the sun into pure light, blasting the daemon-soul inside Lef Yarle into nothing. Since then, she'd realised that the energy of life was everywhere – in the soil and the stone, in leaf and bough – although it was mostly caught in physical objects, hard to be pulled free. Sunlight was the easiest source of power . . . but it was not the only one.

For one who could feel it, the air itself *tingled* with light and energy – and gnostic energy was also a living source of power. By the time she stepped in front of Basia – who seemed to see something in her face or maybe her aura, because she gave ground, her eyes wide – she was ready, and this time she let it stream out through her hands, not her eyes as she had last time, almost blinding herself.

Against a mage, she'd have died a dozen times in the six seconds or so it took to build, and even so, the first of the dead men almost reached her –

– but at last her palms went hot and light blossomed, even as all the candles and lamps went out as she drew on their energy. Her ray of light struck the corpses and each was caught momentarily in a rictus of pain, if they could still feel, then the energy animating them collapsed in on itself and as one they fell, leaving her standing in a nimbus of light and all else in shadow, as if she were the moon itself.

A moment later, Exilium drove a blade through Braeda Kaden's guard and into her thigh. She gave a sharp cry, instantly cut off as his left fist hammered into her jaw and she collapsed.

Lyra looked around for Frankel, hoping he'd still be there, but he was already gone. For a moment she just stood there . . . then the pain in her shoulder overwhelmed her again and she swayed sideways –

– to be caught by Basia. 'Sometimes I don't know who protects whom,' her bodyguard muttered, conjuring a globe of gnosis-light as the main doors burst open behind them and Dirklan swept in, Mort beside him brandishing his great battle-axes.

Lyra felt a flood of relief, then concentrated on staying conscious as they bundled her out of the door. Surrounded by grim-faced men and women, she was borne back to shelter through a night streaked with fire.

'Damn you for a faithless treacher!' Ari Frankel shouted at Tad Kaden, so livid he forgot his fear of the man. 'You've made liars of us all!' he raged, while Tad – bloodied and streaked with ash – leaned against the wall with his head bowed. 'They'll never negotiate with us again!'

'We're not here to bloody negotiate, Frankel,' Lazar said in his chilling voice, but for once Ari wasn't even intimidated by him.

'We are now.' He jabbed his finger at Tad. 'He wants his sister back, doesn't he? So he'll talk now, and sell us out! What were you even hoping to achieve, Tad? You sneer at her "weakness", but Lyra's the only reasonable bastard in the Bastion. If we're ever going to get acceptable terms, they're going to come from her, or no one–'

'We ain't after terms any more,' Gorn growled. 'We never were. We're here for blood. You so fuckin' stupid you don't get that?'

'Yes, I know what *you're* after,' Ari retorted. 'But the people fighting on the barricades? *They* want a better life, not a bloodbath. They *believe* in what I'm offering–'

Gorn stepped in front of him, but Ari's anger sustained him, made him stand straight as the big man balled his fist. 'That won't change anything either,' he said defiantly.

'It'll fuckin' cheer me up,' Gorn growled, pulling back his arm.

'Stop it,' Tad snapped, straightening up and glowering about him. 'It was a chance worth taking and I stand by that. But now I need to get Braeda back.'

'What the fuck does that mean?' Lazar demanded.

'It means I'll offer terms to Setallius,' Tad mumbled. 'I'll pull my people out of Pallas if he frees her.'

'You can't pull out now,' Lazar snarled. 'You keep telling us this is *your* damned movement – you say you've been fighting this fight for generations, so you can't walk away.'

'I can walk away whenever I damn well please,' Tad retorted. 'My family has always played the long game.'

'Well, rukking good for you,' Ari snapped. '*Thousands* of people have committed to this–'

'I sympathise,' Tad said, 'but I have my whole operation to consider. The family can't afford to risk all in this one skirmish.'

'A *skirmish*? This is our life's struggle–'

Tad put his hands on his hips. 'Well, that's your choice. But a man should always be able to walk away.' And with that he vanished through the window.

Rukka ... Damn *him*, Ari thought, but a moment later, Lazar was planting a finger in the middle of his chest, making him catch his breath because Ari hadn't felt him move. 'What about you, Frankel? You going to run too?'

Ari tried to mask the roiling fear inside him. *Disembowelled whilst being hanged by the neck: that's the sentence I'll get: dying in slow agony while people laugh* ... Lazar would get the same, of course, but he looked like he'd welcome it. *He's insane*, Ari thought, finally acknowledging what he'd known from the moment they met.

But he still croaked, 'I'm here to the end.'

'Good,' Lazar said. 'I'm in charge now and the first thing I'm going to do is find Father Germane. We need Ostevan Pontifex's aid, or this rukking rebellion is doomed.'

Coraine, Northern Rondelmar

Her name was Brunelda, Solon now knew, but he didn't use it. There was no need, for they barely talked. Her thoughts and emotions were irrelevant and his weren't hers to know. She was a stopgap in his life, nothing more.

Right now she was kneeling before his armchair, pleasuring him orally – and, he had to admit, showing far more skill and enthusiasm than the real Lyra had ever managed. He'd not meant to return to the House of Lantris that evening, but it was preferable to lying awake, snarling imprecations at faraway enemies – especially when he was still foaming at the news his spies had brought, of an assassination attempt upon the queen.

She's mine, his mind raged while he gripped Brunelda's head and held her in place, allowing her mouth's earthy magic to sweep him along towards climax. '*Lyra*,' he moaned, quivering bodily as he spent himself.

As the moment subsided he shoved Brunelda away so that she sprawled on the rug at his feet, her Lyra-wig mussed and her skin flushed, a little aroused by her erotic duties. He now paid her owners to forbid her other lovers and keep her secluded so that she was his alone. He wanted her pining for him, and evidently that was having the desired effect. And he doubted she'd ever had a lover like him. But right now, when he was burning with rage, it all felt so tawdry.

They tried to kill my queen!

'My Lord?' Brunelda asked uncertainly.

'Go!' he barked, but then he took pity on her crushed face and with an effort, he softened his voice. 'You've done well. But I need to be alone.'

Mollified, but clearly still wanting him, she left and he forgot her instantly, pouring himself a large Brevian whiskey and lounging in the armchair, trying to breathe through his anger.

When Lyra's mine again, I'm going to destroy every man who stood against her.

11

The Test

Fire and Ice

It is instructive that in cold Yuros, fire is seen as the primary element of Lucian, Lord of Hel, while in the hot East, ice is the realm of Shaitan, the Evil One. We see that which is most alien as the chief threat.

HAISAH, JA'ARATHI IMAM, PEROZ 866

The Elétfa
Febreux 936

'*Gricoama! Luhti! Zlateyr!*'

The rotting chamber swallowed Valdyr's cries, draining them of force as the darkness drew in its breath, then exhaled mockingly. He reached for the dwyma, but found nothing there. Alone in utter darkness, his balance failed and he lurched, stumbled and fell – and the rotting wood entombing him cracked and he spun away into nothingness. His limbs flailing as the air whipped by, he cried out in terror, expecting the end at any moment.

On and on he fell, the wind ripping at him while his heart hammered and his screams grew hoarse, the terror magnifying until he felt like his heart would rupture, his lungs would collapse, his head would explode, and in that long moment he realised that he could really die of this *overwhelming* fear, that he was on the edge of seizure . . .

And with that realisation came the knowledge of how to survive, as he had when a youth in the Keshi breeding-houses. He dug deep inside and found what he'd called his inner cave, the place where even Asiv couldn't reach him, where his senses and emotions were dulled beyond numbness, where touch was no longer felt, smells and sounds passed unnoticed and humiliation and hatred were as meaningless as joy. A place to endure until his tormentor was finally done with him. He crawled inside.

How long he was in there, hunkered under a blanket of nothingness, he had no idea, but when he emerged he was still falling . . .

No, floating . . . Tentatively, he opened his eyes, but found pitch-darkness, and panic still lurking . . . and he knew that if he fell into that fear again, this time he'd never stop falling. He clung to the fragile calm, put all his faith in it.

It got me through Asiv . . .

It was a mistake, to think of his abuser.

Instantly, a dark chuckle resounded, so deep it made his whole body vibrate, which became uncontrollable shaking a moment later when his brain caught up and he recognised the mocking laughter. Instinctively he squirmed and shrank, his clothing vanished and his body reverted to that of a naked boy.

A moment later, a big, warm, sweaty hand grasped his bare thigh. He convulsed in shock, thrashing back to the edge of panic as a second hand grasped his other leg and suddenly he was back in the cellar room beneath the breeding-house laboratory, lying on the filthy mattress where all his worst moments had played out. The suffocating sheets were tangled around his face, the ripe perfume of the body crushing him filled the air. He relived the agony of being lanced, the ghastly feeling of having the hated other's sweat and drool and seed soaking through flesh and bone into his very soul.

Panic struck him, vision went red and he screamed, '*Nara – NARA!*'

. . . and Lyra jerked awake, ripped from her dreams of fire and ambush by a vision of a young black-haired youth, one she felt she knew, lying pinned on his front by a grey-haired Ahmedhassan man with Gatti braids, pale brown skin and a pot-belly. She recoiled at the violence in the man's face, the cruel lust shining from his face.

Disoriented, not sure if she was even awake, her reaction was purely instinctive: she sent *herself*, streaming through the dwyma's endless strands until she was wrapping her arms around the boy's shoulders, pulling him into her grasp and shouting into his blank eyes, '*Valdyr –* *I'm here – I'm here . . .*'

His abuser's eyes went black and he lashed out, his long nails ripping her cheeks. She shrieked in pain, almost lost her grip, but clung on, her eyes locked on the boy's – which finally cleared and he saw her . . .

Nara? NARA!

When he saw the blonde woman, fear for her outweighed Valdyr's terror. Guilt for having dragged her into this and rage at seeing her assailed combined; he twisted from his abuser's grasp and slammed his feet into Asiv's chest even as he hurled himself into Nara's arms. The Gatti mage was sent spinning away, but Valdyr was ripped from her arms even as they shouted their relief at finding each other.

He hit the ground, cracking the back of his skull and winding himself. Lying there, gasping and disoriented, he realised Nara was gone and he was himself again, adult and dressed and alone. He sat up slowly, still breathing hard, pulling himself together. When a soft muzzle pressed into his nape, nuzzling him, he stroked Gricoama's unseen head while his racing heartbeat slowed and his shaking subsided.

A faint glow penetrated the darkness: a distant opening along a tunnel of rough wood. Through it he could see the stair continued to spiral up the outside of the mighty tree. He rose to his feet shakily and with Gricoama, walked out of the passage into the open air.

I got through . . .

But that gave him no comfort, because if the test had been to conquer his paralysing terror of Asiv, he'd failed. *Again.* Just the memory was enough to unman him.

I've not outgrown it or overcome it. I still fall apart before him.

That realisation was almost enough to reduce him to a sobbing heap, because he felt as if he'd never be free. For a moment he was tempted to walk to the edge and hurl himself into the black. But instead he gripped Gricoama's shoulders, clinging to the great wolf for strength, for he had none left of his own.

The path up the great tree went on, so he began to climb again, bereft of hope. *I'm sorry*, he whispered his apologies to Luhti and Zlateyr, to Kyrik, to Nara and to the dwyma itself. *Asiv will get me in the end – but while I can I'll keep going, for you.*

Lapisz, Mollachia

Asiv Fariddan jerked out of the waking dream, trying to fathom what had just happened. One moment he'd been standing at a window and then he'd had the most powerful memory-illusion he'd ever experienced, as if someone had thrown him back in time to when young Valdyr Sarkany was impaled on his shaft in his secret den beneath the breeding-house labs. But it wasn't just memory – because he'd also seen Valdyr as he was now, big and brawny with his scarred back and long black hair and moustaches. Not that he'd fought like a man.

He struggled like a child, he smirked. *There's nothing to fear from little Valdyr.*

But who was the woman who pulled him from me?

He kindled a relay-stave and reached out to the Master.

Hegikaro, Mollachia

Asiv's daemon legion was only days away, according to the scouts. The last of the refugees had arrived and all non-combatants had been sent to the beginning of the Registein trail with instructions to press on and beg refuge if Hegikaro fell.

Though Rondians don't shelter 'natives', Kyrik thought bitterly.

He had runners go through the town to announce an assembly in the square that afternoon. If the town was to be properly prepared, there were things that needed to be said. At the appointed hour he walked out onto the steps, wearing a light circlet around his head rather than his heavy crown, and armour rather than courtly attire. Kip was with him, and Milosh Nirabhy. He'd had the middle of the plaza roped off, leaving a narrow aisle that led to a postern gate on his right. Everyone was peering at it in some puzzlement.

A trumpeter blew a short blast as he surveyed the pale, anxious faces below. Eight in ten were men; but there were women too who'd elected to stay and fight – most were hunters' wives, proficient archers in their own right.

Kyrik began, 'My friends, we're living through a terrible season. The East has invaded West and daemons walk the daylight world. All we can do is ride out the storm.'

The gathered crowd nodded fearfully, glancing sideways at each other. They'd clearly expected – and hoped for – words of inspiration, not a litany of their fears.

'In such a time,' he went on, 'it feels like every miracle is a dark one, that all the powers of the world are ranged against us. But I am here to tell you that not every omen is evil. Not every wonder contains horror.'

He waved a hand and a line of big-horned cattle began to file in through the postern gate and down the roped off aisle, walking through the crowd to the central pen.

'Several years ago, a people enslaved by the empire managed to escape. They were a special people, mage-warriors every one of them, and they forged a life for themselves in the wilderness. But the empire continued to pursue them, so they were for ever on the move.'

The Mollachs were looking at each other in puzzlement, eyeing the cattle in the pen before them in confusion, wondering what this herd had to do with their king's tale.

'Are we to have a feast before the battle?' someone shouted. 'Been a long time since I had roast beef.'

Kip snorted under his breath.

'There will be no feasting until the battle is won,' Kyrik replied, 'but listen: for these mighty mage-warriors finally came to a mountain valley, a beautiful land, and decided that there they would stand and fight.' He raised his arm and shouted, 'Do not be afraid! This is a mighty sign from Kore Himself, that He sends us the aid we sorely need: not angels, but the next best thing.'

'Yar,' Kip shouted, unable to contain himself, 'he sends you *the Bullheads—*'

As one, the Mantauri stood on their hind legs as their bodies reconfigured.

The burghers shouted and Kyrik could taste their alarm. He remembered the bloodbath they'd only just averted when the Mantauri had revealed themselves to the Vlpa Clan a few months before and shouted, 'Do not fear!' He conjured light and shields around himself to remind them that he was a mage, to draw their eyes and give them pause enough that no one did anything stupid.

With those at the back as curious as they were fearful, and blocking any at the front who might have considered fleeing, the buzz of scared burghers gradually calmed.

'I introduce the Mantauri,' Kyrik shouted, projecting his voice with the gnosis. 'They are constructs, sanctioned by Empress Lyra herself' – *a white lie is allowable*, he told himself – 'and they have come to aid us in this dark hour.'

In Lantric myth, the Mantauri were the barbaric companions of great heroes. Now he reminded them of that. 'Like Ouros, the companion of the hero Rokalus, the Mantauri hate the darkness. They are here to protect us!'

Kyrik watched his people – fervent believers in Kore to the last – absorb that. *Mantauri from the old tales*, he heard some say. *Ysh, this is possible – but how can they be here? Why are they aiding us?* Then heads began to nod in understanding. *Ysh, that is what Mantauri do*, a few insisted. *The empress sends aid*, others added.

Rationalise it however you like, Kyrik thought. He doubted Empress Lyra cared about Mollachia, but if the thought gave his people courage, all the better. 'Maegogh, why are you here?' he shouted, and the crowd stared, wondering who he addressed.

'Kirol Kyrik,' Maegogh rumbled, stepping to the fore of his beastmen, 'we are here to fight the darkness.' He made a fist and conjured light around it, illuminating the square.

The crowd recoiled again, but not so far, nor so fearfully. A few even cheered.

'*They speak – they're* magi *– they're here to fight for us –*' Now people were babbling wildly to their neighbours, or praying, some with tears streaming down their faces, in thanks for answered prayers.

Maegogh led his people to the stairs, where Kip's Schlessen made a show of embracing them, then they all bowed to Kyrik, demonstrating their willingness to accept his command, another necessary step to gain acceptance with the watching Mollachs. Finally, their weapons were brought forth and brandished and the mood changed again as cheers resounded through the assembly.

'Good,' Maegogh rumbled to Kyrik as they surveyed the townsfolk. 'Now we can work openly.'

Kyrik shook his giant hand and was about to respond when he felt a pulse of gnostic energy above and behind him. He glanced back, then swallowed.

Hajya stood on the balcony overlooking the square, clad in Sydian riding leathers and a Sarkany family cloak. In her hand was her periapt, gleaming pale blue like a luminous sapphire. She must have found it among Asiv's abandoned possessions.

He felt his heart constrict at the murmur susurrating through the gathering in the square. In that moment he felt both incredibly proud and very, very frightened for her.

She's not strong enough for the days to come . . . I should never have brought her here.

After the 'unveiling' of the Mantauri, the pace of work trebled, for their gnosis and sheer physical power made the heaviest tasks so much easier. Even repairing the southern breach went ahead in leaps and bound. Every day was filled with sweat and exertion. The ordinary people, at first leery of getting close to the giant constructs, were soon won over by their phlegmatic nature and immense strength. The more gregarious of Maegogh's people made inroads into winning confidence with shows of good humour and for a while, Kyrik felt an immense sense of possibility.

But the scouts' reports were harrowing: five thousand possessed soldiers were advancing upon them.

'They're more like animals than men,' one reported, but his colleague was shaking her head.

'They're worse,' she said. 'Animals don't kill and torture for pleasure. Beasts don't turn men into more beasts.'

Kyrik didn't try to silence such tales – he needed his people to understand what they were facing – but he countered with stories of his own, telling them how silver could weaken and even kill the possessed; how sunlight disoriented them. He told them that the enemy were *flawed*.

Every night he retreated to the royal suite to tend Hajya. She was horribly sensitive to the approach of Asiv's army and the daemon infesting their souls. Although her body had at last been purged of the ichor, her mind was sensitive to the daemon's incessant vile babble. Every night was an ordeal, drifting in and out of nightmares and waking Kyrik with stream-of-consciousness echoes of the mind of Abraxas. There was no question of resuming life as man and wife, not when she was teetering on the edge of an internal abyss.

Then came the day they'd feared, an hour before sunset, when Asiv Fariddan's forces poured around Lake Drozst with none of the synchronised pomp of a real Rondian legion, no drums, no trumpets, no marching hymns – just a horde who moved in silence.

The watchman on Haklyn's Tower saw them first. He called urgently to his fellows below. Moments later a pair of scouts who'd been brave enough to take horses west along the valley road came clattering through the gates, yelling, 'They're coming – they're coming!'

Kyrik stood with Kip on the battlements. The Schlessen giant pulled on his gauntlets, glaring down the valley with a look of satisfaction. 'I hate waiting,' he growled, before bellowing down to his Schlessens in the courtyard below, 'Minaus calls us to war – do you hear him?'

As if in answer, thunder rumbled in the southern peaks and every superstitious man – which, with soldiers, meant all of them – made some gesture to ward off evil or seek divine blessing. They put tools aside, strapped on helms and climbed up to the battlements to see, while the burghers, from aged men and women to barely grown youths, took up their own weapons and followed.

'How many?' Kip asked.

Kyrik conjured using clairvoyance to gain a closer vision of the foe. Every legionary had black eyes and dark bloody drool around their mouths. Their uniforms were torn and stained and a great many appeared to have discarded their weapons. *Maybe they prefer to use teeth and nails.* The thought chilled him.

He put that aside. In the Second Crusade he'd been a wind-mage, flying skiffs on scouting missions, so he'd learned how to count formations. 'Four thousand in view, more coming. I can't see Asiv . . . no, wait . . .' He focused upon a clump of horsemen who had trotted into view. Asiv could probably have dispelled his conjurations, but he didn't, so Kyrik saw an inhumanely handsome Ahmedhassan in rich velvets and furs riding a black-eyed stallion, surrounded by fifteen wound-ravaged, ebony-eyed battle-magi of the Rondian legion. They hissed as if sensing his scrutiny, but still no one dispelled it.

Kyrik broke the spell before Asiv latched onto it and spoke to him. He had no desire to hasten that conversation. 'He's here, and he's got all the battle-magi with him. they are all possessed.'

Kip scowled and spat. 'We could use a little help, Bullhead,' he admonished the skies, before turning to Kyrik and adding with a lop-sided smile, 'He never listens.'

'Neither does Kore – or the rukking empire,' Kyrik replied.

Kip snorted, then looked pensive. 'You, me and fifty-odd Mantauri,' he said quietly. 'We can hold out a while, but I can't see how to win.'

'Neither can I,' Kyrik admitted. 'A possessed battle-mage is worse than any ordinary mage, from what I've seen – and Asiv is an army on his own. They've got enough men to encircle us, leaving nowhere to run.'

'Minaus spits upon the coward who runs.'

Kip was so much the essence of the Schlessen barbarian it felt almost like an act. *Perhaps inside he's screaming in fear?* Kyrik thought, then he decided that was unlikely. *No, I think he actually loves all this.*

'I just wish Valdyr was here,' he said . . . then he thought about that and corrected himself. 'No, actually I'm glad he's not.'

Kip laid a hand on his shoulder. 'He'll return, Kirol. Let's make sure we're here to greet him.' He hesitated, then asked, 'Will Hajya be able to aid our defence?'

'No,' Kyrik answered flatly. 'It was a mistake to bring her here.'

Freihaafen

Ogre emerged from the trees where he'd been watching the comings and goings of the human women and female Mantauri left in Freihaafen. Their days were mostly filled with tending the children and feeding everyone. He was waiting for Sabina to be on her own; as she was head-woman, that took some time, but finally, around midmorning, he found her standing alone beside the palisade gates, catching her breath.

'Sabina?' he called deferentially. 'May I speak with you?'

Although she was clearly a little frazzled, she waited as he ambled up. 'Ogre, what is it? Have some of the children been in your cave again?'

He smiled. 'I didn't mind, truly. No, it's just that . . . well, I have to go.'

She stiffened. 'Go?'

He dropped his gaze apologetically. 'I've solved the book – I know what the Master intends and I need to tell certain people. I can't do that from here – I have no relay-staves and Mollachia is too mountainous for me to penetrate without one.'

Sabina said, looking worried, 'The truth is, we are comforted to have you here, Ogre, especially when all the other warriors have gone. But of course we'll cope. One warrior more or less will not matter if the enemy find us here.'

'I would not ask this if I didn't believe that time is of the essence,' Ogre told her, 'but I understand his intentions and what he needs for his triumph and I believe there's no time to lose.'

The Master writes of requiring a tamed dwymancer, he reminded himself, *and he's got Jehana Mubarak. It could already be too late.*

'Then you must be careful,' Sabina told him. 'If your old master knows what you've learned, he will fear you and send hunters.'

That the Master might fear him was ridiculous; Ervyn Naxius was above him like the sun was above the sea. 'I'm nothing to him,' he told her modestly, 'but others will know what to do.'

Tarita will know. Part of him wondered if he was just making an excuse to seek her out, but he dismissed that thought. *No, it's necessary. She is Merozain and she has the ear of powerful people.*

'Then I wish you good fortune,' Sabina said formally.

He was waved off an hour later with a small pack, an axe and little fanfare. Faleesa gave him a satchel of flatbread and cured meat and Sabina handed him an argenstael dagger and some silver dust, 'Just in case.'

He walked through the narrow ravine concealing the hidden vale, following the stream that ran from the lake seeking the greater rivers of the Mollachia lowlands. He emerged around the middle of the day into a tangle of trees, where he shed his clothing and packed everything into his pack, then bound it to his back before invoking morphic-gnosis. Shape-changing was something he found disturbingly easy, as if reverting to beast-form was natural. There was pain, and a disturbing flood of heightened scent and hearing as he fell forward onto all fours, emitting a groan that became a whine and then a growl as bones shrank or lengthened, muscles and joints popped and cracked and bristles burst through his skin.

When it was done, the pack was still on his back and he needed only to tighten the straps around his new shape before thrusting the axe through the straps and turning his hands to padded feet. He resembled something like a shaggy carnivorous pony with a bearish pelt and wolverine head, coloured a mottled tawny brown and black. He could smell and see much more clearly, and these limbs would eat up the miles.

Become a beast too long and you'll remain one, the old gnostic texts warned, but as he inhaled the scent of creatures that had passed this way, listened to the birds and the roar of the wind in the trees, he felt the call of the wilderland, the lure of vanishing into another life. But even that wouldn't protect him from the Master's plans, so he resolved to heed the warning.

The landscape beyond the small wood was broken and harsh, with bare stone and streaks of snow on the heights above. High above, eagles circled and in the distance he could hear the bellow of a stag. The scent of spring gave the clear air a lusty tang. The going was hard, but he covered the miles easily, clambering over rock falls and through narrows that a horse could not have managed, keeping under the cover of the trees, hidden from eyes in the air.

His senses tingled and he realised that someone, somewhere, was scrying for him. The peaks around Freihaafen must have blocked earlier attempts. Determined not to be caught now, he strengthened his wards before moving on.

By evening, he'd reached the Osiapa River, where he took his own form again to make a cold camp in the lee of the river bank, guzzling water so cold it froze his gullet. Gulping down food, he estimated progress. Twelve miles, he guessed, good going over such rugged land. It would be easier as he descended. Hegikaro was still fifty miles away as birds flew, two or three days on foot in such terrain, he'd been told.

Do our enemies watch these paths? He gazed up, wondering about the birds. Possessed animals died swiftly, but if Asiv had magi, they might use beast-magic to use creatures as scouts. Hopefully they had no great reason to seek him in this area, but once he reached the main trails, there might be unfriendly eyes. In the end it would come down to luck.

Despite the discomfort, Ogre woke next morning refreshed. Excitable birds squalled in the trees, roused by the kiss of sunlight on the peaks, but the river's music was soothing. He wolfed down the remaining flatbread, then changed shape and got underway, following the west bank of the Osiapa downstream towards the lower valley.

Evening found him wading across a swift-flowing ford, the water up to his furred belly and cold enough to make him shiver. As he reached an eyot midstream, little more than a few yards of shingle, a low rumbling snarl carried from the high top of the cutting. A mountain lion was silhouetted against the ridgeline, looking down at him a hundred yards below. It coughed out a second throaty roar and was joined by another. When it appeared, Ogre could see the second animal was smaller and leaner, a female. They looked scrawny and hungry – it had obviously been a hard winter.

Then both lions rose on hind legs and even across the distance, Ogre could feel the sudden flare of malice as their eyes went black. The male growled and called down in a smug, oily voice, 'Ogre, we've found you at last.'

12

A Place of Refuge

Impersonators

Throughout history, vulnerable rulers have employed impersonators as a security measure, so that others might take the knives and arrows meant for them. A successful impersonator must erase their own identity, forsake the immortality of being remembered – and often also forsake any hope of family and children. I confess, I find this impossible to comprehend: I want everyone to know my name.

ARUN 'ELAN' LANTREY, CRUSADER GENERAL, HEBUSALIM 897

Norostein, Noros
Febreux 936

'Ali Beyrami?' Waqar gasped. 'How dare you assail—'

The Shihadi cleric made a silencing gesture and for all he was not a mage, it had the same effect on Waqar as a spell, silencing him. He watched in dread for the imam's eyes to go black, but he remained clear-eyed, as did his Godspeakers.

Waqar looked around the pavilion, which was full of priests and ex-Hadishah magi, all of them Shihadi men, apart from the young female mage, who'd backed away. No one looked at all sympathetic to him – no surprise, for Waqar had never hidden his distaste for the Shihad or the Amteh fanatics.

None of these men believe I'm worthy of their Paradise . . .

'Prince Waqar,' the imam mused. 'Do you know how much your head is worth right now?'

'I neither know nor care,' Waqar retorted, adding, 'And neither do you.'

Beyrami's all about religion and power.

'Perhaps not, but it would sweeten the pot, when I can already rid myself of a troublesome sceptic whom I have no desire to see upon the sultan's throne.'

That's undoubtedly true. But he's not handed me over yet. He's curious . . . or afraid.

'Would you rather have a cabalist on the throne?' he demanded in response. 'A man whose allegiances are to a renegade mage, the man who murdered Sultan Salim – a man who is possessed by a daemon?'

'Extraordinary claims.' Beyrami sniffed. 'Do you have any proof?'

'If the word of a prince is not enough to –'

'None, then?' Beyrami grunted, straightening and turning to his Hadishah captain, a shaven-skulled man with scars all the way up his bare arms, the marks of self-penitence. Reconciling the gnosis to worship of Ahm was a painful undertaking for some. 'Shaarvin, take him to the sultan and –'

'Wait,' said a new voice, one that sent a thrill through him.

Waqar jerked his head around and saw the face of the young female mage alter from a round-faced, unremarkable woman to the bony features of Tarita Alhani. Her eyes were alight with mirth as she raised her hands, palms empty.

The room exploded into motion, blades limned with gnostic light flashing out, shields flaring as Shaarvin interposed himself between her and Beyrami. For an instant Waqar feared they'd cut her down where she stood, but Beyrami snapped, 'Hold –'

That stilled them all.

Tarita hadn't moved a muscle.

'Who are you?' the cleric demanded.

She kept her hands raised, palms out, as a man behind her placed a blade against her throat. She said lightly, 'I am Prince Waqar's official concubine.'

Beyrami raised his eyebrows. Waqar had vanished from the Shihad camp after the death of his former lover Fatima and being declared a traitor by Xoredh – and the woman's accent was clearly Jhafi dirt-caste. 'Prince?' he asked.

'Ai, she is,' Waqar replied, concealing his doubt on that point.

She flashed him a smile. 'If you will permit, I have something to show you,' she told Beyrami.

Beyrami glanced at his Hadishah commander. 'Shaarvin?'

The Hadishah captain looked like he'd as soon slit her throat and have done. 'A traitor has no voice, and neither does his foreign slut.'

'Mind your tongue,' Waqar snarled, 'lest I cut it out when we're done here.'

'Shaarvin has my protection,' Beyrami warned, before glaring down at Tarita. 'Where's the real Kamilala?'

'She's in her tent, unharmed,' Tarita replied. 'There's a bound man with her. You should bring him in – but be careful not to remove his Chain-rune or bindings.'

Beyrami's eyes bored into her. 'Your name?'

'Reeta,' Tarita lied.

'If there is such a man there, we will bring him, and if there isn't, I'll have you stoned as an adulteress. I may do so, regardless.'

Waqar checked his tongue, marvelling at Tarita's composure and fearing for her survival. Beyrami was not a man to get on the wrong side of. A moment passed until Beyrami's Hadishah returned with a bound and hooded man.

Beyrami conferred with his people, then he signed to Shaarvin, who tore away the captive's hood and removed the gag.

The prisoner's teeth immediately crunched into Shaarvin's hand, blackened saliva spraying everywhere as his teeth tore through skin and cracked bones. The Hadishah backhanded the captive, before cradling the bitten hand, wincing angrily.

The prisoner's eyes were ebony pools. His face contorted into a rictus of hatred as he snarled about him, trying to wrench his way clear of his bindings. Even Beyrami flinched, but he gestured and two of his men leaped on the prisoner's back and bore him down, mashing his face into the mud.

Beside him, Shaarvin swayed woozily as tendrils of black fluid spread up his forearm. He gave a horrified squeak and turned to Tarita. 'What is –?' he stammered.

Waqar looked at Tarita, who stared back, the faintest shift in her expression telling him that she'd given him the tools he needed to persuade Beyrami – no one was going to listen to her, so he needed to think and speak fast.

'That daemon possession I mentioned?' he put in, improvising fast, working hard at keeping his voice calm and clinical, 'it's spread by bodily fluids.'

Shaarvin's eyes went round and his knees gave way. 'Master,' he pleaded to Beyrami, who'd gone pale.

'Join us, pig,' the possessed prisoner leered. 'Help me kill these scum.' Then his face cleared and he rasped, 'Beyrami, bring me the prince and his slut in chains, or I'll slaughter you all.'

The voice was Xoredh's.

Everyone looked at Beyrami in horror, their faces ashen.

In the shocked silence, only Tarita moved: she drove one elbow into the throat of the man who was holding her while her other hand seized his wrist and twisted until he dropped his dagger – which flew sideways into her fingers. Without pausing, she slammed some kind of mesmerism spell into the daemon's skull, knocking him out cold.

'Now you know where Xoredh stands,' she told the imam, then she looked down at the man she'd felled and added, 'You touch me again and I'll break your face.'

Beyrami still hadn't moved.

Waqar pulled out a silver coin and thrusting it at Beyrami's lieutenant, told him, 'Silver is sovereign against the ichor. Press this coin to the wound – do it now if you wish to live.'

Shaarvin looked up at him imploringly, then grabbed the coin and pressed it to the wound. He convulsed in agony, his flesh searing as he collapsed into a shaking heap.

'You're welcome,' Tarita said drily.

Beyrami's Hadishah were waiting for a sign from their leader. At last he shook himself and gestured at his men to put up their weapons.

'Please, Holiness,' Waqar started, 'we should be allies here.'

Beyrami was still staring at his stricken man, watching as the blackness receded up his forearm. 'Shaarvin?' he asked.

'It's working,' Shaarvin croaked, 'but by the Prophet's tears, I swear I have heard the voice of Shaitan himself.'

'Not Shaitan,' Waqar interrupted. 'Abraxas, the daemon is named. His ichor is being spread by servants of Ervyn Naxius, the man behind the Masked Cabal who murdered Sultan Salim.'

Every man in the room made a sign against evil, even though they were mostly magi.

'Explain,' Beyrami croaked.

Waqar would have preferred a private discussion, but perhaps this was for the best. 'The Masked Cabal who slew Sultan Salim are spreading daemonic possession – not just here, but in Pallas and Mollachia as well.' He indicated the black-haired, olive-skinned prisoner. 'This man is one.'

'He was a soldier in the army of the "Lord of Rym",' Tarita put in, moving to stand next to Waqar. 'I found him down the road, where Xoredh has been sending whole divisions of his own men. Your sultan is feeding your worshippers to the daemon, Imam.'

'As you just heard, Xoredh is himself possessed,' Waqar added. 'Sultan Rashid confessed as he died that he'd given his son to become a pawn of Naxius, to further his own goals for Shihad and the crown.'

Beyrami started to protest, but quickly fell silent again. When at last he spoke, his voice was uncharacteristically small. 'What must we do?'

Latif, Ashmak and Sanjeep were preparing Rani the elephant, while trying to conceal that fact. Desertion seemed to be their only option if they were to avoid having to march down the fatal Eastern Road. Around them, the other elephant crews were also busy in the frigid afternoon sun, repairing equipment, feeding or washing their beasts.

Latif paused and gazed south at the walls of Copperleaf looming above them, the sentries visible, half a mile away. *Seth's up there*, Latif thought. *Ramon too, and maybe others I know.* He ached to see them, but uppermost in his mind was the problem of getting out of Norostein. Where could they go? Claiming they'd been reassigned to Verelon, to the east of here, was the best they could come up with, but that would be fraught with perils, especially if Waqar was right about the army being surrounded by possessed men.

He surreptitiously lifted another quiver of arrows into the howdah, while Ashmak slipped a satchel of stolen provisions among the blankets. An officer came by and they busied themselves mending a broken piece of wickerwork until he was gone.

Then an eerie sound filled the air: a piercing wail that echoed all the way from the eastern side of the Lowertown tier, then war-horns blew and men stumbled from bedrolls, a few with frightened camp-women clinging to them, all blinking in the glare of daylight.

'It's the call to arms,' Ashmak shouted. 'Mount up – to arms, men, to arms–'

The cry was taken up on all sides. The elephant crews began preparing their howdahs, but Rani's crew were already ready; they each took a corner of the howdah and with Ashmak's kinesis doing the heavy lifting, got it onto Rani's back. The elephant was flapping her trunk about fussily as they scrambled up, then Sanjeep touched her left ear and she lurched to her feet.

'That's efficiency, you slobs,' Ashmak crowed to the rest as Rani swung round and headed for the north-facing exit.

With any luck we can be away before the officers notice, Latif thought hopefully. They had their route to a quieter gate already planned, and their story for the guards. Rani strode confidently under Sanjeep's guidance, ignoring the calls of the other crews.

Looking up, Latif saw roc-riders taking to the air, wings hammering as they sought lift. Skiffs were rising too, their sails billowing as they caught the wind, and all the while that dreadful wailing sound tore at the air.

It's coming from the Eastern Road. Latif's heart lurched. *It's like the voice of ten thousand daemons . . .*

'Hurry,' he called down to Sanjeep. 'Something's happening . . .'

Officers were bawling contradictory orders from all sides. Rani broke into a trot, the howdah swaying as she tried to shoulder her way through a loose formation of Lakh spearmen all shouting to their many gods as the howling swirled around them. They were forced to haul her nose around, which had Rani trumpeting balefully.

'Who's attacking?' Latif hollered to the Keshi officer.

'No one knows,' came the response, 'but they're coming from the east.'

More men poured in, scared Keshi conscripts who tried to stop when they saw the arrayed Lakh spears, but many more were pushing in behind them, so the Lakh lifted their spears and tried to let them through, despite the officers bawling at them to hold formation.

Then *something* hit the rear of the Keshi lines and total panic broke out. Dark figures were slamming into the milling soldiers, many too large to be human. The impact rippled through the square, men breaking around Rani like water around a rock, while the keening grew in volume, swelling in horror as if Heaven itself were appalled.

'Hold—' the officers bellowed in vain.

'Move – now!' Ashmak shouted to Sanjeep. 'Get us to the gates.'

Sanjeep hauled on Rani's reins, sending her wading through the wavering defenders, trying to force a path downslope to the north road, but a wall of ragged dark-clad men was assailing the soldiers, the ferocity of their attack cleaving a wedge through the press. When a giant figure with a shaggy hide reared up and engulfed the commanding officer, horse and all, the line completely disintegrated. The attackers were both men and constructs, black-eyes gleaming with malice, and that hideous cry pouring from every mouth.

The daemons – they're here!

It occurred to Latif that he and Waqar had triggered this: Xoredh had realised resistance was forming and decided to strike early. 'Go, go,' he urged Sanjeep, 'we've got to get out!'

But another horde was coming up the road to the north, pulling down the fleeing men before battering against the first lines of determined resistance centred around a Keshi mage and some veteran soldiers who'd organised themselves with spears extended in serried ranks, the front line crouching, presenting a wall of jagged steel. It recoiled at the impact, but held.

We're cut off from the north gate, Latif cursed. 'Sanjeep, try going west—'

Once again Sanjeep pulled Rani around and they tried to ram a path through the panicking defenders. Trumpeting, the elephant lurched into a run, battering men aside, even as more of their unit entered the square from the south, knocking dozens more off their feet. Even stalwart Rani staggered, trying to find firm footing as man after man was crushed under the press of bodies.

Ashmak roared a warning, Latif automatically swung about, drawing back his bowstring, as a big shaggy shape leaped onto the shoulders of the packed bodies and sprang at them.

His arrow buried itself in the creature's blackened right eye: the best shot of Latif's life and it tumbled into the press below, a droplet of triumph amid a sea of disaster, for the men were falling in swathes. The elephants were being targeted now and their thrashing and rearing was spoiling their own archers' aim. Ashmak and his fellow magi were firing mage-bolts as fast as they could, but still the enemy kept coming.

'Dear Ahm, what is it we face?' Ashmak wailed.

'Death,' Latif called back. 'Sanjeep, get us out!'

'I'm trying,' the mahout hollered, turning Rani's head yet again, for a path had opened where a brick wall had collapsed at the southern edge of the square and the men were flowing towards it like water from a punctured barrel, carrying Rani with them.

They slammed their way through a wrecked shop, but the curve of the tight-packed streets forced them to keep heading south – towards the Copperleaf walls and further from safety. With thousands of fleeing men sweeping them along, they had little choice but to follow.

'West,' Ashmak shouted to Sanjeep, 'take us west, you idiot Lakh—'

'There is no west – this road only goes south,' Sanjeep shrieked back.

Ashmak glared – he'd never learned how to take contradiction – then he called, '*Chod* – then just keep us moving.'

They'd been climbing as they went and now they could see smoke rising a quarter of a mile away at the gate they'd been making for. Dark figures were crawling all over the tower and shimmying up the walls like ants. An immense banner unfurled beneath the setting sun: a red wolf on a black background. Latif looked in all directions, but options were fast evaporating. Above them rose the Copperleaf walls, where brazen Rondian trumpets were blowing the call to arms.

We're trapped between the daemons and the walls.

'Where's the sultan?' Ashmak raged. 'Where's that *matachod* sultan?' Xoredh's banners were nowhere to be seen; only those wolf banners were visible on all sides. 'We're trapped,' he groaned. 'There's nowhere to run.'

Sanjeep winced, raising his eyes to the heavens, but Latif was still looking left and right, seeking an answer. *I saw Rashid die: I heard his last words and was avenged for my wife and son and my beloved Salim, so perhaps I have no right to demand more of life than this.* But he thought about what Rashid had confessed – what he'd unleashed upon his own people.

No, it can't end like this . . .

He rose and stepped to the edge of the howdah, threw an apologetic look at his comrades – *no, my friends* – and said, 'I have an idea. Don't wait for me.'

Then he dropped to the ground and ran up the rising path to Copperleaf.

'Sir, sir,' Andwine Delton called from the door, amid the blasting trumpets, 'the enemy are under attack.'

Seth was conferring with Justiciar Detabrey, Vann Mercer and those of the Noros nobility who'd distanced themselves from Governor Myron enough to earn a degree of trust. They'd been trying to work out how to deal with Myron's captured cronies when Delton burst in.

'Show me,' Seth replied, hurrying from the room, relieved to escape the tense negotiations.

He and Delton took horses and cantered to the walls, then climbed a watchtower where they found chaos unfolding below. 'What the Hel's going on?' Seth demanded of Era Hyson, whose Royal Guards were on duty here.

'We don't know,' Hyson admitted. 'Suddenly there was this Korebedamned wailing noise, then the enemy started attacking each other. It's slaughter down there,' he added, in awed tones.

The sun was setting, its scarlet glow streaking the scene in blood.

From what Seth could tell, all the movement was from the north and east, as if the attackers were herding the Shihadi soldiers southwest. But the western gates were under a new banner, one he'd not seen before. The red wolf on black reminded Seth of Ramon's tales of the wars in Rimoni.

'The Lord of Rym,' he breathed. 'I think the Lord of Rym is attacking our enemy.'

Is it possible he's on our side?

From the east, a blast of Keshi horns announced the sultan's own cavalry, white-horsed and gaudy. They thundered along the Kingsway leading from the main gates to where he stood; but half a mile away they veered and ploughed into a horde of their own men, cutting them down in a bloody swathe.

'What—? The sultan's *helping* to slaughter his own men?'

'There's been a schism,' Delton exclaimed. 'Should we attack?'

Attack? Should we? But there's ten times our number out there . . .

'No,' Seth decided, 'We hold the walls but don't intervene. We must remain secure.'

Waqar stood beside Ali Beyrami on a rooftop overlooking what had been a marketplace, the latest fall-back position against this sudden assault. It was ironic that a man he'd always regarded as a dangerous lunatic was now his best hope. A few hundred yards to the east, their lines were being ripped apart and it was too late to reinforce. They'd made a fatal error and now thousands of men would pay . . .

We should never have shown Beyrami the possessed man, for of course Xoredh saw everything – but how else could we have convinced him?

'Take courage in Ahm,' Beyrami was calling in his stentorian voice to the massed soldiers below and the archers on the roofs. 'The Prophet blesses you.'

I wish that mattered, Waqar thought, but to his surprise, he could see that it did. That belief was palpably stiffening the resolve of the men below.

For the past hour, he and Beyrami had been rallying units to reinforce their makeshift bulwarks as they were driven westward through the city. The Lowertown lake divided their forces, but it also helped them, for the artificial reservoir was forcing Xoredh's daemonic forces to attack on two narrower fronts. Though man for man the enemy were stronger and more savage, smaller lines were easier to defend. They'd been spreading the word too about the need to decapitate, and to use silver if they had it – but most of these men had never been paid, and what few silver trinkets they'd once owned had been traded months ago for bread.

We're still losing, and now they're behind us, too. The sunset end of the city was aflame and he could hear fellow magi in the aether confirming that they too were trapped. And the Yurosi defenders were sleeting arrows into them if they deployed too close to the inner walls. Perhaps as many as eighty thousand men were packed into a couple of square miles, but they were being overrun.

With a scream, a dozen venators came hurtling across the rooftops from the north. Waqar's heart lifted – but only until the riders started blazing mage-bolts into his lines and he saw that they had also been possessed. A flight of his own roc-riders tried to intercept, but the daemonic possession made the enemy so much harder to kill.

<*Take their heads!*> he blared hopelessly.

He turned to Beyrami. 'Keep them steady, Imam. We must hold here, or all is lost.' He pointed behind them, to the west. 'A quarter of a mile over there is our rearguard, facing the other way and already assailed.'

Beyrami, nodding his understanding, turned back to the soldiers below with eyes aflame with fervour and roared, 'Ahm is waiting for you, my martyrs – his virgins wait to bathe your wounds–'

That eerie shriek sounded again and a mob of black-eyed men poured into the square, their wailing like claws raking the inside of Waqar's skull as they stormed forward. A flight of arrows pierced flesh and sometimes eyes, killing outright, but most staggered on even when hit, striking the spear-wall in a berserk frenzy. The spearmen held firm, impaling the first wave, then slashing at necks and limbs with their scimitars. Waqar saw men wading in where survival was impossible to behead a construct beast.

And still the pressure grew.

He was so caught up in the struggle, preparing himself for his own moment of truth, he didn't notice Tarita until she grasped his shoulder and pointed to a rooftop across the market-square some hundred yards away. 'There,' she murmured. 'It's your cousin.'

Waqar saw the Mubarak banner and the men beneath it on the opposite rooftop. He felt a mix of despair and cold anger seeing Xoredh's gloating face lit by pale blue gnostic shields. The sultan gave him an ironic salute, then sent a mage-bolt searing into the air: a signal.

Keshi horns boomed and three squadrons of white-horsed cavalry came thundering into the square, the horses as black-eyed as their riders. They were preceded by a wave of kinesis that hammered into the lines, knocking men over and weapons askew, then the lances struck. The lines burst apart and suddenly Waqar's position was under direct attack.

13

My Enemy's Enemy

Makelli

Vico Makelli, the Lantrian philosopher, was chief advisor to three princes, switching
allegiances frequently while keeping his neck whole in an era when political murder
was rife. The princes all deemed him too valuable to kill. His career spanned forty
years and his teachings have informed political thought ever since.

ANNALS OF PALLAS, 823

Norostein, Noros
Febreux 936

Waqar and Tarita stepped to the edge of the flat roof, spread their arms
and hurled mage-bolts at a blinding rate into Xoredh's possessed cavalry below, reeling in the intoxication of conjuring and releasing so
much energy. The Hadishah protecting Ali Beyrami did the same, cutting a channel of flame through the men and horses. Daemons thrashed
about, screaming as they were immolated, going up like torches.

But it wasn't enough: the weight and momentum and sheer ferocity of
the attackers overwhelmed the front rank of spearmen defending them
and those behind, shouting in despair that all was lost, began to break.

Waqar and Tarita found their own shields battered by a torrent of
energy from the opposite roof: Xoredh himself, forcing them on the
defensive. Their shields went through purple to scarlet as his attack
built, until Waqar could feel himself going under, just as those below
were failing.

We need more magi – we need something—

But it wasn't magi who saved the line – it was *faith*.

Ali Beyrami had been pulled to the back of the roof by his Hadishah for his own protection, but he descended to join the terrified, milling soldiers. Even over the daemons' wailing, his massive voice, clear and fervent, filled the alleys.

'*MEN OF AHM, YOUR GOD IS CALLING YOU: TO ARMS, MY BRETHREN, TO ARMS!*'

His voice penetrated the senses and slapped the soul. Even Waqar felt it, the sense that the sky was just a silk veil and Ahm Himself was beyond it, His gaze weighing every soul. He found himself needing to prove his valour, to rise above the terror and be worthy of Salvation – this despite a lifetime of healthy scepticism.

To the true believers, the majority of the men below, it was balm to their terror and iron to their spines. They turned, screaming inchoate worship, and counter-charged. It was desperate, ragged and suicidal, but it felt like glory. With Beyrami's booming voice filling their ears – now interspersed with instructions like '*BEHEAD THE DAEMONS*' and '*SILVER IS YOUR ALLY*', they struck back, sheer weight of numbers slowing Xoredh's possessed riders, and as the silver bit, pulling them down.

'We have to keep him alive,' Tarita shouted in Waqar's ear and she launched herself down into the press, landing beside Beyrami and joining her own bright shields to Shaarvin and his lieutenants to protect the imam. She held a gleaming scimitar, the one he and she had retrieved from Midpoint Tower, its blade harder than steel, though without the devastating effect of silver upon the possessed men.

For a few minutes, the daemon cavalry were driven back, possessed men and horses going down biting and thrashing, blood both red and black spraying. Heads were hacked from the fallen indiscriminately.

But Xoredh's attacks were unabating: infected men kept pouring into the square as it became the new keystone of the defence. Spells burst and broke over the defenders and Waqar's rooftop, taking their toll. Bipedal constructs resembling armoured bears were now entering the fray and the tide was turning again. Despite all the fervour and blind heroism, Beyrami's men had no choice but to give ground. The square was so packed that no one could move any more; they just stabbed and hacked until they died on their feet and slipped beneath the surface.

We're still losing. Waqar spared a glance at the Copperleaf walls above them, wondering if the damned Yurosi were laughing at this new chaos – or did they realise that they were next?

We're all going to burn in the Pit. He set his jaw, and raised his blade – coated with Mollachian silver. It wouldn't last long, he knew. *So let's all burn together.*

'Boss, this is insane,' Vania di Aelno murmured. She and Ramon stood on the edge of the parapets, watching the Shihad tear itself in two.

Ramon understood the sentiment, but to him it was all too explicable. His legions had been fighting in Rimoni for four years and during that time the mysterious Lord of Rym had spread his influence from village to village, concealing his true strength or nature, never leaving living witnesses to reveal what it was they fought. Finally the Becchio Mercenary Guilds had fractured and turned on themselves.

'It's Rimoni all over again,' he told Vania. 'We only just got out alive and I still can't rightly say what we faced. Berserkers, some said. Necromantic draugs, said others. Now we know. Clearly the Lord of Rym no longer fears to be revealed.'

The red and black banners of the Lord of Rym were springing up on all sides now while the air reverberated with that spine-sapping howl. They could see constructs of all kinds, every one black-eyed and savage and many wielding the gnosis, and despite the chaos their brutality was clearly controlled by an iron hand.

For now, Copperleaf remained unassailed, but below them all was confusion. Just a quarter of a mile away they could see a massive battle taking place on the shores of the Lowertown reservoir, and all the space between was filled with Keshi soldiers, all singing and chanting to Ahm as they rallied. But Ramon could see the defence on the far side of the lake had all but collapsed and the Lord of Rym's banners were advancing from the west. The remains of the Shihad were trapped and doomed. Above them giant eagles tore each other to pieces in mid-air, while the remaining Keshi windships were burning on the ground.

'We're going to be facing a whole heap fewer Noories tomorrow,' Vania observed.

'Yet somehow I'm not comforted.'

Melicho joined them, his face anxious. 'Boss, what're the orders? We've got Noories straying into the killing zones as they run westwards and the lads aren't sure whether to shoot or not?'

'Only shoot if they try to scale the walls,' Ramon told him. 'There's a plague out there, remember.'

A plague that turns men berserk, engineered by the Lord of Rym?

Melicho saluted, then invoked the gnosis to spread the orders. Ramon clapped Vania on the shoulder. 'Come on, let's get to the aqueduct tower. I want to make sure it's secure.'

They passed along the walls westward, reassuring the men as they went, before joining a queasy-looking Tabia in the cupola of Aqueduct Tower overlooking the elevated water channel they'd crawled up only a few days earlier. Since then, rising temperatures had melted the ice and now the race was full. The sluice-gates had been shut to starve the enemy below of fresh water, trapping millions of tons of water in the mile-long race.

'Boss,' Tabia greeted him anxiously, 'it's the Beast of Rym, isn't it? That's his banner over to the west.'

'Looks that way,' Ramon told her. He squeezed her shoulder in reassurance before moving on to join Pilus Lukaz and his serjants, Vidran, Bowe and Harmon, at the corner of the tower.

'Is Seth nearby?' he asked Lukaz.

'He'll be here soon – he's briefing Legate Pelk,' the pilus replied, pointing at a ballista tower a hundred yards down the lines. 'Left us here 'cause it was just a quick chat, he said,' he added in a miffed voice.

Doesn't like his charge leaving his sight, Ramon interpreted.

'Hel of a show, sir,' Bowe said. 'Can't be bad, havin' the enemy all killin' t'other, eh?'

'That's the Rym Lord's banner, though, innit?' Vidran asked, in tones of mild interest.

'It is. Keep an eye on Tabia,' he asked Lukaz quietly. 'We'll bring up more archers. As the panic spreads, we're going to have desperate men doing desperate things. Keep them out of here.'

'I'm our best shot,' Bowe put in, picking up a crossbow leaning against the battlements. 'They won' get in 'ere.'

The Shihad was being torn apart by an unholy foe, but Ramon almost felt sorry for them, invaders or not, and he couldn't shake the feeling that their own situation was worsening.

After five years, the Lord of Rym finally has my lads cornered.

Suddenly a crowd of Keshi spearmen burst from cover below them, hauling a ladder – a pathetic thing that would barely reach the ramparts. 'Fire!' Tabia squawked, and a flurry of shafts mowed the lead men down. The rest scattered, except one with an arrow in his calf, who fell to his knees.

Bowe put a quarrel in the man's chest as he begged for entry and he folded sideways.

'Dear Kore,' Ramon breathed. 'I hate war.'

But it wasn't over. More tried to scale the walls, some organised and determined, others just flailing about in panic for any escape from the carnage. More arrows flew until finally there was just one man, a ragged archer with a shaft in his right thigh, crawling over the bodies of the fallen and looking up at him with pleading eyes.

Bowe raised his crossbow.

And the wounded Keshi cried out, '*Ramon Sensini!*'

Xoredh Mubarak waded over bodies piled two- and three-deep in the market square where Waqar and Beyrami had made their stand. Odd to think of them, the coward and the fanatic fighting together. But it wouldn't last long.

He had no need to tell his possessed troops what to do; daemons just knew. Inside his skull, Abraxas cackled over this long-drawn-out orgasm of battle, revelling in each death. And hanging over them all was a new presence, one he could see by closing his eyes and looking inwards: a skull-masked woman with a cloud of white hair, who looked equally appalled and enraptured by the killing.

Glamortha, the Angel of Death, the daemon informed him. It was her scream issuing from the mouths of the possessed.

He paused to admire the severed head of the Hadishah commander Shaarvin, caught with his mouth open and screaming at the onrushing darkness, mounted atop a planted spear.

What's the matter, Hadishah? Is Paradise not what you dreamed?

A venator landed on the carpet of bodies and began to feed, while the hulking Lord of Rym leaped off and lumbered towards him. The gleaming emerald-green skull with a scarlet serpent instead of a tongue, the mask of Cadearvo, Angel of Plague, hung from his belt.

'Have you captured Waqar?' he demanded.

'Soon,' Xoredh replied. 'He had the Merozain slut with him.'

Cadearvo bared gleaming canines. 'Did he now? I want her too. We have personal business.'

Xoredh bowed his head and sent a pulse through the shared intellect of his army. <*Attack – and bring me Waqar Mubarak and Tarita Alhani. Kill the rest.*>

Even as Ramon went to yell, 'Cease fire –' Bowe's crossbow sang and the bolt tore through the air . . .

. . . and slammed into the ground, right beside the crawling Ahmedhassan's head.

'Thought you was a decent shot, Bowe,' Harmon griped.

'I was distracted,' Bowe complained. 'Fucker said sumfing, din' he?' He reached for another quarrel.

'Wait,' Ramon shouted, '*wait –*' *How the Hel could the man know his name . . . unless . . .* 'Rukka mio, it's Latif,' he blurted. 'Hold your fire – cover me!'

He leaped from the battlements using Air-gnosis, landed on the muddy slope and skidded, then ran. A Keshi erupted from cover, blade in hand, but he knocked the man head over heels with a kinesis blow, slid to the fallen man's side and studied his pain-glazed face.

He hadn't weathered well – or he'd been through Hel in the last five years. He was grey-faced from the wound, his beard was ragged and he was unwashed and starved, a far cry from the sleek creature they'd captured at Ardijah. But it was definitely Latif, Sultan Salim's chief impersonator.

Pushing numbing healing-energy into the leg-wound, Ramon scooped him up and went hurtling through the air, even as his archers opened up on shapes emerging from the shadows to seize him. He landed on the turret, trying to cushion the impact before lowering the man gently to the stones.

'Get that arrow out if it's safe,' he snapped at Tabia; she might be a weaker mage but she was a better healer than he. 'His life is in your hands.' He straightened as Lukaz and his squad peered down at the fallen Latif.

'Well, rukk me sideways with a batterin' ram,' Bowe exclaimed. 'It's the Sultan of Kesh – y'know – the dead'un.'

Seth Korion hurried into the taproom Ramon's battle-magi were using as headquarters and found Pilus Lukaz and his squad in full battle harness, guarding the stairs – and enjoying a surreptitious tankard of beer. He ignored that, instead hurrying up to the room where a cadaverous, hollow-eyed Keshi was lying. His thigh was heavily bandaged.

This is impossible, he thought. *It can't be him –*

But it was.

He'd never truly known if the man was impersonator or the real sultan, but even as captor and captive, Seth and Latif had become friends for a few intense months during the siege of Ardijah. He forgot all protocol as he hurried to the bed, sat and grabbed his hand. 'Latif? It's really you? It really *is* you!'

'Ai,' the other man groaned blearily. 'Seth . . .' His head lolled, then he rallied and seized Seth's shoulders, his eyes going wide. 'Daemons . . . There are daemons inside the sultan and his men – you have to save us! Please, Effendi, I beg you, for the sake of humanity . . .'

His voice trailed off as he fainted away.

Seth engaged healing-gnosis and numbed the worst of what looked to be appalling pain, then turned to the mage hovering over them, a fragile-looking woman. 'Tabia, isn't it? How is he?'

'He'll live,' she answered. 'An artery was pierced but I got to it in time. He's weak, though.'

Latif groaned and opened his eyes again as Ramon bustled in; he gave the Silacian a weak grin and murmured, 'My rescuer . . .'

What's Latif doing here? Seth had no idea. *Salim, the man he impersonated, is dead. What's he gone through since?*

'Did I see you at the Battle of Collistein Junction?' Seth asked, suddenly remembering a moment during the battle when he'd thought his senses deceived him.

'Ai,' Latif said. 'We thought your line broken, but then there you were – as usual.' He smiled ruefully, then seized Seth's hand again. 'My friend – if we can call each other that – I must ask the impossible of you. Outside, good men are being slaughtered by evil ones. A daemon sits the sacred throne and we cannot withstand him alone – and believe me when I tell you: *nor can you*. And he will come for you next, of that I am certain. But *together*, we have that strength.' He gripped Seth's hand hard, his face pleading. 'Prince Waqar knows – speak to him, please. But you must act now, before it's too late.'

Latif's pleading tore Seth's heart, but his request was insane. His smile froze and his mind swirled. *Daemons? But such beings can't be mass-summoned, and not for so long. It's impossible. I can't just open the gates based on such a tale . . .*

He threw a look at Ramon. *Help me*, he silently beseeched the Silacian.

Ramon put Latif to sleep with a pulse of mesmeric-gnosis, then looked at Seth. 'Well?'

'I don't know – I want to help him, but that's beyond belief, isn't it? Surely it's just a disease, not some kind of permanent mass-summoning of daemons?'

Ramon had a speculative look on his face. 'You know what, I think it *might* be daemons. I fought the Lord of Rym for years and he certainly had a way of making servants of men who'd been his implacable enemies. While plagues stripped the south of people, his armies grew, and they were savage, like those men below. If mass-summoning is possible, and if it's possible to anchor those daemons in flesh, that would explain everything I've faced these last few years.'

They shared a long look, assessing what it was they risked.

'We have no proof,' Seth worried. 'And no time . . . My friend, I have no right to ask, but can I ask you to please, speak to Prince Waqar, see if you can verify this tale. We've probably got no more than an hour or two to get to the bottom of this.'

Ramon gestured towards the walls, where the clamour of fighting was growing. 'Amici, we may only have minutes.'

Waqar set his men's latest fall-back position right below an aqueduct on a ridge of earth overlooking a wall and a road, a scant thirty yards of killing space with not much elevation for defence. He paced behind the lines, exhorting them to courage. Tarita was beside him, her narrow face set and grim.

She'd told Waqar to summon Ajniha and escape, but he'd refused. Now she appeared to feel she couldn't leave either and he wondered why: it wasn't loyalty to Kesh, so it could only be ambition or gain.

Or is it love?

Surely not: even in the throes of coupling, he'd never found the real her. She was a comrade, someone he'd made rash promises to, but he sensed that her heart was unmoved, and so was his, although each moment he admired her more for her prowess and steadfast courage.

Perhaps if we had more time . . . but we won't . . .

Then the enemy's keening wail drew him back to reality, for yet more black-eyed men and monsters were emerging from the maze of alleys. He still had more than twenty thousand men deployed inside these few remaining city blocks, which was a mighty force, but their enemy was implacable; one they couldn't stop. They needed to reform behind proper walls, but Xoredh was giving them no respite.

Dear Ahm, I'm going to die today. We all are.

He tested the edge of his scimitar: he'd melted his second-last nugget of silver from Mollachia to re-coat the blade. It would burn away slaying his first few possessed foes; barely an edge in such a battle, but he'd take any advantage.

With a wild scream the enemy charged, this time spearheaded by ogre-constructs encased in steel who came pounding up the low slope towards them. Hundreds of bowstrings thrummed, filling the air with arrows, but the daemon-possessed constructs, almost a third taller and thrice the bulk of the men they faced, hammered into the lines.

They buckled instantly.

Officers roared at the wavering reserves, '*Stand fast, hold this line –*' as the front rank crumbled. They were pitting mere men against ogre-constructs with outsized weapons, commanding them to stand and fight and die, if only to buy time for others to do the same.

Inhuman courage, religious fervour or bloody-minded perversity, whatever inspired his men, Waqar didn't care. He was caught up in the same fervent game of delaying death, trading hope for despair as he blasted apart the skull of the next ogre in line. He caught Tarita's face as she cut down her own foe, disembowelling a beast that could have been her friend Ogre's twin. Her eyes were glazed over, as if this were a nightmare she couldn't wake from.

He could almost count the seconds until death.

Then a new factor entered the fray from an unexpected source: archers on the aqueduct above began firing down into the charging enemy – and something about their archery was deadly, for every shaft caused the daemon-possessed constructs and men to crumple and fall, howling in agony. He pulled one such shaft out of a corpse and stared. *Silver?*

Waqar threw a glance upwards and swore in disbelief: the archers were maroon-clad Yurosi and there were battle-magi among them, sending volleys of vividly hued mage-bolts that scorched the air.

One of them stepped to the aqueduct's rim, splayed his hands and loosed a torrent of flame over the enemy assailing Waqar's position, torching dozens of constructs – and even better, it had the rest screaming in agony, even those untouched by the blast. That bought a respite, and every Shihadi present cheered, even for a Yurosi.

Tarita grabbed Waqar's arm, her mouth going wide. 'He's an Ascendant,' she gasped, her eyes round as platters. 'That amount of power, he can only be . . .'

Someone like her, Waqar thought. 'A Merozain?' he asked. *Or a Yurosi Keeper?*

Whoever he was, this man's power had broken the latest attack. The enemy reeled away, leaving writhing corpses covering the slopes. 'Behead them,' an officer shouted, and after a moment, men ventured out with axes to butcher the fallen foe. As the defenders rejoiced in their survival and another assault broken, they looked up at Waqar, seeking guidance on how to react to these Yurosi that had come to their aid. Then they all murmured as the Yurosi Ascendant floated down towards them, his sword in its scabbard and his hands aloft, palms showing.

The Shihadi soldiers yelped and waved weapons, but Waqar called, 'Let him come.'

The Shihadi men melted away from him as the Yurosi landed. He gave Waqar a serviceable genuflection, displaying some knowledge of the harbadab.

'Prince Waqar Mubarak, I am commanded to make your acquaintance,' he said formally, in passable Keshi. 'General Seth Korion, commander of the armies of Norostein, wishes to aid you in your current plight, to the betterment of both our peoples. Will you hear me?'

Waqar's heart thudded, but he'd survived the royal court too long to take anything at face value, even this. 'To whom do I speak?' he asked coolly, ignoring the soldiers straining to hear, sensing their lives were in the balance.

As is my own, and I'll not sell any of us fecklessly.

The Yurosi bowed again and said, 'My name is Ramon Sensini.'

The Viper of Riverdown, Waqar thought. An audible gasp ran through the massed Keshi: on the march to Norostein, Rashid had commanded that Korion and Sensini's names be publicly slandered in a bid to motivate his men. Now those lies threatened to destroy this moment.

'Hold,' Waqar shouted again, 'I will hear this man.'

Beside him, Tarita stepped towards Sensini. 'I know your name,' she said, her voice disbelieving. 'Mistress Alhana spoke of you as a brother to Alaron Mercer. She said it was she who gave you . . .' She paused, then finished carefully, 'a special gift.'

'Elena Anborn?' Sensini said, his face softening with wonder. 'Who are you?'

'I am Tarita, Elena's maid . . . or I was. I am Merozain now,' she added proudly.

For a moment Sensini looked flabbergasted, then he laughed. 'Life is truly a mystery.' He looked at Waqar. 'Prince Waqar, we may not have long. Will you trust me?'

Waqar stared, desperately wanting this to be real, but petrified by the man's reputation. Every Eastern mage knew the name: *Ramon Sensini*, the man who'd engineered the débâcles at Riverdown and Ardijah, and as recently as a month ago destroyed the vanguard of the Shihad at Venderon.

But only a few yards away Xoredh's possessed warriors were readying another assault. They had only seconds to make this decision.

'What do you mean? Do you offer sanctuary?' Waqar demanded. 'Must we surrender ourselves? Do you mean to imprison us?'

'This man knows *Alhana*,' Tarita hissed in his ear. 'What more endorsement could you need, for Ahm's sake?'

'It's not that simple,' he snapped. 'We need surety.'

'General Korion offers surety,' Sensini insisted. 'No surrender. You keep your weapons and supplies. We'll give you sanctuary from these daemons in Copperleaf. Kore's Balls, will you die procrastinating?'

Waqar looked at Tarita, then right, where a Ja'arathi Godspeaker was labouring up the slope to join them: Zaar. He had clearly been listening, for he hurried to Waqar's side and murmured, 'Some would say, "Better to die free than submit to the whim of Shaitan's minions". But I would advise that we all choose life.'

'We're fighting Shaitan's minions right now,' Tarita put in emphatically.

Waqar hated being cornered into anything, but he could see no other way. He turned back to Sensini. 'Even if I agreed, how could we achieve this? Our men hate each other.'

'Our men are soldiers, trained to follow orders,' Sensini replied. 'If we set the example, they'll follow.'

Yours might be trained to obey, but in truth, four-fifths of the Shihad are conscripted rabble, Waqar thought sourly. But when he considered the long march here, he realised that they were better than that: the hardships had made them into soldiers. 'How can we get so many men inside with the enemy fast upon us?'

Sensini gave an irritatingly confident smile. 'I know a way, but you'll have to trust me.'

Trust you? You're the serpent who outwitted all of Kesh! But Waqar quelled his misgivings. 'Damn this . . . very well, we're in your hands.'

'Thank you. I'll need to contact Seth. I have a relay-stave in my belt . . .' At Waqar's nod, Sensini pulled out the stave, conjured, then sent and received a series of messages.

Waqar looked at Tarita, who nodded approval, then at Godspeaker Zaar. *He's a moderate, one of those who preach about the 'brotherhood of mankind'*, Waqar remembered. *Perhaps he's someone we need right now?*

Sensini lowered the crackling relay-stave and said, 'We can get you inside, but it won't be easy. If we open our gates, we're going to have to make sure that only your men get inside, or we're all screwed.' He glanced at Zaar, 'No offence, Godspeaker.'

'None taken,' Zaar replied. 'These are desperate times.'

Sensini turned back to Waqar. 'Right, here's the situation. We're on a natural ridge here, beneath this aqueduct that runs right up to the base of the Copperleaf walls – but there's no gate there. You've got to stage a fighting retreat towards our walls, then wind west a hundred yards to the nearest gates. South of this spot is Raathaus Square, where there's a natural embankment some twelve feet high dividing the plaza in two. That's your next fall-back position.'

'What then?' Waqar demanded.

Sensini gave him another of his damnably clever looks. 'You'll see.' He glanced up. 'I must brief my own men.' He gave Waqar an ironic salute, then flashed upwards.

Waqar turned to Tarita and suppressing his fears, told her, 'Find whatever commanders you can and persuade them to retreat to the Copperleaf Gates. Do whatever it takes.'

She nodded grimly, then shot into the air as Sensini had done, weaving into the roofs and out of sight. Waqar turned to Zaar. 'Do whatever you can, Godspeaker, but get the men moving south. I'll cover the retreat.'

*

A few minutes later only a single rank of archers remained, lined up beneath the aqueduct, facing the corpse-littered slopes. Sensini's men were positioned on the aqueduct itself, and to their right, masses of Keshi soldiers were jogging towards Copperleaf, except for one hazara-bam, one thousand of the most fervid Shihadis, chosen by Ali Beyrami himself, who were arrayed behind Waqar's archers, ready to form a rearguard. The imam was at their head, exhorting them with phrases from the *Kalistham*.

They have chosen to be martyrs.

'At my signal,' Waqar shouted to his archers, 'fire every arrow, as fast as you can. Hold nothing back – nothing at all – and then we go: along the aqueduct, towards the Copperleaf walls. *This is an order.* Understood?'

'Ai,' the Shihadi soldiers shouted back, even though he doubted they truly did.

Then Waqar drew on his training and forced all thought from his mind but battle, readying blade and gnosis, body and mind.

Then with a roar, the enemy exploded from the far side of the road – possessed Shihadi soldiers this time. Perhaps Xoredh was dismayed at the losses his constructs were suffering? But it was dreadful knowing that these had once been his own men.

'Fire!' Waqar roared, and the arrows flew thick and true, ripping through the air at eye-level, spearing into the skulls of man after man, sending the first rank reeling and then the second. But the torrent was not sustainable and it faltered as the third wave charged. Above them, the Yurosi, who'd been shooting just as savagely, raised empty quivers and pointed south.

'Beyrami–' Waqar bawled, blazing a signal bolt of blue light into the sky.

As one, his front rank poured backwards down the designated retreat lines, meeting and crossing with Beyrami's Shihadis, who were pouring into the front rank, belting out hymns to Ahm as they came.

Ali Beyrami led them, himself, hands raised to heaven, beseeching his god to intervene. Briefly their eyes met, then the imam dismissed Waqar with a curt nod and gave all his attention to his believers . . . and the sacrifice to come.

Waqar turned and ran, the Yurosi archers pacing him on the aqueduct above, the remnants of his roc-riders swooping overhead. Catching his eye, the lead rider waving to him and he realised Ajniha was with them, flying rider-less. He longed to summon her down and escape all this, but he thrust the temptation aside.

'*ONWARDS,*' he roared, projecting his voice above the clamour. '*FOR THE GATES—*'

Seth watched from the turret of the Copperleaf gatehouse, Lukaz and his men arrayed around him. Beside him, Delton was clutching a relay-stave, sweating from the concentrated exertion of holding more than a dozen lines of communication open. The aether thrummed, the silent vibration tingling in his bones.

'Dear Kore, look't 'em all,' Bowe gasped. 'It's a feckin' Noorie river.'

'Now even Bowe's a poet,' Vidran noted; the only one apparently unmoved by the sight.

Below them, the thousands of men pouring into Raathaus Square were forming up atop the embankment dividing the plaza in two, creating a spear-wall facing north to where the enemy would appear.

If they don't hold, the enemy could sweep all the way into Copperleaf, Seth fretted.

'Tell me the square behind the gate's empty,' he breathed to Delton. 'Tell me it's cordoned so the Noories can't go straight up the high road to Ringwald. Tell me our bloody archers know not to shoot.'

'We're ready,' Delton squeaked, his eyes tightly shut. 'I think.'

Delton was spinning like a top as he got every officer briefed, every contingency covered. But it could still go horribly wrong. The Shihad soldiers were milling about, unwilling to go on: the open gates looked like a trap and they were frightened this was just another way to die. They needed something to push them on, even with death on their heels.

They needed someone to believe in.

Latif, wrapped in a grey cloak and squinting against the torchlight, looked up and saw Seth turn his way and give him a Rondian salute before shaking his head in disbelief.

He felt exactly the same way.

'All right, Sanjeep,' he called. 'Let's go.'

Sanjeep patted his elephant's head. 'Come, my Rani: let us give our men a sultan's welcome.'

Ashmak conjured shields, muttering, 'We're going to die and go straight to the Pit.'

Rani was trumpeting anxiously at all the fuss, but she trudged beneath the raised portcullis, narrowly avoiding scraping the howdah and crew off her back, and emerged into the square full of frightened, directionless Shihadi soldiers caught between the enemy behind them and the Copperleaf gates open before them. Many were on their knees, beseeching Ahm for salvation. The Godspeakers and officers were striding among them, trying to urge them onwards, but order was disintegrating.

Latif stood, casting aside the grey cloak. Beneath, he was clad in the best approximation of Sultan Salim's finery that they'd been able to pull together in an hour, mostly thanks to a madwoman called Vania who'd raided the big house she'd called the Governor's Mansion and produced acres of fine silks. 'He had a mistress with damned expensive taste,' she'd told him, busy turning dresses into robes and scarves into turbans. She'd also kept patting his behind and telling him to meet her afterwards, 'If you haven't been torn limb from limb, darling.' He'd been washed, had his hair and beard trimmed and styled and been given armour with pure gold melted over it like cheap gilt. It wouldn't fool anyone who'd known Salim well.

He prayed it wouldn't have to.

Then Ashmak lit a gnostic light that bloomed around Rani and as he did, a blast of trumpets from the walls made every head spin – and they saw him.

For a moment, there was near-complete silence, an awestruck moment when the Shihadi soldiers took in the sight of a dead sultan, riding an elephant from the gates of their enemy's fastness. Those nearest fell to their knees in shock or reverence or both; those behind stared, gasps and oaths rippling back through the frightened masses.

Ashmak conjured a spell to amplify Latif's voice, which rang out: '*MY PEOPLE, I HAVE RETURNED!*'

The square was a sea of wide-open eyes and mouths, lit by the moon and the flames, hanging on his words. For a moment he was as stunned as they, but then years of training took over: he had impersonated Salim thousands of times – tens of thousands – in the past. All his life had prepared him for this moment.

'*MY PEOPLE, I RETURN IN THE NAME OF PEACE.*'

Peace . . .

The word resounded through the square, eliciting both cheers and confusion – but not rejection. These men had been at war for many months now. They had experienced the visceral, harrowing maelstrom of battle and the deathly menace of winter. They missed their homes and families and the fire of holy war had burned very low. They were frightened and they believed they were going to die.

To them, I am hope . . .

'*BEFORE US ARE THE MINIONS OF EVIL, ENEMIES OF MANKIND, SER-VANTS OF SHAITAN –*'

'Ai,' many shouted, fresh from fighting constructs and black-eyed savages, 'they come from the Pit!'

Latif pointed behind him, to the Copperleaf Gates. '*AND BEFORE US ARE MEN, ALIKE TO US: MEN CREATED BY AHM, AS DISMAYED BY THIS EVIL AS WE ARE. THEIR GATES ARE OPEN TO GIVE US SHELTER. WILL YOU WALK THROUGH THEM WITH ME?*'

He watched hope battle with disbelief, that an enemy could ever be a friend, and the long-held view that Yurosi were as much creatures of Shaitan as the black-eyed monsters behind them. Everything teetered in the balance . . .

But as the men of the Shihad wavered, a warm wind flowed through the open gates, carrying the ripe smell of cooking meat, borne on a wind of some wily mage's conjuring. It hit the soldiers like a spell. Latif saw saliva spilling from hungry mouths, eyes filling with longing.

Then Godspeaker Zaar walked forward, shouting, 'Long live Sultan Salim!' He knelt, placing his forehead to the ground before Latif and Rani, calling, 'Ahm is truly with us –' Then he rose and strode towards the gates.

That was enough. Men surged after him, prostrating themselves hurriedly to Latif and then spilling through the gates into Copperleaf. Those close enough reached out to stroke Rani as they passed, gazing up at Latif in awe. Some called questions of where he'd been, but Latif kept his silence, trying to preserve this delicate bubble of suspended disbelief. Sanjeep turned Rani and they walked back through the gates, leading the army through.

The Eastern soldiers were still half-afraid that that arrows and burning oil would come down on their heads, but Godspeaker Zaar was walking calmly before them and when they poured into the space behind, they found cooking fires lining the edges of another square – and, Ahm on high, there were even some women waiting with platters heaped with steaming food.

That, perhaps even more than the food, sealed it: would an enemy allow their *womenfolk* among them?

There were also soldiers, but Latif doubted the starving men even noticed. They descended on the food in a dreamlike rapture, weeping openly as they left fire and death behind and entered a realm of succour.

'To Peace,' he shouted. '*To the peace of Ahm and Kore.*'

He doubted anyone heard, but perhaps they would remember his words later. He signed Sanjeep to halt Rani and they let the Shihad flow around them, into the sheltering arms of their enemies. He looked back and caught the solemn, shining face of Seth Korion, gazing down from the gatehouse in wonder.

The Eastern men were perfectly behaved, addressing the serving women as if they were queens, and many embraced the Yurosi soldiers, tears running. And the Yurosi didn't dare put a foot or word amiss, perhaps because Seth had officers overseeing it all, but maybe they too could sense the magic of this moment.

Latif leaned down and called to Sanjeep, 'Take us out, now, before the spell is broken.'

Sanjeep looked back at him, his old eyes shining with tears of joy. 'My Rani, she is the Queen of Heaven,' he called proudly. 'She is the wife of Gann-Elephant and will live among the stars.'

'What's he saying?' Ashmak grunted. 'Old lunatic.' But he was crying too.

Then Seth Korion spoke into his mind. <*Is it working?*> he asked, in Rondian.

Latif flinched, but he'd trained with magi under Salim, and quickly recovered. 'Ai, it's working,' he said aloud, knowing Seth would hear.

<*Good – but that's only a tenth of your men! We need everyone inside, so you'll need to get back out there and do it again.*>

Xoredh stalked along the road running beneath the aqueduct, then with a thought rose and flew upwards and landed on the structure. The race was dry and ran all the way to the Copperleaf walls. It entered the wall halfway up, to mitigate the gap it left in the defences. In the distance, he could see soldiers retreating along it – they were Yurosi, confirming the unbelievable.

The Yurosi are aiding Waqar . . .

At first he'd not credited it, being caught up in the fury and exultation of killing. Having the daemon inside him during war was overpowering: it fed *too much* stimulus so that the glorious, blood-soaked carnage was all could see. Strategy, tactics and decision-making had been buried beneath the need to *kill kill kill*, to bury his blade in an enemy's chest, to take heads, to bite and rend, to guzzle blood and gnash upon sinew.

I didn't notice the ruse until too late . . .

Ali Beyrami's fanatics had been last to fall, in retrospect clearly a rearguard action. Xoredh had slain Beyrami himself, impaled him on a spear and held the body aloft like a banner while the old madman died. The joy of butchery had consumed his possessed men until they were all soaked in gore.

But while they'd been so enjoyably engrossed, Waqar or whoever was leading the remnants of the Shihad, had torched the streets behind the front line, creating a barrier between his advance and their retreat. The flames had taken too many, until Cadearvo had stepped in to halt the advance.

Which has given the remnants of the Shihad time to escape . . . into Copperleaf tier.

It was unthinkable. Three Crusades had ingrained an implacable Eastern hatred of the West. It was *inconceivable* to Xoredh that common ground could be reached. *It won't last*, he thought sourly, gazing up at the walls. *It can't last.*

A tall figure lumbered out of the blazing line of houses on the opposite side of the square and came to join him. Cadearvo glowered at the banner of the Shihad hanging alongside that of Noros on the Copperleaf walls. For once, even the Lord of Rym looked perplexed.

'This is unexpected,' Cadearvo admitted. 'But there are still tens of thousands outside the walls. We must press the attack and seek to force the gates while they stand open.'

We've infected twenty thousand men over the past week and slain at least as many today, Xoredh calculated. *Waqar could have no more than thirty thousand, including the baggage handlers and camp-women, left.*

'Yes, we must attack,' he agreed.

Cadearvo made a growling noise, then reached upwards as if summoning a hunting falcon. A giant winged reptile plummeted down to land beside them, spouting gouts of flame from a mouth that was large enough to eat a man whole.

Xoredh felt his eyes bulge. 'Is that . . . a draken?'

Cadearvo licked his lips. 'Ai. I am the Master's most favoured.' He grasped the beast's reins. 'I will hunt down their captains,' he said grandly. 'You will lead the assault down here.'

He didn't wait to debate but snarling to quell his unruly beast, he leaped into the saddle. The beast's wings almost buffeted Xoredh from his feet as it flapped away. He glowered after it, angered at having to serve that abomination and absolutely burning in envy.

Seek their captains then, he seethed. *I pray they bring you down . . .*

You should have run, Tarita berated herself. *You don't owe Waqar anything.*

But she'd committed herself, although she couldn't tell if she'd been swept along by all this 'good and evil' nonsense or whether her heart or her yoni was leading her brain around. *I don't love him and I've had plenty of better sex,* she told herself angrily. *So why am I still here?*

She looked around Raathaus Square. The plaza was built on two levels, the drop of a dozen feet between them the natural barrier to defend. The low safety wall on top would be the new front line. Behind them reared the walls of Copperleaf and to her right was a giant aqueduct plunging down to the Lowertown Lake.

The gates could only admit so many at a time and there were maybe as many as thirty thousand soldiers, labourers and camp-followers jammed into the killing zone. More lives would have to buy time right here to avoid slaughter at the choke-point outside the main gates.

How does dying here help my mistress or my people? she asked herself. *How does it thwart Naxius? We should've left to find Jehana.* But she *was* personally involved now. She couldn't work out whether she truly wanted Waqar, but it was a good alliance – or it would be if she lived to profit from it.

I just wish I loved him.

She didn't, though. Love belonged to her broken past, to Fernando Tolidi – he'd been so young, but he was a mage-noble, and she'd been just a maid, barely old enough to bleed. First love. Coupling with Fernando had been transcendent, as if they'd invented sexual pleasure for their own amusement. Nothing else had ever come close since. Losing him had poisoned everything afterwards.

What's love compared to something solid? Waqar's crown is solid, and so is his gold.

She gripped her scimitar, the gnostically forged relic salvaged from Midpoint Tower, and swore on its edge that she'd get out of this alive and somehow work it all out.

Flames lit up the dusky skies and plumed into the stars as the moon rose. She could hear the approach of the enemy, the heavy tramp of the constructs emerging onto the lower tier of the plaza. Smoke rose behind them.

That the enemy numbered beings like Ogre pained her even more.

She smiled to think of his ugly, amiable face – then flinched as she remembered their sad, foolish parting.

You deserve better than me, she whispered to his memory, *but I'll always be your friend.*

Then she pushed aside all thought but war, for a single shriek was echoing from thousands of throats and the black-eyed enemy was pouring towards them again.

14

A Foe Beyond You

The Angels of the Last Days

*The Angels of the Last Days are grim beings made by Kore to destroy Urte, his cre-
ation. In their allotted hours each shall ravage His works. First comes War, then
Plague and Famine, until Glamortha who is Death draws down the curtain on this
tragedy. Mankind shall beg her protection, but she shall betray them and lay with
Lucian, Lord of Hel, summoning the Daemons to Urte. As Mother of Daemons she
and her dread consort shall rule over Perdition, punishing the unworthy for their
sins, for all eternity. Repent, while there is time.*

PRIOR HENDRY CARVER, KORE THEOLOGIAN, 697

Norostein, Noros
Febreux 936

The sun was going down and still the Ahmedhassans and those few
beasts of burden that hadn't been slaughtered for food continued to
stream into Copperleaf – but it wasn't happening fast enough.

They're moving at less than half the rate we need, and we're doing all we can,
Seth worried. *When the enemy break the lines at Raathaus Square, we'll be out
of time – and I'll have to close the gates – if we still can.* He envisaged that: trying to shut out half the Easterners while the rest were inside. There'd be
a massive outcry, blades would be drawn and this fragile peace would
disintegrate . . .

Dear Kore, let us have enough time . . .

'Look, sir,' Delton called, pointing down into Lowertown, where a
solid mass of enemy constructs had emerged onto the northern edge of

Raathaus Square, facing the final rampart, the last defensible place this side of the walls. It was lined with Keshi archers.

If I send my men out to help them, it slows the rate of people entering, Seth thought, *but if I don't, can they hold?*

'Send battle-magi,' Seth told Delton, 'from my own legion.' When his aides looked askance, he lost his temper. 'Those people are in our care now,' he barked, 'and we'll damn well fight for them.'

They saluted and in moments, three dozen men and women in red robes floated down from the walls and made their way against the tide of humanity flowing towards the gates.

Seth gave Delton a stream of instructions about housing, provisions, accommodation and a raft of other minutiae – until a piercing shriek came from above and he looked up to see a giant winged reptile diving in and raking the square below with flames. To his horror, he realised he'd seen such a beast before, in the last days of the Third Crusade.

A draken . . . holy Kore, they've got a draken . . .

He barely saw the surge of the enemy beginning the final assault, for his eyes were full of this dreadful beast as it turned and dived towards the Copperleaf gates – towards *him*.

He conjured shields, gripped the parapet and began to pray.

Cadearvo sent the draken raking across Copperleaf again, blasting fire into the Shihadi men before the main gates, gleefully lapping up the carnage and the exhilaration of riding such a beast. Never before had the Master allowed him to use the draken openly; too soon, he'd said, for they risked bringing the Imperial Keepers, the Merozain Bhaicara or the Ordo Costruo down on their heads. But the Keepers were destroyed or subverted and the Merozains and Ordo Costruo were far away, trying to save the Leviathan Bridge.

I can win this war on my own . . .

He hauled on the reins and brought the beast around again, for the draken required a minute to rekindle its fires, a kind of liquid regurgitation that ignited as it vented from the mouth: a piece of animagery genius.

They swooped again, his shields battering away the few arrows that came near. A ballista bolt – the one weapon he feared up here – whistled harmlessly by, then he had the draken spew fire over the gatehouse turret, torching the ballista and its crew, then flashed over the second tower, where just one man stood, shielding desperately as the flames broke around him. He laughed aloud as he lifted from the battlements and brought his beast round again to finish the survivor.

Where's the false sultan? he thought. *Where's that damned pretender, whoever he is?*

But then something caught his attention: a stream of rocs lifting from the highest tier of the city and surging towards him, lance-wielding magi on their backs.

Flyers . . . very well, I accept your challenge . . .

The draken banked and he guided it back towards the oncoming rocs. He had no fear: his beast was four or five times their size, with jaws large enough to snap the birds in half and claws that could gut them with a stroke. It blew out plumes of black smoke as it readied another fire-storm.

This is going to be fun . . .

When Waqar Mubarak saw the draken's fires wash over the Copperleaf gatehouse and battlements, he felt a crushing weight slam down on his chest. Around him, the Shihadis wailed in despair – the refuge of Copperleaf suddenly looked like a trap, and the beast was coming around again.

Dear Ahm, he thought despairingly, *haven't you given our enemies enough weapons already?*

He stepped from the lines, waved a concerned Tarita away and opened up his mind. <*Ajniha,*> he called, <*to me!*> He felt the roc respond and come plummeting toward him, trailed by the few remaining flyers of the hundreds who'd begun this holy war.

<*Alramh-Amyr,*> someone shouted through the aether: *the Prince of the Spear.*

His heart rose at the thought of being aloft again. He spun, caught Tarita's arm. 'We have to hold here, but we must also bring that beast down – I have to go.'

She looked appalled. 'You're needed here.'

'Only the Shihad have flyers now and I am their captain – it has to be me.' He turned his back and strode away, found an open space and called to Ajniha, shrieking towards him. The draken was returning and pandemonium was growing around him as the retreat into Copperleaf stalled. Their plan was breaking down, their hopes falling apart, because of this one dreadful foe.

But Ajniha was above him now, her eyes blazing, while the other rocs circled. *Just a dozen left*, he saw in shock. Others were away on patrol, or still in the north, he knew that, but still . . . *So many dead . . .*

He had no time for grief, not with Ajniha hovering above him, her wings beating hard. He hurled himself upwards on kinesis and Airgnosis, landing in the saddle and whipping the buckles into place as the roc clawed at the air. They climbed, the other roc-riders closing around him, and his eyes sought the draken. The sun was setting, casting long shadows and streaking the skies with scarlet, as if the draken had set fire to the heavens.

<Come, my eagles,> he called. *<Tonight we hunt Hel-beasts.>*

Tarita watched Waqar's construct-bird flap away, snarled a thousand curses and turned to the task at hand: *The real task, you* matachod. *Damned glory-hunter . . .*

'Eyes front,' she shouted, brandishing her gleaming scimitar. 'Take aim!'

She had no right to give orders here, but when she bawled 'Fire!' as the black-eyed enemy roared across the lower plaza towards them, bowstrings thrummed in deadly harmony, propelling a jagged wall of feathered steel and wood. Some slammed into shields, but those which found flesh and eye sockets took those enemy down. Then from all along the rampart that divided the upper and lower plaza, mage-bolts and fireballs blazed.

Yurosi magi, Tarita realised, astonished that the slugskins really were helping them.

The defending Ahmedhassans reacted with surprise, but the unexpected aid stiffened them as the enemy scrambled up the bank. The decorative surface had easy handholds and a forgiving angle – but the defenders thrust long spears down into their faces, shouting to Ahm and to their mothers, hurling the black-eyed men and monsters back with desperate savagery.

Tarita joined the fray, took down an ogre-construct, then blazed fire at a wolf-man brandishing a giant axe, sending him screaming back into the press. She shielded as spears were hurled her way, then slashed through the guard of a possessed Shihadi and beheaded him. For a harrowing minute the assault looked likely to sweep over the top – but the enemy recoiled when the setting sun broke through the clouds on the western horizon and shone directly on the plaza. As more Yurosi battle-magi joined the defence, the enemy fell back, snarling and spitting, sheltering their eyes, but they only retreated a hundred feet or so.

As the sun kissed the horizon, more enemy were emerging to fight.

Dear Ahm, we've barely seen their full strength, Tarita realised. *Whatever we do, it's not going to be enough.*

Her mistress would have been furious: she'd been trained that when the odds turn against you, you cut and run. And now even her reason for being here had left to fight in the sky.

I should be with him, she thought, shielding her own eyes and peering upwards, but the draken and the dozen remaining rocs were just distant shapes silhouetted in the heavens.

Then an officer approached her and asked deferentially, 'Mistress Merozain, what are the prince's commands?'

How in Hel should I know? Tarita thought angrily. *The chotia just flew off and left me to die.*

But what she said, calmly and firmly, was, 'Hold here. We hold to the death.'

While everyone else scrabbled to survive, Ramon kept to his plan, barely thought through though it was. Ideas like this streamed through his imagination on a daily basis as he watched the world around him; this one mightn't even work – but it was worth a try. *Just give us a few more minutes*, he exhorted the Ahmedhassans below him in Raathaus Square.

From his vantage on top of the first pillar of the aqueduct, level with the barrier wall that split the square, he called, 'Is everyone in place? Are we ready?'

'Aye,' Postyn, his best Water-mage, called from the sluice-gate.

'Aye,' added Moxie, clinging to the underside of the race with Earth-gnosis.

'And I've got our back, boss,' Vania drawled, from her position beside Melicho at the levers for the next sluice-gate, her crossbow cradled. 'Get on with it, Mel.'

'Yeah, yeah, in a moment,' Melicho complained. 'This isn't as easy as you think, Horseface.' The tower was the keystone to the main lock-pool and Melicho was driving a wedge of Earth-energy into the pillars holding the structure up. 'Fuckin' hare-brained idea, if you ask me.'

'You lot ever heard of a little thing called *respect*?' Ramon griped. Then he returned his gaze to the unfolding struggle in the plaza below. *It's all about timing now . . .*

While his possessed men and constructs hurled themselves at the embankment, Xoredh Mubarak sat his white horse, brooding sourly amid the clamour. If this was truly the Shihad, he would be surrounded by friends and advisors now. Men would be bowing as they passed him and the soldiers would be singing hymns to him as they advanced. But the black-eyed daemon-hosts just snarled and gibbered, ignoring him.

What is the point of rank when we're all one in the hive-mind of Abraxas? he asked himself. If this was a glimpse of his personal future, it was some-what disenchanting. But there was still a war to be won.

The daemon-possessed were suffering from daylight lethargy, impaled by the last rays of the setting sun, but sunset was just minutes away and even now, the gap in the clouds was closing. Darkness was about to rush in and seal his victory.

He raised his arm and ordered the advance, although there was little point when his army ran itself. Feeling hollow, he nudged his mount forward, glancing upwards, where the draken and the rocs were still tearing at each other, but half the eagles were already down, spinning earthwards, torn or ablaze.

We'll sweep right over them, then through the open gates. They'll never stop us.

He lifted his eyes to the aqueduct and noticed movement, focused in on it and stiffened. *Sensini is there . . .* It took seconds to calculate the danger and he blazed a warning through the shared mind of Abraxas.

Instantly a swarm of the possessed launched themselves at the small knot of defenders on the water course, but the tower was high and the pillar smooth.

Magi are needed there . . .

He kicked his horse into motion, his hackles rising and blood in his nostrils.

Waqar nudged Ajniha into a spiralling climb, then with one eye on the draken, took his final lump of Mollachian silver from his pouch, melted it and recoated his blade and spearhead. The construct-beast was about half a mile away, trying to get above them.

His task done, he gave his attention to those with him. *<Who leads this flight?>* he asked.

He was surprised when a female voice answered tersely, *<I do, Prince Waqar.>* He peered, and saw a stick-thin woman. Few of the roc riders had been female, and he'd not known any to be in leadership positions.

<Who are you?> Waqar asked. *<I thought I knew all the wing-leaders.>*

<Joraf died, so I took over,> she answered. *<My name is Amiza. Don't worry, I know what I'm doing. What's going on down there?>* she added.

<Everything,> he told her. *<We're trying to get the Shihad into Copperleaf.>*

<Ai,> she sent back in amused tones. *<So suddenly the slugskins are our friends. This is good, I think.>* Then her voice became authoritative. *<Stay to the rear, Prince, I don't want your death to be on my account. Your family never forgive.>* She called to her flight, *<Split left and right and watch this mata-chod's fire-breath. Forget arrows, stick lances in the chotia's gut.>*

Waqar had been about to say exactly that, so he signalled assent, following Amiza's bird as they soared upwards and then split into two columns of six, surging towards the draken that had given up trying to out-climb them and was now turning at bay. Waqar tried to get to the fore, but the other birds crowded him to the rear, right where the presumptuous Amiza wanted him.

As they closed, he focused on the draken, wondering who rode it. Perspective was difficult at this distance, but the rider looked unnaturally large and he remembered the ogre-being he'd glimpsed inside the volcano in Mollachia. Engaging gnostic-sight, he saw the rider wore a skull-mask.

Dear Ahm, it's the creature who captured Jehana . . .

<*Beware the rider,*> he called to the flyers. <*He's at least as dangerous as the draken.*> But his mind was racing over a mad thought: could he take this *chotia* alive?

The distance closed swiftly and suddenly they were fighting. The draken-rider took his beast straight at them, sending an incandescent blue bolt punching straight through the shields of the lead rider, ripping the roc from the sky – then the draken struck like a cobra, lunging in and plucking another rider from the saddle with its jaws. The roc flailed as the saddle-straps caught, then snapped, but a draken claw had already torn its belly open. It shrilled and spun away, while the rest of the wing scattered around it. Spears glanced off the draken's ridged hide, but another mage-bolt had already burst the skull of a third bird. Waqar hauled Ajniha out of line to avoid careening into the back of the roc in front of him and their attack broke apart in confusion. The other column flashed by impotently, circling back to try and engage. He heard Amiza cursing before she blared, <*Pull up, reform, reform!*>

As they scattered, the draken plunged into a dive to gain speed for another climb, then shot upwards, leaving the roc-riders cursing and swinging in pursuit. They'd all lost altitude in the manoeuvres and were now only five hundred feet above the battle in the city below.

In a few heartbeats, thirteen had become ten and the draken was untouched.

Cadearvo's mount levelled out of the dive and he scanned the skies below. Ten rocs were still pursuing him as he circled above the big square above the Copperleaf gates.

I'll kill these scum, then rake the men below in flame . . .

Then he recognised Prince Waqar's bird among his attackers and laughed aloud. <*Hail, Alramh-Amyr,*> he sent mockingly. <*I am Cadearvo,*

Lord of Rym. I see your sense of chivalry has failed you, Prince Waqar: one against ten? Poor odds. You should have brought more, to make it a decent fight.>

Waqar didn't respond, but Ajniha and the other rocs squalled indignantly, as if sensing their riders' ire. They climbed after him while he circled, letting them expend energy while the draken's complex physical chemistry did its work and readied another bellyful of fire.

Just as they reached him, he banked and picked his target. They peppered him with mage-bolts and spears, but he loosed a concussive wave of kinesis that dashed aside their pathetic missiles and blasted the birds backwards beak over tail. Then his draken spat its fiery torrent, engulfing one bird, then biting another and tossing it aside. Cadearvo surged through the stalled rocs, impaling one on a lance as his draken tore the wing from another.

Then they swept on, and ten was now six . . .

. . . and in front of him he saw Waqar's bird and emitted another blast of kinesis that stalled his prey in mid-air.

His draken crunched into the roc, gripping it in massive talons as Cadearvo craned his thick neck to seek the rider while conjuring energy on his lance. He leaned over in the saddle, the weapon blazing . . .

Waqar was at the back, which saved him from Cadearvo's initial onslaught. As the rocs before him were scattered and torn from the skies, he missed that first stunning kinesis wave, then the draken burst through the stalled flock, ripping three more from the sky, the ogre sent out another blast of energy and Ajniha was slammed to a standstill too. Before he or the bird could react, the draken was upon them, wings buffeting them. Talons big enough to engulf a horse opened over them, then wrapped round Ajniha's torso as she shrilled in fury.

As the draken's giant head reared over them, Waqar tore free of his saddle-straps and launched himself over Ajniha's head – then realised in horror that he was anticipated and heading right for Cadearvo's glowing lance-head. He glimpsed the mask, saw it contort with glee as the weapon thrust through his shields . . .

. . . but he twisted in mid-air like a dancer and it only grazed his thigh – then momentum took him onto the face of the draken, slamming into it right between the eyes, his own shimmering lance in his hands . . .

The spearhead took the draken through the right eye, momentum and kinesis ramming most of the length of the shaft right through into the brain, bringing the draken to an abrupt stop, but Waqar flew onwards, grabbing for his scimitar as he sailed over the beast's impaled head towards its rider. The masked ogre had an instant to register his presence, but as the construct's hand blurred to the dagger hilt at his belt—

—Waqar's scimitar came free. Cadearvo's shields turned scarlet, then the speed and weight of impact burst them open as they smashed together and Waqar's curved blade plunged into the masked ogre's neck, carving through the gorget of chain, and lodging against the bone in a spray of blood – even as Waqar found himself impaled on his foe's dagger.

The mask contorted like a second skin, the ogre's face swelling up and his mouth opening, his eyes bulging in rage – and then Waqar, screaming through the agony of the dagger-blow, placed his other hand on the scimitar hilt and wrenched sideways, cleaving the spinal cord, and the hideous masked visage spun away.

Then the agony struck him and he stared down at the dagger buried in his midriff, gnostic energy crackling as the flesh was seared. He convulsed and almost blacked out, lost his scimitar but grasped the headless torso of his foe as the draken began to plummet. Somehow he hauled the dagger out amid a jet of hot blood. He felt more than saw the draken's lifeless claws lose their grip on Ajniha, who screamed and spun away, trying to flap damaged wings.

<No,> he wailed, <Ajniha—>

Together, the falling draken and the injured ròc fell. The draken began to spin while Waqar tried to think through the dreadful pain in his side and find the clarity to somehow get himself out of this. Below them, the city landscape was roaring up to meet him and some part of him realised that he had to get clear or he'd hit and die – but the thoughts wouldn't connect through the rising haze in his mind.

He tried to move, but debilitating pain shot through him, radiating from his midriff like an explosion of burning lamp-oil. It was all he could do just to cling on – then he saw something like a giant centipede emerge from the neck-stump of the dead construct. He gasped in revulsion and almost swept it away when he realised what the thing was – and instead flashed out his hand and grasped it just below the head and *pulled*.

What emerged was almost a foot long, coated in black and scarlet gore, pincers snapping at him impotently as it emitted a squeal and thrashed in his grip. Then the dead draken fell into a spin and Waqar was flung loose, spinning head over heels –

– and roc talons wrapped around his waist. Above him Ajniha shrieked in triumph as they shot over the rooftops of Copperleaf, barely missing towers and spires. He sensed the roc, like him, was barely holding on, but she clung onto him and sought flat ground, flashing over the battlements of Ringwald and all but crashing into the turf outside the Governor's Mansion.

As the talons released him and he sprawled on the wet grass, Waqar felt a wall of unconsciousness rising. Desperately he wrenched the squirming centipede into the pouch at his belt, clipped it shut and clamped his hand over it, moments before the darkness rose up like an ocean wave and he was swept under . . .

Ramon's team were about a minute from delivering the destructive blast to the aqueduct tower and he was readying the order for his battle-magi to pull back with him – then everything changed.

Someone in that ravening horde below clearly had a mind, because all of a sudden the nearest group of black-eyed beast-men and possessed Shihadis turned from the attack on the upper plaza of Raathaus Square and hurled themselves at the aqueduct tower.

'Rukka, we're seen,' he shouted, as a wave of the enemy swarmed up the embankment, shrieking in fury. 'Moxie?' he called, craning his neck, 'you done?'

The diminutive battle-mage was clinging to the underside of the stone race, checking the last of the glowing pattern of runes he'd etched into the structure to focus a mix of Fire- and Earth-gnosis. But attackers were swarming hand over fist up the stone pillars, clinging like cockroaches,

barely fifty feet below and closing fast; already thrown spears were striking Moxie's shields—

'Just about ready,' Moxie yelled, as Vania came to the rim and shot a
bipedal wolf through the mouth with her crossbow; the quarrel
exploded inside the skull.

'Moxie, *get out*,' Ramon shouted. '*Now*—'

'Gimme a mo—'

Ramon swore and hurled fire at the lead climbers, turning them to
living torches. They dropped in eerie silence onto their fellows below.
'*Melicho*,' he called, to the mage working on the upper sluice-gate,
'*release!*'

'Half a minute—'

Ramon roared, '*Hurry*—*!*' and blazing more energy into the fast-
approaching enemy, cried, 'Moxie, fire it up . . .'

Beside him Vania's crossbow was humming, picking off the leading
climbers with quarrels lit with livid energy, but still the possessed creatures kept coming. Ramon raised his hands to send another blast into
the horde—

—but just then his gnostic perceptions, the mage's early warning
system, screamed a warning and he abandoned the spell and pushed all
his energy into strengthening his shields.

An instant later, something like a dust-cloud of screaming darkness
came from lower down the race and blasted over them – only to fizzle
on his protections. He turned in time to see a lavishly attired Easterner
on a white horse riding up the dry race – and then the air between them
tore open and shadows poured through.

'*Ware!*' he shouted, backing against Vania and hurling up a blazing
ball of light, because despite the suddenness of the strike, he recognised the spell: Jelaska had taught him how to counter it, during the
Third Crusade.

Vania clung to him as the darkness surged around them, crackling
against his light-globe. She fired a bolt blindly into the shadows, seeking
that rider, but it exploded harmlessly somewhere in the race. Moments
later the wave of darkness was burned away, leaving them standing back
to back, ready to face the next attack.

But Postyn, hovering behind the lower sluice-gate, hadn't been so fortunate: he wailed as human-shaped shreds of darkness engulfed him, ripping at him as he flailed on the floor of the race. Then from below came Moxie's voice, a horrified wail that became a receding shriek, overwhelmed by a hungry roar from below. Only Melicho, on the wall above, and Vania, shielded by Ramon's wards, came through.

Cursing in anguish, Ramon dashed to Postyn's side, blasting at the dark shadow-shapes with raw energy until they withered. He went to the rim and saw that the rider below was building to a gallop, even though it was a thirty-foot leap to where they stood.

He wore a Lantric mask of a helmed Rondian knight.

He's a Mask . . . Rukka, he'll make that jump . . .

But Moxie's enchantment hadn't been triggered and without it, the men defending the upper plaza were rukked. Ramon threw a glance left and right, yelled, '*Melicho – release – Vania, get out–*' before grabbing the rim one-handed and swinging himself over the edge of the race, right into the face of the horde clambering up the tower.

Xoredh dug in his spurs – quite unnecessarily, when the beast he rode was possessed, but it felt good – and sent his pale stallion hurtling towards the sluice-gate fifteen feet above. His necromancy spell had winked out unexpectedly early, but he had heard at least two men cry out, so it hadn't been entirely wasted and his slaves were almost at the top of the support pillars, with the rest of his army about to break into the upper plaza, where they would begin the massacre . . .

Hooves crunching on stone, striking sparks as they powered up the slope, he gathered the reins, pulsing his intent into the mind of the daemon-horse, then once again rammed his ornate spurs into the stallion's side and the beast powered into a soaring leap . . .

. . . when a bony-faced, long-jawed woman with tangled black hair suddenly appeared at the top of the sluice, a crossbow in her hands, and discharged a glowing bolt. Xoredh slammed his shields forward with an Ascendant-strength pulse of kinesis that shattered the quarrel in a brilliant scarlet burst, right in front of his mount's chest.

The wave of kinesis knocked the woman off her feet – but it also broke his steed's momentum mid-leap; instead of sailing over the bar-rier, it slammed into the sluice-gate at breakneck speed. He heard the sickening crunch of bone shattering an instant before he himself was hurled against the wall. His face smashed into the stone and he felt his nose shatter and his mask crumple, but his personal shielding held. He reeled in the saddle as his beast bounced and flopped over backwards, and then they crashed back into the dry race with the horse landing on top of him. In a blinding burst of pain, both hip bones and one thigh shattered.

He screamed, clawed for energy, for life, for strength . . . as the crossbow-woman reappeared at the rim. She cocked her crossbow, peer-ing warily – then, calling something over her shoulder, she raised her weapon.

Her bolt flew . . .

Hanging one-armed from the rim, Ramon pasted his hand to the stone-work with Earth-gnosis and swung out, blasting kinesis downwards at the closest attackers, who were already crawling along the outside of the race towards him. Below, he could see a dozen or more black-eyed men ripping Moxie to shreds, but there was no time to dwell on that.

His blast was enough to rip the nearest foes from their precarious perches, but the rain of arrows ripping at his shields turned them scarlet. He breathed thanks to Alaron and Ramita for the potion that had made him an Ascendant mage – any other would be dead by now – and slammed his palm into the middle of the sigils Moxie had so painstakingly inscribed, sending a burst of Fire-gnosis into the wait-ing enchantment.

That triggered a burst of livid red energy, streaming out in veins and turning the stonework super-hot. The men climbing towards him began to fry, hands and knees blistering, then blackening, but still the daemon-possessed attackers kept coming, even as their hands burned to stumps and they dropped into the horde below.

Ramon kicked away, propelling himself back up and over the rim, where he saw Vania taking aim at something on the lower race. Postyn was sitting up, dazed but intact, at the bottom off the race, where steam was now rising from puddles. 'It's triggered,' Ramon shouted. 'Time to go.'

'Sure, boss,' Vania drawled sweetly, 'I'll just skewer this tin-faced twat first . . .'

. . . just as Xoredh opened himself up to the full seething energy of Abraxas, allowing him access to every aspect of the gnosis at once. He let the immense mind of the master-daemon direct the energy flows in a dozen different ways – healing gnosis flowed to hips and thigh; kinesis hurled the dying horse aside, morphism and necromancy transcended the pain.

He rose to his feet, his body still screaming, but his hatred howling far louder. *I am a Mubarak and I am unstoppable –*

He shattered the woman's next bolt in mid-air and hurled her from sight, then wasting no time, he surged on Air-gnosis to the rim of the upper sluice-gate, the royal scimitar leaping to his right hand and energy coalescing in his left as he landed.

The archer-bitch was on her back in the race, thirty feet away, looking stunned, her face a rictus of pain and her foot crooked. At Xoredh's feet was a nondescript Yurosi with thinning hair and straggling whiskers, looking up at him in alarm.

And on his left, a small dark-haired man was straightening as if he'd just landed. Even as Xoredh moved, Abraxas recognised the dark-haired man and started raging. <*RAMON SENSINI,*> the daemon hollered in Xoredh's head. <***KILL HIM!***>

Howling at the agony of motion from his still-mending hips and thigh, Xoredh obeyed, skewering the man at his feet while simultaneously blazing a mage-bolt at Sensini, powerful enough to fry a pure-blood.

The man on his blade convulsed and died – but to his shock, Sensini somehow blocked his gnostic bolt, partially through surprisingly powerful wards and also because he threw himself onto the archer-woman to protect her. She shrieked at the impact, thrashing under him.

Xoredh advanced, snarling through his own pain as he hammered more energy into Sensini, grinning as the Yurosi's shields went scarlet and began to implode. He pushed himself forward, bursting through the smoky residue of the spells with his scimitar flashing downwards, a blow powerful enough to hack both his prey in two.

But somehow the man rose, his blade parrying firmly enough that the scimitar belled and recoiled, almost breaking Xoredh's wrist and stopping him in his tracks.

Unbelievable . . .

'*GO* —' Ramon shouted to Vania and Melicho, who was still working on the sluice-gates. 'I've got this prick.' He lunged from his kneeling position, sword out-thrust and energy punching, and sent the man in the crumpled mask backwards.

He drove forward, enraged by the loss of Moxie and Postyn and terrified for Vania and Melicho. Slashing frantically, he battered at this man's impossibly powerful shields, trying to buy time, conscious that the puddles in the race were now steaming as the stonework heated . . .

'Ramon Sensini,' the Easterner purred, astonishingly calm in this maelstrom, despite his clearly broken body and the black blood seeping through his broken mask. 'I've been hoping we would meet.'

Then he came at Ramon in a deadly whirl of steel, his gleaming scimitar a blur as it hammered so hard at Ramon's guard that all he could do was block and keep his own blade from shattering, all the while trying to withstand an unseen assault of mesmerism. The air around his assailant came alive with frigid blasts of necromancy: his very aura grew raking tentacles of shadow that lashed at Ramon's shields.

He's got too many weapons . . .

Then a kinesis-grip caught him and he was jerked off his feet and thrown a dozen feet backwards. He tried to turn that momentum into a leap, but instead hammered into the stone wall behind him, beneath the sluice-gate. His head spinning, he glimpsed Vania beside him, lying against the wall with a dislocated foot at the very least and nowhere to go. Black-eyed men and constructs were swarming up over the edge of the race, then the masked daemon was looming over him, swinging his blade —

— as the race they stood on came apart in a livid burst of Fire- and Earth-energy.

The spells Moxie had drawn and Ramon had triggered had finally done their job and now Melicho completed the task, for the sluice-gates above smashed open and water came roaring over the top.

Ramon twisted away from the Mask's blade – even as the bottom of the race collapsed at his feet and the first rush of water poured down from above, slamming into the Mask just after his blade cleaved the concrete where Ramon had been an instant before.

Ramon, knowing what was coming, had managed to grab the rim and haul himself sideways, kicking aside the possessed man in his way, but the pillar beneath him was wobbling. He gathered himself to leap – but Vania screamed, some unknown woman shouted, then the pillar collapsed and Ramon began to drop into the ravening horde below – until something wrapped round him, the air shrieked and he was ripped away into the skies.

Xoredh roared in utter fury as a wall of water smashed into him, sweeping him down the collapsing race. The world became a bewildering swirl spinning him in every direction. He shielded, but he was being battered from every side, then flung out into the air . . .

. . . only to crash down to the ground, where the torrent grabbed him again, breaking his barely healed hip and thighs once more.

At last Sensini's flood lost its force and he was able to crawl away from the filthy pool of sludge he'd ended up in. All round him, his soldiers were doing the same. They didn't need air to breathe any longer, and except for those whose skulls had been crushed as they were swept along, most of the battering they'd taken had made little difference.

He rose to his feet, weapon-less. His broken bones were grinding inside him, as was his seething rage. The pain was shocking despite his gnosis: it took him ten minutes to hobble the two or three hundred yards back to the Copperleaf gates, where he could see the extent of this setback.

His own forces were now separated from the enemy by the lower plaza, which was now a flowing tide of water and mud and debris in which bodies floated. Water was still pouring in from the broken aqueduct and now he could see that the river, held at bay all winter, had been released into the city. But the upper tier of the plaza, the level the Shihadi remnants were defending, was clear, standing above the water-level. Their retreat into Copperleaf was already underway again.

Damn them to the Pit . . .

In moments the daemon's thousand-eyed hive-mind was assessing the situation. The river, normally channelled away from the city, was being pushed through the upper reaches of the aqueduct and into Lowertown, which was largely flat and already flooded.

It won't last . . . even that river isn't infinite, and there are elevated roads to the inner walls . . . but it will take days to reorganise and renew the assault . . .

He reached for Cadearvo and found that link utterly silent.

Abraxas showed him why.

So the Master's favourite is dead . . . Xoredh licked his lips, and then slowly smiled, despite the pain in his broken body. *Now it's just me in control here. We'll attack again, as soon as we've regrouped. They can't hold out much longer – they must be short of rations even without two divided armies, and they will have civilians to house and feed too . . .*

Glowering about him, he stalked into the shadows and grasped his periapt. <*Master,*> he called into the aether.

A few seconds later, the gem pulsed and Naxius' face in his youthful guise, perfectly symmetrical features and mane of red hair, bloomed in the darkness. <*Ironhelm. Report.*>

There was no point in gilding the truth. <*Master, somehow the enemy have united against us – the Yurosi are now sheltering the Shihad inside Copperleaf tier. It was Cadearvo's fault: he got himself killed. Then they broke the aqueduct at a crucial moment, driving us back—*>

<*I know all that,*> Naxius snarled. <*I've seen it through ten thousand eyes!*>

But not mine, Xoredh knew: he could shut the Master out, and had been doing so. So presumably had Cadearvo. <*Master, overall it's been a success—*>

<*A success?*> Naxius sneered. <*It's been a rukking mess. Cadearvo is dead – how?*>

Cursing his mistake, Xoredh hurriedly answered, <*Master, I don't know, but he was slain by roc-riders . . .* >

<*Prince Waqar,*> the Master snarled, his mental image coldly furious. <*I ordered that he be taken or slain. I will not tolerate failure at this juncture.*>

<This is no failure: my next assault—>

Suddenly Naxius was unmasked, the callous composure he affected ripped aside, and Xoredh saw something on his face he'd never seen before: fear. *<Your battle is now meaningless!>* the Master shrieked. *<Just kill Waqar Mubarak!>*

Xoredh reeled at the sudden unleashing of emotion and the dismissal of his sacred war. *<But the Shihad—>*

<I don't give a fuck about your petty holy war – it's never fucking mattered,> Naxius screamed. *<A dwymancer can still ruin my plans – so find Waqar and destroy him utterly. He has the potential and that is enough of a threat, especially with both Lyra and Valdyr in the wind. I will not – must not – be thwarted now. Hel awaits us if we fail, Xoredh: do you understand? Your sole task is to destroy Waqar.>*

The contact snapped shut and Xoredh swayed as his whole world turned upside down.

How can this war be meaningless? And what are his plans, if they weren't to conquer Yuros?

Gulping like a beached fish, he staggered away, seeking solitude, and some way to understand.

Ramon twisted in his rescuer's grasp and looked up to find himself cradled in the arms of a woman no bigger than he, a Keshi with skinny arms made strong by kinesis, her narrow face bony and her nose rudderlike, but right now the most beautiful woman in Creation, for any number of reasons.

'Rukka mio, *Amiza?*'

Amiza, Calipha of Ardijah, threw back her head and laughed. 'Ai, Ramon Sensini, it is I. Are you pleased to see me? I heard a man shout your name in the aether and followed the call back to you – just in the twinkle of time, it appears.'

Then she bent her mouth to his, sealed it with her lips and kissed him deeply. After a stunned moment, he reciprocated, because Amiza had been one of his conquests during the Third Crusade – or more accurately, he'd been one of *her* conquests. The half-remembered taste and feel of her mouth was like balm, for she was the lover he'd missed more than any other.

Finally he pulled away and breathed, staring at her in wonder as they overflew the broken aqueduct. He glanced down and saw that this plan at least had been a good one: the loosened waters were still raging through the lower half of Raathaus Square and separating the two armies, allowing the retreat into Copperleaf to proceed unimpeded.

We did it. He twisted again, peering towards the sluice-gates on the walls. He saw two figures standing on the race, one tall and gangly, the other with a tangle of black hair floating on the wind like a banner. *They made it clear, grazie, Pater Sol!* He punched the air triumphantly, then sobered as he remembered Postyn and Moxie.

'Take us down, Amiza-*habibi* – beside the race, if you would.'

She hauled on the reins of her roc and they flashed down to the Copperleaf walls where cheering soldiers lined the parapet. Shihadi soldiers were still pouring in through the gates. The banners of the Rondian empire and the Sultan of Kesh flew above the gatehouse.

Sol et Lune, we did it.

He returned to the miracle of his rescue, clambering behind her, wrapping arms around her narrow waist and demanding, 'Amiza-*habibi*, what in Hel's name are you doing here?'

She threw a confident grin over her shoulder – her poise and strut had always been her best asset . 'Your boring friend – the one who married me when you rejected my proposal – had a tragic accident, so here I am, single again. Having borne a child to a mage, I became one myself, so when this stupid Shihad came I was obliged to join it.' She smirked and added, 'Luckily for you.'

'But you must have known I was in the city?'

'Ai, but what could I do? We were enemies,' she harrumphed. 'And anyway, my spies tell me you're always seen with an *ugly* woman with a face like a horse, so I have contented myself with sitting in my room brewing poison.'

He couldn't tell if she was joking. 'That's just Vania – she's a subordinate – I don't sleep with those.'

'Really?' Amiza sniffed.

'Um, well . . . once a year we both get rotten drunk and end up under a blanket, but that's it.'

'But she's not your wife?'

'More like a favourite sister – except on those drunken nights.'

Amiza gave him a derisive look. 'Men . . . and to think I bore you a son . . .'

That hit him, *hard*. He'd known she was pregnant when the Third Crusade swept them apart again, but he'd never heard more. 'We have a son?'

'A beautiful boy, a little small, but so smart – like his mother. And maybe his father also. I named him Rahmeed in memory of you.'

Rahmeed . . .

'Is he here?'

She snorted. 'In a war? Of course not. If you wish to see him,' she added slyly, 'you must return to Ardijah.'

He stared, grinning foolishly. *Amiza is here . . . and we have a son . . .*

15

The Convent

The Successful Ruler

By what yardstick do we judge a ruler? By the justice of their laws? The victories of their armies? The degree to which they are loved? The magnificence of their court? The longevity of their reign? Their righteousness before God? Wealth? Power? Beauty? I know not. At times all of these things can be a virtue or a bane. Only History can judge a ruler, and History keeps changing her mind.

KOULOUS, RIMONI SCHOLAR, BECCHIO 423

Pallas, Rondelmar
Febreux 936

Lyra had never really seen her father angry until the morning after the attack at the Sancta Esmera Church. Calan Dubrayle looked preoccupied, Oryn Levis shocked, but Grand Prelate Wurther was as furious as Dirklan.

'I told you Frankel would betray your trust,' Dirklan snapped, the moment she took her seat at the council table. 'I *told* you – how am I supposed to keep you safe when you put your head into the first noose they offer?'

'It was idiocy,' Wurther added vehemently. 'Reckless – foolish . . .'

She held up a hand. 'It was a calculated risk. And anyway, I don't believe Ari Frankel meant that to happen.'

Dirklan looked incredulous. 'What? They *wounded* you, Lyra –they could have killed you – and when I catch that damned traitor, I'll–'

'Father, enough!' Lyra interrupted.

For a moment his one eye flared in warning, then he closed his mouth, looking thin-lipped and pale.

Her shoulder was bandaged and painful to touch: scars she'd take to the grave, despite the healers' best efforts. He was right: if the mage-bolt had struck her head, she'd have been dead. But she knew what she'd seen. 'Frankel was as appalled as I was when they attacked: I saw his face. He protested the instant they started.'

Her counsellors looked at each other doubtfully. 'Neither Basia or Exilium saw that, Milady,' Dominius Wurther commented.

'They were preoccupied,' Lyra replied. 'Their focus was on protecting me. They heard Frankel shout, but they don't recall his words. I do: he shouted at Braeda Kaden to stop.'

'Pretence,' Wurther said dismissively.

'Why would he pretend? You didn't hear him: he was truly shocked – and ashamed.'

'Milady, how could you perceive all that amid the attack?' Oryn asked.

'Because I've met the man,' she retorted. 'I've taken his measure. He believes in his cause. He came to talk, not fight. It's his comrades who betrayed us, against his will and knowledge.'

'Then that tells us that he's no longer in control of his rebellion,' Dirklan said. 'Which means he's not worth speaking to. It's the Kadens behind this, probably has been all along.' He pulled out a piece of paper: 'Speaking of which, Tad Kaden has approached us: he wants his sister back and he's willing to pay – and withdraw his people.'

Calan asked, 'Do we negotiate with the likes of the Kaden Rats?'

'To end this damned rebellion?' Dominius said. 'Damned right we should.'

'It won't end it,' Calan opined. 'The commoners will continue to resist.'

'Which means Frankel still matters,' Lyra said firmly. 'Dirklan, string Kaden along. Find out how far he's prepared to go – and when it comes down to negotiation, tell him that I want that talk with Ari Frankel.'

'But Milady—' Wurther began.

She slapped the table. 'That's my final word on the matter.' She looked at her agenda. 'I see that I'm to meet the Argundian Ambassador this afternoon? Lord Dubrayle, you have arranged this?'

'In my role as temporary Imperocrator, Milady,' Calan replied. 'It's to discuss the possibilities of a dynastic marriage to prevent the secession.'

'So they're still interested?'

'He almost bit my hand off when I made the offer, Milady. It appears the one thing they want more than independence is to be the dominant nation in an intact empire.'

'How predictable,' she said drily.

'They'll offer you Andreas Borodium, their Crown Prince: he's currently commanding the Argundian troops in the south, but I understand he's willing to fly here if a marriage proposal is going to be accepted.'

Lyra recalled a tall, strongly built blond man with a handsome, fleshy face and supremely arrogant manner. 'This is the same Prince Andreas who ensured his army wasn't in the field when my late husband needed them most, then marched north when Rashid went south? And isn't he married already?'

'He would put aside his wife to marry you. Argundan law permits this.'

She wrinkled her nose. 'He would destroy one alliance to make another. I like this less and less. Did the ambassador hint at terms?'

'They believe they're in a position to extract maximum advantage,' Calan replied. 'The ambassador said Andreas wants full imperium: the title and privilege of Emperor, replacing you in all executive roles – and the removal of your son Rildan from the succession entirely.'

She remembered her brave words, that she would never accept such terms – but what choice did they truly have? Garod Sacrecour was marching and she was going to have to find the courage and sheer heartlessness to hurl blizzards into their faces, this time without the aid of Valdyr, who was still absent from the dwyma. And Solon Takwyth had the Coraine legions marching too, and those she could not assail, not when they were fathers, brothers and cousins of the men who surrounded her here. And if she refused Prince Andreas, the empire would cease to exist, triggering the civil war that would wreck Yurosi civilisation.

'Do we have any leverage by which we can claw back anything?' she asked.

No one replied and her heart sank further.

'Very well, I shall give the ambassador his hearing.'

The remainder of the meeting passed in a dreary, defeated manner, even though Oryn Levis tried to speak in an upbeat manner about defending the city and sending an embassy to Duke Torun to persuade him to make common cause against the Sacrecours.

Finally she rose. 'Gentlemen, thank you. Calan, I'll hear the Treasury Report in my suite in a few minutes. Everyone else, I know you're busy.'

Dominius Wurther took both her hands in his, before taking his leave. 'Dear Lyra, be brave. It all looks bleak, but while there's life, there is hope. Have faith in Kore's love and go on.' He was so uncharacteristically earnest that it almost made her choke up.

Her Spymaster and Treasurer appeared in her sitting room shortly afterwards and they huddled together to hear the Treasurer's report on his 'little project'.

'Things proceed apace, Milady,' the Treasurer said tersely. 'I had the governors of the Gravenhurst Stronghold bank attend me on a pretext of a briefing, then laid out my intentions.'

'How did that go?'

'About as you'd expect.' He smiled. 'When I told them that I'd be making a silent illegal takeover of their operation and making a loan to the Crown that is around twenty times their bullion reserves, they declared me an "unconscionable criminal who should be dragged before the assizes". They threatened to expose me, so I told them I'd destroy their families and businesses so utterly that it would be as if they had never existed; they told me they'd ensure the market knew so that this utterly tyrannical act would fail, destroying the Crown – and I told them I'd rip out their tongues before they left the room if I thought they'd do that.' He chuckled softly at the memory.

'Dear Kore,' Lyra breathed, seeing no humour in the matter at all. 'What did they say then?'

'They appealed to Lord Setallius, who just smiled. Then they tried begging, and when I told them to be silent they offered a smaller but legal loan that would leave their bank intact if it failed. When I explained that was inadequate, they tried appealing to my honour, but it has already been established that I have none.'

Lyra shook her head. 'Calan, I can't help but feel that you're enjoying this far too much. Did they agree?'

'Well, I then offered them positions as Governors of the Bank of Rondelmar, the institution that will arise from this crisis and become the official Crown-backed bank, one that will dwarf *all* their rivals, thus ensuring their families sit at the highest tables in the land for generations to come – well, provided your Majesty's regime prevails. And then . . .'

He stopped, pausing for effect. When Lyra *huffed* in impatience, a quite uncharacteristic broad grin split his face, and he concluded: 'They accepted.'

Lyra sagged in her seat. 'Thank Kore.' Then she straightened as the implications of their strategy began to hit her. 'We've just bullied and bribed the governors of a bank entrusted with the life-savings of thousands of people, endangered all those funds and broken our own laws. This isn't something to be proud of.'

'No,' Dirklan agreed, 'but it might just save us.'

'It might,' Calan said, 'but there are still logistical matters to sort. We can accept the loan in the form of a promissory note, but to pay people, we need hard currency, more than we can lay our hands on. We're going to have to issue new, debased coinage.'

'Debased?' Lyra asked.

'We're going to have to mint coins that contain far less silver and gold than normal,' Dirklan said. 'You'll need to sign a new law of weights and measures to make them legal.'

Lyra gave him a blank look.

'In the past,' Calan explained, 'a silver coin contained its value in actual silver, by which I mean, if you melted it down and sold it, that was the price you'd get. That went by the wayside centuries ago, but most people still believe it's true. It's particularly important for cross-border trade: when Rondian coins are exchanged for the local currency, traders must believe in a coin's intrinsic value.'

Lyra frowned. 'What will happen if we put out debased coins?'

'Worst case: the market rejects them and our people are left with worthless currency – it would be as if we never paid them *and* they'll feel cheated and resentful.'

'So is there a *best* case?'

'There is: that the coins are accepted for their face value and we live to fight another day.'

'Do we know which is more likely?'

'It's a gamble, Majesty.' The Treasurer smiled drily. 'Your head will be on the new coins, in a very real way.'

'That's not as funny as you think,' she told him, then she sighed. 'Get on with it, please.'

'*TEAR IT DOWN – TEAR IT DOWN –*' Ari Frankel chanted, leading the crowds surging around the marble plinth bearing the ten-foot-tall bronze statue of Emperor Sertain. Everyone who had managed to grab hold of one of the many ropes currently knotted around it was hauling manfully, and a massive cheer erupted as the statue crashed down, barely missing the foremost rope-men.

'*Death to all tyrants,*' Ari hollered, and the cry was taken up, resounding around the small square. Despite this, he felt his personal despair rise.

He'd tried talking passionately about suffragium and people's basic rights, but it was only when he pointed at something breakable that the crowd had truly come alive. *Violence begets violence*, he admitted to himself. *Now we've given the mob permission to destroy, that's all they want to do. My message is being lost in the mayhem.*

He knew it, Lazar knew it. The difference was, Lazar didn't care.

It was Father Germane's preachers caterwauling about the 'Last Days' who roused them now, filling them with a sense that time was running out, so any atrocity was permitted. The former royal chaplain was inseparable from Lazar, and more and more weapons were being smuggled into the docklands.

'Let us fight for a better tomorrow,' he shouted, trying to recapture the crowd's attention.

'There is no tomorrow,' someone hollered back.

'*NO TOMORROW – NO TOMORROW*,' the chant went, and abruptly Ari shut up and jumped off the barrel he'd commandeered. Hardly anyone noticed; they were too busy looking for something else to break. He slipped off through the crowd – until someone grabbed his arm in an iron grip. Heart in mouth, Ari turned to see a cowled figure, one hand out of sight.

Dear Kore, a Volsai assassin – I suppose I shouldn't be surprised . . .

Then Tad Kaden's voice asked, 'Do you still want to speak with the queen?'

His throat went dry. 'I . . . ah . . . yes–'

'Then come with me.'

The late winter sun was setting in a hazy, sullen scarlet blur while darkness stalked in from the northeast. *A metaphor for my reign*, thought Lyra, alone on her balcony. *Everything is unravelling.* Smoke was rising over the docklands, where there were yet more barricades, yet more rioting.

She felt more anxious than hopeful over the banking proposal, and with both Coraine and Dupenium on the march, time was running out. Even if she did agree terms with Argundy – *but oh, I really don't want to marry that oaf –* it was doubtful they could get men here in time to protect the city. The meeting with the Argundian ambassador had been a humiliating haggling session over potential marital terms, but the upshot was simple: either she accepted Andreas of Argundy as her emperor and ruler and disinherited Rildan, or there would be no alliance.

The dwyma was empty and her enemies were closing in on all sides. Nothing was coming of Dirklan's negotiations with Tad Kaden, Solon's men and Garod's army were only days away, so she'd been forced to agree to Argundy's demands. The ambassador, smiling triumphantly, had gone away to begin drawing up the treaty.

I should be calling on the dwyma and preparing to hurl storms at the Sacrecours. I should be making rousing speeches. I should be doing something . . .

But negotiating her own surrender had left her mentally and physically exhausted and utterly depressed. Did she have the right to kill tens of thousands more men just because they were unfortunate enough to have Garod Sacrecour as their lord? Swap uniforms and her own Corani would be indistinguishable from Garod's Dupeni: they were all Rondians, after all.

And what of Solon Takwyth's army? Would her own even fight it?

And what will Rildan say when he's old enough to know that I signed away his throne, so that I could be a trophy wife to a foreigner? Will he thank me or hate me?

'Dear Kore,' she whispered. 'I don't even know any more if you exist. But I'm at my wits' end and I don't know what to do. Every choice is wrong. Everything I do feels dirty. Robbing the churches, corrupting a bank ... Takwyth ... the Mob ... I can't cope any more. If this is power, I don't want it. So please, tell me what to do.'

Kore didn't answer.

Maybe silence itself is the Voice of God. If so, it was of no use to her.

Feeling bereft, Lyra drifted down the stairs to her garden. The guards outside Greengate put hands to hearts when they saw her through the grille and one called, 'Yer Majesty, some fella's been wantin' t'see you. Came an hour ago, but we sent him on 'is way.'

It was unusual that someone would come to this part of the keep at all; the public entrances were on the far side. She was about to ask for details when the dwyma stirred and a young voice spoke, a girl, frightened and alone, who whispered, '*Help me.*'

She instantly forgot the guards and hurried away into her garden. It was almost completely dark, but this was her place: she could find her way by touch alone. Owls hooted as she reached the pool and saw Pearl drinking, shimmering white in the gloom.

'*Help me,*' that voice whispered again.

Lyra had once used the dwyma to heal Coramore, casting out Abraxas and purifying her blood – had that given her the dwyma gift? But it didn't matter *how*: Ostevan was in Dupenium, so the girl must be in terrible danger. She flung herself to her knees and stared into the water – then the reflection of the swirling sunset clouds above and her own silhouette faded, replaced by an outlined shape of a cowled head, and Coramore's voice pleaded, '*Please, help me.*'

'Coramore, I'm here,' Lyra sent back – but in a dizzying swirl her perspective shifted and then blurred, her vision following a trail of liquid light, a silver river winding towards the rising moon.

She's on the Bruin, she guessed – and leaped to her feet as Pearl made a nickering sound in her ear. She whirled and embraced the pegasus, cradling her head while her mind raced. She looked down at herself: she was wearing leather gloves and a thick coat against the cold, and for once she'd put on long boots that day instead of her usual delicate slippers. It was as suitable travelling gear as any she had.

'Milady?' Basia was calling from the balcony; she'd clearly been gone too long for her bodyguard.

They wouldn't let me go . . . but Coramore needs me. She'd come to care for the girl, despite all that lay between them. And if she didn't go, who would?

This is stupid, she told herself. *I have Rildan – and what could I even do to help her?*

But only she could sense Coramore's dwyma-contacts and find the girl. And Pearl was so swift, it wouldn't take long . . .

She knew that her roiling frustration and despair were pushing her to act rashly – but a powerful sense of purpose exploded in her breast and she was suddenly sure that Kore really had spoken to her and *this* was His answer.

Basia limped along Lyra's balcony, peering down into the gloomy darkness of the garden below her. If Lyra was beside her pool as usual, she'd be out of sight around the curve of the wall.

Damn. I just want to sit down . . .

She had good days and bad days and today had been a bad one: even with healing-gnosis, her stumps ached and walking hurt. And it had been hateful watching Lyra squirming through the meeting with the oily Argundian ambassador, selling herself to another man she didn't want.

'Milady?' she called again into the darkened garden, her voice echoing along the walls. There was still no answer. Duty demanded she find Lyra, so putting aside her weariness, she headed for the Rose Bower – and hearing the unmistakable thud of wings, tilted her head to see Pearl rising into the air. Silhouetted against the rising moon was someone with long streaming hair clinging to Pearl's back.

Basia gave a strangled gasp, then cried, 'Lyra? Lyra–?'

Rukka mio, what's she doing?

16

A Vision of Now

Omniscience

There is an adage that 'Knowledge is the greatest power'. Who would not wish to be omniscient, to see as a god sees! But would that knowledge not just heighten aware-ness of all that we cannot change? Unless we also have omnipotence, would not omniscience drive us insane? Ancient Lantric philosophers used to say: 'All the gods are mad, and hence the world they made . . .'

KOULOUS, RIMONI SCHOLAR, BECCHIO 424

Osiapa Valley, Mollachia
Febreux 936

The tiny eyot shrank to the whole of Ogre's world as the bipedal lions leaped easily from the low cliff to the eastern riverbank. The powerful male was almost his height and the female was only slightly smaller, a weird blend of muscular naked woman and furred cat.

As they stalked forward, Ogre's mind was racing. *They're possessed magi, they have to be – which means one bite and I'm done for . . .*

There was no time for him to resume his normal form, but he did what he could, shedding the pack before turning his fore-feet to clawed hands, straightening his spine and grasping the shaft of his great axe.

The pair of man-beasts wading towards him were kindling gnostic shields and drawing long thin blades from sheaths strapped to their own backs.

Ogre drew in a massive breath and bellowed a ferocious warning that reverberated through the narrows, bouncing off the cliffs and sending birds scattering. The lions didn't flinch but came bounding through the water, the lithe female gliding sideways, seeking an opening, while the male came straight at Ogre, his flickering sword demanding all his attention. He was swift, slashing high then low, but Ogre parried the first and caught the low blow on the shaft of his axe, almost losing fingers as the sharp blade slid down the handle, then he short-armed the axe-head at his foe's face, forcing him to give ground.

The flaring of power warned Ogre just in time to throw kinesis at the female, enough to jolt her backwards and send her mage-bolt awry so it just sprayed weakly over his shields – but that was enough to tell him her blood-strength was at least his own. It was Kyrik who had realised that magi infected with the ichor didn't become stronger – only the Masks were of Ascendant strength – but their range of skills became complete for they were able to access all sixteen studies of the Gnosis. But for all their snarling bloodlust, this pair were fighting tentatively . . .

They want to take me alive, Ogre realised. *I have to end this . . .*

He went on the attack, circling left to stay out of the female's reach before smashing an overhead blow at the male that went awry, exposing Ogre's flank. The lion-man saw the opening as he darted aside, and lunged –

– but Ogre had left the gap deliberately and now he slammed it shut, cutting short his swing and instead using the butt of his axe to deflect the blow, then lashing out with his taloned hind foot, ripping into the male's chest and bowling him into the shallows. Instead of following up, he spun and leaped with all his power straight at the startled female, crunching straight through her shields and bearing her down.

He landed on top of her with the axe-haft wedged into her windpipe. Jaws that could break a man's skull crunched beside Ogre's face and her talons raked Ogre's flanks, snagging fur and ripping, but her eyes were bulging and her breathing gurgled weakly. He glanced at the male, who rose in the swift stream, his fur plastered to his body, raised his hands and conjured energy. With counterattack imminent, Ogre redoubled his efforts, pushing the axe-shaft down as hard as he could, crushing the lion-woman's neck as she fought for air, her hind legs still seeking leverage to flip Ogre off him – then the male's mage-bolt blazed . . .

. . . and Ogre twisted, finally letting the female's attempt to throw him off succeed. He flipped sideways and she rose – and her mate's savage bolt took her from behind, blasting open the back of her skull.

She flopped to the ground.

Ogre was already hurling her body to one side and hefting the axe in readiness, but the male had pulled up short, his eyes blazing. Whether any kind of emotional bond still existed between them, Ogre couldn't say, but when the beast-man spoke, his voice was cold and callous.

'Can you feel the ichor bite, Ogre?' he snarled, pointing to Ogre's torn side. 'Soon you'll be like us.'

Is he right? Ogre turned his senses inwards, dreading to feel an alien presence.

'Can you hear Abraxas in your skull, Ogre?'

Almost as if they'd been waiting for those words the voices began, at the very edge of hearing, and Ogre, realising the daemon-mage was right, leaped at him with a one-handed sideways blow. His foe arched away from it, letting the axe pass by his nose, and his narrow blade lanced towards Ogre's chest, but it was an obvious blow and after battering it aside, Ogre whipped out his massive paw and caught the male's wrist. His enemy's face swelled in fright – a moment before the axe arced back around and cleaved the leonine skull, the silver sizzled and the ichor in the daemon's veins turned to ash.

The lion-man collapsed, kicking and thrashing into stillness.

Ogre pulled his hand from the ichor-stained blade as the inner wave of daemonic voices hit him. '*Ogre,*' they hissed, '*Ogre . . .*'

'Silver,' he croaked aloud, yanking off the coin hanging around his neck and with a sharp cry, pushed it into the worst of his wounds. The pain was enough to knock him to his knees, but he wasn't done yet. He crawled to his pack and found Sabina's pouch of silver dust. When he dusted the lesser wounds on his flanks, the daemon voices fell silent.

Gathering a little morphic-gnosis, he used it to numb the pain, but he knew his fate depended on the silver. *Maybe I've been lucky?*

He rose shakily, thinking how strange it was, the way once the fray was over and danger past, wound-shock could strike. But he managed to stay upright through the dizziness and quickly regaining command of his faculties, surveyed the carnage for a moment. He shook himself back into action and beheaded both of his foes, just to be sure.

They're all mentally linked, so Asiv knows I'm here now. The Master too . . .

He reverted to his natural shape, the better to think, and once dressed, shouldered his pack and with axe in hand he set off again, not wanting to make camp anywhere near. Using animagery to erase his scent, Earth-gnosis to smooth his tracks and night-sight to find his way, he covered another four or five miles before exhaustion claimed him. He clambered into the roots of a giant oak and slept, awaking at sunrise barely rested, but determined.

After breaking his fast he pressed on, unsure where the path led, but the Osiapa River was still audible away to the west. Ogre glimpsed flocks of crows flying into the river valley from the west and his hackles rose.

Possessed birds? Such creatures would burn out in a few hours – but they need not necessarily be possessed, just compelled. A competent animage could make them hunt him, though not for long, nor over a great range – which meant the animage must be near.

That meant he had to move on, fast, working southeast to escape the air-borne spies, staying under the deep forest canopy, which hampered his speed. Finally the birds dissipated, but now he heard baying hounds, although they were well to the west. He prayed the river had erased his scent.

The sun was going down when he topped a hill to see smoke rising from the direction of Hegikaro, a thick black pall coming from the south side of Lake Drozst.

The attack's begun . . .

Despite his weariness, he set his jaw and began to run.

Hegikaro

Asiv Fariddan scowled down at the lakeside town from his vantage point on a hill half a mile from the outskirts of Hegikaro. The castle was wreathed in smoke from the burning cottages surrounding the outer walls. Concealed pits filled with silver-tipped stakes had cost him a dozen men, not that he cared, but two of those had been possessed magi, which was enough for him to pull back and torch the outer buildings, in case of other surprises.

With those damned bull-constructs they've got more magi than I have . . .

But what really troubled him was that in the deep south, Ervyn Naxius was doing *something* far more important than this. *Why haven't I been recalled to the Master's side?* The possible answers to that question frightened him far more than anything Kyrik Sarkany or even his dwymancer brother could do.

Why am I stuck in this frozen backwater? 'Find Valdyr Sarkany and Ogre,' I was told. 'Bring them, and you may return.' But where are they? Surely Ogre was just a slave? Then he paused and thought about that.

'A slave in the Master's laboratories,' he said aloud. *So what does the beast know?*

He was mortified that he'd actually had Ogre in his hands – and used him as a make-weight in a hostage exchange – and now he'd not only escaped again, but killed two of the magi he'd sent to find him.

As for Valdyr, his former catamite had vanished at the volcano, not fallen in, but disappeared into the air, which made absolutely no sense. He'd gone back twice and found nothing at all.

So it was with no great enthusiasm that Asiv felt his Master's gnostic call and saw the translucent image of his face – the unnaturally youthful redhead guise he currently favoured – forming before him. As always of late, unease filled him.

Nevertheless, the Gatti mage genuflected, touched his forehead to the soil and didn't rise.

<*Asiv, report,*> Naxius growled, clearly in grim spirits.

'Master, I have burned out the hovels outside the walls, in preparation for the assault. We will move in as the smoke clears.' Breathing fumes made no difference to possessed men, but reduced visibility opened up the possibility of more tricks and traps.

Naxius replied in a flinty voice. <*Where is Valdyr Sarkany? Where is Ogre? I want them: dead or alive. Everything is at stake, Asiv – find them.*>

Despite Naxius' hauteur, Asiv sensed that the Master feared something, that he needed to hear good news. *Somehow, they're a real threat to him – to us*, Asiv finally realised.

'Kyrik is inside the keep. His plight will draw out the brother, Master. And Ogre has been spotted in the Osiapa River Valley.'

<*Do not fail me,*> Naxius warned. <*Your future is at stake, Fariddan. Will you rule Gatioch, your homeland, for ever; or scream for all eternity in the belly of Abraxas?*>

Then the image dissolved and the Master was gone, with no salutations, no promises. Asiv remained kneeling, seething with indignation and worry. *The Master has some huge purpose, but I'm here cleaning up loose ends.*

With a grimace he rose, and strode to the nearest daemon-mage. 'Attack at sunset,' he growled. 'Take their leaders alive and bring them to me.'

The daemon turned on its heel, walking away as the aether crackled with orders. Asiv turned back to the keep, wondering what hand he should take himself. There was no one inside who could defeat his gnosis, but war was more than just gnostic skill or raw power. Unseen missiles and subtle blows could down the mightiest mage. War was chancy and he'd always hated risk.

Let others die to clear my path to victory . . .

'They're coming,' someone said tersely, drawing Kyrik's attention from the silhouette framed by the window in Haklyn Tower, where Hajya watched anxiously.

Stay there, be safe, he prayed as he shifted his gaze to the burning buildings below. Dark shapes were emerging, careless of the toxic air. Along the battlements, men and Mantauri huddled behind the crenulations, their faces wrapped in scarves against the thick smoke.

'Be ready for anything,' he shouted, lifting his eyes to the night sky, seeking airborne magi or even possessed birds, but the sky looked empty.

The gnosis favours defence, but only if you know the attack is coming . . .

'Prepare,' he called, and his archers – Mollach hunters and their equally adept wives and elder children – lined up their targets. The dark shapes resolved into Rondian legionaries, but with no sign of their usual spotless precision; instead, ragged groups of black-eyed, blood-stained men snarled in the torchlight. They formed up at the edge of the shadows beneath the walls, at the foot of a sharp slope. Amid them were a dozen blue-wreathed battle-magi.

'Hold fire,' he called, listening through the aether to Kip and the Mantauri around the castle; every flank was reporting movement: this was the beginning of an all-out assault. Those burghers who couldn't find space on the battlements were huddled in the courtyard below, ready to reinforce as needed. How many would find the courage to do what was needed, he couldn't say.

He had a moment to wonder, *Where's the Vlpa clan? Is Freihaafen safe? Can we hold?*

Then like the onset of a thunderstorm, bolts of energy blasted from the magi below as the black-eyed attackers charged up the slopes.

'Fire!' Kyrik shouted, and a volley of arrows scythed into the advancing men, silver-tipped and potent – several staggered and fell – but most came on. His own shields flashed red as bolts struck and the two men on either side of him, both young farmers, screeched as they pitched backwards into space, their faces scorched into unrecognizability. Shouts filled the air along the walls, but the enemy scrambling up the walls like limpets were silent.

'Stay under cover,' Kyrik shouted, as mage-bolts from below sought out any defender foolish enough to lean out. 'Spears at the ready–'

He heard scrabbling on the wall and nodded to the axeman beside him when an arm reached over the lip . . .

Kyrik lunged, his blade punching through a helm's eye-slit and into the brain. The possessed legionary fell silently away, but he was immediately replaced, only for that attacker to take an axe-head to the chest. The defenders also hacked at limbs, not fatal, but enough to dislodge, sending the attackers crashing back down, although they simply rose up and assailed the walls again.

The black eyes, the silent snarling and the lack of reaction to pain and maiming were all unnerving, but the Mollachs and their allies fought with grim determination. Minutes passed like hours and still the attack intensified.

Then a possessed battle-mage flew out of the darkness, black-eyed and snarling. He landed atop one crenulation and blasted fire along the fighting platform, torching several men and punching a hole for the daemon-solders to swarm over the battlements. Though the reserves tried to counter, more enemy magi appeared, setting the air alight as they blasted mage-bolts into the throng below.

'Hold on!' Kyrik shouted: these moments were critical. Shielded Mantauri hurtled along the walls, hacking down attackers and exchanging spell-fire, but the battle-magi were stronger. Kyrik heard one daemon cackling in glee as two bull-men roared in agony and tumbled to their deaths.

Kyrik pulled aside a teenage girl who staggered, then folded over a sword-thrust, her determined, fearless expression fading to confusion. He destroyed her killer with a kinesis-aided stab of his argenstael dagger, then leaped in on the blindside of the daemon-mage who'd begun this breach, hacking his sword blade through both ankles and sending him toppling away.

He was immediately assailed by a black-haired battle-mage barely clad in the torn, bloody remnants of her robes; she hurled a crackling bolt of raw energy before lunging at him. They traded blows, steel clanging, then her foot lashed out; had he not been ready she would have pitched him over the edge, but he struck back, slashing down on her sword arm and breaking it, then thrusting his dagger through her raging mouth into her brain. As she fell, ash bursting from her eyes and mouth, Maegogh closed in from the other side, pitching two foes over the edge with one mighty swing of an enormous hammer.

But all along the outer walls, Kyrik could see the relentless assault was breaking through. Stairs were clogged with the bodies of his men who'd been blasted as they tried to plug the gaps. He saw a Mantauri hacked down from both sides, and another who'd been buried in biting, tearing, ripping men, emerging with black eyes and hate on his face.

We're losing . . .

'Fall back to the inner keep,' he shouted, kinesis fuelling his leap to the roof of the stables. Hearing a thump behind him, he turned in time to catch a blade meant for his back, battered another thrust aside, deflected his foe's sword up and then slashed sideways, beheading the man and kicking his body off the roof.

His cries to retreat were taken up and those who could fled down the stairs, trying to dodge the fire raining down on them from above.

Kyrik leaped to the courtyard, fast filling with bodies and blood, joining the rearguard alongside Kip and Maegogh just as the next wave of enemy struck. They fought shoulder to shoulder to keep the attackers back, shielding the retreat into the inner bailey.

When a torrent of silver-tipped arrows from the keep walls above slammed into the next wave of possessed, checking their impetus, Kip shouted, 'Go!' and they took to their heels. They were the last through the keep gates, which were then slammed shut.

Kip's normally confident expression had disappeared, worn away by the rapid loss of the outer walls and the dozens of men and Mantauri already dead, but Maegogh gripped the Schlessen's shoulder and for a moment the pair pressed foreheads together, fortifying each other.

Then Kip looked at Kyrik and demanded, 'Where are your Vlpa?'

'No idea. They can't contact us without betraying themselves – you know that.'

'They'd better get here soon,' Kip said grimly, then he straightened his spine and called to his men, 'Bullheads, to the walls – Minaus is watching us.'

The Schlessens regrouped swiftly, their years first as legionaries, then as mercenaries telling. They joined the archers above, packing the ramparts.

Kyrik saw his own people's despair and fought down the same emotion. 'To your posts,' he shouted. They'd prepared for this moment, but no amount of practise could overcome the shock of experiencing a reverse, let alone the realisation that there was nowhere else to fall back to.

I have to give them hope, he told himself, and just as Kip had done, he stiffened his spine. 'Men and women of Mollachia, we *can* hold,' he told them. 'The fields of fire are narrower here. We can defend in greater depth. Now, move!' He brandished his sword in their faces. 'For Mollachia – for all those you love.'

It wasn't much, but it sufficed. He saw dread on many faces, but they too sought courage within themselves. They took up their positions, many praying aloud as they went, as he hurried to the top of the gatehouse, which was filled with hunters.

Then a shout of horror went up as the church across the square, the site of his bloody coronation, burst into flame – and the air was filled with the screams of those townsfolk who'd taken shelter there instead of in the keep.

Dear Kore, no . . .

The flames rose swiftly, fanned by the wind whistling across the lake which set sparks streaming upwards, glass shattering and fiery tongues licking through the portals. The possessed legionaries ringing the square were ghoulishly lit by the lurid flames.

A few of the archers were firing, while spitting out curses.

'Hold fire,' Kyrik shouted. 'Save your arrows for the next rush when we can do some good.'

As his archers stilled, a silent ripple ran through the possessed men and without a word, they melted back into the alleys until the square was empty of all but the wounded and dead.

The screaming inside the church reached a crescendo when the roof crashed down in a roar of flame and Kyrik found himself fervently praying, *Kore and Ahm, take them up, I pray you.*

A dark shape stepped from the smoke surrounding the burning church, walking nonchalantly among the flames. Kyrik presumed it was Asiv Fariddan, although the robed figure wore a Lantric mask: the long-nosed, bird-like visage of Beak, the meddler.

'Kyrik,' the dark voice called, 'how do your people fare?'

The defenders fell silent, until someone muttered, 'I can hit him . . .'

Kyrik didn't need gnostic sight to know the Gatti mage was wreathed in shields. 'Hold your fire,' he said, then called, 'Is this a parley, Asiv?'

'Call it what you like. I just wanted to show you something.' He gestured, and four of his possessed legionaries dragged a bound body into the square. Kyrik's throat seized up. He threw a horrified look up at Haklyn Tower and saw the window was shattered.

Hajya . . . He must have gone up there, in the midst of the fight . . . and what of the four men with her . . . ?

Asiv's laughter filled the square. 'Perhaps we should talk?'

Kyrik felt all hope wither inside him. It took three tries before he could fill his lungs enough to speak. 'I do not hold the life of one woman above those of my people,' he shouted.

'Of course you don't, O Noble King,' Asiv sneered. 'But do you hold your own life above hers?' He gestured, and the ropes around Hajya moved like tentacles, hauling her to the charred spar over the well from which the bucket normally hung and tethered her there, upside down.

Kyrik could see she was aware and struggling in her bonds.

Asiv stepped in front of her and gestured widely. 'Come and get her, Kirol Kyrik, if you have the courage to fight one duel, Brave King: with me. Or better yet, let me offer a simple exchange: your queen for your brother.'

A dark titter ran around the men lining the square as the daemon voiced its approval through hundreds of throats.

'It's a trap,' Kip told Kyrik, stating the obvious. 'I will fight him—'

Kyrik shook his head and asked the Easterner, 'My brother is not here – and why would I accept a duel knowing you'll storm the keep afterwards anyway?'

Asiv chuckled. 'Why should I? All I want is your coward of a brother.'

'My brother is not here,' Kyrik repeated.

'Then where is he hiding, while his people suffer?' Asiv's voice was full of contempt. 'I see women fighting, children fighting – but not your cowardly catamite brother. Come down here and prove me wrong – or are you as feeble a woman as Valdyr?'

'Why would I put my head into your trap?' Kyrik asked again.

'Just the sort of pathetic response I expected.' Asiv turned to the possessed man guarding Hajya and calling, *'Butcher the queen.'*

'No—' Kyrik couldn't stop himself wailing, as every hard-won moment of joy he and Hajya had shared swam before his eyes. 'No – wait – I will fight—'

Kip gripped his shoulder. 'Don't,' the Schlessen growled. 'You know he's too strong – you're throwing away your life for nothing. He won't let any of us live, you know this.'

Kyrik pressed his forehead to Kip's, as he'd seen the Schlessen do with the Mantauri, as if seeking strength, but what he murmured was, 'He's the key. Remember at the hostage exchange, how these possessed men became a rabble when their leaders fell? I have argenstael – I know it's unlikely, but one good blow and we're back in the game.'

Kip made a rumbling sound, then, 'Yar . . . yar . . . Minaus approves, Kirol Kyrik. Fight the duel.'

They shared a grim look, then Kyrik shouted, 'Very well. We shall fight.'

'Goodness me, have you actually grown some testicles?' Asiv taunted. 'I didn't think you Sarkanys had those. You have half an hour to prepare yourself, Sarkany. We will fight before your own gates. If you kill me, you can cut her down and my army will leave.' He snorted dismissively. 'Not that you will. No, you will die . . . and I will renew the assault until Valdyr Sarkany crawls from his hole to give himself up.'

The masked man strode back into the shadows.

The men on the walls were all looking at Kyrik, and he could see the question on every face: *Where's Valdyr . . . ? And why must our kirol die for his brother?*

The Elétfa

Valdyr gripped Gricoama's ruff, caught up in the wonder of the Elétfa. Hanging in the branches all around were glowing spheres of translucent light, each containing some tiny detailed scene of a lake or a city, a meadow or a mountain. When he got right up close, he could see tiny shapes were moving.

These are visions of now: these are real places . . . It was breathtaking, beautiful, eerie and frightening. He was petrified of what would happen if he touched, or worse, broke one.

And he still had no idea what to do, other than to keep moving, so he and the wolf soldiered on, the meal at the Keshi farmstead a long-digested memory. Each step required more effort, but the light growing brighter above pulled them onwards. The leaves now surrounding them were huge and minutely detailed, thousands of blades of green slowly scything the air, blown by some vast cosmic wind.

Then the stairs took them though a cleft between two massive branches, taking them inwards, a sharp ascent to a flat place – not the very top of the tree, but the top of the trunk before it forked off into the highest branches. The inside of the tree trunk was revealed, a hollow shaft in which a huge globe, bigger than all the others he'd seen, slowly rotated. Around it spun two more spheres, dimly lit, one large and closer, the other smaller and further away.

It's Urte, Valdyr realised, as the largest globe's surface resolved into continents: Yuros, the eastern half covered by darkness, the western region streaked by cloud and the north coated in gleaming snow. He saw rivers winding across plains, a patchwork of farms and the dark stain of forests. *And those two lesser orbs must be Luna, and Simutu, the Wandering Star . . .*

Gricoama looked up through the branches, growling. When Valdyr followed his gaze, he saw the Elétfa was hanging in a void, a light in an eternity of darkness; but following it were dark shadows which looked to be feeding on the trailing sparks.

Ghosts, he guessed. *Or daemons.* It occurred to him that they might be the same thing: Death feeding on Life – and trying to *re-enter* it. They looked like floating clouds of eyes and mouths and limbs and organs, for ever forming and reforming, merging and coming apart, resembling a flock of dark crows circling a tree they couldn't land upon.

Words from the *Book of Kore* came to him and he whispered, 'And in the Last Days, dark shall become light and the sun shall turn black. *Crows shall alight in the branches that break.* The sky shall be torn apart and the daemons shall be summoned by their Mother, the Fallen One, Glamortha who is Death. Thus the eternal night shall begin.'

Is that what's happening right now . . . ?

His head spun at the enormity of that thought, that these were indeed the Last Days, that all of Urte was about to end, that Kore was

279

coming in judgement, to take the Deserving to his Paradise and leave the rest at the mercy of the daemons who would inherit the world.

Does a broken man deserve the Mercy of Kore? he wondered. But the *Book of Kore* had nothing but condemnation for men who'd endured the sins Asiv had wreaked on him. *He's still inside me. The wounds are cauterised, but the venom still burns. Why did the dwyma chose someone as unworthy as me?*

But he wasn't the only dwymancer. *Nara is surely more worthy than me.*

But she wasn't here and his thoughts went back to his family, to Kyrik . . . and his brother's name sent his awareness swooping across Yuros at a bewildering speed, arrowing down – and when his vision cleared he saw Hegikaro. The lake was iced over, although his dwyma senses told him the thaw was coming. The castle was smouldering on its promontory, even the church was aflame.

Dear Kore, the whole town's ablaze . . .

Then he saw the dark shapes packing the alleys around the inner keep – and men and women, shining with life, besieged within.

It's their last stand, he thought frantically. *Asiv has them cornered – Kyrik –*

That panicked thought sent his perspective right to ground level. The gates were swinging open to reveal Kyrik, ashen-faced, his eyes seeking a bundle hanging upside down above the well – Hajya, gagged and barely conscious.

Asiv Fariddan stood beside her, armoured for battle.

A duel, he realised. *It's a duel for Hajya's life. Oh, my brother . . .*

Asiv shouted, 'Last chance, Sarkany: where's your craven catamite brother?' The Gatti mage raised his curved scimitar to the skies. It gleamed with dark energy sent from the daemons outside the Elétfa. His voice echoed with a thousand voices as he shouted, 'If Valdyr won't come forth, I'll make do with you, weakling.'

Kore's Blood, Kyrik's doing this for me.

Valdyr went to tear at the air when a woman's hand gripped his hand. 'No,' Luhti begged, appearing beside him, young and timeless. 'No, you failed the test – you aren't ready.'

'But my brother –'

'This isn't why you're here,' she shouted in his face. 'You must go to the empress—'

The empress? 'No,' he roared back, 'Kyrik needs me.'

He wrenched himself free and turned back to Kyrik – and realised that in this place where time was fluid, his delay had been a deadly mistake, because his brother was already down.

17

Wings of Pearl-White

House Sacrecour

Mikal Sertain, the first Rondian emperor, took the family name Sacrecour when he was crowned. That family has held the throne ever since, which is not the feat it sounds when you consider that Sertain himself reigned for another two hundred years, and all of his line have the longevity of the pure-blooded magi. Ironically, the only reason Mikal Sertain was among the Blessed Three Hundred was because he'd run away to join Johan Corin's followers in rebellion against his tyrannical father. Blood will out.

GRAND PRELATE DOMINIUS WURTHER,
HOLY PRECINCT, PALLAS 931

Bruin River, Rondelmar
Febreux 936

Lyra's flying west up the River Bruin, Basia de Sirou thought frantically, watching the dot that was Pearl and her rider merge with the darkness. *She's run away – dear Kore, she must have decided it's all too much . . .*

It was tempting to scream the palace down, but she realised that that would be the worst thing to do: if people knew the queen had left, panic would set in and half the city would rise up in rebellion. So instead she sent, <*Vasingex, to me!*> into the aether and conjuring mage-light to illuminate her path, went tearing back through the garden.

As she ran, her mind cleared enough to ask the obvious question: *Why is she flying towards her worst enemies?* To that, she had no immediate answer.

She hurtled up the stairs to the balcony and barged into the apartment to find Exilium looking around in puzzlement at the empty suite. 'Basia?' he exclaimed. 'Where's the queen?'

She ignored him and ran to the nursery, expecting to find it empty, but there was Nita, sharing a blissful look with Rildan as she fed him. The maid turned, smiling. 'Milady Basia – are you all right?'

Dear Kore, Lyra didn't *take Rildan . . . Why wouldn't she take the son she loves?* She just stood gaping, half-turning back and forth as tried to think. *If she's left him behind, she must surely mean to return.*

'I . . . um, sorry,' she panted, backing straight into Exilium.

He grabbed her forearms – the first time he'd ever touched her, part of her noticed – and stopped her. 'Basia, where's the queen?'

Her brain stalled – then she heard a shriek outside as Vasingex answered her call; the wyvern was circling outside the southern towers of the Bastion, no doubt causing much consternation on the walls.

She pulled herself free, gripped her periapt and stared out the window, her mind questing. <*Dirklan? Dirk?*> She got a wordless, irritable response – the spymaster was busy. But she persisted. <*Respond, damn it!*>

Unable to wait, she swung back to face Exilium, whose expression had changed from perplexed to worried. 'Come with me,' she told him. She shut the nursery door and dragged him into the next room before blurting, 'Listen, Lyra's just taken Pearl and she's flying east up the river – I don't know why, but I've got to follow her . . . Keep it quiet, but tell Dirk – he'll know what to do.'

'But–'

'There's no time: just do what I say, *please*.' She spun and ran out onto the balcony again so she could call Vasingex nearer, then using Air-gnosis and kinesis, she hurled herself from the railing and landed on the battlements with a thud, seconds before the guards below crying out in alarm heralded the wyvern's arrival.

'Don't worry,' she shouted, though they'd probably heard her calling Lyra's name earlier and were already putting things together. 'Volsai business,' she added, a warning to mind their own.

She darted beneath Vasingex's right wing, pulling off her day cloak and rolling it up, then clambering up his reverse-joined knee onto his back, placing the folded cloak over his spinal crest so she could sit there without having a ridge of bone torturing her. Gripping the largest of his spinal plates, she ordered, <*Go —* >

The wyvern's wings thudded; without a saddle or straps, she had to grip with kinesis as he leaped, his wings caught the air and they lifted with a surge – then they were off.

How the Hel is Lyra coping? she wondered suddenly. *She's not got a ruk-king saddle either, has she?*

Vasingex, a wyvern construct, part reptile, part bird, was faster than a venator and could normally catch a pegasus, but Lyra had a head start on her. She wasted no time, whooshing down the slopes of Roidan Heights barely ten yards above the houses before shooting through the smoke over Kenside and arrowing up the river. The rising moon reflected in the water formed a ghostly path eastwards.

<*Basia?*> Dirklan shouted into her mind. <*Sorry, I was with Wurther and Dubrayle – I couldn't respond in front of them. Exilium's in a panic over the queen vanishing – what the Hel's going on?*>

<*I don't know yet,*> she sent back, plaintively. <*She was already in the sky when I saw her and she's flying straight towards the bloody Sacrecour army.*>

<*It's your damned job to watch her,*> he said angrily.

She'd never heard the boss so enraged – or frightened – but he had every right. Lyra was his daughter and she'd blinked when she should have been vigilant.

<*I'll find her, I swear, Dirk.*>

<*We should have locked that damned pegasus up the moment it arrived,*> Dirklan fumed. <*If you can't find her by dawn, there's going to be the biggest panic in imperial history!*>

<*I know – just help me track her down.*>

<*I'll have men in the air in a few minutes to follow you – find her, and guide them in, Basia. And good luck.*>

They broke the connection and she gave her attention to the sky. Clouds were rippling in from the north on a rising cold wind; it was going to be a bitterly cold night. She tried to scry Pearl, but the dwyma murk encasing Lyra was preventing any contact.

Lyra's never flown before – and pegasi can be capricious, even Pearl. If she runs into a Dupeni aerial patrol, she won't stand a chance.

Then the clouds swallowed the moon and she was left flying in darkness. Gnostic night-sight was short-range and risking a light would make her a target herself, so all she could do was go on flying blind, pulsing out a signal to those following and praying fervently for some kind of lucky break.

Dear Kore, Lyra – what on Urte possessed you? Yet again she wondered if Lyra had simply gone insane. Wasn't that what dwymancers did?

I must be mad, Lyra thought as she and Pearl followed the river weaving its way eastwards in broad, sweeping bends. The frigid air was making her eyes tear up and her frozen fingers were numb. She wondered if Pearl could even see, then remembered Ril had told her winged constructs were bred with a transparent membrane beneath the eyelids to protect the eyes while flying. She knew magi used the gnosis to warm their mounts if they had to, but she couldn't do that, so common sense demanded she take the pegasus down and find shelter before a night of flying through the freezing winter killed them both.

She had no reins, so the only way she could tell Pearl which way to go was through the tenuous communication they somehow managed.

She drank from my pool – it must be the dwyma permitting this understanding. That was some comfort.

Listening to the dwyma gave her no updates on Coramore and there was no response when she called the girl's name – and then she remembered another risk: Oryn Levis had told them the Sacrecours had skiffs and constructs flying ahead of their army, which meant there was a very real possibility of her blundering into an enemy patrol.

This night flight is madness, she decided, wiping her streaming eyes with an icy sleeve, then thumped on Pearl's back and jabbed her finger downwards. 'Pearl, take us down,' she shouted. 'Come on, Pooty-girl, we need shelter. We'll find her tomorrow.'

To her immense relief, the pegasus went into a smooth spiralling descent. Lyra strained her eyes, using the barest glimmer of Luna that was piercing the clouds to identify some reference point, then a fortuitous moonbeam illuminated a copse in a snowy field below, with a broken-down building on the edge. *'There –'*

Again Pearl understood and glided in with wings outstretched. The ground was coming up terrifyingly swiftly, then Pearl's hooves crunched into the frosty grass and the jarring landing tore Lyra's hands free, she spun off the pegasus and fell onto her back in the snow, winded and gasping – and hugely relieved there was thick grass underneath.

'Dear . . . Kore . . . Oh my Lord . . .' she panted.

Pearl's long head loomed over her, her hooves clomped down beside her shoulder and she licked Lyra's face as if in apology.

Lyra lay there, panting helplessly for breath. When she could breathe again, she said, 'Did . . . I say . . . that I've . . . never done . . . this before?'

Pearl whinnied as if amused and licked her face again.

'Rukk you too,' she groaned, sitting up, trying to assess if there was any real damage, but thankfully, she couldn't feel anything more than a bit of bruising, although her burned shoulder felt excruciating, despite the numbing cold.

And of course you flew off without bringing the pain-softener the healer left, she scolded herself ruefully. She clambered to her feel and looked around. Pearl had interpreted her wishes perfectly: they were only a few yards from the building, which turned out to be an old barn. She draped an arm over Pearl's neck and together they walked to the ruin. An owl shrieked and flapped away when she entered; in the mess of rotting hay, vermin scuttled.

She led Pearl into the corner that still had a bit of roof, then pulled off her cloak and rubbed the pegasus down to get her coat dry, the way she'd seen Ril do. The pegasus accepted the attention while crunching ravenously at the dry hay.

This must be one of the farms Calan told us about, abandoned because of the raids by soldiers from Fauvion. I hope the owners are safe . . .

Only a few minutes later she heard a shrill cry in the sky above; she was terrified she'd been discovered, but she wasn't going to risk going outside. A few minutes later the sound repeated, further east and more distant. She had nothing to eat, but she found an old bucket that was full of rain water and brought it over. Once she'd pulled Pearl to the ground, draped the cloak over her and crawled beneath her wing, she drank deeply, then gave the rest to the pegasus to finish. Her last coherent thoughts as she drifted into a confused dream were of Coramore, wondering where in the world she might be.

Coramore peered furtively over the side of her coracle from her hiding place in the reeds, watching the barges laden with soldiers float by: Uncle Garod's men, apparently marching in the name of her brother Cordan. She wondered where her brother was, if he was as frightened and miserable as she was.

He can't be, though, because he hasn't spent a night lost on a giant river, hunted by a daemon . . .

She'd woken up freezing to find the coracle drifting through the predawn mists. Thankfully, it had been a clear night, although the hills were white and the air was bitterly painful to inhale. Her legs were numb and her fingers locked rigid, but she rubbed and chafed them back to life as she continued drifting on the current. When she heard a shrieking sound above, she used the pole to push herself deeper into the reeds. The flight of giant venators soaring overhead petrified her – but evidently the flyers weren't looking down, for they swept by and were quickly gone.

It had been a timely warning, however, because only a few minutes after she reached the shelter of the reeds, she heard shouting from upstream and a line of barges came into view. She had no choice but to remain hidden for the rest of the day, for the flow of boats and barges was constant.

They're going to Pallas to kill Lyra.

She'd guessed by now that the dwyma was waking in her; her vision would blur at times – then she could lose minutes gazing at a leaf, or the swirl of the river-water shot through with rainbows of light.

Kore's Love, it's beautiful . . .

Then a harsh male voice broke through her reverie and set her heart thumping. 'No, over *there*,' he called. 'They reckon whatever it was, it was in them reeds there.'

A worried man answered, 'What're ye thinkin', Serjant? If'n it's a Volsai Owl, we ain' goin' near 'em.'

'Our bloody orders are to beat out this section, Jobbers, so if it turns out there's rukkin' Owls in there, we'll call for help, won't we.'

'Be too late for the poor fuckers what found 'em, boss.'

'Just do as you're rukkin' well told,' the serjant called.

Coramore peered through the reeds and cringed at the sight of a pair of longboats, which had paddled into the reed-bed where she was hiding. They might be hunting Volsai scouts, but they'd be happy to grab her damned quick.

If they get too close, I'll have to leave the boat . . .

She peered doubtfully over the edge. The water was murky so she couldn't tell how deep it was – if it was more than five foot deep, she'd be over her head. And it was going to be utterly freezing. *But if I wait too long, they might see me . . .*

Then she heard a watery *thwack* as someone struck the reeds only a few dozen yards away, and more voices started shouting. She flinched, feeling like a cornered animal. *Any second now and they'll see me . . .*

Stifling a moan, she edged to one side, making the coracle tip alarmingly, then flipped her legs over the edge, yowling silently as her legs were immersed in the icy water. Her eyes bulged as the bitter water reached her waist, then her feet struck muddy silt and she almost slipped and went under, gasping despite herself.

'Oi – what's that, then?' someone shouted.

'Quiet, lads!' the serjant bellowed, and the searchers stopped beating the reeds.

Coramore clung to the side of her little coracle, a silent, agonised stream of curses and prayers pouring from her lips as she tried to be still and let the splashing around her subside. Every second was a hideous, frozen lifetime.

'Nah, there's nothing,' someone said eventually, alarmingly close by.

She planted her legs and once she was sure of her balance, she slowly let go of the coracle and with deliberate care dropped until just her eyes and nose were above the surface. She waded towards the bank, only a few yards away, trying desperately not to make the reeds move, sidling between clumps as she made for a tangle of willows on the bank.

Then someone shouted, 'Oi, sarge, look't this – it's a little dinghy, innit.'

She had to fight not to run as the soldiers poled their longboat through the reeds to her coracle. *Don't see me*, she told them, over and over. *Just let me get ashore.* She was crawling through the clinging silt and green slime at the river's edge. The bank wasn't high here, just a broken shelf of ice-blackened grass. Her teeth were chattering and her flesh was so numb she couldn't feel her toes, but she crawled ashore and slithered towards a place where the tangled tree roots had made a bit of a cave. She slipped in, put her back against the earth and curled into herself, cowering and clenching her teeth to stop them chattering.

'Careful, lads: eyes peeled, innit. Rukkin' Owl could be bloody anywhere' the serjant bawled, probably terrifying his men. She wished she really was a Volsai and had the gnosis so she could deal with them all with one deadly spell. But her clothes were soaked, her heart was hammering in fear and shock and she felt a long way from being a mighty mage. The rational part of her brain, sharpened by weeks of having the daemon inside her, knew she was still in deadly danger if she didn't get warm and dry quickly. She had to move.

The bank had a narrow strip of bare bushes and trees; through the naked branches she could see low stone fences and hedgerows, which meant farmland, which meant people, which meant things she could steal. *Come on*, she told herself, resisting the urge to curl up into a ball and close her eyes. *Move, you silly little chit!*

While the searchers still beat timidly at the reeds, she slithered away until she found a track leading inland and crawled along it, avoiding the deeper grass and the old snowdrifts, trying not to leave a trail. At last she lost sight of the river behind her, there was no shouting following her and by the time she reached a wooden stile over a stone wall, she could no longer hear the hunters at all. She risked revealing herself as she darted over the stile, but dropped safely with a crunch into clump of frost-covered grass.

Made it . . . She huddled there, panting heavily, savouring her little triumph, before looking up at the sound of a distant bell chiming sonorously over the fields: two rings, marking the second hour after dawn. Her stomach was screaming with hunger, but she was feeling bleary and unfocused, as if this was happening to someone else, not her.

You're going into shock . . . You need warmth and food . . .

She rose and staggered on, following the echoes of the bells, trying to think, to pray, to reach out of herself to someone, to Kore or Cordan or . . . *Lyra . . . Help me, Lyra . . .*

She walked across the undulating, frost-covered land and as she staggered along she fell into a blurred reverie in which nothing coherent happened, just flashes of memory, until she came to, to find herself standing before a trio of brackenberry trees, the biggest she'd seen – and they were laden with berries. They each leaned into the other, their branches entwined in an intricate weave that somehow formed a Brevian knot-pattern of incredible intricacy. And she could *smell* the power of the place.

This is like the bush in the graveyard in Dupenium but magnified a hundred times, she thought, lifting her head and hands to embrace the energy flowing from the place. *Aradea brought me here*.

She hesitated a moment, but the tree branches rippled as if welcoming her in. The rich loamy smell of the earth blended with the sharp scent of the berries and her mouth salivated. Then a dark shape entered the tree's shade on the other side and she caught a glimpse of a deer's head in silhouette, a doe with small twisted horns and luminous eyes – then she realised that it was walking on two legs.

'Aradea?' she asked, stumbling into a faint. 'Lyra?' she whispered as leathery but gentle hands caught her. Someone tipped water down her throat, flavoured by crushed berries, waking a warm glow inside her. She was lowered to the ground, a woman's earthy odour filling her nostrils, and cool lips touched her forehead. The moon shone down through the canopy of leaves, light dancing through the knots and whorls, mesmerising and beautiful. The silhouette of the doe-headed woman hung above her, fingers brushed her eyelids and closed them, pulling her down into sleep . . .

. . . Lyra . . . ?

It was Coramore's voice again and it came from somewhere *that* way: towards the northeast, towards Dupenium and Garod's army. That was all Lyra knew, that and the weary desperation in that mental call: the sound of someone so far past terror they'd fallen into resignation.

It gave Lyra the spur she needed to move again. Despite her fears, she'd slept well, warm against Pearl's flanks, but the dawn air was frigid. For the first time she thought guiltily about her father and Basia – they probably thought her kidnapped, or worse.

In the cold light of dawn, it was hard to remember the fervour she'd been in as she set out. What on Urte had she been thinking, venturing out alone on a mount she barely knew how to control, seeking a Sacrecour child on the eve of war? But she could sense Coramore more clearly now, somewhere ahead on the river.

She stroked Pearl's soft head, then rose and donned her cloak before teetering to the doorway on stiff limbs. It was gloomy, the cloud hanging thick and low, which was probably in her favour if the Dupeni had mage-knights in the air. Fog was hanging over the Bruin snaking by a mile away. Thick frost crusted in the long grass.

Pearl stood and unfurled her wings, shaking them vigorously, then nuzzled the empty water bucket. Lyra's stomach growled as the pegasus looked at her expectantly.

'Sorry, Pooty-girl,' she murmured, 'but I don't have any feed for you – nor me.'

The beast snorted reproachfully and nosed through the damp grass. Lyra wished she could eat grass herself, but had to content herself with slurping water from a puddle, like a beast in the fields. Next she had to find a place to relieve herself, awkwardly pulling her skirts out of the way as she squatted.

Some bloody queen, she chided herself, before chuckling at the indignity. At least there was no one around to see her humiliation.

Once she was ready, she hauled herself onto Pearl's back and settled herself as best she could. With a boisterous snort and a quick gallop, Pearl launched herself into the air. It was still alarming to be airborne, but Lyra trusted her mount. Now she just had to guide the pegasus to Coramore.

Please let us find her soon. The rushing air was chilling her already dangerously cold body and she worried that she couldn't endure much more of it.

They swooped through the fog hanging over the river and out the other side, heading northeast, and as she flew, Lyra called into the dwyma, *Coramore, I'm coming . . .*

Whether the girl heard or not, she had no idea.

Basia de Sirou glared down at the fog in utter frustration, wrestling with calculations of air-speed and probability. How far could Lyra have got? Was she somewhere still ahead, or had she overshot while Lyra and Pearl had taken shelter? Was she even still alive?

She'd flown all night and seen no sign of them, but she'd seen *hundreds* of barges on the river and every moment heightened the risk of being spotted by Dupeni patrols. Exilium's men, on the slower venators, were still miles west of her, but she and Vasingex were both exhausted despite her drawing on the gnosis for endurance.

I'll try a sweep north. She slapped the wyvern's left shoulder and Vasingex banked and arched round, just as Dirk's terse voice crackled into her mind.

<Any news?>

<Not yet,> Basia sent back. *<If we knew why she ran off, we might know where to look.>*

<We still have no idea,> Dirklan admitted, his voice sounding as weary as Basia felt. *<You're certain she went upriver?>*

<Where else would she go?> She bit her lip then asked, *<What if Ostevan got someone into her garden? We've believed it too well-protected for that to happen, but what if he managed it somehow and used Pearl to escape?>*

<Then she's already in Garod's hands,> Dirklan groaned. *<But we can't give up yet.>*

<I'm not: I'm going to try northwards – perhaps she left the river and flew directly to Dupenium?>

<Garod's got men in the air as well,> Dirklan warned. *<Wait until Exilium reaches you, then travel in force.>*

<Numbers will just attract attention,> Basia sent back. *<I've got a better chance of evading detection on my own.>*

She felt Dirklan hesitate, then give a tired mental shrug. *<All right, but keep Exilium informed. He's got Patch and Briggy and a few others with him. If you're seen, shout.>*

The contact broke, leaving her wincing at the gnostic exertion. She'd been burning through her energy to keep Vasingex warm and exhaustion was setting in. And the rolled-up cloak was utterly insufficient: she felt like she'd never be able to sit comfortably on anything, ever again. *I should've kept this ugly brute saddled . . .*

Then moving shadows caught her eye and she looked down to see three dark spots following the river-fog upstream, just above the swirling mists. She was too far away to identify them, but all her comrades were west of her, so she watched them warily – and when they suddenly banked and shot away to the north, she caught her breath.

It wasn't anything like a clue, but maybe these were enemy and they had news of Lyra?

Bereft of other ideas, she brought Vasingex around and telling Exilium what she was doing, she set off in pursuit, thousands of feet above and behind. <*It's probably nothing,*> she warned him, thinking, *But it could be everything . . .*

Dupenium

Ostevan Pontifex sat bolt upright on his throne, staring into the shimmering image of a florid, thickset Sister of Kore in a deep blue habit fringed in white, hanging in the air before him. 'What?' he demanded.

The Abbess repeated her greeting, her voice crackling from aetheric distortions, 'Holiness, we've found a lost girl and we think it's Princess Coramore. At least, that's who she says she is. We found her in a grove at the edge of our gardens, asleep and almost frozen. I can't get any sense out of her; she's delirious.'

'And you're *who* again?' he snapped. 'And where?'

'Abbess Lyfrasia, of Sancta Pontelia Abbey,' she repeated forthrightly. 'We're about twenty miles west of Fauvion, on the Bruin.'

Why are rural abbesses always such formidable women? Ostevan wondered, then, *If it is her, the girl managed to float past the entire fleet unseen. Or maybe she was ahead of it . . .* 'Are you sure it's her?'

'Almost certain, Holiness,' Abbess Lyfrasia said. 'I've seen the girl from a distance in Fauvion, and she's wearing a signet bearing the Sacrecour seal.'

This is perfect, Ostevan mused. *Anyone but clergy would have gone directly to Garod.*

'You've done well to contact me directly, Abbess Lyfrasia. The girl is indeed missing and we've been most anxious. There's a rich bounty,' he added slyly. 'Keep this silent until I can reclaim her and I will ensure the rightful reward goes entirely to your abbey.'

The abbess' fleshy face took on a glow of satisfaction. 'That would be most appreciated, Holiness. It's not easy in the borderlands between the Corani and the Dupeni.'

He sent a pulse of thanks and gratitude, warned her again to tell no one else, then broke the connection and sat back, thinking hard. *Find the little bitch and kill her*, the daemon inside him growled, but he blocked Abraxas's awareness to his deeper thoughts and pondered, chin in hand. This had to be handled right or he risked losing access to the girl. It had to be his people who collected her, but knowing what the dwyma could do to a possessed man made the matter delicate.

No, I need unpossessed *men. Lyfrasia is a mage and I doubt she's a fool.* He tapped the table feverishly. He had plenty of unpossessed men, including mage-knights, who'd follow his orders loyally, thanks to his rank, and some of those had the necessary discretion. *But I need that girl in my hands as soon as possible . . . Lyra could start hurling blizzards at Garod's army at any moment . . .*

Best I do this myself.

He dredged up names and faces, settled on one and sent his orders, then rose and striding from his chamber, started snapping orders to his servants. 'Ready a flight of venators,' he told the commander of his personal guard. 'I want a steed for me and a dozen of your best, ready to fly in twenty minutes.'

Sancta Pontelia Abbey, Bruin River Valley

Coramore woke with a start to find two faces looming over her. She stifled a squeal as the newcomers resolved into a pair of young nuns, Sisters of Kore in white-trimmed blue robes. Her peripheral vision told her she was in a small room, the only ornament a Dagger of Corineus on the wall. Distantly, she heard the sound of female singing, a hymn to Kore.

A nunnery . . . She had jumbled recollections of people fussing over her, of warm water and bare skin, of hot gruel and bread . . . and a blur of words.

What have I told them?

'Uh, who –?' she said timidly, while she tried to think. *Have I been recognised? Have I – Kore forfend – even told them who I am? And where am I?*

Fortunately, this guileless pair told her everything she needed to know, blurting 'Majesty' and 'Highness' in awestruck voices. *I blabbed, rukk it! But who have they told?*

Then a thickset woman in finer robes with a periapt around her neck waddled in and curtly ordered the two nuns to, 'Be about your duties, Sisters.' She stared down at Coramore like a cat at a bowl of cream. 'Princess, it's good to see you awake,' she purred. 'I'm Abbess Lyfrasia. I imagine your guardians must be worried sick.'

There was no sense in denying her identity – but where did this woman stand on the question of Ostevan?

'It was probably foolish, but I ran away,' Coramore said, watching the abbess closely.

'It's not unheard of for children to do so,' Lyfrasia observed. 'We take in strays more frequently than you can imagine. We'll have you back with your family in no time.'

'Don't you want to know why I ran?'

'Your reasons are your own, Highness. My duty is to return you to their protection.'

'My family don't protect me,' Coramore said plaintively. 'Not from that sort of . . . *abuse.*' She dropped her eyes and made her lower lip quiver, hoping she wasn't overacting.

The abbess' body tensed. Her voice softer, she asked, 'What do you mean, child?'

She's genuinely concerned – she might look like a greedy hog, but she does have a heart. But Coramore knew not to get her hopes up. *She can't protect me, not from someone like Ostevan.*

295

'There's a man,' Coramore started, the horrible memories she'd experienced under Abraxas' thrall giving her too much inspiration. 'He comes into my room when everyone's asleep . . .'

Lyfrasia gasped and made the sign of the Dagger over her heart. 'Kore forfend – not your uncle?'

'No,' Coramore said. She put every ounce of conviction she could manage into her next words. 'It's Ostevan.'

The abbess blanched, clutching at her ample breast in anguish. 'Dear Kore – I spoke to him myself only an hour ago.'

Coramore felt the blood drain from her face. 'What did you tell him . . . ?'

Before the abbess could answer, the door opened and one of the young nuns burst in, excited and anxious. 'Holy Mother, there are men on dragons circling above us!'

Coramore gripped her sheet, her skin ice-cold. She looked up at the abbess pleadingly. 'Holy Mother, you have to save me – they've come to take me back to that *dreadful* man . . .'

Basia took Vasingex in lower as the three venators she was trailing dipped towards an old grey stone building set amid a white patchwork of fields and gardens: a monastery or an abbey, she guessed. When she closed in she saw the riders wore black and white tabards: Kirkegarde.

An overwhelming sense of aching loss seized her suddenly. At first she didn't understand – then she remembered a similar scene, six years ago, descending upon just such a place, flying alongside Ril and the Joyce brothers, with Kirkegarde foes below. Ril had rescued a young woman from imminent death – Lyra Vereinen.

In that moment I lost Ril, before I even knew I wanted him, and everything we're suffering now was set in motion . . .

The enormity of it stole her breath, the sense that Fate was a real thing – and that it was laughing at her. *How ironic it would be, to die here.*

Then she saw the three Kirkegarde were trailing someone else: a white pegasus with a blonde-haired figure in a purple cloak clinging to the winged horse's back as it tore down towards the abbey's courtyard.

Rukka mio, it's Lyra!

Fear for Lyra overcome all other thought. She sent Vasingex into a dive, lining up her shadow with the hindmost Kirkegarde so that if he looked back, she'd be nothing a blur in the sun. As the ponderous vena-tors closed in on Lyra and the abbey, her lighter, faster mount brought her above and behind. With their attention firmly fixed on the pegasus below, her prey never saw her coming . . .

When they were within ten yards of the rearmost man, Basia com-manded, <Now – >

Vasingex drew back his head, then lashed forward, spewing a torrent of flames – wyverns might not breathe fire in the mythologies, but con-structs were subject only to the skills of the animagi breeders and in Vasingex's case, they'd achieved a very great deal.

The Kirkegarde knight had been concentrating on flying, not even bothering with shields: he never knew the danger until too late. The flames burst over him, fiery phlegm clinging to man and venator alike. Thrashing in agony, they screamed as one and nosedived.

Basia and Vasingex flashed onwards. The two flyers below her had seen her and split up; one went left, the other right. She blazed mage-bolts at both, wishing she was lashed to a saddle and had a lance. Her foes shielded strongly and though her bolts turned the translucent pale blue cocoons crimson, the enemy emerged unscathed. She followed the one angling left. It was too soon for Vasingex to breathe fire again, but she had to maintain the initiative.

Below them, her first victim hit the ground at a frightening velocity and sprawled brokenly on the frosty ground. Her two foes roared out defiant threats as they sought to catch her in a pincer, but Vasingex spiralled out of the trap and climbed.

Basia craned to check on Lyra, but she was safe, for now, at least: she and Pearl had landed safely in the abbey courtyard. Basia remembered the nuns six years ago who had tried to kill Lyra to keep her out of Corani hands; if history repeated, Lyra was on her own.

Her job was to keep these Kirkegarde rukkers away. Pulsing mage-bolts left and right, she tried to keep both men occupied – and one bolt got lucky, punching through frayed defences and striking the venator's head. Suddenly blinded, it dropped dramatically and careened into the outer wall of the abbey, breaking its neck – but the rider had already severed his saddle-straps, leaped and hit the ground running.

Then the remaining airborne venator came straight at her, swerving into her path with jaws gaping. Shouting in alarm, she took Vasingex into a sudden climb, but her foe, a Kirkegarde grandmaster from his plumes, came after her – and he did have a lance. Their flight paths intersected and she managed to haul Vasingex aside barely in time to batter away the lance with her sword. The two reptiles got close enough to rake each other with their claws; Vasingex emitted a throaty yelp and she glanced back to see bloody furrows along the side of his belly, below the wing joints. Pain started bleeding into her brain from his.

<*Hold on,*> she sent, bringing him round again. The grandmaster's venator was ponderous, but it was bigger and stronger, and he was better armoured and armed than her too, and at least her match as a mage.

Kore's Balls, Lyra, what are you doing here? Is it worth our lives?

Pearl tried to land gently, but at their speed they slammed in hard, the legs of the pegasus jarring and almost buckling, and even with her arms wrapped around Pearl's neck, Lyra was still thrown free. This time when she hit the ground she rolled away from the steel-shod hooves that smashed down beside her, and came to a halt, a little winded.

Spitting out snow and gasping for breath, she muttered, '*Rukking* landings – I hate them.'

But she had to move. She pulled herself upright and staggered towards the nearest building. Female voices were squealing in alarm as blue-clad nuns flapped about like startled birds.

'Cor . . . ah . . .' she choked out, as they stared at her with frightened eyes.

'Cora–' she tried again. '*Cora* . . .'

'Lady?' one of the nuns squeaked.

If I tell them who I am, they'll think I'm here to kill her . . .

'Must . . . *protect* . . . Cora,' she panted, looking for the right door. Like legion camps, Kore abbeys tended to have identical layouts. She spotted what she was looking for and tried to run on wobbling legs.

Then Pearl neighed a warning and everyone looked up. Her heart punched the inside of her ribs as she recognised Vasingex, wheeling above with two venators.

Dear Kore, it's Basia –

'Those men mean her ill,' Lyra shouted, and in a moment of inspiration, added, 'They are not true Kirkegarde.'

The nuns looked aghast, but no one moved until a stout abbess appeared, shouting, 'Lady, the princess is here – come with me, please.'

Lyra had no choice but to trust the woman. She gathered her skirts and the nuns parted to let her through. The abbess had a periapt on her ample bosom, and shrewd eyes.

'Lady, do you come from the duke?' Her eyes flashed over Lyra's clothing, seeing the imperial emblems embroidered on her clothing.

Lyra hesitated, not sure how to answer, but a girlish voice interrupted, calling, 'L . . . uh . . . *Lena*?' Coramore came hurtling down the stairs with arms spread. 'You've found me!'

Any doubt must have evaporated, because the abbess stood aside and even managed a smile, watching Lyra sweep the skinny little girl into her arms.

'Cora, Cora, it's all right, we have you–' *Dear Kore, she's nothing but skin and bone.* Lyra looked heavenwards, praying Basia was holding her own above.

Then she turned to the abbess. 'We have to get her ou–'

Someone screamed, and they all turned back to the courtyard to see a dark shadow crunching into the abbey's outer wall, just thirty yards away. It was a venator and it flopped to the ground, obviously dead – but a Kirkegarde knight had landed beside it and the moment he spotted the women milling about, he raised his hands and blazed mage-bolts at the sisters. Two women were struck; they crashed to the ground with blackened holes in their chests.

As the rest froze like deer before the hunter, he fixed his eyes on Lyra and shouted, 'Seize her – she's the empress!'

For a moment, Lyra's limbs locked as well, then the abbess gestured with a chopping motion like a butcher hacking into meat and the man was bludgeoned backwards.

'Get inside,' she shouted, backing up and shielding as Lyra and Coramore and the terrified sisters fled for the chapel doors. She was last in, then she slammed the doors with kinesis and light bloomed as wards locked into place.

'Is there somewhere safe?' Lyra asked.

The abbess looked at her curiously, perhaps noting her lack of gnostic shields, but all she said was, 'This is no fortress, Lady, but a sanctuary.' She looked at Coramore, who was still clinging fervently to Lyra, which seemed to reassure her. 'I am the abbess, Lyfrasia, and I will protect you both.'

Then something battered into the door with a crunching, splintering sound and the sisters shrieked, then they all dropped to their knees to pray. Lyra almost copied them, her childhood as a novice overwhelming her, but she thrust those memories aside and instead, gripped Coramore's hand and reached for the dwyma as the door was battered again . . .

Basia gave Vasingex free rein, letting the wyvern pick his path through the storm of mage-bolts unleashed by the Kirkegarde grandmaster. Her shields were holding and thanks to her mount's speed and erratic weaving, she was being struck only by glancing blows.

But we're one square hit from disaster and I can't get close to the bastard . . .

All her strength was going into shielding while she clung to the wyvern's back, but from the pulses of gnostic energy echoing below, the knight who'd crashed into the abbey was still alive, which meant Lyra was facing dangers she couldn't survive alone – and who knew whose side those nuns were on? Somehow, she had to find a way to strike back.

<*Got to try it some time,*> she sent to Vasingex, along with a series of visual images: of a manoeuvre they'd practised, but never tried in a real fight. <*Now!*>

The construct made a hungry, snarling sound, pinned his ears back and with smoke streaming from his mouth, flashed into a spiralling turn before swinging over the venator's flightpath: a barrel-roll that caught the grandmaster by surprise. Basia was clinging on for grim life as they swung up and round, right under the venator's tail. They closed in as the venator twisted in the air, trying to keep them in sight, the grandmaster squirming around in his saddle, seeking a clear shot, but in doing so, reining in his venator and losing them height and airspeed. The beast stalled – and Vasingex scorched in under the venator's body, whipping his tail upwards.

Giving Vasingex not only fiery breath but also the mythical venomous sting of a wyvern's tail-tip was a triumph of animagery. Basia watched the tail spike lash upwards, plunging into the beast's belly and gushing poison into the wound, wishing those far-sighted animages could see their ingenious work in action.

But there was no time to stay and gloat. Basia smacked her hand down and Vasingex obeyed, dropping instantly away, so the jaws of the venator crunched together a foot above her head as she flashed by. They barely avoided ploughing into the ground, but a moment later were banking hard and climbing, just in time to see the venator vent a tortured shriek before it thudded into the snowy field. The great construct bounced and lay still, about three hundred yards from the abbey.

But the grandmaster had survived and was already tearing free of his saddle-straps in a burst of kinesis, his enraged cry echoing through the aether. He landed on both feet, blade in hand and bawling at them as they flashed by.

'*You, come here,*' he roared, aloud and in the aether. '*Come and fight me!*'

I don't think so, honey, Basia thought as she took Vasingex back towards the abbey, leaving the grandmaster fuming and swearing. The courtyard was empty but for two figures lying motionless on the snowy paving stones – and the door to the main building was shattered.

They're all inside . . .

Vasingex slowed enough for her to float down on Air-gnosis. The moment she hit the ground, her knee stumps protesting as the wooden lower legs struck, she was running for the door.

Then the aether reverberated and the grandmaster smashed through the main gates of the compound like a giant's fist, splintering the timbers without slowing down and roaring towards her. Even fully armoured, he'd covered three hundred yards in around fifteen seconds.

She gulped, snapped off a mage-bolt that barely turned his shields pink, then planted her wooden legs before the stairs as the man steamed towards her.

'Seventeen years I had that construct,' the Kirkegarde grandmaster snarled. 'Seventeen years, egg and beast—'

'So old and slow, like you,' she couldn't stop herself replying. But beneath the bravado, she felt drained from the exertions of the night and this sudden deadly fight.

The next moment his big broadsword was battering against her slimmer blade. When he punched at her with kinesis, plucking her from the ground and slamming her back into the stone walls, only her shielding kept the back of her head from turning to paste. He thrust again and this time his sword lanced through her guard and into her side, emerging as blood spurted. Her sword arm went numb, the blade falling from her fingers, and for an instant all she saw were stars as she slid down the wall.

A sword-point kissed her throat. 'Not so old and slow, then,' the grandmaster rasped.

Then a Southern-accented voice said, in very earnest tones, 'In my country, it is considered the height of dishonour for a man to assail a woman.'

Exilium.

Basia's vision cleared through the haze of agony, enough for her to see the gnostically imbued blade-tip touching her leather breastplate. The grandmaster, a grey-bearded man with a battered, homely visage, looked like a tower of steel and fur, and though he was panting from exertion, his sword arm was steady as a rock.

Beyond him was Exilium Excelsior, standing in the middle of the courtyard. His venator was on the roof of the gatehouse behind him and more Volsai were swooping in around him. The Estellan was composure itself, not a hair out of place, but Basia could hear the tension in his voice and his eyes were watchful.

Kore's Balls, you've got wonderful timing . . .

'She killed my steed,' the church knight rasped. 'Do not lecture me on honour.'

'I saw. It was a fair fight, with both sides risking loss. I counsel you to consider your standing with Kore.'

The grandmaster clearly did consider, including the fact that he was presently going to be alone against many. 'A duel, for her life,' the grandmaster offered in a grave voice.

'I accept,' Exilium said instantly.

I am not a rukking prize for men to scrap over, Basia absolutely did not say. Her eyes met Exilium's and she sent him all her luck; he responded by saluting with just the faintest touch of irony, then turned to face the grandmaster.

With a grimace, the knight pulled his sword away from Basia's chest.

She shoved the pain aside, flicked her wrist and a sheath-knife slid into her palm: she lunged and drove it into the back of his left knee as he turned away. It would not normally be a fatal blow, but the blade was coated in the same venom Vasingex secreted.

The grandmaster gave a choked cry; his arm lashed round, but she ducked the flashing blade. Then he gave an agonised cough, his eyes bulged and he collapsed on the stones, dying a moment later, his eyes looking at her in betrayal.

'*Basia*,' Exilium exclaimed in mortification, 'did you not understand? We had agreed a *gentlemen's* duel.'

'Supercilious wanker,' she gritted, as her vision blurred.

'That's unfair: he was a true knight—'

'Wasn't meaning him,' she snarled, then she indicated the broken door. 'Lyra . . .'

She tried to move, her stomach screamed and the world turned into a red blur. Exilium laid a restraining hand on his shoulder. 'Stay here,' he told her. 'I will go.'

A moment later, the Volsai who'd landed behind Exilium came bounding in – bluff, burly Brigeda, who caught her in muscular arms. 'Here, Bas, just you lie down a moment,' she said, her usually brusque voice gentle.

'But I'm fine,' Basia slurred, then the adrenalin that had been sustaining her until now ran out and everything faded . . .

*

'You are the queen and you are my prisoner,' the Kirkegarde knight said crisply as he pushed through the shattered door of the strong-room. Abbess Lyfrasia was lying in a scorched heap while the nuns were on their knees, cowering against the wall amid piles of boxes, barrels and chests and stacked altar plate.

Lyra knelt with them, staring up at the blonde nun in the middle of the room dressed as her. A moment before the door was broken down, the young woman had torn Lyra's purple cloak from her back and was now wrapped in it. Coramore, huddling behind Lyra, was enveloped in a habit someone had quickly thrown over her head.

The ruse couldn't last – and it would surely cost someone else their life, so Lyra couldn't let it go on. She took a deep breath, ready to confess her identity before anyone else was hurt – then she sensed a trembling in the aether and realised that any delay could be vital. She exhaled, waiting her moment.

The nun in Lyra's cloak somehow had the courage to lift her head and face the knight with the bloody sword. 'What is your name?' she asked, perhaps to buy a moment of precious life.

'I am Jaron Parelle, knight of the Kirkegarde, and –' He broke off, tilting his head and frowning, then going pale as something in the aether reached him. 'Grandmaster –?'

He sagged and for a moment looked lost, then he straightened, his features grey. 'Lady, I regret to inform you that you must die. Do you have any last words?'

Lyra only heard *you must die*. She stared as her brain roared silently, thinking, *No, this isn't right . . .*

As Parelle lifted his sword they all heard boots pounding through the building. Gnostic light flared along the steel and he flexed his arm –

'No,' Lyra shrieked, 'I *am the queen* –'

And the room suddenly erupted: someone else was shouting, '*No, I'm the queen* –' and then another, woman after woman, and Parelle's gaze moved from one to the next in bewilderment – until his eyes narrowed and he focused on the kneeling Lyra.

'It's you,' he whispered, raising his sword. He strode forward –

– and a crossbow bolt slammed into his back.

The nuns gasped in shock and buried their faces as the Kirkegarde knight dropped bonelessly to the flagstones, the energy in the bolt burning his over-zealous heart to ash.

Lyra looked up at the barred window high on the chapel wall and saw a well-known face: the straggle-haired, whiskery ruffian Patcheart, one of her father's Volsai. To her, right then, he looked like Corineus the Saviour. He gave her a thumbs-up and vanished.

Exilium burst in through the shattered doorway. 'Majesty, are you well?' he asked. Then he saw Coramore and his eyes widened. 'Princess?'

Lyra clambered painfully to her feet, her shoulder screaming in pain, but she reached for Coramore and hugged her, then knelt before the sister who'd briefly – *crucially* – impersonated her.

'Sister, I owe you my life.'

'I just . . . I . . . um . . .' the young nun stammered.

'You don't even know me and yet you offered up your own life – I will reward you in any way I can.'

'No man can come in here to kill a woman and say he's doing Kore's work, ma'am,' the nun said, blushing bright red. 'T'ain't right.'

Then everyone turned as Abbess Lyfrasia proved herself not entirely dead by groaning and rolling on to her side. In moments she was swamped by her sisters and Lyra was touched by the love and concern on their faces.

The Church has not always been good to me and my faith is now clouded in doubt, but there are those within whose belief in virtue is true.

Exilium joined her and dropping to one knee, said, 'Majesty, it is a joy to see you. But where you go, so must I.'

The reprimand was clear and justified, but Lyra, clinging to Coramore, knew she'd just saved someone who shared the dwyma and that was worth a great deal, perhaps even all these lost lives, though guilt pricked at her.

'Circumstances did not allow, Exilium, but your arrival was indeed timely,' she told him, more primly than she'd intended, but his formality was infectious. 'Where's Basia?'

Patcheart appeared at the door. 'She's outside, Milady, a little roughed up, but she'll live.'

The Volsai helped see to Abbess Lyfrasia's comfort before leaving. Lyra took Coramore's hand, receiving a shy smile in return, and they let Exilium lead the way through the abbey. The familiar scents of incense, candle wax and damp stone filled her nostrils and all those hours on her knees, the earnest prayers, the wondering why Kore tested her so, all came flooding back, and so too did the comfort of knowing whatever cruelties the outside world contained, her existence inside had been a simple one.

I was never truly alive in my little convent, but I wasn't dead either, and I had my books. And I believed, then.

Outside in the courtyard, she found Brigeda tending to Basia. The two dead nuns were being wrapped in cloaks and taken into the chapel. The nuns following them outside wailed when they saw their fallen sisters and again Lyra felt a stab of guilt.

She swallowed, then raised her voice. 'Sisters, please know that we came here by accident, not design – and I knew not what would befall us when we came. We did not intend to bring harm upon this holy place. I know it is no consolation, but although the men who did this were only following orders, they chose to kill, and that was evilly done. I will make what reparation is due.'

The nuns looked at her in wet-eyed silence and a few touched hand to heart in the imperial salute. Then a mocking handclap rang out and Lyra whirled. When she looked up, she saw a dozen armoured men lining the rooftop surrounding the courtyard. All of them wore Kirkegarde tabards and had drawn swords. They were silent, save for the man above the gates in heavy black velvet robes and a tall mitre.

Ostevan.

Lyra pulled Coramore closer as his black gaze transfixed her. Around her, the small group of Volsai, their eyes bright and faces pale, strengthened their shields. They were outnumbered, and overmatched.

'What a pretty little speech, Lyra,' Ostevan said. 'Almost an epitaph of your reign: "I knew not what would befall us when I came". Blood is what came, Lyra: a trail of death.' He gestured toward her and said, 'Kill these traitors, but the princess and the queen are mine.'

The eyes of his knights narrowed. Lyra realised that they weren't daemon-possessed, but she saw no pity on their faces, either. She started to speak, trying to find words that might make them pause, but Ostevan gestured and her throat was gripped by unseen fingers, choking her.

The knights shouted a Kore war-cry and leaped from the roofs, blazing fire . . .

18

Forever Broken

Mystic Healing

*One of the least understood aspects of the gnosis is Mysticism, which deals with the
inner workings of the mind. It can be used benevolently to heal distress and trauma
and correct abhorrent habits. But it can also be used malevolently, and such damage
is far easier to inflict than to rectify.*

SOREN BASCO, HOLLENIAN MAGUS, DAMSTADT 790

Hegikaro, Mollachia
Febreux 936

Hajya had been drifting in and out of awareness, but those moments
were growing longer, her hold on the *now* strengthening. When she did
finally pull herself from the mire of unconsciousness, it felt like she'd
been plunged into Kore's Hel.

She was hanging upside down over a round bricked shaft with the
reflection of water below. Her limbs were bound and her mouth gagged,
but she could see the town square before the inner keep, with the
church ablaze and corpses scattered across blood-slick cobbles.

Hegikaro – on fire?

Memory vomited up a slew of hideous images: bodies ripped apart in
her own bedchamber, and Asiv, black-eyed and cruel, gloating as he
loomed over her.

Not again . . . please . . .

Then she heard the Gatti shouting in Rondian, his voice echoing
around the stone walls; it took her a moment to make out his words.

'—owardly brother will not come forth to save your queen, I shall make do with you, *weakling*,' he was bellowing.

She couldn't see Kyrik, but she heard his clear voice when he replied, 'My brother is not here, but he is no coward and you will not defame him.'

Is this some kind of stupid duel? she wondered suddenly. Could Kyrik – a quarter-blood mage at best – really be going up against Asiv – which meant going up against Abraxas – for her? She felt loved and horrified in equal measure – but such a fight would be bloody and *brief*. Opening her eyes again, she saw Asiv, brandishing his scimitar arrogantly.

'Can truth be defamatory?' Asiv sniffed, lowering his Beak mask over his face. 'Your brother is a craven catamite who parts his buttocks at the drop of a coin – all should know this truth.'

Hajya struggled against her bonds, but they were too strong and her gnosis was bound in a Chain-rune.

And her heart almost stopped when Kyrik appeared at the castle gates, sword in hand, ready to fight his foolish duel. Ready to die.

'This is foolish,' Maegogh rumbled in Kyrik's ear. 'You're throwing your life away.'

Kyrik ignored him and gestured at the guards to pull open the gates, watched by pale-faced Mollachs who didn't see why their king would sacrifice himself for a Sydian woman, much less defend a cowardly frocio, brother or not. A dishonoured man wasn't worth defending.

They don't question Asiv's accusations. To them, Valdyr is still a stranger . . .

He steeled himself for his own end. He would uphold whatever honour the Sarkany name still retained and he would die before his wife was murdered.

'Throwing one's life away needlessly is a time-honoured tradition in Mollachia,' he told the Mantauri chief, then, showing them his argenstael dagger, 'It's our best chance of lopping off the serpent's head.'

The giant Mantaur understood, but he still didn't approve. 'Good fortune to you: but if you fall, your people's resistance will collapse. Who will lead them with you gone?'

No one, Kyrik admitted to himself, but he could not let Asiv's words go unanswered, for that would be to tacitly accept them, which would be just as damaging.

To stay silent is to corrode us all. And in any case, I hate this bastard and I want to hurt him. And I'm right – this is the only chance I'll get at him . . .

'A king must shoulder these burdens,' he replied, looking round. 'Where's Kip?'

'Busy,' the Mantauri chieftain told him.

Kyrik's eyes narrowed. 'I forbid him to intervene.'

Maegogh's inflexible face gave away nothing. 'Shield for all you're worth and move fast, human. Make the fight last.' He clapped Kyrik on the shoulder, almost knocking him over, then the doors swung open and Kyrik's vision became a tunnel that ended with Asiv Fariddan on the far side of the square. The Keshi, wearing his Beak mask, was drawing a dark mist about him as he walked past the well where Hajya hung.

Kyrik took a deep, deep breath, then walked through the gates, his boots echoing on the cobbles. He drew on the gnosis, calling shields and kindling energy on his straight sword. It felt like a tiny spark amid a canopy of night, or a snowflake in Hel.

He felt the same heightened sense of reality he'd experienced in previous fights, intensified because he had no illusion about what he faced. *Tarita might have had a chance against this man, or Waqar: Ascendants and pure-bloods. Not me . . .*

But his hackles rose as he saw the smug face of his foe. He focused on Asiv's blade and feet, the way he moved. *Not a swordsman*, he decided, *but it's barely going to matter . . .*

He put aside Maegogh's cautions and advanced; his good steel sword in his right hand, and a brittle but deadly argenstael dagger in his left.

As they closed, Asiv's left arm came up and Kyrik hurled himself to the left as a wall of force punched towards him; it clipped his shoulder, spinning him sideways, instead of flattening him. He smacked into the ground, rolled and kicked off to his left as a mage-bolt flashed past; a second bolt scorched over him as he threw himself flat with a gasp, then rose and crabbed to the right.

The Gatti mage hadn't moved but was flexing his left hand again–

– and this time a kinesis punch smashed into Kyrik's shields, shoving him twenty feet across the square until his backwards rush was halted by a corpse. Winded and gasping, he threw himself behind, an instant before flames bloomed and engulfed him and the dead man. The body in front charred coal-black with a ghastly stench of cooking meat. Kyrik's hair crisped and his vision turned to dazzled scarlet, but he darted the other way, towards the well.

Asiv still hadn't shifted but his masked face was following Kyrik's jagged advance. His blade hung unused at his side, but his left hand still crackled with energy.

'Come on, Majesty,' he taunted. 'I thought this was supposed to be a duel?'

Move, move, Kyrik told himself, sucking in air, then he stutter-stepped, leaping to the side to avoid the bolt of lightning that cut across his path. He tore at Asiv, swinging his sword in the desperate hope that his foe had used all he had on that bolt, but judging by the kinesis punch that crunched into him an instant later, sending him head over heels and emptying his lungs, Asiv had plenty of juice left in him. The back of his helm crashed against stone and he saw stars.

A mage-bolt sliced through his shields and for a few seconds he jerked and convulsed in agony, dimly aware of Asiv advancing, his clawed hand extended and laughter on his lips.

He dimly heard shouts of dismay and arrows rattled down from the keep battlements as his people forgot the rules of the duel in their despair, but they just shattered impotently on the masked mage's shields; he barely noticed them.

'Too easy,' Asiv remarked, 'barely long enough to be enjoyed. But *this* will be fun – for me, at least.'

The colour of the energies in his left hand changed to pale yellow, then lanced into Kyrik's eyes and suddenly Asiv's voice was inside his head, cackling. He screamed airlessly, his mind imploding as his body went limp . . .

'*Nooo*,' Valdyr howled, grabbing Luhti and hurling her aside. Reaching over his shoulder, he hauled out his zweihandle as the air parted with a tearing of sparks, a gash that billowed into a rent large enough for him to leap through.

He hurtled into the fire-lit square and landed over his brother's broken body, swinging his zweihandle at Asiv's head. The mage's shields went through blue to scarlet and burst apart, but they held enough that the blade only crunched into the copper mask, crumpling it and shattering the Ahmedhassan's right cheekbone and jaw, rather than beheading the man.

The daemon-possessed mage rallied instantly, peeling the smashed mask from his face and conjuring healing energies. His pulverised face began reknitting, but Asiv was laughing.

'Valdyr, little Valdyr, is that all you've got?' he slurred, spreading his hands mockingly, inviting another blow. 'I've had slaps from girls that hurt me more. *But then, you always were my little bitch.*'

His dark eyes flashed and suddenly he was inside Valdyr's head, pulling out those paralysing memories of humiliation, the abuse and rape of a boy who had never known such foul acts even existed. Valdyr felt as if his skin were being peeled aside, his soul displayed for the mockery of the world, and fell to his knees. His blade clattered on the stones as he fell to his knees, helpless and unmanned again, just like every time.

You failed the test. Luhti's voice echoed in his head again. *You're not ready.*

That made him angry – at himself, because he'd come so far and yet gone precisely nowhere. What was the point of the dwyma, of channelling energy and light and life, if you fell apart before your *real* enemy?

You haven't forgiven yourself, Luhti had told him, and she was right, of course, he hadn't forgiven himself, even though he'd been a boy in manacles up against a fully grown man, a half-blood mage who could do whatever he wanted unchecked.

It was not my fault.

That thought, conceived in anger and pain, led to the sudden realisation that weakness of the body does not mean weakness of the soul.

But he was already too late, for Asiv had him locked in a kinesis grip and was standing over him, raising his scimitar for the killing blow . . .

*

Despite his massive frame and hard-earned musculature, Fridryk Kippenegger was the weakest of all magi: a sixteenth-blood who wouldn't even pass the gnosis on to his children. But sometimes, if applied at the right time and place, a little power could go a long way. His old friend Ramon Sensini had taught him that.

Earth- and Water-gnosis were his affinities, and exactly what he needed. From the instant he'd seen Kyrik react to Asiv's challenge, he knew what would happen, and what he needed to do. That half-hour wait gave him just enough time.

Now it was all about how swiftly he and Bromed, a Mantauri who shared the same affinities, could widen the holes that needed widening, how swiftly they could slither through the drains –

– and come up the well-shaft beneath Hajya.

Light was already flashing in the circle of light above and he could sense Asiv's cackling in the aether. Speed was needed, but he kept his draw on the gnosis gentle as he clambered hand over hand, bubbles pouring from his mouth as he rose through the water.

<Tend the woman,> he told Bromed, mind to mind. *<Make her safe, then help me – if Minaus has left you anyone to fight.>*

They went swarming up, propelled by kinesis and raw strength, up to the rim of the well beside a wide-eyed Hajya – and right behind one of the possessed men, who was avidly watching the duel, black saliva running from his torn mouth.

Kip drew his heavy dagger and plunged it overhand through the top of the man's skull and into the brain. The man dropped with a clatter as Kip erupted from the well and hurled a kinesis punch at Asiv's back just as the Ahmedhassan's blade swung at Valdyr's neck.

If Asiv had been ready, he'd not even have staggered – but all his thoughts were bent on the culmination of his conquest of this one victim.

The weak kinesis blow slammed him sideways, the scimitar flashed past Valdyr's crown and buried itself in the stonework with a flash of dark light – and Kip thundered towards them, howling, '*Minaus – blood for Minaus!*'

*

Valdyr saw Asiv fly sideways and the blade that should have left him headless instead plunged into the ground and wedged between two cobbles.

He lunged for his zweihandle as Asiv staggered and turned to face a huge shape that had burst from the well: Fridryk Kippenegger, roaring to his Bullhead God. For a moment he dared hope that Asiv would be too slow—

—and he called upon the dwyma, still wrapped about him, and felt it bloom as swiftly as the gnosis responded to a mage. Light pulsed along his blade as he rose to one knee and launched himself at his nemesis, even as Asiv hurled Kip backwards with a burst of kinesis . . .

Asiv hurled the Schlessen barbarian backwards, roaring in thwarted rage – when a movement caught his eye and he realised that Valdyr was attacking – but he was no longer the little boy he'd pleasured himself upon, but a furious brute of a man with a zweihandle in his hands . . .

But I am an Immortal of Abraxas . . . He recovered his balance, the gnosis cradling him as he evaded Valdyr's blade – then he felt the burning chill of *dwyma* on the blade flashing by him. He leaped aside with kinesis, the fastest response he had, his hand flashed out and he wrenched his scimitar from the cobbles. He gave himself a moment to send a bolt at the fallen Schlessen to keep him down; the blast hammered into the barbarian's torso, searing his armour, and the accompanying burst of mesmeric-gnosis silenced the savage's brain.

'It's just you and me now,' he told Valdyr, taking his guard.

Valdyr roared, swinging at him, and Asiv found himself parrying a blow of real power, but he riposted, slashing the young man's arm and forcing Valdyr backwards.

'Oh, this just gets better and better, you *weakling*.' He prepared a deadly mage-bolt to cripple his foe and take him down so he could end this travesty once and for all.

Around them both, his possessed slaves were erupting from cover to meet the bull-constructs and Mollach fighters pouring from the gates. A storm of arrows sleeted from the battlements, shafts snapping and pinging around him or breaking on his shields: what had been a duel was now open battle –

– and with a savage shriek and thunder of hooves, the warriors of Clan Vlpa poured through the open castle gates, plunging lances through the backs of the possessed legionaries or slashing down at them.

Chaos was erupting on all sides, but Asiv kept his eyes on Valdyr, whose glowing blade was really the only thing here that could hurt him. The young Mollach was moving painfully, his left arm bloodied, but the zweihandle still pulsed with dwyma-energy.

He hurled his most powerful bolt at the young Mollach –

– and stared as the blast dissipated, absorbed by the power that Valdyr had wrapped himself in.

That should not be – can dwyma counter the gnosis? he wondered. *Surely not?*

He tried again, blasting a mage-bolt at Valdyr's head, but again the energy fell apart somewhere after leaving his fingers, and for the first time, Asiv was worried. He howled for his men to protect him, then focused on the thing that mattered: killing Valdyr, as the Master had commanded, and regaining favour . . . and power.

The arrival of Clan Vlpa made Valdyr's heart soar. *Hajya's people*, he thought wildly, *our people*.

Suddenly, this battle no longer felt impossible.

He went at his foe, sustained by the dwyma and by rage, and discovered the two were not inimical. He hacked away at his foe's guard, great bludgeoning two-handed blows that Asiv's scimitar could barely repel. Asiv was no swordsman and stolen knowledge didn't transfer battle reflexes.

I have the dwyma and his daemon powers can't reach me if I don't let them. Our powers have cancelled each other out . . . so this is about blade-work now.

Once in the Dhassan chain-gang, he'd been manacled to another man and made to fight to the death by bored guards. The other man had been driven mad by the sun and brutality, and Valdyr had been petrified – until the first blows. Then he'd fought with as much savagery as his assailant, finally managing to get his hands around the other's throat and holding on through gouging fingers and knees and kicks and punches, until he broke his neck. It was only in Asiv's presence that his courage failed.

But with his brother dying only yards away he refused to fail again.

He battered blow after blow into his foe's guard until he broke through, bypassing a parry that was too slow and plunging his six-foot blade into Asiv's torso, below the ribs. The Ahmedhassan spat blackened blood as the steel lodged in his guts – then and dwyma, life-energy, bloomed in the wound like liquid sunlight, making Asiv's face contort in agony. His black-limned blade fell, the dark energy winking out.

Valdyr lashed out with his boot, caught Asiv in the groin and the Ahmedhassan's face bulged as he folded forward, falling off the blade in his gut and sprawling.

You don't gloat over vipers or rats, his father had once told him. *You just kill them.*

Valdyr gripped his hilt and swung, cleaving through the neck and crunching into the stones, while the severed head rolled away, black blood spraying.

At once every possessed man screamed and faltered, wavering on their feet as the mind controlling theirs was snuffed out. The Mantauri, the Mollach burghers and the Sydian riders rallied and started cutting down their opponents as they reeled helplessly.

Valdyr staggered from the fray and fell to his knees beside his stricken brother. 'Kyrik?'

Kyrik's eyes fell open and he gave him a dazed, disbelieving look. 'Val—'

Then his head fell sideways, but he was breathing.

Thank Kore. Valdyr rose, gripped the zweihandle anew and strode towards the knot of Rondian legionaries still trying to defend themselves. His long blade became a slab of sunlight and without Asiv to counter it, the power ran free as never before.

An hour later, sometime around midnight, Valdyr finally had a respite. Unbelievably, and perhaps barring a few possessed men lurking in hiding, Hegikaro was free.

He looked down from the steps of the keep where he sat, watching

Schlessens, Sydians and Mollachs embracing, pounding each other's backs, sharing food and drink, laughing in the exhilarating relief of unexpected victory and survival. Even the towering bull-headed Mantauri were mingling freely in the glow of aftermath. It was a bawdy, boisterous and beautiful thing, enough to make his eyes sting.

Upstairs, Kyrik and Hajya were unconscious in the royal suite, under constant attention from those with healing skills. Patrols were going door to door, hunting down enemy stragglers, while townsfolk were reuniting families, sharing the relief and the grieving. It was a flowering of every seed his brother had planted here. Music was playing and he spied Rothgar Baredge and Korznici, the Sydian Sfera-witch, dancing slowly, eyes on each other. His smile deepened.

A pair of heavy hands fell on his shoulder, then Kip dropped down on his left and Maegogh on his right, giving the six-foot tall Valdyr the unusual sensation of being dwarfed.

'To the victor,' Kip toasted, raising a tankard of ale and clapping another into Valdyr's hands. 'Minaus is with you, Valdyr Sarkany.'

They all looked up at Asiv's head, spiked above the gates. His body was already ablaze on a bonfire in the market place. Valdyr would as soon have burned the head as well, but trophies mattered here. Though even now, he couldn't quite lose the fear that the head would start speaking.

'You proved him a liar,' Kip added, clanking mugs and taking another giant mouthful.

Did I? I killed him, certainly, but his accusations were mostly true. Then he chastised himself. *No, they weren't: I'm no coward and nothing he did to me was consensual or welcomed. He's gone and now I'm free. My life starts now.*

19

Step Into The Light

Strategy and Tactics

*No strategy survives first contact with the enemy intact: there are too many varia-
bles on the field of battle. This or that attack or defence will fail, units must be
shifted, goals altered. This is the mark of the true commander: not how well he
plans, but how well he improvises when his plan disintegrates.*

GENERAL KALTUS KORION, BRES 914

Bruin River, Rondelmar
Febreux 936

The first few moments were deadly.

As Ostevan's Kirkegarde knights leaped from the rooftops into the
courtyard, most of the Volsai did as Volsai generally do in a fight and
lunged for cover. Apart from Exilium, they were lightly armoured and
trained for stealth, not hand-to-hand combat, nor were they pure-
blooded magi. Lyra reeled in horror as those who could neither shield
nor evade, the nuns and the weakest of the Volsai, went down in
moments.

But Exilium's pale blue shields enveloped Lyra and Coramore; they
instantly went crimson, allowing heat to blaze right through, until
Brigeda stepped over Basia and linked her shields to Exilium's. Between
them, *somehow*, they held.

Basia grabbed Lyra's skirt, hauled herself to her knees and was dazedly fumbling for her blade – then she shrieked, '*Run –*' and shoved Lyra
towards the door behind them.

Lyra clasped Coramore's hand and they obeyed, just in time, for a
dark shape had stormed through the smoke and flame, a battle-axe
cleaving the air where they'd been standing moments before. Exilium
ducked, spun and lashed out; his sword flashed through steel, flesh and
spinal cord and the enemy knight fell backwards. His head rolled in the
other direction, but the Estellan was already flowing into another move,
this time slicing off the sword arm of another knight before kicking
him out of the way to protect the queen's retreat.

Lyra saw Patcheart and, flinching as a mage-bolt flashed past her
face, thrust Coramore towards him. Ostevan was in the courtyard
behind her, plunging his crosier's sharpened tip through the body of a
burned-past-recognition Volsai. Brigeda was hurled through a window,
vanishing in a crash of wood and glass. Then Basia lurched upright
beside Exilium, pale as a ghost, and parried a Kirkegarde; their blades
crashed together – until a blow from behind slammed into her helm
and she collapsed, and suddenly Exilium, beset by two more knights,
found himself being driven back. Basia lay unmoving in the bloody
courtyard as the fighting surged past her.

'Basia!' Lyra shouted, but Patcheart had Coramore in hand and was
hauling them inside.

'Is there a strong-room?' the Volsai captain asked.

'I don't know.' They picked a corridor and ran, followed by Exilium,
guarding their rear from a knot of Kirkegarde. His shields throbbing
scarlet, he twisted athletically, somehow avoiding a massive zweihandle thrust at his chest, which instead plunged into the wall and stuck,
giving him time to dispatch his opponent in a gush of blood.

'Exilium, this way!' Lyra shouted, terrified that Basia was dead
already, and that in a few moments they would be too. But the impera-
tive to survive drove them on.

Patcheart lit a gnosis-light and they ran along the corridor, seeking
anywhere that might offer a chance of refuge. Coramore was screaming
alternately for her brother and for Aradea – and that thought prompted
Lyra, who started calling, *Aradea!* with her mind as they pounded into
the refectory, scattering chairs and tables, with what felt like a never-
ending stream of Kirkegarde at their heels – and hit a dead end. Lyra

flailed left and right, seeking an exit, as Patcheart and Exilium slammed the doors and warded them—

—only for the timbers to explode in their faces. Patcheart lurched drunkenly, a foot-long splinter of wood protruding from his side. His face went white and he fainted away. Exilium was ten feet away, battered against a pillar, his eyes rolling backwards into his skull.

From outside came a measured tread Lyra knew only too well.

Aradea, she pleaded, *help us*.

The green coil of light in her heart bloomed and with it came energy, a surge of glorious *life* running through her. The sensation was like the day she'd summoned light and slain Lef Yarle, but this was different, drawn not from the sun but from *everything*: the people with her, the flowers on the altar, the offerings of fruit and bread and wine, even the air itself.

She felt her aura swell.

Then Ostevan Pontifex stepped into the chapel, smiling beatifically. Exilium tried to rise, but Ostevan backhanded the air, sending a concussive thud of kinesis into the Estellan, whose head cracked against the pillar again and he went still. Coramore gave a small squeak and hugged Lyra's waist.

'Well, Lyra,' Ostevan purred, 'didn't you always know your story would end in a chapel?'

Lyra clung to the dwyma as Ostevan advanced. His eyes shone ebony as he raised his hand and fingers of kinesis sprang half-seen towards her, large enough to engulf her and the princess—

—only to dissolve around her, leaving them both untouched.

For a moment Ostevan snarled in thwarted fury, then he flashed forwards and punched Coramore as she tried with heroic foolishness to protect Lyra, sending her sprawling limp and motionless across the tiles.

The black-eyed cleric focused on Lyra. 'So it appears the Master is right: a full dwymancer's power does cancel out the gnosis when roused,' he said conversationally. 'I guess that just leaves us as we are: a man – and a *weak* woman.'

She reached for her argenstael dagger, but Ostevan was already on her and wrenching the dagger from her grasp, then driving a fist into her stomach. She folded, vomit clogging her throat, and dropped to her knees, gashing them on the stone, her grip on the dwyma wavering. Ostevan yanked her up and threw her onto her back with a snarl, then fell on top of her. The coil of light in her heart was smothered by a vile tentacle of darkness, as Ostevan reached inside her soul, pouring in the emptiness beyond the dwyma, the void of the daemons. It gripped and squeezed, cutting her off from all that she could be, as the man who'd nearly succeeded in seducing her pinned her down and ground himself against her.

'I could kill you with a thought now,' Ostevan gloated, 'but where's the fun in that?'

From outside the chapel came the sounds of screaming women – the last nuns being pursued by the Kirkegarde – but all Lyra could see was Ostevan, his darkly handsome features now perfected to such an extent that he scarcely looked human.

All she felt was utter revulsion.

'Remember our kiss, Lyra?' he purred. 'You should have been mine. All this talk of the Last Days, of daemons ruling Urte? The Master is planning something, you know. "Mother of Daemons", he said to me – and he has *a dwymancer* in his power. So tell me, Lyra, what can he do with a dwymancer in his power? *What can he do?*'

Lyra stared at him, bewildered by the desperation lacing his hunger and lust. Behind the exultation of victory, the possessed priest was clearly *terrified*, but she had no idea what it was he wanted.

'I don't know,' she panted, screaming inside at the touch of his cold hand caressing her cheek while he kneed her skirts up her rigid body.

'What is it Naxius wants? Ostevan demanded, dark drool running from his mouth as he gripped her bodice, ready to tear it open. '*Tell me.*'

She shook her head, squirming in his grip, furious but despairing. How could any *loving* god let one being have this much power over another?

'Life *is* unfair,' Ostevan jeered, hearing her thought. 'Have you not yet learned that lesson? Why does the Master need a dwymancer, Lyra? *Why?*'

321

He ripped open her bodice and gripped her breast painfully. As she stared at him, his face changed: he had reached a decision. With deliberate slowness he pulled her head aside, bent over her throat and elongated his canines – and then he lunged at her and *bit*, those hideous teeth plunging through her skin. Hot ichor gushed into her, sending her into shock.

He murmured, a sensuous exultation that revolted her, as if he'd just climaxed inside her, then stared down at her, straddling her triumphantly.

She tried to fight, but he snuffed out her dwyma effortlessly. 'Dwymancer blood, the sovereign protection,' he jeered, licking his lips. 'Can you feel the ichor inside you, Lyra? Abraxas is coming for you. "The Queen of Death shall lie with Lucian, Lord of the Pit, and become the Mother of Daemons, thus beginning the Last Days",' he quoted. 'In a moment, dear Lyra, you'll finally be my willing queen: my whore.'

In the teeth of utter defeat . . . lay her last, wholly unexpected chance.

With dwymancer blood in his mouth, Ostevan acquired the subliminal knowledge required to cut off Lyra from the dwyma – but when his ichor entered her veins, she gained the same thing.

Immobilised beneath him, fighting a rising tide of daemonic voices, Lyra felt his gnostic grip on her fail, so only his physical dominance remained. He was still stronger than her, but her arms were suddenly freed–

–and lying on the ground close at hand lay the little weapon Ostevan had so contemptuously thrown aside.

Lyra seized it and stabbed it into his breast with all the strength and hatred in her heart.

The *argenstael* dagger pierced his chest – and she pulled it out and stabbed again, and *again and again and again*, roaring in fury and rage and dread for all the horror this man had wrought in her life, rolling onto him and hammering the blade into him *over and over and over again*, at something that spat and snarled and wailed and babbled and pleaded and clawed at her ineffectually, while the dwyma burst back into her and the blade went glowing white, and still she struck, *over and over and over* . . .

Gentle arms wrapped round her from behind and pulled her away, leaving the argenstael stiletto buried in what had once been Ostevan Pontifex and was now nothing but a burned and blasted husk, his face a blackened skull howling at the oncoming darkness. As she watched, his ribcage crumbled into ash. Inside it lay a daemon-spawn, immolated and lifeless.

'Lyra, daughter,' her father said in her ear, 'he's dead. *Ostevan is dead.* You killed him.'

It took a moment to process that, and another to understand that it was Dirklan holding her, with a crowd of fresh faces at his back, and that pulled her back to the present, and the realisation that the daemon was silent, that somehow its ichor had burned away inside her.

She didn't know how – not yet – but it felt hugely significant.

Life is stronger than death, she thought dizzily.

She tried to speak, but instead collapsed into her father's arms. His voice filled her head, something like balm flooded her brain and drew her down into a soft, pillowed darkness –

– until she surfaced again, blinking, to find herself sitting upright on a pew in a chapel, her father's arm over her shoulder, supporting her. Someone had dressed her, somehow managing to mend her ripped bodice, and her bruises and grazes were gone.

Lyra looked around and saw Coramore was being tended by Mort Singolo. Exilium, propped against a wall, was talking to Brigeda with what looked remarkably like camaraderie. Only when she saw a body-shaped mound covered by a tablecloth on the floor did she remember her berserk frenzy.

Ohmigod dear Kore he –

'Hush,' Dirklan said. 'Don't think about it. I've done what I can, but you need to keep your mind quiet. The best mystic-healers in Pallas will attend you on our return.'

Her grim father looked as steely-eyed as she'd seen him, completely the *Wraith*, oozing menace and vengeance – but that malice was entirely directed at the dead Pontifex.

He's used mysticism to suppress my reaction, she realised. *He's numbed the memory . . .*

She could remember the broad facts: she'd been bitten, then killed her assailant. But she didn't *feel* like she had gone through these things, or at least, not recently; it was like a distant memory, a very bad thing that had happened a long time ago. She didn't know how she might feel about that in the future, but for now it was a relief, because her sanity felt very, *very* fragile right now.

Then Basia limped over to her, awkward with concern. 'Milady?'

'Dear Kore – Basia, are you all right? Should you be walking?'

Basia gave a sharp cackle. 'You should see the other bastard. Got him good.' She glowered around the room, then she pulled aside the tablecloth and studied Ostevan's corpse, with the argenstael dagger still planted in his blasted chest. 'All hail the mighty letter-opener,' she intoned gravely.

She hugged Lyra, then teetered towards Exilium, shooing Brigeda away. 'Don't worry, I'll have this idiot up and daemon-slaying again before you know it.'

Dirklan helped Lyra stand, then went to Patcheart's sprawled body. He held a hand to his throat, then breathed a sigh of relief. 'If we were paid by the wound, we'd be rich men,' he remarked. 'Ostevan's minions became disoriented when he fell, but they'll recover soon enough and we're miles from safety. I'm sorry, everyone, but we have to get out of here.'

Lyra made herself look at Ostevan. *I killed him*, she reminded herself, *and he deserved it, ten times over*.

She took a deep breath,. 'Let's burn the bodies of our enemies and go.'

Basia winked at Brigeda. 'Coo, get her.'

'Bloodthirsty bitch, that one,' Brigeda smirked. 'Wanna join the Volsai, Majesty?'

Lyra felt something like the fellowship she sometimes felt around the council table when everyone agreed – but somehow, this was purer.

She grinned. 'No way – I've heard the boss is a right bastard to work for.'

PART TWO

The Masquerade (The Puppeteer)

The Night of Ghosts

In the Book of Kore, the Last Days is preceded by the Night of Ghosts when it is said that all the dead shall return to life to face the judgement of Corineus, which will determine who will ascend to Paradise and who will be left on Urte as the prey of daemons. We pray for the coming of that Blessed Night, when we who are true to our Lord shall ascend to his side.

ARCH-PRELATE ACRONIUS, PALLAS 452

Rym, Rimoni
Martrois 936

The lean, redheaded man with the perfectly symmetrical face strode into the middle of the small theatre, a glowing worm of light linking his hands to a quill floating over a piece of parchment ready on the lectern. The semi-circular row of seats facing him was entirely empty.

He lifted his hands, cleared his throat and began to declaim – and the quill began to write by itself, capturing his words for posterity, just as the Rimoni senators had used scribes to record their speeches and render their words immortal. The more vainglorious of those senators had even published speeches they'd never given, just to reveal their intellects.

I am a giant, compared to those puny inbreeds, Naxius sneered inwardly. *My words will resonate for ever – and I'll be around to ensure they do.*

He lifted his head and addressed the empty room – and eternity.

'Most men have small dreams,' he began, 'but I, Ervyn Naxius, have always dreamed *large*. Such genius is often misunderstood, even ridiculed.' He drew himself up and placed his hand on his heart, proudly enumerating his feats. 'The empire rejected me because I would not genuflect to their mythology of Kore and Corineus and the divinity of the magi – even though I wrote half their damned *Book of Kore* for them.'

He laughed at the irony, his mirth echoing around the empty theatre.

'Even the Ordo Costruo, who claim to serve knowledge, hated me, so mired were they in their hypocrisy, betraying me with their petty jealousies and lily-livered envy. Like cooks afraid to break an eggshell, yet still believing they could learn the recipe of Creation. Only a few of them were worth a damn and they were hounded as I was.'

He raised his eyes to the ceiling and asked the silence, 'What difference is there, really, between experimenting on people and experimenting on animals when humans *are* animals, after all. Why waste effort and materials testing on rats, when bipedal rats trundle past our doors every day? Most humans add *nothing* to the sum of life – those whom I utilised did at least contribute to the wider pool of knowledge.'

The silence seemed to understand.

'Once – and yes, I will admit it – I hated my Ordo Costruo colleagues, especially that pompous, supercilious craven Antonin Meiros. But I am above such feelings now: why should a god envy? Why should an immortal hate? No, that would be wasted energy.' He raised a hand to the heavens and shouted, 'Let the "gods" envy me.'

He chuckled at his own sly wit.

'Of course, there are no gods, just men who imagine them, and daemons who are really just the ghosts of men come back to haunt us.' He tapped the *Book of Kore* sitting on the lectern beside the scratching quill. 'I myself wrote the passages about the Last Days. At the time I saw them as a morality story to make the ignorant tremble in fear, a whip to hold over their psyches: *Obey the emperor or the daemons will come – worship my imaginary God or you'll suffer for eternity.* What utter shit . . .

But when I was cast out, first from the Church and then the Ordo Costruo, I thought, *Why not?* And my instincts were sound: life is a brief flame and only the dark is eternal. Therefore, the only lasting allegiance worth giving, is to that darkness.'

He licked his lips, and beamed. 'Let's be clear: there is no Kore, no Ahm, no Vishnarayan or Sol – there are only the mighty hive-minds of the aether, *the daemons*. They are the ultimate outcome to which all life proceeds, *and we exist to feed them*. Their ascendancy is inevitable, so to resist is futile and self-defeating. But to seek accommodation with that inevitability? In our ignorance, that is the step the world hesitates to take. Only a true genius has the wit to *embrace* it.'

The room fell silent as he contemplated this revelation.

'When I was rejected by my peers,' he added, 'I resolved to bring my own prophecy into being: to end life as we know it and bring about the reign of the daemons – with myself as their king, just as I "foretold" in the *Book of Kore*.' He chuckled. 'I dare to dream large.'

The quill stopped moving as his words faded into the air. He bowed, then left the theatre, silent applause ringing in his ears.

The quill fell lifeless onto the parchment.

An hour later Naxius emerged from a steaming bath and stopped before a mirror to examine the lean, redheaded man with piercing eyes smiling back at him. *Strange: when given the choice of any body at all, one gravitates to one's own features and form, however imperfect*. Though he'd made improvements, of course; he'd never been quite so rakish or toned in his youth.

He dressed and walked into the next room, where Jehana Mubarak, skull-masked and white-haired, was writhing in the grip of the endless daemon-visions. Judging by her appearance – her shift was stained with blood, piss and faeces; vomit was caked around her mouth and gashes scoured her arms where she'd torn at herself – her senses were clearly overwhelmed with whatever murder, torture, rape or infection she was currently experiencing. A gurgle escaped her mouth, the closest she could come to a scream when her body was parched and shaking with weakness.

He studied her for a moment without pity. *Much more will likely kill her.*

With a careful touch to the mask, he dissipated the spell linking her to the master-daemon Abraxas and fed her energy to aid her recovery. Her shaking subsided, then slowly, fearfully, she opened her eyes.

He enjoyed watching her expression change as the horror of recognition bloomed. She shot backwards like a frightened beetle, fell from the pallet and huddled in a foetal ball on the floor, whimpering and shaking.

He summoned possessed slave-women. 'Yes, you're back,' he told her. 'You need sustenance before you return to the daemon's mind.'

'No . . .' she pleaded weakly, looking up at him with haunted eyes, trying to express something. He bent his ear to her mouth and heard, *'Please, make it stop.'*

'I'm afraid I have no choice, my dear,' he told her, an entirely false note of regret in his voice. 'All of Urte must suffer, and you must bear witness. That's how this works – unless you've changed your mind?' He stroked her arm gently, thinking that even broken and disfigured, she was a lovely creature: a worthy queen. 'When the daemons rule, only the sinners will suffer. Wouldn't it be better to allow the deserving to ascend to Paradise and let the End of Time begin?'

He gestured, and one of the slave-women gave Jehana water. Once she had soothed her raw throat enough to speak, she rasped, 'What must I do?' Her voice was laden with despair.

He smiled warmly. *At last, we're making progress.*

20

Against the Omens

The Limits of Divination

The Gnostic Study of Divination concerns communing with the spirit world to ascertain the most likely outcomes of human interaction. It predicts a future, but it makes no claims that the future is set in stone. How do we reconcile this to the Book of Kore, which reveals a fated end? According to the Book, the main passages of which predate the gnosis by centuries, Urte is pre-destined to destruction in the Last Days – and yet divination predicts no such ending.

COVIS BALDYN, HOLLENIAN MAGE-SCHOLAR, DAMSTADT 817

Pallas, Rondelmar
Martrois 936

With the Volsai on their venators arrayed around her, Lyra took Pearl swooping down to land on Sertanus Parade, the huge flat grounds outside the walls of Pallas. She was still traumatised by how close she'd come to extinction – or worse. Every time Ostevan's leering face flashed into her mind, paralysing her, she had to remind herself, *It doesn't matter what he nearly did. He's gone now.*

She could feel an almighty collapse waiting inside her, but so far she'd managed to hold it at bay. There was too much at stake, too many urgent things to deal with, so right now, she had to keep moving. She could break down once she'd saved the empire . . .

Pearl's hooves struck the ground lightly and they went from gallop to canter to a gentle walk until Lyra, feeling battered, could slide off gratefully – her first successful dismount.

I'll never ride without a saddle again, she vowed. *Never.*

Dirklan and Basia landed, gave their own beasts to the waiting attendants and joined her. She clung to her father as they walked towards the waiting carriages, Exilium following with Coramore in his arms.

'Do not *ever* leave us like that again,' her father was admonishing her.

'I didn't think I had time–' she tried to say, but all she managed was 'I didn't think . . .' which probably summed things up more accurately. 'But we got Coramore back,' she added.

'A successful outcome doesn't forgive the risks you took,' her father growled. Then he fell silent as a bulky shape emerged from one of the carriages and Grand Prelate Dominius Wurther waddled towards them, his face anxious.

'Your Majesty? You're safe, thank Kore. Setallius tells me nothing.' As he neared, he asked, 'What happened?'

She gestured to Coramore. 'Somehow she escaped Dupenium and managed to call me through the dwyma.'

Wurther's eyes bulged as he made the sign of the dagger to absolve her heresy. 'She shares your . . . er . . . gift?'

'I think perhaps when Aradea cleansed her of the daemon ichor after Reeker Night, she marked her for the dwyma,' Lyra told him. 'She has the potential. Thankfully, Ostevan didn't kill her when he had the chance.'

Wurther's face looked apoplectic and he stammered, '*Ostevan was there? Then–?*'

Dirklan turned and called Brigeda, who was trailing them, lugging a large box in her arms. She caught up and flipped the lid, revealing Ostevan's head, blackened and eyeless, but the hair and shape rendered it recognisable.

'Kore's Blood,' the Grand Prelate blasphemed, his face swelling with pleasure. 'How?'

Lyra felt a sudden overwhelming sense of martial pride, unlike anything she'd ever experienced, and she rather shocked herself at the ferocious satisfaction which filled her as she said, 'I killed him – I stabbed the rukking bas–'

Her voice broke and she had to turn away and hug her father until she regained composure. 'I'm sorry, Grand Prelate, my language . . .'

The stunned Dominius stepped in and engulfed her in stiff brocade and wine fumes. 'You are truly the answer to all my prayers, my Queen.'

For a moment, Lyra wondered what the watching soldiers and servants were making of queens and prelates and Volsai lords hugging each other, then decided she didn't really care. Despite all the treacherous, self-serving things Dominius had done, he'd always been her favourite 'Uncle'. She let him fuss over her, his care cleansing her just a little more, which gave her the strength to straighten her back and ask Brigeda to close the box.

'Put it on a spike,' Wurther said. 'We want the whole world to know he's dead.'

'See to it, Briggy,' Dirklan said. 'Put it on the Traitor's Nails above the main gates to the Place d'Accord and we'll issue fresh proclamations of Imperial support for the rightful Head of the Church.'

'Indeed,' Lyra agreed. 'You must reunite your Church, Grand Prelate, behind our respective thrones.'

Dominius inclined his head, his eyes were twinkling at the prospect. 'By this evening, there won't be a clergyman in the empire who does not cleave to you as our ruler, my Queen.'

She gave his hand a squeeze, then Dirklan helped her into one of the carriages. A grey-clad healer with milky eyes and a kind smile wrapped a thick blanket around her and placed fingertips against her temple.

The rest of the journey to the Bastion was a blur.

Lyra woke to a strange, hollowed out feeling inside. It took a long time to remember who she was, where she was, who the sweet-faced girl holding a tray of food was and what anything she'd just said meant.

After a while she recognised that she'd been bathed and smelled of rosewater – and somehow the blood and violence of the night had been washed away as well.

The strange-eyed healer-mage sat beside her on her bed. When she stroked her forehead, Lyra felt something like a finger inside her head, caressing her senses. 'There, your Majesty,' the healer said, not quite looking at her. 'You may feel a certain emotional distance for a few days and the recollections of last night will be hazy for a while, but it won't last. In time you'll recall the events clearly, and you must deal with those memories – I can help you through that. What will matter is that you endured and triumphed. You've been through some harrowing times, Majesty, but you've endured.'

'Somehow . . .' Lyra conceded, 'although some days it feels like everything I do is a mistake.'

'We all have those days, Majesty.'

'What's wrong with your eyes?' Lyra asked, unthinkingly.

'I was born blind,' the healer replied tolerantly. 'The damage was irreparable, but the gnosis is versatile, so I manage. There have been bad times, but I too endure.'

'What's your name?'

'Selea, Majesty. I was House Fasterius until I took my vows as a Sister of Healing.'

The Imperial Healers take vows to heal any person, regardless of who they are, Lyra remembered. *But nevertheless, I've just been healed by an 'enemy'. How wonderful.*

'Thank you, Selea.' She smiled, feeling further cleansed knowing that she was not alone in believing political allegiances meant less than bettering lives.

But the day wouldn't wait: Selea was replaced by Nita with Rildan, giving Lyra a few precious moments salving her emotions with her son's cherubic face. She could have spent all day that way, but she returned him to Nita and dressed, then joined Dirklan and Basia on the balcony, where they were watching the smoke hanging over the city like a shroud.

'The riots are getting worse,' Dirklan told her. 'They're not even bothering with speeches to incite the mob any more. It's virtually open war. Our soldiers are chaffing at not being permitted to strike back.'

'Then convene the Royal Council, Lord Setallius. The Dupeni and the Corani renegades will reach us very soon, the city is ablaze and the Pontifex is dead. We have a lot to do.'

Dirklan hesitated. 'Lyra, if you can't face –'

She tried not to let her annoyance show. 'I'll be fine, Father, as long as I'm active.'

'Of course.'

While he instructed an aide, Lyra asked Basia, 'How is Coramore? And Exilium . . . and you? How did you even survive?'

'The girl's sleeping and Exilium's already on his feet. And I'm fine,' Basia replied, despite the fact that she looked battered. Healing-gnosis had at least faded her bruises to yellow-purple. 'Dirk's lads broke in seconds after you and Exilium got out, so I was never alone.' She handed Lyra an envelope. 'This was handed to the guards at Greengate. I don't know if it's genuine.'

The name on the envelope read 'Lyra Vereinen' with no titles. It was still sealed, for whatever that was worth. She opened it and read aloud.

Lady, I must speak with you. I swear the attack at the church was not my doing. I beg you, please meet with me. Leave a note with the guard at the place I left this. Ari F.

Lyra looked at Dirklan, feeling both surprise and vindication. 'I told you Frankel only wanted to talk.'

'That may be, but this could still be a trap. I counsel you to ignore it.'

'I'll think about it.' She pocketed the note. 'Allow me an hour, then we'll sit down and prepare for the council meeting.'

When Lyra entered the council chamber, she found her counsellors already gathered. Dominius Wurther was gnawing on a roasted pig's trotter with an expression of smug contentment. Calan Dubrayle, in contrast, looked pale, tense and harassed. Oryn Levis was drained, and her spymaster was yawning.

'Gentlemen.' She smoothed her favourite green Corani gown and settled on the throne. 'I think you all know that this morning, I was assailed by Ostevan Pontifex while protecting Princess Coramore Sacrecour at an abbey in Bruinland. With the aid of my bodyguards and the Volsai, we were able to rescue Coramore – she's resting now, after her terrible ordeal. And most of all, we slew the false Pontifex.'

'All Koredom praises your name for that,' Dominius said boisterously. 'Heaven praises your name.'

'Indeed, we all give thanks,' Calan added.

'A great victory,' Oryn agreed. 'Though the risk–'

'Yes, it was a rash adventure,' Dirklan put in sharply. 'One we should not repeat.'

'If I hadn't heeded Coramore's call, you would never have allowed me to go to her,' Lyra said, unrepentant. 'Why should others always take risks on my behalf?' Knowing there to be a welter of valid arguments against that stance, she moved straight on. 'Tell me what's happening in the city.'

Oryn answered. 'Majesty, we have only seven legions left: two Corani and four imperial and one Kirkegarde. Garod has nine and Takwyth seven, including four of Hollenian mercenaries. At seven against sixteen, that's less than one to two odds, which might still be considered sufficient if we held the city properly. But the Kirkegarde are in the Celestium—'

'Where they belong,' Dominius put in. 'I am just as much a prize for our enemies as you, Majesty, and Garod could assail either side of the river.'

'We've also got one of the imperial legions on the Southside,' Oryn interjected, 'which leaves just five to protect Pallas-Nord, except that right now two of our legions are trying to keep the rebels penned in Tockburn and Kenside. If we are to free them up, we must crush this rebellion. Please, give me leave to treat these arsonists and vandals as enemy soldiers.'

'They are our citizens,' Lyra shot back. 'No, we continue to contain them.'

'They're wearing red roses, Milady, signifying that they are willing to bleed for their cause; and they're being armed by smugglers. My men are beside themselves with frustration at this policy of restraint.'

'No.'

Oryn looked skywards, the most open dissent the usually placid knight had ever shown, but he went on doggedly, 'We have only three units to defend Pallas-Nord – and most of our Corani don't wish to fight against Takwyth's men – their kinsmen and comrades, Majesty. They are begging us to find common cause with him.'

'Common cause?' Lyra asked sharply.

Oryn looked away. 'They wish you to repair relations with Lord Takwyth and Duke Torun, Majesty.'

'Marry him, you mean?'

'Some are saying that, yes. Others just want you to bury your differences.' He looked down miserably.

It's what he wants too . . . Her hackles rose. 'I will never, *ever* marry that man. I will never look at him again, unless it's at his head on a spike beside Ostevan's. *Never*, you hear me?'

When Oryn nodded sullenly, she pointed out, 'I thought we agreed you were to bring your men to my way of thinking, not you to theirs.'

'But Corani shouldn't fight Corani, Milady,' he tried. 'Surely some compromise can be found?'

'That man tried to *enslave* me – and he still wishes to do so. Why is that so hard to understand?' She sighed, and changed the subject. 'What of Argundy?'

'The ambassador has prepared a proposal, Majesty,' Dirklan told her, his voice flat. 'Prince Andreas has flown to Delph in anticipation and the Argundians have their barges ready on the Siber River. They could have their legions here before the Sacrecours if we come to an agreement today.'

Andreas. The thought of yet another man left her cold. 'I need to think,' she told them. 'Tell the ambassador I will give him a firm answer tomorrow.'

'But tomorrow—' Oryn began.

'Tomorrow,' she snapped. 'Last night I had other things on my mind, gentlemen. You must give me time.'

They all looked at the spymaster as if to say, *She's your daughter, you talk to her.*

'With respect,' Dirklan started unwillingly, 'tomorrow may be too late.'

'Dear Kore, it's midday and I've just killed a man who violated my brain and was about to destroy my soul! When have I even had a chance to think of a *rukking* marriage?'

She put her hand to her mouth, appalled with herself, because she *never* used to swear. 'I'm sorry – I'm so sorry. I'm not myself.'

'We're all under pressure, Majesty,' Dominius rumbled, bless him, 'and indeed, we hear your anguish. Let the world await your pleasure. A decision such as this must be correct, as well as timely.'

Correct ... meaning Andreas ... 'Do we have a choice?' she asked plaintively.

'Only an alliance with Argundy will truly alter the equations, Majesty,' Calan replied.

'Unless you are able to once more unleash the force of nature upon Garod's men?' Oryn put in quietly.

She flinched. 'No, I . . . I just can't. I still have nightmares about that night.'

'Milady, if you are unwilling to fight them your way, we must fight our way – and men will die, including those loyal to you.'

'I know.' She bowed her head. 'Tomorrow. Give me tonight to think and tomorrow I will decide everything.'

Abruptly, she felt exhausted, unable to go on. The next most pressing matter was the banking proposal, and only Calan and Dirklan were privy to that line of action. 'Gentlemen, I know there's other business: I give you leave to discuss it and report to me later. I must rest.'

She stood, making them all do the same, then wearily shuffled out.

'They'll manage without me,' she muttered to Basia, standing guard at the door. 'I need rest.' But Rildan would be asleep and she was loathe to disturb him – then she realised what she really needed. 'Let's go to my garden.'

Lyra went ahead, wanting space to think alone, and Basia was content to clip along behind as she wound through the keep to her garden, then drifted through the twisted roses. They were stark and bare, but birds were twittering avidly, and once a fox appeared, tossed its head then flitted away silently.

Beside the pool at the heart of the garden, they found Pearl, grazing placidly. Lyra stroked her head and flanks, then turned back to Basia. 'Could I have a moment, please?' When Basia hesitated, she added, 'I won't fly off again, I promise.'

The bodyguard reluctantly returned to the seat in the roses, while Lyra knelt, cupped water and drank, which helped as much as any mystic healing to make her feel whole again. After communing a while with the dwyma, feeling Aradea in the wind and water, she opened herself to the dwyma, and distantly sensed Valdyr of Mollachia, but she didn't want to see him just yet, not so soon after the horrors of the night. So she soaked up the weak sunlight, breathing deeply as calmness stole over her.

I endured. I will endure.

When Lyra rose stiffly, she found herself shivering. Clouds now hemmed in the remaining blue and Pearl had flapped away, hopefully to the stables. Basia had dozed off and Lyra had to shake her awake, which made her smile and embarrassed Basia hugely.

'Thanks for keeping watch,' Lyra teased. 'Go and rest – Exilium will be waiting upstairs for his shift.'

Basia gave her a grateful look and hurried off. Lyra was making her way to the stairs to her balcony above when a muffled voice called out from Greengate, 'Milady?'

She looked around and saw the two guards had a man with them. He was heavily wrapped against the cold, most of his face hidden by a scarf.

'Yes?'

The man went to call again, but one of the guards cuffed him around the ear. 'Oi, shut it,' he growled. 'Her Majesty don' talk to the likes o' you.'

Lyra peered at him curiously, then stared. *Dear Kore . . .* She knew she should be shouting, *It's him – arrest him–*

Instead, she croaked, 'Admit him.'

The guards looked at her in surprise. 'Majesty?'

'Test him with silver, take any weapons, then admit him.'

The two men shared an uneasy look. 'Lord Setallius, 'e'll 'ave our guts if'n we let a fella in 'ere, Milady.'

'I think *I* was still queen, last time I checked?'

The two men swallowed. One pulled out a large silver coin and pressed it to Ari Frankel's face, but there was no physical reaction. The other patted him down thoroughly before reluctantly – *very* reluctantly – letting him in.

Lyra greeted him in a low voice, for his ears alone. 'So, Master Frankel: you wish to talk?'

*

Ari followed the queen up the wrought-iron spiral stair that led from Greengate to a balcony two or three storeys above. *This is the Royal Suite*, he realised.

He hadn't truly believed she would see him; instead expecting to be locked up, especially as he was right now, unwashed and whiskery and jumping at shadows. But he'd had to try. Being admitted to her private rooms, warm, sweet-smelling and full of beautiful things, was surreal. He felt like a wild animal that'd somehow wandered inside.

A serving girl carrying a grizzling child in her arms came in. She looked at him with disapproving surprise but no recognition as the queen indicated a chair, then accepted the baby. 'Tea, please, Nita,' Lyra said.

'Shall I tell Exilium that you've . . . um . . .'

'Got company? Yes, please.'

'I'll let him know. Lord Setallius has repaired Basia's legs and Exilium is seeing to her.'

Lyra laughed. 'Exilium is *seeing to* Basia?'

Nita went scarlet. 'I m-mean, helping her, um, adjust them,' she stammered.

'I'm teasing,' Lyra told the maid. 'Tell him I'm in no danger.' She waited until Nita had gone, jiggling and comforting her child until he settled, then she looked at Ari. 'I'm not in any danger am I, Master Frankel?'

Ari shook his head firmly. 'You've never been in physical danger from me, Lady.'

'Yes, that's right: you threaten only my crown and my neck,' Lyra said drily. She dandled her son, cooing. 'And this little fellow's future – indeed, his very life.'

Ari blushed. 'That's not very fair, Milady.'

'Isn't it?'

They fell silent as Nita returned with a tray laden with cups and a steaming teapot, then slipped out. Ari felt his mind begin to engage. He'd been hiding with Tad Kaden as the streets turned to chaos; he couldn't waste this opportunity.

'Why should one baby have his future guaranteed?' he asked. 'Everyone else must struggle.'

'So your politics are those of envy, then?'

'They are the politics of justice – one man –' He saw her eyes narrow and interrupted himself. 'One *person*, one vote: a meritocracy, based upon suffragium. If your son proves his excellence, then he will win that ballot and take his *term* as ruler.'

'If my son doesn't inherit, it'll be because his mother is dead, and all those who protect him. I've got two armies marching to claim my throne, Master Frankel. They don't want suffragium, they want my bloodline to perish.'

'But your *people* want suffragium,' he told her earnestly. 'Tens of thousands of people have heard my words, maybe *hundreds* of thousands. Every day we take more of the city. Don't you see? This isn't a movement about dynastic squabbling. The people are the nation and they deserve their fair share.'

She threw him a bitter look. 'Your mobs are destroying the city and making damn sure that our defences will crumble when Garod or Takwyth arrive. And I've got bad news for you: those bastards are even less likely to give you what you want than I am.'

She and Takwyth were lovers not so long ago, Ari thought. He'd seen it in their body language the day he'd been reprieved from execution. *What happened?* he wondered, then thrust that thought aside. 'But you acknowledge that I might persuade you?' he asked nimbly.

'I wouldn't get your hopes up. I've fought with all my being against more implacable enemies than you. Some days I hate what I must do: I wish most devoutly that I'd been forgotten in my obscure monastery. But that didn't happen. They're all counting on me – all my Pallacians and Corani, all my loyal subjects. And my son.' She stroked the child's head, her eyes moist and her voice fragile. 'What's it all for, if not for him?'

'Is this truly the life you want?' he asked gently. 'And for your son?'

'What *I* want doesn't matter. Empires don't fade, they fall, and so do rulers. The red carpet before the throne is coloured with the blood of rivals – everyone knows that. I must hold the throne or I'll end up with my head on a spike, and Rildan's too. That's the savage truth. Rulers don't let rival claimants live.'

'The task itself is killing you,' he told her. Up close he could see the crow's feet and furrows: more lined than a young woman's should be. *She's ageing before my eyes.* 'You aren't a natural ruler.'

'Am I not?' she retorted angrily. 'Kore's Blood, I've read every treatise on kingship ever written and I have learned on the job. I've had counsellors betray me and assassins shoot at me. I've had Reeker hordes climbing my walls and I've come *this close* to death' – she held her thumb and forefinger just a hair's-breadth apart – 'as recently as this morning. But you know what? I'm *good* at it this rukking *impossible* job. I can read the accounts and understand what they're telling me. I can see through Dubrayle and Wurther's shenanigans and I can puzzle my way through a bill of law. I can speak to a crowd and address a court and I can tell a just decision from a corrupt one. So don't bloody tell me I can't do the job –'

'I don't say you *can't* do it,' he said quickly. 'Quite the opposite. I've learned of late that you do it as well as anyone ever has. But it's the whole institution of kingship that's morally wrong and utterly inefficient. How many good kings have there ever been? Most are venal, bloodthirsty nepotistic tyrants who treat their people as slaves and expend all their energy on self-aggrandisement and conspiracy.'

'I'm not like them.'

'I know that now: you're a flower among thorns, Lady, truly, or else we wouldn't even be having this conversation. But don't you think that the people should have the ruler they *want*, someone who actually wants to rule *for* them, not *over* them? Is that not what Kore would want? What decency and humanity demands?'

She stared at him with hollow eyes. 'You're dreaming, Ari. In the real world, men with swords and the gnosis take whatever they want.' She shuddered, looking away. 'This morning, I was attacked by a mage. He gripped me in a kinesis-spell, held me utterly immobile while he . . .' Her voice tailed off.

She shuddered, then rallied. 'I stabbed him to death. He'll never misuse another being again. But Takwyth would do the same to me, and so would Garod and any other of these "noble" lords. Men with swords take whoever and whatever they want: *that* is the world we live in.'

He shuddered in sympathy, trying to find words to reach through that horror. 'Lady, I was once a priest. The *Book of Kore* says those with the most must serve those with the least. For all the flaws of that book, I still hold to that sentiment. To rule must be to serve – and only suffragium can give that to society: a system where men are willing not just to take up authority, but to also lay it down in turn, according to the people's will. If political rivals accepted that their contest should be with votes, not sword, that regimes can change without blood, would it not be better?'

'You're even more naïve than I thought,' Lyra said bitterly. 'No one willingly surrenders power.'

'Milady, I'm not naïve.' Ari sat forward. 'There's only one way your rule can be preserved through the coming crisis. You've got just days before your enemies arrive, and you don't even know if your own soldiers will fight. Your forces are divided by the river – and Dominius Wurther can't be trusted; everyone knows he's only concerned with his own survival. Argundy could intercede, but Rondians have always hated Argundians and the moment you announce any kind of alliance with them, you'll instantly lose half your support and any troops Argundy sends will be besieged in the Bastion while Pallas burns. Garod will never reach accommodation with you, and I imagine Takwyth has only one use for you. You've got one chance. Me.'

She stared silently at him, her eyes narrowing, and he was struck again by her incredible tolerance, because anyone else would have had him dragged off to the dungeons by now.

'What *one chance* is that?' she demanded at last.

Her voice told him that he must deliver now, or he'd lose her.

'Join the rebellion,' he told her.

'*What?*' She reached for her bell.

'Wait – please, think about it, Milady – Lyra. Right now you're fighting on too many fronts: Takwyth, Garod, us . . . You're outnumbered *and* having to watch your back at every stage. But what if you commit to *reform*: to dismantling the monarchy and instituting the regime the people want – a *res publica*? Then you'll no longer be facing *internal* enemies: Pallas will be united behind you. Your enemies will be the ones who're outnumbered, outside the walls.'

He watched her think, her journey from instinctive refusal to consideration, until the narrowing of her eyes signalled real recognition of opportunity.

Seeing that, he pressed on: 'To create a true suffragium, with all senior public offices subject to a ballot, takes time – but you could start tomorrow by allowing citizen representatives onto your ruling council and setting a date for elections.'

She stared at him, then said, 'Not so naïve after all, are you?'

'I'm learning as swiftly as I can, Milady.' This wasn't a new thought, after all; he'd been talking ideas through with Tad Kaden and to his surprise, the mage-thief had been supportive, if less than optimistic.

'Milady, we know that Garod Sacrecour and Solon Takwyth despise our movement, but I believe you are sympathetic to the plight of ordinary people. Lives have grown harder since your reign began' – he raised a hand to still her retort – 'because of the mess the Sacrecours left after the Third Crusade. We all know that. There is huge energy for change, Milady. If you harness it, perhaps you'll be able to ride this out.'

She held up her hand in turn, so he fell silent, and tried the tea untouched in his cup. It was lukewarm, but easily the best he'd ever tasted. He looked longingly at the pot, then returned to studying his adversary.

Or ally.

He stiffened as her face hardened and she picked up her hand-bell and rang it. A moment later, Exilium stepped in. He guessed he'd been listening at the door, because he expressed no surprise at seeing him, only frank distaste.

'Milady?'

'Tell Dirklan I wish to see him.'

A dark shadow with silver hair covering half the face appeared behind the bodyguard. 'As it happens, I'm also here, Majesty. I was informed you were entertaining and thought I might be required.'

'Do I have no privacy?' Lyra asked tartly.

The spymaster glided into the room and fixed Ari with his single cold eye. 'You ignored my advice to leave Pallas, Master Frankel.' The Volsai commander's gaze was as chilling as Lazar.

But Ari didn't flinch. 'I have a mission.'

'And I have a job.' Setallius turned to Lyra. 'What is it you want, Majesty?'

'Your opinion.'

The spymaster glanced meaningfully at Ari and the queen nodded. 'Master Frankel, Exilium will take you to my waiting room. If you require more tea – or something stronger – just ask.'

Is that all the time I get? Ari thought indignantly. *This is my whole life's purpose and you spare me no more than a few minutes?*

But he recognised that pressing her further might alienate whatever tentative rapport they'd forged. He bowed and followed the bodyguard to a small room dominated by a portrait of Magnus Sacrecour, Lyra's grandfather. It reminded him that while she represented a new dynasty, she also represented continuity with the men and women who'd ruled the world for five centuries.

He took a seat on a small sofa and looked up at the man closing the door.

Exilium leaned against the wall. 'How many people have died because of you, you smart-mouthed piece of shit?' he asked, his voice bitter.

'A fraction of those who've died under the repression of the mage-nobles,' he retorted, probably unwisely. 'The queen mentioned a drink?'

He scowled, but walked to a low cabinet. 'You know if they find against you,' he said, as he poured two glasses, 'then the next significant walk you'll take is to the gallows?'

'Then make it her best Brevian whiskey, please.'

Lyra looked at her father, relieved despite her earlier comment that she didn't have to reiterate Frankel's proposal. 'So, Father? What do you think?'

His one eye glinted in the lamplight as he looked at her. 'You're tempted, aren't you? Not just by his offer to bolster our defence, but by his arguments for this "res publica".'

'I am,' Lyra admitted. 'Ever since we put him on trial, I've had his voice in my head, telling me that the system I'm fighting to protect is wrong.'

'Makelli would argue that a ruler should never listen to either conscience or sentiment.'

'I've read Makelli, Father: he was a nasty, cynical soulless creature,' Lyra retorted, 'full of wonderful advice for oppressive murderers whose sole ambition is to crush anyone they suspect of being a threat.'

'Very effective advice, for all that,' he remarked.

'I'm sure – but shouldn't we be more than that? Wouldn't Kore expect us to be more?'

'Kore doesn't exist.'

'Perhaps not, but the ideals of Kore are good ideals. If everyone on Urte lived as Makelli suggests, a kingdom would consist of one man sitting on a throne surrounded by slaves. And don't try to tell me that Makelli's approach works, because rulers should not be *exploiting* their subjects. They should be *serving* them.' She jabbed a finger at him, although she was arguing as much with herself as her father. 'We're not lions, gorging on meat, or we shouldn't be.'

She paused then, thinking. 'If we put the morality aside, is he right? Are all his people burning things and chanting obscenities because they want a fairer system of government? Or do they just like burning things and swearing?'

'A bit of both, I imagine. But if enough of them are soldiers of a cause, not wanton vandals, then perhaps they are the manpower we need. When Garod and Takwyth arrive, we'll be in a hopeless situation. But with a united Pallas behind you, everything changes.'

'We could double our army overnight, so we wouldn't need Argundy,' Lyra said, her heart lifting.

'And Makelli would counsel that drawing the ringleaders into the open will make it easier to dispose of them after the danger is passed,' Dirklan noted.

'Father,' she reproved, 'I couldn't do that.'

'Well, you say that, but if they play you false?'

She bit her lip. 'Frankel is genuine. I trust his intentions.'

'But the people behind him? Tad Kaden – do you trust him? Or this madman, Lazar? Believe me, Frankel is not the strategist of this movement; he's just the mouthpiece.'

Lyra groaned. 'Dear Kore, this is a maze.' She rubbed her forehead and stifled a yawn, although she was wide awake. 'And then there's the question of what happens to me, I suppose. Frankel is right: the people are only going to believe in this if I commit to abdicating. I'd no longer be queen – and then what? I own nothing personally; all I have belongs to the Crown. I have a son whose birthright is a throne that I'd be giving away. Would Rildan ever forgive me?' She looked at her father: 'Would you?'

Dirklan looked at her steadily. 'Lyra, I've given my life to preserving the Corani, mostly not knowing you existed. Finding you gave my role a deeper purpose, but I've never believed that returning to Pallas was in our best interests. Pallas is a death-trap for a provincial House like ours. We've tried to entrench ourselves, but we're still outsiders. And now Pallas herself, finally free of the Sacrecours, is flexing her muscles. Our only chance of survival may be to align ourselves with Pallas. All of which is to say that I'll support you working with Frankel if it gets us through this crisis and allows us to deal with things properly later.'

Lyra knew her father's reputation: that he'd tempered his ruthlessness during her reign, even when he thought her too merciful. That was a form of love, too.

'If I abdicate, how would the vassal-states see it?'

'As license to secede. The empire will collapse.'

'And the bloodbath would begin?'

'Almost certainly.'

Lyra hung her head. 'We're going round in circles.'

Her father looked at her steadily. 'There is another solution.'

Coraine, Northern Rondelmar

Ostevan is dead. Solon Takwyth stared at the messenger. He found he was quivering and breathless. *That vicious pile of silk-wrapped excrement is dead* . . . 'You're certain? Absolutely certain?'

'Aye, Lord, ' the legion scout replied fervently. His name was Hulvyn; he'd been recently reassigned to a role akin to Setallius' Volsai after Solon had beheaded the first Volsai to turn up pretending to be loyal and no one else had stuck their head above the parapet. However, that left him without anyone experienced in covert missions, so he'd been forced to recruit from the army.

'You've seen the body?'

'His head's on the Traitor's Nail behind the Place d'Accord,' Hulvyn told him. 'I seen it meself.'

It wasn't like Lyra to proclaim something so boldly unless she were absolutely certain. *Garod must be shitting himself,* he thought exultantly. *That's the support of the Church, gone in a flash!*

'Well done, Hulvyn,' he told the man. He fished in his pouch for a very special ducal token; it could set a man up for life. 'Take this to Duke Torun and he'll reward you.'

Hulvyn looked suitably awed and very grateful as he backed out, bowing and gabbling.

When he was alone Solon poured a Brevian whisky, sat in his armchair and took a deep, slow breath. He hadn't realised how much he'd been afraid of what that snake Ostevan might do. His one encounter with a Mask had left him broken and near-dead; he'd been dreading sending his boys up against Garod if Ostevan was at hand. That he was dead was a boon.

I don't fear you, Garod. I only feared Ostevan and now he's gone. Victory will be ours . . .

He sat for a long time going over his plans, then stood, peeled off his gown and entered his bedchamber. Brunelda lay naked in his bed, sleeping on her stomach, her shaven skull gleaming in the candlelight. Her wig was discarded on the floor. He'd purchased her from the House of Lantris; now she lived in a maid's room near his suite during the day and at night, she kept his anguish at bay, despite being merely a substitute for the woman he really wanted. Even so, every night as their bodies and auras coupled, she became more and more his, and in truth, he was growing somewhat fond of her. Most nights, now, it was to Brunelda he made love, but tonight his thoughts were of another and he didn't wish to see her true face.

Climbing into the bed, he gripped her hips and pulled her into a kneeling position as his member stiffened. As she realised who it was, her sleepy protest turned to welcome. Either she was a consummate actor, or she was becoming infatuated with him. That could happen to ordinary mortals who made love with magi, unless the mage shielded their aura. He'd never bothered to do so.

Either way, she was fulfilling her purpose. As his pleasure mounted, he groaned, 'Lyra—' so Brunelda would understand who she was tonight. 'Lyra . . .'

I'm coming back to you, my love.

21

Imposter

The Kalistham and the Last Days

The Kalistham, the holy book of Ahm, is remarkably similar to the Book of Kore concerning the final days of Urte. Both speak of a time of suffering, when the chosen people must endure hardship and privation, after which a messianic figure returns to life to gather the righteous for the final struggle. But the Kalistham holds that the Army of Light will defeat the unholy dead and establish the Kingdom of Heaven on Urte while the Book of Kore cedes Urte to the daemons.

ORDO COSTRUO COLLEGIATE, HEBUSALIM 841

Hegikaro, Mollachia
Martrois 936

Valdyr looked across the table at Ogre, bruised and battered after being assailed on his journey to Hegikaro. He'd arrived the morning after the duel and Asiv's death; when he'd asked to speak to Valdyr in private he'd been brought to the council chamber.

Kyrik and Hajya were still recovering, leaving Valdyr nominally in charge. Outside, those fit enough were burning the bodies of the dead, or guarding the surviving possessed men, who'd been penned in a sun-lit stockyard to attempt their rehabilitation.

At least we know how now, Valdyr reflected, *thanks to Ogre. I barely know him, but Kyrik trusts him. That's enough for me.* 'What is it?' he asked gravely.

'Prince Valdyr,' the big construct said formally, 'these past weeks I have been studying the *Daemonicon* of my old master. It was encrypted and in an unknown language – but I have deciphered it.'

Valdyr stared. The construct was seven foot tall and built like a Mantaur – one who'd been crudely moulded from clay. Such intellect was unexpected. 'Then you are a scholar.'

'I was trained rigorously,' Ogre rumbled, 'and now I know what the Master purposes. He has been seeking a captive dwymancer for his plans and I fear he has one.'

'Jehana.' Valdyr sighed.

'The Master proposes to destroy our world and leave himself the ultimate ruler. Any who remain alive will be daemon-possessed. That is his stated intention, written twenty years ago in his *Daemonicon*, before it fell into Ordo Costruo hands. They failed to decipher it, but Ogre did not,' he concluded, with a hint of pride.

Valdyr blinked, stunned. He'd been expecting something more earthly: seizing the Imperial Throne, maybe – but this sounded like something from the Last Days.

'Can he do such a thing?'

Ogre's big purple tongue emerged to lick his cracked lips. 'He can. He has a way that he believes will work. Only a dwymancer can stop him – one such as you.'

Valdyr caught his breath. *I barely stopped Asiv – surely Naxius is beyond me?* Then he paused, because he wasn't alone. 'There's also Nara of Misencourt,' he told Ogre. 'I'm not the only dwymancer.'

'Then you need to warn her,' Ogre advised. 'Tell her now. The Master has everything he needs and he may have already begun.'

Nara, Valdyr called into the dwyma from the platform on Haklyn Tower, *please, I must speak with you.*

The Elétfa was immense to his inner eye and his grasp of it more secure than ever before, a legacy not just of the time spent there, but also of killing Asiv Fariddan. He had a new sense of certainty now he had forgiven himself for past weakness; he finally felt worthy of this great gift.

But there was little time to dwell on that accomplishment, for thanks to Ogre he now knew the enormity of what was at stake. Ogre was sitting opposite the brazier, next to a sleeping Gricoama; the wolf's tail was twitching as he dreamed. The new moon overhead was a glittering scythe in the cold, still air.

Nara . . . Nara . . . ? He'd felt her presence at times, like a doe flitting through a forest, quiet and elusive. This new reticence to speak to him was troubling: this was the third night he'd tried to reach her without success. With a sigh, he abandoned the effort.

I can't put this off any longer, he decided. *I can't wait on her . . . she might even be dead.* Although he thought he'd have felt it in the dwyma if she'd died. He banished the horrible notion, opened his eyes and looked up at Ogre's lugubrious face as he concentrated on roasting a rat on a stick over the fire. It was amazing what you could get used to when the granary was empty.

'What do I do when I'm in *there*?' Valdyr wondered.

'You just look like you're talking in your sleep,' Ogre replied, taking an exploratory bite of the rat. He heaved a deep, dissatisfied but resigned sigh and took another mouthful. 'You reached this Nara?'

'No. I think we're on our own.'

'Then we should go and find Tarita – she might be able to convince the Merozain Bhaicara to aid us.'

Ogre's open face was easy to read: he wanted to see Tarita, even if it hurt to do so. Valdyr felt a surge of sympathy, but said nothing; Ogre didn't need his pity.

'Can't you just contact her with the gnosis?'

'The distance and the mountains prevent that,' Ogre rumbled. 'I might with a relay-stave, perhaps, but neither the Master nor the Ordo Costruo trusted me enough to show me the art. So unless you have one –?'

Valdyr shook his head. 'Kyrik never learned that either,' he admitted. 'Well, I guess that's what we must do,' he decided, placing his own skewered rat into the flames. 'We might know what Naxius is doing, but we're only guessing where he is and we don't know how advanced his plans are. I don't think the odds-makers would give us a good price on our success.'

Ogre smiled, lighting up his misshapen face. 'The odds-makers don't know us. They would have placed money on Asiv, or Semakha, or Alyssa – and lost it every time.'

They shared a grin, which faded as Valdyr looked across to the main tower, where his brother and his wife were still recovering. He felt wretched at the thought of leaving when Mollachia needed him. *But I fear we must: it's all of Urte at stake.*

He felt a sudden empathy with Ogre, for all their differences, and an urge to admit something he seldom spoke of. 'Ogre, I spent my formative years in the Keshi breeding-houses–' his voice broke and Ogre touched his forearm, his big eyes surprisingly sensitive.

'You don't need to tell me,' he rumbled.

He ignored that and went on, 'Those girls I had to mate with – they were no more willing than I. They chained me down and gave me drugs to perform. Those poor women had to humiliate themselves to get my seed. Most were in tears. It was truly Hel on Urte. Something like what Naxius is going to create . . .'

'And yet you survived,' Ogre noted. His face betrayed his own pain. 'As did I, despite being an abomination Master Naxius created as a slave.'

Valdyr stared as a long-supressed memory resurfaced. 'Of course . . . Ervyn Naxius . . .'

'Ai,' Ogre rumbled, his eyebrows twitching. 'You know of him?'

'Know him?' The memory set Valdyr to trembling again, but this time as much with excitement as horror. 'Naxius used to visit the man who imprisoned me – Asiv was his acolyte.'

Their eyes met and Valdyr felt a powerful sense of shared history with this construct creature he'd never met before. They were flies in the same web. He could see that Ogre felt the same empathy. *We understand each other. We comprehend what each other has been through.* That felt incredibly meaningful. He extended his hand and they solemnly shook. His own big hand was dwarfed, but he didn't flinch. 'I offer you my friendship, Ogre.'

The big construct's eyes lit up. 'Friends,' he growled warmly. 'Friendship is precious.'

It surely is. With that thought, Valdyr rose. 'Goodnight, Ogre. We'll leave at dawn – we've a long way to go.'

Valdyr woke next morning to Gricoama's wet tongue on his cheek. They tussled playfully for a few moments, then he rose, sluiced icy water over his face and scarred body, dressed and buckled on his zweihandle and dagger.

When he emerged into the square, sunlight was slanting through the charred timbers and broken walls of the outer bailey. The castle was crowded with refugees, with families even sleeping in the eaves of the wreckage. Many were awake, watching his departure curiously.

Kyrik was waiting too, his battered face full of concern. He'd finally come to the previous night. 'Brother,' he said, placing a shaking hand on his shoulder, 'I wish that–' Then he stopped himself. 'No, what I really wish is that I could come.'

Valdyr put an arm around his brother. 'No, you don't. You've got to get better yourself, then work on making different tribes one, feeding and housing your people and loving your wife back to health. You don't want to leave them behind.'

'Ysh, I know – but who's going to look after you if I don't?'

'Like you did when you accepted that stupid duel?' Valdyr reminded him. 'Brother, I need to know you're here, putting our home back together. Without that, how will I find the strength I need?'

Kyrik pulled him close. 'I *will* rekindle the home fires. They've burned very low.' He chuckled, 'It's like one of the Fey Tales. You've killed your draken, Sir Rynholt, so now go and rescue the Skydancer.'

Kyrik bent and hugged Gricoama, which the wolf permitted grudgingly, then a low growl resounded through the square, and everyone drew back a little as a something halfway between a horse and a wolf stalked out of the stables. It was saddled, with baggage tied to its back.

Valdyr wasn't at all comfortable about riding his companion, but Ogre had insisted, and he had to agree it would certainly make passing through hostile lands easier.

So he gave Kyrik one last hug, whispering, 'Kiss Hajya for me.' He mounted Ogre's back and without fanfare, departed through the town gates.

Kyrik watched his brother ride off in silence, crushed by sadness, but proud too. When he'd found Valdyr after so many years lost, he'd been a wounded animal. But now he rode tall in the saddle and looked the world in the eye.

Kore and Ahm be with you, brother.

He looked around him, overwhelmed by the sheer enormity of all that needed doing. But he wasn't alone – he had the strength of Kip's Bullheads and the Mantauri to draw on, as well as the manpower of the Sydians and the good people of Mollachia. The farms were recoverable, the mines were still operable and the pastures would thrive as spring advanced. It would take time and they might never know true prosperity in his lifetime, but Mollachia would recover.

It has to.

Sensing eyes on him, he turned to see Hajya leaning on the door-frame, a shawl about her shoulders and squinting in the sunlight – but she wasn't flinching from it. She still looked dreadfully thin, a shadow of the robust, self-assured Sfera headwoman he'd first known, but her lived-in face had regained some of its old imperious command as she called, 'Husband, will you join me for breakfast? I'm ravenous.'

His stomach rumbled at the thought. 'Me too.' He gathered her in his arms and felt the tentative beginnings of his world being hammered back into shape. 'I could eat a bullock.'

'Don't tell Maegogh,' she advised wryly, then she stretched, arms wide. 'By the Stallion, I love the sun.'

'Do I have to add the Sollan Faith to the religions of Mollachia?' he laughed.

'Why not?' she chuckled. 'I hear their priests lay with virgins every Solstice – that's my kind of religion. It makes us Sydians look positively staid.' She stroked his face the way she used to and forgetful of the people watching, they kissed, at first tentatively, then with passion, drinking in the tastes and textures they'd missed for too long.

In that moment, Kyrik finally found his wife again.

Norostein, Noros

How can a person be right here with you and yet miles away? Waqar wondered, watching his lover's face as it turned in every direction except towards him. *Any other woman would be fussing over me, trying to cement my gratitude at the very least – but she's barely here . . .*

He was naked and lying on cool cotton sheets – but that was as romantic as things got. Tarita was squirming on the small stool beside the bed, bored and clearly anxious to be elsewhere. In her lap lay Cadearvo's crumpled mask, retrieved after the construct and his dead draken had crashed into a mansion in Ringwald. Waqar hadn't wanted the ugly thing, but Tarita was fascinated by it. She'd even tried repairing it.

And she'd helped repair Ajniha too, resetting bones broken by the draken's claws, and for that Waqar was profoundly grateful. The roc was recovering faster than he was, by all accounts.

I slew Cadearvo . . . But it didn't feel like a victory, not when his body was so ruined. Cadearvo's dagger had gone in under Waqar's ribcage, sliced, then cauterised his stomach muscles and punctured a lung. He'd almost drowned in his own blood. The mage-healers – the Rondians had far more power and expertise than any of the Shihad's magi – were saying he was lucky to be alive, but it was doubtful that he'd ever fully recover.

And Tarita had no use for him any more – she wasn't entirely heartless, he knew that, but being here was a torment to her. He knew that after spending more than a year paralysed, she'd developed a real horror of sickbeds. But that was only part of her discomfort.

She wants to continue the search for Jehana – and whatever we had feels like it's over.

'What are you thinking about?' he asked, to break the silence.

'Latif,' Tarita replied absently, gazing up at the painted ceiling, a gaudy scene of Kore saints and angels. 'I helped him escape from the massacre of Salim's household and here he is on another continent, passing himself off as Salim again. What a strange life.'

'It's no stranger than a maid who becomes an Ascendant mage, joins the Merozains, spies for Javon and becomes the concubine of a Keshi prince,' he replied, forcing a laugh. 'If that's still what you want?' He wasn't sure what he wanted her answer to be.

'I suppose,' she said absently.

He couldn't work out which she was replying to: his initial statement, or his question. *Should I just get my rejection in first?* he wondered. 'Where's my sister?' he asked instead. 'Why can't we find her?'

'We've tried everything we can,' she answered tersely. They'd even used the blood-scrying and still got nothing. 'She's being veiled too strongly, or she's deep underground.' She sat up. 'The mountains, a wall of stone thousands of feet high, are just south of us. The scrying spells that led us here were directional – what if we got the southerly readings before she passed beyond our reach and now it's the mountains blocking us?'

'Then what else can we do?' he demanded.

'Cross the mountains and scry again.'

'In case you haven't noticed, I have a pierced lung.' He sagged into his pillow. 'Take some of my blood and go,' he said, trying very hard not to sound bitter. If he didn't recover fully, he would never be sultan, and Latif's ruse wasn't sustainable, which meant Teileman would claim the throne – maybe he'd even fly his court home and abandon the broken Shihad to its fate.

But what if Teileman's also a Mask? he thought suddenly, his heart going cold. *There's still a possessed army outside our walls – and Xoredh's still alive.*

Since the Yurosi and Shihad forces had united, almost a week ago, and he'd killed Cadearvo, there had been no further attacks. Xoredh's daemon army had retreated to the plains outside Lowertown, which were still flooded. The sultan's banner flew, but he'd not been seen since that night.

'You should go,' he told Tarita. 'I need to rest.'

She looked at him squarely and he could almost hear her words before she said them. 'I've thought about our agreement, Waqar,' she started. 'We both know your people would never accept a known Jhafi spy in the court – I'd be a danger to you, and to myself. And anyway, turns out, I don't want to be a princess. Who knew?' She sighed. 'I'm happier on my own.'

He tried to sit up, but a jab of pain racked his chest and he ended up coughing up more blood instead. By the time his vision had cleared, she was standing over him, clearly torn between her desire to leave and genuine concern. She placed the mask on the bed, but he waved it away.

'Take it,' he croaked. 'I don't want it here.'

Then he dissolved into another coughing fit and when his eyes cleared Tarita and the mask were gone. In her place was a white woman with kindly eyes who held his hand, gifting him her healing energy.

Tarita slipped out of the sickroom, waved to the Rondian healer-woman and walked onwards blindly, feeling odd now the words had been said. *Thank Ahm it's over*, she thought morosely, and then, *What's wrong with me? I just jettisoned a prince, for Ahm's sake – and a handsome one at that.*

She went to his suite and after eating and bathing, stared in the mirror at herself naked: small and skinny, maamehs too big for her size. Normally she was proud of her body, but today she felt ugly. She tugged on undergarments and men's clothes, better for fighting than woman's skirts, tied up her hair and packed her things, wondering what came next.

The common factor in all my failed relationships is me.

Someone had once told her that infatuation lasted nine weeks and love for nine months – the time that it took to birth a man's child and for him to look for the next conquest. Eternal love was a myth.

Most of my affairs last between nine hours and nine days.

Since the Shihad's retreat into Copperleaf, the Ahmedhassan leaders had been given a disgraced nobleman's palace as their headquarters, but Waqar and Latif had accepted guest rooms in the Governor's Mansion. Since then there had been little integration, but no outbreaks of serious violence either. Thankfully, Xoredh hadn't attacked either, although why, she had no idea – perhaps he needed time to mop up resistance.

The peace within the walls here was entirely due to Latif – *Sultan Salim* – and the Rondian general, Seth Korion, who seemed a decent man for a slugskin. Remarkably, he and Latif knew each other; they'd told her, laughing, that Korion, believing Latif to be Salim, had captured him during the Third Crusade.

Such things could make me believe in Fate, Tarita thought.

Her own Fate lay elsewhere, though. She strapped on her sword-belt and hefted her small pack – and as an afterthought, packed the Cadearvo mask. Then she went to find somewhere else to sleep.

She found space in a building on the opposite side of the square, a tiny storeroom above a refugee dormitory full of frightened camp women and their infant children, She'd barely settled herself when a Noro-man runner found her – so someone was obviously watching her movements.

'General Korion requests your presence, Lady Merozain,' the man said formally.

She hesitated, almost went to decline, then decided she needed to keep busy, so replied in fluent Rondian, 'When would he like to see me?'

'Now is ideal, the general said.'

She sighed and followed him back across Ringwald Square, where thousands of Shihadi were now encamped, around a central space lined with a handful of remaining Rondian windships and the remaining half-dozen rocs, to the Governor's Mansion. Waqar had told her hundreds of Keshi windships were still manning the supply-lines back to Ahmedhassa, but it was hard to forget that *vast* windfleet she'd seen crossing the ocean. She was still reflecting on the devastating losses this war had inflicted on her own people when she was shown into General Korion's offices. The Noroman guards were looking at her warily, but she also sensed that her presence offered them hope. That made her uncomfortable, that they thought she was here representing Alaron Mercer and the Merozains. *But they're wrong.*

Inside were most of the important leaders of both sides – all men, she noted – discussing the situation of the city over steaming pots of coffee. They fell silent when she entered.

'Good morning, Magister Tarita,' Seth Korion greeted her. His blond hair was newly trimmed, but his eyes looked tired.

That she, a dirt-caste upstart, could be honoured with the title of 'Magister' by a Rondian general still amused her.

She was served coffee by the general's aide, an earnest man called Andwine Delton, and as she took a seat, Korion introduced the Rondians – the clever-faced Ramon Sensini; the terribly serious Royal Guard commander Era Hyson; some legion commanders whose names she didn't catch, and two civilians, a Justiciar called Vorn Detabrey and some kind of representative of the people, Vannaton Mercer, who turned out to be the father of Alaron Mercer, although he wasn't a mage. *Mistress Alhana's brother-in-law*, she realised, giving him a reverent curtsey.

Opposite them sat Latif, still clad in his mock-finery, with Admiral Valphath, now Senapati of the Shihad forces inside the city, some junior officers hastily promoted in the field, and a young kalfas named Chanadhan, who was acting as translator. The last member of the Eastern entourage was Godspeaker Zaar, the only clergymen present.

Tarita tried the coffee. It was weak, badly roasted and someone had ruined it with milk – clearly Yurosi knew *nothing* about real coffee – but it helped, despite its inadequacies.

'Thank you for joining us,' Seth Korion addressed the room, before adding in Keshi, 'Sal'Ahm, sadiqaa,' while touching his right hand to head, then heart in greeting.

Tarita was sure that for a mere general to speak ahead of a sultan or a prince – even if he was a titled nobleman – was a dreadful breach of etiquette – but then, their side of the table was nominally headed by a man they all knew to be an impersonator. *It'd take a specialist in the harbadab to work out that riddle, and personally I don't give a shit, as long as they don't steal our supplies then hang us out for Xoredh to slaughter.*

'Sultan,' Seth Korion began, pointedly using Latif's false title, 'how are your men settling in? Have there been any fresh incidents?' He spoke in Rondian; Latif and Tarita were both fluent and the scribe Chanadhan rapidly translated for those Keshi without the tongue.

Latif glanced sideways at Admiral Valphath before replying, 'I'm told there have been seventeen separate brawls, a stabbing over a woman, numerous instances of theft and complaints – but Admiral Valphath tells me this is normal, no worse than when a Dhassan warband shares camp with Keshis.'

Tarita thought of Latif when she'd met him in Sagostabad, the night his family was slaughtered. She'd lost him in the confusion and presumed him dead, but somehow he'd endured and now here he was, back at the centre of things. Clearly, Salim had trained him well, because he spoke before this potentially fractious gathering with ease and authority.

'It's just as bad when a Rondian legion encounters Argundian soldiers,' Seth observed. 'I think it's going well: both sides are respecting the new alliance, we're getting everyone fed and there's been no open fighting. But if we're to hold the city, we must integrate our forces.'

'The example must be set from above, General,' Latif replied. 'Our officers must walk together and act as one to clamp down on indiscipline. You and I must inspect every unit. Only by displays of unity can we become one fighting force.'

Tarita saw the various legates and hazarapatis pull faces, but Korion was immediately supportive. 'Yes, exactly: we here must set the example, starting with you and me. It must be our highest priority.'

Tarita recognised that a genuine friendship existed between Latif and Seth Korion, but Latif wasn't letting that undermine his position: he knew when to be firm or conciliatory, and he had a sound grasp of the necessities of leadership. *This is a man Waqar needs to learn from*, she thought, wondering how she could bring that about.

'General Korion,' Latif responded, 'clearly your men understand the defensive positions inside this tier of your city and we don't. If we're to share the burden, your officers must brief ours and let us take control of some of the walls.' Then he added with a disarming smile, 'Not that we don't appreciate the rest.'

This was an understatement: the Shihad soldiers had been starving, frozen and exhausted; almost all their stores had been used for the riotous celebrations of Xoredh's coronation, leaving little for the future.

Because Xoredh knew they wouldn't need food, Tarita reflected grimly.

Latif's words were conciliatory, but the matter of trust was a major sticking point. Tarita heard Valphath muttering something to an aide before grumbling, 'When will you show faith in us?' in Keshi. Korion was not the only Rondian to understand his words.

'I am sure it's not a question of trust,' Latif replied sharply. It was the diplomatic thing to say, but they all knew he meant the opposite. This was *all* about trust – and could anyone blame the Rondians, for the Shihad *had* invaded their lands and killed thousands upon thousands of people, and displaced or enslaved many more . . .

The argument went round in circles, the Rondian commanders questioning the Shihadis' readiness while the Keshi commanders played their own games. Some, like Valphath, wanted to be given responsibilities, while others were quite happy for the Rondians to take all the risks. Tarita fancied a few still looked to a future when, having defended the city successfully, they might seize control of it.

Don't they realise the Shihad is over? We stand or fall with these Yurosi now.

She quietly fumed, until Ramon Sensini looked at her pointedly and asked, 'Are we boring you, Magister?'

Her temper flared at being singled out. 'Ai, you are. I am bored because you talk in spirals and do not say what you mean.' She jabbed a finger at the Rondians. 'You think we are a shambles who will run when the enemy attack, or even help them.' Then she turned on her own kind. 'And you – you are either vainglorious or hoping to let others fight while you wait to pick up the pieces. Only two men here truly mean well: Seth Korion and Latif. You others should piss off if you're not ready to work together.'

Eyebrows shot up and almost every man in the room looked offended – except for Sensini. The fleeting smirk on his face told her she'd said *exactly* what he'd wanted her to – and amused him along the way.

If his intent was to unite them all, it worked, because they all rounded on her, men of both sides, demanding to know what right she had to be there and what she knew about anything anyway.

'I am the pupil of Elena Anborn and I could wipe my feet on any of you,' she shouted, coming to her feet.

'Just because you drank a potion and didn't die doesn't make you a fighting *man*, Merozain,' a Noroman named Sir Tonald Grace sneered.

'What do you know about command? Have you even drawn blood in a fight?'

'You want to find out?' she shot back, and the knight went pale.

Sensini lightly touched her shoulder and she calmed a little. No one liked Tonald Grace, she realised.

Seth and Latif were telling everyone to sit down and be silent and abruptly she felt silly and out of her depth.

It was Sensini, having provoked her, who picked up on her points. 'Frankly, I'm with Lady Tarita. We must agree what part the Shihad will play in the defence of Norostein – *now*.'

Tarita gave him a hard stare. *Cunning* matachod, she thought. *And as for 'Lady'* . . . she smiled despite herself and found herself wondering if he was single. *I really am faithless,* she decided unrepentantly, *but I do like a man with strut.*

Finally, things started happening. Korion agreed that Ahmedhassan units would start rotating onto the walls; Latif told his people they would cooperate or be replaced. The meeting broke up with a pledge that every Shihad officer would have toured the walls by evening and their men would be assigned defence positions in the event of attack.

Her interest in Sensini terminated almost immediately after the meeting, when a skinny woman with a deep desert look clad in Khotri silks swept up and took his right arm imperiously.

Probably just as well, she thought, feeling somewhat morose as she drifted back to her new hidey-hole. She found a broom and spent the afternoon trying to make it more homely. She was bored and edgy and wondering when she had last smiled. *I wish Ogre was here,* she thought suddenly. *He'd make me laugh.*

Announcing that Latif's suggestion – which they'd already agreed privately – would be implemented immediately, Seth and the sultan led their commanders and hazarapatis on a tour of the defences that very afternoon, from Ringwald Gate down through the length and breadth of Copperleaf. Their respective escorts mixed uneasily, Rondian battle-magi and Hadishah, sworn enemies, forced to cooperate. The horses were made skittish by the miasma of smoke and death clinging to the smouldering buildings, which were being picked over by squads of soldiers, white and dark-skinned alike, faces wrapped in scarves.

Whenever they passed his men, they stopped to thump their chests and call 'A Korion, a Korion!' his old family war-cry; and not to be outdone, the Easterners turned to face their sultan and went down in a waves of genuflections, hands to hearts.

Then one Keshi looked at Seth and called, 'Sal-Ahm alaykum, Senapati Korion.'

Seth knew the Ahm gesture, the rippling movement of the hand from heart, to forehead to the palm-up extension of the right hand, and managed it passably, while asking Latif, 'How do I respond?'

'What do you want to say?' the impersonator asked.

'That I thank them, and wish them well.'

Latif fed him a string of words and Seth rattled them off, eliciting first a hesitant response of 'Ahm Akbar,' and then scattered laughter and touches to the forehead. 'What *did* I say?' Seth asked Latif suspiciously.

'You told them they are beasts in battle and you tremble to see them.'

'Good on me,' Seth snorted, throwing a general salute about him then urging his mount on, Latif keeping pace effortlessly. 'Really, I'm glad to have them with us. No one shoots like an Ahmedhassan.'

'And no one defends a rampart like a Rondian legionary,' Latif responded graciously.

Their eyes met, thinking of a place called Riverdown almost seven years ago. Both shuddered.

Seth subtly pulled a flask from his belt-pouch and showed Latif. 'Have you ever tried Brevian whiskey? It's like smoke and honey.'

'A good Amteh man does not drink alcoholic beverages, Effendi.'

'That's not how I remember you.'

'I never said I was a good man,' Latif said, with a wry grin. 'But when I was your captive, none of my people could see my transgressions. Here I am the sultan and must set the example for all my men.' He looked away, then winked at Seth sideways. 'So best no one sees.'

'In an hour, in the governor's lounge?' Seth suggested, suppressing a grin.

It took longer than that, of course, for Seth had to take reports from all sectors and deal with the usual array of complaints, decisions and delegations before he could leave the legion commanders to guard the walls. Once he'd managed to get away, he disarmed and retired to the governor's private lounge, where Latif was studying the room. He had good cause: as an exercise in conspicuous consumption it was second to none. The room was panelled in polished Bunavian holzetta wood marbled with gleaming amber and hung with heavy velvet drapes, with a ruinously expensive Rimoni-style mosaic on the floor. Oil paintings filled the walls and statues of ivory and ebony stood in every corner. It was a sumptuous place of relaxation for the office of the man who'd been the real power in Noros for more than two decades.

Seth poured them generous measures of the Brevian and settled into one of the armchairs in front of the fire. The mock-sultan sipped the whiskey, winced a little, then nodded. 'An acquired taste, friend Seth, but one I may become used to.' He raised a toast. 'May we hold, and our men become true brothers in arms.'

'The Copperleaf walls are a strong bastion,' Seth commented. 'In the Noros Revolt of 909–910, this city held out for months against a Rondian army led by my father. It didn't surrender until all hope had passed. Mind, Father always said he'd been told to take the city intact.' He pushed aside the painful memory of Kaltus Korion and asked, 'So, Latif – I've been dying to know but we're never alone: how on Urte did you end up here?'

Latif's tale amazed him: masked assassins, murdered family, an involuntary conscription and a trek across half of Yuros, all the time hiding his identity and biding his time. 'But I was right there as Rashid died,' Latif concluded. 'After all I'd been through, I heard from his own lips what he'd done before I watched him die.'

'He sold his own son into daemonic possession,' Seth breathed, shaking his head.

'Who could do such a thing?' Latif asked, just as dismayed.

'My father would have, I don't doubt,' Seth answered. 'To him, I was only ever a disappointing footnote to his illustrious career. He was going to disinherit me, but died before it could be effected.'

'I never knew my parents,' Latif reflected. 'I was an orphan until the sultan's people saw that I resembled Salim, then my life changed utterly. Education, luxury, even a wife . . . and a son.'

Whom the Masks slew in cold blood, Seth thought. 'Naxius has much to answer for.'

'Ai, he must be ended. But what of you?'

'I have a wife, Camilla Phyl – she was a healer in my legion during the Third Crusade. We have two daughters.'

'I remember her – the shy one, pale hair, ai? She used to visit to make sure I didn't fall ill, royal hostages being rather precious. So you seduced one of your staff, Effendi? Or was it the other way round?'

Seth coloured. 'It was more . . . um . . . organic than that. On the journey home, we rather fell into each other, and it turned out we were near neighbours. My mother was appalled that I'd marry any but a pure-blood.'

'But it was love, ai?' Latif chuckled, toasting him again.

Was it love? Seth wondered. 'I suppose. We're comfortable together . . .' He fell into an awkward silence, then picked up his tale. 'Despite my father's plan, I inherited his titles and became Earl of Bres – the highest nobleman in Bricia – but like Noros, we're ruled by a governor, appointed by her Majesty in Pallas.'

'I envy you your happiness.' Latif looked down at his brocaded coat and sighed. 'I don't know how long we can retain this fiction. Salim's reign was backed by Rashid, a man all revered. With him gone and Xoredh exposed for what he is, there will be war in Kesh, regardless of whether any of us return there alive after this débâcle.'

'What of Waqar Mubarak?'

'An obvious candidate, but he is second in rank to Rashid's younger brother Teileman, who leads the northern army. Neither have the experience – or in Teileman's case, the personality – to unite an empire. And any exertion right now could kill Waqar.' He looked at Seth. 'What of your empress? I hear nothing but contempt for her – and I'm told your own empire is falling apart?'

Seth thought about Lyra Vereinen. 'I've only met her once. She spoke well and she seemed to be a decent person. But her allies are deserting her and the old Sacrecour dynasty will probably regain power.'

'How will that effect you?'

'I don't know.' Seth sighed. 'The empire is likely to break up – our army split in half because I was the only one prepared to defend Norostein. The Rondians and Argundians were happy to see Rashid come here unopposed.'

Latif whistled softly. 'Your retreat here doomed the Shihad, Effendi. So many men died because of your decision to come here.'

'We didn't invade' – Seth raised a placating hand – 'this time. But we have been the aggressors and some would say we richly deserve your retribution. Honour demands vengeance.'

'Ai. *Honour* does . . . But we need peace more than we need honour. War is mass-murder, my friend, and no one wins. It's peace we both badly need.' He pushed his glass away and rose, a little unsteadily. Seth rose too and they took a couple of quick steps together and embraced. 'You and I need to set an example, my friend,' Latif told him. 'While we can.'

He kissed Seth's cheek and for a moment they inhaled the same air. Seth felt a gentle chime, a thought that this was how things should be: enemies embracing as brothers.

Xoredh stared across the frozen plains from the front of his pavilion to the walls of Norostein. This was where Rashid had pitched his tent a month ago. Lowertown was flooded; the water still pouring in from the broken aqueduct had overflowed the lake inside the walls and turned the streets to thick mud. He'd left men in there to ensure it wasn't reoccupied by the defenders, but he had no intention of staying in that swampy sea of ruin himself.

With Cadearvo dead, it was truly *his* army now, although he was at something of a loss as to how to proceed and awaiting the Master's next contact with considerable trepidation.

But the hour had come. He let out his breath and returned to the pavilion, where he set out his scrying bowl and the specially enchanted brazier. He darkened the lamps and conjured the link, homing in on the Master's secret sigil.

Naxius' face appeared in the brazier's smoke in his youthful guise, with copper-red hair and an implacable stare. Thankfully, he looked calm, the rage he'd unleashed the day Cadearvo died back under control.

'Ironhelm, report,' he said, his voice crackling from the distance.

'The enemy are coexisting without open violence,' Xoredh admitted. 'The walls of Copperleaf are intact and well-manned. I'm not sure of our ability to get inside.'

'It matters not. We have a higher mission.'

'I don't understand, Master.' Xoredh was wondering what secret purpose they'd all been serving. *Did he ever care about this sacred war at all?*

'The game has moved on,' Naxius said carelessly. 'The purpose of the war has been fulfilled: it has drawn my real enemies into the open, just as I desired. I have always had a deeper intention, Ironhelm. This conflict has been amusing enough and I'm sure everyone's thoroughly enjoyed the chance to spill heathen blood and settle scores, but it was only ever about revealing the dwymancers and bringing them into my grasp. I now have one of them – your kinswoman Jehana. She's what I needed all along.'

Jehana? Xoredh frowned. 'But I could have taken her any time before the war–'

'Indeed.' Naxius chuckled. 'Ironic, isn't it? When I thought her of no value, she was easily in our reach – but by the time I realised her importance, she'd vanished, and so millions have died. Life is pure comedy at times.'

The Shihad was for more than your amusement, Xoredh thought coldly. *It was right and just.* But he knew better than to reveal his disquiet. 'What is our goal, Master?'

'The same as it's always been: making the world our own. But just as Jehana is my key to victory, the other dwymancers who could have offered me the opportunity I sought are also our greatest threat. Now that I have Jehana, the rest must be eliminated, lest they interfere. Your own task is to kill Prince Waqar.'

'Ai, Lord. Thy will be done.'

The contact was broken and Xoredh sat alone, head bowed uneasily. *Of the eight original Masks, only I survive.* They'd all thought to rule the world; now they were daemon-fodder. *So who will be hunting the other dwymancers he's spoken of?*

He felt a strange weariness, but sleep brought nightmares of his own demise, so horrific that he shunned rest. However, brooding must now be put aside: his task had been made clear.

And I can't afford to fail again.

22

Angel of War

Macharo

The Last Days begin with the rise of Macharo, the Angel of War. Before his dread gaze, the armies of the Unrighteous shall wilt and his daemons shall destroy all defences, laying Urte bare for conquest.

BOOK OF KORE

Pallas, Rondelmar
Martrois 936

The Place d'Accord – the name was from old Frandian, meaning 'Forum of Union' – was the historic site of the founding of the Rondian Empire. Today it was thronged with people, just as it had been when the Sacrecour emperors hosted grandiose parades to display their might, lavishing spectacles on the masses.

Such extravagances had always been beyond Lyra's regime – but this gathering wasn't about impressing the Pallacian burghers; they'd not been lured by promises of drink, food and entertainments. Instead, heralds had been going through streets daily, distributing leaflets and proclaiming in their booming voices: '*Come to the Place d'Accord on the first day of the new moon, the first of Martrois, when Empress Lyra will address her beloved people concerning the future of her kingdom. All are welcome, all are summoned.*'

Lyra had feared a poor attendance, that the people wouldn't trust her enough to come – but she needn't have worried. The Pallas Mob poured in like a sea, all sporting embroidered red roses on their breasts to signify their support for Ari Frankel's *res publica*. Men and women of all ages brayed slogans and sang new songs of rebellion and freedom. Kensiders chanted insults at Tockers; docklanders shrieked derision at Esdale soldier families, and they all roared their disapproval of the middle-class families of Gravenhurst and the northern slopes. It was Pallas at its most visceral and raw, a seething stew of influences and interests, like the empire in miniature.

Smoke hung heavy in the air like the threat of open violence. She'd lost control of half the city and still refused to let Oryn Levis send in his men. 'Minds aren't won by battering heads,' she told him, but the Knight-Commander was at the end of his tether – and quite possibly at the point of mutiny. She suspected that if this went badly, he'd be opening the gates for Takwyth himself when he arrived.

Which is only days away . . .

Lyra entered the Place d'Accord wearing a white gown with a gold brocade cloak and ermine collar. The crown was weighing heavily on the coils of blonde hair which had been carefully back-combed and pinned into place to make her look regal and imposing.

Exilium and Basia, flanking her, were somewhat recovered, their bruises concealed by paints and powders, much to the young Estellan's disgust. 'What warrior ever went out made up like a woman?' he grumbled.

'I do, every day,' Basia had twinkled, tweaking his nose and telling him he looked pretty as a peach.

Behind them were Dirklan, Calan, Dominius and Lumpy, there to lend their weight to her address. All of them looked grim, for this was her last throw of the dice. If it failed, she'd likely have to flee.

Ranks of battle-magi and soldiers guarded her passage from the gates to the podium overlooking the square. Towering over them all was the one-hundred-foot-tall statue of Corineus; the dagger was glowing in the Sacred Heart. Some had jumped onto his stone feet, seeking a vantage, and the noise was a physical thing, a cacophony she had to wade through, amid screams for her to 'Go hang yourself, heretic–' or 'Rukk off back "oop narf" ', Corani bitch.' And some, insidiously, started chanting, 'Takwyth, Takwyth . . .'

That made her shiver, but she climbed the steps to the podium, none the worse for the harsh words or the occasional pieces of rotten fruit spattering harmlessly over the gnostic shields surrounding her. She felt like she was perched on a precipice above a seething lake of faces and hands all punching the air as they shrieked in derision – but there was support, too: she spotted a core of green-clad Corani to her right, stoically singing, 'The Green Hills of Coraine' at the top of their voices.

She took a deep breath, trembling at the enormity of what she meant to do here at the heart of the empire, the nexus of all that was good and ill in Rondelmar, the corrupt and the well-meaning, the splendour and the squalor. She raised a hand to quieten them and began to speak, her voice amplified by a gnosis-wielding herald standing nearby. Two hundred thousand souls could squeeze into this place, she'd been told, more than the population of all but a few Yurosi cities. Not all fell silent, but her voice carried clearly over the vast crowd.

'People of Pallas, people of Rondelmar,' she began, her voice echoing around the plaza. 'The following speech is now being read in every imperial city. It has been written by me, Queen Lyra Vereinen, in my name and in the name of Prince Rildan, my son and heir.'

As she paused for breath, the chants and slogans rose again, but less vociferously, for somehow, people began to sense the importance of what was happening. Craning their necks to see, they began to shush noisier neighbours.

'I have heard your voices,' she went on, 'your demands for greater freedoms and for your own voices to take part in governance. I have heard Master Frankel speak of *suffragium* and the *res publica*. His words resonate with me.'

At Ari's name they cheered, and she wondered where he was; she'd not seen him since their meeting. But most just stared upwards, wondering where this was going.

'But I have also seen houses burn and good people suffering,' she told them. 'Fear has ruled the streets of my home, spread by criminals in the guise of freedom fighters. I have watched peaceful protests turn to bloodshed and death.' She swept her pointing hand across the square, encompassing them all. 'I see a people divided: the unstoppable desire for freedom in collision with the immovable walls of empire. One must fail, but both are suffering from the impact.'

That took some unpacking, but the crowd were now murmuring as they worked it out.

'The world is always changing, but institutions like the Crown or the Church resist change. Pressures grow, until they are released violently.' She raised her voice. 'We *must* resolve this. Immovable objects must move and unstoppable forces must come to rest. I will not have my realm burn.'

She removed her cloak – to reveal a *red rose* embroidered on the left breast of her gown. Those who could see gasped, and a confused cheer gusted through a crowd who couldn't quite believe their eyes. Behind her, a new banner was unfurled: her personal ensign, the Winter Tree against Corani green, but with a huge red rose emblazoned above it.

'People of Rondelmar, I, your Queen, sanction your *res publica!* As *ongoing* Head of State, I give you the right to appoint the Royal Council and to take executive leadership: your people, chosen your way. Suffragium, just as Master Frankel has espoused. Your *Res Publica*, your nation.'

They'd fallen almost silent, but this time when she paused, there was an incredible shriek of joy and the *suffragium* chants resounded as Pallacians started jumping up and down, whooping and cheering themselves hoarse. She saw open mouths, bewildered and joyous faces, heard raucous cheering that blew away the threat of violence in a wave of exultation.

But she also saw consternation and dread on the faces of her Corani.

She raised her arms again. This time it was several minutes before she could be heard again. 'My people, we are aboard a ship adrift on the tides of history and her name is *Rondelmar*. I have been her tillerman, but we all sail on her. If some of us row while others burn the sails, we *all* go down – but if we pull together, if we fill those sails, we will prevail against the storms.' She turned her palms out, in an offering gesture. 'I give you this gift, my people: my promise of change. Let your representatives come forth and join me in steering this ship.'

Then she stabbed her right hand to the north and then the east – towards Takwyth and Coraine, and Duke Garod in Dupenium. 'Because make no mistake: the storms are blowing in, marching on us even now – and you may believe me when I tell you, *they will grant you no such rights*: for they are *Empire* men, every one of them, and they want to rule.'

'So do you,' a sceptical voice shouted. 'You're just like them—'

'Me?' Lyra laughed. 'I'm just a mother, one who longs to leave the daily business of empire to those better qualified,' she replied. 'I told you I have been a tillerman, but I would much sooner be the figurehead on a more seaworthy ship.'

'No one gives up power,' that same voice railed, and she could see people turning to look at the dissenter.

'I do,' she retorted. 'I *choose* to step aside – but I'm not leaving this ship, and nor are the magi close to me.' Her voice was now deliberately defiant. 'I am giving you this *res publica*, but I will be its first defender and *any* who try to topple it, any who try to pervert it into tyranny, will have to come through me ... and through the Volsai and the Church and the Royal Guard. Do not squander this gift.'

That quieted the heckler and sent a ripple of intrigue through the crowd.

Take that, Makelli, and your sophisticated brutality.

She pointed to the rose on her breast. 'I pledge my life to serving the Res Publica of Rondelmar. Who here will do the same?'

That engendered another roar and suddenly the mood was all excitement again, a positive energy based not on resistance and violence, but on the notion of serving something bigger than oneself.

She raised her hand once more and the cheers started dying away. 'I am speaking now to the people of Argundy, of Brevis, of Hollenia and Andressea, those who wish to secede from our union. I grant you that secession, uncontested. People of Midrea, of Noros, of Bricia and Estellayne, of Mollachia and Rimoni, Silacia and Lantris and all the kingdoms of Yuros: hear me. *Your lands are your own.*'

For a moment it felt as if the air had been sucked from the giant plaza – then voices rushed in, uncertain now. Rondians were *proud* of their empire – surely this threatened their status in the world? Lyra didn't care overly about that, but she didn't dismiss their fears.

'To our Rondian kindred in Coraine, Dupenium and Aquillea, we remind you that you are our blood, our kith and kin, part of the greatest nation in Yuros, the keystone of the West. You might hear my words and believe it best you go alone, but remember this: in numbers lie strength, wealth and prosperity. Together we are strong – alone, you are vulnerable.'

Think on that, all you Dukes. Will you stand alone and small, or be part of something that can still be dominant, even if it's no longer an empire?

'LONG LIVE RONDELMAR – LONG LIVE QUEEN LYRA,' came the shout, right on cue, from Dirklan's Volsai, seeded among the crowd. The chants spread quickly through the Place d'Accord as the crowd regained the fever of a victory won, the hope of something new and better for themselves.

They still see themselves as the greatest nation on Urte. If that helps them accept this moment, so be it.

She waved to all sides then stepped back as the crowd began chanting, 'FRANKEL, FRANKEL –'

A few moments later the rabble-rouser himself was pushed forward to the lower steps of her podium. He looked up at her and touched his heart.

Yes, I kept my promise to you, she thought, proud of that.

Then he turned to face the people, his face alight with joy and excitement, and began to speak, his unamplified words cracking with the strain of being heard. Lyra didn't listen, too exhausted by the emotional effort.

I've just ended the Rondian Empire. I've just relinquished executive power. I've taken away my son's birthright – quite possibly, I've sanctioned a bloodbath . . . But perhaps I've saved us all.

The next few days would show whether this was her greatest triumph or her worst mistake. And right now, all her enemies would be reacting to her pronouncements and getting reports from the mage-spies who were doubtless hidden among this vast throng.

Are Solon and Garod laughing at me now, or are they beginning to doubt?

She left almost unnoticed, surrounded by her counsellors, as waves of sound buffeted Ari Frankel. Dirklan gave her a measured, approving look. This had been his compromise: a constitutional monarchy, he called it: not quite the full *res publica* that Frankel had wanted, but something he could agree to and sell to his adherents.

Dominius looked far more at ease than she'd expected – but then he probably saw this as a victory in the centuries-old struggle between Church and State. *He's reuniting the Church, while the Crown is fragmenting – of course he's happy.*

Calan had been the hardest man to sell it to: all he foresaw was lost tax revenue, new borders for tariffs and tolls to destroy trade – and *amateurs* trying to meddle in his Treasury. But if the alternative was mobs of ravening burghers rampaging through his offices with torches and knives, he was prepared to let it play out.

Oryn Levis was the one who worried her. Military men didn't debate, they issued orders. Generals were like emperors and kings, and they didn't deal in compromise unless cornered. So far, the big, placid Knight-Commander appeared to be acceding to her requests, but Solon wasn't at their gates yet . . .

Her father had been adamant. '*If Oryn wavers, he goes.*' He didn't mean into exile, either.

She took Dirklan's arm gratefully, her legs suddenly wobbly as the enormity of her actions hit her like a blow. She barely noticed the weeping servants, bowing and curtseying as she hurried past them.

'I need to hold my son,' she told her counsellors. 'I must pray for his forgiveness.'

An hour later, she could still hear the triumph reverberating through the city, despite the high Bastion walls. Rildan was asleep on her lap while Dirklan relayed reports from his agents spread across Yuros.

'Duke Kurt Borodium has proclaimed a Kingdom of Argundy,' he said, brandishing the relay-stave. 'Our imperial legions in Delph have left the capital for Aquillea: they report no trouble yet, but desertions are rife as non-Rondians are electing to return to their own countries. The general mood is triumphant – although privately, the Borodiums are furious at being blindsided. Safe to say you won't get to marry Andreas.'

'What a shame,' Lyra said drily. 'What of Aquillea?'

Dirklan smiled. 'The Duke has told his people they stand with Rondelmar.'

Yes, Lyra thought, clasping her hands before her. *Thank you, Kore – and Duke Salinas.*

'And Garod?' she asked, taking strength from the good tidings to deal with the bad.

'As expected, he's denounced you as mad and a traitor to the empire – he's vowed to place your head on a spike when he restores his nephew Cordan to the Imperial Throne, and to order a Crusade to bring every nation back under the Imperial yoke.' He smiled. 'His pronouncements were apparently received rapturously in Dupenium and in Fauvion. The Sacrecours have never permitted men like Frankel to speak in their lands. The average Dupeni believes concepts like freedom and equality emanate from the Lord of Hel.'

That sounds typical, she thought bleakly. 'And Coraine?'

'Ah.' Dirklan gave her an intent look. 'Solon refused to let the royal heralds speak, so the people of Coraine know nothing about this. Remember that Solon has publicly announced that you're virtually a prisoner and that he's marching to free you and restore Corani rule. I doubt he has any idea how to tell them that you're virtually abdicating.'

'I'm *not* abdicating,' she said sharply. 'I have a veto on *everything*, and a *hereditary* crown. The monarchy part of this "constitutional monarchy" of yours is no less important than the constitutional part.'

'I know that – but I doubt Solon understands the nuances,' Dirklan said. 'Our people will get word out swiftly enough, although I expect Solon will tell them the Mob have bullied you and only he can restore order.'

She thought about that. 'Will people believe him?'

'Undoubtedly – but it doesn't matter. What does matter is that there were thousands of men with legion experience in that crowd today and tomorrow we'll be recruiting like mad. We have a chance.'

So long as Lumpy and the Corani inside Pallas don't side with Solon, she thought grimly. 'And what about the Pallacian mage-nobles and battle-magi?' Lyra asked. They were her greatest worry right now.

Dirklan smiled again. 'Do you mean your courtiers – who

wholeheartedly believe it when the *Book of Kore* tells them their gnostic powers come directly from the hand of Kore Himself, making them divinely mandated to rule?'

'Yes, *them*. If they're against this, Solon may still arrive to find our heads on spikes.'

'My people are watching them.'

With knives drawn. Lyra shuddered. They shared a taut look, then with an effort she put that to one side. 'I've been neglecting the dwyma – I really should refresh myself in the garden. Have your grandson for a while.' She handed Rildan to Dirklan, planted a kiss on each head, then took the stairs from the balcony to her garden. It had been days since she'd opened herself to the dwyma and she craved it, suddenly.

Forgive me, she murmured. *I've had too much to deal with here.*

As she trod the familiar path Pearl trotted over, nickering, and nuzzled Lyra amiably.

She's eaten all the rose buds, she noted, more amused than annoyed. *Ah well, more will grow.* Somehow the pegasus-construct embodied her lost husband and his wayward charm and made her feel that he was still with her. She stroked Pearl's head as they wandered together to the pool. Both drank, then the pegasus looked around with strangely wise eyes.

She's drinking from a pool blessed by a genilocus, she thought. *What's that doing to her?*

The pegasus looked down at her as if to say, *What do you think it's doing, silly?* Then she gave a sprightly neigh and trotted off into the late afternoon gloom, her pearly coat swiftly lost among the foliage. An owl hooted and a squirrel darted onto a branch of her Winter Tree sapling and stole a berry.

Letting the dwyma bleed into her heart, she closed her eyes and listened . . .

<Nara?> a male voice called into her head almost immediately and Valdyr's gaunt, moustachioed features appeared in darkness, lit by firelight. A dark shape squatted beside the Mollach, far too big to be an ordinary man.

In the moment it took her to wish it, she was sitting on a log beside him.

<*Valdyr,*> she greeted him, touching his arm, which felt as real as flesh and cloth despite her spirit-state.

<*Thank Kore,*> Valdyr responded. <*It's been days – I've been worried.*>

She felt surprisingly warmed by his closeness. *I missed him*, she realised, *and he missed me*. That made her heart thump and her throat tighten with nerves. She'd not thought she could feel warmly about any man, not so soon after Solon, but she and Valdyr had already shared a lot in a short time. Her breath quickened and she momentarily forgot what she meant to say.

Then she blurted, <*I'm sorry, there were things that took up all my time.*> She squinted at the dark shape across the fire and saw that it had to be a construct – but it looked part-human, and that was illegal, surely. <*What is that creature?*>

<*He's a construct,*> Valdyr replied. <*His name is Ogre and he's possibly the most important person in Yuros right now. He's discovered exactly what Ervyn Naxius is doing.*>

Lyra shivered. <*Which is what?*>

<*He's going to destroy the Elétfa and usher in the Age of Daemons.*>

<*He's what?*> She felt her jaw drop. <*But . . . but he must be stopped—*>

<*Of course—but there are only two people in the world who can: you and me, the last dwymancers.*>

<*Oh no . . .* > She bit her lip as a fresh weight came crushing down on her soul. *Dear Kore, haven't I enough already?*

Valdyr was staring at her, imploringly, but she couldn't face him. <*I can't,*> she blurted. <*I'm already dealing with too much.*>

She tore herself away and opened her eyes, to find herself kneeling beside her pool, shaking and blinking back tears. *No*, she thought, *it's too much. My battles are here.*

Bruinland, East Rondelmar

Cordan Sacrecour clung to his saddle as the column jolted down towards the banks of the Bruin. The river, a mile wide and gleaming like a strip of beaten steel under grey skies, dwarfed the fleet of barges clinging to the shores. It was late afternoon and his whole body was aching from the hours on horseback. He'd always thought riding was really just sitting down and letting the horse do the work, but it turned out, it used *all* his muscles, even ones he didn't know he had, like in the small of his back, and every night he collapsed and slept like the dead, only to be roused at dawn, still exhausted and stiff as a corpse.

'No snow and no storms,' Uncle Garod crowed, a few feet away. 'She's lost whatever she had.'

'Lyra can call a blizzard out of clear skies,' Uncle Brylion growled, 'and we're still sixty miles from Pallas.'

'Nonsense – those blizzards were already on their way. She's too weak to do it again,' Garod replied. 'Kore's sake, Brylion, perk up. The men need to see confidence.'

They had been having the same argument all the way from Dupenium and Cordan was sick of hearing it. The one thing that mattered was that Coramore was with Lyra. Messengers had told them that – and the incredible news that Ostevan Pontifex was dead.

She ran away . . . Ostevan went after her and died . . . It's wonderful, Cordan thought to himself, although he'd never let his uncle know; he and Brylion hadn't seen it that way. They were furious, mostly because the Kirkegarde legion in Dupenium had immediately shut themselves in their keep and refused to march, costing them vital men. But neither man was grieving; both had feared the priest.

I'm glad he's dead – and I'm glad Cora's safe with Lyra. Perhaps she can stop this war.

It made him angry that this campaign was being waged in his name when the only person in Dupenium who didn't want it was him. But young princes didn't get a say.

Is this what it'll be like being emperor? If they even let me rule . . .

He had no idea what to make of the other news from Pallas, although Uncle Garod just called it 'arrant nonsense'. He said the idea of a *res publica* was a travesty, but Cordan didn't know enough to decide, though increasingly, if his uncle was for something, he was against.

Once he was crowned, his uncle would rule as regent until Cordan was eighteen – but a little voice kept whispering in his ear that he'd never get that old. *No one gives up power*, he'd read that in the book by Makelli he'd been given. *It's always taken from them at sword-point.*

He followed his uncle down to the river bank, the cavalcade of nobles and mage-knights at their heels, to where a barge was being unloaded so the rankers could camp for the night. When the soldiers saw them they raised their swords, shouting, 'Hail! Hail to the Sacrecour!' in booming voices.

It sounded ugly, like the trumpets and the drums, but he had to play this game; to do less would 'betray his lineage', as Uncle Garod kept saying. His uncle had vowed to get Coramore back and to put Lyra's head on a spike – that was what emperors did – so he saluted the soldiers, shivering, as the drums began to hammer yet again and the hymns of death rolled out across the river and all the way downstream to Pallas.

Coraine Road, Northern Rondelmar

The road is a river, Solon Takwyth mused as he watched the columns tramp past, singing Corani marching songs to the beat of the drums. It was rare for a poetic notion to enter his prosaic mind, but he enjoyed turning it over in his head – although inevitably thinking of rivers led his mind back to logistics: the Dupeni were on the Bruin and making better time than he was.

We're forty miles from Pallas, but they'll arrive in better shape, and sooner.

That didn't trouble him overly: he was confident of his military prowess, certainly compared with men like Garod and Brylion, who only knew one way to fight.

Steam rose like fog from the marching columns and went snaking through the cold landscape – the snow was heavy here in the uplands, but not so bad it required his weather-magi to intervene. Best of all, Duke Torun had decided to stay in Coraine, leaving Solon unequivocally in charge. And Endus Rykjard was proving an amiable enough companion on the road, although right now the mercenary was pensive.

'What's on your mind, my friend?' Solon asked him.

Rykjard glanced over his shoulder, looking northwards towards his homeland, somewhere behind the mass of distant snowy peaks. 'It's this news out of Pallas – the break-up of the empire? My agents in Hollenia tell me that the Imperial Governor has already left Damstadt, and there's an almighty fracas brewing as every mercenary captain and noble – mind you, in Hollenia that's mostly the same thing – are grabbing what they can. But I'm here . . .'

'And set to be a power in the restored empire,' Solon said firmly. 'Help me win this battle, Endus, and I'll see you raised high.' He meant it, too. Rykjard was clearly an able legion commander and men like that were gold dust.

'If we can get it done swiftly, I can perhaps do both,' Rykjard mused.

'We'll do it all at my pace,' Solon insisted. 'We don't rush things and we don't go charging in with our armour half-strapped. But it'll be resolved quickly, I assure you.'

The Hollenian didn't argue the point, but he fell silent as they trotted onwards.

Solon returned his thoughts to the scarcely believable news from Pallas. *She gave power to the Mob in exchange for some kind of honorary status? Incredible . . . An elected Assembly will dominate her Royal Council and govern the country – and Wurther and Dubrayle let her do this? What the fuck were they thinking?*

No doubt it was all a sham. *Afterwards they'll renege on everything*, he sniffed. *Even the fool woman's father wouldn't let her carry this idiocy through.*

Comforted by his reasoning, he turned his mind to how he would conduct this battle. He had to move fast, clearly, or he'd be stuck outside the walls with Garod Sacrecour inside.

It all comes down to my people inside Pallas, he reflected anxiously; he'd always hated being in the power of others. *If they come through, I shall yet be emperor.*

Failure was not an option.

Rykjard said something, startling Solon out of his reverie. 'What was that?'

The Hollenian indicated Solon's own carriage, which was trundling past. 'You brought a woman with you,' he observed. 'I thought your prize was the queen?'

Solon smiled awkwardly. In truth, he'd intended to leave Brunelda behind him – after all, she'd fulfilled her purpose, giving him someone to ease his nights until he had Lyra in his possession. But on the morning of departure, he'd not wanted to let her go.

She rukks better than Lyra ever did, he'd told himself, *and she doesn't complain afterwards.* She might be a whore, but she was better company than Lyra too: she didn't argue or harbour stupid dreams. *I'll put her aside once Lyra's in my hands*, he'd decided, and so here she was, part of the army streaming south.

'This road's too damned cold for an empty bed,' he told Rykjard.

'The Crusades ruined my resistance to cold too.' The Hollenian laughed. 'That's why I keep four wives.'

'You heathen prick.' Solon guffawed. 'I might follow your lead.'

Brunelda gazed out of the curtained window of the carriage as it rattled and shook its way over the rutted, ice-encrusted road, jolting fit to shake her teeth out. But her eyes were on the hillside, where her lord rode alongside the Hollenian.

What's happened to my life? she wondered.

Like every other man, woman or child of Coraine, she'd idolised Solon Takwyth, the Saviour of Coraine, the pinnacle of manhood, without ever expecting to meet him. She'd not even been born when he'd resurrected House Corani after the massacres of 909; all her life he'd been a living legend. She'd screamed his name from the cheap stalls at jousting tournaments, worshipping him for his victories, for his handsome manliness and his utter mastery of the art of war. More than even the ducal house, Solon *was* Coraine.

She'd been sixteen when he went into exile in 930; like most of the duchy she'd hated the queen for choosing that southern rake Ril Endarion over her hero. She'd bought tapers to pray for Solon's return and wept for joy when he had.

And now here she was, in his bed: a dream beyond imagining – but caught up in something far more complicated than she could fathom. That he'd made her pretend to be Lyra, well, she could understand that: he loved his queen, but he couldn't be with her, so he needed someone like her. There were times when she saw the great man inside him – when he showed her kindness, or encouraged someone to be better than they were; that was the man she loved.

But more often he was a bully who exhausted her and left her humiliated and wondering why she didn't run.

All her life she'd been told she was stupid. No one had ever bothered to teach her much more than how to speak and how to count the coin she earned – but she was good at reading customers, and good at giving them what they needed. 'You're not much,' her mother told her every holy day, when Brunelda visited to drop off whatever she could spare, 'but you're a good whore, may Kore have mercy on your soul.'

I am a good whore, she breathed, gazing up the slope, *so good that the invincible Lord Takwyth chose me, and now he owns me.*

But he frightened her sometimes, especially when he took her by surprise, pinning her down and using her violently, all the while roaring the queen's name. Or when he tossed in his sleep, sweating at some nightmare, clutching at the marred side of his face: even though the scars had been all but magicked away, his wounds ran deeper than skin.

I want to love him. I want him to love me . . . but me, *not Lyra. Me.*

She was also terrified about this war: her own brothers were in the queen's army, in Oryn Levis' legion, and she was frightened for them. Every night she prayed they would see sense and desert, for Solon would destroy anyone who stood in his way, she knew that.

But what happens to me when this is done? she wondered. *He'll have his queen – but what will I have?* And more chillingly: *I don't know if I can live without him any more . . .*

Pallas

The throne hall wasn't full and that worried Lyra – and her paranoid father – more than the armies of Dupenium and Coraine right now, because the pure-blood mage-nobles of Pallas all believed that but for a quirk of history, they could have been emperor.

Now I'm asking them to give up that dream.

Thankfully, Dirklan, Calan and Dominius had been working the Great Houses with their trademark blend of negotiation, cajoling and threat.

'Do you really think Takwyth or Garod will favour you when you haven't done a thing for them in six years?'

'The Dupeni don't see you as a potential ally: they see you as a treasure hoard.'

'The Church has blessed this new regime; do you really want to be on the wrong side of them?'

'There's a Mob out there: do you want explain your objections to them? We have only to give them your name.'

And perhaps most tellingly, although Lyra didn't like it, *'You've got every advantage, Milord: mage-blood, wealth and education. Play your pieces right and you'll own every seat on this new elected Assembly.'*

Lyra ignored the gaps and focused on those before her: old mage-knights sporting dated finery; dowagers of centuries-old dynasties; brooding lords with plump wives, their figures ruined by pregnancies and indolence. These Houses had ruled for hundreds of years. They were here to renew their fealty to her – but mostly to find out what she'd given away.

The next family was led by a florid knight with a pregnant wife half his age, trailed by a lanky bastard son, a mage-knight with intense eyes. Her herald whispered their names in her ear.

'Do you, the Blessed of House Misen, swear to serve the Republic of Rondelmar?' she asked them.

Simplifying *Res Publica* to 'Republic' had been Calan's idea; the new word rolled off the tongue much better than the clumsy Rimoni term. Frankel wasn't happy – of course he was a linguistic purist as well – but Calan had pulled rank, enjoying his petty victory during this 'surrender'.

The moody Lord Misen, positively simmering with resentment, went down on one knee, followed by his kin behind him. He placed his hand on the *Book of Kore* and in a surly voice intoned, 'I, Tybor Misen, Lord of Misencourt, do pledge the allegiance of House Misen to the Republic of Rondelmar.' He kissed the giant sceptre with a sour expression, as if it was coated in vinegar.

'Thank you, Lord Misen,' Lyra said, smiling at the thought that she'd inadvertently masqueraded as this man's kin when she'd chosen the pseudonym Nara of Misencourt. 'Rondelmar sees and hears.'

Behind her right shoulder, Grand Prelate Wurther recited, 'Kore sees and hears. May he bless your loyalty with riches and curse infidelity with eternal loss.' He made the sign of the Sacred Heart over the kneeling family. 'Go forth to serve and protect.'

The family rose and turned and Lyra let out a small sigh of relief: another House pledged, although she'd not have trusted her life to any of them if she'd been left alone in the room.

Then the young son surprised her by turning back and kneeling again. This time he lifted his empty scabbard in both hands, as if in offering. 'Kore bless you, Majesty,' he said hoarsely. 'Let me serve you.'

Lyra saw the rest of his family rolling their eyes, but the young man either didn't notice or didn't care. 'Sir . . . ?' Lyra asked.

'I am Sir Argus Misen,' the young man cried, his shining eyes fixed on her.

Oh dear, another admirer. 'Sir Argus, I'm sure you'd be welcome in the Royal Guard,' she started, but his father was glaring.

'A Misen does not serve with guardsmen or common soldiers,' Tybor Misen sniffed. 'No son of mine—'

'My Queen,' his son interrupted, 'let me serve you – and your republic – as a knight.'

'But—'

Lyra stopped when Dirklan bent and whispered in her ear, 'You've not inaugurated any new knightly orders – this is an excellent chance, and will perhaps get us some badly needed support.'

'How?' she whispered.

'Just decree it – you have the right. Servants of the Realm, paragons of virtue, protectors of virgins, that sort of nonsense. Who knows, it might channel the young bravos' energy into something useful.'

She gave her father a reproving look, then turned back to the earnest young knight. 'Sir Argus, I am moved,' she told him, making his face glow. 'Our republic does indeed have need of brave and virtuous men, pledged to protect the traditions of knightly honour, loyal service and ... um ... protecting virgins,' she blurted – *damn you Father, for putting those words in my head* – then trying to recover by adding, 'and of course, *all* women, from harm.'

Even queens. Especially queens.

'You shall be the Order of Misencourt. Your patron shall be Saint Nara.' There really was a Saint Nara, a martyr to Kore in the early Rimoni Empire. 'Your head shall be Sir Exilium Excelsior, a paragon of virtue and proud servant of the realm. All mage-knights of the Blood are invited to join.'

She turned her head and looking up at Exilium, said quietly, 'I really don't need two bodyguards.' Seeing the uncertainty on his face, as if he feared his service had been rejected, she announced to the hall, 'Sir Exilium Excelsior, will you become my First Sword of Rondelmar?'

He swelled up, then burst out with, 'Praise you, my Queen –' and came racing around to kneel at her feet and kiss her hand. 'The Knights of Misencourt will become famed for our piety and our loyalty: we shall be the strength of your arms.' He stood and drew his sword, walked to the still kneeling Sir Argus Misen and touched the young man's shoulders with the naked blade. 'You will be my second, Sir Argus.' He glared around the court. 'Who here has the courage to join us?'

For a moment Lyra feared the answer would be *no one* – then a knot of young men standing among the Corani loyalists looked at each other, all youngest sons living meagrely, sniffing *opportunity*. Traditionally, knightly orders provided equipment, lodgings and a stipend, which was more than a provincial lord gave.

Someone called out, 'I will join.'

When he strode forward, his friends followed suit and within minutes, the Order of Misencourt numbered almost fifty mage-knights – mostly, Lyra realised, at the cost of the Great Houses' private warbands.

Dirklan winked at her, but she could see dissatisfied faces among the mage-lords.

She walked to Lord Misen and smiled at him. 'Lord Tybor, as honorary patron of the Order that bears your name, you will need to see the Treasurer about assistance in extending your halls.'

Lord Tybor's face, which had gone through annoyance to rising anger, suddenly cleared. 'Misencourt is honoured, my Queen,' he proclaimed, striding forward and placing a proud hand on the shoulder of his illegitimate son for possibly the first time, judging by how awkward it looked for both. 'Long live Rondelmar!'

As the court echoed his shout, Lyra smiled wryly. *With your son a part of my first knightly order, you have no choice but to be firmly on our side now.*

She took up the heavy sceptre and raised her voice. 'Let the badge of the Knights of Misencourt be the Winter Tree, the Vereinen emblem. Let your colour be red, for the rose of the republic. May Kore bless and keep you.'

She told Exilium to stay with his new men. 'Take command of them, marshal them and make arrangements for them – you'll need to quarter them in the Bastion for now, until the halls of Misencourt can be readied.'

Misencourt is miles away, somewhere south of the river, she remembered. Her new knights wouldn't be going there any time soon, not when she needed them right here.

She stood, which meant everyone else but Dominius had to kneel, and swept from the room, feeling like she'd just won a minor victory.

Taking Basia, she headed for the council rooms, her counsellors and Ari Frankel trailing after them. Servants poured wine, then withdrew. It had been a long, tense day and Lyra sipped her glass gratefully.

'Gentlemen,' she began, 'that seemed to go well. Forty-seven of the sixty Pallacian Houses took the oath – and we formed a new knightly order, which stole fifty men from those Houses. A good day's work.'

'They're mostly half-blood bastards,' Dominius put in.

'But many will be better warriors than their pure-blood kindred,' Oryn commented. 'The pure-blood heirs tend to spend more time with quills and coins then blade or periapt. It was well done, Milady.'

Lyra was warmed by the praise. 'Credit goes to Dirklan, who saw the opportunity before I did.'

'What of the absent Houses?' Calan asked.

Dirklan's good eye glinted. 'Six of them were planning to aid either

Takwyth or the Sacrecours. We raided them separately last night and arrested the key plotters.' He glanced at Calan. 'If the treachery is proven, their treasuries are yours.'

'Every coin is a drop of blood in our veins,' Calan said – a quote from one of his own speeches, if Lyra recalled correctly. He tapped his pile of papers. 'And we have the signatures of five of the six major banks. Loans are forthcoming. We are, technically, solvent.'

'Through some of the most dastardly tactics of financial malfeasance known,' Dominius rumbled. He'd found out about the State Bank legislation that morning and had deduced the rest: but it was a *fait accompli* and as they'd left him no time to get his money out, all he could do was mutter about it.

'Is that reproval or envy I hear?' Calan smirked.

'Dread.' Dominius sniffed. 'Is nothing is safe from your predatory avarice?'

'I do hope not.'

Lyra's spirits lifted to hear these implacable rivals bantering, after all they'd done to each other. She turned to her Knight-Commander. 'Oryn, how is the recruitment going?'

'Latest reports are good,' he said. 'This morning the recruiting stations were inundated with volunteers. Many have never fought before, though: we're trying to separate out the veterans so we can arm and assign them first.'

'Mix the new men with the old,' Dirklan advised. 'Let them learn by example.'

Ari Frankel raised a hand. 'Spirits are high, Majesty, and the city was quiet last night.'

'But what about Lazar?' Dirklan wanted to know. 'And Tad Kaden and his gang?'

Ari shifted uncomfortably on his seat. 'Tad helped me reach her Majesty. I saw him two days ago, and he told me he would be leaving the city as soon as his sister is freed.'

Lyra had granted Braeda's pardon, but she would not release her until this crisis was over. Kaden might resent that, but for once she held the upper hand.

'Where will they go afterwards – to join our enemies?' Dominius growled.

'I know not,' Ari replied. 'As for Lazar . . . perhaps a pardon, or an amnesty . . . ?'

'No,' Lyra said firmly. 'I will not reward violence.'

'He would say that nothing would have been achieved without his actions,' Ari argued.

'I agree with her Majesty,' Dirklan put in. 'It's too soon. His sort are never satisfied unless they are burning or killing. Reform was their excuse – trust me, they'll quickly find another.'

Oryn put in, 'I'm reassigning one of the two legions who've been penning the Mob in the dockland to the walls. The other needs to stay in place, I think, until the two armies arrive.'

'It would be a show of faith to withdraw both,' Ari put in.

'But Lazar's still out there,' Oryn retorted. 'What do you know about military planning anyway, scribe?'

'I know what the people think,' Ari replied, not at all intimidated. 'The City Guard were sufficient before, yes? So let them return and the legions go and fight.'

Lyra looked at Dirklan, who nodded faintly.

'I take your point, Oryn, but I'm inclined to agree with Master Frankel: we need a visible show of faith,' she decided, which made Oryn scowl. 'Let us demonstrate our belief in the unity of the city. At the moment Lazar has no pretext to act against us, so let's not furnish him with one.' She clapped her hands. 'Moving on. The secession?'

'Same as yesterday, but more so,' Dirklan responded. 'Argundy, Estellayne and Lantris have publicly declared their own sovereignty, while informally their ambassadors thank her Majesty and express the desire to keep diplomatic channels – and trade links – open.'

'What of military alliance?' Oryn asked.

'Too soon, but we'll get there – as long as we survive Solon and Garod.' Dirklan produced a piece of parchment. 'This is a letter from Duke Salinas of Aquillea, reaffirming his commitment to Rondelmar, but proposing new terms: a halfway house position giving them favourable treatment in return for supporting the throne – but he's careful not to specify who is sitting on that throne.'

'Worm,' Dominius sniffed.

'It's what I'd do,' Calan objected.

'Like I said.'

'Gentlemen,' Lyra reproved. 'What about the South?'

'Midrea, Noros and Bricia are silent,' Dirklan replied. 'Midrea have Imperial Armies shielding them from the Shihad just now and don't want to upset us; Noros is occupied by the Shihad and Bricia's most powerful man is Seth Korion, who's penned up in Norostein. Don't expect responses from them anytime soon. Hollenia is disintegrating into factions, as is Brevis. And Andressea is scared they'll get no protection if Schlessen raiders emerge from the forests. They'll want to stay allied with us, at the very least.'

It was about as good as they could expect: no one was going to help them; but there was enough doubt about the outcome that few were siding with Garod Sacrecour or Solon Takwyth either.

Lyra looked down the table, thinking, *I'll miss this. Four of these five men could still betray me before this crisis is over, but I do like them.* She rose. 'I believe the rest is logistics, and I've had a long day. Lord Setallius, please attend on me.'

She made a point of thanking each man personally for their support, even though Dominius and Calan had both acted against her at times and Oryn and Ari still might. *It's the end of an era – if six years can count as an era.*

'Gentlemen, I've decided in the coming days it would be better for me to remain in the background. Father has convinced me that I'm too important to risk myself needlessly, so we're turning the Royal Suite into even more of a fortress. Pass all messages through Basia de Sirou, if you would. Oh, and our Lord Spymaster has been assigned a special mission, so he too may not be as visible as usual.'

'He's not usually visible at all,' Oryn muttered.

'That's my job,' Dirklan told him.

'It's sensible, Majesty,' Calan told her.

'Unusually so,' Dominius agreed suspiciously.

Lyra smiled. 'Quite. Good luck, gentlemen.' *We're going to need it.*

She left the council room, clutching her father's arm and praying for the strength to do what must be done.

23

Three Armies

The Ill-Omened Number

In Rondian culture, three is the unluckiest number. While two people can be in har-mony, add a third and that harmony will be destroyed. There is no place for three bodies in a bed, or three armies on a battlefield.

DARUN TRINHURST, DIARIST, PALLAS 881

Pallas, Rondelmar
Martrois 936

Basia de Sirou felt like all her life had been preparation for this moment. For years she'd been champing at the bit to show Dirklan what she could do. Now the enormity of it left her breathless.

Dear Kore, I'm effectively the Commander of the Volsai.

Dirklan always said controlling spies was like herding snakes: the deadly men and women tended to lash out when cornered. But he'd worked hard to instil camaraderie into his people, and a feeling of fam-ily. She hoped they saw her in that way too.

Right now her eyes were spread right through the city, hunting down leads on Sacrecour spies and Corani traitors. There was something being planned by men loyal to Solon Takwyth and her agents were clos-ing in, but Takwyth was only a few days away now, and the Sacrecours were even closer. They'd be outside the walls the day after tomorrow.

On the plus side, the priests, dissidents and street-preachers were finally singing from the same hymn-sheet: *Kore protect the Queen and the Republic.* The news from the wider empire was encouraging and the Sacrecour cause felt isolated; none of the newly ceded states wanted their return. The royal legions were integrating the veterans among Frankel's dissidents as swiftly as could be hoped, and Exilium's new 'Knights of Misencourt' were drilling hard in mounted combat.

Leaving the Royal Suite in Brigeda's hands, Basia went to the central stairs to intercept Exilium, who was armoured up and heading for the stables and another day's training with his new unit. He was limping and his really rather gorgeous face was marred with fresh bruises.

'What happened?' She *tsked*, stroking his cheek, then blushed as she realised what she'd done.

His face took on the confused state it usually had around her. 'There are some good fighters among the knights.'

'Did someone beat you?' she asked archly.

'No,' he said, his quietly dismissive voice saying more than boasting, 'all three of them are in far worse state than I. But they'll recover, I'm told.'

Holy Kore. She knew he was good, but three men at once? 'Try to leave some standing for the battle.'

'I shall,' he said earnestly, then he asked, 'Is there news?'

'Of course – we Volsai know everything first.' She leaned closer and dropped her voice. 'Takwyth's Corani are three days away on the north road, while Garod Sacrecour's men are a day closer, thanks to their river-barges.'

They both knew the numbers: Takwyth had four of his own legions and two of Hollenian mercenaries. Garod had nine. Lyra had seven, now that the dissidents had joined them, some 35,000 men. Ordinarily, fortifications were meant to count for double in military reckoning, but the outer walls of Pallas were poor. The empire had been at peace for centuries, and walls an expense that successive emperors had felt they could forego.

Once the armies get inside, they'll run amok, fellow Rondians or not. She shuddered, remembering 909 and the Hel that had cost both her legs – remembering Ril . . . and above all, Brylion Fasterius. It was a rare night that the stink of his alcohol-breath and the weight of his body on her

394

back didn't rip her from sleep, leaving her crying aloud from remembered pain and terror. With difficulty, she thrust the image aside and clapped Exilium's arm. 'On the bright side, Rolven Sulpeter is marching north with six Corani legions—'

'—and on the dark side, we don't know whose side he's on,' Exilium finished for her.

'Ours, I hope,' she replied, but she doubted that; the old lord would despise Lyra's new *res publica* and in any case, his son marched with Takwyth. 'He's making his way to the Siber to take barges north. He should reach Pallas a day after Takwyth.'

'Then what will we do?' Exilium asked.

'That's what's about to be decided,' she told him. 'I'm heading for an army meeting now.'

Exilium made the Sign of Corineus over his chest. 'We have the blessing of his Holiness, and our Sacred Queen as our banner. We will prevail, for Kore will light our path to victory.'

I won't burst his bubble. 'Get your men ready,' she told him. 'I'll see you later.'

They met each other's eyes briefly. *He means well and he's a decent man*, she thought. She suspected that he was seeing her with fonder eyes now too, but his faith was still a barrier between them. She'd never met a man more fervent about his religion, even among the priesthood.

'Kore go with you,' he said as they parted.

She entered the council room to find Oryn Levis already there, standing with a mix of Pallacian and Corani legion commanders. They'd all been appointed by Lyra and were loyal up to a point – except that they'd all served Solon Takwyth first. None of them looked pleased to see a Volsai interrupting their discussions.

'Lady Basia,' Oryn Levis greeted her. 'Do you have fresh intelligence?'

'I do,' she replied. *Unlike the stale intellects I see here.* She quickly outlined the latest reports from Volsai overflying the armies converging on Pallas. She finished by saying, 'Garod Sacrecour has brought siege-engines on his barges – including catapults. Those could cause great destruction inside the walls.'

'The housing is close-packed in Esdale and the eastern parts of the city,' Legate Cornelius, a Corani veteran, noted. 'If he sets the place alight, we could lose half the city.'

'The walls will be taken in half a day,' Oryn Levis predicted gloomily. 'Better we don't rely on them at all. We should march out and choose the field of battle. There is high ground east of the city we could defend.'

The other men nodded in agreement, while Basia tried to think it through. 'Won't Takwyth circle behind us?'

'Neither Garod nor we can afford that, so Garod would be forced to attack immediately,' Legate Darmonieu of Gravenhurst countered. 'One day to converge with Garod, one day to fight and if we're victorious, we'll be back behind our defences before Takwyth can engage us in the open.'

Basia blinked: she hadn't anticipated this proposal and Dirklan was out of reach on his own mission. 'I would need to consult the queen,' she said, stalling for time.

'With respect, the queen does not have military expertise,' a Pallacian mage-noble named Viron Bondeau replied tersely. 'We need to decide, not her.'

They were right about that, but it was a Hel of a gamble. 'One day's delay and we're stranded outside Pallas, leaving Takwyth to march in,' she said, wondering if that was what Oryn wanted.

'It's no bigger a gamble than waiting inside the walls for two armies to arrive,' Oryn replied. 'Military history tells us that when you face two armies, the one thing you can't afford to do is let them unite.'

Put like that, it sounded reasonable. 'It's your decision,' Basia conceded. 'The queen will back you. But how quickly can you march?'

'We've been preparing to march for the last two days,' Oryn said. 'Just in case it became appropriate.'

Really? 'So you could have mentioned it earlier,' she complained.

'It was a contingency only: it required confirmation that Takwyth and Garod would arrive on different days,' Darmonieu told her. *Leave the war to us, girl,* his eyes added.

How does Dirklan cope with this responsibility? she wondered. Just a few days in charge and it was driving her mad.

Deciding she could brief the queen later, she headed for her next appointment at the Imperocracy, enjoying the feeling of breezing past the officials and guards without being stopped, now they all knew who she was. She joined Calan Dubrayle in a meeting with forty-odd richly dressed Pallacians – all male, all grey or balding, and all looking sceptical. They were bankers and traders whose assets were irrevocably tied to the city, which was why they had remained here when Jean Benoit and half the Merchants' Guild fled to Dupenium.

Calan was holding up a coin: the first coin minted in the name of the new Republic of Rondelmar. It bore Lyra's head in profile with the Dagger of Corineus on the reverse, and around the edge were the words *Res Publica di Rondelmar, 936.*

'This will be the new coin of the realm, gentlemen,' the Treasurer was saying as Basia slipped in through the side door. 'My people are calling it a "lira", thanks to the happy coincidence that the old Rimoni word for "pound" is libra, and of course it's similar to the name of our queen. It's worth the same as the imperial auros and will replace the auros in due course; it will be exchangeable one for one from the Crown Bank of Rondelmar. I urge you to take it up, as the Imperocracy will begin to make its use mandatory in payment of all duties and tolls within six months.'

This was greeted with consternation, and it was a few seconds before someone piped up and asked, 'The Crown Bank of Rondelmar? Who are they?'

'The Treasury have taken a controlling interest in Gravenhurst Stronghold Bank, whose governors are now Arch-Legates of the Treasury,' Dubrayle replied evenly. 'We are now, as of today, the largest bank in Rondelmar.'

His words were greeted with stunned silence – and then an angry babble broke out, before a red-faced banker stomped forward, snapping, 'This is *infamous*. The statutes of empire prevent the Crown from banking – it's explicit in the Deeds of Trust for our banks that the Crown will not interfere –'

'Indeed, Magnus Jusst,' the Treasurer said evenly, 'but that *was* the empire. *This* is the Republic, which is under no such constraints. Consider your Deeds of Trust superseded.'

The bankers and merchants looked at each other with purpling faces as the racket rose, then another man, bald, austere Kaspar Ankargild, raised his voice. 'This is criminal,' he said in a querulous voice.

'Only under Imperial Law,' Dubrayle replied. 'Not all of those were carried into the new republic.'

He knows he'll hang if we lose in the field, Basia thought, admiring the Treasurer's gumption. *Perhaps he feels he's got nothing to lose.*

'You can't change the laws behind our backs,' Ankargild railed. 'You're playing games in front of a forest fire, Dubrayle – and the wind is rising behind it.'

'I have every confidence that the Republic will vanquish the Sacrecour army again,' Dubrayle replied, with far more certainty than Basia felt. 'Those who have backed Duke Garod's revolt had best look to their assets.'

The threat hung in the momentarily silent hall and Basia saw the bankers suddenly remembering the storms Lyra had summoned the last time Garod marched.

They'll have a bet either way, Calan had predicted at yesterday's council meeting. *They'll squeal, then pretend to support us. It'll all come down to whether we defeat Garod and Takwyth.*

Then why do this now? Dominius had asked, once he'd recovered from his own apoplexy at the announcement of the new Crown Bank being set up behind his back and likely to throw the Church's wealth into chaos. *Why risk alienating them?*

Because it gives us money now, Calan had replied. *It makes us a player in the back-room deals again.*

Basia couldn't pretend to understand it all, but she could see that the Treasurer's predictions were correct: the bankers might be grumbling, but they were also making a show of grudging acquiescence.

When Calan declared the meeting over, she approached him. 'What happens to the bank if we lose?' she asked, leading the way through a high-pillared marble hall.

'Tens of thousands of people will have their life savings plundered to enrich Garod or Takwyth,' he sniffed, 'including Jusst and Ankargild and all those other silk purses back in that hall.'

'I never knew you were such a gambler,' Basia remarked.

'Our lives are at stake, Mistress de Sirou. I'll use every weapon, as will you. We're not so different.'

'Were they right about the legality?'

'Of course – but they also know that it's the winners who write the rules. Victory in the field will make us into saints; defeat will cast us as devils incarnate.' He shrugged. 'I shall enjoy the former and I won't see the latter, so it's really not such a gamble.'

'And you have the money you need?'

'I do finally have a war-chest worthy of the term. The game is on. Now, if you'll excuse me, I need to explore ways to spend it . . .'

Pallas-Coraine Road, North Rondelmar

The camp was rising, but Solon had been awake for hours, although he was still on his back on the small pallet, with Brunelda on top, her hand planted on his chest to keep herself upright as she ground against him in wet, rhythmic intensity. Their ruddy skin was bathed in sweat and she was moaning through another climax as he built towards his own. When he closed his eyes, she was Lyra.

Then a metallic rattle came from outside the tent-flap and someone called, 'My Lord?' in a tentative voice.

It had to be fairly obvious what they were doing, which meant the matter was urgent. 'One minute,' Solon called, looking up at Brunelda's bouncing breasts, her face contorted with the intensity of their coupling. He sat up, turned her over and finished her with a powerful series of hip-thrusts, then gazed down at her tear-stained, worshipful eyes.

'You're weeping,' he noted.

'Sometime when I climax, my eyes leak,' she said apologetically.

'So it's a physical reaction, not emotion,' he clarified, climbing off her and tipping a jug of water over his head.

'Yes, Lord.'

'Good,' he decided. 'You've done well . . . um, you're good at . . . erm . . .'

'I'm a good whore,' she said shamelessly.

'Quite.' Her subservience pleased him. *Maybe she can teach Lyra a few things . . .*

But the day awaited: he put her from his mind and left the tent, barking orders for it to be dismantled within the hour. An aide was waiting outside – he should have known the youth's name, but there had been too many new faces recently. 'What is it?'

'A messenger from the city,' the aide replied.

Ah, Solon thought, his attention focusing, 'from *inside* Pallas? Bring him.'

The messenger was a mage-pilot fresh from his skiff and flushed about the cheeks from the icy wind. His terse update was mostly good news: Pallas was rife with rumour over the impending arrival of House Dupeni and House Sacrecour and confused by the queen's speech about a *res publica* – a foolish notion, it'd never work – and Oryn Levis was preparing to march out, which was predictable. But one thing did prick his attention.

'You say Setallius has dropped from view?' he clarified.

'The man I met with says he's vanished, and Basia de Sirou is acting in his stead.'

Solon was perturbed by this. When they were all working together, Setallius had only ever left court when something big was happening – and he'd always reappeared precisely where he was needed. *Like the night we took the Celestium back from Ostevan.* His disappearance left Solon uneasy.

But everything else was playing out the way he wanted. He dismissed the mage-pilot and looked around him; he was on a low rise above the road, as his men readied themselves for another day of marching. The weather was milder today, with spring in the air, no storms had been forecasted.

My lads are in good spirits. They believe we're in the right. I wonder how those serving Lyra feel?

Endus Rykjard sauntered up, gnawing on a chicken leg. 'They're a quiet lot,' he observed, glancing back at Takwyth's aides, who'd been studiously ignoring him.

'You know how magi get when they've known each other for years, Endus,' Solon said. 'It gets so nothing needs to be said aloud.'

They both knew the real reason was that mage-nobles held merce-naries in contempt.

Rykjard made an affable 'it's no matter' gesture. 'What did the mes-senger have to say? Is all well?'

'Better than well, my friend. We have solid intelligence that Oryn Levis is going to march the bulk of his forces out of Pallas to meet the Sacrecours in battle. There's a town called Finostarre, four miles east of Pallas, beneath a low ridge. It's open ground, favourable for battle with an advantage to those who hold the high ground.'

'Wasn't that where you won a jousting tourney and regained your place at court?'

'Aye,' Solon said, 'I vanquished the shit-smear Lyra married and engi-neered my return.'

'Won't Garod just sail right past Levis and dock in the city?'

Solon shook his head. 'His barges would be sitting ducks: they'd be slaughtered. No, he'll land his men east of Finostarre and give battle. Nine legions to five: he'll believe his victory inevitable.'

'There's no such thing as inevitable,' Rykjard observed.

Solon clapped his shoulder. 'I couldn't agree more.'

Finostarre, Rondelmar

'I know this place,' Brylion Fasterius grunted. 'Finostarre.'

'Finostarre,' Cordan echoed. 'Where the Grand Tourney was held?' He'd been a prisoner of the Corani during that event, but he'd lapped up news of the tourney like milk.

'Aye,' Uncle Brylion growled, his swarthy features ugly with displeasure.

'You were beaten in the semi-final by Sir Solon,' Cordan went on blithely.

Brylion smacked him hard on the ear, making it ring. 'Keep your shitty mouth closed.'

Tears stung his eyes but Cordan gritted his teeth through the pain. 'I'm sorry,' he said in a small, choked voice, railing silently, *I'm going to be emperor one day*. Brylion scared him: the man absolutely seethed with fury these days and was never far from lashing out.

Uncle Garod gave Cordan no support and everyone else always pretended they hadn't noticed. Now Garod's retinue, thirty mage-nobles of varying ages and kinship, studied the terrain before them from their position at the edge of a small wood. They could see a wide expanse of grass before Sancta Lucia's Abbey, a small hamlet beyond that and a gentle rise where Corani and Pallacian banners fluttered in the gentle breeze, above lines of green-and-white-clad legionaries, half a mile away.

The Queen's army, Cordan thought, and for a spiteful moment he hoped someone would kill Uncle Brylion, *dead as dead*. But he buried the thought and asked his uncle, 'Is there any news of Coramore?'

'She's sequestered with the queen in the Royal Suite,' Garod said quietly. 'She's a prisoner, of course. They'll threaten to hang her if we don't turn back,' he added cruelly.

Cordan's heart fluttered. 'But . . . you wouldn't let that happen, would you, Uncle?'

'She ran away,' Garod reminded Cordan, 'straight to rukking Lyra Vereinen – and left our ally the Pontifex dead.'

Cordan looked away. *I hate you all – and I'm glad creepy Ostevan is dead.*

Lyra had been good to him – so had Ril, and Basia, and even Solon Takwyth. He didn't understand why Solon was now at war with his queen. And he really didn't know who he wanted to win.

I just want to live, and for Coramore to be safe.

Garod signalled a herald and trumpets began to blow on all sides as Sacrecour soldiers, men of Fauvion and Dupenium and the surrounding countryside, tramped out of the woods, freshly disembarked from the barges.

Nine legions – and they have only five. He set his jaw. 'Dear Kore, protect my sister,' he whispered. 'Protect all those I care about.'

None of whom are with me now.

Exilium bowed his head in silent prayer. Around him, the chapel rang with the voices of monks and nuns, chanting hymns of praise, the familiar, comforting sound grounding him, salving his soul.

'Great Kore, who gave the powers of life and death to the Blessed,' he prayed, 'forgive me for invoking your Holy name. I know that you are a loving God, for whom war is anathema. But this is a just war, to preserve the Church of your name and the Crown that unites your Chosen People. Look favourably on our endeavours.'

Except we're all fighting in your name, he reflected uncomfortably. *The House of Kore is at war with itself.*

The rightness of the Queen's cause was indisputable, though: he had seen her himself, alight with holy fire as she blasted the daemon from the body of Lef Yarle. The false Pontifex Ostevan was similarly destroyed. Lyra Vereinen was a Living Saint, that was clear. And Dominius Wurther, for all his faults, still backed her. Set against that divine mandate, Solon Takwyth and Garod Sacrecour were unholy traitors.

Heartened by his logic, he raised his voice for the final verses, leading his knights in a rousing chorus of the battle-hymn, 'One with my Maker'.

He took a final look up at the imposing icon over the altar – ironically, Sancta Lucia, better known as Mater-Imperia Lucia Fasterius, grandmother of Cordan Sacrecour – then left the front pew and marched down the aisle, his knights falling in behind. Their mounts waited outside, but before they rode off, he addressed them.

'Men of the Order of Misencourt, we are called to war. This will be our first battle as an order, so let us win glory in it. Let our names strike fear into the enemy hearts.'

He knew they thought him a rigid, pompous foreigner, but at least they respected his sword. He'd won that from them, beating them two or three at a time to show his prowess and right to lead.

He'd appropriated the war-cry of the legendary knight Sir Rynholt and now he shouted, 'Rise up, rise up – bloody deeds await us, but we shall wash our hands in the sacred fountains of Kore. Misencourt for the Queen!'

'We rise,' they shouted back fervently, because they might doubt the will of Kore, or even His existence, but they could not deny that they were about to fight for their lives.

They took up position in front of a small rise a hundred yards from where the queen, veiled and flanked by Volsai guards, was mounted on a white horse. The air about her crackled with half-seen webs of shielding and wards. She turned and raised a hand in blessing as the knights saluted her, hands on hearts, before facing the enemy.

Exilium muttered a prayer for her Majesty, but his eyes were drawn to Basia de Sirou, standing stiffly at the queen's side. When she saw him staring, the bodyguard threw him an ironic salute.

If only Basia would embrace Kore as her Saviour, he thought sadly. *She would be a fine woman if she exchanged her pride for piety.* Then he coloured and gazed across the fields, because staring at enemy soldiers was easier than thinking about Basia's unsettling charm.

The Sacrecour legions in imperial purple were arrayed just half a mile away across the old tournament grounds, in the lee of a long narrow piece of woodland. Farms dotted the landscape, but the fields were fallow and the herds had been relocated. The Sacrecour left was near the Bruin River, a distant gleam of dull silver. Their right stretched towards the hills, half a mile to the north.

Exilium joined Sir Iles Kraal, the veteran mage-knight he'd appointed his marshal; the man would stay clear of direct combat to ensure he was kept apprised of the battle's tides. They trotted up to join Oryn Levis' commanders, who were gathered around the Knight-Commander.

'Sir Exilium,' Levis greeted him. The Knight-Commander was sweating heavily, but he spoke firmly enough as he turned back to his commanders. 'Today, we have the higher ground but we are fewer in number, so we must defend, and counter-attack if the opportunity presents itself,' Oryn lectured them: textbook tactics and easily predicted, not that Exilium would have done anything different. The question was whether they could hold – and whether Oryn would know when to counter.

Once the legion commanders had confirmed their placements, Exilium asked, 'Where shall my knights deploy?'

Oryn pointed to a flat piece of slope to their left, north of the centre, where a gentle rise climbed to an uneven low ridge, along which a double rank of pikemen were lined up, backed by crossbowmen. 'Behind them. Bolster them if they break, and counter if the chance presents – once my permission is given.'

'Any delay could cost the opportunity,' Exilium noted.

'And a false charge could cost us everything,' the Knight-Commander said curtly. 'You will await my orders before any attack.' He threw a salute, then turned away, making it clear the discussion was over.

Exilium nudged his horse back into motion, past the arrayed rankers of Pallacios IX, who looked him over with interest but little liking.

'It's that Estellan bastard they say's better'n Takky hisself,' he overheard, to which another man said, 'Nah, Takky rukked him over in the yards, I 'eard.'

There was way too much reverence for Takwyth in their voices for Exilium's liking.

We need to give them new heroes.

He and Iles Kraal joined Argus Misen at the fore of the Misencourt knights and he filled in the minutes inspecting his knights, learning a few more names and getting a feel for their temper. Mage-knights were notoriously difficult to lead: they generally considered themselves to be both the best warriors on the field and too valuable to lose. Exilium had seen that in the Inquisition and the Kirkegarde and these men were no different. Being members of the Great Houses, they had the added charm of being arrogant, entitled pricks. But he'd whipped most of them on the training fields and there was no one who didn't accord him grudging respect now.

From across the fields, the first drums rolled, and the Sacrecour legions began to march forward at the walk. The time had come.

Exilium bowed his head and whispered, 'Kore, I commend my soul to thee.'

'They haven't got a prayer,' Brylion Fasterius growled, slapping Duke Garod on the shoulder. Cordan watched the two men exchange a confident handshake, then the hulking knight swaggered off towards his warhorse.

Is it wrong to wish my uncle dead? Cordan wondered.

But regarding the battle, he'd decided that it wasn't wrong to hope for victory. His side were fighting for the preservation of the empire. *My empire.* Even he felt betrayed by Lyra – the empire had stood for more than five hundred years; who was she to throw that away? How could a *res publica* ever work when men were palpably unequal? One mage was worth hundreds of men on the battlefield, so how could anyone say a commoner could be their equal before the law, or worthy of a voice in court?

I'm only fourteen, but even I understand this better than Lyra.

When he was emperor, he would forgive her. She'd treated him fairly, and in truth, she was very pretty for an older woman – but she was being foolish now. Or she'd been misled. *It's that scary Wraith who's to blame, I'm sure. And Fatty Wurther.*

Then the trumpets brayed, the drums hammered and each centurion, pilus and serjant echoed the order: 'Forward . . . march!'

Cordan gripped the hilt of his sword, his heart beginning to pound. *I'm going to see a battle and maybe I'll have to kill someone. I might even be killed.* The thought sucked the air from his lungs, but he gritted his teeth and whispered, *Dear Kore, make me brave.*

It's too beautiful a day for war, Basia thought. *We should be laying trestle tables with food and ale on a day like this.* She glanced to her left, where the blonde woman in the crown was fidgeting nervously, her face veiled against the glare. Basia hadn't wanted her here, but the queen had to be visible, a banner for her men. She wore Pallas blue, like the sky.

Kore, watch over us, she thought, the irony not lost on her. *I don't even believe in Him, so who am I praying to?*

The Royal Guard were arrayed a hundred yards in front of them, five ranks deep and bristling with javelins. Officers in crested helms were barking orders and encouragement, reminding the men of who they were, of why they were here. *Kore save the Queen*, she heard, over and over.

Then her eyes crept to Exilium, mounted at the head of his knights. *Be safe,* she wished him, knowing he wouldn't be.

But the enemy were closing in now, in the brisk, business-like manner of the Rondian legion: methodical, inevitable and hard-hearted.

Exactly the same orders were being rapped out on both sides: *Hoist javelins – shields high – steady.*

She scanned the cloudless, serene skies, taking in the lush greens of the spring growth breaking through the greys of winter, marvelling at the beauty of a starling's song lilting in the trees somewhere behind her and basking in the pallid sunlight. She blinked at the gleam of light on the dew-laden grass in the moments before it was trampled underfoot.

It's such a lovely day, but it's going to turn ugly very quickly . . .

In her mind she counted down the seconds before the carnage began as the purple-clad Sacrecour rankers closed in, shields and javelins high, their stance mirrored by the green-cloaked defenders. She focused on one face, a young crossbowman with the beginnings of whiskers, cranking his bow, placing his bolt methodically, sighting over the heads of the rankers in front and below him. When she squinted, she could see that those deft hands were shaking, the crossbow quivering erratically as he peered along the shaft.

Most men aren't killers, she remembered Dirklan saying once. He was, of course. *So am I.* She gazed towards Brylion Fasterius' banners directly opposite her position, thinking that she would give the rest of her legs to see him dead.

Then the orders rang out – '*Ready . . . arms back . . . and throw*' – and the killing began.

The javelins soared up from both sides, flashing in the morning sunlight like rays kissing the river, and then hammered into the ranks before them, leaving both sides recoiling in shock from the impact. A dozen men had gone down right in front of her; the lines were rippling as replacements stepped in and shields fouled by bent and broken javelins were thrown aside.

The attackers were also reeling, but the cries of the officers were relentless: '*Swords out – second wave, advance –*'

With a roar, more javelins flew, battering the defensive wall again, and now mage-bolts blasted between knots of battle-magi, shafts of pale blue light like rips in the world. Shielding crackled red under stress as the aether filled with soundless concussions. Swords flashed, hacking at the defenders' pike-shafts and seeking to close in, while trying to fend off the points and blades of their foe's longer weapons.

The Sacrecour front line hit the Royal Guard and all along the lines identical conflicts broke out as the ranks came together and recoiled, every man probing for weakness. So far, the casualties were light, despite the armies being in touching distance.

The queen made a small sobbing sound, but she remained steady as the war-cries turned into the screams of the maimed and dying. Prayers and bellowed orders melded with the hammering of steel on shields and the belling of blades.

Basia's eyes flashed about, seeking direct threats.

Windskiffs and venators were now flashing above them, duelling for supremacy of the skies. Bursts of flame and lightning lanced across the top of the embattled lines, magi fighting from behind their own rankers, separated by hundreds of men but still able to reach each other. The crossbowmen kept pumping out bolts, carving rents in the fabric of the lines. Wounded men tried to crawl out of the press, faces contorted in agony and fear. The grass was already reduced to churned blood and mud, a dirty scarlet colour.

Abruptly, the first assault was over. The Sacrecour officers shouted, '*Retreat at the walk, eyes front* —' and their men broke off in a ragged fashion and started staggering backwards, breathing hard, shields raised if they still had them.

A volley of crossbow bolts instantly slammed into them, hurling any exposed man to the turf, and those remaining lost their nerve, turned and ran.

Paths immediately opened in the defensive lines and Levis sent cavalry streaming through, hunched behind shields as they bore down on the fleeing men. A few went down under a volley of arrows from the distant Sacrecour archers, but most planted their lances in the backs of the fleeing rankers, then their warhorses reared up and came stamping down on the next men. Even from here Basia could hear the sickening crunch of broken bones. She saw Exilium's white and gold tabard at the head of the red-clad Misencourt knights, his gnostic shields flashing as shaft after shaft broke on them or deflected away.

For a minute or so the horsemen ran amok, then trumpets blared and they pelted back, shields of gnosis and wood now deployed behind them as they sought shelter behind the lines. The infantry cheered, waving their pikes aloft triumphantly.

We held, she thought dazedly.

But the trumpets blared again, the drums pounded and the next Sacrecour attack began.

Exilium pulled off his helmet, accepted a waterskin and drank deeply as sweat ran down his face despite the chilly air. His fellow mage-knights did the same, gasping in relief at another sortie survived. Thrice now he'd led counter-charges as the enemy assaults broke, cutting down running men from the back. It didn't feel glorious in the least.

Twice, Oryn Levis had sent an aide, reprimanding him for charging without orders. The first he'd screwed up, the second he'd passed to Sir Iles Kraal, who'd read it aloud, making the men laugh. Oddly, that was the moment when he felt things change.

They're with me now. We've shared danger and misdeeds, like boys stealing from an orchard, becoming brothers united by our shared sin. For the first time in his life, he felt a sense of belonging. He'd always kept aloof in the Inquisition and the Kirkegarde, seeing the other men as rivals, and unworthy ones at that.

All war is a sin, he thought, *but it's how legends are made.*

He looked towards Oryn Levis and saw the Knight-Commander staring at him across the quarter-mile – but the older man just touched fingers to temple and Exilium returned the salute. There would be no more reprimands. Most of his knights saw the long-distance exchange and remarked on it.

'*Misencourt for the Queen*,' someone growled.

Exilium glanced back to the hillock behind the lines, a couple of hundred yards away. The queen was still on horseback, Basia beside her. Seeing them lifted his heart.

But the trumpets called again and they turned as the front lines readied for yet another attack.

'Are we winning?' Cordan asked anxiously.

For three hours men had been tramping forward, only to be sent reeling back. The queen's knights were causing havoc whenever they charged at the retreating soldiers and there had been no breakthrough.

But Duke Garod looked calm enough, his haggard face pinched, but not anxious. He saw everything, from the crumbling of another assault on the right, to the lonely death of a wind-pilot above when his skiff went down in flames.

'It's coming,' he drawled. 'This is attrition. When they break, we'll sweep them away.'

'Why don't we send in our cavalry?' Cordan asked.

'You don't send cavalry against massed pikemen, *boy*,' Garod sneered. 'The bellies of the horses will be ripped open and the men cut from horseback before they can strike a blow.'

'But we've got mage-knights—'

'And they've got battle-magi among the ranks. A lance wielded in the charge is all but unshieldable – but that same impact-speed can allow an ordinary man to punch his pike through a gnostic shield. *We do not charge pikemen.* Now be silent, watch and learn.'

Stung, Cordan shut up, feeling resentful: the aides had all heard the exchange, men he'd one day rule. *Uncle Garod should have shown me more respect*, he thought angrily. But he swallowed his pride, glad to be far enough away that he couldn't see the blood, though the steady stream of maimed and dying men being hauled past him towards the rear was hideous enough. War had been far more palatable when played with painted lead miniatures across his table.

He resolved to throw those toys away.

The stink of blood, metal and glory filled Brylion Fasterius' nostrils as he walked his horse forward, surrounded by his knights. The hot stench made his nostrils flare and inside him, Abraxas growled hungrily. It was all he could do to not let his eyes go black and turn the daemon inside him loose.

The time had come to take a hand, to catch those damned royal knights – the Misencourt Order or whatever – when they next emerged, and cut them to ribbons. To that end, he'd edged his riders forward under cover of smoke from Fire-gnosis, masking their advance.

'Send in another wave,' he growled to the legion commander. 'I don't care what happens to them, as long as they lure out the enemy knights.'

The legion commander saluted and hurried away, orders were relayed and another assault began. This one was half-hearted and ineffectual, but Brylion salivated as they began to break, then came pelting back down the slope. The taste of ichor filled his mouth and he lowered his visor.

Rukk it, the daemon can have full reign, he thought. *Come one and all: I'm going to eat your souls.*

A shrill trumpet called another charge, those annoying knights came galloping through the queen's lines and out into the field again, ripping into the retreating rankers with fire and steel. Exilium Excelsior was at their head.

'Forward!' Brylion roared, jamming his spurs into his mount's flanks and with his entire force bursting into a gallop behind him, they bore down on the suddenly exposed foe.

Inside him, Abraxas shrilled with ravenous glee.

24

Broken Lines

Cadearvo

Cadearvo, the Angel of Famine, will arise in the wake of the reign of war. With their armies broken, the Unrighteous shall see their peoples decimated by hunger and thirst. Bellies will shrink and the breasts of mothers run dry, until proud kings gnaw upon their thrones and the poor eat their kin.

BOOK OF KORE

Finostarre, near Pallas, Rondelmar
Martrois 936

In the heart of the mêlée, Exilium's overextended gnostic awareness screamed, his shields pulsing with every threat his subconscious perceived. His immediate foe, a grey-bearded mage-knight, launched a crunching blow with a flanged mace that struck Exilium's buckler and had him reeling in the saddle, but he lashed back with that same buckler, catching his foe with the steel rim which shattered the man's nose in a spray of blood – then Exilium's blade thrust through steel and leather into his chest. When he fell, his horse screamed and reared, flailing iron-shod hooves inches from Exilium's face.

He hauled on his reins to find space and realised they'd got too far from their own lines – then he saw a phalanx of Sacrecour knights under the Fasterius banner, lances couched at full gallop, come ploughing into the mêlée, crashing a full dozen of his men to the ground – then riding right over them, heading straight for his banner – and him.

'Misencourt,' he shouted, 'fall back–'

– but the first of the Fasterius men had reached him and somehow he managed to flick away the lance-head, a bare moment before the man's warhorse crashed into his. Exilium kicked clear as both animals went down; he had an instant to see his enemy's leg was trapped and shattered, but the next mage-knight was already on him. Exilium hurled himself aside as another rider ploughed through the space, staggered against the flank of Iles Kraal's horse and almost lost his head to a lance that arced past him, missing by an inch –

– but piercing Iles Kraal, impaling him and left there, thrown by Brylion Fasterius himself. The pole broke off inside Kraal's body, but the Sacrecour Knight-Commander careered on, not even noticing Exilium, on the ground and fighting to draw his own sword.

But Fasterius' attendants *had* seen him: they closed in, horses rearing, their blades flashing down . . .

Survival became pure instinct. Only the strength of Exilium's pureblood shields kept him alive as he parried a mad flurry of blows from all sides. No sooner had he felt a blade glance off his armour than a steel-shod hoof smashed into his shoulder-plate. He fell, rolled under a horse, rose and stabbed, piercing a Sacrecour man's groin, found himself beside Kraal's mount again and this time flung the dead man from his saddle. Blocking a longsword, he used kinesis to get into the saddle. The horse panicked, bucking madly, but somehow he clung on, parrying and riposting until the beast's training took over and at last they were moving as one.

Only then did he see the extent of the damage. The Sacrecour knights – *How did they get so close?* – were galloping through the gaps that had been left in the royal lines for Exilium's charge and all across the centre the supposedly faltering assault was being renewed. And worst of all, Brylion's banner was being borne by a knot of steel-clad riders who were thundering straight towards the exposed hillock where the queen watched, with only Basia and a few guards around her.

<*Basia!*> he shouted, driving his new mount into the fray. He cut down one Sacrecour knight from behind, then another, desperation overriding any notion of chivalry, until a gap opened and he hammered his spurs into the beast's sweating flanks and the horse surged forward –

– as a cluster of Sacrecours yelled, 'There he is – *kill him!*'

And suddenly Exilium was fighting for his life again.

Basia de Sirou had already seen Brylion Fasterius coming for them when she half-heard a frantic warning from Exilium in the aether, but her awareness was barely here: despite the battle's bloody clamour, she had been snatched back to another place and time when she'd been *that* girl, the sparky one who'd been everyone's friend at the Arcanum, relishing her new life in the giant city of Pallas and wondering if that sweet-looking boy Ril Endarion might be someone she could lose her heart to. She'd been drinking stolen wine and giggling with like-minded girls in the well-garden on the night the Sacrecours took back Pallas.

909.

The children of other rival Houses had opened the gates and joined in as the Sacrecour knights poured in to destroy the flower of young Corani magehood.

As Brylion's never-forgotten, brutal face bore down on her now, she remembered those Hel-ish moments, being held over the edge of the well while Brylion raped her. On either side of her were her friends, also being raped. Fasterius might have been a young man, but he was already immense, a fearsome sight, and he had singled her out – she had no idea why. Once he'd used her, he'd slashed her throat and pushed her into the well, thinking her dead. When they'd realised she'd survived, although Kore knew how, they hurled spells at her, and rocks, and finally the bodies of her friends . . .

Which was when Ril, fighting for his own life, had plummeted down beside her. Somehow, badly injured and trapped below ground, they'd hung on for days, until Setallius' people had found them.

We survived: we were broken and maimed, but we got out and I've longed for vengeance ever since. She drew her longsword and kissed the hilt. *Thank you, Kore, for giving me this chance . . .*

'Get out of here,' she told her charge. 'Your Majesty, *get out* –' She glared at the other guards until they grabbed the reins of the white horse and hauled her away, then she nudged her own mount into motion and, sword extended, rode to meet Brylion and his thugs. She recognised most of them; they'd all been there that night . . .

From somewhere on her left, horns were echoing in the hills, but whatever was happening, it didn't matter, for the man she most hated in the entire world was *here in front of her*.

With a feral scream, she went hammering down the slope to meet him.

The clarion call of the horns floating out over the foothills north of the battlefield at Finostarre came rolling over the smoky battlefield. The sun was bright but the air was cold. The distant roar of the battle was music to his ears.

Solon Takwyth drew his broadsword and rode along the front line, using the gnosis to make his voice carry to the furthest ranks.

'I have asked you to remember always that you are Corani,' he roared. 'Down there is a Corani army: one led by a misguided queen in the thrall of traitors – but they are still Corani. Are we to stand aside while our brothers fight?'

'*No!*' the soldiers roared to a man.

They'd marched all day and night, taking back roads past the farms and estates of the rural nobility, spurning the chance to seize Pallas almost unopposed to reach this place in time. He was pretty sure they'd given the watching scouts the slip; they'd left behind a single legion, pretending to be an army.

No one knows we're here . . .

He stabbed the skies with his blade. 'Will we rescue the queen and destroy the Sacrecour tyrants *for ever*?'

'Aye – *aye!*'

'Then advance, my brothers, advance to conquer: for the Corani, and for the empire –'

The horns shrilled again, this time signalling the advance, and from the foothills overlooking the fields of Finostarre, Solon's men came swarming down to hit the exposed right flank of Garod's army.

*

Brylion grinned savagely as he recognised the skinny freak screaming like a burning witch as she came galloping to meet him, longsword extended and eyes blazing. They were through the royal lines, which were disintegrating behind them as the officers tried to close the gaps. The air was a cacophony of horn blasts and battle-cries, the aether crackling with frantic calls, but he barely heard, so filled was his mind with visions of 909 as Abraxas sifted through his memories of that glorious, *viscerally* bloody night, chortling over the best moments.

'She's mine,' Brylion roared, snatching a fresh lance from his squire. 'You two – with me; the rest of you, take the queen – and don't let the bitch get away: I want her *alive* –'

He jammed his spurs in again and his closest cronies came with him, all three lances aligned on the single rider pelting towards them. With shields flaring and lances tips aglow, thundering up the rise and onto level ground, they hit top speed as Basia de Sirou shrieked towards them.

He could already picture how this would play out, the freak skewered on three poles, then *ripped* apart – *And then we'll take our time with the convent girl* . . .

It all happened in a blur of motion that Basia barely comprehended.

Barely ten yards from impact – a matter of half a second – dark figures rose from the ground ten feet on either side of her and a cord suddenly stretched across the turf, a foot above the ground and right in front of the hooves of the three Sacrecour knights.

Brylion's showy warhorse caught its leading leg in the rope and went over in a blurring tumble, the beasts flanking him tripping a moment later and suddenly she faced not levelled lances but a tumbling wall of steel-clad horses and men – but the animals' heads were striking the ground with sickening crunches, while the riders flew onto the turf, landing with equally bone-crunching force –

– and Brylion was thrown straight at her, arms splayed, back-arched and weapons askew.

She barely had time to correct her aim before they collided. Her longsword, blue with gnosis-fire, punched right through his visor and was torn from her grasp as he fell away. The impact snapped her wrist, sending a blaze of numbing agony up her arm – then someone's horse smashed into hers and she was hurled backwards, head over heels, but calling on well-honed instincts she rolled herself into a ball just an instant before she struck the muddy turf. The broken wrist *screamed* and just for a second she blacked out.

A moment later her vision cleared enough to see a bloody-faced Brigeda and a smirking Patcheart sitting astride the prone Sacrecour knights, lifting their chainmail gorgets and methodically opening throats.

'Wha . . . th . . . fuh–' she managed to gasp.

'Just keepin' an eye on you, honey,' Brigeda told her. The burly woman blew her a kiss.

'Queen out here, thought you'd need some back-up,' Patcheart added smugly.

Basia looked around dazedly and saw Brylion – who was well and truly dead. His head had been blasted by the energies in her sword, which was still buried in the skull, the hilt sticking out of the visor, the point protruding from the back of his head, puncturing the iron helm.

Strangely, she didn't feel a thing. It was as if all her emotions had gone into charging, leaving nothing left for victory.

She turned away. She didn't need to see any more.

At his death, Brylion's knights broke off their chase and pelted back towards their own lines, allowing the queen's party to get away.

Thank Kore, she breathed. *Thank you, Life . . .*

Then she became conscious of something else.

To the north, on the left flank of the queen's army, newcomers were pouring onto the field in fast-moving columns, rolling up the suddenly beleaguered Sacrecour forces. For a moment even her heart soared as the Corani Badger banner swung in the breeze. Then she cursed.

Takwyth, she breathed. *Rukking Takwyth's here to steal our victory.*

She climbed dizzily to her feet as the Sacrecour knights and infantry fighting below the hillock were suddenly recalled by blaring trumpets, shrieking out the notes of the retreat. She looked towards Oryn Levis, on the knoll to her right, and saw that the Knight-Commander was calmly dispensing orders, almost as if he'd known this was coming all along.

And everywhere, she could hear the royal army screaming, '*TAKW-YTH, TAKWYTH –*'

And it wasn't just Corani men. The Pallacians were joining in.

The bastard . . .

She looked around for her horse, but it was dead, big eyes staring sightlessly up at the sky, its neck broken in the collision. Cradling her wrist, still panting, she limped over to Brylion. With her left hand she yanked out her blade, then with a sudden shriek, poured kinesis and raw energy into the sword and severed his neck in one blow.

'*Got you!*' she screamed to the ruined skull in the blackened helm, spitting on it, then staggering away.

'Good job,' Brigeda told her, taking a turn to add a gobbet of her own spittle. 'Patch and I are going to reel in the queen. We've got horses in the copse behind this hill. None for you, sorry.'

'Go on,' she told them. 'I'll catch up somehow.'

Basia was still looking around for a riderless horse when she saw a white-clad knight, spattered in blood, emerge from the fray, horseless and limping – and one of Oryn Levis' aides riding up to the young Estellan and saying something . . .

Exilium shook his head – and the aide drew a sword, levelling it at his chest.

Shit – he's arresting Exilium . . .

But the Estellan was already moving, blurring under the man's blade and seizing his arm, hurling the aide bodily from the saddle and into the ground. The aide flopped limply and went still. A moment later the Estellan was mounted on the other man's horse and glaring up the slope at Levis, raising a fist.

Basia's eyes swept over the plain: Takwyth was now on the field, being mobbed by men from Lyra's army, cheered to the hilt: *hail the returning conqueror.* Garod's soldiers were running, and his noblemen too. The battle was all but over.

But the war for control is still very much on.

Exilium was still staring up at Oryn Levis' retinue, his face livid. She shouted to him with voice and mind and flung out a hand, pointing towards the queen's fleeing party – and Briggy and Patch, pelting after them.

He galloped up and swept her into the saddle behind him. She squirmed into position and grabbed his waist as he turned to follow the queen's party. 'We've got to get her to safety, Basia shouted in his ear. 'Rukking Takwyth's stealing *everything . . .*'

Exilium dug in his heels and the horse put on a spurt. As they ate up the turf, she clung to his back, craning her neck so her face was alongside his. Then she realised he was weeping.

'I lost them all,' he sobbed. 'I didn't even see the counter-attack coming . . .'

Experience, she could have told him. *They let you show your hand, then struck.* But that was no consolation. Vengeance was owed. 'Lumpy has betrayed us, the damned toady. He threw you out there when he knew Takky was coming. This is now Volsai business.'

They pounded onwards, but they were not alone: a detachment of Oryn Levis' House knights were in hot pursuit – until a trio of venators ridden by mage-knights in Corani colours swooped down on the queen's escorts. The queen's horse reared, throwing the rider to the ground – and moments later the venators were rising, leaving behind two corpses and three riderless mounts.

Exilium threw Basia a shattered glance and reined in. She looked behind to see their pursuers had drawn off, content to let their dangerous quarry go now that the queen was in their hands.

Basia sagged in the saddle. *Everything's falling apart.*

As the remnants of the Sacrecour army streamed eastwards, flinging aside their weapons so they could run faster, Solon walked the lines, which dissolved into a cheering horde as the two armies came together and became one.

Solon felt monumentally triumphant. He rode through the ranks, alternately punching a fist aloft or reaching down to shake a soldier's extended hand. Lyra's army had fallen apart as surely as the Sacrecour one, the Pallacian legionaries backing off uncertainly in the face of Corani unity.

Oryn Levis came through the press – *Good old Lumpy, you came through* – and they clasped hands, a gesture full of symbolism. *Yes, this is our triumph, and we outmanoeuvred Setallius' backstabbing sneaks to do it.*

'Well done, my friend,' Solon boomed, and Oryn's round face was suffused with pride and pleasure.

'My Lord,' Lumpy replied loudly.

Lyra thought she had an army, but I only loaned it to her. He drew close to Oryn and whispered, 'Where's the queen?'

That triggered uncertainty on Lumpy's guileless face. 'Uh, we have the prisoner in a pavilion, hidden and—'

'Good,' Solon told him. 'We don't want her making some tragic scene now. Keep everyone out – and make sure she doesn't pull some dwymancer fuckery. She needs to know what's what before we parade her in public.'

Oryn leaned in close. 'You need to see her *now*.' His voice held a very clear warning.

Solon nodded to show he understood, wondering why the moment was souring. *What is it?* But he set about milking it anyway, letting everyone know exactly whose victory this was. That suffragium bullshit still had to be crushed, but it did hold one kernel of truth: popularity was a path to power. So he kept pumping hands, leading fresh waves of cheering, letting the relief of victory wash over him.

'His scars have faded,' someone remarked. 'It's a sign of divine favour.'

Yes, let them think that.

It was some time before he could win free. Dismounting before Oryn's pavilion, he waved one last time at the hordes of happy soldiers and strode into the tent. Oryn was already there, together with Lord Rolven Sulpeter, who'd flown in by windship, along with a clutch of House Corani peers. They were all standing silently in a ragged circle around the pale-faced, weeping blonde woman, the only person seated. Outside, the cheers still rang out, but in here there was perfect silence. Even Oryn wouldn't meet his eye.

Solon pushed through and lifted the queen's chin.

You bitch, he told the *absent* Lyra Vereinen. *You snivelling,* cowardly *bitch.*

Somehow his self-control held, although he was trembling in rage. 'Nita, isn't it?'

The queen's maid looked up, plainly terrified, with *damned* good reason. 'Uh,' she squeaked.

'Where's Lyra?'

'I don't know,' Nita whispered, tears starting from her eyes again.

'How long has she been gone?'

'Nearly a week.'

Nearly a rukking week? Kore's Blood . . .

Something inside him snapped – the suppressed tension of the past months, or the never-resolved fury at what Lyra had done to him, rage at being thwarted yet again, when victory had appeared his. As if by its own volition, his hand rose, kinesis boiled over and he slapped his open palm across the girl's upturned face – *no* – *too hard* – and with an audible *crack* that reverberated through the pavilion, her neck broke and she was hurled to the ground, flopping like a ragged doll.

He stared at his hand print, scarlet on her left cheek, as her eyes emptied and his fury disintegrated into appalled shame.

Dear Kore . . . I killed her . . . I murdered her . . .

He dropped to his knees, shouting, 'Healer – healer –' People crowded around her, while people shouted contradictory orders. Oryn pulled him away.

'I didn't mean to . . .' he began.

Roland de Farenbrette shouldered his way over and grabbing his shoulders, shouted into his face, 'It's not your fault, Solon, understand? *Lyra* did this, *she* abandoned her cause and left the stupid trollop in her place – it's not you, man, it's her – *all* her –'

Is it? Was it? I didn't mean to . . .

Nestor and Oryn were ashen-faced, the other knights wide-eyed, open-mouthed, *silent.*

Roland gripped his head and screamed, 'This is Lyra Vereinen's fault, Solon: that girl's blood is on her hands, not yours –'

'Aye,' someone said, and others took it up, stronger. 'Be it on the queen's head,' another added, and the pavilion filed with denials and platitudes.

'What man could contain his wrath at such cowardice? It's Lyra's fault.'

Yes, he thought, still stunned at himself, *yes, what man could restrain his anger?*

Somehow, composure returned. 'Aye,' he snarled, 'this is on *Lyra's* head.'

Nestor laid a cloak over the corpse of the broken-necked maid while Solon scanned the tent, seeking hints that any here weren't still his, heart and soul. 'A man cannot be blamed for a woman's perfidy,' he growled. 'This – this does not leave here. It never happened. Bury the girl in the woods, and . . .' He floundered, but then inspiration struck. 'Bring my personal carriage, *now*.'

They looked puzzled, until he shouted, 'Now–' and everyone leaped into action.

Solon gave Roland a thankful nod. 'Well done, Blacksmith,' he murmured. *Roland always hammers a problem into shape.*

A few minutes later, his carriage rolled up and Brunelda was bundled into the tent, pale and frightened. When she saw him, she flew to his arms, weeping with relief. She didn't notice the way the knights all gasped in shock – no one had ever seen her properly before; they'd no idea how closely she resembled the queen, especially dressed as she was now in a green velvet dress with a coronet on her perfectly coifed wig.

'On your knees,' he growled at them over Brunelda's shoulder.

'You survived,' she was whispering. 'Thank Kore thank Kore thank Kore . . .'

'Hush,' he hissed softly, then turned her, murmuring, 'Take their homage, my Queen.'

She looked up at him, at first not understanding . . .

To her credit, she reacted with admirable poise, straightening and giving him *that* look – the one she'd been schooled in, the 'Lyra' look of tremulous but defiant determination – then turned to face the men.

'Gentlemen,' was all she said, as Lyra did.

Most surely knew it wasn't Lyra, but their eyes widened, flashing from her to him and back again, and then they knelt as one. 'Hail, Queen Lyra,' they chorused.

'Well done,' Solon told them all. 'Now, lads, get out there and take control: we have two armies that must become one.'

When they were gone, Brunelda collapsed against him, choking back sobs, but he had no time for womanly weakness. 'Wipe your eyes,' he told her as Nestor and Roland went to the dead maid and wrapped her more securely in the cloak someone had flung over her. Nestor took her head, Roland her legs and they carried her out.

'Who was that?' Brunelda murmured as one of Nita's hands flopped down and dragged on the ground a moment before the two men vanished with her through the tent flap.

'No one,' he told her, turning her face to his. 'Just a foolish nobody who got in the way.'

That's all she was, he told himself insistently. *That's all she was.*

'Stay in here,' he told her. 'I'll post guards until I return. We'll spend the night at Finostarre Abbey.' He stroked her face, the relief of surviving another battle stirring his blood – although in truth he'd only been peripherally involved in the fighting. *She can do this until I get my hands on the real Lyra.*

He pulled her hands from him and sat her down, then left her there and found Oryn Levis, waiting outside with Rolven Sulpeter. 'It's an old ploy, the impersonator,' Solon reminded them. 'Lyra's just a woman surrounded by cowards. We shouldn't judge her by our standards. But let's be discreet: we've got an army out there who think we're holding the real queen. Let them carry on thinking that.'

'When do we move on Pallas?' Lord Sulpeter asked. 'My legions are still a few days to the south.'

How long will I need to find her? If Setallius had Lyra hidden, it could take weeks – time he didn't have. That decided him. 'We'll move tomorrow, take control of the Bastion, purge her people and restore the empire.'

And after being paraded from a few balconies, 'Queen' Brunelda can be tucked away while I decide what to do with her. Maybe I'll even declare the 'real' Lyra an imposter and watch the empire reform around me.

'Find Basia de Sirou,' he snapped. 'She'll know where the real Lyra is.'

Pallas
Five days earlier

Lyra turned and left the Royal Council room, swallowing a lump in her throat. Dirklan took her arm as Basia closed the doors and followed. 'Did I sound too final?' she asked quietly.

'I don't think they guessed,' he replied. 'Come, we have a lot to do. I'll meet you at second bell after sunset, all right? That's just under two hours.'

He hurried away, leaving Lyra and Basia by the stairs to her suite. The bodyguard was quiet and withdrawn, clearly unhappy, but knowing her arguments would fall on deaf ears. They ate in silence, serving themselves while Nita was off having her hair cut and dyed.

'Well,' Lyra said to Basia, 'let's get started.'

Basia helped her dress in close-fitting breeches, a padded leather jerkin and leather boots. Her sword-belt had two dagger-sized scabbards, one bearing *Papercut*, her precious argenstael stiletto. 'All hail the deadly Letter-Opener,' Basia intoned solemnly as she buckled it closed.

Lyra felt very strange, weighed down by the weight of the jerkin, which had chainmail sandwiched between the leather layers. She added a wool-lined steel cap and a thick scarf, a heavy fur-lined cloak and the odd-looking glass discs set in moulded leather Basia handed her.

'They're eye-glasses, to protect your vision while flying,' she said. 'The Noories came up with them – we've been wiping our eyes or using weird gnostic spells for centuries while they show up and solve the problem right away, the bastards.'

'A lesson for us all,' Lyra noted, looking in the mirror at the stranger staring back: a blonde adventuress with the weird eye-glasses pushed up over her forehead.

A knock on the door announced Brigeda, leading a white-faced, amazed Nita – only this Nita now wore Lyra's favourite Corani green gown and had the royal circlet set on her newly blonde locks. She had clearly been weeping, although whether for joy or sorrow wasn't clear.

Lyra clapped her hands in applause, then took the girl's hands. 'Thank you, my dear,' she said warmly. 'Basia will protect you, and so will Exilium and all his men. You'll be safe as can be.'

Which may not be very safe at all, she thought guiltily; this part of the plan gave her the most misgivings. *I will never forgive myself if she's hurt or killed.*

Nita stammered, 'I st-still d-don't un-understand . . .'

'I have to go away,' Lyra told her, 'to stop a very bad man.' That was the most they could tell her, for if she was taken, they knew she would quickly confess anything she knew. She hugged the girl and promised, 'You'll manage. No one will suspect.'

'But Lord Solon—'

'Will perish outside our walls, as will Duke Garod. Have faith, dear Nita.'

The girl nodded meekly. She had agreed with her usual undemonstrative courage.

Basia was no happier at being left behind. *Lyra's absence is easy to conceal,* Dirklan had argued, *but you're distinctive. Where you are, people assume Lyra is – so you're staying.* He was right, and in any case, he was her boss, but she was still resentful.

'Don' ye worry, Majesty,' Brigeda told Lyra now. 'I'll look after these girls an' see 'em right.' Along with Basia, she and Patcheart, the three of them the spymaster's ablest lieutenants, knew the truth.

Nita fetched Rildan and Lyra spent her remaining time cradling her son, smothering him in kisses and weeping until his nightdress was soaked. Finally, and yet far too soon, the second night bell rang. It was dark outside and she could hear the wind moaning.

Patcheart knocked on her balcony door. 'It's time,' he called softly.

Lyra took Rildan to the nursery and hugged him one last time, upsetting him because he didn't understand why she was crying, so her last sight of him was bawling in Nita's arms.

At the top of the stairs, she turned to Brigeda. 'I hope that this will be resolved swiftly,' she said. 'I don't want Nita in peril for a second longer than necessary.'

'You won't want to miss us lopping off Takky's big 'ead,' Brigeda chuckled darkly, before blurting, 'You look after ol' One-Eye, yer Majesty, okay? He's a good boss.'

The idea of her looking after her father was comical, but Lyra promised, 'I'll do my best.'

'I'm sure you will,' Brigeda said seriously. 'Five years gone, I wouldna hae given a copper for you lasting six weeks, but 'ere we are, right enough. You probably don' give a shit what some ol' saffy thinks, but I reckon ye're awright.'

Lyra blushed, and patting Brigeda's heavy right arm, said, 'Thank you . . . Briggy.'

'Majesty,' she said, tugging a forelock. 'Hate these emotional partings,' she added drily. 'Get off wi' ye, now.'

Lyra followed Patcheart down the stairs into her garden, her eyes streaming.

She paused to drink at her pool and beg Aradea for her aid, then made her way to the lawn at the far end where two winged beasts paced, ready for travel. The wyvern, almost identical to Basia's, was hissing at the small team of Volsai strapping packs to its saddle harness, but Pearl had been waiting quietly, until she caught sight of Lyra, when she whinnied impatiently.

'Hello, Pooty-Girl – all set?' she murmured as she checked the saddlebags; everything looked to be in place, as far as she could tell. She could still feel the tears on her face, but she was catching Pearl's mood and was suddenly eager to begin.

Dirklan strode into the clearing, his eye gleaming with some kind of protective spell; he disdained the Easterners' eye-glasses. 'The others are in the air,' he said tersely. 'Sooner begun, the sooner done.' But he paused to touch Lyra's arm. 'Are you all right, Daughter?'

She nodded mutely, wiping her eyes.

'I'm proud of you,' he told her. 'It takes courage to step away.'

'To be honest, it's a relief. Frankel was right: ruling is best left to the willing.'

'I disagree: often, the best rulers are those who take power reluctantly. You've served your people well, no matter what others might say. But if you're the only one who can stop Naxius, then we have to go and do it.'

'I still can't quite believe that you're letting me,' she confessed.

Her father smiled crookedly. 'I do think saving the entire world is a little more important than just saving Pallas.' He tapped her arm. 'Mind you, if this Valdyr is wrong about all this, I'll string him up by the scrotum.'

Lyra blanched. 'He's not wrong, Father.'

'He'd better not be.' He reached out and tucked a stray lock into her cap. 'To be honest, I'm not sorry we'll miss the fighting here. These mass battles aren't my style: I'm far happier sneaking around than facing an armoured mage-knight full-on. I'm far too old for all that carry-on.'

He turned to his wyvern. 'This is Domitia,' he said. 'She's from the same brood as Basia's Vasingex: faster than a venator, with fiery breath and a temper to match.'

The wyvern hissed at him, but held still as he climbed into the saddle. Lyra turned to Pearl and mounted, then lowered her eye-glasses.

A moment before Domitia's wings thrashed and she leaped into the air, Lyra waved to Patcheart, then touched Pearl's flanks and the pegasus-construct eased from a trot to a canter and then leaped up, her wings spreading to catch the wind. Beating hard, they skimmed over the walls and swept upwards.

Lyra turned her head and caught a glimpse of Nita, with Rildan in her arms, standing with Basia on her balcony. Coramore was with them, risen from her sickbed to wave goodbye. Lyra lifted her arm, wishing them every good fortune, then she faced forward and concentrated on the mission as her eyes began to sting again.

We're off, she thought. *Farewell, Queen and Empress. I never wanted to be you anyway.* She'd loved the *Fey Tales* growing up. The faery Stardancer had been her idol: with her mortal lover Rynholt she slew the Widowmaker and saved the kingdom. That old dream made this moment feel a little surreal, as if she'd stepped out of Urte and straight into Aradea's realm.

Perhaps I have. But I'll come back, she silently promised Rildan. *I swear I will.*

Pearl followed Domitia to where five more beasts, all durable venators, circled. Two had riders, Rhune and Sarunia, Ventian scouts in

Dirklan's service; the other three were laden with baggage. The Ventians were brother and sister – or maybe husband and wife; Lyra wasn't entirely clear on that – and they'd protected her before.

Lyra took one last look at Pallas glimmering below her, dark except for the lights around the plazas and churches and taverns, and prayed silently, *Dear Kore, protect Basia and Exilium, and especially Nita.*

Then Dirklan shouted and pointed south and they all banked, then went streaking across the sky together and suddenly exhilaration replaced fear. Finally, after so much chasing of shadows and reacting to unseen dangers, they knew their real enemy – his name, his purpose, and where to start looking for him.

It's started, she thought. *The Quest of the Stardancer has finally begun.*

25

Stronger Together

On Brotherhood

I speak now of Brotherhood – but do not limit what I say to just the male gender. By Brotherhood, I mean that all people are one, united by a bond that transcends kinship, nation, religion or even friendship – though it can encompass any or all of these things. It's the banding together of the like-minded in common cause, for mutual protection and achievement. We possess few finer instincts.

ANTONIN MEIROS, HEBUSALIM 696

East Midrea
Martrois 936

Valdyr Sarkany groaned as Ogre began ascending yet another tortuous goat-trail. It had been a long day in the saddle and Ogre's gait was more akin to Gricoama's lope, nowhere near as comfortable as a horse. By now his body was begging for respite. How Ogre felt, he had no idea, for in beast form he couldn't speak.

Ahead of them, the wolf sniffed about, alert as any scout. Since their journey through the Elétfa, Gricoama's awareness of his surroundings had become positively preternatural – no one was going to be taking them by surprise.

Between us, perhaps we'll manage to evade both armies' patrols in Augenheim Pass, he hoped, perhaps a little optimistically.

They'd abandoned the heavily settled lowlands soon after leaving Mollachia; there were too many patrols from both the Imperial Army south of them and the Earl of Midrea's men, who were also in the field.

Midrea lacked the stark beauty of Mollachia: the hills were lower, the thawing ground muddy, the thick forests full of short deciduous trees with none of the towering majesty of his own lands. The ruined farm-steads everywhere suggested men had tried – and failed – to cultivate the land. But it was warmer than his mountainous homeland and spring was already evident in the green buds and the bleating of new-born animals. They'd raided one lonely farm and stolen two lambs last night; he'd felt a guilty about that, but only a little. *Midreans have plenty*, he'd reasoned. *They won't miss them.*

Ogre made a grunting sound as he topped the difficult climb; he was holding up to the arduous task he'd set himself, but that morning, they'd agreed they would all walk the following day. They were five days out of Hegikaro.

Valdyr hadn't heard anything from Nara, although he'd largely stayed out of the dwyma himself, for he'd had an uneasy feeling that someone was hunting him in the aether.

Nara's decision to stay in the north hurt, but he couldn't blame her. *We'll do this ourselves, Ogre and I – and perhaps Waqar and Tarita will join us? We'll have to be enough.*

When they descended from the small ridge they found a dell with a tiny stream, a bank to shelter under and a poorly covered fire-pit. Some-one had camped here, but some days ago, by his reckoning. Valdyr threw his leg over Ogre's back and slid to the ground, wincing as his numbed legs took his weight.

'That's enough,' he groaned. 'We'll rest here tonight.'

Ogre sloughed his beast form in an impressively fluid release of gnostic energy, straightening painfully as the saddle and baggage dropped past his waist and clattered to the ground around him. He immediately cast about for his clothing; Valdyr had discovered that Ogre was sensitive about his man-made body, though he couldn't quite stop himself gawking the first time. Constructs were rare curiosities, especially humanoid ones. Ogre was eight feet tall when he stood straight and his hefty frame had been getting increasingly leaner as the journey burned any fat away, revealing formidable muscles. His manhood was concealed by thick black hair, but his scrotum was the size of a man's fist. Altogether, he made

Valdyr – six foot and well-built – feel puny. Ogre was an alarming sight, despite his gentle and surprisingly erudite nature.

Realising he'd been staring, Valdyr belatedly averted his eyes and instead studied the campsite. 'A mounted patrol was here four days ago, by the state of the dung. These tracks are old and the fire-pit's cold. I think we can risk one night.' He paused as Gricoama appeared, his tail was wagging. 'Gricoama thinks we're alone too,' he added.

Ogre had just finished dressing when something shrieked overhead. They all looked skywards to see a large winged shape circling far above – then it peeled off and they realised it was speeding down towards them.

'Rukka,' Valdyr cursed, 'under the trees – quickly.'

He raced to the dropped baggage and grabbed what he could, Ogre hot on his heels collecting the rest. They scrambled into the undergrowth, Gricoama behind them, backing up and growling like the rearguard of an army at bay.

'Shhh,' he hissed at the wolf. 'Quickly, come.'

They'd barely made the cover of the trees when they heard wings thumping and a dark shadow fell over the dell. They pressed themselves flat to the ground, but Valdyr could clearly see their hasty passage, the torn aside vines and disturbed vegetation. Anyone with eyes would see the signs too . . .

If we need to run, we'll have to ditch our gear. He tentatively reached for the dwyma, wandering if he could unleash anything in time. There was nothing in the serene grey clouds above to work with, but perhaps this forest contained something?

But it was too late: his throat tightened as a winged beast touched down, some kind of reptilian bird with large hind legs and a whip-like tail with a wicked spur at the point, wings formed of spines and membrane and a large, long-nosed head with ridges and tiny horns. A sinister grey-robed figure slipped from his mount's saddle, kindling pale-blue gnostic shields as he did so.

Then another, utterly different shape swept down: a gleaming white horse with pearlescent wings, ridden by a young man. It reared as it landed, looking more like someone's coat of arms than anything. Valdyr watched as he fumbled with some straps, then dismounted, groaning as his legs took his weight, clutching at the saddle to steady himself. He was clothed in bulky furs and his eyes were concealed behind strange glass discs.

Then he lifted the discs from his eyes and Valdyr saw the shape of the face and his heart lurched.

Although she surely couldn't see him in the near dark, she turned unerringly to him, calling, 'Valdyr? It's me – Nara.'

A pulse of emotive energy welled up inside him, a sudden lifting of anxiety that made his heart hammer. 'Nara?' he gasped. Ogre grunted in surprise, but Gricoama was wagging his tail as Valdyr rose from concealment and strode towards her, his arms opening to embrace her before he could even consider whether that was too forward.

She came to meet him, a broad smile opening her face up, and he swept her into a thankful bear-hug, lifted her off his feet and held her, his face buried in her hair as he inhaled her, finding that she felt and smelled and sounded exactly as she had when they'd met in the dwyma. That told him that this was real, that *she* was real, and her grip around his chest was just as tight.

It felt magical.

'Nara, Nara,' he couldn't stop saying, as if she were the answer to everything. *Maybe she is.* He remembered the way it had felt when they'd called down storms together, how powerful they were in unison. She had been the first woman since the breeding-houses who didn't scare him, or dredge up horrible memories.

It occurred to him that he was perhaps a little in love.

But she's a noble of Pallas . . . don't be foolish, he chided himself, finally remembering his dignity enough to lower her back to the ground. He looked down at her face, upturned and flushed and looking as joyful as he felt. He wished he had the courage to kiss her . . .

. . . and then he found that he did. His mouth closed on hers before he had the chance to think about it – and although she stiffened for a moment, she melted into him, the taste just as his senses recalled from their one stolen kiss inside the dwyma.

He waited for the old familiar guilt and panic to rise – but Asiv was dead and, like grave-goods, all his old weakness and self-loathing had been buried with him. He felt nothing but exhilaration and possibilities –

– until a dry – very *masculine* – cough brought him back to the here and now and they both flinched and stepped apart. A lean man in grey robes with long silver hair and an eye-patch concealing his left eye emerged from behind the reptilian bird creature.

'Lady Nara,' the man drawled coolly, 'perhaps you might introduce us?'

Nara flushed. 'Dirklan: this is my *friend*, Prince Valdyr Sarkany of Mollachia.'

'Erm, Lord Dirklan?' Valdyr managed a sketchy bow, his face burning scarlet. 'Please excuse my forward behaviour, but this is a reunion – um . . . of a kind. I am, uh, honoured to meet you, sir.'

'Good to meet you,' Dirklan replied, measuring him with his single glacial eye before turning to Nara. 'Reunion or not, remember your station and recent events, Milady.'

Nara went an even brighter red and nodded meekly. Valdyr wondered what he was referring to. *She told me that she was the consort of a powerful man in Pallas,* he remembered. *But she never speaks of him. What's happened?*

In the sky above, four more giant beasts were circling lower, calling to each other in shrill voices. Dirklan glanced behind Valdyr at Ogre and Gricoama, who had emerged from the undergrowth. 'And these are?'

Valdyr belatedly recalled that Ogre, a sentient, gnosis-using construct, was illegal. He'd told Nara about Ogre – had she told anyone else? 'This is Ogre, the researcher I told Nara of. And the wolf is named Gricoama.'

'A researcher?' Dirklan repeated doubtfully.

'Among other things,' Ogre said in his gravelly baritone. He conjured fire in his left hand and hefted his axe in his right. 'Perhaps Lord Dirklan wishes to enforce the Gnostic Codes?'

For a moment tension crackled, until Nara stepped between them. 'Ogre, Valdyr's told me so much about you,' she exclaimed, extending her hand – which bore an imperial signet ring. 'I understand that we have you to thank for our knowledge of the enemy?'

Ogre was immediately disarmed. His gnostic flame winked out and he lowered the axe as his misshapen face creased into a shy smile and he mumbled, 'The Master is a threat to us all. We must stop him.'

'Indeed.'

Nara's manner was authoritative but not overbearing, reminding Valdyr of Kyrik. *She has my brother's relaxed sense of command.* He was impressed anew, and a little embarrassed at their impetuous kiss. *But she returned it . . .*

'Perhaps we should make camp?' he suggested, looking at Lord Dirklan. 'We were just about to – night is falling and we're leg-weary.' He indicated the undergrowth where they'd hidden. 'We have supplies we can share – and much to discuss.'

Dirklan scanned the skies, where the other flying beasts were still circling. They all looked to be laden, with riders or perhaps baggage. Then he agreed, 'Aye, let's camp here.'

While Dirklan tended to his wyvern – they'd quickly discovered Domitia wouldn't let anyone else touch her – Lyra, who knew nothing of cooking, helped Rhune unloading the venators, leaving dinner to Sarunia. It was nigh impossible to tell the Ventians' ages, for they had similar narrow faces, smooth tanned skin and the silver hair of their race. Lyra heaved down a saddlebag and was hauling it across the clearing when she was nearly knocked off her feet by the friendly head-butt of the immense venator. Rhune took the bag from her, lifting it effortlessly, and gave her a grin as he set it down.

'Rhune,' she panted, 'may I ask you: is Sarunia related to you?'

She'd seen them kiss like lovers, but there was no privacy on a mission like this and the pair had maintained a polite distance, sleeping under different blankets.

Rhune gave her a lopsided smile which made him look even more like his . . . *sister?* 'Private,' he replied in a droll voice, and sauntered off to get the rest of the baggage.

Feeling useless, she took a pail and went to scoop up water from the shallow stream trickling through the glade. A moment later, Valdyr joined her, lugging a pair of waterskins.

'How did you find us?' he asked. 'I've stayed out of the dwyma and Ogre hasn't sensed any scrying.'

'I just knew where you were,' she replied. It was the best way she could express it.

She knew some of his history, the pain he'd endured as a child in the Keshi breeding-houses, but there was a sense of ease about him that she'd not felt before. He looked like a man who'd conquered daemons.

He said that the Mask, the man who tormented him, is dead . . . as is Ostevan, who tormented me. The symmetry was encouraging.

She told Valdyr what had been happening in the north in broad terms, careful not to identify herself – she trusted him, but the empire had been no friend to Mollachia. 'But now the false Pontifex is dead. We don't yet know what the outcome of the battle for Pallas was, if they've fought yet.'

'Is the man you . . . um, your lover . . . is he in the fighting?' Valdyr stammered, his voice a little sour.

With jealousy, or distaste? 'No,' she said, worried he thought her a harlot.

'I daresay such arrangements are common in Pallas,' Valdyr responded cautiously. 'In my land, a woman is a virgin until she marries – and that is for life. Men of Mollachia must often work apart from their families, you see: in the mines, or hunting and trapping. They need surety of their wife's virtue, that their children are their own.'

He does think I'm a slut . . . Lyra looked away, feeling her usual despair when it came to matters of the heart. *You've only just met him,* she chided herself. *Who did you think he was – Rynholt himself?*

'Things are different in Pallas,' she said. 'Men have all the power and women need protectors. My patron was a bully: he turned against me when our politics clashed and tried to force me into servitude. Now he marches against the Empress,' she concluded bitterly.

'You say women have no power, but you have an empress,' he noted.

'She has a lot less power than you imagine,' she told him. 'She has to juggle this against that, find allies and keep them. Her life is privileged, but hard.'

She realised that she'd raised her voice and promptly shut her mouth.

'You care about her,' Valdyr said. 'To us, she is a distant tyrant.'

When he'd told her of Mollachia's problems, she'd discovered the Pallas-appointed tax-farmers had been ravaging his kingdom, far over-stepping the laws. 'When the Empress found out what was happening in your kingdom, she made all tax-farming illegal,' she reminded him. 'If she survives, she will make reparations, I swear.'

'You speak for her, do you?'

'I know her,' Lyra blurted. 'I have attended on her at times and I know her mind. She doesn't always make good decisions, but she cares about her people.'

Something in her vehemence must have satisfied him, because he made a placatory gesture. 'I've seen the sort of decisions my brother must make,' he replied, in a gentler voice. 'Some of them have been very complicated and alienated a lot of people.'

'No one can please everyone, all the time. That at least I've learned.' She blinked, and added, 'From observing the queen, as well as my own life.'

He didn't appear to notice her little slip. They fell silent, just looking at each other. She wished they could return to that initial moment of joy – *and that kiss* – but there was too much going on for that. It would have to wait.

That resolved, she regained her emotional balance. 'It's good to finally meet you, Valdyr,' she said formally. 'Dirklan needs to hear what Ogre has learned first-hand and so do I. Let's join the others.' She rose, hefted her bucket and left him.

This is a time for level heads, she told herself firmly, *not wayward hearts*.

Ogre looked at the fire-pit, which was burning well. Unless they were overflown or someone stumbled right into their dell they were pretty well hidden. The Pallacians had brought supplies, so the meal had been fresh and filling, the best he'd had in weeks. Gricoama was hunting for himself, the giant venators were gnawing on haunches of meat and the beautiful pegasus was peacefully grazing, a vision of magic come to life.

All eyes were on him, though, as he related what he'd learned from the *Daemonicon di Naxius*. 'The Master claims that Urte is a sphere of stone spinning in a void,' he said. 'It teems with life – and that living energy, constantly renewing, is what keeps the void at bay.'

'So say the Arcanum scholars too,' Dirklan agreed.

'All magi agree that the void isn't empty: daemons dwell there – perhaps they were once living souls. Wizards can summon them, but only for a few hours, before they're cast back. But the Master changed that.'

He thought about Naxius, always scratching away at the surface of reality.

'Master Naxius created *ichor*, a substance that anchors a daemon in the living world. The ichor is a distillation of living tissue and daemonic essence – and it's spreading. The Master wants to infect every living person with his ichor.'

Nara shuddered, but Dirklan shook his head. 'Everywhere it appears, we've defeated it.'

'For now,' Ogre agreed. 'Master Naxius admits the ichor has vulnerabilities – silver, argenstael, sunlight, these are some of the remedies we've discovered – but he believes that these can be overcome. But he fears *dwyma* – he wrote that in a war of Life Magic against Death Magic, here in the Living World, Life has the advantage.'

'I've used pure light to kill daemons,' Nara put in. 'And I've burned ichor out of my own blood.' She shuddered at the memory, while Valdyr glanced at her admiringly. That Valdyr was in love with Nara was as clear to Ogre as his own love for Tarita, but something told him that she wasn't ready to open her heart, despite their earlier kiss.

'This is so, but the Master has found a way to give the daemons the edge. He purposes to poison the dwyma. In the *Daemonicon* he details his hunt to find a dwymancer to put to use for that effect.'

'And now he's captured Jehana,' Valdyr put in darkly.

'Jehana *Mubarak*,' Dirklan said, emphasising the notorious family name. 'Is she a willing accomplice?'

'Jehana is no more desirous of the end of our world than any of you,' Ogre told them. 'I have travelled with her: she is a good woman. But the Master knows how to break a person's soul – and the *Daemonicon* says all dwymancers are vulnerable to madness, because at some point they must face this dilemma: that humanity, which burns forests for fuel and breeds animals for meat, is the enemy of Nature and the source of the daemons.'

They all fell silent. Nara and Valdyr shared a troubled glance.

After a moment, Ogre went on, 'The Master *will* break Jehana and she *will* destroy the dwyma, and when she does, the barriers between the Living and the Deathly will collapse. Daemon spirits will pour into this world: this is what Master Naxius writes, and he is never wrong. Every living soul will be conquered by daemons in the greatest mass-possession of all time. It will be irreversible and complete. Daemons will rule this world, feeding on all life, then cannibalising each other until Urte becomes a lifeless rock, populated only by daemons, and ruled by the one who controls them all: Master Naxius.'

'Dear Kore,' Dirk breathed. 'What madman could desire such a thing?'

'And why?' Nara added plaintively.

'Because when he's done with this world, he'll find others,' Ogre told her. 'The Master knows that Urte is not alone in the void. When it's a discarded husk, they will move on, taking this knowledge and leaving nothing behind.'

He stopped then, watched them all make self-reassuring gestures, hugging knees or casting eyes skyward, lips moving in prayer. He lifted the waterskin to moisten his dry throat.

'What can we do to stop him?' Dirklan asked.

'We must find him and kill him,' Ogre said simply. 'And if she's too far gone, we must also kill Jehana.'

'How long have we got?' Nara asked.

'I don't know,' he admitted, 'but he's had Jehana for several weeks now and she won't be able to resist him for long. No one can.'

'Where's his lair?' Dirklan asked, his single eye intense.

'I do not know precisely where it is,' Ogre admitted. 'It's somewhere in Rimoni, but I've never been there. But I know a way to find it, for which we must travel via Norostein.'

'Why?' Dirklan asked. 'What's there?'

'*Who*: Jehana's brother, Waqar Mubarak, who is also a potential dwymancer. It may be that only he can reach his sister. Familial blood can break through scrying wards better than anything else.'

'But if she's a dwymancer, can't we find her through the dwyma?' Nara asked.

Ogre patted the *Daemonicon* again. 'We can try, but if the Master is correct, her dwyma will change, and may already be doing so. Naxius intends to attune it to the void – "dark dwyma", he calls it – and if successful, she may not share your concerns for life any more.'

'But the dwyma rejects the ichor,' Nara protested.

'That's true,' Ogre replied. 'When he wrote his *Daemonicon* – which was taken by the Ordo Costruo twenty years ago – the Master believed the ichor would corrupt and enslave any person, but we now know that he misjudged. At Midpoint Tower last year, Sakita Mubarak was used to destroy the tower through a feat of dwymancy, but it destroyed her.'

'Another Mubarak,' Rhune observed. 'Does the family serve Naxius?'

'Not Waqar, not Jehana,' Ogre replied sharply. 'The Master wrote of using his agents – Masked men and women infected by daemon's ichor – to propagate strife and draw out the dwymancers so that he could capture and use them. That was his main purpose for this whole war. Some of the Shihad leaders are likely to be his servants – but Waqar and Jehana are not.'

'Tell us more of them,' Dirklan asked.

'Waqar and Jehana were born to be both mage and dwymancer,' Ogre told them. 'The Ordo Costruo found that when Sakita, the first dwymancer in centuries, had children by a mage, they fused the potential.'

He watched those around the fire take that in. 'They're uniquely powerful,' Dirklan breathed. 'With them leading the Shihad, we could be annihilated.'

'Neither of them wish that,' Ogre told them. 'Jehana isn't warlike and she doesn't support the Shihad. Waqar is also of the peace faction, although he has fought, as his duty decrees: he is, after all, a royal prince. Neither have gained the dwyma – indeed, Waqar has shown reluctance to do so. His only real concern is the safety of his sister.'

He glanced round the circle, stopping at Nara, who was looking stricken. 'My son . . .' she whispered. 'He will have the same potential, won't he . . . ?'

She has a son? Ogre noted that Valdyr must be aware of this, because he didn't react with surprise, just awe.

She looked up at him. 'You've given us too much to think about, Ogre,' she said, but she smiled. 'And Os–' She stopped, then restarted, 'My comfateri was a Mask who sought to capture me when he learned that I was a dwymancer. Naxius also pursued me, in spirit form. Things he told me chime with your tale, Ogre.' She looked at him directly. 'Your Master is an evil man, but you deserve the highest praise.'

To be complimented by a beautiful Pallacian noblewoman was enough to make Ogre stammer into silence, but he'd told them all they needed to know.

Now they just had to decide what must be done.

The camp settled into sleep after the usual awkwardness of finding private places and working out how to share the small circle of warmth around the fire without sticking feet or elbows in someone's face or snoring and disturbing everyone. Lyra, quite unused to such deprivation, found the discomfort almost impossible; she barely slept despite her exhaustion. Her mind was churning and the ground was hard as stone – and Valdyr's presence made it worse.

Dirklan took the first watch, with the Ventians volunteering for the middle and dawn shifts before settling down a little apart. Beside the fire, Ogre rumbled and snored like a volcano, quite ruining Lyra's sleep, until all she could do was gaze through the flames at the Mollach prince's face as he too tried and failed to sleep.

What do you think of me? she longed to ask him. *Do you see a pampered, wayward fool? Do you understand that people can make mistakes – but that they can learn from them?*

But eventually she closed her eyes and drifted away . . .

Next morning, one of the pack-venators was assigned to Ogre; his affinity for animagery enabled him to quickly bond with the creature. Instead of mounting up behind Rhune, Valdyr walked to another of the riderless constructs and Lyra felt his dwyma entwine with the beast, who permitted him to mount. Within minutes, he was riding as if born to the saddle.

Gricoama emerged from the undergrowth and Dirklan was issuing instructions on how to get the wolf safely onto the last pack-venator, when Valdyr barked something in Mollach and the wolf vanished into the trees.

'What did you say?' Lyra called to Valdyr.

'I told him to meet us in the south,' he replied. 'He'll find us, don't worry.'

Dirklan frowned, but he muttered to Domitia and the wyvern shot into the skies. Lyra sent Pearl cantering in their wake, feeling the wind stinging her face as she looked back to see the venators rising behind her. The thrill of flying rushed through her again.

'Norostein, here we come,' she shouted. Valdyr drew alongside, upright in the saddle and peering about him in wonder. She'd intended to be proper today, to be a lady – but instead, she waved merrily, kicked at Pearl's flanks and shouted, 'Catch me if you can!'

They tore across the skies, her heart soaring with her.

26

Armoured From Within

The Riddle of Armour

A knight girds himself for battle, coating himself in chainmail and plates of steel. But do be not deceived: unless his heart and mind are armoured with courage, he may as well go forth naked and unarmed.

BOOK OF KORE

Norostein, Noros
Martrois 936

Tarita's little attic room was dimly lit through the domed glass turret by a sliver of the new moon. The besieged city was as silent as it ever got, but she couldn't sleep.

I should be tending Waqar and begging his forgiveness. Or trying to find Jehana, if she really is somewhere south of the Alps.

She couldn't decide between those two impulses, or find any rest, so finally she sighed in exasperation, threw the Cadearvo mask she'd been examining onto her blanket and went to the window. In the plaza below, the remaining windships were tied down against the strong northerly blowing cold over the city. A few lights shone in the Governor's Mansion opposite and she wondered if Waqar was awake. If she went to him now, would he welcome her?

'All quiet,' she heard one watchman call to another.

It was her third night alone in this little room, which had become her refuge. It had an eerie beauty when the moonlight lit the coloured glass dome, shafts of red and blue light carving through the dust motes and cobwebs, almost solid enough to touch.

She yawned. It was just before dawn and the sliver moon was hanging low in the sky, basting the misty square in pallid light that glistened on the dew. It was still bitterly cold, but no longer freezing. Winter was passing.

Then something dropped from the darkness above and the square came alive. She dimly heard shouting, but no alarms rang out as five venators landed, followed by two more exotic constructs – a flying horse and a winged reptile that walked on hind legs. *Pegasus and Wyvern*, she remembered from the Yurosi myths Mistress Alhana liked to tell her.

Guardsmen swiftly surrounded the newcomers, five grey-cloaked human forms – and one larger shape she couldn't quite make out, until he stepped into the moonlight and her heart thudded so hard she gasped.

'*Ogre?*'

She didn't bother with the stairs but threw open the latch, lifted the sash wide and hurled herself into the air, gliding down on Air-gnosis and the sudden lightness in her heart.

Ogre hung back as Dirklan and Nara confronted the guardsmen swarming around them, ringing them in crossbows and spears. He peered around fearfully, keeping his cowl over his head and waiting for the inevitable outcry when they saw what he was.

The miracle of flight had brought them five hundred miles in two long sessions, the first by day as they traversed the foothills of the Matra Ranges to avoid the Shihad and Imperial Army's aerial patrols over the Augenheim Pass. They'd rested for a day before approaching Norostein by night to avoid the main Shihad army's flying patrols. In the event, they'd seen none and had landed inside the city's upper ring unopposed.

But now what? Will they see us as friend or foe?

He'd asked to remain hidden in the countryside, but Dirklan insisted he'd be needed to persuade Waqar of his sister's plight. Right now that felt like a mistake.

Then it happened. 'You there,' someone shouted, levelling a crossbow at him. 'Come out where we can see you.' When Ogre reluctantly complied, the man swore. 'Rukk me, it's one of those damned constructs –'

He's seen others like me? Ogre was stunned, then horrified. *The Master is the only one who makes constructs like me . . .* He showed his empty hands and called, 'Please, I'm on your side.'

The man's eyes went round. 'It talks – the bloody thing talks!' He raised the crossbow, but Valdyr stepped in front of it.

'No. He's with us.'

'And who in Hel are you?' the crossbowman demanded as others crowded in, shouting a bewildering volley of orders. 'On your knees,' an officer bawled over the top of them, while Dirklan tried to protest.

Suddenly a small bundle of shadow came hurtling through the press, light bursts of kinesis battering guardsmen and battle-magi aside, then Tarita collided with his chest squealing, 'Ogre – *Ogre*, you're *here* –'

The impact nearly knocked him off his feet, but he automatically caught her and clung on – although he did at least manage to instantly slam his shields up as well, just in case some idiot did loose a crossbow. To his surprise Tarita was pounding his chest, crying and laughing, and his own eyes were filled with stinging tears so that the whole world became a blurred smear. 'Ogre, Ogre,' she kept saying, her voice like light on water.

'Ogre is here,' he mumbled hoarsely, and then he amended it. '*I* am here . . .'

He was vaguely conscious that in his peripheral vision, torchlight was glinting on blades and arrowheads, while officers were barking orders of restraint, then an authoritative voice cut through the din. 'What's happening here?'

'I'm Lord Misen, General Korion,' Dirklan replied quickly. 'Hopefully you got my message?'

Ogre blinked his eyes clear and saw a tired young man with a serious face. Despite the early hour, he was fully dressed and armed. *Seth Korion, presumably.*

The man conferred hurriedly with Dirklan, then said, 'Stand down, Captain. These are emissaries from the north. I need to speak to them.'

While the Yurosi general spoke to Dirklan, Ogre looked down at Tarita's upturned face, still smiling broadly, squeezed her gently then lowered her to the ground. She looked tired and dishevelled and utterly wonderful.

'I missed you,' she whispered, making his heart sing. 'Except your snoring, obviously.'

'I was just about to say the same,' he mumbled. 'Except your farting.'

She wiped her eyes, then gazed admiringly at his venator. 'You flew on your own?'

'Not as comfortable as your windskiff, but more fun.'

She grinned impishly. 'Always do the fun thing,' she advised. 'But what are you doing here? With Valdyr? And who are these other people?'

Ogre indicated the blonde woman: 'That's Nara of Misencourt and the one-eyed man is her protector, Dirklan. The other two are their guards.'

'Nara – the dwymancer from the north? Have they come to help us?'

'To defeat the Master – yes. I deciphered the *Daemonicon*,' he added.

Tarita's eyes widened, then she took and squeezed his huge hand in her little ones. 'You clever, wonderful man.'

Ogre felt his chest swell and all the stress and misery of the past months fell away. He was with his friend again, and he'd won her praise.

This is the best moment of my life.

Valdyr returned to Nara's side as the tension around Ogre dissipated, although the soldiers were still glaring at the giant construct with mistrust, and at Tarita for so thoughtlessly swatting them aside.

The Rondian general, Seth Korion, issued orders for their steeds to be cared for before leading them up the stairs into one of imposing buildings surrounding the plaza.

Rhune and Sarunia had dropped their cowls, but Nara kept hers over her head and her face averted. 'Are you all right?' Valdyr whispered, talking her arm.

'Fine,' she murmured, bowing her head as they passed into a well-lit foyer.

She's worried about being recognised, Valdyr realised. He supposed that

445

the mistress of a powerful lord would be well-known in courtly circles. He glanced behind him, saw that the eight-foot-plus Ogre was still holding hands with five-foot-nothing Tarita; the construct's eyes were everywhere as he took in the majestic building, while Tarita was strutting defiantly as if daring someone to pass comment on her outlandish companion.

Seth Korion led them four flights up a grand sweeping staircase of highly polished oak, halfway up the immense well, and into a large council room decorated in blue and white.

Dear Kore, there's more wealth in this room than the whole of Hegikaro Castle, Valdyr thought, staring about him. His brother's throne hall was smaller than this side-room – and this building didn't even belong to a king.

'Send for Capitano Sensini, Sultan Salim and Prince Waqar,' General Korion told a messenger, 'and tell them it's urgent – bring the prince on a stretcher if necessary. We'll need coffee and tea and hot bread; let the kitchen know – quickly.' He bowed to Dirklan and said apologetically, 'We'll all join you in fifteen minutes.' He hurried away, leaving his aide to see to their comfort.

The man introduced himself as Andwine Delton. He lit the fires with gnosis, frowning up at the high ceiling and muttering, 'These rooms are pretty enough, but they're cursed hard to heat.'

'You should see the Bastion in Pallas,' Dirklan replied. 'Damn place is an ice-box.'

The two men conversed gently while everyone else gazed about uncertainly. Nara was the only one still cloaked and she made no move to lower her hood as she clung to Valdyr's arm – not that Valdyr had any objection. Rhune and Sarunia went to the windows, as did Ogre and Tarita, who were still holding hands, almost as if they'd forgotten they were doing so.

Nara watched them curiously. 'Do you know the *Fey Tales*?' she murmured. '"The Lay of Hobokin"? He was a Troll: he fell in love with Glymahart, the Stardancer's sister – he was ugly, but she saw his true heart and kissed him.'

Valdyr, seeing Ogre's lumpen visage lit by a radiant smile, said, 'That's nice.'

'Not really,' Nara replied. 'She'd been cursed so that her kisses brought only sorrow. Hobokin went mad – in the end, Rynholt had to kill him. Glymahart set his head in the skies, where it became Simutu, the lesser moon.'

'So you think she'll break Ogre's heart?'

'How can she not?'

The sun was beginning to rise, the golden light streaming through the windows and illuminating the blue and white décor. Food and drink, steaming in the frigid air, was served and they all ate greedily, for it had been a long night. The hot meal got them chatting, Tarita teasing Ogre about the huge platter he devoured, and Valdyr was gratified to be able to serve Nara, buttering her a scone and pouring tea.

'I'm not helpless,' she scolded lightly, 'but thank you.'

Then Seth Korion returned with a clever-faced young man with olive skin and a dark goatee, followed by a limping, wheezing Waqar Mubarak clinging to a healer-mage; he collapsed into a chair with relief and looked around, ashen-faced.

Valdyr noted that he and Tarita barely looked at each other, but she dropped Ogre's hand, which made the construct's face fall.

'What's this about?' Waqar asked gruffly, then he took in the presence of Valdyr and Ogre properly and his eyes widened. 'What are *you* doing here?' he demanded. 'Is Jehana found?'

'No, but we've come south to find her.'

'Tell me,' Waqar demanded – or tried to, as he suddenly doubled over, coughing up blood.

Before Valdyr could reply, another Easterner arrived, this one immaculate and richly attired, despite the hour. Seth Korion announced, 'May I present Salim, Sultan of Kesh.'

There was a low gasp of surprise from everyone in Valdyr's group.

'What's the *dead* Sultan of Kesh doing here?' Dirklan wondered, for once mystified.

'I'm a guest, along with what's left of my army,' the sultan replied, speaking better Rondian than most Yurosi. 'The army outside the walls is an enemy to us all.'

Dirklan looked flabbergasted. 'Clearly I've been out of touch too long,' he muttered sourly. Then he glanced at Nara before turning back to the sultan and the general. 'We should introduce ourselves. You must be wondering who we are and what we're doing here.'

'Certainly, Milord,' Seth replied. He turned to the young man with the goatee. 'This is my friend, Capitano Ramon Sensini, Commander of the Retiari Freeswords of Silacia. And some of you know Prince Waqar Mubarak,' Seth went on. 'And this is Tarita Alhani, of Javon in Ahmedhassa.'

'Lady Alhani has no status here,' Waqar grumbled. 'She should withdraw.'

Valdyr looked from the prince to the Merozain, wondering what had broken their liaison so swiftly.

'Lady Tarita has links to both the Merozain Brotherhood and the Ordo Costruo and I value her presence,' Seth said firmly, and prince or not, that was that: Waqar was overruled. The general turned to Dirklan. 'And your party, Milord?'

The one-eyed man bowed. 'Of course – although I would like to clarify first that this is an official Embassy representing the Crown of Rondelmar, with all assumed privileges. Is this understood and agreed?'

Seth went to agree, but Waqar raised a suspicious hand. 'Wait, what does that mean?'

'An ambassador may not be detained for any reason, nor any of his retinue, even in times of war,' Dirklan replied. 'Surely the Keshi have similar protections?'

Waqar looked sour, but made a dismissive gesture. 'Ai, it is known.'

'Excellent,' Dirklan said. 'In that case, I present Valdyr Sarkany, Prince of Mollachia. With him is a construct, Ogre. So that you understand fully, Ogre was bred by Ervyn Naxius and he is both fully sentient and a mage.'

Waqar already knew this, but Seth and Ramon clearly didn't. 'And so *you* understand fully,' Ramon replied, 'we've fought hundreds of similar beings over the past few weeks.'

'Ogre guessed, from your men's reaction,' Ogre growled. 'The Master called Ogre a "proto-breed": a test. He has bred more, of course.' Then he lifted his head. 'But only Ogre was educated, to explore his capability to reason.'

Valdyr couldn't imagine talking about oneself as a gnostic experiment. It was bad enough to have been treated as one by Asiv – and he didn't want to think about his dead abuser at all.

Seth exchanged a look with Sultan Salim that implied considerable empathy between the two men, then he turned to Ogre and said, 'Rest assured: I accept your place in Milord's embassy, Ogre.'

Dirklan turned to his Pallacians. 'These are Rhune and Sarunia, of Ventia. And this is –'

'Allow me,' Nara said coolly, releasing Valdyr's arm. Stepping fully into the light, she flicked back her hood and turning to Seth, said, 'General Korion, it's good to see you again. We chose well in you.'

Valdyr stared as Seth's jaw dropped.

The general blurted, '*Your Majesty–?*' in an incredulous voice and began to drop to his right knee, then checked himself, while his face swirled with emotions.

Beside him, Sultan Salim frowned, puzzled by the general's reaction, while Ramon Sensini snorted softly.

'Who is this woman?' Waqar asked, voicing the same question Valdyr was suddenly asking himself, all at once the ground was swept from beneath him.

Dirklan said, in a voice of dry irony, 'May I present Lyra Vereinen, Queen of Rondelmar.'

'*Nara?*' Valdyr croaked softly, while Salim, Waqar and Tarita went pale. Waqar went so far as to lay a hand on his scimitar; when Ramon Sensini put a warning hand on his arm, he shrugged it off angrily.

But Valdyr had eyes only for her as she turned to him, her expression apologetic. 'I'm sorry, Valdyr,' she said, her voice composed. 'I'm sure you can appreciate that I could hardly reveal my true name under the circumstances. I hope we can still be friends.'

Friends? he thought. *Dear Kore, you're* more *than my friend . . .*

He felt hurt on so many levels. She'd lied to him, led him on, beguiled him into trust . . . *And the beginnings of love*, he admitted, flushing red.

Part of him wanted to rail at her, or to storm out like a hurt child, but a lifetime of suppressing his emotions in the name of self-preservation had made him stronger than that. And the things they'd shared *mattered*, whatever her true identity.

And she's right, a small voice inside him whispered. *She couldn't have told you her name. You share a heretical power – and you'd have run a mile as soon as she told you.*

The room had fallen silent, every eye on the blonde woman with the soft but determined face – and then on the sultan, who was staring at her as if she were an apparition.

Here were the rulers of East and West, in one room.

Ramon Sensini chuckled dryly. 'Then can I assume you to be Dirklan Setallius, the Volsai commander?' he asked Dirklan. 'We liaised via the gnosis when I extricated Lord Dubrayle from a certain . . . um . . . problem, a month or so ago.'

Volsai? Valdyr thought, a little sickened. The empire divided opinions, but the imperial spies were universally loathed.

The room fell silent as everyone digested these revelations. Valdyr found his eyes dragged back to Nara – *No, she is Lyra Vereinen, the Kore-bedamned-Empress*. He remembered their past interactions in the dwyma and over the past few days, trying to comprehend how he could have missed such a glaring fact, but she'd always contacted him from her garden and there had never been any intimations of crowns or titles.

Dear Kore, I've kissed the Empress of Yuros.

'I would have told you if I could, I swear,' she said. 'I hated deception – but I had no choice.'

'We've been travelling together for two days,' he reminded her, his voice angrier than he intended.

'We were never alone. I was seeking the right time, but it never came.'

'And *this* is the right time?' he glowered.

'No, no it isn't. But it could no longer be avoided – General Korion has met me before.' She turned back to address the room. 'My apologies for the surprise. But this isn't a social visit, or even a diplomatic one. We're here on a matter of the utmost importance. It concerns a renegade mage who wishes to destroy us all – by which I mean not just this city or even the Rondian Empire, but all of humanity. I speak of Ogre's former master: Ervyn Naxius.'

Everyone looked to the sultan, her natural counterpoint. The sultan glanced at Seth, then said, 'Please – there is more than enough evidence that this war has been conducted by a mutual enemy of both East and West. I am eager to know more.'

'Yes, we do all need to hear this,' Seth agreed, 'but first, could your Majesty please explain the despatch that arrived a few days ago? In it, you renounced the title of Empress of Yuros and offered secession. As you can understand, besieged in the only remaining free city in Noros, we're unable to make any decision, or even to formulate our questions. But are you our empress?'

'I was your empress, but I am no longer,' she replied. 'I'm just a queen, whose role is to be limited by a constitution that's still being written. But right now, I'm on a quest to save the world.'

Despite his hurt, Valdyr could appreciate her grace and wit before such a gathering and at such a time. He watched the others: the Javonesi, Tarita, was nodding appreciatively, as if she recognised spunk when she saw it. Sensini was clearly similarly impressed, smiling wryly as he exchanged a glance with the more strait-laced Korion.

Waqar, however, was not happy. 'I won't confer with those who launched Crusades.'

'I didn't,' said Lyra evenly. 'That was my predecessor. And I understand, Prince Waqar, that you have a certain potential? It's one we share.'

Waqar's eyes bulged. He shot a glance at Valdyr and finally understood. 'You're *Nara* of whom Valdyr spoke?' He put his hand to his mouth and then his forehead. 'Ahm on High. And you're here because of Jehana?'

'We are.'

Waqar set his jaw and then made a courtly gesture, full of graceful swirling hands. 'Then I apologise, Majesty,' he said in subdued tones. 'I am at your service.'

Lyra gazed around the table, struck again by how unique this gathering was: men and women, West and East, magi and dwymancers; all working together despite so many past wrongs.

Outside, the daemon-possessed attackers remained sullenly encamped, so at no stage was General Korion called away. They were all able to give Naxius their full attention, but it was a long day.

Ogre spoke first, repeating for the newcomers what he'd learned in the *Daemonicon di Naxius*, after which his conclusions were dissected at length. The construct spoke well, handling the questions with patience and real intellect, and Lyra noticed that whenever he floundered, he would look at the diminutive Tarita and she would murmur something that grounded him again.

Hobokin and Glymahart, Lyra thought again. *He's Earth, she's Air, and it'll end in tears.*

After Ogre finished, they all reported their own encounters with Naxius' Masked Cabal, then came the difficult discussion about dwymancy – not everyone present knew of it, and there were long discussions about its nature, its status under Church Law and what it could and couldn't do. Lyra was proud to declare her power, and Valdyr too, but Waqar was reluctant to discuss his own potential, or that of his captive sister.

Then Salim told them of the dying words of Rashid Mubarak, of how he'd let his own son, Xoredh, be infected by some new kind of ichor to gain power in the East: a daemon's bargain, if ever there was one. They spoke of the Masks and all they'd done, and Ramon Sensini described his long battles against the so-called Lord of Rym, who they'd only recently discovered to have been another of Naxius' pawns.

'Naxius deliberately destabilised both Yuros and Ahmedhassa and launched us all onto a collision course,' Dirklan concluded. 'Masked cabalists with unrivalled gnostic power, daemonic ichor spreading through the veins of our peoples – and all of it traceable back to Naxius himself.'

'And thanks to Ogre, we now know what Naxius wants,' Tarita piped up. 'Let's stop him.'

Lyra glanced at Valdyr, still wishing she'd managed to tell him the truth sooner, but he seemed to have forgiven her, at least partially, and that mattered more than she'd thought.

'I'm convinced by what I've heard,' Seth told them. 'I believe we must aid your mission, your Majesty. If dwymancers are required to prevent Naxius from using Jehana Mubarak for his foul purpose, then we must speed you on your way with whatever support we can give you. I will place magi at your disposal, if you wish. But we must still defend Norostein, I deem. We have tens of thousands of refugees, and Xoredh's army is still formidable.'

'And for my part, any man of mine you need is yours,' Salim told Lyra.

Lyra glanced at Dirklan; they had discussed this at some length. 'Thank you, your Majesty, my lords. It is indeed our purpose to hunt down Naxius; but to do so we will have to rely on speed and stealth. We must leave Norostein unseen and find Naxius without our approach being detected, so we can't be a large group. Valdyr and I must be there.' She glanced at Valdyr and was pleased that he was nodding firmly. 'I'm unable to dissuade Lord Setallius from coming, and Rhune and Sarunia tell me they're indispensable.'

'We are,' the Ventians chorused drily.

'You lot have power to burn, but you can't make camp, tend animals or cook to save yourselves,' Sarunia added in a sultry drawl.

'Those are the only people I can speak for,' Lyra concluded. She turned to Ogre. 'I have no right, but—'

'The Master made me,' he rumbled. 'I know him.'

'And I'm coming too,' Tarita put in. 'I've been on the trail of these damned Masks from the first. And I'm a Merozain, so try and stop me,' she added, with a cocky smirk.

No one contradicted her, but they all looked at Waqar.

The Keshi prince grimaced and threw a rueful look at himself. 'I'm told that any kind of exertion could kill me. I badly want to come, but—'

'But he can't, and that's that,' piped up the healer-mage, sitting against the back wall. Her voice brooked no argument. 'He's operating on one lung. I refuse to let him out of my care.'

'We'll find her for you,' Tarita said, and Waqar nodded gloomily.

Seth turned to Ramon. 'My friend, you know I'd rather you were here, but it's your call.'

Waqar scowled. 'Why him?'

'Because I'm an Ascendant mage,' the Silacian capitano replied casually. He tapped his fingers on the table thoughtfully while the room digested that little nugget. These days Ascendant magi were almost unheard of outside the Merozain brotherhood. Since the demise of the Keepers, there were none in Pallas.

Finally, Ramon turned apologetically to Lyra and said, 'Majesty, we still don't know what the enemy will do next, and everyone I care about is here. My lads have marched with me for five years on a losing campaign against the Lord of Rym. I can't abandon them. They're my family.'

Lyra had formed an opinion of the young Silacian as someone with more craft than will, but the gravity in his voice belied that. 'I honour your decision,' she told him, while reflecting that another Ascendant mage would have been a godsend on their quest. But at least they had Tarita.

There was nothing else to decide. 'Then we have our party,' she sighed. 'Just a handful to find and destroy Naxius and save Jehana.' She put her head in her hands, already exhausted from the long road to this moment.

The room fell silent, then Seth Korion asked Lyra, 'Majesty, from your tale, you have experience against what we face. Silver, argenstael . . . we can work with those things, but is there aught else you can do to aid us?'

Lyra glanced at Valdyr, then at her father. She knew both well enough by now to know how to reply. 'Sunlight gradually purifies the body of those lightly infected. They can all be saved. But if we do anything here, our presence will be revealed . . .' Her voice trailed away and she looked at Valdyr. 'Perhaps . . .'

They all fell silent, then he and she shared a smile. *Yes*, she thought, *we can do that.*

Dirklan spoke up. 'Then we must rest, but not for long. We'll leave tomorrow morning, to give ourselves daylight to cross the Alps. The possessed men have better night sight, so we've higher odds of evading them during the day. We can't spare any more time – indeed,' he added gloomily, 'we may already be too late.'

Rym, Rimoni

Ervyn Naxius took his seat opposite Jehana, studying her with admiration. His slaves had pampered her, washing her hair and skin, grooming her until her bone-white hair was lustrous and gleaming, then dressing her in a silken shift of scarlet, form-hugging and revealing. He'd outgrown lust, by and large, but an aesthetically pleasing woman was always an ornament. He'd preserved the bodies of all his past concubines in his private quarters, each posed as if still living; their souls had been imprisoned in the bodies for him to talk to.

Jehana's upper face was hidden by the skull-mask of Glamortha but her expression was clear: she was suicidal, just as he desired.

A window showed the ruins of Rym, painted in jagged silver and deep shadow by the waxing moon: a stark, beautiful outlook that spoke of the futility of existence and the passing of all things.

Naxius took a sip of wine and asked, 'Jehana, do you understand all that I've told you?'

She responded slowly, her voice hollow, distant, as if she thought this conversation might be just another vision inflicted by Abraxas. 'You say that life engenders energy that binds bodies and rocks and plants and water and animals, flame and sunlight. That this energy creates a self-renewing cycle, like a tree whose branches are joined to the roots.'

'A tree, yes. Some call it the "Elétfa", the Tree of Life – but others see veins circulating around a heart, or waters flowing from rivers to oceans to clouds to rain and around again.'

'But what's it for?' she asked dully.

He didn't mock the question: philosophers had been asking it since the dawn of time. 'Life isn't *for* anything, Jehana. It means nothing *except* what we chose it to mean. There's no cosmic lesson, no Creator putting us to the test or Evil Lord trying to corrupt us. Nobody waits to punish us for our sins or reward our good deeds. There's only the void.'

'The void,' she echoed with a shudder. 'But the void isn't empty.'

He leaned forward. 'No, indeed. When we die, there is a part of us that detaches from the body, which decays and is fed back into the energy flow – the Elétfa. The part that detaches is our "soul" or "spirit". It flows out from the system, if we have the self-awareness to cling to sentience. It goes out into the void.'

'It goes to Paradise,' the girl breathed, more in hope than belief, by her tone of voice.

'It goes straight down the throat of the daemons: the already-dead souls, waiting in the aether to swallow others, to prey on their energy and vicariously live other lives.'

She clutched her chest. Naxius could almost smell her heart-blood. 'Abraxas . . .'

'Yes, Abraxas is one of them – one of the Great Ones, a prince of his kind. There are many others, just as mighty. However, Abraxas was the first one visionary enough to ally himself to me.'

'I see you,' she breathed. 'You have shadows all round you.'

'You see the daemons linked to my aura, feeding me their power and perceptions,' he boasted. 'They don't possess me – I possess *them*. You see, dear Jehana, by liberating myself from morality I have become the most powerful man alive. There is nothing I will not do to perpetuate myself, and that frees me: heart and soul, body and mind.' He reached across and enclosed her limp hand in his. 'You can do the same.'

She didn't wrench her hand away, which suggested he had succeeded. He was strangely moved to realise that this was the closest thing he'd had to a consensual relationship.

'If we're going to be future daemons, Jehana, isn't it better to be lords of their kind? Why accept domination when you can dominate? Become what I am, help me destroy the Elétfa, and we – you and I – will rule Eternity.'

'But you say the dwyma and the daemonic are inimical,' Jehana murmured, 'so I don't understand how this can be.'

He studied her masked face. Was it possible that this was an act, that she was feigning subservience to try to find a weakness in his plans? But he doubted she had the guile, and her time inside Abraxas' mind had clearly broken something. It took a very special mind to emerge unscathed from such ceaseless sensory overload – he hadn't.

'I spoke truly – the dwyma is the essence of life, and daemons are the embodiment of death. When Alyssa Dulayne tried to contain them both within her, she was destroyed, consumed by that which she sought to control. But *you* could do it: by taking on both together, in a controlled way. Because life *is* part of death, and death of life: when we die we just become another form of life, like bricks taken from a ruined building to build another. Alyssa sought to gobble everything at once and she couldn't contain and control that contradiction – but with my guidance, you can be the one to reconcile the daemonic to the dwyma, the one to embrace both and ease the return of the daemons to Urte.'

She shuddered. '*Embrace them* . . . dear Ahm, you don't know what they're like . . .'

'Oh, I do, my girl, I do indeed. There's nothing you've endured that I haven't gone through myself.'

For pleasure.

She finally looked at him then, her eyes going wide. 'Oh my . . .'

Sympathy . . . She thinks I'm some kind of victim . . .

It was almost enough to make him laugh, but he overcame that urge. 'I have gazed upon the Void, Jehana. I know what you've been through.'

She looked stricken.

It really was too funny to bear, but it did at least confirm the key to breaking Jehana was empathy, which shone inside her, despite her royal upbringing and brittle imperiousness.

'The daemons aren't evil,' he told her now, relishing his own cleverness, 'they're in pain – insane with it – because they once had life. They circle us in desperation, wanting to rejoin us. They succumb to envy and hate, but a true *daemonist* could heal them. She could bring them surcease and return them to life, create a new paradigm of existence in which nothing dies and we all live in harmony.' He leaned forward. 'Think of it, Jehana: a Paradise on Urte, where all beings are immortal. When one's body dies, we simply create a new one for our soul. No one need ever suffer or die.'

Hilarious.

He rose and left, leaving her to contemplate that without having her captor in front of her.

She's coming round.

Naxius returned to his own chambers, his awareness pricked by a gnostic sending, but the identity was masked. That was in itself puzzling, but he picked up a relay-stave and conjured a field of energy in the midst of a gnostic circle. Inside it, a translucent, shimmering image appeared of a man in the robes of a Kore monk, but over his face was a mask . . . Macharo.

Macharo is dead . . . I felt Brylion Fasterius die . . .

'Who are you?' he demanded.

The man pulled the mask away to reveal a blandly handsome, tonsured blond man. 'My name is Germane. I served Ostevan Pontifex.' Then his eyes turned black with ichor. 'And now I serve you.'

Naxius blinked, then reached into the hive-mind of Abraxas and found the connection . . . This man had been flitting in and around the royal courts, meddling on Ostevan's behalf. 'How did you learn my contact sigil? And where did you get that Mask?'

And how come you to have the ichor . . . ?

Germane smiled smugly. 'When Brylion Fasterius died, they didn't realise what he was, or what was lodged inside his chest. But I did. I joined the burial party and found what I sought.

He took the daemon-spawn into himself . . . Naxius licked his lips, impressed by the man's determination to pollute himself in the name of power. *And this means I still have an agent in the north after all.*

'What news?' he asked hungrily.

Germane spoke swiftly, concisely. 'Solon Takwyth has seized power, arriving on the battlefield and attacking the Sacrecour army, joining his forces to those of the queen, but usurping control. He now has her and he marches upon Pallas. Word is the city is now divided – many desire to open the gates, but as many fear him.'

'He's taken the queen? Lyra is his?'

'Yes, my Lord,' Germane replied unctuously.

'Will he use her?' Naxius demanded.

'Most thoroughly, I am sure.' Germane smirked.

'No, I mean, will he harness her dwyma for himself?' Naxius asked, then he realised that this Germane probably had no idea of the queen's true nature.

But that was instantly disproved. 'I have no doubt that having a pet dwymancer will be very much to his liking,' the priest drawled.

Ah: then Lyra might swing Takwyth to her side, so there is still danger to my plans. 'Get close to them,' he ordered, 'and kill her.'

'That's not so simple,' Germane replied. 'I'm an outlaw now. Of course, with my new skills, that's not a big impediment, but I'm unsure what I face . . . ?' He paused meaningfully.

He wants something, Naxius' temper rose, but he said carefully, 'I can aid you.'

Germane's face took on a slightly martyred aspect. 'Ostevan confided in me that he believed there was some great matter in train, something the death of the queen might prevent. He, of course, thought to use her to place himself above you, but I am not so ambitious. All I seek is a place at your side.'

'Not so ambitious' . . . amusing fellow. But he could be vital. 'Kill the queen and then we'll talk.'

Germane smiled. 'Of course . . . Master.'

The contact went dead.

Naxius sat back, both perturbed and exhilarated by this latest development. Though the Masks had never been more than pieces in his private tabula game, their deaths had left him without agents in key locations, so if this Germane could fill part of that gap, well and good.

But now Jehana was very nearly ready, perhaps only hours from complete breakdown, so soon he would have nothing at all to fear. As long as the dwymancers remained distant and ignorant, they were no threat.

A day or two more and this filthy, random world will be purged and set to rights – and I shall be its first real god.

27

Sunlight Through Glass

The Fourth Dwymancer

Dameta was, with Eloy, Lanthea and Amantius, one of the four early dwymancers who engendered great panic in the early Rondian Empire, when Emperor Sertain feared them as potential rivals. He feigned friendship and then destroyed Eloy; the other three fled. Amantius was subsequently slain, but the fate of the two women was never truly determined, for they simply vanished. They say Lanthea went native in Sydia, but Dameta was rumoured to haunt the Veronese Alps for centuries after.

ORDO COSTRUO COLLEGIATE, PONTUS 738

Norostein, Noros
Martrois 936

Lyra sighed in frustration, too tense to sleep, and rolled over again, trying to get comfortable. The unfamiliar guestroom creaked as the wind moaned through the eaves and hidden draughts chilled her skin and made the candles dance. They'd been housed away from the Governor's Mansion to limit prying eyes.

She was exhausted, wanting desperately to sleep, but rest wouldn't come. Her mind kept churning over the dwymancy she and Valdyr had exerted that evening, a subtle drawing of energy quite unlike the tumultuous storm-riding they'd done previously. *Did we get it right? Would it be detected?* And she was anxious about the day to come, when they would fly south to set themselves against a madman of unknown powers to prevent an event prophesied in the *Book of Kore* itself.

Dirklan says the holy book was written by men, but surely Kore Himself guided them?

If that was so, their mission was already doomed.

Outside, it was still night, and deathly quiet. Occasionally, she heard soldiers assemble and tramp away, doubtless to relieve the watches along the walls. Messengers came and went, briefing General Korion and Sultan Salim – who turned out to be an *impersonator* . . . Seth Korion had told her the full story, which was weirdly ironic, given what she'd done; it set her to worrying about Nita and events at home.

The Sacrecours will have reached Pallas – they might even have fought by now . . .

Part of the price of their secrecy was no news: the aether was never perfectly safe from listening minds, so Dirklan had decreed no contact at all with the north.

This is hopeless, she thought at last. She wrapped her cloak around her shoulders, then crept to the door and slipped into the lounge, where she found Rhune and Valdyr, lying beside the dying fire. The Ventian was snuffling softly, but Valdyr saw her and sat up. She gave him a tentative smile, then headed for the servants' door, opened it quietly and slipped through to a smaller room. She sat on the window's padded seat and looked down at the square below.

'I can't sleep,' she yawned to Valdyr, who slipped in behind her. His breath was steaming too.

'Neither can I.' They sat together, peering out at the moon lowering towards the southwest, silhouetting the peaks of the Veronese Alps which towered over the city. 'It's nearly dawn anyway.'

He turned to face her and for a while they just gazed at each other. From a distance, he looked grim and forbidding, the touch of frost at his temples and drooping moustaches making him look at least forty, but this close, it was clear he was much younger, around her own age.

He's had a hard, hard life, she thought. *He's been through Hel.*

She reached out shyly and stroked the moustache: it was softer than she'd expected. 'These are awfully out of fashion in Pallas,' she teased. 'No one wears just a moustache. It's either clean-shaven or a full beard.'

'In Mollachia, moustaches have always been a sign of masculinity – and beards are for married men.' He smoothed his facial hair self-consciously. 'You don't like them?'

'Well, maybe they take some getting used to,' she confessed, 'but I'm not criticising.'

'Good, because they're not going away.'

She pushed aside the urge to kiss him; she knew so little about him, so here was her opportunity. She asked him about his homeland and family, drinking in what he told her.

Then it was her turn, and this time she held nothing back, talking first about Rildan and his father and her infatuation with Ril, her handsome, heroic rescuer. Then, despite feeling deep embarrassment, she confessed how close she'd come to letting Ostevan seduce her, and then her ill-fated lurch into Solon's arms.

'It's hard to trust my feelings,' she confessed. 'Ostevan played me like a harp . . . and Solon was overpowering: a bully, emotionally, physically . . . sexually. At first I thought I was proving something, you know? Becoming the sort of woman that men demand . . . but I hated him in the end.'

He looked down at his hands for a moment, gathering strength for his own soul-baring. 'Lyra, I was a child when I was sent to the breeding-houses . . . I've lain with hundreds of women, maybe even thousands, but I've never made love. I have never been with someone who wanted me for myself . . .' He paused before adding, 'And nor do I expect to, until we've dealt with Ervyn Naxius.'

'After that,' she agreed, relieved not to be pressed.

Valdyr took her smooth hands in his callused fingers. 'You are still queen of a mighty nation. I have no expectations.' He hesitated, then smiled. 'But I'm not discouraged. Asiv is dead and you cannot imagine how this lifts my soul.'

'I think the death of Ostevan left me feeling something like that,' she told him. *Although my violence scared me . . .* 'Dirklan believes we can reach Rym in two days, so this may all soon be over, one way or the other. If . . . if we live, who knows what might be possible?' She considered. 'Under the new constitution, I will be sharing the responsibilities – I will have more time for myself. That's not a luxury I've ever had – Kore is a demanding Master too – you have no idea how much praying a nun's expected to do.'

'My brother will need me in Mollachia for some time,' he replied, 'but not for ever. And once I've done what I need . . .' His voice trailed off and they shared the silence again.

Lyra could not stop herself from leaning in, or touching her lips to his . . . and sinking into him, until she was lost in his taste, his warmth, and the solid bulk of him that promised real dependability.

Ogre stared at the wall of the chamber he'd been allotted. For all it was small, it was still the most luxurious room he'd ever slept in, although his mind was not on the softness of the mattress or the smoothness of the linens but on the journey to come.

We're hunting the Master, yet even the Ordo Costruo failed to find him. He couldn't escape the fear that he was going to die – but his life, begun as an animagery experiment, had disproven the view that someone like him could only ever be miserable. Since his great adventure began, there had been many memories he would cherish: victories of body and mind, times of connection and laughter. But most of his best moments had come when Tarita had burst into his life and immediately offered friendship; the times they'd rescued each other; the shared joy and relief of companionship – even the gift of watching her sleep, pressed to his side and utterly trusting.

It's of these things I will be thinking as I die, he told himself.

He was a half-blood mage: he had no illusions about how he'd fare against the Master's mightiest servants. Once periapts were kindled and blades drawn, he'd not last long.

He gave up on sleep and crept into the corridor, ignoring the staring guard outside as he tried to orientate himself and work out where he wanted to go. *Somewhere with a view,* he decided. He finally found a narrow spiralling staircase and, peering up, caught a glimpse of a faint glow above suggesting he might find a view of the sunrise.

He had to bend double as he clambered carefully up steps too small for his feet, but his reward was to emerge through a half-open door into a chamber beneath a dome of chequered panels of red and blue glass.

Cobwebs clung in the corners, but it looked like someone had brushed the worst away. The wooden floor barely creaked as he walked out into the chamber and gazed upwards, to see the moon refracted through the glass dome in scintillations of colour.

He smiled slowly in appreciation.

'It's lovely, isn't it?' Tarita commented.

Ogre spun, his heart thudding, a rush of embarrassment washing over him that she'd taken him by surprise – and that she might think he'd been looking for her.

Weren't you? the dry voice in his head asked.

She was sitting up against a wall in the darkest part of the chamber, wrapped in blankets. Her clothes, boots and weapons were piled beside her.

'Didn't they give you a room?' he asked indignantly.

'They did – with Waqar,' she answered, her voice indifferent.

'Oh.' He floundered, then settled for, 'I'm sorry.'

'Don't be. I got bored being a concubine – and now he's sick. I hate sickrooms – and anyway, we've got a job to do.' She patted the floor beside her. 'Sit here. The sunrise paints the walls all colours. It's quite lovely.'

He hesitated, then settled a foot away. She ruined his attempt to keep his distance by scooting across and worming into the crook of his arm.

'What's wrong?' she asked, looking up. 'Something's up.'

'We might all die,' he mumbled, because that was easier than, *I love you and it's killing me.* 'Or we may be possessed and enslaved by the Master.'

'That all?' she teased, patting his forearm. 'Come on Ogre, you're not usually put off by a little pain and death. And if we don't do this, who will?'

'Yes, but . . .' He groaned heavily. 'I've lived for twenty-one years, but only this year under open skies. This has been the best year ever.'

'Apart from all the people trying to kill you.' Tarita giggled. She wrapped her blanket tighter against the chill, then squirmed against him.

'Even that. At least I felt alive. Before this, there were just tasks, books, people who hated me, people who treated me like an exhibit or an experiment gone wrong ... and the Master.' He hung his head. 'I don't want it to end. I've got too much to do.'

She patted his thigh. 'Listen to you talk: you say "I" now. It used to be, "Ogre says" and now it's "I say". You've come so far – I'm very proud of you.' She punched his arm. 'The Ordo Costruo really wasted you, hiding you away like that.'

'They were kind–'

'They were cruel. I think they were ashamed that they'd been taken in by Ervyn Naxius, and scared people would hear of you. They should have found a better place for you.'

He didn't like to think about that: to his mind, the Ordo Costruo had been merciful. 'But anyway,' he mumbled, 'I've not done enough with my life.'

'How can you say that?' She sounded indignant. '*You* unravelled Naxius' plans and because of that, you've given us a chance to thwart him. That's not nothing.' She wriggled around to face him and kneeling in front of him, face upturned, said firmly, 'You're a warrior, my hero and my very good friend.'

Just looking into her eyes made his throat seize up. 'The last thing is the best thing,' he croaked.

She came to her feet with easy grace. 'Oh no, she said, a little throatily, 'being a warrior is important too: you're big and strong and bold, like Kip's men.' She reached out and playfully grabbed a handful of his long straggling dark hair. 'You need warrior braids, like a Schlessen Bullhead.'

Ignoring his protests, she combed through his tangled hair, ignoring the fact that he'd gone rigid at the touch of her fingers. After a while he relaxed enough to savour her nearness, while trying to ignore that she was only wearing a blanket and *probably* a nightshirt. She was completely unselfconscious, humming to herself as she worked deftly, gathering his lank tresses and weaving them into braids.

Another memory to take to my grave ...

'There,' she said, pulling the new braids into a loose topknot. Giggling, she ordered, 'Pull a fierce face, Ogre.'

He growled, she squealed, then exclaimed, 'Pull another—'

And suddenly he was all right again: they were the two teasing friends, sparking off each other, and he put aside vain wishes and enjoyed what was.

'Look,' Tarita said after a moment. 'The sun's rising.'

She sat in his lap, careless – or ignorant – of the fact that he was completely besotted, and tentatively he slid his arms around her. Together, they watched the brightening dome until shards of coloured light speared through the room, each filled with dancing dust motes.

He blinked and looked down at her, lit by the ethereal light and timeless, like a pixie from the *Fey Tales*, delicate and unearthly. He imagined that he looked like an old troll. 'I still love you,' he whispered, unable not to.

'I know – but you'll get over it.' Abruptly she rose and he cursed himself, for breaking the spell. 'Come on, Ogre,' she said, 'best we gird our loins.'

He felt himself go red. 'We what . . . ?'

'It's a Rondian phrase: it means "prepare for battle" or some such. There's nothing wicked involved, damn it.' She grinned and skipped across the chamber to pull on her clothes. 'Let's get breakfast – I'm hungry enough to eat a horse. Or even a pegasus? Do you think they taste better than horse?'

'Mmm, yes. the queen's mount looked very tasty,' Ogre observed solemnly, averting his eyes from her bare legs and arms and slipping back into their routine. 'I bet the wings taste like chicken.'

'You pluck, I'll cook.'

She pulled on her tunic and leggings, belted on her weapons and piled the bedding in a heap, then turned, ready to go. But Ogre noticed something glinting in the blankets and reached in to pluck it out. His eyes went wide as he saw it was a skull mask, akin to the ones he'd seen in Mollachia worn by the Master's servants. This one was green, with a red snake protruding from the mouth like a tongue: a visage he'd seen in the *Book of Kore*.

'Cadearvo,' he rumbled.

'Waqar killed him,' Tarita replied. 'You shouldn't touch it – I think there are enchantments—'

'It's the Master's work,' Ogre interrupted, turning it over in his hands. He closed his eyes and listened to the way the artefact resonated. 'It's part of a set – can you feel how it calls, each to the others? But there's no response . . . No, wait . . .'

He turned slowly, then opened his eyes and pointed. 'That way. The Master is that way.'

Tarita tilted her head, a grin creasing her face. 'South, towards the big mountains,' she exclaimed. 'Bring it with you. That Dirklan only had a rough idea where to find Naxius, but with that, you can lead us to his doorstep.'

They looked at each other in growing realisation that this quest might just be possible after all.

'Dear Ahm, it's good to have you back, my friend,' Tarita exclaimed. 'Ogre and Tarita, *still* trying to save that damned princess.'

Waqar was woken by a wet nose snuffling around his face. He opened his eyes drowsily – and went rigid.

An immense wolf almost as large as a horse was standing beside his bed. The reek of wet fur and rancid meat filled the room, but it sniffed at Waqar and wrinkled its nose as if he was the one that smelled.

'Gricoama?' Waqar said uncertainly. *How in Hel did this beast get here?* The wolf looked up at him with big, mesmerising eyes. 'By the Prophet, you're magnificent, aren't you?' He reached out to stroke an ear –

– as the beast's jaws opened and crunched shut, teeth punching through the back of his hand and he convulsed in anger, gnostic energy flaring . . . and collapsing . . .

The beast released his now bloody hand, still staring at him with those impassive, searching eyes.

Waqar started to speak when something inside smote him and the world fell away.

Valdyr and Lyra slipped out of a side door, followed by Dirklan, Ogre, Tarita, Rhune and Sarunia. He was looking round for Gricoama when the wolf materialised from the shadows and bounded toward him.

He yelped and ran to greet the wolf. 'How fast you got here,' he exclaimed, but the wolf just looked at him loftily.

Gricoama walked the Elétfa with me and probably got more out of that than I did. He's probably more spirit than wolf now. But when Valdyr hugged him, he still felt as warm, shaggy and, well, *doggy* as ever. 'I'm glad you're here,' he told the wolf.

Those big, wise eyes said, *Of course you are. Now feed me.*

'I'll see what I can do,' he promised, and followed Lyra and the others into a small square behind the administrative building where their constructs were being readied. The venators were grumbling and squalling and the queen's pegasus neighing restlessly until Lyra went to her. He found an aide who promised to feed the wolf, then went to his own venator and helped rub him down.

Then he noticed Ogre, tending the mount beside his, and peered quizzically. 'Ogre, what have you done with your hair?'

'Warrior braids,' he said proudly. 'Schlessen warriors wear them.'

'And Mollach virgins,' Valdyr said drily, making Tarita shake with silent laughter.

Dirklan left his wyvern and called them together. 'All right, pay attention. The sun's high enough and shining at a good angle: it'll blind anyone in the old Shihad camp who might be looking our way. We're going to fly right under the cliffs to the south, then go westwards seeking the southern passes. It's a tough route – no one lives up there, and there can be sudden storms – but all being well, by evening we'll be in northern Silacia.'

'What then?' Lyra asked.

'We'll scry, using Waqar's blood, and the mask. Without the Alps to block us, it should work.'

'And if it doesn't?'

'Then we have a problem,' Dirklan admitted. 'But what other choices do we have?'

'Ysh,' Valdyr growled, 'let's get on with this.' He looked at Lyra as he said, 'Sooner it's done the better.'

'We are ready,' Ogre announced. 'We have girded our loins.'

Tarita shrieked with laughter and the big construct joined in until they were both shaking with mirth.

What's that all about? Valdyr wondered, but their laughter lifted the group and everyone was exchanging grins as they mounted up.

Dirklan's wyvern bounded into the air first, followed by the queen's pegasus; Tarita, sitting in front of Ogre, took off next, then the two Ventians. Valdyr rose last, shouting to Gricoama to meet him in the south. The wolf looked up, seemed to nod, then went back to the bloody haunch of meat he'd been provided with. Valdyr took that as agreement.

After a few nervy seconds when he was sure the sluggish venator wouldn't clear the roofs, they were all spiralling upwards, the cold air seeking bare skin to sting and then numb as they left the beleaguered city behind.

As one, the flying beasts banked, caught a thermal from the walls of the Alps behind them and flowed into the next valley, seeking the high passes that would take them into Silacia and Rimoni.

Waqar drifted through dreams, vaguely conscious of the healers hovering over him, voices and auras washing over him. He meant to rouse himself and speak to them, to soothe the anxiety in their voices, but he kept getting distracted by the collisions of galaxies, or the way a fly's wing hummed, or the diffusion of light into rainbows through his eyelids.

It's beautiful, he sighed. *Let me stay . . .*

'His one good lung is filling up with blood,' he heard someone say in Rondian in a worried voice.

I wonder who they're talking about?

'Put him on his side,' a female voice said tersely. 'Get that tube inside him.'

The world lurched and something pushed uncomfortably down his throat. He saw a pottery bowl, admired the way the enamel gleamed in the sunlight streaming through the open curtains, then a torrent of red fluid splattered on it and he lost himself trying to read the patterns of the splashes.

There are omens written in the shapes, he thought. *I can see my future . . .*

But before he could understand those scarlet marking, his future faded and vanished.

*

Xoredh stared from the shadow of the pavilion out across the stark landscape. When the Shihad had arrived, these fields had been lush thanks to the autumn rains, but three months of trampling and foraging had turned the land around Norostein to bare mud beneath a cold sun.

There's no cloud . . . for the first time in months . . .

His magi servants were all daemon-possessed now, both more and less than they'd been, but this unlooked-for change in the skies was pinning them inside their tents and hideaways. He'd tried manipulating the weather with the gnosis, but someone inside Norostein was resisting, and the defensive always trumped the offensive in such matters.

Open skies and sunshine . . . and the full moon is almost here.

It was a good thing the Master no longer cared about the war; because for the next couple of weeks pursuing it would be impossible. So he put strategies aside, and bent his mind to his new mission: the murder of Waqar . . .

28

Triumphal

On Defeat

When are we defeated? When we surrender, or when we die? Neither. I contend that we are defeated when we lose sight of who we are and always have been: the children of Ahm.

GODSPEAKER HAIDAK, PEROZ CONVOCATION, 904

We are human, and we have adapted as the times change. Better we survive in a new world than perish clinging to an old one.

PRINCE OMAR KABARAKHI'S RESPONSE, PEROZ CONVOCATION, 904

Pallas, Rondelmar
Martrois 936

'Oldgate is open, Lord,' the messenger said breathlessly. 'The city is yours.'

Yes, Solon thought, meeting the man's eyes and clenching one steel gauntlet in victory.

Behind him, Oryn Levis, Roland de Farenbrette, Rolven Sulpeter, Endus Rykjard and the rest of his retinue cheered hoarsely and the tension that had hung over this final leg of the march began to lift. There would be no fighting, no need to lay siege to his capital. His march into Pallas would be triumphal.

He turned in the saddle and called to Lord Sulpeter, 'Pass the word, Milord: Pallas spreads herself like a good whore.' His retinue – all male, all Corani – guffawed and whooped. He turned his horse and trotted back down the line, taking the rising cheers of his men, peering back along the column.

His eyes lighted on his carriage, trundling along in the rear of the advance guard. *Speaking of good whores*, he thought, *someone had better get my little queen ready.*

He waved in the sour-faced nun who'd been appointed to look after Brunelda. She trotted up, riding her mare gracelessly. 'Sister Virtue, yes?' *She probably does still have her virtue, too, with a face like that.*

'Aye, Lord,' she replied, her eyes downcast.

'See to Milady's attire and appearance. She will be required once we're in the Bastion.' He rode on to the two prison-wagons and pulled alongside the first. Peering through the bars at the morose, grey-haired man inside, he called, 'Duke Garod, you'll be pleased to know we'll be entering the city inside the hour – unopposed.'

The Sacrecour didn't look at him, just spat through a split lip and hung his head. A Chain-rune constrained his gnosis and his scabbard was empty. His finery was smeared in mud and blood and his forehead crudely bandaged where it had been split open – not that he'd actually gone down fighting; he'd been captured unharmed – but Roland de Farenbrette had paid him a little visit.

Justly so, Solon thought, smiling grimly.

'Enjoy the ride through the city, Garod,' he taunted, then trotted to the second rolling cage. Rolven Sulpeter joined him, frowning. 'What is it, Rolven?' Solon enquired coolly. Sulpeter quite clearly had one eye on the pending appointments to the Imperial Council.

'What do you intend for the second prisoner?'

'I haven't yet decided,' Solon said, knowing he needed to make up his mind.

This prisoner had been granted a seat, a blanket and a piss-bucket, and he hadn't been roughed up.

When Solon peered in, a pair of mournful eyes stared out, widening in recognition.

'Sir Solon,' Cordan Sacrecour bleated hopefully.

Solon studied the boy: fourteen years old, a student mage, his natural lack of athleticism accentuated by puppy fat and lack of exercise. But he was the rightful emperor, according to some.

Kill him and only Coramore will be left with a legitimate claim on the Sacrecour side. After them they're down to distant relatives and sundry riff-raff no sane man would bend the knee to.

'Bear up, boy,' he advised, not quite meeting those frightened eyes. 'Show courage.'

The boy sniffled and Solon, always uncomfortable with weakness, hauled on his reins and cantered away, Rolven at his heels. Oryn Levis joined them, his bland face lined with worry.

'Kill Garod, but show the boy clemency,' Rolven said, as they slowed to a walk.

Garod was going to die: that was a cast-iron certainty, and a moment Solon was looking forward to, but he still wasn't sure about the boy. He'd grown somewhat fond of Cordan when he'd been Lyra's prisoner: he'd been positively worshipful, lapping up tales of battle and the tourney. There was a man lurking inside the dumpling.

And that's why I'd be wisest to take his head. Clemency is for women.

'They're traitors to Rondelmar,' he growled, to see how his advisors reacted.

'In that case, you should have just killed them on the battlefield,' Rolven declared.

'They surrendered,' Solon snarled. 'I've built my reputation on chivalry and hard justice.'

'But what they did in 909 –'

'I know what they rukking did in 909 and they'll damn well pay for it.' He spat, then asked, 'Did your men find Brylion's head?'

Rolven's nostrils flared, but he bit back whatever retort he might have wished to utter and said in a sour voice, 'Aye, but it's basically just a helm full of charcoal. Eye-witnesses say the Stick Insect nailed him good and proper.'

Basia de Sirou got her revenge after all, Solon mused. Turning to Lumpy, who was bringing the latest despatches from their informants within the city, he asked, 'She's in the Celestium still?'

Oryn leaned closer. 'Aye, they all are. Wurther's taken in Basia de Sirou, Exilium Excelsior, Princess Coramore, a few of the legion commanders and battle-magi . . . and Prince Rildan, of course.'

Another child I may have to kill, Solon thought grimly. 'I trust we have the Celestium encircled?'

'From the air and the water, and we've sent four legions south of the river. The Holy City is under embargo: nothing and no one in or out.'

'And the docklands?'

'Still barricaded and babbling about Lyra's "Republic" and chanting "Death to all tyrants".'

Solon bunched a fist as blood thumped in his temple. *Damned rabble*. 'There'll be no barricades in *my* city,' he snapped. Then he unclenched his fist, staring at it. *With this hand, I broke Nita's neck*, he reflected. That horrific moment, that hideous snapping of self-control, haunted him still. *I never knew I had that in me.*

But there was no room for weakness, not now. 'We'll offer them one chance,' he told Rolven, 'then we'll break them. Once we've got the lads into the barracks, issue ale, wine, whatever, and have our loyal magi listen to the talk. Next morning, I want lists of dissenters, doubters, loyalists and whingers. I want their bloody names.'

Rolven's eyes went round. 'But it'll be used as a chance to settle scores and—'

'I don't care,' Solon interrupted. 'Better a few innocents go down than any bad apples remain. Rot spreads.'

Oryn grimaced, then nodded, but that was enough to make Solon's heart go cold. *Dear Kore, don't you dare become part of the problem, Lumpy.*

'Lady?' a terse female voice called.

Someone rapped on the carriage door, startling Brunelda from her reverie as she gazed through the curtained window at the marching soldiers, feeling very alone. She didn't feel much better when it was the plain-faced nun, Sister Virtue, who opened the door and stepped in, carrying a bundled-up cloak.

'I'm not a lady,' Brunelda muttered.

'I know that, dear,' Virtue said drily. 'Neither am I.' She plonked

herself onto the opposite seat, where Solon usually sat if he joined her.
'Now, I'm commanded to tell you that you need to be dressed in royal
finery.' She unwrapped the cloak, revealing a pale blue dress with white
lace cuffs within.

Dear Kore, Brunelda thought, recognising the fabric and lacy cuff. *It's
the dress that dead woman was wearing – the one they carried from the tent.*
That had been horrible enough, before she'd realised the dead woman
must have been the queen.

'Not that dress . . . I can't–' *He's going to dress me up as her, for real . . .*
She clutched at her breast. 'I . . . I don't want to do this . . .'

Sister Virtue surprised her with a sympathetic look. 'It's just a dress,
dear. We've washed it.'

'Was she stabbed?'

'No,' Virtue said, and Brunelda sagged in relief until the nun added,
'but she soiled herself as her muscles loosened and there was blood on
the collar from where Lord Takwyth struck her cheek – and broke her
neck.'

Brunelda burst huge, frightened convulsive tears, cowering in her
corner, not wanting to emerge, *ever*.

Sister Virtue surprised her by moving to sit beside her. Putting an
arm around her shoulders, she cooed softly, 'Hush, dear.' Her voice was
soft but her eyes were hard. 'You'll ruin that milkmaid complexion and
then *no one* will be fooled. Now, dress, in that *dead* woman's frock.'

Brunelda's gorge rose uncontrollably and she vomited over the floor
of the carriage.

The entrance into the city was like the triumphal marches of the old
Rimoni emperors. Solon rode at the head of it, bareheaded but for a lau-
rel circlet, waving to the crowds lining the road from Oldgate, through
the legion quarter in Esdale, then circling north through Gravenhurst
and up onto the Roidan Heights via the steep Arcanus Road, used for the
Palace Guard's monthly Changing of the Duty Legion. That meant fewer
crowds, but it avoided traversing the edges of Tockburn, which was still
in rebellion.

For now. We'll deal with the rabble next. Lyra had been too soft with dissenters, scared of being called a tyrant. They'd soon realise that he was no squeam: retribution would be swift and harsh.

For now it was enough to take the cheers of the good citizens as they entered the Bastion through Soldier's Gate. *It's apt, because I'm a soldier first*, he mused. *My lads will see it as proof that I'm one of them – not an admission that I don't yet control the whole city.*

Trumpets blared and drums rolled as he rode into a parade ground filled with Corani legionaries. He'd told Lumpy to have the Palace Guard stood down – they were Pallacian and likely to be loyal to Lyra. *We'll break them up – I want only Corani around me.*

He waved and the rankers cheered hoarsely, then he turned to the steps of the Bastion, which were filled with Pallas nobility. He could sense their fear as he dismounted, which made his hackles rise. These were the weaklings Lyra had tolerated: milksop men who wore fashionable silks and velvets, women with low-cut dresses and lower morals, spiders and snakes the lot of them – and all candidates for the purge he planned.

My court will be one of real men: an austere and godly court, a centre of power, not frippery and vice. He strode up the steps, his commanders behind him, and surveying the crowd, found the ideal target for his simmering anger: Lord Tybor Misen, whose son had fought for the queen at Finostarre. *And died.*

'You,' he said, pointing at the nobleman, 'get off these steps.' Then he glared about and picked a few more at random, men he just didn't like, the sneering, hoity-toity, more-fashionable-than-thou set who frequented soirées and shows and sent others to fulfil their Houses' military obligations. 'And you – and you – in fact, you can all get off these Kore-bedamned steps: this dais is for the victors and I see no victors here.'

They goggled at him, faces blanching or colouring, wide eyes flinching and mouths bleating, so he roared again, '*Get off these stairs –*' He placed his hand on his hilt as Roland and Nestor joined him. Of course the cowering weaklings melted away to the foot of the steps, leaving him standing triumphant above them.

He turned to face the rankers, aware that at every window were the faces of servants and staff, while the space around his men was crammed with imperocrats and secretaries and scribes and runners, the people who infested this fortress-cum-palace-cum-cesspit.

He raised his fist. 'This is our victory,' he began triumphantly. '*My* victory. I have never been defeated, and no Sacrecour scum were ever going to. Corani For Ever—'

The rankers roared in unison, punching their fists in the air towards him. '*CO-RA-NI! CO-RA-NI! CO-RA-NI!*' He led the chant for a minute, while glaring about him, impressing on everyone here exactly who was master.

He gestured for silence, got it instantly. 'This city is riddled with gossip and lies and always has been, but there is one source of truth you can rely upon – my voice. Remember that in the days to come. Cleave to me and you will hear only truth. Ignore that false cleric Dominius Wurther and the worms who cower beneath his robes – Dubrayle, Wilfort, de Sirou and the rest. Clutching a newborn child to their cowardly breasts and claiming that they rule Pallas – *pah!* – what do they rule? Nothing but a gilded mausoleum, a refuge for craven sots, backstabbing spies and whining frocio. Where were they when I united two armies and won back *my* queen? On their knees in a sanctuary, when real men strode the battlefield like colossi: real men like you, my faithful Corani—'

'*CO-RA-NI – CO-RA-NI,*' they bellowed back, while the courtiers cringed. He thought he sensed some disquiet at his impious dismissal of the Church, but he was past caring.

'Bring forth the queen!' he shouted and right on cue, Brunelda's carriage rolled to the bottom of the steps and Sister Virtue helped a blonde figure in a pale blue dress from the cabin, her head bowed.

Wave, girl, he thought.

But Brunelda kept her head down and shambled up the steps with nothing like Lyra's composed grace. The nun was having to hold her arm firmly to keep her steady. When they reached the top, he gripped her forearm and had to conceal a wave of distaste as he smelled vomit. She was white as a spectre, her eyes red-rimmed and glassy. Fortunately, having cleared the steps, there was no one close enough to see her features except Roland, Rolven and Nestor, who were already privy to the secret

'Wave to the crowd,' he commanded her quietly. 'Show your joy.'

She looked like she was about to faint, but swallowing hard, she forced one arm up. Her eyes were leaking tears. He glared at Sister Virtue for letting her out of the damned carriage in this state, but somehow the girl rallied and managed a tremulous smile, while he murmured, 'Good girl, good girl,' as if she was a puppy.

His Corani cheered Lyra's name while the courtiers murmured sullenly.

'Get her inside,' he told Sister Virtue. 'Now.'

When Brunelda had gone, he turned back to the cheering crowds and with a confident smile, declared, 'Not all gossip is untrue. One tale I can credit – that the queen and I have been *lovers* – in every sense of the word: Queen Lyra owns my heart, and I hers. Others kept us apart for our union threatened their own ambitions, but true love will always triumph.'

The men cheered lustily, while the Pallas foppery squirmed.

'And now only one thing threatens our happiness: Dominius Wurther holds her son hostage in the Celestium. But not for long, for I will rip the Holy Gates from their hinges if I have to, for the sake of my love. The true queen is restored: give her son back, Grand Prelate –' By now he was punching the air with fury, while the rankers shouted their support.

He fixed his eyes on the craven courtiers beneath him. 'The winds of change are blowing free, people of the empire. I'm here now, and any who harbour conspiracies against me will be swept away. The old age of Sacrecour decadence is gone and our queen now has by her side the one man she needs to set things right. I will purge the Imperocracy and create a better society, based on true Kore values: a place where men protect their women and women serve their men. If you're a good, Kore-fearing man, you've nothing to fear. But if you thrived under the Sacrecours and managed to hide your treachery for these past five years, know this: we will find you, we will root you out, and we will expose you as the traitors you are.'

The walls echoed back his words, but the square was utterly silent, the courtiers beneath him *trembling* – then his rankers raised their voices, this time chanting, 'Takwyth – TAKWYTH,' and '*CO-RA-NI – CO-RA-NI – CO-RA-NI.*'

With that, he spun and strode into *his* palace.

The Celestium, Pallas

Basia huddled over a fire in a small, smoky room, scratching the aching stump of her right leg. She looked up as the door opened, admitting Exilium Excelsior – who flinched when he saw her stump and the artificial leg on the floor, shuffled awkwardly and went to leave again.

'Oh, sit down,' she drawled. 'The other one's just the same,' she added, tapping her knee. 'If I'm not embarrassed, you have no right to be.'

Exilium sat, still studiously looking away. She'd shed her armour and was clad in just her smallclothes and a loose shirt, showing far too much skin for the prudish Estellan knight. Not that she minded; offending him was about the most fun to be had these days.

'Wurther will see us soon,' Exilium said. 'His secretary told me. Once he's done praying.'

'Praying,' Basia snorted. 'He's got a whole army of priests to do his praying for him. I imagine he's probably trying to negotiate a price for getting us off his hands.'

'He's the Grand Prelate,' Exilium protested.

'That'll help his haggling,' Basia sniffed. 'Are these suites secure?'

Exilium slumped. Defeat had drained his stiff-backed self-belief and his eyes were dull. 'So far as I can manage,' he mumbled, 'but we're at the Grand Prelate's mercy.'

He took his new knightly order into battle and got most of them killed, Basia thought sympathetically. *He doesn't believe he's invincible any more.*

'So long as all the entrances to this wing are guarded and warded, we've done all we can,' she told him. 'You still have a few men, and we've got the Volsai here – those who aren't undercover in Pallas-Nord.

We've got Rildan and Coramore and we know that whoever it was Takwyth paraded today, it *wasn't* Lyra.'

Dear Kore, I pray it was Nita.

She reached out and patted his knee. 'We can weather this.'

Exilium sagged, hanging his head. 'Can we? I was entrusted with men's lives and I lost them all. A true knight would fall upon his own sword rather than face this shame.'

That annoyed her hugely. 'Why, can't "true knights" face shame?' she snapped. 'Can't they deal with setbacks and loss?' She threw a hand out in the rough direction of Finostarre. 'In 909, Brylion Fasterius raped me, cut my throat and threw me down a well. When Dirk pulled me out three days later they had to amputate my lower legs. I waited twenty-seven years for the chance to ram my sword into Brylion's face, living with *shame* for all that time. So you fucking swallow that shame like I did and come back fighting, you hear me?'

She glared at him, hoarse and frayed and wanting to scream – and praying she'd said the right thing. She didn't deal in absolutes often, but if Exilium didn't react to that, she was absolutely finished with him.

I like your face, but I need to see your backbone.

It took him a few moments – everything did, except in battle – but his spine straightened and his gaze cleared. 'I still have my sword and my God,' he said steadily. 'In them I trust.' He hesitated, colouring slightly, and added, 'And I believe in you.'

Basia found she was shaking, because the façade of strength she was throwing up was pretty damned flimsy, not that she was going to let him see that. 'I believe in you too,' she told him, and not just because she suspected he needed to hear it. 'Solon Takwyth and Roland de Farenbrette tried to break you in the training arena, remember? They only do that to men they fear. It won't take you twenty-seven years to get your chance at them, I swear.'

They traded a look of shared purpose, until someone knocked and a curt voice called, 'The Grand Prelate will see you now, Lady Volsai.'

'Lady Volsai,' she echoed sarcastically. 'Let's go and see what that old hog wants to sell us for, shall we?'

*

480

Dominius Wurther sat on his throne, slurping red wine and occasionally belching, while Grandmaster Lann Wilfort of the Kirkegarde rattled off the military dispositions. 'Summarise, Lann,' Dominius interjected, as the grim-faced knight paused for breath. 'I don't need every name.'

'We've got two legions crammed into Southside, one Kirkegarde, one Pallacios,' Wilfort growled. 'We face almost twenty now that Rolven Sulpeter's men are arriving by barge.'

The Kirkegarde were loyal and the Pallacios legion, comprised of Pallas natives drawn from here on the Southside, could likely be trusted, Dominius reflected. He ran his eyes around the council table. As well as Wilfort, there was the new Inquisition Princeps, Vikal Cobas; Basia de Sirou and Exilium Excelsior; Legate Gael Fend, an ageing man with a tangled mane of greying yellow hair who was commanding that Pallacios legion. And there at the end of the table, fingers steepled, sat his old sparring foe, Calan Dubrayle.

I could just about buy my way out of this by handing over de Sirou, Excelsior and Dubrayle to Takwyth, he mused. That temptation had been growing these last two days, from those panicky hours when the refugees from the defeat at Finostarre had poured into Southside to the fateful moment when Basia had shown up with Rildan Vereinen in her arms and Coramore Sacrecour at her side, seeking sanctuary.

But Lyra's out there somewhere, and so's bloody Setallius . . .

When one side held the Bastion and all the manpower, it should have been a simple choice. But he'd seen Lyra survive Reekers and assassins, face down mobs and freeze the Aerflus – along with Brylion Sacrecour's army. And he knew that no one, anywhere, was safe from Setallius.

In any case, he doubted Takwyth had any desire to work with him. His agents had reported that inflammatory speech, word for word – 'that false Grand Prelate, Dominius Wurther' – and he knew Takwyth meant every word. *He wants my head.*

So he had to play for time if he was to find a way through this maze. He needed sanctuary, somewhere where the faithful still took precedence over the secular rulers – somewhere like Estellan – and if it meant grovelling to foreigners, so be it.

'What are our other assets?' he asked the table.

'Justice and righteousness in the eyes of Kore,' Exilium said instantly.

How I've missed that blind fervour, Dominius mused wryly.

'The knowledge that the real Lyra will return,' Basia added. 'The Pallas Mob heard Takwyth's speech and they're not happy. Tockburn and the docks are still barricaded.'

'He'll send in the Corani – or the Hollenian mercenaries,' Legate Fend replied.

'His army is as much Pallacian as Corani,' Basia noted.

'Those legions are drawn from Esdale and the east end of Pallas-Nord,' Fend stated. 'They won't care if a bunch of Tockers and Kensiders get their noses bloodied, much less Southsiders.'

'Do we have contacts inside Tockburn? Who leads now?' Wilfort asked.

'Some say Lazar, others Frankel or even Tad Kaden,' Basia said, scowling. 'We can't rely on them – they're fragmenting as we speak – and Legate Fend is right, Takky will deal with them soon anyway.'

That's about how I see it, too, Dominius thought glumly. He cheered himself up with more wine.

'But we do have money,' said Calan Dubrayle. 'Rather a lot of it, if we work together.'

'Most of "your" bullion was mine to start with,' Dominius glowered.

'What ends up with the Treasury, belongs to the Treasury,' Calan replied calmly. 'In any case, I have secreted caches worth enough to buy the loyalty of a Hel of a lot of manpower, if we can find the right people.'

How Calan had done it, moving money out of the Treasury in the few hours he'd had after Finostarre, Dominius had no idea. *I'd love to know.* But he'd been shown a mix of gold and promissories and he believed the rest. The Treasurer had stripped his own Treasury and Takwyth was probably screaming at the heavens right about now.

'You're right,' he admitted, 'the problem is *who* to buy.'

They all looked at each other.

'Argundy?' Legate Fend suggested. 'The queen has kin there.'

'And Prince Andreas hoped to marry her,' Calan put in. 'Argundy could well see this as their chance to seize control of the empire.'

'I don't want a swarm of Argundian dullards ruling my city,' Dominius growled.

'That's not helpful,' Basia said. 'We need to bury our differences, not dredge them up.'

'This is *my* throne hall,' he reminded her, even though she was right. 'What can we offer them? We have an imperial princess up our sleeves, for example.'

'Coramore represents a rival dynasty to Lyra's,' Basia said dismissively. 'That's not what we need right now.'

'Then what use is she?' Fend asked.

She's a potential dwymancer, Dominius thought uneasily. At their private meeting yesterday, Basia had told him the truth. 'I see no problem with noising her availability around,' he said aloud, looking at the Volsai, 'but I imagine it would be a complex and protracted negotiation.' *Read between my lines*, he urged her silently. *The negotiations will go nowhere, but they'll stall a few of our enemies.*

Basia did catch his meaning, because she made a show of conceding the point. 'Our priority is to keep Rildan safe until Lyra returns. Once she is able to openly oppose Takwyth, his support will divide and we'll be able to rally any open resistance.'

'When will that be?' Wilfort asked the question very much on Dominius' mind.

'We don't know,' Basia answered, 'but it'll be days, not weeks or months.'

'Then in the meantime, what do we do?' Fend grumbled. 'Sit on our hands?'

'We protect the integrity of the Holy City,' Dominius said firmly. 'Right now, Takwyth is in the flush of victory: he thinks he can bully everyone into submission. Let him get a taste of what *real* rulership entails. People were baying for Lyra's blood when she was gentle with them. Let's see what they do when things turn bloody.'

Coramore peered from the shadow of the door out across the brightly lit turf to the bare mound in the middle of the triangular lawn. The open skies above scared her, especially as venators bearing Takwyth's knights circled overhead. They were high up, just dots, but she knew if they dived, they could be on her in moments.

They'll snatch me up and lock me in a cage with Cordan, she worried. *Dear Kore, protect my brother.*

Solon Takwyth – a man she'd *never* trusted – had Cordan and meant to kill him. If she could wish anyone dead, it'd be Takwyth, *right now*.

'It's all right, girl,' said the gruff, stolid woman with her: Brigeda, one of Basia's Volsai, who patted her arm. 'You can't see them, but there are wards, and those men on the walls have heavy crossbows, and there's at least three ballistae in the turrets overlooking this garden. And I'll be with you.'

Brigeda offered a thick-fingered, strong hand and Coramore took it tentatively. 'I want to see inside the mound,' she said. 'Lyra says it's an important place.'

'Then let's go.' Brigeda led the way across the lawn to the cave-opening in the side of the mound. Coramore looked up at the top, where the burnt-out stump of a tree lay surrounded by blackened turf: the Winter Tree, which Lyra said was the heart of dwymancy in the north.

'I'll go down alone,' she said firmly.

Brigeda frowned, but let her go, lighting the torch in the holder at the entrance and handing it to her before lecturing her on not burning herself or getting sparks in her dress. She looked distinctly uncomfortable being there.

Magi are scared of dwymancy, Coramore realised, her heightened perceptions reading the other woman like an open book. *She's a safian and she's been rejected by her family and her old friends, but the Volsai are her family now. She still believes in love, and she'd die to protect me if those venators attacked. I can trust her.*

'I'll be all right,' Coramore told her.

The Volsai grimaced and said, 'Don't be long.'

Coramore took the steps spiralling down into a chamber thirty feet or more below ground. There was a fire-pit and some old blackened bones on the floor, but the walls were what caught her attention: they were coated in some kind of translucent substance like amber, the colour of dried honey. When she held up her lamp, she saw dark, wispy shapes like men or women, caught in the surface.

It's me, Coramore, she told them.

Coramore . . . Coramore . . . they whispered back.

A bead of amber liquefied and ran down the side of the wall. She scooped it with a finger and sucked it down, savouring the bitter taste as she watched the shapes in the amber change to the shadow of a giant tree stretching to the stars.

Then her thoughts returned to Cordan and for a moment she saw his face, pale as a ghost, his eyes red-rimmed and swollen, and darkness all round, closing in hungrily.

She cried out, but he didn't hear and the vision faded.

The Bastion, Pallas

Cordan Sacrecour wiped his eyes and for the first time, really looked around. But there was little to see other than the stone walls and iron bars, a wooden pallet with a thin, hard mattress of straw, a water jug and a piss-bucket.

Much of the past day had been a blur. His rattling cage had been pelted with rotten vegetables and buckets of piss by the taunting crowds, and when they'd arrived he'd been dragged from the cage, stripped and doused in cold water before having his smallclothes returned to him. Now he had nothing against the cold in this frigid cell in a tower of the Bastion but a thin blanket.

He'd been determined not to cry. *Lyra wouldn't have done this . . . or would she? I thought Solon was my friend . . .* Ironically it'd been Takwyth's words – 'show courage' – that had got him through without collapse, but once he was alone, the humiliation had been too much and all his tears and terror came out.

Lyra gave me a proper room – she even had her people teach me the gnosis. They let Cora and me play together.

'I didn't even want to be emperor,' he whispered to the darkness, but no one heard.

But next morning, he was dressed in his own clothes, from when he'd been a prisoner here, and two burly soldiers half dragged, half carried him into a big room where a grim-looking justiciar told him he was a traitor to the empire. Solon Takwyth sat at the back, stony-faced, surrounded by other equally stern men. When he tried to beg mercy, they gagged him with the gnosis.

The queen wasn't there.

'You will be beheaded at the next assizes,' the justiciar pronounced, then paused to allow Solon to grant clemency, but the emperor-in-waiting said nothing, so he concluded, 'Use your remaining days to make peace with Kore for your crimes.'

If he could have screamed or cried or begged, he would have. *I haven't committed any crimes*, he tried to cry, but only gurgling emerged. *I never wanted to be emperor.* Then they dragged him away.

Outside, he saw Uncle Garod in manacles, his eyes blackened and nose crooked, lips split and welts on his cheeks. When Garod shouted, '*Cordan –*' they struck him down.

They carried Cordan back to his cell, where he fell into the darkness again.

29

At Bay

On Courage

Courage is not the lack of fear – that's called stupidity. True courage comes from acting even though you have full appreciation of every dreadful thing that is confronting you. Revere the lowly who struggle on more than the battle-mage whose valour is found in his inability to conceive of failure.

BROTHER THOMON, KORE PRIEST, MISENCOURT 622

Pallas, Rondelmar
Martrois 936

Solon rose from the royal bed, casting an eye over Brunelda's sprawled body, tangled in the damp sheets as she slept. *Thoroughly used*, he thought, *and perhaps even with child*. She was fertile this week, which troubled him. He hadn't intended a by-blow, but he needed her in his bed. *Whatever happens, I'll look after it.*

He threw on a robe and went out onto the balcony, wrinkling his nose at the acrid smoke below. Knowing they were connected to the dwyma, he'd had some Fire-magi go in and burn out the Winter Tree sapling and drain Lyra's favoured pond.

I want her weakened until I know she can be trusted. We'll hold the life of her son over her if necessary.

He was quite sure, however, that once he'd bedded Lyra the way he used to, she'd come back round to him, the way Brunelda had – and if not, she'd be withdrawn from the public eye, becoming nothing more than an ornament he occasionally wore.

He turned his gaze to the Celestium, shimmering in the morning sun just a mile away across the Bruin. *All my enemies are there*, he thought, wishing he had spies in the Holy City, but of those he'd tried to send in, only tokens had come back.

The Volsai are in there . . . and Dubrayle, that cunning prick. And others too stupid to see the way the wind is blowing, like Wilfort and Fend and Excelsior. But they had Coramore and they had Rildan, which gave him pause, because Lyra and that snake Setallius could be anywhere right now. *Surely they're in there too . . .*

But would Lyra unleash the dwyma on Pallas to protect her son?

No, he decided. *She wouldn't want to risk 'innocent' lives.* Women weren't strong enough to take the hard decisions. *She'd have shown clemency to Garod and Cordan, but I won't.*

That resolved, he decided there was no point in holding back. *First the docklands, then the Celestium . . .*

Solon and Roland de Farenbrette dismounted in front of Sancta Zunas Church in Esdale, near the west end of the docklands, and walked over to the knot of senior officers and centurions gathered round a sheet of parchment nailed to the doors.

'So what is it, lads?' he asked as they saluted, then parted so he could see the notice.

'They went up all over the city, middle of the night,' a centurion told him. Solon tore down the parchment and read it.

The Tyranny Begins

People of Pallas, we are betrayed!
Lyra Vereinen put on a red rose and
claimed to be one of us. She promised
reforms and elections of public officials.
She asked us to rally to her.
But when Solon Takwyth manoeuvred
in behind her at Finostarre,
she forgot her promises.

488

> *Who rules us now? Who rules her?*
> *Rise up, Pallas!*
> *They are going to steal your every*
> *hard-won freedom.*
> *Rise up!*

Beneath the words was a woodcut of himself screwing Lyra from behind – pretty much what he'd been doing all night – *Except it's only Brunelda* . . .

He snorted and showed Roland. 'A good likeness, you think?' he chuckled.

'Of her, maybe – you aren't so fat,' Roland laughed, handing it back.

'It's Frankel, obviously,' Solon declared. ' "Rise up" – that's high treason. I want him publicly hanged, drawn and quartered – and no trial, either; he had his day in court.' He turned to the officers and waved the parchment – no doubt they'd read it already. 'Bring me Frankel alive. Break or burn every barricade in your way.'

'There are women and old folk on those barriers, Milord,' a centurion noted.

'No, there are only rebels and traitors,' he snapped. 'Anyone taking a soldier's part gets treated as such.'

'There'll be blood,' that same man muttered.

'Name?' Solon asked icily.

The centurion, a balding man in his forties, solid and competent-looking, flushed at his tone. 'Renco, sir, Fifth Century, Third Maniple –'

'This is your only warning, Renco,' Solon interrupted. 'All of you, take heed: we're at war still. You think because Garod's in chains, the struggle is over? We've got Argundy on our borders and a mass secession to unwind, so unless we get our house in order damned fast, the enemies of Rondelmar will descend on us like wolves. If that means a few stupid people have to be dealt with, so be it. You hear me?'

'Aye,' they all chorused, including Centurion Renco.

They just need someone to think for them, he reminded himself. He saluted, then took Roland aside, muttering, 'If that man says anything else against this, deal with him.'

The Blacksmith grinned savagely. 'I'll see to it.'

Ari Frankel emerged from the doors of the tavern where he'd been concealed, Lazar's thugs closing around him. His hood was raised against the windskiffs roaming the air above Tockburn and the docklands; they'd been circling ever since Takwyth occupied the city.

'Morning, Counsellor,' said a ragged man bent over a small blaze of twigs and dried dung, before adding with a bitter chuckle, 'You even still a counsellor now, heh heh? Takky sent for you yet?'

No, but he's put a price on my head.

Others recognised him as they scurried by, ordinary folk setting up their stalls in the squares. Small cooking fires blazed, roasting nuts, vegetables and thin strips of meat from creatures best left unidentified. Shopkeepers scraped ice from their shutters, while criers hollered the latest rumours. He could taste the smoke and anxiety filling the air of Tockburn.

Lazar joined him as they waited at a corner for a Guard patrol to move on. 'Takwyth sent a maniple of the Twelfth into Kenside last night,' he snarled. 'Seven dead – two was women.'

Ari, like most of the city, torn between anger and fear, asked, 'Any word of the queen?'

'Takky's parading some blonde bint, but she's only ever seen from a distance and ne'er speaks,' Lazar growls. 'Can't be the real Lyra, cos she never shut up. An' that Volsai bint with the stick-legs insists the real queen's in hiding.' He scratched his stubbled chin and spat. 'Can't see it matters. Takky's emp'ror in all but name.'

'This is a city of a million people and he's got just a few legions,' Ari replied. 'A few thousand men.'

'That's all he needs,' Lazar growled. 'Folks was fine with marchin' an' all when they thought Lyra might listen, but they know Takky won't: with him, it's going to be cracked skulls and blood.'

'We need this republic,' Ari insisted.

'Do we? Old empire got us by. Daresay even a broken-up empire'll still work.'

Ari was struck by the flatness in Lazar's eyes. His cold monotone never changed, but his gaze no longer harboured purpose. *He's given up. He's killed a few people, lined his pockets and now he'll slink away . . .*

Ari hung his head. Since Finostarre, it'd been too dangerous to speak publicly and without his words to breathe air into the lungs of change, no one was going to fight for the concessions they'd won from Lyra.

I don't think any kind of speech can help us . . . Words like 'freedom' and 'representation' and 'suffragium' are too insubstantial in a world of blood and steel. There were warrants out for him, offering a large reward. Sooner or later someone would be tempted – maybe even Lazar, this morning . . .

The moment I speak in front of any kind of gathering, the magi will be told where I am, and this time there'll be no escape. Tad Kaden won't act, because he still thinks his sister will be released. The only people who might help us are penned up in the Celestium.

He sagged wearily, denied the only things that truly energised him: a crowd and a platform.

The word came down – the patrol had moved on – so they stole across the small plaza. A few more blocks took them to the Tockburn docks, where masses of men, women and even children were labouring to unload and distribute the supplies that were still arriving by ferry from across the Aerflus, brought in from the countryside west of Pallas, from crofters who'd sided with Ari's rebels.

'This way,' Lazar muttered, pulling Ari to some steps leading to an open balcony after making sure their cowls were raised and the bandanas covering their lower faces hadn't slipped. Faces turned their way and a few waved and cheered hoarsely, but the tension reduced even that to a low buzz.

He pointed away north to the edge of the open space. They had a narrow view down the street to the edge of the distribution point, where a barricade of broken furniture and old bricks and broken chunks of masonry had been erected. Behind it, lines of redcloaks were forming up. Ari shuddered at the sight of the legionaries' serried ranks and locked shields.

'They broke up the barricade three blocks onwards, at the edge of Tockburn,' Lazar said tersely. 'They're preparing to rush this one now.'

'We're all Rondians,' Ari said weakly.

'That's Takwyth's Corani out there. They don't give a shit 'bout anyone else.'

Rough-clad men on the barricade armed with bows and crossbows were peering out at the soldiers, lining up their shots, but they'd barely slow any determined attack. Ari could hear orders being barked above the buzz of the people in the square. People here were desperate for food to eat and the orderly queues of the past month were breaking down as everyone tried to grab what they could and get out before the soldiers attacked.

'I need to be down there,' Ari told Lazar. 'I need to calm them. People are getting hurt.'

Lazar snorted. 'You don't calm people, Frankel. You rile 'em up.'

'But if those soldiers attack—'

'Then there'll be a shit-storm. Folks'll see what Takwyth's really made of.'

'I pray nothing happens,' Ari gulped, 'but I must go down there.'

'We can't protect you down there, Frankel. Don't be a rukkin' martyr.'

A martyr . . . Dear Kore, I'm no martyr. Ari remembered that day he'd railed at the queen herself, staring down death in the most horrific manner but so fired up that he didn't care – and it'd been Lyra who blinked first.

But Takwyth won't blink. 'I must go,' he said thickly. *I got everyone into this.* Abruptly, he clasped Lazar's cold hand, then turned and pounded down the stairs. He threw back his cowl and almost instantly, the crowd stirred to life, people murmuring, '*Ari Frankel,*' with respect and even awe. Hands extended, some patting his shoulders, others clasping his. One woman stinking of sweat and fish even seized and hugged him as a low chant went up: 'Frankel, Frankel . . .'

'We must stay calm,' he told them. 'They won't kill defenceless people – we're just feeding ourselves. Stay in line. There's enough for all.'

Incredibly, it worked. People visibly calmed down and someone called, 'Counsellor Frankel, can you get us more food?' as if he had some sway with Takwyth.

'Speak to the queen for us,' a few exhorted. 'Tell her to remember us.'

Can I tell them that it's not the queen up there? What will that do – harden their resolve or break it? He decided that piece of information was too volatile, too unpredictable.

He was surprised to find that he'd travelled sixty yards into the press and was near the supply wagons. People were pulling him forward, calling, 'Speak, speak–' with the same hunger he felt. Crowds fed him – and he fed the crowds. 'Ari, what's going to happen?' they asked. 'Tell us what to do.'

He glanced back at the balcony and saw that Lazar was still watching him, his cowl falling back from his face as he gave Ari an ironic wave – and then he half-turned and made a sign towards the barricade, to Ari's left.

At once, someone over there roared, 'Fire –' and a dozen burning pots were hurled over the barricade towards the legionaries.

Ari's jaw dropped and he stared in disbelief at Lazar. The rebel saluted him again, then raised his cowl and vanished inside. Trumpets blared beyond the barricade and moments later the redcloaks started climbing up the other side. Lazar's archers fired two rounds, then scattered. A man cried out in fear, a woman screamed and the crowd recoiled, but the alleys were narrow and already jammed.

Then the barricade went up in flames with a hideous whoosh, black smoke and oil and roaring orange flames threw a wave of heat across the square. Ari saw the legionaries on the burning wall reel in shock, leaping away just in time, and he thanked Kore that none of them looked to have been caught in the sudden inferno.

'Stay calm,' he shouted, 'hold steady and keep together –'

But he was just one voice in the din of frightened, trapped people. The shrieking became ear-splitting as some lost balance, went under and were trampled in the panic. A windskiff swooped overhead and an archer in the foredeck fired at a man on a roof, who dodged and shot back.

Then a massive blast of gnostic energy punched open the barricade, hurling burning wood and broken bricks into the press behind. Ari was slammed painfully to his knees as the crowd shoved from all sides. He put his arms up to protect his head as something hammered into his side, then a body fell on him, an old man, wheezing for breath. For a moment there was no air, then Ari struggled upwards like a drowning man, pushing for the surface in desperation, rising alongside a terrified woman clutching a screaming child in one hand and clinging to a young man in a butcher's apron with the other.

'Here they come,' someone shouted in his ear. 'Kore save us all . . .'

Ari threw a look towards the broken barricade, where redcloaks were swarming through and forming up on this side, shields locked and spears projecting through, butt-first. The alleys were disgorging yet more soldiers, pinning in the thousands of people in the square. Realising their danger, the crowd had started backing away as best they could towards the supply wagons and the shoreline.

This was well planned, Ari thought. *They've got us trapped.*

A knight rode through the smouldering barricade, a young blond man with a glowing periapt on his chest. '*Silence, rabble*,' he shouted, his voice amplified by the gnosis so that it rang off the buildings.

Ari looked around and saw that Lazar's men had either escaped, or dropped their weapons and faded into the crowd. The balcony was empty. *Lazar does want a martyr . . . me.*

'I am Nestor Sulpeter,' the young mage-noble brayed, 'and I am commanded by your ruler, Solon Takwyth, to seize these illegally imported goods and break up this gathering. Resist, and . . .' He glared about, the threat implicit.

More trumpets rang out, more boots thumped on cobbles, more people were trampled underfoot as they fell. Ari's thoughts raced through words he knew wouldn't sway this young knight, nor the hard-eyed centurions behind him.

One youth tried to dash through the cordon, but a ranker smashed a spear-butt into his face and he collapsed bonelessly. A young woman screamed and fell onto him, howling up at the soldier, 'Get away from him, you northern bastard!'

The ranker blanched but roared something back. Complete chaos was a heartbeat away.

'Hold together,' Ari shouted, and those around him took it literally, grabbing each other, family and friends, complete strangers, all linking arms so that no one else would fall.

'Hold together,' others called. 'Hold together—'

'Together we are strong,' Ari shouted. 'Together we are Tockburn.'

Men and women around him took up the chant. 'We are Tockburn – we are Tockburn—'

The roar became deafening as Nestor Sulpeter screamed for silence, turning red in the face. He raised a hand and blasted kinesis into the faces of those before him – the whole crowd recoiled, but their locked arms held, for the most part, and they raged back.

'Get out of Tockburn—'

'—rukk off, you Corani cock—'

'Piss off back north . . .'

Kore's Balls, the moment one of Lazar's lot fire another shaft, there'll be a massacre, Ari thought wildly. 'No weapons,' he shrilled. 'Don't attack, just hold together . . .'

'Centurion, seize those wagons,' Sir Nestor ordered, and one hundred men marched forward, spears high, trying to ram their way through the mass of Tockers – but they held together grimly. Ari could barely see what was happening through the constantly shifting press, but he could hear fishwives and dockers alike shouting, 'Our children must eat—'

Nestor tossed back his head and screamed, 'Break them!'

The centurion shouted, the soldiers reacted and people started going down as spear-butts were rammed into faces and chests and bellies. The soldiers hammered forward and the crowd tried in vain to scatter. A grey-haired blacksmith went down, pole-axed; the young woman clutching his arm launched herself at his assailant – and another ranker panicked and stabbed his shortsword into her chest, so hard it protruded from her back. The soldier holding the sword, seeing what he'd done, started wailing and let the weapon go. Someone scooped up the girl, then a burly fishwife wrenched out the sword and thrust it through the ranker's chest. As he fell wordlessly, the woman took two spearheads in the chest. Similar fights were breaking out all over the square.

Finally the crowd burst apart as those at the back started hurling themselves into the river. The pressure eased and the crowd found themselves swept inexorably along, past the wagons and down to the docks. Ari fell, tried to rise and was knocked down, then a man hauled him to his feet and wrenched him through an opening in the lines to the edge of the wharf. Ari chanced a glance back to see Sir Nestor, encased in flashing shields, was waving his sword around ineffectually while his men cleared the square of the few left standing.

Smoke and noise filled the air. Blood splattered the stones. And *hundreds* were down, injured or dead, he couldn't say.

Ari found he was weeping – had been for some time – and he was not alone. He hugged the man who'd got him out of the square, then staggered away, his brain whirling.

This is my fault: I encouraged them to dream . . .

Nestor Sulpeter was leading some House Corani cheer, pumping his fist aloft as if this was some great victory.

I hate you, Ari thought furiously, impotently. *You are everything I despise.*

But he was no mage and his thoughts couldn't kill, however much he prayed they would. The Corani soldiers stood in a ragged line facing down the slope, many wide-eyed in shock. A few were yelling, 'Thieves, traitors–' as if trying to justify their own actions, Ari sensed, but gradually they pulled apart, leaving new hatreds freshly bred to add to the centuries-old feuds already festering in the city.

'We just wanted food,' a stolid fishwife was wailing, alone on her knees a few yards before the line of men. 'My children are hungry – we've nothing to eat . . .'

Nestor Sulpeter nudged his horse through the lines of men and strutted arrogantly towards her. His lip curling, he spat, 'You've never been hungry in your life, you fat cow. You're nothing but a greedy traitor. If you truly have children, I doubt you know their fathers' names.' He raised his sword to those Tockers still milling about on the wharf and cried, 'Begone, rabble.'

A few shouted abuse back, but not many, and those who did ran as soon as they'd spoken.

Dear Kore, strike him down, Ari prayed fervently.

But Sir Nestor wasn't struck down, just went right on preening and shouting encouragement to his men.

There was an escape route now, along the bank of the Lower Bruin. Ari pulled up his cowl again and let the crowd sweep him along. He tried to find words to express his rage, but all he could see were the shocked faces of the girl who'd been stabbed and the soldier who'd killed her, the hate and fury and the stupidity of it all.

He wept at the futility of trying to change the way the world was run. *I believed in you, Lyra Vereinen – where are you?*

'Where's the queen?' Rolven Sulpeter murmured, standing with Solon as the throne hall filled with courtiers, some grave, others triumphant. 'She should be here. It looks wrong to have her absent, Milord.'

No, it doesn't, Solon thought. *What looks wrong is me leaving that throne empty.*

'You know why my pet whore can't be here,' he whispered. 'Find me the real queen and I'll consider it.'

He wasn't going to sit in the Prince-Consort's throne, the one Ril Endarion used, placed on the right hand of Lyra's imperial throne. *Using it is demeaning: Endarion was nothing compared to me.* So, as the trumpets rang out and a herald declared the Imperial Court of the Rondian Empire to be in session, Solon boldly rose and took Lyra's throne.

Silence fell like a collapsing tower and every eye fixed on him.

Yes, he thought, *I am the true power here and I'm not afraid to state that fact.* He glared around him, seeking dissenters. There were more than a few, but no one said a word.

They love me or they fear me and I don't care which. He felt an almighty swelling of glory as he stroked the carved wooden arms and thought of all the men – and one woman – who'd sat here. Sacrecour scum, mostly, but by Kore, they'd been powerful.

And I'll be the greatest of them all.

'Pallas belongs to me,' he began, stating a fact. 'The insurrection is broken. This morning my legions crushed the Mob, seized their supplies and burned their barriers. Their leaders are being rounded up as I speak.'

They'd better be, he thought, watching the reactions in the room.

'The true hero of the day,' he went on, 'was the young man who retook Tockburn. It will be no surprise to you that I am speaking of Nestor Sulpeter, the son of my dearest counsellor, Lord Rolven. The best men breed the best sons. Lineage is the only reliable pre-determinant of greatness. I tell you all: young Nestor here is destined for the highest distinction. He broke the barricades with his Kore-given gnosis and faced down the Mob almost single-handed. When assassins sought his life, he took theirs. He is a true hero of Rondelmar!'

Nestor, his eyes shining, took the plaudits, and Solon let him savour the moment, then added, 'Such are the men who serve me.' Because this was still *his* moment, after all.

'Where's the queen?' a spindly mage-noble of the Pallas Imperocracy called.

Who're you? Oh yes, Lord Sisam.

Solon fixed him with a firm look. 'The queen is distressed that the clemency she once showed the rabble was thrown back in her face. She's asked me to deal with the matter while she concentrates on her natural role as a mother.'

'Are you legally our emperor now?' Lord Sisam dared to ask.

Space began to clear around him.

Solon mentally added Sisam's name to his list. 'We're in a state of emergency, Lord Sisam, and the queen has granted me executive power. The legalities will catch up in due course.'

'But could she at least attend this court to endorse –'

He's heard the rumours about Lyra being in hiding and he suspects they're true. 'When she feels able, perhaps she can allay your *doubts*, Milord.'

'I, er, have no doubts,' Sisam stammered, suddenly noticing that he stood alone.

Solon let him squirm, then turned to face the room. 'Today, we have reclaimed Pallas-Nord. Our remaining enemies are in the Celestium, cowering behind the skirts of the Grand Prelate. Dubrayle, Wilfort, de Sirou, Excelsior and the rest of those traitors are surrounded, and if they don't surrender, I shall have no choice but to march in and take them. I will not let the clergy shelter my enemies.'

Even knowing him, he saw the disbelieving, fearful looks, the furtive hands making the Sign of Corineus over their chests. *Yes, I'm prepared to storm the Holy City. Lyra did, and you all cheered.*

'Let me make myself clear, my Lords. This empire has new leadership. My queen has done all she can, but now a man's strong hand is on the tiller. I will regain all she lost – starting with control over this city. Then comes the Kingdom of Rondelmar. Dupenium and Fauvion will be brought to heel, and the rest will follow. Secession will be met with war. There will be no "republic" and no break-up of this Kore-given empire.'

He glared around the hall, letting them see and feel his certainty – then, abruptly, he was sick of them.

When I've broken the clergy, I'll start on these sycophants. I'll sweep them all away.

'Lord Rolven, Lord Oryn – attend me. The rest of you, be about your affairs. We have an empire to save.'

He strode through the bowing audience, found a conference room and stalked to the window. Rolven and Oryn, behind him, avoided looking at each other. They were an ill-suited pair, the haughty and conservative noble and the diffident military man – and neither were irreplaceable in the longer term.

'I need to appoint a council,' he told them. 'Oryn, you'll continue as the Lord Commander – but military only. I want a new position – head of security – and I'm going to appoint Roland de Farenbrette. The Volsai will be his – when we have some. Rolven, I want you as my Imperocrator. Find me a man who's good with numbers for the Treasury – one of those bankers from Dubrayle's Bank of Rondelmar. No clergymen. Let the priests stick to praying.'

The two men shared troubled looks. 'The Grand Prelate has been a fixture on the Imperial Council since the dawn of the empire,' Rolven said in a troubled voice.

'That's because the Sacrecours lacked the balls to cast them out. I don't.'

'But the people—'

'The people don't matter – do you really think they care about councils and suffragium and all that shit? Frankel was delusional and the queen was weak. The mob just want bread and beer and to know a strong man is looking out for their security. Basic needs are all basic people aspire to. I want this empire run like a legion: a known hierarchy, each in their place. Accountability. Rules. Order.'

Rolven smiled thoughtfully, while Oryn wavered, then nodded.

Solon scowled at his initial hesitation, but went on, 'Wurther probably thinks I need time to consolidate before turning my attention to him – that I'll negotiate first. Rukk that! I want the captured Sacrecour barges readied upstream of the city. Oryn, you'll fill them with rankers and storm the Celestium while we bring Rolven's legions up overland from the south to prevent anyone escaping. We'll give Wurther's rats nowhere to run.'

'What about the city?' Oryn asked uncertainly. 'The ringleaders are still in hiding.'

'We've got Tad Kaden's sister, yes? Braeda? Announce her execution will take place in three days – she's to be hanged, drawn and quartered, then beheaded. That'll draw Kaden out of the woodwork.'

'But she's a woman—' Oryn gasped.

'She's played a man's part and she can die a man's death,' Solon snapped. *Lumpy's getting softer by the day.*

'It's unheard-of . . . it's dishon—'

Solon slammed his fist down on the table. 'These scum *have* no honour. Let the punishment fit her manifest crimes. And when her brother raises his head to plead for her, we'll take him too. They can share a scaffold.'

Oryn went quiet, but Rolven nodded approvingly. 'This realm has been too lax of late,' he said. 'Thank Kore you've returned to take control.'

It sounded like flattery, but at least it showed Rolven knew which direction the wind blew. 'Tell me of the Treasury, Milord,' Solon invited.

Rolven coughed, suddenly awkward. 'Er ... Milord, the Treasury is empty.'

Solon felt his eyes go wide. '*What?* What about the Church raids? The formation of the Bank of Rondelmar – the loan ... Dubrayle said we were solvent ... I heard him say it ...'

'When Dubrayle went to ground, somehow, if there was money, he made it vanish, the slimy prick.'

Rukka ... rukk-rukk-rukk. Solon balled his fist and slammed it down on the table again. 'Two days – no more than that – I want those barges here and I want my people in the fucking Celestium in two days. We'll get that bastard's money if we have to disembowel him to find it. *We attack in two fucking days* – understood?'

Seething now, he stamped away, almost breaking the door as he slammed it shut. The guards blanched and stepped back, but he didn't care about being seen angry right now. *Dubrayle and Setallius have all that blasted gold – I know they've got it. They could be buying support right this rukking minute. I've got to move fast. No delays.*

He strode through the Bastion, the look on his face sending anyone who saw him fleeing in the opposite direction, until finally he found himself in the royal suite. Brunelda was being readied for him, her wig teased into some elaborate coif. A pair of maids squealed in surprise and then curtseyed as he entered.

'Out, out,' he rasped, and they fled. He poured a large Brevian, then sprawled in an armchair. 'Come here,' he told Brunelda, 'and earn your keep.'

But when she came to him, he found that all he really wanted was someone to listen, so he let her sit at his feet while he told her what he faced. 'Once they know me, they'll understand that I know what they need,' he concluded, through clenched teeth. 'I can't be weak: it's only my strength that's holding back the chaos.'

She looked up at him and stroked his knee. 'I know,' she said. 'Sometimes your eyes shine as if you see something none of us can.' *Only I see this in you,* her expression added wordlessly.

But she was only a whore, so how could he trust even that?

Pallas-Nord

'Wake up, girl,' Sister Virtue's harsh voice urged, tugging Brunelda up from a deep, dark dream. *Wake up, wake up, wake up . . .*

She realised the nun had been speaking for some seconds, that in her dreaming, she'd been repeating the same thing – *Wake up, look around, see . . .* She rolled over, groaning as all the aches hit her, from her chaffed, raw nipples to the bone-deep bruising in her groin.

Surely pleasure shouldn't hurt, she thought blearily, looking up to face the nun. *He knows it's hurting but he won't stop until he's done. Why don't I hate him . . . ?*

'I don't want to know,' Virtue said drily.

Oh, Kore, did I speak?

'I'm sorry,' Brunelda mumbled, staggering naked from the bed and teetering to the garderobe to piss. She didn't care what the holy sister saw. 'What time is it? I thought I could sleep today.'

'No, you're needed in an hour,' Virtue said. Was that a hint of sympathy in her voice? 'The emperor wants you to be with him on the dais in the Place d'Accord while he executes Garod and Cordan Sacrecour.'

Oh Kore, Brunelda thought. Her stomach rebelled and her bowels gushed liquid.

'Garod's an old snake,' Virtue mused, 'but poor Cordan's just a boy. Your predecessor rather liked him.'

'I'm too sick,' Brunelda moaned, staggering to a chair and collapsing into it, dizzy from exhaustion . . . and maybe morning sickness?

'Cordan's just fourteen,' Virtue went on absently. 'He likes playing with toy soldiers and talking about the jousts – he *idolised* Takwyth – but his Imperiousness is going to lop his innocent little head off.'

'Shut up!' Brunelda groaned, thinking of her womb. She'd only missed one course and it wasn't certain. *Another child . . .* Where was the daughter they took away? *And do I really have to cheer on the taking of a boy's life, while carrying his executioner's baby?*

Sister Virtue stood, walked to the wardrobe doors and swung them open to reveal the glittering dresses that didn't quite fit Brunelda.

'How about red?' the nun called. 'That's a good colour for executions.'

Brunelda almost made it back to the garderobe before she vomited again.

Solon waited impatiently in the vast reception hall of the Bastion. The marble monstrosity was hung with banners and shields and icons designed to overawe visitors. It was almost empty this morning, cleared so that he could make his grand exit to the podium overlooking the Place d'Accord, two hundred yards east. Outside, a carriage awaited him and his queen.

'Where the Hel is she?' he grumbled to Roland de Farenbrette again.

Roland shrugged and resumed admiring his new state robes. Rolven Sulpeter stood beside Nestor, both still basking in the son's new-found glory. *Thinks because he waved his sword at a few rebellious burghers, that he's some kind of hero*, Solon sneered inwardly, remembering Corani heroes of the past. *There's no one left but me fit to lace those men's boots.*

The city had been sullen overnight, with only a few arsons to disturb the night watch. The armies were moving closer, the barges sliding down the Bruin. The day after tomorrow, the Celestium would fall.

But first, this . . .

'Damn it, where – ah, finally!' he exclaimed, as Brunelda appeared, clutching Sister Virtue's arm. He ran his eye over the nun – she was plain and stocky, not at all to his taste, but apparently she was a strong mage and she did her duties well. *Anyway, she's a nun; she doesn't have to be pretty.*

He walked thrice around Brunelda, making sure that she resembled Lyra as closely as possible today. 'Don't speak,' he told her, 'just wave and smile.' He pinched her cheek. 'You're too pale, even for Lyra.'

'I'm not well,' Brunelda said weakly.

'The child?' he whispered, and she nodded.

If this was the real Lyra, he'd be trumpeting his virility, but he was told boasting of a child out of wedlock with the empress would alienate certain conservative supporters. *Old men with limp cocks. Yesterday's men.*

When he took her arm, she blurted, 'Please, I don't want–'

'Lyra would attend,' he interrupted. 'There are too many whispers already.' He pinched her cheeks again, to make them ruddy. 'Don't you want to live in luxury? Don't you want our son to rule after me?' At her nod, he said, 'Then do this, for me – for us.'

He took his 'queen' to the carriage and they drove the short trip to the gates in silence. Brunelda was silent, but she hardened her face as the doors were opened and they were hit by a wall of noise. She even managed to look regal as she joined him below the imperial dais.

He'd taken care to ensure only his most rabid supporters were here: those Corani families, nobles and soldiers who'd cheer him to the hilt even if he declared himself to be the Lord of Hel incarnate. As he appeared they roared his name: '*Takwyth, Takwyth.*'

'Wave, girl,' he muttered, raising his own hand, and Brunelda did too, then he escorted her up the stairs, using subtle kinesis to impel her. She looked overwhelmed to be standing before so mighty a crowd in such a vast place. The giant statue of Corineus the Saviour towered over them and the sound smote them like waves on the coastal cliffs. He fed her energy so that she didn't faint, comparing her unfavourably to Lyra's quiet dignity when in public.

His men closed in around him as they climbed to the top of the dais and waved to their supporters. The plaza could hold a hundred thousand people . . . but now he noticed it was only a third full and his smile faltered.

Rolven told me it'd be packed – he's let me down.

But he forced another smile and waved again before taking his queen to the thrones and seating her in the lower one with a fine show of gallantry, hissing, 'Don't you bloody faint, Brunelda. Remember what's at stake.'

Striding to the front of the dais, he pointed to the gallows he'd had erected in front of the thrones. A hooded headsman waited at the top of the aisle roped off for the prisoners to walk between the ranks of watchers.

'Today marks the end of the Sacrecour rebellion,' he shouted, and paused to take the cheers that rose in response. 'Today, we chop the head off the snake who wished to rule us!'

'*Takwyth – Takwyth –*'

'Today we end the threat of tyranny!'

'*Takwyth – Takwyth –*'

'I take no pleasure in this,' he shouted, quite untruthfully. 'But justice must be seen to be done. My men and I are labouring to make you safe. We must purge this empire of traitors – and this is just the beginning. We will expose the disloyal wherever they are and root them out.'

The cheers died momentarily as the people below took in his words. Then they returned: '*Takwyth – Takwyth –*'

The echoes bouncing off the stone walls surrounding the giant plaza made the chorused voices sound oddly hollow. Irked, Solon turned to Roland. 'Bring them out.'

Roland signed and from the lesser gate to the Bastion rolled two prison-wagons, the first bearing Garod Sacrecour and the second, Cordan. Garod was sitting with bowed head, but the boy was clinging to the bars, crying uncontrollably.

Damn it, they're supposed to have given Cordan something to calm him . . .

He gritted his teeth, wondering who was at fault, watching the wagons ploughing up the aisle. His supporters among the crowd were venting their hatred, hammering on the cage bars and hurling rotten vegetables – but too many were hanging back for his liking.

He glanced down and saw that Brunelda was white as a sheet, clearly not far from fainting. He spied sour-faced Sister Virtue among the flock of aides and sent tersely, <*Attend upon the queen. If she passes out, I'll fucking de-frock you and throw you to the streets.*>

The first wagon reached the steps, the cage door was pulled open with a screech and burly soldiers pulled the compliant Garod from the cage and marched him up the stairs.

The second carriage stopped, but Cordan was left inside the cage, which had been Rolven's suggestion.

Solon strode down and ascended the gallows, probably offending some tradition or other, but he wanted to witness Garod meeting his end up close. He towered over the duke as he was hauled up the steps, his legs barely functioning. His robes were torn, his visible skin scabbed and his lank grey hair matted. At close quarters, he stank.

'Loser,' Solon jeered softly.

Garod gave him a hollow stare as he was shoved towards the executioner's block and the headman, who was hefting the massive axe. The two men holding Garod turned him to face the crowd for the customary final words. Tradition allowed such speeches to be as long as the condemned wished, but the headsman, a mage, was under orders to stop Garod after a few words.

The duke raised his head. 'House Sacrecour . . . true rulers of Urte,' he tried to call out, but his jaw was broken, so not much was understandable. The crowd murmured derisively, then Solon flicked a finger.

The guards pushed the would-be ruler of the empire to his knees, the axe rose and fell and the head thudded into the basket in a spout of blood that sprayed the skirts of Solon's robe. He grimaced, remembering finally that as ruler he should be on the throne above, not down here on the gallows. But he was here now and it would look foolish if he were to leave. Impatiently, he signalled to the men on Cordan's wagon.

They unlocked it as Cordan wailed, 'No, please, no, no . . .'

The crowd hushed and shuffled as the boy clung to the bars, screaming, 'Cora – Cora –'.

'He calls for his sister,' a woman exclaimed, as if this was some sign from on high.

'*Cora*,' Cordan wailed, then he saw Solon. 'Sir Solon – please, Milord – you said we were friends –' He broke off as the soldiers finally dragged him out of the cage, thrashing and kicking.

Rukka, Solon scowled, *shut him up*. He glared at the men holding the boy, but the imbeciles didn't seem to realise what he meant.

'You said we were friends,' Cordan shrieked again as they hauled him up the steps. The crowd was silent now, and some of the women were hiding their faces . . . and some men too. 'You gave me toy soldiers,' the boy wailed. 'Mercy, Milord Solon, mercy –'

Damn it, do I have to do everything?

Solon grabbed the boy's face and sealed his mouth with his hand. Staring down at the huge, wet eyes, for a moment he saw that same hand kill Nita. The gallows seemed to lurch.

This must be done, he snarled at himself. *Weakness is unacceptable*.

But he was shaking, he was stunned to realise: shaking with guilt.

No, not guilt, with weakness. That was intolerable. He lashed himself onwards. 'Do it,' he snarled at the soldiers, taking a step back so they could pull the boy to the block. Cordan kept struggling like a slippery eel and they all slithered and nearly slipped in Garod's blood, but at last the boy was forced to face the block.

'No speech, just keep his rukking mouth shut,' Solon rasped – and in the silence, his words carried over the crowds, causing an increasing murmur of disquiet. He swore again, under his breath this time, and nodded at the headsman.

Cordan twisted as soon as the soldier removed his arm to try and bow him down. Looking up at the thrones, he cried, '*Lyra, mercy, mercy –*' Then his eyes bulged. '*You're not Lyra – you're not the real queen,*' he screamed, as loudly as he could. '*You're not the queen!*'

Brunelda was rigid and open-mouthed, Sister Virtue muttering in her ear, then she shrieked, 'Mercy – *mercy!*'

Rukka, Solon fumed. The queen had the right to give clemency – but he'd never told Brunelda that, for this very reason. *Did that rukking nun tell her?* He shot Sister Virtue a murderous look. *<Did you tell her to grant clemency?>* he sent silently.

<She knew,> the mage-nun sent back tersely. *<Perhaps her confessor?>*

Damn them all, I'm being betrayed. But the damage was done: he'd look exactly like a tyrant if he went through with this now.

'The queen has spoken,' he said hoarsely. 'Take the prince back to the Bastion. Give him . . . his old rooms back.'

He could see his partisans were angry at having their blood spectacle snatched away. This moment, his long-dreamed-of revenge for 909, had been transformed from sweet wine to rancid vinegar. Seeking to retrieve the moment, he reached into the basket, lifted out Garod's head and held it high. 'So ends the Sacrecour tyranny,' he shouted, spraying drops of gore as he brandished it. He was dimly aware that some of the women had fainted – and that there were few cheers.

He dropped the head and stormed down from the gallows and up the steps to the dais. 'Get the *queen* to her rooms,' he snapped at Sister Virtue, then he gestured to Roland to join him. 'What a rukking disaster,' he muttered. 'Who organised it? Whose damned fault was it?'

Roland flicked a glance at Rolven Sulpeter. 'The old windbag.'

Solon glowered at Sulpeter, who looked away. *Dead wood. I need to take an axe to it.*

But thoughts of axes only drew his gaze back to the bloody block and then to the crowd. There was no hero-worship in the eyes of the women now, no idolising young knights, just horror . . . and *fear.*

Makelli said, 'They don't have to love you as long as you're feared.'

'Cordan should have died too,' he told Roland – told himself. 'She had no right . . .'

'Say the word and I'll finish him,' the Blacksmith growled back. 'On the quiet.'

'They heard him denounce Brunelda,' he whispered. 'Was he believed?'

'It doesn't matter – deny, deny, deny,' Roland advised. 'You're the emperor – the truth is whatever you say it is. They understand what you're about, Milord: you're going to make us great again.' He clapped Solon's shoulder. 'We're stronger because of this.'

Solon took a deep breath. *Roland's right,* he told himself. This was necessary. 'Let the boy live – for now,' he growled. 'We'll ensure he doesn't see another year. And get rid of the queen's confessor.' He glared about the plaza. 'Get the gallows washed down. The dungeons are filling up and we need to make room.'

The Celestium

The girl was inconsolable, but for all she wasn't used to dealing with young people, Basia tried. Holding her seemed to be helping a little. 'Coramore, shush,' she murmured, 'he's not dead – they didn't kill him.'

'I know,' Coramore sobbed, 'b-but Coñ would've been so f-f-frightened . . .'

Outside, the full moon lit the night sky. 'Take me to the garden,' she whispered, and Basia twitched uneasily but acquiesced. Like the queen's sanctuary, the Celestium's Winter Tree garden was an eerie place, especially when Coramore was in it. The princess had been spending most of her time inside Saint Eloy's burial mound of late; she'd told them Solon had burned out Lyra's garden, so presumably the dwyma had told her.

They made their way through the secluded guest wing to the back of the great cathedral, past the guards at the gate to the lawned garden. The silver moon hung heavy overhead, casting shadows like pools of emptiness.

The walls were manned by a double watch of both Kirkegarde and her own Corani, but Basia was still uneasy as she let Coramore go below on her own. Unease prickled at her skin and she scanned this way and that, sure someone was watching, though she couldn't see anyone.

I could kill her, right now, Father Germane mused, clinging like a venomous spider to a low parapet just a few yards from a sentry. *But why is Lyra not here as well? I've seen that girl several times, but never the queen . . . Surely a dwymancer would come here all the time?*

He quivered, sorely tempted to make his move, but even with his new powers, this garden gave him a queasy sense of peril. The daemon inside him whispered of other possessed men who'd tried to enter such places and come to very permanent ends. The danger might not be clear, but it was palpable. Glimpsing his prey was tantalising, but the perimeter was riddled with gnostic wards and had dozens of guards including magi. The oppressive sense of menace hanging over everything was the dwyma, he presumed.

Reluctantly, he crept away, slithering down the wall and flitting into the shadowy warren that was Fenreach, where half the hovels were now abandoned. He emerged soon after with a new face and new clothes and walked brazenly back to the Celestium, joining the other cooks for their long, hard shift in the kitchens.

He needed to get into the guest wing if he was to find Lyra and her entourage and kill them all – then he could join the Master in his grand project, whatever it was. He told himself he'd heard too many 'Last Days' sermons of late, but the feeling that time was slipping away wouldn't leave him.

There'll be a way, he told himself. *For someone like me, there always is.*

30

A Sea of Fog and Ruin

Lines of Defence

*Generals speak of layered lines of defence, but to me the first line of defence is
absence. If you're not on the battlefield, they can't hurt you. Move in shadows,
strike from behind. War isn't about honour, it's about winning. If you really care
about looking chivalrous, write the history afterwards.*

GURVON GYLE, GREY FOX LEADER, NOROS 909

Rym, Rimoni
Martrois 936

Jehana followed Ervyn Naxius down crumbling hallways lined with
broken colonnades and fallen statues, through collapsed mansions
open to the skies, across debris-strewn plazas. Nothing grew there, even
centuries after the Rondians had taken the city, Naxius told her, thanks
to gnostic blights. There were no weeds, no insects or rodents, no sound
but the wind, no smell but old dust and grit. The dust-covered desolation was soul-sucking.

Jehana barely noticed, though, for her attention was focused inwards,
where her nascent dwyma was slowly being poisoned by ichor. Alyssa
Dulayne had tried to take on the dwyma whilst wholly infected, but
Jehana was to be more slowly transfigured. As the dwymancers were
the masters of the natural world, she was to be the queen of the daemonic: a hideous proposition, with her psyche still racked by the
linkage to Abraxas.

But if I see it through, can he still control me . . . ? she wondered.

That was the hope she was clinging to: that she could pass through the fires and then unleash them on this *evil* bastard. It had led her to this strange kind of truce as they felt out each other's weaknesses. That she was barely a woman and Naxius was a centuries-old mage wasn't forgotten; and that she was no use to him without the dwyma also hadn't escaped her. She was playing with the deadliest of fires, but she believed if she could open herself to the dwyma fully, she would find a way to break free. Naxius seemed to believe she couldn't – or wouldn't.

One of us is going to be utterly, disastrously wrong . . .

But in any case, she couldn't take any more of the daemon's never-ending procession of iniquity and depravity. It left her soul raw and bleeding as memories that weren't hers screamed through her mind. Faces she did know and love – her mother, her brother, her friends – became warped and entangled with the horrors Abraxas fed her, until it was either break free or die. And now that she knew exactly what lurked in the darkness beyond death, there was no way she wished to die, not ever.

They know my name and Abraxas is waiting for me. So I will jump before I fall, while I still have some self-will, and – somehow – *I will grow wings.*

They emerged onto a low promontory jutting out into Lake Patera. The flat, sullen expanse spread before her, the murky surface covered in fog which danced, swirling like old cobwebs, as they moved down the steps into a dell right at the edge of the water. The far shore was lost in the mists. The sun hung low in the sky, but whether it was morning or evening, she couldn't tell, for she couldn't work out if she was looking east or west.

'Behold,' Naxius said grandly, gesturing to the cliffs behind him, and she turned to see a big tree clinging to the edge like a wooden spider. It was covered in prickly little emerald leaves and small red berries. Then she caught her breath as her half-wakened dwyma-senses saw the tree was pulsing with strange energy, like a distorted version of the dwyma filled with hunger. She saw bones of birds had been caught in the twisted branches as if snared. She sensed the tree's eyeless regard watching her approach.

'What is this?' she breathed, at once drawn and repelled.

'When I realised what the Winter Tree in Pallas was – a nexus of the dwyma – I stole a cutting,' Naxius said smugly. 'It's a brackenberry – I planted several, using sylvan gnosis to accelerate the growth, and leached ichor into the soil, to make them more amenable to my aims. Most died – the ruination spells on this city are particularly virulent – but I fed this one blood and it thrives – indeed, it has grown voraciously.'

Jehana shuddered, her courage faltering as she saw the way the tendrils of the brackenberry stroked the air menacingly, coiling and uncoiling as the tree reacted to her presence. *It fears and wants me too,* she sensed. *We are each other's threshold* . . . Her mouth went dry but her heart was thumping. 'Wh–What must I do . . . ?'

'Go to it,' Naxius invited, his hooded eyes giving nothing away. 'Eat some berries.'

The berries contain essence of both the dwyma and the daemonic. She hesitated, perceiving the tree as more creature than plant. *It fears me . . . It hates me . . .*

'You could bring some to me,' she said weakly.

'I could, but that would achieve nothing,' Naxius said. 'The berries are not enough. I have been feeding them to you while you slept: they have already given you all they can. More is needed to awaken you. Go to it.'

'But–'

'Must I compel you, girl? I thought you resolved?'

'I . . . I am . . .' she stammered, wavering.

She took a hesitant step forward, then another, stopping a few feet from the longest of the writhing branches as she tried to work up the nerve to take that last step. The tree quivered, reaching for her, then recoiling, as frightened as she was, but drawn nevertheless . . .

She reminded herself that without this, there would be no escape. She'd been initiated into the dwyma, but without a firm bond to a genilocus, all she could do was listen to it, *feel* it, almost *taste* it, but without the fulfilment of union, she had no hope of anything but death . . . and the waiting Abraxas . . .

She gathered her courage and murmured, 'Ha'ana . . .'

Here I am . . .

She stepped forward.

The tree shuddered, its branches rippling and the leaves hissing, whorls like eyes fixed on her face as she took another step, then another . . .

And then branches were whipping round, ripping her off her feet and jerking her into the tangle of foliage . . . She opened her mouth to scream—

—but a rope-like tongue had burst from nowhere and rammed into her mouth and down her throat, gushing something like sap into her. She fought for air and lost, drowning, going blind as her clothing was rent and tendrils plunged into her skin. Stars exploded in her head, dark shadows rushed in and she floated . . . then faded . . .

Naxius watched the tree curiously. Its jerking movements were subsiding but the inner branches were still wrapped tightly around Jehana, lofted high up the trunk. The air began to throb and his whole being tingled with excitement and that intoxicating *frisson* of risk.

My enemies think me a cruel manipulator, someone who lets others take the real dangers . . . They don't understand that every experiment I essay is risk, and that failure is fatal . . .

But for now, the die was cast and the girl was in the hands of this thing he'd made of dwyma and daemon, life and entropy. If – *when* – she returned, she would be something else, a dweller on the threshold of life and death. She might even exceed him . . .

If I could, I would have taken this upon myself . . .

But only she had been bred to be both dwymancer and mage. There was the brother, of course, but he'd promised Rashid that Waqar would not be touched and by the time he felt ready to disregard that pledge, Waqar was out of reach.

The girl will suffice . . .

He watched a while longer, but the tree had settled down into still-ness again, savouring its new prey. He lifted his head from his musings and scanned the lake, which was once again tranquil. The northern shore was lost in the fog rolling down the river valley and in from the

513

eastern coast as well. His gnostic senses revealed no weather-gnosis . . . but the other dwymancers were still alive.

Lyra's in the north . . . but where's Valdyr?

None of his enemies *should* be a threat any more: the Ordo Costruo and the Merozains were mired in the fruitless struggle to save the Leviathan Bridge, and the dwymancers knew too little. Mollachia was far away, and in any case, Valdyr was ignorant of the true stakes. He and Lyra might have evaded death, but the window of opportunity for them to thwart him was slamming closed.

The process has begun . . . tonight will be the night.

Dirklan Setallius led the six venators in, skimming the surface of the vast fogbank Lyra and Valdyr had conjured, seeking a place to land. Finally he jabbed an arm downwards and they swooped towards a dark patch of earth.

It had been without doubt one of the coldest and most uncomfortable journeys of Ogre's life, but he barely cared, for his blood ran hot and his chest swelled to be so close to Tarita.

But now the Master waited . . .

They were all frozen and painfully stiff from so long in the frigid air, which cut pitilessly through even the heaviest layers and had them continually scraping ice from the eye-glasses as they came skimming down river valleys. It was a mercy now to glide in Dirklan's wake to a wreckage-covered plaza, an island amid the fog.

They disembarked awkwardly; the magi were able to feed heat and energy to their limbs, but all Lyra and Valdyr could do was stamp around, chaffing their numb fingers.

Tarita's eyes gleamed with gnosis-light as she scanned their surroundings. 'All clear,' she called softly, the other magi nodding agreement, then they all fell silent, taking in the dreary emptiness. There was no birdsong here, or even the moan of wind over stone. The mist swirling from their steeds' wings gradually stilled.

Ogre's heart was speeding. Ever since his rescue by the Ordo Costruo, the central fear of his existence had been that he might fall back into the Master's hands: it was the source of his nightmares and his waking dread. And now here he was, willingly seeking the Master's lair, when all he wanted was to go with Tarita to some faraway place and hide for ever.

But if I do that, the Master will destroy everything . . . and he'll still find us. In his head he knew it was better to do this and die, rather than attempt to run and hide, but glimpsing the maze of desolation that had once been the greatest city in the world chilled him to the soul. It felt like a foretaste of the Master's plans for Urte.

'Hey, big boy, even you should be able to move unseen in this place,' Tarita said slyly. 'Just so long as you don't fart and blow the fog away.'

'Ogre will be silent,' he answered gloomily, unable to rise to her teasing.

The others joined them in the middle of the rock-strewn plaza. 'Is Gricoama joining us?' Lyra asked Valdyr.

In response, the Mollachian turned to face the wall of fog to the north – and out of the mist trotted a dark shape the size of a pony, its fur sleek and amber eyes faintly aglow.

They all stared at the giant wolf padding up to Valdyr and nuzzling him, then looking around with what Ogre thought was something remarkably like a grin.

'Ysh, he is with us,' Valdyr chuckled.

Ogre's heart lifted, and he shared a look with Tarita and saw she felt it too: a sense that Urte itself was responding to the threat of the Master. They weren't alone.

But are we in time?

Dirklan took charge. 'Rhune and Sarunia will remain here with our mounts, ready to bring them to us if we find we're in the wrong place,' he said. 'We five – and Gricoama, of course – will go on. It's been four days since we left Pallas and almost two since we left Norostein and I fear we're running out of time.'

'Yes,' Valdyr said firmly, 'let's finish this. The rest of our lives await.'

The sun was setting behind the fog, marking west for them with a glow of gilt and rose. Rhune and Sarunia helped them prepare, shedding travel gear and donning armour or heavy padded vests, checking weaponry, tucking pouches of dried food, waterskins and essentials into deep pockets.

As night closed in and the ruined city woke, the five humans and one wolf crossed the plaza and began picking a path through the rubble.

Despite Gricoama's advent, Ogre felt a sense of impending doom, borne of living his whole life in the shadow of his creator – they were too few, they were in the wrong place, Waqar was not with them. They faced the Master, the genius even Meiros and the Ordo Costruo had not been able to defeat. So it was hard not to feel that they'd already lost.

But equally, he felt a rising determination to see it through to the end.

Mount Fettelorn, Veronese Alps

Waqar felt the light seep from the grey cloud enveloping him as the day surrendered to the night without a whimper. He paused, clinging to his walking staff, shaking in weakness. All round him the icy rock dotted with deep pockets of snow mocked his efforts. He, a child of sunlight and heat, could die in this frigid place from nothing but the cold, he realised.

Where's your strength, mage? the wind hissed. *Where's your mighty gnosis now?*

All but burned out to get me this far, was the answer. He cast a look back over his shoulder, but visibility could only be measured in yards. The air was thin, and so cold his nose burned at each inhalation. That he was even here was insanity – but from the moment Gricoama bit his hand, he'd fallen into delirium, barely understanding what he was doing, let alone how he'd got here – wherever *here* was. All he knew was that he must go on.

I have to climb . . .

There was a stairway carved into the bedrock, winding back and forth across the almost sheer face. Some of the steps were so thick with ice he had to hammer at them with the staff or melt with the gnosis before he could risk stepping on them. The wind whistling across the cliff-face tore at his clothing, but his sense of urgency was growing, for the sound of Jehana's voice came on the moaning, shrieking winds.

Sister, I hear you, I'm coming . . .

But night was coming faster, like the last night of the world.

He'd collapsed within seconds of Gricoama's bite, utterly bewildered at this betrayal. The wolf's eyes haunted him as he fell, those teeth dripping *his* blood as he tumbled to the infirmary floor.

What felt like only a moment later, he woke to find Gricoama was licking his face.

'*Madha . . . ?*' he slurred. Gricoama nuzzled him, then turned and padded out of the door, nudging it until it closed and the gnostic locks clicked back into place. Waqar stared after him, then a dust mote crawled across his vision like a cloud of stars in the night sky and he was caught up in raptured awe at how light could speckle on the tiniest of spots, that light was the eye of Ahm, seeing all, striking all, terrible and beautiful . . .

The light shifted across the room—

—and then something crashed, *bang bang bang*, the door rattled and voices reverberated, the tongue too foreign and too loud to comprehend. A woman shrieked in alarm and then there was fuss, bustle and confusion and people were lifting him and liquids were tipping into his throat in a breath-taking cascade, the moisture in his mouth like rain in a desert, and everywhere the light danced, through opened curtains, in the eyes of the people bending over him . . .

. . . and all the voices . . .

There were a thousand voices, ten thousand – no, beyond millions, a deafening, overwhelming cacophony that was both music and discord – until he found himself looking at the ceiling, his eyes piercing the roof as his awareness soared up, up, up to where a light shone.

An oil lantern hung from the hand of a grey-bearded man, robed and cowled in brown like a monk of Kore. He was standing on an outcropping, the air swirling with snowflakes, each one a miniature masterpiece. His eyes were gold, like his lamp, or Gricoama's eyes, and he was waiting.

Waiting for me . . .

Some time later, Waqar woke to find the afternoon sun gleaming through the open curtains, but somehow he could still see that golden lamp, high above and – he paused to get his bearings – southeast of him, in the heights of the Alps. The old bearded man's visage flashed across his mind again – as if he was waiting for him.

A bustling Rondian healer-mage in pale blue robes came and went, but he couldn't concentrate on what she was saying because he was so captivated with *how* she said it: her words ran together into music and meaning eluded him. He wept at the timbre of her voice, wanting to capture it and listen to those notes for ever. But they faded, so he closed his eyes, dreaming of a pearly-white winged horse sipping from a mountain stream and an owl in a northern garden that someone had cruelly torched. He saw Gricoama padding through a river valley in thick fog, moving like a shadow –

– and a tree coiled about something of flesh and blood, in the throes of feeding, or mating, or giving birth . . . or all three, and from it came a voice, screaming his name–

Jehana!

He sat up, heart thumping, with the sound of his sister's voice ringing in his ears. She was snared and helpless, her shrieks harrowing – but the vision was gone and he was alone in this darkened suite, his heart thudding painfully, his lungs gasping for air.

But if he looked upwards, *just so*, the man with the lantern was still gazing down, still waiting.

He moved in feverish bursts, flinging himself upright and hauling on clothing and boots. He found his thick flying cloak, his eye-glasses and gloves, his sword and his periapt. *I have to help her*, resounded over and over in his mind. *I must help her.* He didn't know how, but he was full of the conviction that the old man did. *I'll go to him . . .*

He left the room, ghosting past healers and nurses too busy with the wounded to notice, until he reached a bustling lobby and saw big doors leading outside. Faces turned his way, mostly pale Yurosi who scowled or peered at him curiously. 'Wanker sleeps while his men work,' someone murmured as he passed, but Waqar had no idea what that meant. Only Jehana mattered.

Someone, dark-faced and exhausted, fell to one knee as he passed and murmured, 'Sal'Ahm, my prince.' Waqar hurried by, mystified why anyone would kneel to him.

Then he heard a piercing cry and a name flashed into his mind: *Ajniha*. He broke into a run, pounding along the halls, bursting through the open doors as a contingent of soldiers entered.

'Prince Waqar?' someone shouted, but he ignored them: *there was no time.*

Ajniha, his mind called, and the bird shrieked again. He felt a painful heaviness in his chest as he ran and he was panting for breath – *What's wrong with me?* – but he was outside in the huge fountained plaza before the Governor's Mansion and a dark shadow was falling from the twilight sky. Moments later, a huge eagle landed before him, buffeting him with the wind of her wings, and he knew her.

'Ajniha, good girl,' he praised, leaping to her back. Someone had been tending her, although there were still bare scarred patches on the bird's flanks, and she too seemed distressed, her breath also short and rasping. He vaguely recalled being told that the draken had broken her ribs when it had caught her.

We're a pair, he thought dazedly, but even his beloved roc couldn't be spared, for Jehana needed them.

He didn't bother with saddle-straps but nudged her into motion and they rose clumsily into the air, sweeping into a southeast heading, riding an updraft around the northern face of Mount Fettelorn, which stood like a sentinel over Norostein. Glancing down, he had a flash vision of a startled Xoredh staring straight up at him, although his cousin was two miles away in the Shihad camp. Then Ajniha rounded an outcropping, dipped behind a ridge and Norostein and Xoredh were both gone, excised from his eye and his mind.

High, high up on the southern flank of the mountain, a golden light shone like a low-hanging star.

'There,' he told Ajniha. '*There!*'

*

That was hours ago and now he could scarcely remember why he'd come.

Somehow, flying had become impossible. The higher they went, the thinner and colder the air grew until it was so bitterly cold he realised that Ajniha could never make it even if she were fully healthy. Straining his eyes, he saw the stairway carved into the snow-streaked slope and he realised what he had to do. He took Ajniha down, got off, then sent her away. She went reluctantly, crying mournfully as she dived, and the swirling snow snatched her from sight.

He looked upwards and saw that golden lamplight far, far above. He could picture the lined, weather-beaten man, half-lit by the lantern as he peered down at him, waiting. Then he caught another glimpse: of a place beyond the lamp, a swirling carpet of light stretching all the way to the stars: all the way to Paradise.

Gricoama howled distantly. An owl hooted softly, and Jehana sobbed his name . . .

A wooden stave was lying beside the path as if waiting for him. He picked it up, gripped it two-handed and burned the ice away from the next step, then using it as both crutch and probe, he began to climb.

Even with ichor in its veins, the cold-blooded venator could go no further. Xoredh cursed as the flying beast convulsed, brayed mournfully, then went rigid and began to career downwards.

He ripped himself free of the straps and leaped, moments before the beast spun into a ravine. It vanished, but Xoredh engaged Air-gnosis and floated down onto a snow-covered outcrop, landing on one knee, blade drawn and eyes roving.

Nothing else moved on the lifeless stone. Once assured there was no threat, he rose and sheathed his blade. Mount Fettelorn loomed above him, lit by the immense face of the moon painting the night in monochrome swathes of white, grey and black—

—except for one golden pinprick of light, hanging high on the icy peak, well above the snowline. There was a black, waving line that climbed towards it: a stair.

There: Waqar's up there . . .

Xoredh trawled the daemon's knowledge of the dwyma: drawing on the experiences of others, now dead and gone: *Asiv Fariddan trailed Valdyr Sarkany to a volcano where the dwyma was strong . . . There's a dwyma garden in the Rondian queen's castle, and one in the Holy City of Kore . . . So this must be another such place . . .*

That suggested the danger to him was real, that he must cut down Waqar before he reached his destination, so he sprouted wings on his back, built up his lungs and chest muscles, pulled in energy and turned it to heat – and with a snarl, he leaped into the air, caught an up-current and skimming the slope, flew upwards to where his cousin laboured . . .

31

A Night to End All Days

Glamortha and Lucian

Theologians have long speculated upon the nature of Glamortha, the Angel of Death and Mother of Daemons. Why would Kore create an Angel who would betray Him? Does she have free will, or is her part in the Last Days fated? And why is it that the two greatest cosmic crimes, those of Glamortha and Corinea, are committed by women?

OFFICIAL RECORDS, CONVENTION OF PRELATES, PALLAS 723

Rym, Rimoni
Martrois 936

Jehana's eyes flew open, but her sight remained fixed on the vistas playing inside her skull. The first moments, caught in the coils of the tree, had been hideous, but she was numb to such things now, for her time inside the daemon's mind had shown her far worse.

Something bitter had been forced into her mouth – not ichor, but a liquid caught between the twin poles of the dwyma and the daemonic. When it reached her heart, the beat changed. At first she'd thought she was dying, but now she felt as if she were swimming back from the deep waters towards an emerald sun.

Her vision cleared. The fogbound city and the lake were gone and instead, she hung in space, slowly revolving around a glowing orb, a world wreathed in cloud through which blue waters and green and brown lands could be glimpsed. Like her, it was caught up in a vast tree floating in the starry void – or was it a heart encased in veins, or a fountain feeding itself?

She wasn't alone in this void: she recognised the other beings floating around her as daemons. *What a foolish name for such beauty*, she thought. They were always in motion, glittering constellations of awareness shifting, reforming, joining and separating: fleeting wonders that kept reconfiguring into a new shade of emotion. The closer she looked, the more she saw: the faces of the dead and the never-alive joined by a single need: to return to the world of being. They fed on orbs of light that came from the tree – the Elétfa? Some burst right through the daemons, seeking to engulf them, and disappeared into the void, but most were devoured and joined to their new host to become part of a greater whole, like ants being swept up by the tongue of an anteater.

She floated among the vast clouds full of constantly changing mouths and eyes and limbs, their names whispering through her mind: Abraxas, Gorvial, Hrogath, Inaryon . . . as a student she'd seen these same names in ancient daemonicons.

Their shifting forms made her wonder if she could do the same here: she imagined herself as a bird – and she was; and then a snake, then a cat, a man, a jackal, then she lost interest and was herself again.

Where are the apsarai? she wondered. *Where there are daemons, there should be angels*. She looked to the outer limits, seeking whatever might lie beyond: a giant light hung far, far away in the void – the sun, she realised, which was really just the nearest star . . .

'There's nothing out there,' a melodious voice said and she spun around to find one of the daemons watching her closely: a serpent, which became a lion, which became a glowing, naked man, his face serene perfection, filled with curiosity . . . and *hunger*.

As he spoke, a majestic marble palace formed around them, with green gardens where tigers roamed with peacocks and fish flew like birds. She ignored it and focused entirely on the one daemon who dared to approach her.

'Then where do those who escape your kind go?' she asked.

'Paradise, or the Pit?' he replied indifferently. 'Our nets are incomplete – some slip through.'

'Holy men? Saints? Godspeakers?'

The daemon laughed, a sound of crystalline loveliness, entrancing as music. 'Broadly speaking, they are no more or less easy to catch than any other. It's those who have lived a full life we struggle to contain: they're the tastiest, the ones we love to pick apart, but they're the hardest to trap.'

'So those who elude you are all out there somewhere? Do they feed the apsarai?'

'Apsarai? Angels? I've never seen one, nor heard of any who have.' The daemon made a rippling, shrugging gesture with all his body. 'Perhaps they just burn away. I care not – my concern is *that*.' He pointed to Urte, his voice hungry with desire. 'And right now, *you*.'

He drifted closer and although they were just ghosts, they were also male and female. She felt a tinge of unease because he was just *too* beautiful, radiant as a morning star.

'Who are you?' she asked.

'I have been called Abliz . . . Lucian . . . Yama: names bestowed by the ignorant. In truth, I'm the greatest of our kind.' He gestured at the other daemons.

She shuddered at that. *The Lord of Hel in Urte's religions*, she thought with a thrill of fear. *The opponent of Ahm, of Kore and the Lakh gods: the Great Enemy. Shaitan.*

And yet she felt no immediate threat. They stared at each other, looking past bodies, because those were just light and illusion, infinitely mutable; only their eyes gave substance to who they were. His were entrancing, deep pools to dive into, promising all knowledge, all wisdom and every experience; wells of mysteries to a girl who'd barely begun to live. Enticing, *dangerous* eyes . . .

'The greater question,' the shining daemon said, 'is who – and what – are you?'

She'd not yet got around to wondering that herself. *Am I dead and floating in the aether, waiting to be devoured?* But she'd never felt so alive. Perhaps she should be running, but she sensed there was no escaping him here. And if she was ever to find a way to defeat Naxius and his hideous plans, surely it was here and now?

'I'm Jehana,' she began, but that was inadequate – it meant nothing. Words failed: here others' lives were *experienced*, not told. Tentatively, she extended a hand, a shimmer of light and shadow, offering that experience.

Was there a flicker of uncertainty in his glowing red-gold eyes? Perhaps, but then he raised his own hand and slowly, like galaxies colliding, they pushed them together . . .

Through the scrying orb he'd conjured in his Chamber of Wizardry, Ervyn Naxius watched Jehana from a mile away, deep inside his palace. He saw her rise from the branches of the poisoned dwyma-tree to be caught in the vortex of energies concentrating around her. She was lying on her back, floating in mid-air facing the skies, where a giant shadow was forming in the mist, the shape of a man . . . or a monster.

Lucian's ichor flowed in his own veins now, so he saw with the Daemon Lord's eyes as the copper-skinned, white-haired woman floated upwards to meet him. He raised his hand, in total sympathy with his host.

It's a curious thing, Naxius thought, *this letting one's birds fly free*. He wondered if this was how parents felt. He'd never wanted children; his work had always been enough for him, and in any case, companionship was for weaklings: *empathy destroys rationality*.

But seeing this young woman made other parts of him awaken. 'And *Glamortha shall lay down with Lucian and beget the new race of daemons*,' he said out loud. He'd written it and now he would make it so.

I hope some part of her appreciates my genius . . .

He had a glimpse of what empathy might feel like as he willed her to succeed, to *become*, to fulfil all her promise – that in doing so, she would be condemned to eternity inside Lucian's mind was incidental.

It had been decades since he'd last enjoyed a woman, natural desires subsumed by his passion for research, but as the two daemon bodies fell into each other, Lucian took substance and form – and Naxius was right there, inside the daemon lord, as it reached for her . . .

Cloaked in mist, Lyra and her companions slipped through the ruined city, a vast emptiness of broken stone, tumbled colonnades and smashed statues. Her mind churned over what Dirklan had told them, of how the

Blessed Three Hundred, their ancestors, had visited fire and destruction on the pagan south.

The first magi slaughtered the almost helpless Rimoni soldiers and civilians, then salted the earth for a hundred miles around so no one could live here. Millions were displaced, a whole race stigmatised: was that truly Kore's will?

She found it ironic that once they'd destroyed the Rimoni, the Rondians set about imitating them; Rym architecture and art proliferated in the north and they'd copied virtually every Rimoni law and institution. She'd not even realised the first magi had 'Rimonised' their names, so Baram became Baramitius; Fastæ was now Fasterius, and so on . . . and yet the fate of Rimoni was still invoked to cow resistance to the rule of Pallas.

No wonder everyone hates us, Lyra thought, following Dirklan and Valdyr down a shattered street. No birds sang, no animals stalked the desolation, not even windblown weeds grew here in this eternal wasteland.

Tarita and Ogre were flanking the group, the little Jhafi woman skipping through the ruins like a haunting sprite, the lumbering Ogre almost silent despite his size. She could sense they were mentally linked, feeding each other information – and banter, judging by the occasional chuckle. And Gricoama ghosted through the ruins like a wraith, a shadow come to life.

Dirklan stopped and bent over something, then waved them forward. 'Hoof prints,' he breathed, pointing to some almost obliterated marks in the dust; they were heading deeper into the city. The spymaster turned to Ogre. 'Can you tell if this is the right way?'

Ogre looked around, although they could see little in the thick mist. It wasn't one she and Valdyr had summoned to conceal them; perhaps the fogbanks were natural here.

Finally Ogre conceded, 'I don't know. The Master never brought me here. But in the *Daemonicon*, he writes sometimes of gazing across Lake Patera, and of the sunset silhouetting the old Rondian watchtower on the *far* side of the lake in spring. That tells me he has a window looking west across the lake. We need to find the lake and work along the shore, seeking signs of activity.' Then he pulled out the dented lacquer mask Cadearvo had worn. It glowed in his hands and he pointed southwest. 'That way – but the closer we get, the less precise the reading becomes.'

Lyra was fascinated at the construct's thoughtful nature, such a stark contrast to his lumbering body and misshapen skull. He and Tarita were so very much in tune that it made her wonder if Hobokin and Glymahart might ever end well. Then she shook herself.

End well? It's likely going to end completely today, if we ever find his Master . . .

She glanced at Valdyr, suddenly struck by the fear that they might never have a chance to find out what was growing between them – that she'd never hold Rildan again . . . that she'd lose everything and everyone, for ever.

Stop it, she berated herself. *Be brave*.

Dirklan made them all wait while he tracked the hoof prints across the plaza. He came back to tell them they'd vanished down a street running west. 'We'll take the more southerly exit. The mist is hiding us, but we're likely to encounter some kind of perimeter watch soon and it'll almost certainly be possessed, so we must somehow bypass or eliminate them unseen. And there may be gnostic traps too, so I'm going to go ahead and seek them out.' He turned to Tarita. 'Lady Merozain, will you come as second scout? Ogre, stay with Valdyr and Lyra and follow us in five minutes.'

He and Tarita vanished into the mist, veils of illusion wrapping around them. A few moments later Gricoama padded in and nudged Valdyr with his muzzle, then took up guard over their tiny group.

Lyra, Valdyr and Ogre huddled in silence on the steps of a building with a cracked marble façade: a courthouse perhaps, or an imperocrat's administrative headquarters. At last Tarita returned and laying a hand on Ogre's shoulder, announced, 'The plaza's clear, as is the first part of the southern path. Wait three minutes, then Ogre will lead you on.'

In the Fey Tales, Lyra thought, *heroes journeyed together for months. They became like brothers and sisters. But we're going to have learn to trust each other despite still being strangers.* She looked at Valdyr and smiled cautiously. *At least you're not a stranger to me.*

He took her hand and they silently communed, trying to ignore Ogre watching them with big, sad eyes. A minute or two passed, then he muttered, 'We must go.'

Tarita flitted through the misty streets, reflecting that of their group, only she could match Dirklan's stealth. The queen moved like a court lady, while Ogre and Valdyr were just too big for sneaking around. *Leave it to 'Lady Merozain'*, she thought, following the old Volsai's footprints as the fog stirred and broken pillars and statues loomed eerily into view. It was easy to imagine eyes watching her from the gloomy shadows.

Then she heard a rattle of stones from the northern approach to the crossroads she was about to enter and sank behind a low wall an instant before a dark shape detached from the fog: a rider on a black horned horse, a khurne of Rondian myth. It had natural eyes, she noticed, so it wasn't possessed.

She wondered about that: perhaps these daemons refused to bear each other? She was struck by something she'd not considered before: despite their shared intellects, the possessed men she'd fought had never fought as a *team*: they passed information and took orders from their masters, but although they might share sensations, they remained essentially selfish. *They're not really one intellect at all: they're yoked together – and I bet they hate it.* Given that, an independent but subservient mount made perfect sense.

She moved her attention to the rider, who had a goat's head with two curling, bone-coloured horns, a hunched torso and backward-jointed legs, shaggy below the waist. It slid from the khurne's back and started sniffing the dust, emitting a low braying sound, then glancing left and right.

It's spotted traces of Dirklan's passing – and the others will be here in a few minutes. If it doesn't move on, I'll have to do something . . . She weighed her choices and smiled. *Ai, that might work . . .*

The goat-man and his mount began to track Dirklan's faint footprints in the dust, and she ghosted along in their wake. Mistress Alhana had prepared her meticulously for stealth missions: her eyes moved constantly, assessing every footfall, until she ducked behind a low wall barely thirty feet from her prey.

She opened her senses to the sound of the daemonic host: the vile whispering, snarling murmur in the aether came off the possessed construct in waves. Tuning into it with clairvoyance and mysticism, she concentrated on the feel of it until she was satisfied she could recreate it herself.

The possessed goat-man moved on and she rose carefully, spotting Dirklan behind a nearby pillar. His eyes met hers as he drew a stiletto.

If he sees Dirklan, all his kin will know . . .

She gestured for Dirklan to go still, then conjured illusory black eyes and created an echo of the daemon's voice in her mind, before casting a veil over her deeper self. Then she rose and said, <*You, hold.*>

The goat-man spun, face perplexed, and she felt his abrasive, churning intellect scrape over hers – and meet the daemonic mental mask she'd built, maintained with an Ascendant's strength. He brushed her mind and withdrew – and there was no change in his visage.

'See, a possible intruder,' he growled hungrily, indicating the footsteps in the dust.

She feigned the same animal hunger. 'Show me.' She moved closer, with the total certainty of one who knows the other being is the same as them and no threat.

It worked: the goat-man stepped aside and showed her Setallius' boot-prints. *What the spymaster's making of this I can't guess,* she thought as she made a show of examining the tracks, then met the daemon's gaze . . .

He had no defences raised, so with a sly burst of mesmeric-gnosis, she wrapped his mind in coils and fed him a lie of being alone in the city. The goat-man succumbed silently as she locked kinesis around him, then conjured Air- and Earth-gnosis, letting the swirling rock dust envelope him, calcifying even as she knifed a Chain-rune into his psyche, instantly shutting down his gnosis. Within a few seconds, he was just a crude statue of a misshapen goat-man, locked inside stone and powerless to move, while an illusion looped ceaselessly through his mind, for that was still linked to the daemon Abraxas and his vast interlocked awareness. By the time her illusion dissipated, the goat-man would have suffocated and died.

She stood and turning to face the shadows, collapsed the illusions she'd wrapped herself in. As the black eyes and subsonic litany of malice vanished, she called to Dirklan in a low voice, 'You can come out now.'

The one-eyed spymaster slipped from behind his pillar. 'You almost had me believing you'd been taken,' the Volsai said, his voice a mix of awe and uncertainty.

She pulled out her argenstael dagger and placed it to her cheek. 'Just illusion.'

'Impressive. You might have shared that little trick with us before.'

'I only just thought of it,' she admitted.

Dirklan gave a low whistle of appreciation. 'Then you really are damned good. Would you like a job?'

'After this, I'm going somewhere it doesn't rain where I can walk around naked and never again feel the cold.'

'Then perhaps I'm the one who should be asking you for a job,' he laughed, then he gestured west. 'That way's a dead end – I was just coming back when I saw that creature. Let's try another.'

They tethered the khurne, aware it would die if they never returned, but not wanting to let it wander. Leaving a mark in the dust for Ogre at the crossroads, they turned south, where they found yet more remains of ancient statues, caved-in temples and mausoleums and the stumps of pillars jutting into the sky. *All empires come to this*, the ancient city seemed to whisper.

'I grew up in Coraine, where it's often misty,' Dirklan commented. 'My sister and I called fog "The Nothing". When it swallowed up the ground around our house, we imagined it was eating up the world.'

'Cheery,' Tarita replied. 'No wonder you turned out a Volsai.'

Within five minutes they were scrambling through a gap between two immense palaces subsiding into rubble, their leaning towers like the broken ribs of a stone giant, towards the shore of the lake. They could see no horizon, just a few feet of black water lapping coldly at their toes and extending away into the murk.

As they waited for Ogre's group, Tarita examined the shoreline, although there was little to see beyond a tumble-down mess shrouded in Dirklan's Nothing. The air remained still and silent, barely lit by the pallid sun floating above the mist.

A few minutes later, Gricoama formed out of the mist, Lyra, Valdyr and Ogre behind him. When they gathered round, Dirklan reported what they'd found. 'This is a bay on Lake Patera: we can go due west and we'll likely hit the northern point of the cove, or we can follow the coastline south. There's no sign of life so far, apart from a scout Tarita dealt with.' He looked at Lyra and Valdyr. 'Can either of you reach Jehana?'

Lyra closed her eyes for a moment, then said, 'No, I can't sense her – and the dwyma is weak here. There's so little life . . .' She turned to Valdyr and he faced her. They both closed their eyes and linked hands.

Tarita groaned inwardly. *They could be gone for hours* . . . She turned to Ogre. 'What about you, Big Man?'

Ogre pulled the crumpled Cadearvo mask out again. 'I don't like using it, not so close,' he murmured, but he stroked the lacquered copper, listening for the harmonics of the gnostic link built into it. 'Nothing,' he muttered. 'I can't fix on a direction now . . . but maybe . . .'

Before Tarita could stop him, he placed the mask against his face – and the metal gripped his skin—

Ogre acted without thought, on impulse. When the lacquered copper tingled and then adhered to his skin, a wall of sound struck him, the hate-babble of a daemon, and a tangle of imagery overwhelmed him, some hideous but most prosaic, just visions from other eyes – and none of them reacted to his presence.

That calmed him, although he was aware he was breathing hard. Tarita had seized his hand and was speaking to him, but the words washed past him – he raised a finger to still her, then listened with all his being, feeling the way, trying to sense distance and direction . . .

There . . .

He raised a hand and pointed, though he was too caught up in the link to know which way he was indicating. He heard gasps of triumph from his companions and felt Tarita's small fingers squeeze his hand.

Then he heard a voice – his Master's voice, declaiming as if to an audience, '– *never been a valid reason not to push the boundaries of knowledge. Only I have truly seen this truth. So called "great minds" like Meiros and Baramitius were hamstrung by their own morality – a form of cowardice, in my view. But on this day – the Last Day – their lack of vision will be made clear . . .'*

Ogre pulled the mask from his face, the copper releasing his skin reluctantly, and blinked in the dim light. That loathed rasp faded from his senses, but he shuddered at the intense memories, wondering to whom the Master spoke.

At times he would lecture empty rooms, Ogre remembered, *debating with people who weren't there. Is he doing that again?*

'This way,' he rumbled, looking along his still extended arm. It was pointing southeast.

'Well done, Ogre,' Dirklan said.

When Tarita breathed, 'You're the *best* –' he felt himself go scarlet.

Then Valdyr and Lyra stirred and they all turned to see what they had learned . . .

To Lyra's inner eye, she and Valdyr were floating above the city. There was no fog, so she could see the full expanse of the shattered ruins, like the bones of murdered giants, scattered beside a still, dark lake. It was a chilling vista, but she took comfort from Valdyr's presence and the feeling that the whole weight of their world wasn't just on her shoulders. Together they focused on the dwyma, but with no flora or fauna and even the soil lifeless for many feet, the dwyma was all but smothered by the poisonous miasma.

When the magi destroyed this place, they were beyond thorough.

But water and light were two of the building blocks of life and not even the ancient magi could extinguish that spark for ever. The threads were tenuous, but present enough for them to tap into a current of deeper energy. At last they realised that one knot of dwyma wasn't weak at all, just *different*. Focusing on it, they plunged in – and recoiled immediately, appalled by an overwhelming sense of wrongness. To Lyra it felt almost familiar: like her Winter Tree after Ostevan poisoned it. And there was a groaning female voice . . .

They opened their eyes. 'She's that way,' Lyra said, raising an arm – and saw that Ogre also had an arm extended. His pointed southeast; hers pointed west.

'But Naxius is that way,' Tarita insisted, indicating the direction Ogre pointed.

'I heard the Master,' Ogre whispered. '*He said the Last Day is today.*'

They all fell silent, staring at each other.

'West or south?' Dirklan mused. 'Together or separate? And why are they not together?'

They all floundered, unable to unpick the tangle.

Then Valdyr spoke up. 'A dwyma place isn't safe for magi,' he said, 'and all the wrongness comes from there.' He looked at Gricoama, who growled softly and nodded his big head. 'I don't think Lyra and I can help you against Naxius; nor can you help us.'

Dirklan set his jaw. 'Then we must separate, and Kore grant we're doing the right thing.' Abruptly he pulled Lyra close, hugging her tightly. 'Do what's needed, Daughter, and come back.'

'You too, Father,' she murmured, trying to hold back her tears. 'You too.'

Tarita and Ogre shared a surprised glance and Lyra belatedly realised that they'd broken their unspoken agreement to conceal their true relationship. She was further mortified to see Valdyr colour, then look away awkwardly. 'Sorry, I was going to say . . .' she mumbled apologetically.

'Anything else I should know?' he asked caustically.

She shook her head, then turned to Tarita and Ogre and said, 'Please, be safe.'

'Safe is dull,' Tarita told her. 'Let's just be victorious.' Ogre growled in agreement.

Dirklan shook Valdyr's hand, his one eye skewering the Mollach prince like a lance. 'She's in your hands,' he told her, his voice somewhere between plea and threat. Then abruptly he turned away and led Tarita and Ogre into the mist.

She turned to Valdyr – and Gricoama, watching her with ancient, wise eyes. 'I did mean to say,' she began, 'but . . .'

'It doesn't matter,' he said, with some restraint. 'But no more secrets, please.'

She impulsively stood on tiptoe and kissed his cheek. 'I'm sorry, it's a secret we conceal from almost everyone, because he's not meant to be my father. It weakens my legitimacy for the throne, and – well, it's a long story.' She pointed to the westward shore. 'Are you ready?'

'As I ever will be.' He hesitated, then asked, 'Do you think he approves of me?'

Her heart lifted. 'I think so,' she told him, smiling despite the gravity of the moment. 'But it's my opinion that matters, not his. And it's something for tomorrow, not today.'

He straightened. 'Then let's make sure that there is a tomorrow.'

32

You'll All Fall With Me

Shadow Lives

Emperor Sertain reigned for centuries and outlived four sons. The third, utterly overcome with hatred for his apparently immortal father, rebelled against his future as a living footstool. He gathered followers and attempted a palace coup and when that failed, he burned down his home with his entire family – and himself – within. Such is the agony of life in another's shadow. The closer you approach the pinnacle, the more you yearn for it, until the one thing you can't have is the only thing you desire.

THE BLACK HISTORIES, 776

Paldermark Forest, south of Pallas, Rondelmar
Martrois 936

Birds chirruped in the pines, low cloud swirled on the stiff breeze and everywhere ice and snow melted, drip by drip. The forest path was thick with pine needles and slushy from the melt; an eerie place, not least because it was here that Brylion Fasterius' legions had been buried by Lyra's blizzard. There were still a multitude of bodies being slowly uncovered by the thaw, many so uncorrupted they looked newly dead.

Oryn Levis rode with Endus Rykjard behind him, their steeds picking their way through the woods nervously. Rykjard was humming to himself, but Oryn was almost oblivious, caught up in an unfamiliar mental struggle as he wrestled with doubts he'd never felt before.

The military life had always been his home: do your duty, don't question your officers: that had been drilled into him from an early age, removing all the difficulties of choice. Everything made sense if you just followed orders.

I'm a good soldier. I've risen because of that. People know they can trust me.

While the Corani were undivided, that had been enough, but when Lyra became empress, he'd found himself conflicted: why couldn't she have just retreated to the nursery like any other goodwife? It was a man's place to lead and a woman's to support him.

She drove Solon to this . . .

But Lyra's culpability didn't absolve Solon of his. The man Oryn had grown up with and fought alongside had been noble, courageous and magnanimous. That man would *never* have broken the neck of a helpless girl, or put Cordan through that hideous ordeal, or made a woman his chattel. He would never have plotted the invasion of the Holy City or locked up good men for speaking truths.

This is not the Solon I love.

And now he'd been sent here in some convoluted game of Solon and Roland's devising.

They don't trust Rolven Sulpeter, so they've sent me to take over his legions – but perhaps they don't trust me either, because they've sent Endus Rykjard with me. We've both been separated from our own legions. Even a blind man could see that Roland de Farenbrette wanted Oryn's job. *And some of our escort are Roland's new Volsai . . .*

He straightened in the saddle as they topped the rise and surveyed the camp below, hundreds of tents erected in a field at the edge of the trees. This was the army Rolven Sulpeter had brought north, sheltering in Paldermark Forest, lest Lyra unleash winter on them.

But Lyra wouldn't do that. Oryn recalled how shaken she'd been that night – the very night she'd first taken Solon to bed, in fact.

Right now in Pallas, Solon was overseeing assizes against officers accused of treachery – accusations that were anonymous and possibly – *probably*, he had to admit – groundless, levelled at truth-speakers who'd dared to point out facts Solon didn't like.

'It isn't right,' Oryn mumbled.

'What was that, Milord?'

Oryn jumped, forgetful that he wasn't alone. 'Rykjard! Sorry, I was miles away.'

The Hollenian mercenary captain nudged his horse closer and they both dropped their voices to exclude their escort, waiting a dozen yards away.

'An auros for your thoughts, Milord?' Rykjard murmured as they reined in and let their horses stand. 'Or perhaps a "lira"?'

Oryn grunted mirthlessly. 'You overpay for my paltry musings.'

They shared a tentative smile, then Rykjard said, 'It's a bad business, this marching against the Holy City.'

'Empress Lyra raided churches all over the empire,' Oryn replied.

'So she did, but folk liked her anyway. She didn't lop off heads or arrest people on the say-so of snitches.'

This coincided uncomfortably with Oryn's thoughts. *Don't think about it*, his instincts warned. *Just keep your head down and do as you're told.*

'An' I don't like going up against a man like Lann Wilfort, neither,' Rykjard went on. 'He and I fought in the Third Crusade together, in Javon. Got our arses handed to us by a queen who everyone underestimated, as it happens. We were lucky to get out alive.'

'Wilfort has sided with Milord Takwyth's enemies.'

'Oh, I expect he's just following orders too,' Rykjard drawled. 'Only Lann's orders come from the anointed Voice of Kore himself.' He shrugged. 'Anyways, soon as this is done, I'm taking my earnings and marching my lads back north. Folks I'm not fond of have taken up residency on the Hollenian throne and I'm no longer convinced Lord Takwyth will deliver on his promises to me of rank here in Pallas.'

'Solon doesn't have the coin to pay you,' Oryn blurted. 'Nor can he afford to lose your men.'

Suddenly, the mercenary wasn't looking so relaxed. 'What do you mean, "doesn't have the coin"?' he demanded. 'He's just grabbed the fucking Treasury, hasn't he?'

'Which Dubrayle had already emptied,' Oryn confessed, knowing he shouldn't be divulging such things, but needing someone to share his fears with.

The mercenary commander fell silent, then laughed humourlessly. 'Well, that clears up my motivations.'

Have I just betrayed my lord? Oryn wondered miserably.

After a few more minutes of sideways thoughts and rising fears, they touched heels to flanks and trotted down the slope to take command, their escorts jangling behind them.

The spot between Oryn's shoulder blades began to itch . . . and it wouldn't stop.

The Bastion, Pallas

Solon woke and rolled over to find his bed empty. He heard Brunelda groaning in the garderobe, the pervasive stink of vomit wafting into the chamber: morning sickness again, thanks to his child growing inside her.

Torn between pride and frustration, he quelled the lustful urges that had built while he slept and swung from the bed. He pulled on a robe, jerked open the curtains with a gesture and peered through the barred windows across the river to the Celestium. The dome was gleaming in the morning sun.

By nightfall, it'll be mine.

It had been a week since his masterstroke at Finostarre and he'd already broken the dissidents in the docklands. At night he ploughed Brunelda senseless in Lyra's bed, though the illusion of screwing her as Lyra was wearing thin. Since he'd let her regrow her hair, a fine dark brown down now covered her scalp. It didn't matter, because he had no intention of parading her in public again.

If only she were the real Lyra . . . He was haunted by the dread that he could wake tomorrow to find his city locked in ice, or worse, but it hadn't happened yet.

Where is she?

The question was unanswerable, and today he could afford no doubts. So he went inside, where a basin of hot scented water waited to wash away the odours of the night. A servant shaved him before he put on his harness in readiness for the day to come, then strode in his martial glory through the palace.

'What news overnight?' he asked Roland de Farenbrette and Rolven Sulpeter, who fell into step with him.

'Levis and Rykjard have taken command in the Paldermark,' Sulpeter reported. 'They'll march north and should reach the Celestium by nightfall.' His voice betrayed his uncertainty at having his forces given to other men, but Solon was perfectly content to let him squirm.

'What about the assizes?'

Roland nodded in satisfaction. 'Seventeen centurions and junior officers, three battle-magi and twenty-eight public officials have been charged. All were overheard voicing complaints.'

'A complaint isn't treason,' Sulpeter put in.

'In times like these, the slightest grievance is treason,' Roland growled. 'Rankers hear officers gripin', it turns mutinous.' He lowered his voice and added, 'I've separated the two Hollenian legions, in case they cut up nasty when they hear their boss's down. I've put the legions barracked beside 'em on alert.'

When you couldn't afford to pay mercenaries, you made sure their commander wasn't around to wave his contract in your face – that was standard practice. Lord Sulpeter didn't look easy with it, but he said nothing.

Too old, Solon thought again, *too set in his 'honourable' ways. This is a dog-fight, not a joust.* 'Does Oryn know?' he asked.

Roland shook his head. 'He'll be able to plead ignorance if he needs to,' he sniffed scornfully. He leaned in and murmured, 'I'm looking forward to Rykjard's Noorie wives. Never had darkie purse before.'

You're an animal, Solon thought, as he slapped his friend on the shoulder. *But I can rely on you.*

They strode out into the lobby, where Solon took the bows of servants and soldiers passing on their various duties, mounted up and headed for the barracks, their escort closing in around them.

'What about the city, Blacksmith?' Solon asked.

'It's quiet,' Roland replied. 'We raided a few houses, broke some jaws. They know there's a real ruler now.'

'And Frankel?'

'Still in hiding, the prick – and still leaving leaflets – handwritten and badly copied, because we've smashed all the printing blocks.'

They'd sent men into the mercantile quarters of Gravenhurst and Nordale to wreck every woodcut printer they could find. They'd all sworn they'd never printed anything seditious, that they were being ruined – and that might be the case, but Solon was happy that the usual broadsheets were no longer circulating around Pallas.

I'll produce all future news, he thought suddenly. *People will believe whatever I tell them.* Cheered by that moment of inspiration, he set his horse to a fast trot, eager for the day's work to begin.

Wurther, you old hog, I'm coming for you next.

The Celestium, Pallas

'We should just have left,' Basia told Exilium. 'Now we're penned in the least defendable bolthole in Pallas.'

'This is the heart of our faith,' Exilium replied stolidly. 'Kore Himself will protect us.'

'He didn't rukking well protect anyone when Ostevan made himself Pontifex just a few months ago.'

'Ostevan's dead,' Exilium told her in an unassailable voice. 'Kore is patient.'

They strode through the doors to the Great Dome to find the great and good, those of the Great Houses who had sided with Lyra to the end, already there. They were a dwindling number. Across the river, Solon Takwyth had installed Rolven Sulpeter, Roland de Farenbrette and Oryn Levis as his new council and issued lists of proscribed persons: those for whom a reward was offered, dead or alive, including everyone here.

They're frightened, and rightly so, Basia thought grimly. Dangling bodies and severed heads now decorated the Place d'Accord and the Pallas Mob had melted into the woodwork. Wurther offered up public prayers for peace every day, clinging to the sovereignty of the Church, but the Holy City was surrounded.

It's only for fear of alienating some of his key supporters that Takwyth's not assailed us yet. That's not going to last . . .

Her primary fear was that Wurther would cut a deal. There was no news of Lyra's mission, which was probably the only thing staying Wurther's decision. The wily old hog never committed to anything rashly.

As Basia and Exilium entered the Grand Prelate's hall, all eyes turned towards them, anxious for information. A hundred mage-nobles representing just forty or so Houses remained loyal. The room stank of desperation.

'What news?' someone demanded, but Basia ignored him; they didn't need to be told what had happened, for the aether had been humming with rumours since the victory-cum-defeat at Finostarre.

A young clergymen bowed unctuously and led her through the press of worried faces. *The queen is in Takwyth's hands*, everyone was saying. Basia kept denying it, but she couldn't say anything else. Talk of the Last Days was everywhere.

And they don't know the half of it, Basia thought grimly.

They found Dominius huddled on a throne in deep discussion with Calan Dubrayle and the grizzled Kirkegarde Grandmaster Lann Wilfort. Wurther saw her and his face tightened. 'What news, Mistress Volsai?' he asked stiffly.

He blames me for losing Nita – perhaps he's right. 'Takky's still pretending he has the real queen. We're still besieged, more estates are being seized and the latest proscription lists include everyone outside this room. I'd say someone's spying, reporting names.' She bit her lip then, and added, 'And there are rumours that they've captured Ari Frankel.'

'Good riddance,' Wurther rumbled.

'Is his head on a spike yet?' Calan Dubrayle asked. 'Unless you've seen it, don't believe it.' Basia rather fancied that Dubrayle had enjoyed Frankel's upsetting of the natural order – or at least saw opportunity in it.

'How are the people reacting?' Lann Wilfort asked. The Kirkegarde grandmaster was grim-faced, but he remained stalwart.

'After Takwyth took his Coraini legion into Tockburn and killed or injured hundreds of people, they're saying "things just got out of hand"

and "perhaps this is for the best",' Basia replied. She didn't like Frankel's ideas all that much herself, but she'd hoped for popular support to help defeat Takwyth. That was evaporating in the face of his unexpected brutality.

'What of your knights?' Wilfort asked Exilium, then asked, 'Do the knights of Misencourt still even exist?'

'Another two deserted last night,' Exilium confessed. They all knew that left just a dozen men. 'But those who remain are steadfast,' he added.

We'll see, Basia reflected. *The poor mutt's really having his eyes opened the hard way.*

They all fell silent, cogitating, then Wurther turned to Basia again. 'You see the situation we're in: it's been a week now and there's no word of Lyra or Setallius. My prelates in Argundy and the rest of the empire are carving out their own fiefdoms. The Church is fragmenting while I'm pinned here. Takwyth's talking about a war to reunite the empire – such a conflict will bring Yuros to her knees, but he doesn't care.'

'Dominius is right, for once,' Dubrayle put in. 'For my part, Takwyth has left my new Bank of Rondelmar intact – in fact, he's backed the new coin as leverage over Jean Benoit and the Merchants' Guild.' He smiled wryly. 'Probably because he doesn't have any money.'

'Because you've got it,' Basia replied tersely. 'But what are you doing with it?'

'I've got feelers out, but these things take time.'

'We don't have time,' she snapped, but the Treasurer just shrugged dismissively.

They fell silent again until Wilfort said, 'Grand Prelate, the Kirkegarde will remain loyal, to the death if needed. Their faith is strong. But will you sacrifice them, if push comes to shove?'

Wurther hung his head. They all knew the odds were insurmountable and the Celestium itself was indefensible. 'I pray it won't come to that, even if I must form a court in exile,' he rumbled morosely.

'Only until Lyra returns,' Basia said, and Exilium nodded encouragingly, even if no one else did.

'For my part, I'm under a death warrant,' Dubrayle put in. 'Takwyth's already appointed a new Treasurer – Sulpeter, if you please – the man's a dilettante. But I suppose I should pack my bags.'

'The sooner the better,' Wurther exclaimed, but then he smiled glumly. 'I'll miss you, you slimy prick.'

'And I you, you glutinous swine.'

The two antagonists shared an odd look, then turned aside as if embarrassed.

'Then it's settled?' Basia asked, as her spirits shrivelled. 'We must all leave?'

Wurther made a gloomy, apologetic gesture. 'I can't shelter little Prince Rildan and hope to keep my Church – and in truth, I may well have to escape here myself. Let me loan you a windship – unless you'd prefer to use winged constructs, or leave on foot?'

'A windship wouldn't get a mile,' Basia noted. 'If we take flying beasts, we'll still have to fight our way out, but at least no one else need risk themselves. We'll leave tonight, if that's your will.' It was an hour before dusk.

'It's for the best,' Wurther rumbled. 'I'm sorry.'

They all hung their heads, until Basia asked, 'What of Coramore?' In the wake of Cordan's near-execution, the girl had only left her room to commune with the Winter Tree.

Wurther steepled his fingers. 'Crudely put, she's one of the best bargaining assets I have. She'll remain here, under my protection.'

Until you can get a price for her, Basia thought sourly. 'May I visit her before we go?'

Wurther looked at her doubtfully. 'To what end?'

'Because she's my friend,' Basia snapped. 'Lyra and I risked our lives to recover her.'

The Grand Prelate's eyes narrowed, but he could think of no polite excuse and he still appeared to want to appear gracious, which was wise of him – but then, he must suspect, and rightly, that she had Volsai inside his clergy.

'Of course, by all means say your farewells,' he said, with a show of benevolence.

Basia and Exilium left the other three to lay their plans. She'd been afraid Wurther might seek to detain them, but Wurther respected the Volsai enough to do no more than speed her on her way.

'Gather your remaining knights and assemble them in the Chamber of the Holy Script behind the main dome,' she told Exilium. 'Call it a prayer meeting or something, but make sure they're ready to travel – and to fight. There's something I need to do before I join you.'

The Estellan looked curious, but there wasn't time for explanations. She sent him off, then clipped along to the suite where Coramore was kept. The guards outside her doors were wary, but after consulting with a mage-priest, she was allowed inside.

The Sacrecour princess was sitting beside a heavily barred window, staring out across the river to the Bastion silhouetted against the northern sky. Her face was pale, her red-gold hair matted and her eyes red, but she managed a wan smile when Basia appeared.

'Is there news?' Coramore asked, as she always did. 'Will they free him?'

Basia looked hard at the mage-nun who was the girl's constant companion until the sister rose stiffly and went into the next room. Then Basia hugged the princess hard. She'd never felt maternal in her life, but increasingly, she wanted to keep the girl safe. 'Coramore, are you ready?' she said quietly, 'It's got to be tonight. Wurther's going to cave to Takwyth's demands and he's told Exilium and me to leave.'

'Tonight?' the princess squeaked.

'Aye. Are you ready for that?'

'I . . . I think so.'

'You have to be, dear.' Basia gripped the girl's hands, and added, 'Be ready at dusk.'

She embraced the girl again, then stood and left, pausing at the door and looking meaningfully at the nun waiting outside, a pallid woman with a square, hard face. 'Sister Lanyr, yes? Look after her.'

The nun gave her a narrow-eyed look, but said merely, 'Of course.'

Basia slipped out the door and hurried away. There was a lot to be done.

The Bastion, Pallas

Solon was laying down the law with his legion commanders ahead of the following day's action when a messenger sidled in and handed Roland de Farenbrette a snatch of parchment. The Blacksmith read, then gestured to Solon.

He clapped Rolven Sulpeter on the shoulder. 'Take over here, Milord,' he said grandly, then drew Roland aside and read the note. *The church rats are growing wings*, was all it said. 'What does it mean?'

'It means that Wurther's given his "guests" an ultimatum: get out, before he's forced to arrest them.'

'Then he's about to capitulate?'

'Aye,' Roland said, with a satisfied glower. 'Not like him not to just cash them all in, but perhaps the old hog's turned sentimental.'

Solon decided it was a bet both ways by the Grand Prelate, which annoyed him, but Wurther had supported him in his bid to force Lyra into marriage and he was prepared to be magnanimous – in victory.

'They'll go tonight,' he reasoned. 'Strengthen the perimeter, but delay the assault until they move,' he told Roland. 'We might get everything we want without having to shed blood after all.'

Roland's face creased in disappointment.

'I only meant in terms of the common clergy,' Solon chuckled. 'We're still going to storm the Celestium, my friend. I don't just want de Sirou and her guttersnipes. I want Wurther, Dubrayle, Wilfort . . . the whole damn lot of them. There will be blood, I promise you. Let's ready the men; I'll take charge personally.'

Roland looked askance. 'Should you risk yourself, Milord?'

'Don't be such a mother hen, Rollo,' Solon told him. 'A leader is not just a figurehead. I lead from the front, and as Emperor-elect, I will lead our march into the Celestium – the symbolism of that moment will define my rule.'

He turned, called 'Carry on–' to Sulpeter, then he and the Blacksmith hurried to the horses.

Tonight, I'll take that Basia de Sirou and break her. She'll tell me where Lyra's gone and I'll end that threat too. Either she marries me, or she dies. He contemplated that, then shrugged. *Brunelda might just end up being Lyra for the rest of her life.*

The Celestium, Pallas

Fear, that ever-present beast, was gnawing at Coramore's stomach as she rolled over in the small bed and sat up. The chamber was austere, meant for nuns, not princesses. She'd glimpsed the prelates' suites: they had been real luxury. She trusted Dominius Wurther about as far as she could push him, but it was better than being in Takwyth's hands.

Dusk, she reminded herself. *Basia's coming at dusk . . .*

Then Sister Lanyr entered, holding a piece of parchment that she thrust into Coramore's hands. 'Dress, Highness,' the nun said urgently. 'We have to leave, now.'

The note was from Basia . . .

Coramore caught her breath, staring up at the nun. 'But you . . .'

Lanyr's not a nun, she's a Volsai, she suddenly realised. She didn't look like a Volsai, but that was probably the point. Swallowing her questions, she stripped and dressed while Lanyr threw clothes into a bag.

Fat Wurther doesn't want us, and bloody-handed Solon is coming . . .

She wished there was something monumental she could do, something Lyra might have done, like freezing the city into a block of ice. Right now, killing a million people meant less to her than rescuing her brother. But she hadn't the skill or the power . . . in fact she had less than the merest novice mage. That helplessness nearly drove her to tears again.

Sister Lanyr gripped the bag and took her hand. 'Are you ready?' she asked, with calm assurance.

'I am,' Coramore pretended, gathering her courage.

Lanyr took her to the locked and warded door and used thin metal rods and the gnosis to open it. Outside, they found a maid slumped against the wall. Coramore sucked in her breath. 'Is she –?'

'One of Wurther's spies, pretending to be a servant,' Lanyr told her, adding drily, 'She'll live.'

They tiptoed past and descended several levels, traversed a dusty old corridor and emerged in a small chapel, where Exilium Excelsior was kneeling in prayer before an icon to the Sacred Heart. He rose when Coramore entered and bowed.

Lanyr caught her sleeve. 'Be safe,' she whispered.

'Is Lanyr your real name?' Coramore asked. 'Oh, I suppose I shouldn't ask.'

'No, you shouldn't,' the woman said tartly. She walked to the door and was gone.

'She'll maintain the illusion that you're still asleep in your suite,' Exilium told her, looking awkward at the thought of even such a small subterfuge. 'Come, please.'

He took her bag and led her through another wing of the maze-like building, then broke the wards on a locked door, revealing stairs going upwards. Exilium handed her the bag and when she'd put the strap over her shoulder, handed her a coin lit with a gnostic light. 'Upwards, Princess,' he told her, 'right to the top, force the hatch and wait on the roof.'

It was frightening to be left alone, but Coramore had managed before, so she took the coin and used it to light the way up the dusty, cobwebby spiral stair. She went round and round, losing count of the steps, until she finally reached the hatch Exilium had described. Pocketing the coin so that it wouldn't betray her, she emerged onto the moonlit open-roofed turret, which was some fifteen feet square. She stayed low, shivering as she muttered prayers and complaints. Princesses shouldn't have to go through such things.

But she'd had Abraxas crawling through her brain and that really had been Hel, so she decided she could endure it.

Wurther came to see them off. *Probably to make sure we leave*, Basia thought sourly.

'Thank you for your hospitality,' she said, with a touch of sarcasm.

The Grand Prelate winced. 'I do wish things had worked out

differently,' he claimed. 'I'd rather deal with your mistress than a bull-headed thug like Takwyth.'

'I'm sure,' Basia drawled. 'Women are so much easier to push around.'

She didn't give him time to retort and the doors slammed behind her: apparently Wurther didn't want to be seen waving them off.

She walked to Exilium's side and pecked his cheek for luck – and because it confused him horribly – then went to Vasingex. The wyvern was busy scolding the venators towering over her. 'Don't worry, girl,' she told the construct, 'we'll be flying in a moment, leaving these lumps behind.'

She swung into the saddle and strapped herself in as the knights did the same. She was pleased to see Exilium was still scarlet from her kiss. Then she gripped the saddle-horn as the wyvern leaped into the air, flapping gracelessly but climbing quickly. In moments they were level with the walls, then moving higher, the venators rising behind her. She circled, staying low, until all were aloft and Exilium sent a command through everyone's heads. They swung south –

– except for Basia, who sent Vasingex winging towards the old tower. She came in hard, stalled steeply and dropped onto the crenulations, and a moment later Princess Coramore was pulled onto the wyvern and settling onto the saddle behind her. She strapped in, just as they'd practised, then clung to her back as Basia touched her heels to Vasingex's flanks and a few seconds later they were airborne.

She heard angry shouts, but no blasts of gnosis or searing ballista shafts came at them. Exilium's men closed around her and in moments she was in the middle of the formation as they swung south.

'Cora, are you all right?' she called over her shoulder.

'Never better,' the princess chirruped, her face alive at the intrigue and danger.

Basia threw her an encouraging smile as they all rose on the stiff breeze.

Then Exilium barked, <*Beware – flyers–*>

Twenty winged shapes had appeared above and before them, blocking their flight path, and shrill cries resounded through the darkness. Basia didn't need to hear the war-cries to know who they faced; she'd

already recognised the Corani pegasi hurtling towards them with levelled lances. Solon Takwyth, resplendent in a crowned helm that glinted
in the moonlight, headed them on a griffon.

Velocity, elevation and the ideal weaponry: Takwyth had every advantage.

Exilium read it before she did, and shouted, 'Scatter!' aloud and
through the aether.

Coramore squealed in terror as Basia took Vasingex into a tight turn
and tore away from their attackers.

Dominius Wurther had returned to his office after seeing off his unwel-
come guests and was in the midst of ordering his evening meal while
reflecting that the fortunes of his long reign as Grand Prelate could be
read in the quality of the cooking. It was surely no illusion that everything had tasted better a decade ago, before the Third Crusade, when
the Sacrecours' grip on power had been unshakable, as had his.

*Emperor Constant was a moron and his mother was the bitch to end all bitches,
but we knew where we stood. All this bloody stress gives me acid reflux . . .*

He'd given express orders to be left alone – he didn't want to know
what happened when Basia de Sirou and her band tried to escape Takwyth's blockade – but inevitably the door crashed open.

'What the fu–' he began, as Lann Wilfort stormed in.

'Language, Grand Prelate,' the Kirkegarde grandmaster admonished
reflexively as the noise from outside – running feet, shouted orders and
frightened responses – flooded into the room behind him. 'The attack's
begun.'

Dominius' stomach lurched. He swilled the red wine – who knew if
it would be his last drop? – and stumbled to his feet. 'Is my windship
ready? Can we empty the strong-room? What about–?'

'No point flying; they'll just bring us down,' Wilfort answered. He
grabbed Wurther's arm. 'Dignity, Dom. This is the invasion of a sacred
place. The people will see that.'

'They'll see my head on a spike,' Dominius moaned.

But Wilfort was right: running was for thieves and pretenders. 'Very
well.' He raised his voice to his major domo, lurking outside. 'Connswa-
ter, my best robes!' he roared. 'Bring me the pontifical sceptre. I will not

be the worst dressed man in the room when that arsehole Takwyth arrives.'

The twelve Misencourt venators did precisely the right thing, veering away from suicidal head-on contact. Solon snarled under his breath as the knights shot away in all directions, but he kept his focus on the one who mattered: Basia de Sirou's wyvern, with *two* figures in the saddle . . .

<The Stick Insect is mine,> Solon told his riders. *<Kill the rest.>*

Instantly his guard fanned out, picking their targets, while Solon spurred his griffin after the wyvern, pouring additional strength into his beast to augment its speed. Griffins were unwieldy beasts, but they were aggressive and capable of frighteningly fast bursts; they'd always been his favourite beast in the jousts. He levelled his lance.

Speed, elevation and aim – the old jousting mantra.

His knights tore after their foes with the advantage of speed and elevation . . . but the Misencourt men evaded skilfully, most of them spiralling out of reach with only two losses from the initial contact, then both sides began circling for height. Solon's guardsmen shielded his flanks and he shot through the chaos unchallenged, his eyes set on the wyvern. Around him, his men collided again with Exilium's.

He glimpsed horrific impacts – lances impaling men and beast; two constructs colliding in mid-air; a Corani pegasus with broken wings plummeting – but the Misencourt venator was also falling in a dazed glide, the rider reeling. The air was streaked with vivid bursts of energy, flames and lightning, men and beasts howling in fury and agony, and a third of those aloft went spinning away.

But Solon was on Basia's tail, riding her slipstream as the wyvern weaved frantically. He could see Princess Coramore clinging to Basia's back and heard the girl's childish squeals as she saw who was pursuing her.

Then a warning flashed into his mind and he reacted instantly, making his griffin corkscrew left just as a lance grazed the shields around his right shoulder, jarring off in a burst of red sparks. A moment later a venator's bulbous head reared over him, its jaws opening wide enough to rip him from the saddle. He slammed a kinesis push upwards, causing the teeth to crunch shut on thin air, but for the next few seconds he and his griffin were spinning groundwards.

He caught a glimpse of the knight riding the venator: *Exilium Excelsior – who else?*

One of his men flashed in on the knight's flank, making Excelsior almost stall in the air, but somehow the bastard hauled his beast aside, leaned out and let the guard's pegasus impale itself on his lance. The Corani knight and beast fell into the shadows below, ripping away the weapon, but Excelsior had kicked his mount back into motion and was wrenching out a longsword, his moonlit face focused to the point of serenity.

Damned fanatic, Solon thought, his own battle-fever rising. Slamming his spurs into the griffin's flanks, he righted its flight and got his bearings. They were south of the gleaming Celestium over marshland, moonlight catching in the icy pools below. Duelling flyers swooped across the moon's face and more gnosis-fire flashed.

Two more of his men went down, caught in their saddle-straps while their flying beasts plummeted, but another Misencourt knight was dead in the saddle too; he could hear the man's mount bleating with loss. The fight remained in the balance, but his men still had the numeric advantage.

Solon stayed focused on Basia de Sirou's wyvern as she ducked and weaved with creditable grace and speed, coaxing the best from her beast. Every time he closed in, she somehow managed to wheel away, and his griffin was tiring – but so was her wyvern . . .

Abruptly, Basia flashed around and headed back towards the Celestium.

Wurther won't take you back, and anyway, you're too late: Rollo's got the lads moving in even now . . .

Then the rukking Estellan caught him up, so he had to haul his poor griffin about yet again to avoid getting taken in the back, sending him spiralling into an uneven hopping climb. Excelsior circled in front, between him and the fleeing Basia.

Fine. I want to go through you anyway . . .

But his two guards, who had been striving to catch up, finally arrived and streaked past him to close in on the Estellan, their lances aimed.

When the Estellan levelled his blade and shot forward to meet them, Solon could see his men would converge on a trajectory that would see them strike a good six seconds before he would.

But I may still get the killing blow, he thought with a fierce grin, and lowering his lance, he jabbed his spurs and all four beasts raced into the same airspace.

The Estellan's venator turned sluggishly to confront the first guard to reach them; the guard's lance plunged towards the mount, but the construct banked and the leading edge of the lizard's wing crunched into the guardsman, breaking his neck and ripping him from the back of his pegasus, while the venator took the winged horse's throat – a second before it took the second guard's lance in the chest. Excelsior's beast croaked out a despairing cry as it went plunging downwards.

The second guard flashed by, punching the air.

Solon was about to follow, to finish off the Estellan for good, when he caught a glimpse of something below and his heart thudded – so after blazing a command at his guardsman to finish Excelsior, he sent his griffon streaking after Basia and Coramore.

They're heading for the Winter Tree Garden ...

Lyra had once told him that old tree was the heart of the dwyma in the North – and now a golden radiance was emanating from the mound where the unnatural tree had grown, as if that mysterious power was coming to life.

Is Lyra there?

There was no way to know, but suddenly he was afraid of what might be unleashed, from ice to gales to lightning from above ... But what was clear was that it was Basia and Coramore's destination, which meant he needed to stop them.

He raked the griffin's flanks viciously and they dived, faster and faster, in the wake of the fleeing wyvern.

Exilium's venator plunged from the sky, limbs limp and heart still, and he went with it, still strapped in the saddle as the beast plummeted.

There was nothing he could do but tear himself loose from his straps but they'd tangled, he'd lost his blade in the impact and had run out of sky. Far above, Basia and Solon rocketed away from him.

I should've learned to joust . . . He'd always regarded the sport as lunacy, a symptom of noble inbreeding that was beneath a warrior of Kore. *Too late now* . . .

Then a sharp cry sounded behind him and he turned, his heart thumping, only now realising that the second flyer had pursued him down and was only seconds behind him.

He tried using kinesis to manipulate his dying mount's wings to somehow check their fall, but to no avail. A bare second before impact he rolled himself into a ball on the saddle and was shielding with all his strength when his mount smashed belly-first into the swamp, spraying freezing muddy water in all directions. Even shielded, the impact almost broke Exilium's spine. His tangled saddle-straps ripped and he spilled from his perch, his body numbed and barely responding.

Moments later a winged shape reared over him and landed, an armoured man dismounted and waded through the knee-deep muck towards him. Exilium was too dazed to react as a war-hammer rose against the moon, then slammed down and the darkness became complete.

'There, there—' Coramore kept shouting, right in Basia's ear, pointing at the glow of rose-gold light emanating from the mound within the Garden of Saint Eloy behind the Celestium. The burnt-out remains of the ancient heart of the dwyma were alight with pale golden foxfire.

Chancing a look over her shoulder, Basia saw a griffin streaking after her, and other pegasi converging on them. It was going to be a near thing – and what they could do if they got there, she had no idea.

Well, I guess it's as good a place as any to die.

Exilium was down too, his venator nowhere to be seen, which gave her a pang of regret for her idle fancy that one day she might mean as much to him as his faith. But regrets were for the grave; she had the living to worry about. She urged Vasingex on and once again, the wyvern responded with a fresh burst of speed, tearing over the rooftops of Fenreach and

Southside and into the Winter Tree garden. Her pursuers were just moments behind now and battering her shields with mage-bolts.

'Beside the mound,' Coramore called frantically, '*hurry –*'

They came in too fast: the wyvern's clawed feet carved deep ruts in the muddy grass as they skidded and almost rolled. The force was straining the saddle-straps almost to breaking point, but the moment they were still, Basia and Coramore ripped themselves clear and scrambled down. Vasingex reared over them protectively, flames licking his jaws in readiness.

One wall of the triangular garden was the back of the Celestium, another formed part of the outer fortifications and the third wall topped the bank of a canal leading from the Bruin River to Lac Corin. The guards on every wall were staring down at them and alarm bells were ringing within the Celestium – and in the sky, a knight on a griffin was plunging towards them.

'Help us –' she shrieked at the guards, '*help us –*'

But before anyone could respond, Takwyth's griffin had flashed over the walls, followed by two pegasi-riding palace guards, all swooping towards them.

Basia turned to the princess and shoved her, screaming, '*Cora, run –*'

They tore towards the mound, where the sapling Lyra had planted to replace the destroyed Winter Tree was outlined stark against the moon. The golden radiance they'd seen emanating from the cave was flickering fainter and Basia's heart sank.

It's fading, she realised. *That can't be good.*

One of the guardsmen was flying directly at them, just a foot above the earth. Coramore froze, but Basia pushed her aside and threw her dagger in one smooth, practised motion: the blade slammed into the neck of the pegasus, which shrieked and faltered, sinking just far enough for its hooves to catch on the grass. It ploughed into the ground and flipped, slamming its rider headfirst into the turf.

The sound of his neck snapping cracked through the night air.

One.

'Run, Cora,' she told the frightened girl behind her, '*run –*' but the girl just stood there, paralysed with fear.

Cursing, Basia turned at bay, shielding the princess as Solon and the other man landed, slipping from their saddles and thudding heavily toward her.

Vasingex snarled and hissed at them, flames licking his jaws.

Solon Takwyth was radiant: his scars were all but faded and he shone like a vision of pure chivalric might. His sword looked like it could cleave Urte in two. And Basia knew the other man too – Sir Del Briarson, with whom she'd sparred and even flirted. He looked pale, but resolved: there would be no mercy from him.

'Solon,' she pleaded nevertheless, 'please – this is a holy place –'

'Holy?' the Corani champion snorted. 'The Celestium may be, but this garden is a place of abomination and I'm going to destroy it and all the heretics who wield such powers.' He raised his blade. 'Will you die by the blade or at the end of a rope, woman?'

Basia kissed her thin blade and bade her life farewell. 'I'm not going to die at all.'

The broken woman against the greatest knight of his generation and his power far greater than hers could ever be? He snorted dismissively and closed in, Briarson moving to flank her.

Go down fighting – don't let him take you alive . . .

Coramore finally burst into motion, taking everyone by surprise as she went sprinting for the opening in the mound. Briarson tried to catch her with a kinesis leap, but Vasingex lunged, spouting fire an instant before his jaws snapped shut, clamping right over the knight's breastplate and lifting him into the air, teeth punching through the steel plate. Briarson was screaming, piercing cries growing more agonised as fire engulfed his body, and the wyvern's jaws crunched tighter.

But Solon had ignored his companion's plight, and was coming right at her. Basia blazed a mage-bolt at him, powerful enough to jar him backwards, then parried his overhead swing and diverted it, riposting with a low thrust that forced him to back up. She pivoted and raised her blade to guard, breathing sharply, slightly surprised to still be alive. Vasingex threw the broken Briarson away and started snarling at Solon, seeking an opening to lunge in.

The would-be emperor hesitated.

'What, no Rollo the Blacksmith to hide your old age?' Basia taunted him.

Solon grimaced and backed up another step . . . then he thrust out an arm at Vasingex and the air pulsed: a burst of mesmeric-gnosis that hammered into the construct's psyche, making made the beast reel . . . then collapse behind her.

Basia swallowed, then realised that Solon had drawn deeply to stun the wyvern and was now slightly dazed and reeling himself, his shields weak.

She hurled herself into the attack – and for a few heartbeats, she had him on the rack; her lighter blade went whipping around his face, administering swift thrusts and cuts, the steel sparking off his shields and rattling off his helm, then she opened him up and lunged, seeking to skewer his right eye-socket–

– but somehow the veteran warrior rallied, battering her blow aside, and the near-miss galvanised him. He straightened, roaring in defiance – and then he was on her, blasting a mage-bolt that lifted her off her feet and slamming an overhead blow into her guard.

Basia parried – *somehow* – and dared a riposte, which almost cost her sword arm. She blocked a flurry of muscular blows aimed at her chest and head, each one rocking her backwards until she couldn't hold her guard, couldn't protect herself . . .

She saw the gap open up in her defence as if time had stood still.

Solon saw it too.

His blade whipped across, brutally fast, slicing through her lower legs, just below the false knees, and in a flash of blue light they shattered. She went down, agony jarring up her thighs, and tried to whip her left arm around and surprise him with a falling thrust, but he battered it aside effortlessly, smashing the longsword from her hand, then planted a boot on her chest.

'Some protector,' he sneered, just like those jeering boys who'd mocked her crippled limbs when she'd finally emerged from the infirmary, the heartless bullyboys who riddled *decent* society. Takky was just that sort.

'You're just a pitiful half-woman,' he told her. 'You're not worthy of *my* blade . . . but the noose will do nicely.'

He bent and slammed his fist into her jaw and the world exploded in a burst of stars.

Coramore sped down the stairs, her last sight of Basia de Sirou facing the Knight-Commander. She knew how that would end. She knew how *everything* was going to end.

He's going to kill me, then Abraxas will eat me for ever.

She couldn't let that happen – but the impulse that had driven her here was giving her no clue about what she should do. The glowing amber encasing the stairs and chamber contained ghostly shadows that were pressing close. The fire-pit was dead and the roots poking through from above into the chamber were lifeless and charred – save for one, which contained a green shoot, hanging from which was a single drop of amber. She caught it on a finger and following her instinct, licked it and swallowed.

'Aradea.' She whispered the word like a prayer – and *something* heard, because the amber walls immediately began to glow and as the golden radiance grew in intensity, she felt a honeyed warmth blossom in her belly and spread, and the shape of a giant tree aglow with stars appeared in the walls.

Then she heard boots on the stairs and whirled to see a man in armour appear only a few yards away: Solon Takwyth, sword in hand, triumph in his eyes.

Descending into the golden glow of the underground chamber was far more frightening than facing a charging knight. Solon knew what he was dealing with when it came to warfare, but the dwyma was a mystery. There were shifting figures in the walls, and when the chamber opened up before him, he saw Coramore facing the wall, and the shape of a tree . . .

'Coramore,' he warned her, 'don't move.' He conjured a kinesis grip and went to unleash it –

– as Coramore faded into the amber glow – and was gone.

The gnostic energy fizzling through his fingers ebbed away and he stared at the unearthly wall as the human shapes within it slowly vanished. If he strained, he thought he could hear voices whispering . . . *daemon* voices, he was sure. He was scared to remain, like a child who'd stumbled upon something deadly.

He backed up, then turned and fled up the stairs, only regaining his composure when he emerged onto the grassy space. By now his men had caught up and three men were standing around Basia de Sirou, binding her gnosis in a Chain-rune. An animage was securing her wyvern.

Reports were hissing through the aether: his legions were inside the Celestium and had Wurther cornered, and Wilfort too. *Yes*, he thought, raising his head, *this is another great victory*. He straightened, enjoying the brief moment of glory, before turning his mind to the question of clemency.

A ruler must take care not to be overly merciful, Makelli had written. *A little can be a sign of strength, but too much will be seen as weakness. Err on the side of brutality in all things.*

Oryn Levis shuffled into the large chamber where Grand Prelate Wurther had been found. He was cornered in his study, but Oryn felt nothing but misery.

Dear Kore, I've led men into the Holy City to depose the Grand Prelate. Surely I'm damned . . .

Of course, he'd done the same at Lyra's behest, to depose Ostevan – but Ostevan had been a daemon-possessed cabalist, while Dominius was the true ruler of Kore's holy church. There was no comparison.

I wish I were a thousand miles away.

His battle-magi looked no happier. They were lined against the near wall, facing Wurther and Wilfort and a dozen Kirkegarde soldiers. The grandmaster had his sword drawn, his grim face simmering.

Someone, presumably Wilfort, had burned a groove across the wooden floor and the dozen Corani soldiers were arrayed on this side of it, facing the clergyman and his protectors on the other. Both sets of men bristled with loaded crossbows and they all looked fidgety enough to fire at the least motion.

But Wurther was slumped in his huge chair, pouring himself a goblet of what looked like Brician merlo. 'Ah, Lumpy,' he drawled as Oryn entered. He raised the golden goblet in an ironic toast, then set it aside. 'You're in on this crime too, eh?'

'Holiness,' Oryn said miserably, dreading a tirade.

'I hope that this monstrous act will destroy your master, and you with it,' Wurther commented coldly. 'All of Koredom will hear of this outrage.'

'You have harboured traitors,' Oryn mumbled. 'The Crown cannot tolerate—'

'Traitors?' Wurther snorted. 'Rivals, perhaps, although only in the paranoid space between your master's ears. But you know the truth of it, Lumpy: we were allies only weeks ago, before you betrayed your queen and changed sides.' He gestured offhandedly to the men lined up behind Oryn. 'You've sinned and blasphemed enough tonight. Call them off, before something truly regrettable happens.'

Oryn hung his head and studied the burned mark on the floor. 'What's this?'

'That's the line thou shall not cross,' Lann Wilfort growled.

Oryn looked at his men, who looked nervously back at him. He motioned them back and listened to the reports crackling through his head – Exilium Excelsior was down and taken, so too Basia de Sirou and most of the battle-magi who had remained loyal to Lyra. Only a few had escaped.

There was only one major name missing. 'Where's Calan Dubrayle?' he asked Wurther.

'He left hours ago,' Wurther rumbled. 'He always did have the instincts of a rat, as you'd suppose.'

'Where's the money?'

'What money?'

Oryn paused. As always, Wurther was almost impossible to read. Was he going to be ambiguous and ironic to the last? *Does he know that Dubrayle emptied the Treasury?* he wondered. *Should I reveal it? They were always enemies . . .*

He was still wavering when the door slammed open and Solon Tak-wyth stormed into the room, his face a mask of thwarted fury, as it always was these days. His sword was drawn and energy sizzled in his left hand.

Oryn took a step back, thankful to be able to abdicate responsibility, but anxious to avoid bloodshed. 'Solon—' he began.

'Shut your face, Lumpy,' Solon snarled, facing the Grand Prelate as the tension in the room, which had been ebbing, suddenly flared again. 'Where's fucking Dubrayle?' he demanded. 'Hand him over.'

'I don't have him, Solon,' Wurther said evenly.

'You lying pig,' Solon grated, looking down at the line, then belligerently stomping across it. Wilfort raised his sword, an old lion at bay, and the men behind him aimed their crossbows. Solon didn't appear to notice.

'I am the Voice of Kore and cannot lie,' Wurther said calmly.

'You're a corrupt old windbag and you lie with every breath.' Solon extended his sword towards Wilfort. 'Back off, Grandmaster. You're too old for a real fight.'

'Big talk, when you don't have de Farenbrette to hide behind,' Wilfort spat back.

'Kore's Balls, Solon,' Oryn breathed, eyeing the crossbows in full awareness that at this range a bolt could punch right through the thickest steel plate – and gnostic shields would fare no better. Thinking of his grandchildren, he pleaded, 'They're not our real enemies—'

Solon gave him a look of cold contempt. '*Everyone* is an enemy, Lumpy,' he murmured, before turning to face Wilfort and Wurther again. 'Grand Prelate, I'll ask you one more time: where is Calan Dubrayle?'

'Gone.'

'Where's Lyra?'

Wurther snorted complacently. 'Isn't she supposed to be in your bedchamber, Solon?'

Solon went to speak, then stopped, turning puce. Behind him, his own men fidgeted uncertainly. He swore under his breath, stamped a foot, then whirled and stormed out.

Oryn stared across the room at those deadly crossbow bolts, shaking with relief—

– until Solon burst back into the room, a crossbow in his hands that blazed with energy as he released it, sending the bolt searing through the air, slashing through half-lowered shields and crunching through Lann Wilfort's breastplate, exploding inside the casing and hurling the Grandmaster onto his back.

Crossbows flew on both sides, something punched Oryn in the chest before he could rekindle his shields, a blow that knocked the air from his lungs. He staggered, looked down in disbelief at the stick of feathered wood sticking from his left breast as the strength went from his legs, the ceiling tilted and the back of his helm smacked into the floor.

All around, men had dropped to the floor, dead or groaning. He saw Roland de Farenbrette striding into the room, roaring, 'Infamy, kill th–'

But the sound was fading until all Oryn could hear was his granddaughter's laughter . . . and then that too was gone.

Solon examined the dents and scratches on his armour and the blood seeping from his right shoulder where a bolt had grazed him. The chamber was filled with the dead and the dying, but more of his men were finishing off the last of the Celestial Guards.

An ashen-faced Dominius Wurther was staring at his fallen Grandmaster, his composure broken at last. 'For all that's holy, Solon,' he croaked.

'You don't fuck with me,' Solon told him. 'I thought you knew that.'

Dominius slowly raised his eyes from the bloodied corpses, and whispered, 'You're going straight to Hel.'

'There's no such place.' Solon gestured to Roland. 'Take him in an unmarked wagon. Put him in the dungeons of the Bastion and if he hasn't told you where Dubrayle is by dawn, he's dead.'

The Grand Prelate was too shocked to protest, even when the Blacksmith hauled him off.

Then Solon saw Oryn Levis lying on the floor, a single crossbow bolt jutting from his heart. His big, gentle face was contorted in shock, his eyes empty.

Oh, fuck . . . Oddly, his first reaction was relief that a difficult conversation had been avoided, but then came the regret: Lumpy wasn't made for times like this, but they'd been comrades for a long, long time.

But that was war: he'd lost many friends over the years.

He signalled to a waiting serjant. 'Oryn Levis was a Corani hero,' he said thickly. 'Take his body to the Bastion morgue. He'll receive his due as one of our best.' Then he turned his back on the carnage and walked out of that blood-spattered chamber, breathing hard.

If Wurther knew where Dubrayle was, he'd have said. The man's no hero. The crown was so close he could almost feel it on his brow – except that rukking Lyra had taken it with her. *I'll have a new one forged and I'll place the damned thing on my own head if I can't find a worthy priest. There's nothing and no one left to stop me . . .*

He headed for the door, his mind on the morning to come. *Wurther, de Sirou, Excelsior . . . I'll behead them all at dawn.* There'd be no trials, no more embarrassments like the Cordan incident. Brunelda wouldn't attend, the executions would be almost private. Lyra and Setallius were still out there, and so was Dubrayle. He had to act swiftly to consolidate all that had been won and deny them potential allies.

That decided, the familiar rush of adrenalin from surviving combat struck him, the relief and the triumph pumping blood through him, opening his pores and filling his lungs. Life was for the living, for the victor. He picked up his pace, waved Rollo to his side and together they strode through the vast entrance hall of the Celestium, where Corani soldiers cheered as he passed. He looked around and spied the Hollenian mercenary captain, Rykjard.

I did well to separate that man from his legions, he thought, eyes narrowing, *but without Dubrayle's treasure trove, I still can't pay him.*

'Capitano Rykjard,' he boomed, nevertheless. 'Well done, sir. Fine work.'

The mercenary captain flashed him a wry salute, then indicated the wooden crates his men were hauling past. 'The Grand Prelate's wine cellar,' he remarked cheerily. 'I'll have the best sent to you, Milord.'

Solon laughed, saluted in return and swept on, murmuring, 'Rollo, deal with the Hollenian tonight. Make it quiet. And make sure I get that rukking wine. Have one yourself. We both deserve it.'

'The spoils of victory,' Roland chuckled. 'A bottle of wine – and that wanker's Noorie wives . . .'

Solon snorted at his friend's unquenchable lust for life. 'A bottle and a whore . . . I think I'll do the same.' He clapped Rollo's shoulder and left him there, while he went out to take the acclaim of the troops.

33

The Last Night

Stalemate

There comes a point in the game of tabula when you are no longer playing to win but to not lose: to achieve gridlock and force a draw. This can be achieved, even when one side is vastly overmatched, by skilled deployment of your remaining pieces. But it's a risky ploy and defeat is only ever one misstep away.

EMPEROR SERTAIN, PALLAS 458

Rym, Rimoni
Martrois 936

Dirklan was scouting somewhere in the mist ahead while Tarita and Ogre huddled together in the lee of a huge broken pillar. Ogre was thoughtfully turning over the Cadearvo mask in his hands.

'Seeing that thing on your face scared me, Ogre,' Tarita admitted. 'It reminded me too much of Semakha – and of what you might have been if the Ordo Costruo hadn't rescued you.'

'I wish I could say that I would've been different,' he replied, 'but who knows?'

'I do,' she told him firmly. 'Some people succumb to temptations, but others rise above them. You're the only good thing that madman ever made, Ogre. Never think otherwise.'

He ducked his head humbly, but she saw his eyes lighten a fraction, which lifted her spirits too. At the Merozain monastery she'd been the black sheep, the rebel; she'd seldom seen fit to praise another. *I was an immature bitch, basically. Ogre, you make me a better person.*

Dirklan arrived with news of an entrance to Naxius' hidden lair. He led the way into the sunset, scrambling along the shoreline. Fog and darkness closed in on all sides.

Tarita listened for daemonic voices in the aether until she could make out at least one sentry ahead – she also sensed a heightened state of alertness and anticipation.

'They believe this is their time,' she murmured. 'We need to hurry.'

They topped a rise overlooking a walkway that had quite clearly been carved through the rubble. There was a ramp on the right leading into the lake; on the left was an archway opening into darkness.

'This is as close as I dared come,' Dirklan whispered. 'When the Rondian Empire controlled this region, the city was patrolled regularly and such earthworks would have been noticed.'

'The Master fears no one now,' Ogre put in softly.

Tarita squinted into the shadows beneath the arch and realised there was an ogre-construct there, standing guard. *Yes*, she thought, *this is it: Naxius' lair. But how do we get in without them knowing?*

They drew back to confer. 'Can you deceive this guard as you did the scout?' Dirklan asked her.

'I don't know,' Tarita admitted. 'I got close enough to look him in the eye and because I'd made mine look black, he was deceived. This one will see me coming – he might recognise me before I get close enough.'

'Then either we get closer, or we strike fast and move fast, accepting that the alarm is raised,' Ogre rumbled.

'I don't like that,' Dirklan replied, and Tarita agreed. 'We don't know how much of a garrison he has either,' Dirklan added. 'I know he's had to be discreet, but the empire lost control of the south years ago. He'd be stupid to have less than a legion, and we all know he's not stupid.'

They considered that in silence, then Ogre said, 'The Master is never stupid, but there's no food here, no supply routes, no farms. Even these possessed men must eat – we learned that in Mollachia. He'll have guards, but maybe not so many.' He paused, then smiled. 'I know how to get close.'

He outlined his plan and Tarita thought it through, matching skills to tasks. Ogre's affinities were all Earth and hermetic, about the body.

and what was solid; Tarita's were all Fire and flash. *Yes, his plan might work. Between us we have what we need.*

She pecked his cheek impulsively. 'You and me, Ogre,' she said, a little more emotionally than she'd intended.

Ogre blinked; Dirklan raised an eyebrow but said nothing.

'What?' she flared at them, to hide her embarrassment. 'So, are we doing this?'

Ogre's misshapen face creased into a slow smile. 'Yes . . . you and me.'

They made their hurried preparations, then she scrambled onto Ogre's back, hooked her arms around his neck and conjured an illusion to disguise herself as a leather pack. Then Ogre rose and clambered over the rocks, effortlessly bearing her weight, and dropped into the cleared passage.

To their right, the water lapped gently at the shore, but they ignored it and strode purposefully towards the archway where the possessed ogre stood sentry. As they walked, Tarita overlaid their auras with the false daemonic aura and began channelling the hate-babble of Abraxas through her mind, while Ogre narrowed his eyes to hide their colour.

The sentry stepped from the shadows to confront them, an axe-headed halberd held in giant arms. 'Yes?' it asked, a little uncertainly, as if they puzzled him.

'I have something for the Master,' Ogre boomed.

Ten yards apart . . . eight yards . . . seven, six . . . five!

Tarita struck, unleashing a net of mesmeric-gnosis that caught the guard's gaze and blinded it, throwing his intellect into the snare she'd readied and deadening his senses. He stumbled as she locked into his head the image of the ramp and the water lapping at the shore, so it was all he could see.

Got you.

The sentry's lumpen face emptied of hostility and any other expression as it slumped against the wall, staring silently at the lake.

Tarita slipped from Ogre's back and grinned. 'Done.'

He puckered up. 'Do I get another kiss?'

'Don't push your luck,' she advised, sashaying through the archway and peering into the dark to make sure they really were alone. The tunnel extended out of sight.

Ogre studied the sentry. 'He and I could be brothers,' he muttered in a morbid voice.

Dirklan joined them. Waving a hand before the sentry's blank face elicited no response. 'We could have used you in the North,' he told Tarita.

'Of course – I'm the best,' she replied. 'This way.' She pirouetted, pointing at the passage into the darkness. There were no torches and the rubble-strewn tunnel exuded a sour, rotting smell, but it had been guarded so there was *something* down there. 'If I was an insanely powerful mage, I'd have a nicer house,' she commented. 'This place is a pigsty.'

Ogre chuckled. 'You *are* an insanely powerful mage – but you don't have a house at all.'

'True,' she admitted.

'Maybe you're just the insane part?'

They poked tongues and touched fists, then she led the way into the dark.

Mount Fettelorn, Noros

Waqar had to consider every single step, which was a labour in itself. He pulsed heat through his stave into the ice coating the slate, blasted it away and clambered up, all the while using kinesis to keep from having the winds rip him away. There was snow in his hair, ice in his nostrils and beard and every inch of exposed skin stung.

He'd tried using Air-gnosis to fly from one outcropping to a higher one, but the gales smashed him hard against the cliff-face, all but dislocating his shoulder. After that he stuck to climbing. At times he caught a glimpse of the golden lantern, waiting above him like a beacon. It felt like he'd been struggling for hours, but surely it had only been a thousand feet or so above him when he started – he should have reached it by now . . .

Glancing back down the sheer cliff, he could no longer see the bottom, just the endlessly swirling cloud – and a vast, hungry pit beneath his feet.

He shuddered and turned his attention back to the task at hand: moving his feet, step by step. His senses were still in turmoil and the hand Gricoama bit was throbbing. At times the sleet looked like blurs of rainbow light and the mountain he was climbing looked more like an immense tree, like the one he'd glimpsed in Cuz Sarkan, he suddenly realised . . .

Then suddenly, with no warning, he arrived. He had been crawling hand over fist up a steep chimney, the steps barely wide enough to take his toes and the ball of his feet, the staff more impediment than aid, but as he topped it, clinging on against the wind raking the outcropping, he found a small platform crudely hewn into the rock.

The man with the lantern was standing in front of a cave. Torches lit a tunnel that curved out of sight into the mountain. His brown robes were as stained and weathered as his skin. His hair and beard were white and his eyes gleamed gold in the lamplight.

'Prince Waqar,' he called in a rough voice. 'Sal'Ahm.'

Waqar stumbled forward, staggering as the wind buffeted him, until he reached the lee of the mountain, and for the first time in – *days? hours?* – was able to stand upright and look around properly. The cave mouth was an arch, hacked into the stone, with four strange symbols carved into the apex.

He focused on the lantern-bearer, who was solidly built, with no sign of wastage in his shoulders and a face like leather stretched over granite. *Yurosi . . . old now, but he's been a warrior.*

'Where are we?' Waqar asked, speaking Rondian.

'You don't know?' the man replied, clearly taken aback. 'Then how are you here?'

'A dog bit me,' Waqar grumbled, holding out his left hand. 'Well, a wolf.'

The man looked amused. 'At times the river finds the sea; other times the sea finds the river.' He raised the lantern, indicating the tunnel. 'She's waiting.'

'Who's waiting?' Waqar asked, a little exasperated.

'Dameta.' When Waqar still looked blank, the man said, 'How do you not know this? Dameta was one of the four great dwymancers, with Amantius, Eloy and Lanthea. This is her refuge . . . or at least, a way to reach it.'

Waqar remembered something Valdyr said on the way to Cuz Sarkan, when he'd asked how the Mollach prince knew where he was going: *'I'm told the gnosis is logical, that this happens because of that. The dwyma is more like a dream, in which everything is connected if you follow the right thread.'* Follow your impulses was the lesson.

No doubt the journey's more important than the destination, or some other mystic rubbish, Waqar grumbled internally, but aloud he just asked, 'Who are you?'

'I'm Caedmor, her son. Please, enter quickly – someone pursues you.'

Waqar blanched. *Xoredh? Who else could it be?* 'Then we should hurry,' he said.

'The path leads to her: she's waiting. My place is here.'

'You don't know what you'll face,' Waqar warned. 'It's my cousin, Xoredh – he's daemon-possessed, as strong as an Ascendant and with access to every Study of the gnosis.'

Caedmor nodded gravely and parted his robes: beneath, he was armoured in chainmail and leather, with a Rondian longsword strapped to his belt. 'He doesn't know what he faces either. In any case, I cannot follow you.' He pointed to the symbols above the arch. 'I'm bound here.'

Holy Ahm – what is this? 'Dameta bound you here? What kind of mother does that?'

'The kind for whom purpose matters more than familial ties, Prince Waqar. I'm sure you know what I mean.'

He thought of Sakita, his own mother, and of Rashid. 'What kind of life is that?' he mumbled in sympathy.

'My life ended long ago,' Caedmor said evenly. 'Enter; no one else shall. The journey–'

'Matters more than the destination?' Waqar suggested wryly.

Caedmor snorted. 'Rukk off,' he said gruffly, snuffing out the lantern. 'And good luck.'

The man's grave demeanour told Waqar the matter was closed, so he inclined his head in thanks, took a lit torch from a wall-bracket and entered the tunnel.

Within ten paces, the cave mouth had vanished. But the sound of the wind growing louder and louder was moaning with his sister's voice.

Xoredh burst through the grasp of the wind, punching through the turbulence with arms extended, fists first, like an arrow shot into the dark. Snow and ice crusted his hands and face as he hunted that elusive golden lamp he'd glimpsed from below. It was no longer visible, but he was certain he had the spot fixed in his mind.

There . . . there's a flat place . . . and a crevice behind . . .

He landed and leaped again, powered by kinesis and burning through energy at a rate that even he, fuelled by a daemon, couldn't sustain for long. The frigid air was thick with snowflakes that looked like lace but were jagged as broken glass, but he tore through them until he slammed into a stone platform and landed with his scimitar out and his shields shimmering.

A moment later a straight sword flashed out of the darkness; he parried by pure instinct – and was almost knocked from his feet and over the edge. Again and again the heavy steel hammered into his guard, then a boot augmented by kinesis slammed *through* his shields and propelled him off the precipice ten feet behind him. He was dashed against the cliff-face, his face *crunched* and teeth shattered as he bounced and fell into a crevice, breaking his left thigh when he landed awkwardly. Agony screamed through him and he convulsed and howled at the pitiless night.

Then healing-gnosis bloomed in his body. He peeled himself off the ground and hauled his broken leg from the crack. He crawled until the bone had reknit enough that he could walk, then he found the steps and climbed. This time, he found a brown-robed man with a drawn sword at the top of the steps.

By the time he reached the ledge again, Xoredh was fully healed. He kindled gnosis-fire and blazed it at the man as he continued advancing purposefully across the space, but to his amazement, the mage-bolt dissipated to nothing and once again he found himself frantically parrying, darting aside from another vicious kick, then lashing out as an opening appeared –

—and the longsword swept his scimitar aside and his foe's left fist smashed his nose again. He staggered, barely parried a chop at his neck that would have ended everything, then took a boot in the ball-sack that hurled him off the cliff again. The wind smashed him into that same crevice, this time breaking his right shoulder, and his sword spun away.

No—he gasped as pain racked his broken body. He pumped more healing energy in, crawled sobbing back to the steps and clung to them as he gritted his teeth, pulled his scimitar back to his hand from a cleft a hundred feet below and, when he was ready, rose again.

Abraxas showed him memories of Ostevan unable to use the gnosis against someone actively channelling the dwyma . . . and Asiv Fariddan, on a peak in Mollachia, where a kind of fog prevented the daemonic from entering . . . until ichor poisoning opened the way.

He used a sharpened fingernail to open a vein and ran blood and ichor into the gutter of his scimitar.

Right, you matachod . . . *let's find out what you've* really *got.*

Rym

Ogre glanced back at the archway and the mesmerised sentry leaning against the wall. From what he could tell, the passage had been bored through the rubble, then shored up. The rough-hewn ceiling dripped water, moss clung to every surface and the air smelled mouldy and dank. He followed Dirklan and Tarita forward with only the faintest mage-light to show the way, dread seeping back into his soul. This was his Master's lair.

After fifty yards, the tunnel turned a sharp right and ended in another archway and a locked door. Dirklan examined it, then announced, 'There's no way we can open that door quickly without whoever cast the ward knowing it's been breached.'

'Three magi and we're held up by a locked door,' Tarita grumbled.

Dirklan smiled wryly. 'I feel your frustration. I'm sure I could pick it undetected, but it would take an hour or so.'

'Do we have an hour?' Tarita wondered.

'Who knows? It's either that or we go back and look for another way in – or we break through and sacrifice stealth for speed from here on.'

'Any other entrance is going to be the same,' Tarita pointed out, 'and probably better guarded.'

Ogre raised the mask and placed it onto his face. He was immediately assailed by a cacophony of exultant hissings and snarling, so triumphal it was nauseating to experience. And Naxius' dry voice was still in full declamatory mode: '. . . *only true regret is that so few will comprehend what I've done sufficiently to realise my genius . . .*'

Ogre ripped the mask from his face, shuddering. 'Something is happening: the daemon is agitated, very excited . . . and the Master is speaking of the end of all things. We must act.'

'Then it's decided,' Dirklan said. 'This doorway feels to me like a side entrance to an old Rimoni palace complex. They were built like legion camps, always much the same layout. I think Naxius has collapsed the upper levels to conceal it – even though he's not had to worry about imperial patrols since the Rimoni governor lost control of this region, he'll still have feared the Ordo Costruo or the Merozains finding him, hence his continued secrecy. So this complex won't be huge and it won't be heavily manned: his safety required secrecy more than force of arms. So we do have a chance, even with just three of us. I'll get the door open. Tarita goes through first and after that we're improvising – fast.'

They clasped hands, then looked to their weapons.

Shyly, Ogre turned to Tarita. Her narrow face was set, but there was a question in her eyes when she faced him.

Rukk it, he thought, clasped her head gently and pulled her face to his and kissed her properly, as he'd only ever kissed one other. But this was *nothing* like kissing Semakha.

When he pulled away, Tarita was still frozen in place. Ogre felt both exhilarated and emptied, but she remained unreadable as she wiped her mouth with the back of her hand and said, 'Mind on the job, Big Man.'

Then she gave him a little wink. 'We'll talk later.'

I can die now, he thought, soaring inside.

Dirklan was looking at them with a hint of amusement. 'Hobokin and Glymahart,' he remarked.

Ogre knew the tale and the comparison didn't entirely displease him, although the sad ending did. *I don't care what you think,* he decided. *I tried, even if her heart didn't melt. I didn't conceal my feelings, nor hide from them.*

'Are we ready?' Dirklan asked drily as he removed his left eye-patch, revealing a faceted crystal set in the scarred socket. It kindled with a pale, menacing light. 'Then let's go.'

The spymaster went to the door, touched the handle and slowly, deftly, began working the gnostic lock. Ogre, following it with a mage's eye, admired his sure touch as he dismantled the strong ward with speed and skill – but its caster would surely sense it happening. The spymaster laid one hand on the handle and held up a finger. Then a second . . . when he lifted the third, he whispered, 'Now—'

He yanked the door aside, Tarita darted through, swinging her blade and a dark shape crumpled, black ichor spurting. A goat-head bounced wetly and rolled aside.

Ogre saw another goat-man on the other side of the door and crashed his axe down on the horned skull, cleaving through the crown into the brain and it too dropped like a stone.

There were two more running towards them from the corridor to the left. Tarita tore forward, lancing blue fire at them, Ogre pounding after her, terrified she'd leave him behind. Her bolts cut them down like blades of grass, but two more erupted from a side door.

'*Merozain,*' one snarled, then, '*Ogre.*'

Crunch. His axe sliced straight through a raised arm and the neck behind. The other construct staggered, then fell as Tarita's blade cut him in two. Ogre threw a glance over his shoulder and saw Dirklan hurrying after them.

'Come on,' Tarita whooped, her face taut and eyes blazing.

They reached a T-junction and a possessed mage-woman with a leprous face appeared from the left. There was a brief exchange of mage-fire until the Merozain unleashed fully, immolating the mage-woman's skull.

Dirklan pointed to the right. 'The central courtyard should be that way.'

This time Ogre took the lead and saw the courtyard ahead, just as Dirklan had described it: a mossy, flag-stoned expanse open to the skies. He glimpsed movement, but there was no shouting, no alarm bells – such things were unnecessary when the defenders were mentally linked. A pair of emaciated men emerged from a door, but he'd cut the first in half before he'd fully registered their presence, while an argen-stael stiletto flew from Dirklan's hand and the second fell, a cloud of ash bursting from his eyes and mouth.

In the centre of the huge square courtyard was a broken fountain, long since run dry, guarded by a statue of a Rimoni sea-god. Doors and corridors led off in all directions.

Ogre listened to the daemon voices and threw out a hand. 'This way,' he shouted, just as a possessed goat-man emerged with a crossbow right in front of him. A blast of kinesis sent the construct spinning and the bolt flew wide, then he buried his axe in the dazed creature's skull.

Onwards.

Now there were more of Naxius' minions appearing from all over; he could sense Dirklan and Tarita firing mage-bolts backwards as they dashed along the shadowy corridors. At the next junction he found stairs and stormed up them, hurling a possessed guardsman off the landing at the top into an empty space – he glanced over the rail. It was a three-storey fall.

Ogre didn't wait to see the construct as it crunched silently into jagged stone and lay broken; he stormed onwards, found an unlocked door and burst it open.

The crash echoed around a dark space – then gnostic lamps flared and Ogre came to an abrupt halt, gaping around the room.

'By every god,' Dirklan breathed behind him, staring.

The circular chamber was a hundred feet in diameter, descending in a dozen tiers to a central circle, the whole a good forty feet across. Arrayed around it on each of the dozen tiers were dozens of stone slabs, and on every one lay a construct, part human, part monster from Yurosi or Ahmedhassan myth.

Ogre, overawed, thought, *This is how I came into the world.*

He saw dozens of his kindred lying amid rows of the horrific and the lovely: slender alvarai from the Northern tales lying beside swamp-beasts of Ventian folklore, lamiae and draken-men, and so many others, all slumbering . . . or lying in wait. There was one nearby who looked exactly as Semakha had when she was new-born and innocent.

'Vessels,' he guessed aloud, 'made for daemon souls.'

'Do we . . . ?' Tarita asked, kindling fire in her left hand.

'No,' Ogre protested, 'there's no time . . . and–'

'Ogre's right,' Dirklan interrupted, 'there's no time. Which way?'

Tarita peered through the door behind them, shielded a bolt, then slammed the barrier shut and warded it. 'There's only onwards,' she drawled, pointing across the chamber. 'Let's go.'

She hurried past Ogre, though she flashed him a sympathetic look. 'Come on. We can deal with this later.'

They took the opposite door, crossed an empty lecture hall beneath a glass dome through which they could see swirling darkness, as if the night sky were being sucked into a tornado . . . that was held in the bower of a great tree.

Ogre's heart thumped, as he realised what it meant. 'It's begun . . .' he said weakly.

'Are we too late?' Dirklan breathed.

Even Tarita froze.

Words from the *Book of Kore* filled Ogre's head.

The sky shall fray like a veil torn aside, and the door between Life and Unlife shall be cast open. The belly of Glamortha, the betraying angel, shall swell up with the seed of Lucian, then give birth to the living darkness. Daemons shall she beget, thousands upon thousands, and the torment of those sinners left behind on Urte shall never end . . .

Ogre cast about, seeking some way to intervene, but this was just a scryed image. Wherever this was truly happening was somewhere else beyond their reach. *We should have gone with Lyra and Valdyr*, he realised. *Only they can stop this . . .*

*

575

Having summoned the fog themselves didn't make it any easier to dissipate it, but it helped hide them, so Lyra and Valdyr let it be. As night fell and the moon rose, the ghostly glow made every direction seem the same, but they clung to the lakeside, clambering their way westwards, towards the pull of the dwyma. Gricoama was somewhere ahead of them, at one with the mist.

They heard a sudden clatter behind them and darted into cover, just in time to avoid a party of twenty goat-headed men, armed and armoured, thudding past, their cloven hooves pounding the broken paving. They were heading the way Dirklan's party had gone and didn't notice their footprints in the dust. Moments later another cohort thudded by.

The others have been discovered, Lyra thought. *Father* . . .

But they'd made their choices.

When all was quiet again, she and Valdyr cautiously slipped from their hiding place, sharing an anxious look, then hurried on. They could feel the pull of the dwyma ahead strongly now.

Aradea, Lyra whispered, *are you here?*

Nothing responded. For several days now, her grip on the dwyma had felt unexpectedly frail and she'd dreamed one night of her garden, burned out and ravaged – but however depressing that thought, her garden was just a focal point. She'd grown beyond being able to function as a dwymancer only in that one place.

Suddenly the land ran out and water was hemming them in on both sides. Gricoama was waiting for them on the low promontory, growling softly at the fog ahead. Valdyr laid a hand on the wolf's shoulder as the mist swirled and the lake lapped at the dirty shore, streaked in greenish slime.

Sharing a fearful look, they advanced into the murk, sensing what was distressing Gricoama: a dark shape growing in the mist as they approached.

Lyra stared. *A brackenberry—*

But this one was full grown, twisted and bare, the branches contorting around a dark shape within the branches. Even as they registered that, it changed, and something like the great Elétfa was towering over them – but this wasn't the Elétfa Lyra and Valdyr knew: this one was a shadow version made of darkness. They stood at its feet staring up the towering trunk to the branches that covered the heavens.

Jehana was held in the upper branches of the shadow Tree of Life, visible even though she was far, far above them: a naked giantess with bone-white hair. Her right hand was extended, palm upwards. Above her was a vaguely human form of gleaming ebony, drifting down onto her, and as they watched, they merged, her light flowing into his darkness, his shadow flowing into Jehana's hand and up her arm.

Dear Kore, Lyra thought, *Glamortha and Lucian? It really is the Last Day.*

'Today,' Ervyn Naxius told the empty lecture chamber, 'is the Last Day, foretold and now brought to be by *me* – so I ask you: on what level am I *not* a god?"

He let the silence digest that, imagining the way an audience would stir, struck by his perception and genius, and then begin to applaud, hammering feet on the floor or clapping hands together. He could picture the open mouths, the widened eyes, the amazed rapture.

Yes, yes, I have achieved this.

'Even as I speak, she succumbs,' he told the emptiness. 'Thinking herself the mistress of her own destiny, she twists and turns in the silken web, not knowing that everything she does is according to my will. She hears the knock and she opens and lets in the spider. See the mandibles I forged, dripping with venom; marvel at the tensile strength of the silken snare I wrought: this is *my* triumph . . .'

His imagined audience was captivated: *astounded*.

'Like the pyramids of ancient Gatioch, stones are piled on stones and beings upon beings, each resting on their lessers. Mine is the apex stone: I am the Master of the Future: the Master of Creation. As the world ruptures and the daemons rush in, all humankind will be possessed; each daemon subsuming thousands of men and all subject to a master daemon, who is in turn subject to a daemon prince: and all of that breed will be subject to *me*.'

It's so close now, he thought, trembling a little. 'In the branches of the dwyma tree that I grew,' he told the room, 'the very fabric of Creation is being unpicked: I will be the one who re-stitches it.'

He paused dramatically and turned to the stage, where he conjured an image of Jehana Mubarak unknowingly surrendering herself to Lucian. She was floating on her back, her white hair spread around, her skull mask shifting as her expression changed from fear to wonder. Above her, the darkness became a darkly beautiful man, falling through the heavens to take her like an offering.

Their hands moved together, then through each other. The daemon's hand went straight to her left breast, even as her hand went to his. She convulsed as if struck and her eyes flew open . . .

Yes, Naxius breathed, *yes . . .*

It was happening just as he'd intended – just as he'd written.

. . . and Glamortha, the Angel of Death, shall lie down with Lucian and beget the Age of Daemons . . .

The aether was silent, the voices of the daemons stilled, all their attention upon the slow melding of their ruler with his offered consort: the union of life and death.

Open her up, Naxius urged him, *make of her a passage from the aether into this world: begin the End.*

His own preparations were all done: he had Lucian's ichor in his veins and through that he would control every daemon the moment they entered this world.

Mine will be the kingdom . . .

'Let him in, Jehana Mubarak,' he whispered. 'Let him in.'

The shadow descended on the floating girl and engulfed her . . .

Then something below the great tree caught his eye and he shifted the focus of the conjured image . . . and saw Valdyr Sarkany and Lyra Vereinen beneath the tree he'd grown, on the peninsula just a mile away, their faces wide-eyed with fear and wonder.

And at the same time Abraxas whispered, *Intruders, in the western wing.*

They can't stop this, Naxius thought coolly. *They're already too late.* Speaking directly into the mind of Lucian, he whispered, <*Now.*>

Then he strode from the empty chamber, blazing a call into every one of the construct daemons that guarded his hidden lair: <*Intruders in the west wing – kill them all.*>

To Jehana, it was like falling into a sea of cold stars and liquid darkness. There was no gravity, no sense of up or down, just her and him as she fell through Lucian's skin, penetrating him as he penetrated her, her senses awash with millions of fragmentary lives all bound together. It was horribly fascinating – but the dread of losing her own identity kept her from plunging her awareness into this sea of lives as Lucien showed her endless images of sublime beauty and pleasure purloined from countless thousands of souls.

He's no different to Abraxas or any of the others, she realised: *he's another swallower of lives, just better at it.* That silenced any remaining shred of doubt and stiffened her resolve.

From the moment she'd awakened in Naxius' grasp, she'd been seeking a way out, but she'd finally realised there would be only one chance, at only one moment, when she might just be powerful enough: here inside the dwyma.

Now, as Lucian flooded her, flowing into her, around her, over her and inside her, she shrank ever more into herself, seeking in the darkness for a way to gain control.

But the Prince of Daemons struck before she was ready–

What had been a *merging* became a *forcing* as his spirit-body changed from a man to a tentacled horror, dozens of appendages erupting from his body to grip hers, lashing her arms and legs, forcing them wide, as his now bestial face loomed over her. A black, spiky tongue shoved into her mouth as below, something equally hideous tore her womanhood open and the snarling daemon rammed itself inside her, his eyes alight with triumphant lust – and inside those eyes she saw Naxius, gloating.

About them, a dark typhoon began spinning madly above her. The tail descended, a tendril of midnight reaching down, striking Lucian's heaving back, piercing him – and flowing through him and into her, tearing her open–

Jehana was choking, her throat blocked by a monstrous tentacle distending from Lucian's fanged maw, and all was agony. She panicked, thrashing helpless beneath him as the daemon lord filled her; the only respite was the growing sensation of icy numbness spreading from her loins as his seed spread. He was so hideous, so horrifying that her mind froze, her sense of self frayed and dissipated . . .

You are the gateway through which my kind will enter this world, Lucian crowed into her skull.

If emotion were a weapon, she would have lashed out with hate, but emotion was no weapon, even here, and even as she screamed vengeance, he drove himself deeper inside, laughing all the while . . .

She didn't think anything could get worse, until he became a serpent and flowed into her belly. It distended sickeningly as he vanished inside and she stared aghast, seeing it was filled with swirling, gnat-like shapes: every daemon in reach, pouring into her ballooning stomach, and then her ribs spread out, and her breasts became engorged, as something forced its way up her throat, pushing blood and spittle before it as her mouth convulsed open –

– and a torrent of darkness like a million insects erupted from her mouth, and into Urte.

Naxius cried aloud in triumph, '*Done – it is done!*'

Mount Fettelorn, Noros

The old man is a riddle I must solve, Xoredh realised, once again hammering away with fire and blade, only to be continually parried, evaded and then smashed backwards. Teetering on the edge of another fall, he managed to twist away from a deadly sweep of the man's blade – but his riposte was immediately, *impossibly* parried, the old man flashed back a dozen steps in a heartbeat, spinning his blade, and took guard again. He couldn't get anywhere near him and the ichor he'd pasted to the blade spattered away harmlessly.

Xoredh reeled, then stormed forward, with a new plan: he kept his defences high and his stance aggressive, going for the head – and meeting a defence so perfect the man could as well have been a wall – and then came the expected riposte.

Let it through . . .

He took the blade right through his belly, roaring in agony, howling as the old man tore the blade sideways and it lodged against his spine. He lost all feeling in his lower body . . .

. . . but his arms still worked. He dropped his own blade and as he toppled forward, his guts spewing through the rent in his abdomen, he caught the old man's arm. With the last of his vanishing strength, he pulled that arm towards him . . . and *bit*.

Then he crawled away to pull in healing gnosis as the old man tried to fight the ichor – the blood of the dead – and he failed, because he too was already dead.

'No . . .' the old man whispered as he realised the inevitable, and then, '*Mother –*'

And then he was gone, clothing and weapon lying lifeless on the snowy rock, his body collapsing into pale smoke that blew away.

Got you, khinzir . . .

It was a long time before Xoredh could move again, though: the gnosis was hard to reach here, even with the old man gone. By the time his flesh had reknit and his spine reset, too much of his blackened blood stained the frosted stone. But he managed to stagger upright, pulling on Abraxas' powers like never before. He could feel the very aether quivering, as if lightning strikes were pulsing through it, a rhythmic discharge of energy that grew ever stronger. It felt as if all of creation were being unravelled.

It took him a moment to realise – and then he screamed in fright, '*The Master has begun – it's TIME, and I'm nowhere . . .*'

Hauling himself upright on kinesis, morphic-gnosis and sheer will, he reclaimed his blade and staggered for the tunnel: surely the place Waqar had come to find.

In a few paces he was striding; in a few more, he was running on limbs that shrieked for mercy, his leg-bones, shattered by three falls and barely reknit, grinding agonisingly. But he had to go on.

Waqar must die . . . I must do as the Master commanded, or I'm lost for ever . . .

*

Waqar ran, pounding down the tunnel as it descended past stalagmites and stalactites, a path smoothed with Earth-gnosis zigzagging past ancient rock pillars and around still pools of luminous water.

Behind him, he heard blades hammering together, the clanging of a dozen blacksmiths.

Xoredh will prevail, logic told him. *Caedmor can't hold against the daemon.*

His breathing was ragged, his head beating dizzily as he tried to take in more air – the healer hadn't been lying; he was a long way from battle-ready, but he had no choice.

He lost the sounds of battle as he plunged deeper into the mountain, until all he could hear were his own gusting breath and the slapping of his boot soles. He rounded another bend – and staggered to a halt in a wide-open space like the inside of a volcano, open to the sky.

There was no lava pit, though, but the roots of a vast tree extending up into the heavens. '*The Elétfa*,' he gasped. *Valdyr's tree.* He looked into the branches and saw a green and blue orb wreathed in white, spinning slowly in the bower of the branches. The whole of it was impossible. Already too vast for the space that contained it, it grew as he approached.

Above it he could see a naked man and woman locked together, coupling in the skies. It took him a moment to realise the white-haired skull-faced woman was Jehana – and her face was contorted in horror and revulsion.

He cried out in shock and rage even as he realised that an old woman clad in a simple dun shift was standing before the tree, her arms raised in rejection and horror.

She turned to him, her face wild with desperation, and shouted, 'You must make her stop!'

He barely registered the woman, for his eyes had locked on his beloved sister, writhing in the dark other's grasp, her head thrown back as she cried out in agony and dread.

He pushed past the old woman – then turned back to her to beg her aid, because he knew nothing of the dwyma or what was needed. *I should have stayed with Valdyr Sarkany at Cuz Sarkan*, he realised belatedly. *I should have embraced this power, not run from it . . .*

But even as he opened his mouth to speak, a dark shape flashed from the shadows and scythed the woman down: a double-handed slash of a scimitar passing right through her waist and spilling her in two pieces on the ground, sending blood spraying all round her. Her body dissolved into speckles of glittering dust that was sucked into the Elétfa . . .

Leaving Waqar alone with his cousin.

Xoredh extended his blade, then gazed upwards, his face alive with wonder – and fear. Waqar extended his own weapon, but he could barely hold the scimitar, so badly were his hands shaking with exhaustion and horror. It was painful to drag his eyes from Jehana's torment in the vastness above him, but he had no choice.

'Xoredh,' he said, 'we must stop this–'

'*Stop it?* You jest, Cousin – what *I* have to do is to take your head and ensure it happens, for my place in Paradise – the reward my Master promised me – depends on it.'

He lunged with his blade, Waqar parried and the fatal dance began . . .

Xoredh tried to kindle gnostic energy and failed, only then realising that this place was too steeped in dwyma for his daemon-enhanced power.

Waqar could still use the gnosis – his shields were intact – but he was already wheezing, and his spittle was bloody . . . He was almost dead on his feet.

But physically, Xoredh wasn't a lot better off – from the moment he'd entered the chamber, all the spells repairing his battered body had begun to fail, forcing him to take the initiative. He battered Waqar's blade aside, lunging in, his belly straining the newly healed scars holding him together even as he began to bleed internally again.

But Waqar countered, again and again, and as Xoredh's limbs started to wobble, he suddenly realised that this was not the foregone conclusion he needed it to be . . . but immortality and eternal might were at stake. Xoredh roared and attacked again, worked an opening and then thrust in, *hard*, with all his fading strength–

–only to be blocked by Waqar – and this time the stomach wound inflicted by the old man's blade *did* split and Xoredh howled at the pain ripping through his abdomen and grabbing at his belly, trying to prevent his intestines from bursting out again.

Then Waqar's boot lashed out, kicking him in the thigh, and the barely reformed bone snapped again. Howling in despair and traumatised by unspeakable pain, he fell to one knee, the impact jarring through him. He lost his grip and dropped his scimitar, then Waqar kicked it away even as he tried to lash out with a spell that never caught.

The old man beat me after all . . .

He looked up at Waqar's blade kissing his throat, reeling in disbelief that all his careful plotting and limitless dreams could end so.

'Mercy,' he croaked, knowing there would be none.

Waqar drew back his sword arm.

'Do you know,' Xoredh croaked through the pain, 'that when Naxius gave my father a place in his cabal, for any of his family, he considered offering you? Ironic, ai?'

Waqar's blade flashed.

Xoredh felt a wave of icy coldness and his vision spun. The floor smacked into his head and he lay blinking . . . three feet from where his neck stump was pumping black ichor onto the rock.

'I think Rashid chose well,' Waqar said, as Xoredh plummeted into a well of darkness.

34

The Fall

Inevitability

The sucker-punch that wins the bout. The hidden card that scoops the game. The dazzling riposte when all looks lost: these are what fire our dreams and make us imagine that on any given day, anything could happen.

But the truth is that we only remember these moments for their rarity. In reality, in the arenas that truly matter, the powerful have all the weapons and hold all the cards. The outcome is preordained by the years of preparation that have gone into reaching that moment. The result is inevitable.

ERVYN NAXIUS, FATE: A LECTURE, RYM 935

The Celestium, Pallas, Rondelmar
Martrois 936

<It's done,> Roland de Farenbrette sent. <Endus Rykjard is dead.>

He kept the link open a moment longer and received Solon's response: <Well done, Blacksmith. Enjoy the spoils.> Then the emperor-elect's presence winked out and Roland opened his eyes and let out his breath . . .

. . . and stared at the knife-point poised over his right eyeball.

'I did it,' he panted. 'It's done. You promised to release me.'

'So I did,' drawled the lean, whiskery Volsai holding the dagger. Pat-cheart turned to the watching Endus Rykjard, who was looking very much alive. 'Are you satisfied, Capitano?'

Rykjard considered while Roland waited, unable to breathe, let alone think past that silvery steel tip filling his vision. Then the Hollenian nodded. 'Yes, release him.'

Patcheart nodded – and then the point slammed into Roland's eye-socket in a blaze of searing, brief pain, that ended a moment later.

'And so is he released from this mortal torment that is life,' Patcheart remarked casually, pulling out the dagger and wiping the blood on de Farenbrette's tunic before sheathing it. The knight hung lifeless in his bonds, blood running from the ruined socket. 'Are you convinced, Capitano Rykjard?'

Rykjard looked round the room at his second-in-command, Hanzi Bochlyn, a bluff Hollenian with a priestly demeanour, at the stolid Brigeda and finally at Calan Dubrayle, a small, dapper figure in the corner.

'De Farenbrette did just as you said he would,' Rykjard admitted. 'And Takwyth has indeed isolated my legions, one inside Esdale and the other outside the northern gates, also as you predicted, so clearly you were right: they had no intention of paying me – or letting me or my men leave.' He drummed his fingers angrily, then turned back to Dubrayle. 'You swear you can buy off the Pallacian legions?'

The Treasurer answered, 'They can see how Takwyth's reign is going to be: their kin are being starved in the docklands and only Corani are being advanced. People say Pallacian soldiers are Esdale men, but they forget it's the poor who join the army – and that means docklanders. Esdale men are just transplanted docklanders – and they're furious about the brutality Takwyth's meting out on their kin. They've heard his rants – and they heard the Sacrecour prince's words about his false queen when she pardoned him. They know Takwyth's seized the Celestium and they're hearkening to the rumours that he'll even execute the Grand Prelate, an act of utter infamy and sacrilege.'

'And don't forget that Lyra promised the people a place at the table of power and now it's been snatched away,' Patcheart put in. 'The whole city is seething right now. With the right nudge, that'll overcome their fear.'

'The right nudge being?'

Dubrayle smiled coolly. 'I've secreted away enough bullion to buy off every Pallacian legion commander in the region. For the right price, they'll swing. But we need you too, Capitano Rykjard: two legions, ten thousand men already on site – that's enough to make a huge difference. You've seen how Takwyth wishes you dealt with – wouldn't you rather be on the winning side – and paid?'

Patcheart glanced at Brigeda, hoping.

'Where's the queen in all this?' Rykjard asked. 'I accept your claim that the woman Takwyth is keeping isn't her – but where's the real Lyra?'

'In hiding,' Dubrayle replied. 'Deepest concealment. I can't say more.'

'That's the truth of it,' Patcheart threw in, although Basia hadn't seen fit to tell him, so he didn't actually have a clue.

'She'll come out when she's ready,' Brigeda added.

Rykjard's fingers rattled the table again, then he said, 'I can't go back to Hollenia right now, so I may as well dig in. But I want the Knight-Commander role – with commensurate land and titles – as well as the money. And Takwyth gets the axe: no reprieves, no exiles, no mercy. He ordered de Farenbrette to kill me. And Lann Wilfort was my friend.'

Dubrayle considered his demands, then smiled. 'I think the queen would welcome a non-partisan presence as Knight-Commander after all this. Capitano, I accept your terms.' He rose and extended a hand. 'Thank you, *Lord* Rykjard.'

The mercenary captain smiled.

Patcheart grinned at Briggy. 'Let's be about it,' he drawled. 'We've got some rabble to rouse.'

Tockburn, Pallas

Ari Frankel came awake from the grey misery of another nightmare in which the bodies of his family and friends dangled just above his head, covered in feasting, fighting crows. But as the dream faded, the cawing of the crows was replaced by a boisterous chanting sound that carried to his below-ground hideaway.

'*BRING OUT THE QUEEN,*' he heard. '*BRING OUT THE QUEEN —*'

What in Hel? He pushed aside the blanket and stood on tiptoes to peer through the shuttered window above his head. The people marching past were just dark shapes smeared with the red of the setting sun, but their tramping feet made the stones quiver, sending tremors through his bones.

'*BRING OUT THE QUEEN . . .*'

People say the woman in the royal suite isn't Lyra — that's what they say the Sacrecour prince screamed on the gallows . . . What if it's true?

He emptied his water cup and stood, dazed from lack of food. There had been no food brought into the city since Takwyth sacked the docks. But the chanting woke him, the irresistible lure of the crowd.

They're angry, they're hungry and they're desperate.

He couldn't have resisted if he had wanted to. He had nothing left — no money or food — and his refuge was empty, for Lazar's men had vanished, slipping away into the countryside like the brigands they'd always been. All he had left were *his* people, his Sufferers.

He fumbled on his clothes then clambered up the ladder and pushed open the cellar hatch, which felt like a monumental effort, for he hadn't eaten more than a morsel of bread in three days. But when he stumbled out into the street, the *frisson* of rebellion revived him enough that he could seize the shoulder of another man and shout along; 'Bring out the queen—' while he tried to get his bearings.

Ahead of them was Roidan Heights, a black silhouette against the setting sun. *We're marching on the Bastion,* he realised. For a moment he was terrified, then the energy of the crowd took him up and he managed to stand on his own, punching the air in time with his comrades, screaming, 'Bring out the queen . . .'

'*Bring out the queen . . .*'

'*BRING OUT THE QUEEN . . .*'

'Ma, ma, look—' a child said in an awed voice. 'Look — it's Ari Frankel—'

Bodies closed in and he felt a surge of terror as hands grabbed him, pulling at him, and he opened his mouth to cry for help — but then he was hoisted on a burly young man's shoulders and he found himself above a sea of faces, big eyes shining in the fiery light of dusk, and mouths were calling his name: thousands of faces, streaming before and behind him, emerging from every alley, every side, all shrieking, '*FRANKEL —*'

'*FRANKEL, FRANKEL, FRANKEL . . .*'

He clasped hands, applauded them, punched the air, babbled incoherently as all reached up to touch him, crying his name as if he were Corineus Himself, come down from on high to save them all. Tears streamed down his face and his heart swelled to bursting.

I'm home, he thought wildly, irrationally, honestly. *I've come home . . .*

The Bastion

I don't understand . . . Solon stared down from the turret of the gatehouse overlooking the Place d'Accord. The fiery glow of sunset was fading into night and the full moon dominated the eastern hemisphere, shining down on the giant square like a second sun. Mater Lune, as the Sollans called her, the Mother of Madness, was reigning tonight.

The massive square was a sea of torchlight and upturned angry faces – and worse, every gate and postern of the Bastion was reporting the same thing. The entire city had risen, from the docklands to Esdale, from Gravenhurst to Nordale and every block and square between. Men, women and children, craftsmen, dockers, labourers, all with their families in tow – and worse, there were soldiers too, in their uniforms and armed.

'*BRING OUT THE QUEEN,*' they were chanting. '*BRING OUT THE QUEEN —*'

They know, he thought helplessly, sweat beginning to soak his armpits and the hair beneath his helm and running into his eyes. *They know.*

These are the same people who called my name in praise just a few days ago. I saved them from the Sacrecours and now I'm saving them from themselves – how can they be so fickle?

'Where's fucking Rollo?' he demanded of a quaking Nestor Sulpeter.

'Kore's Balls, if he's with that Hollenian's wives right now, I'll have his testicles hacked off.'

'I can't reach him,' Sulpeter bleated.

Dear Kore, how on Urte did I ever think of him as promising?

He turned and planted himself squarely before the young man. 'Then. Try. Again.' He sprayed spittle over Nestor's face. 'I want him here. *Now.*'

Nestor stammered something incoherent and fled. The tribunes and battle-magi arrayed around him all shuffled awkwardly. Solon glared at them, flung his arm wide to encompass the crowd in the square below and roared, 'Look at them–' He amplified his voice above the clamour below. 'Pallacian *ingrates* – we saved them from tyranny and still they want more. Dear Kore, I wouldn't trade a thousand of the spineless, lying mongrels for a single true-hearted Corani lad. I'll *break* them: they can hammer on my door all they bloody like, but they'll get nothing from me: *nothing* – I am Solon Takwyth and I concede not one thing: they can all go to Hel–'

As he ran out of breath, his tirade petered out and he heard his words bouncing off walls. The crowd below had fallen silent as he began to shout and he suddenly realised he'd amplified his voice to carry right through the plaza. He spun and strode to the parapet, planted a foot and glared down.

So they're willing to listen now, are they?

He raised a hand. 'People of Pallas, I am your emperor and I command you to return to your homes. There is nothing for you here.'

Heads turned, the massive crowd buzzed and hummed . . . and then a hooded figure raised his head and a familiar voice rang out, 'Return home, Milord? To what? There's no food in the larders and no fuel to burn: not since your brave soldiers plundered our houses.'

I don't believe it. Ari rukking Frankel . . .

'Mark him,' Solon growled at the nearest crossbowman, then he lifted his voice. 'They brought it on themselves,' he bellowed, 'by their rioting and arson – incited by *you*, Frankel: they brought it on themselves and it's your rukking fault!'

'How so?' Frankel dared to reply. 'These good people merely asked to be treated as human beings, as equals of your high and lordliness, instead of being pissed on from above. And our *good queen* listened to them – so bring her out and ask her to explain this sudden change of heart.'

You pissant, Solon snarled under his breath as someone plucked at his sleeve. He turned his head and glared furiously at Rolven Sulpeter, sweating and red-faced.

'Don't debate with him,' the old nobleman whispered urgently. 'Don't dignify his words with a response.'

What he means is, you're not up to debating with the likes of him, Solon thought. He almost punched the old man for his treason, but contented himself with shouting, 'I'll be damned if I back down from this arsehole–'

'Please, Solon,' Rolven begged. 'I've just heard – Rykjard's alive and de Farenbrette's head is on a pole. The Hollenian mercenaries and the Pallacian legions have united against us: we're trapped in here, Solon, and unless we move carefully, this could be another 909.'

Solon stared at him: *Rollo's dead . . . The bastards . . .*

His face contorted again and he whirled back to face this *murdering rabble* again. 'The queen was stupid not to hack you apart, Frankel,' he screamed, 'and as for equality . . . ? Ha! Can you do this?' He raised a fist and blazed flame into the sky. 'Or this?' He sent a blue mage-bolt searing over their heads. A few recoiled – but then the masses below roared back in fury, deafening whatever Frankel was shouting. Fists were raised, hands pointed in unison, voices caught fire:

'*DEATH TO THE TYRANT – BRING OUT THE QUEEN –*'

His temper snapped and he tried to roar above them, but even gnostically amplified, his words were lost in the ocean of sound, until he realised that all he was doing was screaming, '*Fuck you all, fuck you all –*'

He stopped abruptly, though the red mist in his eyes still burned. He whirled upon the crossbowman. 'Do you have a shot?' he demanded. 'Take it!'

The archer lifted his gaze from the seething, dancing, swirling sea of bodies below and blanched. 'No, no Milord, I don't have the shot . . .'

'Bring him down–'

'Do not,' Rolven Sulpeter rapped out. 'No one fires.'

Caught between orders, the soldiers floundered, staring white-faced from one to the other. A few made the Sign of Corineus on their breasts.

Solon whirled and slammed his fist into Rolven's face, the blow bursting through flimsy shielding that did just enough to prevent a broken jaw, but smashing the old man over backwards, sending him sprawling like a child.

For an instant, Solon was standing over the broken-necked body of the maid, Nita.

Dear Kore . . .

'I . . . I didn't mean . . .' he stammered. 'I didn't – I swear . . .' He put his hand to his face, his mind numbed by the roaring defiance around him, paralysed with uncertainty; he'd never been like this on a battle-field. *I'm* not *like this*, he thought, horrified. *I don't do these things. I'm about chivalry, honour – everyone knows that . . . I'm the greatest knight of the age . . .*

'*BRING OUT THE QUEEN,*' they kept on, '*BRING OUT THE QUEEN –*'

All at once it was too much: he clutched his ears, screaming for silence as he stumbled away, the soldiers staring at him, gaping with huge, staring eyes.

He had to get away, lurching to the stairs and down the steps, seeking some place where no one could demand the impossible.

As he fled, all he could think of was Lyra, facing down the mob with poise and eloquence outside St Baramitius Cathedral, on the dawn of the first raid, and that image was like a spear through him, shaming his weakness.

We kissed that very morning, after I saved her from the assassins. We were in love . . . everything was as it should have been.

The memory ripped his heart in two and sobbing, he ran through the vast entrance hall, pushing aside confused and frightened Corani peti-tioners. 'Get away from me!' he shrieked when one tried to stop him, and he launched himself on Air-gnosis into the stairwell.

Lyra, he thought wildly, *I need you –*

But it wasn't the real Lyra . . . only Brunelda was waiting. His steps faltered.

The icon of the Sacred Heart hung above the doorway to the Royal

Chapel, the red lamp proclaiming that the royal family's comfateri was in situ. *Yes,* he thought, suddenly, *I need to Unburden. The weight of this – it's too much for me.*

He hurried to the door and panting for breath, pushed it open. The soft glow of the lamps burnished the carved wood of the pews and kneelers, illuminating the painted ceilings and marble pillars.

The chapel was empty and the curtained booth stood open. He lurched towards it, fell to his knees and stared through the veiled divide at the silhouette on the other side of the booth: the comfateri, whoever that was these days.

'Ave, son of Kore,' the priest intoned. 'Be at peace, for your God is listening.'

Solon almost collapsed in relief. 'Thank Kore,' he blurted. 'I have never needed His benediction as I do now. Never in all my life.'

'Tell me what troubles you,' the priest said, his voice vaguely familiar. 'Tell your God.'

I don't even believe in your *God,* Solon almost said, but the need to explain himself when that *damned mob* outside just wouldn't *listen* was overpowering. He needed to rebalance himself, to find his way through this maze.

'I don't understand what's happening,' he blurted. 'Ever since she walked away from me I've been so *angry* – not just at her, but with *every-one.* Why don't they realise my worth? I've been the greatest knight in Yuros for more than a decade – don't they know how *hard* that is? Every man dreams of being the one to beat me to my knees – the pressure is *intolerable,* but I live with it because I'm strong – because I'm *needed.* The Corani *need* me – the empire *depends* on me. *She* needs me and she doesn't even rukking *know* it – but *why not?'*

The words poured out, echoing through the silent chapel, but the priest didn't speak.

'Don't these people know how stupid it is to say all men are equal when it's so clearly untrue?' Solon pushed on. 'Magi are greater than men. Men are greater than women. Humans are better than animals: there's a natural order and I'm at the Kore-bedamned pinnacle of it,' he shouted at the silent curtain.

Silence . . .

This is the true voice of your God, he thought contemptuously, *because he doesn't exist.*

But then the remorse that had driven him here reared up again and with his voice breaking, he admitted, 'Or I thought I was . . . but look at me. I've had four lovers in my life . . . my wife loathed me; Medelie played me like a puppet on a string; Lyra was frightened of me and–' He stopped, then mumbled, 'I don't even know what Brunelda feels . . . Brunelda . . . It's not Lyra in my suite, just a . . .'

He caught on the horrible word he'd been about to say: *whore.*

What have I become?

'. . . just a young woman whom I *own.* How can that be right? Dear Kore, even the Sacrecours banned slavery, but every night I force her to submit . . . And Nita . . . I killed her, Father, with these hands . . .' He stared at them, expecting to see blood dripping from the pores. 'Everything I do turns to ruin . . .'

He looked at the curtain and it seemed to become a reflection of the wreckage of a sinner.

'I've never been insufficient before,' he told that mirror, 'but I'm inadequate for this. I thought I knew how to rule but I can't. I'm *damaged.* I saw my Corani brothers and sisters murdered in 909 and I've never got that out of my head or my heart. The blood stains my soul and all the blood I shed in return only makes the nightmares worse. The empire needs peace and union but all I have inside me is hate. Lyra . . .' He choked on her name, then carried on, 'Lyra is right – Frankel is right . . . *they're all right.* I've failed . . . I'll leave, on my own, and pray Lyra can put this right . . .'

His voice choked up and he couldn't speak any more, just slumped on his knees, weeping uncontrollably. For how long he wept, minutes or hours, he had no idea, but finally he ran dry.

I'll step down, he told himself. *I'll issue an amnesty and then I'll just go . . . My people don't need me any more.*

'Thank you,' he told the silhouette of the priest, behind the curtain. 'Thank you for listening.' He rose stiffly and walked to the door, feeling strangely calm.

The booth opened behind him and the priest said, 'Where the *fuck* do you think you're going?'

Solon turned and recognised Father Germane, Ostevan's pawn, emerging from the curtained booth with clawed hands and jet-black eyes. He tried to grasp the gnosis, but he was too late, for a blast of kinesis was already ripping him from his feet and hurling him backwards. The stone wall smashed the back of his skull and his head burst apart . . .

. . . And he came round, groaning, to find his hands locked in manacles formed by twisted wrought-iron torch-holders. He reached for the gnosis, but something effortlessly snuffed it out. He blinked his eyes clear and faced his captor, trembling to be so helpless.

Germane's austere face was blazing with contempt. When he opened his mouth, Solon could see his elongated incisors were dripping with black ichor.

No—his mind clamoured.

'So the mighty Solon Takwyth awakes,' Germane sneered. 'By Lucian Himself, what a *pitiful* display – no wonder you can't handle rulership. You're pathetic, nothing but wind farting through an empty suit of armour. Listen to yourself: about the only true thing you said was that there's a natural order – but it's *me* at the pinnacle, not you. There's a new dawn coming, *Takky*, and my Master is the rising sun.'

'No . . .' Solon breathed.

'To think the Master offered you the chance to join us – and you refused?' Germane jeered. 'You fool: no one gets to refuse my Master.'

Solon strained against the bonds, wrenching so hard he thought he might snap his joints, but nothing gave.

'Where's the real Lyra?' Germane demanded.

Solon couldn't take his eyes off those terrifying teeth. 'I . . . I . . . I don't know . . .'

Help me, someone . . .

'If you don't know . . . who does?'

Germane leaned in, making Solon recoil from his foul breath – and suddenly his courage, the one thing he'd thought unbreakable, snapped.

'Basia de Sirou, she knows, she knows . . .' he babbled, unable to shut his mouth, feeling the thud as his soul hit the bottom of the Pit.

Grinning savagely, Germaine drew Solon's sword from his scabbard and raised it.

Solon didn't move – he couldn't. He didn't even flinch, because this was just. 'Do it,' he whispered.

Germane licked his lips . . . then he lowered the sword and caressed Solon's face with his *disgusting* hands. 'No, Solon, I truly think the Hel you live in now is a more fitting fate.' He bared his teeth and with a vicious wrench, twisted Solon's face to one side and bit his throat, puncturing his neck muscles with teeth that felt like shards of ice. 'You rejected the Master, fool, but he still chooses *you*.'

In moments, the acid burn of the ichor struck and a wall of daemonic voices hammered into Solon's skull.

'Enjoy your final hours, "Emperor",' Germane giggled. 'Your enemies will find you manacled here – and you know the rest. And Abraxas will be waiting on the other side.'

Then he slammed his fist into Solon's face, stars burst and darkness roared in.

Germane studied Takwyth: the would-be emperor was hanging from out-spread arms, his wrists bound like Corineus the Saviour in popular Kore iconography.

Amusing, when he's really just a puppet of his own rage.

He dropped the royal sword – it was unnecessary and too conspicuous – and hurried to the doors. *If she's here, I'll find and deal with her.* But his mind travelled further. *What if she's guessed where the Master is? Then she could be a real danger to him . . . and to me . . .*

He closed, locked and warded the chapel before hurrying through the near-empty corridors to the back stairs, seeking the dungeons and Basia de Sirou.

Basia groaned and rolled over on the floor of the cell, coughing as the stale air filled her lungs. The Sacrecours had used their dungeons extensively, filling them with all manner of torture equipment, but Lyra had barely needed them, so everything iron, from the bars to the devices, had rusted, and the closed-in subterranean air was dank and foul.

That hadn't stopped Takwyth from opening them up and hurling her in, along with any number of other people who'd 'disrespected' him. They were all bound by manacles that had been enchanted with Chain-runes to prevent use of the gnosis and shackled by the wrists to the walls. The open-fronted cells were just ten feet by ten feet. They'd been stripped to nightshirts, so they could piss and shit without fouling themselves, but they gave little protection from the biting cold. They wouldn't need to endure the indignity for long, though, for at dawn, the axe waited – unless they betrayed Lyra.

The trouble is, we don't even know where she is. And if we did, it would get back to Naxius and doom us all . . .

All she wanted at this stage was a swift and painless death. *We won't get trials, but who cares? I'm glad to be spared that bullshit*, she told herself. Her artificial legs had been smashed, but for some reason she'd been thrown her spare pair – they hurt abominably, but at least she could walk. *Just spare me from having to crawl to the executioner's block*, she pleaded with the silence. *Give me that dignity.*

Exilium was chained in the opposite cell across the narrow passage, right beside the main doors to this level. He'd done nothing but pray. Diagonally opposite her was Dominius Wurther, who'd been wounded and looked dreadful. He didn't appear to be terribly interested in pray-ing. Perhaps as the most holy man in Koredom he didn't need to. He'd barely moved or spoken either.

There were another three dozen cells on this level, occupied mostly by Pallacian officers who'd backed Lyra – or not backed Takwyth sufficiently – and there were two more levels below, each level progres-sively worse. She'd been told every cell was full. The slime which covered the walls had soaked their thin clothing; they were all shiver-ing constantly now.

Her bleak thoughts were interrupted by a sudden thumping on the rear door, at the far end of the corridor. 'Guard,' a voice rasped through the eye-slit. 'Open up.'

She and Wurther looked at each other across the narrow way, as the duty gaoler – Willum – lurched from his stool at the front door next to her cell and headed down the passage, shouting, 'Who is it?'

'Father Comfateri, to hear their confessions,' the voice replied.

Basia looked at Wurther in sudden alarm. *Since Germane, there's been no comfateri . . .*

'Willum,' she called, suddenly scared, 'don't let him in.'

Willum was more intelligent than his brutal looks might imply. He stopped and looked back at Basia. 'But he says he's –'

'There *is* no Father Comfateri,' Dominius called. 'Keep that door locked, Willum: your life depends on it.'

Exilium stopped his litany of prayer and twisted his head to look as that fist struck the door with a jarring *boom*. 'Open this door,' the voice came again. '*Open* –'

'It's warded,' Willum muttered, backing away towards them. Two gaolers came up the stair from the lower level, swearing at Willum for not dealing with the racket.

'It's only a rukking priest,' one snarled, swaggering towards the door.

'A *mage*-priest,' Basia called, 'and an *imposter*.'

That gave them pause – but these weren't men used to thinking too hard about what prisoners told them, even prisoners as illustrious as these. They held a muttered conference as the door crashed again – and this time the iron bands buckled and the timbers cracked. The three gaolers backed away, Willum, the rearmost, a touch smarter than his fellows, casting a wild look at Dominius. 'Holy Father . . . ?'

'Sound the alarm,' Dominius snapped, coming to his feet. 'Now –'

But before anyone could act, the door at the end of the corridor came apart, foot-long splinters flying everywhere. The two gaolers at the front, brave or foolhardy, tried to rush the intruder, running out of Basia's sight, until gnostic energy pulsed and she heard them both shriek and fall. Willum stopped in front of her cell, fishing at his belt – and a mage-bolt slammed into his shoulder, spinning him round. The next bolt punched through the back of his head and he collapsed into the rushes, spilling something that glinted into the sodden mush in front of Exilium's cage.

'Where's Basia de Sirou?' the intruder snarled, and Basia recognised the voice of Father Germane, who'd taken her confession before he'd been unmasked as a traitor and vanished. More energy surged as his footsteps approached; she could picture him, blazing mage-bolts into each cell as he passed, murdering for the sheer fun of it.

He was Ostevan's pawn . . . dear Kore, he must be infected too.

Exilium suddenly moved, lunging with his bare feet, reaching under the bars until his toe hooked the thing Willum had dropped: his hoop of keys. Basia's chest thumped in terror as he reeled them in.

Germane was advancing down the passage, still out of sight, and with every few steps he took, more energy pulsed and more men screamed and fell. She heard those still to die pleading, begging.

'Where is she?' he snarled, but no one answered – in truth, few of the prisoners could see each other; they likely didn't even know she was here. Two more flashes. Two more dead men . . . and he was now only yards away.

But Exilium had got the keys and was contorting to push his feet to his right hand. Basia stared in amazement, watching his toes moving like fingers, gripping the key and thrusting it into the lock of his manacles.

'No, no, no–' someone shrieked, and light blazed, just four cells down the corridor.

Basia rose and tried to rip her own rusted manacles free: metal flaked and shrieked, but they held. She would have screamed in frustration – but she knew better than to make a sound. Opposite her, Wurther was hurling himself across the cell, trying to use his massive bulk to rip free – and incredibly, that's what it took: the Grand Prelate's manacles tore from their mounts, sending him crashing against the opposite wall, bellowing in fear and pain.

'Where–' *Flash.* 'Is–' *Shriek.* 'She?' Germane's voice carried down the corridor.

Kore's blood, he's nearly here . . .

Cold water splashed over Solon's face and he spluttered back into consciousness, Germane's words echoing among the hideous babble of the daemon Abraxas, snarling inside his skull. 'No . . .' he groaned, 'no, get away . . .'

'Solon?' a horrified female voice exclaimed.

He opened his eyes and saw Brunelda, his false queen . . . his lover . . . his whore . . . staring up at him with huge wide eyes, so many emotions coursing through her face that he couldn't tell whether he saw hatred and loathing, or pity or . . . something else entirely. She held a chalice with a few drips left of holy water, but it spilt from her hand as she took in what was happening to him. He looked down at his bared arms and saw blackened veins spreading like the veins of a poisoned leaf.

'Brunelda,' he croaked, 'get away from me – get away–'

'Solon?' she squeaked again, reaching out, then she wavered. 'What's happening to you?'

'Get away,' he shouted, 'go – please, *go!*'

But she snatched up a steel rod used to open the upper windows and wedged it into the metal loop made by the twisted torch-holders, while he babbled at her to *run, run, run . . .*

With a screech of metal and crumbling plaster, his right hand came free and he fell forward, hanging painfully by his left, almost pulling from the socket. 'Brunelda,' he shouted up at her, 'get out!'

She's carrying my son . . .

But instead, swearing like a labourer, she rammed the rod into the other makeshift manacle and ripped it free, sending him sprawling onto the carpeted floor – as a blaze of hatred and fury coursed through him.

Kill her take her pollute her, the daemon shrieked and half his muscles clenched to obey. But he resisted, going rigid and clutching at the carpet hooks in the floor, howling to Kore for strength and imploring her to run. Then his vision darkened and he reared up–

. . . as something punched into his side, making his whole body scream. He convulsed as someone barely half his body weight landed on his back – and miraculously the daemon's voice went from a shriek to a whisper and suddenly he could think his own thoughts again . . .

'His eyes,' Brunelda said shakily, 'they went dark, but now . . .'

'Are they clearing?' a crisp female voice snapped.

'Sister Virtue?' Solon croaked, while his mind connected the ichor's reaction to the dagger and shouted *silver* at him. 'You have a silver dagger?' The thing was still lodged inside his midriff. 'Keep it in me,' he begged.

'What the –' the nun – if that's what she was, with her silvered blade – started, her voice horrified. 'Get back,' she told Brunelda. 'He's a Reeker.'

Brunelda's eyes went wider still and she clutched at her belly just as Lyra used to, but instead of fleeing, she exclaimed, 'The silver ... my cousin was infected on Reeker Night and Queen Lyra cured him. He needs sunlight.'

Solon clung to that thought. *Dear Kore, can I be saved?*

But there was no time. He twisted and looked up at the nun on his back. 'Sister Virtue, you have to raise the alarm. It's Germane – he's possessed – he's heading for the dungeon – he might already be there – he's going to kill Basia after he's learned where the real queen is . . .' His voice trailed off as he realised how many lies he'd just revealed. He waited for confusion and the need for lengthy investigations.

But Sister Virtue just snorted, as if she knew all that. 'I've been waiting a week for the chance to knife you, you prick, but either you're surrounded by toadies or sealed off in the royal suite behind all those wards.' She paused to twist the silvered knife in his side, making him gasp in agony. 'Tell me why I shouldn't kill you.'

'Germane's a Mask,' he panted. 'He's like an Ascendant ... find a pure-blood – find ten, twenty ... but kill him, before he learns where Lyra is . . .'

Even in this state of extremis, he saw the way Brunelda's composure crumpled when she realised that this was still all about Lyra. But she stayed.

'He's only been gone two minutes,' she said. 'We were waiting outside the chapel for you – I saw you go in, you were distressed and I was worried . . .' She swallowed, then went on, 'When the comfateri left before you, we were confused, so we drew aside and he didn't see us.'

'Everyone in this rukking castle is on the west side, overlooking the Place d'Accord,' Virtue cut in. 'There's no one to warn.'

Solon groaned as the daemon voices rose again, urging him to fling off the nun and *shred her take her rip her to pieces*, but he fought them down and put his hand over hers, keeping the dagger in the wound. Part of him wondered if at some point the level of ichor in him would turn critical . . . and the silver would blast his blood into ash . . .

But if she removes it, it'll take me sooner.

'Then it's up to me – to us,' he panted, resolving to fight until his last breath. 'Who the Hel are you anyway?'

'The name's Veritia,' the nun replied, assessing him coldly, then her expression shifted decisively and she let go the silvered dagger and rose. He immediately grabbed the hilt and, wincing at the pain, made sure it was still jammed inside the wound.

'I've got argenstael as well, you prick,' she rasped. 'If I could've seen your face properly before I attacked, I'd have used that and you'd be dead already.'

'Thank Kore,' Brunelda moaned, clutching at him. Her face was so full of emotion as to be unreadable . . . but there was no hatred, for all he richly deserved it. 'Solon, hold on!'

Dear Kore, I held her as a prisoner and used her for my own ends, Solon thought incredulously. *She can't actually care . . .*

'You can heal,' she pleaded, and he knew she wasn't just talking about the ichor.

'Yes, I can,' he told her, matching her every meaning. He gripped her shoulder. 'Listen, I free you. Go, pack your things and go. Take care of our child, and . . .' He choked then managed to add, 'I'm sorry – for everything.'

She looked at him, her eyes welling up. 'Don't die,' she whispered. 'Please –'

'Kore's Blood,' Veritia barked urgently, '*come on* –'

Solon gritted his teeth, snatched up his discarded sword and with his left hand over the hilt of the silvered dagger to keep it in, he faced Brunelda. While he floundered for words, she seized his face, kissed it, then fled.

He stared after her, until Virtue – *no, Veritia* – grabbed his shoulder. 'Come on!'

'Are you Volsai?' he asked, as they hurried to the backstairs.

'Freelance – sometimes Kaden Rats, sometimes Grey Foxes . . . but yeah, now I'm Volsai.'

Two of the worst gangs in history . . . or three, if you counted the Volsai. But Solon was relieved: she'd know how to fight. 'You've got argenstael,' he managed, staggering in her wake. 'If the daemon overcomes me . . .'

'It'd be my pleasure,' she said tersely. 'Now come *on*.'

She hurled herself over the balustrade and plummeted down to the entrance hall and he followed suit as the daemon voices rose further, becoming clearer . . .

Germane strode to the next pair of cells, looked left and right. At last: one was female. He got rid of the male first, a torrent of energy turning him instantly to charred meat and bone, then faced the woman, who was kneeling on the stone floor, clad in a filthy nightdress. Her short dark hair had been hacked into tufts. Her head was turned away.

Short dark hair . . .

'You,' he called, 'stand up.'

She didn't move. Further down the row of cells, somewhere out of his line of sight, he could hear the sounds of struggling, but he wasn't concerned; all the magi here were Chained, manacled and behind bars and no one had yet raised the alarm.

'I said, *stand*,' he rasped, and conjuring kinesis, ripped the woman from her kneeling posture and hurled her against the wall. She gasped in pain as he crushed her against the stone, studying her . . . and then he laughed at himself; he should have seen right away that she wasn't his quarry: she had legs. 'Who are you?' he demanded.

'Braeda . . . Kaden . . .' she groaned.

He saw a strong face, more handsome than comely, but with a certain truculent charm – certainly desirable, had there been time for such pleasantries – the daemon inside him loved such things. But right now the only thing that mattered was that she wasn't Basia de Sirou – so he snapped her neck with kinesis and she slumped lifeless in her manacles. Then he moved to the next pair of cells – where he stopped and stared.

'Why, Grand Prelate, how *wonderful* to see you.'

The head of the Church of Kore was standing in the middle of his tiny cell, empty but for a piss-bucket, his obese frame barely covered by a tent-like nightshirt, bare feet standing on the wet stone in the muck. His wrists were shackled to four-foot-long chains that he'd somehow wrenched from the wall – an impressive display of strength, Germane had to admit. His jowls were quivering with resigned fury.

'It must be every priest and nun's dream to see you thus,' Germane gloated. 'It is mine, certainly – even before I had the ineffable good fortune to join my Master's cause.' He slowly raised his hands, which were crackling with energy. 'There will be dancing in the streets when your fate is known, you vile piece of corruption.'

'That's rich, coming from a daemon,' Wurther rumbled.

'Even your own holy book prophesises our ascension to glory,' he pointed out with justification. 'Truly, our time has come.'

'"Prophecy"?' Wurther snorted. 'Don't you know that the *Book of the Last Days* was written by a demented madman and included only because Sertain thought it made a better stick to beat down the people with than some fluffy poetry about Paradise? I hate to disappoint you, but you're going to float in the void for ever.'

Abraxas screeched through Germane's soul, making Germane blast a deliberately weak bolt of gnostic energy into the Grand Prelate's naked feet.

As the Grand Prelate collapsed to his knees, howling in agony, Germane cried, 'Kneel, "Holiness", before me.' Still moving slowly, enjoying the naked terror in Wurther's eyes, he gathered energy for the kill. 'Are you ready to burn?' he asked, raising his hands and grinning widely, before saying, 'for this, Grand Prelate, is our final farewe—'

The word was left uncompleted – from the corner of his eye, Germane glimpsed movement – a man bursting from the next cell, snatching up the fallen gaoler's sword and charging. The dark-haired man's lunge was blindingly fast, the steel blade aimed unerringly at Germane's chest—

– but the daemon's own preternatural speed saved him, locking his shields and deflecting the sword even as he was hurling kinesis at the swordsman, smashing him aside into the bars of the opposite cell. He blazed a mage-bolt, but the swordsman ducked under his blast, rolled away and smoothly came to his feet.

Exilium Excelsior, Germane noted, *which means Basia de Sirou is close . . . most likely in that other cell.*

The Grand Prelate could wait. He turned and pulled another of the dead gaolers' swords to his hands. The blade was blunt and nicked and he knew little of fighting, but Abraxas did, so he met Excelsior's leaping attack with a strong parry and a crunching blast of kinesis that pushed the man away so hard that he smashed the iron-banded door open. He took a step forward, glanced right and saw exactly what he'd hoped to see: Basia de Sirou, trying to insert a key into her manacles – which glittered with enchantment. If she succeeded, she'd free her own gnosis, which would be troublesome, even though she'd be no match for him.

He used kinesis to wrench the keys from her grasp and into his own hand before knocking her unconscious with a kinesis blow – then turned as Excelsior, now desperate, hurled himself forward once again. Germane slammed him into the stone wall and this time – *finally!* – the Estellan flopped bonelessly and didn't move.

Those threats dealt with, Germane burst the bars of Basia's cell, strode in through the shower of rust and iron splinters and gripping her by the hair, yanked her face to his. He had to hold the daemon at bay as he slapped her several times to bring her round, for Abraxas wanted to make her *suffersuffersuffer . . .*

'Where's your queen?' he demanded. 'Where's Lyra?'

The woman's eyes were frightened, but still she defiantly clamped her jaw shut, so he dragged her to the passage and showed her the unconscious Excelsior. Kindling energy in his left hand, he snarled, 'Tell me, or he dies.'

'No,' she said flatly.

She probably knew Exilium Excelsior was dead no matter what she said: she was Volsai and she knew the game. *Well, there's one way to make sure I find the bitch queen.* He bared his teeth and elongated his incisors. 'I think you need a change in motivation.'

He bent to her, stretching his mouth as she cried out in fear, still struggling, for all it was not the blindest bit of use –

– when he was ripped away from the woman and hurled against the bars by a giant figure who'd leaped over the fallen Estellan and was storming toward him. He had a longsword blazing in his grip and pale shields had crystallised around him.

Takwyth . . . ? Rukking unbelievable –

For a moment he feared the man had somehow defeated the ichor – then he saw the blackened veins and realised Takwyth was holding a blade rammed into his own side. *It must be silver . . . clever.* But the blood running from the wound was not entirely red and his clumsy gait showed he was succumbing.

I just need to wait him out . . .

Takwyth went straight on the attack, bludgeoning with all his immense gnostic and physical strength, but Germane surrendered control to Abraxas and with the knowledge of the souls of a thousand swordsmen and the power of the ichor he parried and blocked, all the while watching Takwyth's veins darkening, until at last the ichor reached his eyes –

– and Solon Takwyth, the greatest knight in Koredom, cried out in utter despair and fell to his knees, his sword clattering to the flagstones.

'Slave,' Germane purred, 'get up and follow me.'

His mastery assured, he turned back to deal with Basia de Sirou.

An instant later, something cold and sharp punched into Germane's left buttock and he felt the most excruciating burst of agony, as if all his blood were on fire. There was no time to drew breath and scream, for the roof tilted and his eyes burst into flame, blasting his awareness away . . .

Takwyth groaned and rolled up onto his knees, as Veritia sidled warily through the door, examining him carefully. He withdrew Veita's argenstael punch-dagger, which had been concealed in a spring-loaded sleeve scabbard, from Germane's body.

'Good plan,' he conceded, 'although I didn't think the illusion would hold. I was sure he'd sense it.'

'I had every confidence,' she said drily, unstrapping the dagger.

He pressed the silver dagger deeper into his side, groaning at the pain. The blood-flow was increasing and now he could hear the daemons as clearly as he could hear the Volsai. 'I'm losing it,' he warned her. 'It's time – I don't think I can–'

Veritia loomed over him and he didn't flinch as she raised the argenstael dagger . . . which she reversed and smashed into his temple.

The world cracked open and he spun away.

A distant sound troubled the void, light trembled at the edge of darkness and Exilium woke up.

He was lying on grass, water was trickling somewhere nearby and leaves rustled in a cool, refreshing breeze, somewhat spoiled by the smell of ash. The moon hanging overhead was a glowing milky orb shining through misty clouds. Somewhere nearby, a man was vomiting.

Had it not been for the noisy purging of someone's guts, he'd have assumed he was in Paradise. Then a wave of pain washed over him and told him that he was assuredly still mortal – and still alive. His whole body ached, and when he tried to move his right arm, he felt the grind of bone on bone in his shoulder. Gritting his teeth against the pain, he sat up, looked around and found Basia sitting beside him, a blanket covering her hips and legs. Their eyes locked as utter relief blazed through him.

She's alive, she's alive.

He hadn't realised how precious she was, how much he relied on her being *her*, pricking at him, questioning him, making him think about things he'd never even considered.

He glanced past her to see Solon Takwyth, bent over a pool and pouring water down his throat, turning away to vomit horribly, and then repeating the actions. He was being tended by two women, a nun and the false Lyra. A few feet away he saw the Grand Prelate, drinking from a wineskin. He finally recognised where they were: Queen Lyra's private garden. The foliage was burnt black, but the pool was still clear and somewhere, a night bird was singing its heart out, not quite drowned out by the distant sound of cheering swirling about the high walls.

This is impossible. Perhaps I am dead? But when he stammered, 'Kore's Blood, what's happening?' everyone looked at him and smiled.

'Patcheart's just come from the walls,' Basia told him. 'Sulpeter's capitulated: he's pledged to Frankel's constitution and is marching the Corani legions out of the city. Rykjard's Hollenians are taking control of the Bastion and Frankel's leading some kind of singalong in the Place d'Accord.' She smiled shyly and concluded, 'The world's gone mad.'

His heart thudded and he reached out and clutched her hand. 'And Takwyth . . . ?' His eyes turned to the Corani knight, who was now sobbing in the arms of his fake queen.

'He's surrendered,' Basia told him. 'We survived. *Pallas* survived—'

But her words were cut off by a great crack of thunder, so loud it made the ground shake. A howling wind rushed in out of nowhere and the night sky was suddenly covered in boiling blotches of darkness which came pouring out from the dark places between the stars, blocking them out. Something like a massive claw raked the translucent canopy above, as lightning split the sky like jagged tears in the fabric of the universe.

The dark shapes took form: giant figures with wings and claws and burning eyes . . .

'Oh no,' Basia breathed. 'Lyra's too late. It's begun.'

The Last Days.

Exilium grasped her fingers tighter as everyone looked up in awe and despair.

We must pray, he thought wildly. *We must beg Kore's forgiveness – the Doors of Paradise are closing and we are outside among the sinners. We must repent.*

Then indignation set in. 'How can this be?' he demanded. 'It's not fair – we prevailed . . .'

Basia, her face an inch from his, was gazing up at the lightning raking the sky. 'Ah, Exilium, life never was fair,' she breathed, turning away from the ruptured skies and facing him. 'We never get what we want.'

Then she kissed him as an earthquake rumbled, shaking the city. He barely noticed. Utterly stunned, he found himself responding, kissing her back with all the pent-up passion of a life of repressing every sinful impulse, drinking her in, tumbling with her to the wet ground and falling into her while the world collapsed around them.

35

The Last Hour

Paradise Now

Imagine a world in which we conquered only with love: a place where we embraced our brothers and sisters across barriers of race, nationhood and religion, shared the fruits of the world fairly and raised each other up with all our skill, knowledge and compassion, so that all were equal in possessions and status. Would that not be Ahm's Paradise made real on Urte? And why do we not already have this?

GODSPEAKER ILAM, JA'ARATHI PREACHER, HEBUSALIM 922

Mount Fettelorn, Noros

Waqar turned from Xoredh's decapitated body, his cousin already forgotten. His blade dripping ichor, he stared past the breath taking, terrifying vista of the giant tree with the world cradled in its branches to the giant form of Jehana floating above it. Sunlight lit her, but the darkness went on for ever.

He shouted, *'JEHANA!'* but there was no sign that she'd heard. The darkness continued to engulf her, the sky swirling around her as she writhed, her head thrown back in a silent scream as a dark vortex erupted from her mouth.

Then he saw that Lyra and Valdyr were also standing at the edge of the cavern – how they'd got there he had no idea . . . unless it could be reached from other places? But the *how* didn't matter: he needed them, and this time, when he shouted their names, they did hear. They looked shocked, but an instant later, they and Gricoama were standing with him.

Together they realised the dwyma was fighting back – and they were its weapons. Valdyr and Lyra grasped Gricoama's fur – and after a moment's pause, ignoring the sudden sharp ache in his hand, Waqar reached out and did the same. The Rondian queen was wide-eyed, her hands white-knuckled, but Valdyr's flinty face was steadfast.

He's been here before, Waqar remembered.

The Mollach prince shouted something and instead of the wolf, Waqar found himself with a hand on Ajniha's feathers, while beside him, Lyra had her arms round the neck of her pegasus, but there was no time to wonder: they threw themselves onto their mounts and instantly they were flying.

'*Jehana*,' he shouted, '*we're coming.*'

They shot upwards, weaving through branches wider than rivers bearing leaves big enough to blot out the sky, while around them things like the husks of huge insects swooped onto beads of light rising from the immense tree – and as each was snared, there was a piteous shriek that swiftly faded.

Those aren't insects, Waqar realised, aghast, *they're daemons . . . eating* souls . . .

There was a malevolent hiss as the immense spectral insects *saw* them and came shooting at them with mouths opening around malformed, ever-changing heads, a cacophony of clamouring voices from their throats –

The dwymancers killthemsnarethemtakethem . . .

– the nearest of the giant creatures lunged, claw-like appendages erupting from its shifting maw, and Ajniha banked to the right, shrieking, Pearl shot the other way, while Gricoama *leaped*.

Waqar bellowed in alarm as the creature reared over him, taller than a palace, and instinctively blasted at it with a puny mage-bolt, expecting nothing – but he was Sakita Mubarak's son, bred with the potential for both gnosis and dwyma: the bolt exploded from his hands and struck like a meteor.

The daemon shrilled as it collapsed in on itself.

I can use the gnosis here – ai, aiee – but Valdyr was already shouting, 'Go – go – *go!*' as more daemons burst through the leaves, swarming over them . . .

Mount Fettelorn, Noros

'They're massing again,' Dirklan called from his position at the right-hand walkway, the secondary approach to the door they guarded. This was the last place they could make a stand.

Tarita threw him a grim look. They'd not found Jehana or Naxius and now they were trapped while the skies above boiled with apocalyptic shapes, nightmarish visions come to life in the heavens.

We've failed.

On the walkway and the wide steps leading to it were strewn the corpses of the successive waves of possessed constructs that kept hurling themselves at them. They'd barely survived the last rush; only her torrent of mage-fire, punching holes in flesh and bone, backed by Dirklan and Ogre's own mage-bolts, had kept them away: it was wholesale slaughter, but each rush was getting closer, and there were more of them with every attack.

It's only a matter of time now. She looked at Ogre, sheltering behind a pillar on the other side of the walkway. 'Hey, Big Man,' she called softly, realising this could be the last chance they had to speak. 'I've got a new theory.'

'About what?'

'About love.'

They could all see movement on the ramp below, and hear the tramp of more feet.

'What theory?' Ogre rumbled, gripping his axe and flexing his shoulders.

'Well, as you know, I've maintained a strict policy of sleeping with random men and neglecting my friends, which has mostly led to misery and worse, embarrassment.'

'And?'

'It's time I stopped neglecting my friends.' She let him digest that, then added, 'Ogre, you're my very best friend and I love you, too.'

His spine straightened, he mumbled something hoarse and his eyes gleamed wetly before he turned away. Then a bestial howl echoed and the next wave of daemons came streaming along the footway while a dozen more burst over the top of the rubble-packed roof and threw themselves down from above.

I failed.

Yes, you failed.

You used me.

Yes. You are our puppet.

This is all my fault.

Yes, for you are weak: just an orifice, a threshold, an open door.

Jehana floated in stars, locked in the hideous embrace of the daemon as a torrent of spiny, clawed, bestial shapes, ever-shifting but always vile, poured through her. Daemons spewed like insects from her mouth, the dead and the never-alive, pouring down into Urte which hung before her tortured gaze, while her nethers disgorged venom that covered the root-soil of the Elétfa, bad blood poisoning the veins of the world's heart, fouling the rivers of life.

She was helpless. She was nothing.

No, not nothing, that gleeful voice gloated, *you're one of us now: the Mother of Destruction. We will keep you with us, our vessel to poison world after world, until all Creation belongs to us.*

She tried to flee from that dreadful thought, but there was nowhere to run to, nothing that wasn't Lucian, nowhere He wasn't already present. He was *in* her. He *was* her and she was just an extension of Him.

The giant Tree of Life began to wither.

All things fail, Lucian – Naxius – crowed. *Everything but us. Only Entropy is eternal.*

Waqar, Lyran and Valdyr came to rest on a branch in the bower of the Elétfa, their mounts bathed in sweat, their wings shaking. Their riders were scarcely stronger. The deadly pursuit was barely a minute behind them and there was nowhere else to run.

But before them, they saw a stunning vista: Urte, their world, a blue-green planet half-lit by a distant sun, hanging in the gauzy branches of the tree. And from all sides, immense clouds of darkness were beginning to cover it, emerging from a hole in space – a gateway from the aether to the physical realm, Waqar guessed. A shrieking sound vibrated through the air, through the tree, through his skin and bones. Then his gaze shifted, or the stars did, and he saw that the hole in Creation was a mouth, and that the stars around it formed the outline of a face – one he knew.

'*Jehana . . .*' He looked back to see the daemon swarm closing in.

Lyra ran to the nearest branch, plucked three berries, wolfed one down and handed one to Valdyr and one to Waqar.

The Mollach prince stared. 'What is this?'

'Does it matter? What have you got to lose?'

'Put like that . . .' He bit, tasting acrid juice, then swallowed. 'What . . . ?'

'Hopefully, it'll give you what you need to reach Jehana,' Valdyr said. 'We'll give you every second we can – she's beyond the reach of anyone else . . .' Then he gripped Lyra's hand and they turned away to face the oncoming daemons.

Waqar turned his awareness inwards, hoping for a miracle.

At first, nothing happened to him other than the bittersweet berry taste seeping down his throat – then his vision blurred and cleared – *No, it's more than cleared*. He caught his breath: everything was brighter, more intense, and he had the strangest sensation that he was living a death-dream, that somewhere else, his body lay dying.

How can any of this be real?

But the daemons were real enough, of that he was certain, and so was what was happening to his sister. He shouted with voice and mind, <*JEHANA!*> and this time he felt his call rippling out through the space between them – then the stars around her flashed, her eyes flew open and *she saw him*.

But the daemons heard him too, and they roared in like a swarm of giant locusts, an avalanche of living ice, a torrent of ravenous crustaceans. Lyra uttered a wordless cry, echoed by Valdyr, and a bolt of light coruscated from the distant sun and flashed around them. The daemon cloud convulsed—

—and then broke over them like a wave of hate. Jehana's face vanished, but Waqar clung to the memory, calling her name again as mage-bolts burst from his hand in a last futile gesture of defiance.

Gnostic energy burned, kinesis surges blasted out and the next wave of the daemons was hurled back, Tarita's Ascendant strength making the stairs a place where nothing could survive. She used a wizardry binding to paralyse the possessed constructs, so that they were caught defence-less in her next spell, a torrent of fire, while those leaping from the roofs were dashed aside by Ogre and Dirklan's kinetic blasts, winning another respite.

They heard a querulous voice shouting, '*KILL THEM* —' aloud and into the aether.

'Rukka te,' Tarita snarled. 'That's *him*, isn't it?'

Ogre's face went flaccid with shock, and he mouthed the word *Master*.

With a mad shriek, she went pelting down the stairs, hurdling the piles of blackened and burning corpses, in the direction of that voice. She heard Ogre cry out her name, then he roared, his big feet hammering into the stonework as he pursued her, followed by the sound of Dirklan's boots close behind.

She had no plan, just an insane desire to strike first, instead of waiting to be overwhelmed. No more caution, no more waiting: '*It's time to die!*' she yelled as she tore along, Dirklan and Ogre pelting behind her. Thunder rumbled and the corridors burst into life around them, a giant horned Mantaur bursting from a door in front of her and other constructs right behind it, larger still than any they'd fought.

Tarita skidded under its giant axe and rammed her silvered sword up into his groin. The Mantaur howled in agony, but a moment later, Ogre had beheaded him, leaving the body to crash to the ground in a spray of blood and ichor.

They exchanged a wild-eyed look: she saw that Ogre got it completely, that he was with her until the end, and she loved that. But there was no time for anything more: Dirklan had flashed by, his false eye blazing as he hurdled the swinging hammer of a giant ogre and plunged an argenstael stiletto into its shoulder. Its howl turned to a torrent of ash pouring from its mouth as it collapsed.

Tarita took the lead again and burst into a courtyard and a flurry of flashing blades. Between them they downed seven constructs in as many moments with argenstael, fire and silvered blades – and to their gratified shock, the rest broke and fled, the daemon's control overridden by the sudden explosion of death. Tarita sent a mage-bolt laced with necromancy after the hindmost; his head withered in the blast, dust pouring from the disintegrating skull.

'Effective,' Ogre rumbled, panting hard.

'Always, darling,' she told him, wondering, *So where's Naxius, and what's between us and him?* She cast about and caught sight of a spotlessly clean corridor leading off the courtyard. 'That way, or I'm a virgin.'

They raced on through increasingly silent halls and she worried she'd got it wrong, until she saw an archway which bore the motto *Knowledge is the only true power.*

'Is this it?' Dirklan asked, breathing hard, and she realised that despite being a mage, he was also an old man, and a lot older than he looked.

'I bloody hope so: I don't want to be a virgin again.'

'He's here,' Ogre growled. 'That's his personal motto.' He looked terrified but determined.

'Are you ready to face your old Master?' she asked him.

He met her gaze solemnly, his face resolute. 'So long as you are with me.'

She squeezed his hand. 'To the end, Ogre.'

He straightened and his voice grew stronger. 'To the end.' He reached past her, grasped the handle and stared as the lock instantly clicked open. 'He didn't erase my gnostic aura from his wards,' he said in a puzzled voice.

Because he believes he still owns you, Tarita thought. *Old fool.*

Ogre pushed open the door and led them through.

Ogre's first step into Naxius' sanctuary was, in a horrible, soul-crushing way, like coming home. Even though he'd never been here – he'd been bred in another of Naxius' secret lairs – he *knew* this was the Master's chambers the moment he inhaled, for Naxius' rooms in Verelon had smelled the same – sterile and faintly musty.

He gripped his axe, quelled the sudden hollowness in his limbs and stalked down the corridor towards the only light, which turned out to be a central hall. Tarita and Dirklan were with him, but this was *his* confrontation: Master and slave.

They stepped into the light, blinking in the glare and trying to make sense of what they were seeing. The room was circular, with a stone slab like an altar of polished marble in the middle. Above it floated a skull-masked woman with long hair the colour of bone: Jehana Mubarak. Something like a shadow made flesh was ravishing her naked body. Her mouth, caught open in a rictus scream, was spewing out smoke or insects or filth.

A gnostic image, Ogre realised: a projection, so that Naxius could watch the culmination of all his scheming unfold.

'*And Glamortha shall lay with Lucian, Lord of Hel, and beget the Last Days . . .*' he murmured, his heart turning to lead in his chest.

Then he saw a small figure beneath the image, staring up at it with rapt eyes.

The Master . . .

In that same moment Naxius saw them, a flash of mild irritation crossing his face. Dirklan and Tarita attacked, one darting left, the other right, but Naxius splayed his fingers, sending a burst of shockingly strong kinesis laced with webs of light that caught them both and hurled them against the walls. Dirklan hit hard, his skull smashing into the marble with a sickening crunch, and at once he went limp, blood running from the back of his head, scarlet against the silver.

Tarita's arm had snapped at the elbow, and another twitch of Naxius' finger cracked a kinesis blow into her jaw, breaking that too. She lay there glassy-eyed and moaning.

Naxius laughed.

He didn't touch Ogre at all. There was no need.

The Master looked radiant: youthful, perfected, a compact body with a noble face beneath a mane of red-gold hair. His eyes glowed like small suns. As he walked, the very stone beneath him seemed to ripple at his passing.

'I'm beyond you all now, Ogre,' he purred. 'I am the sum of all things.'

Ogre badly wanted to run to Tarita, but he knew he was a finger's twitch from instant death himself.

'All that power up there?' Naxius drawled, gesturing to the streaming shadow slithering in the ceiling dome above. 'That's just a fraction of what I can reach now. I could walk into the Merozain Halls in Hebusalim and destroy them all with a word. I could walk into the Bastion and kill every soul therein without a moment of personal peril. I am a God, and I have the power of life and death in my hands.'

As if to emphasise his point, he suddenly flicked his wrist – and Ogre choked back a cry of horror as he heard Dirklan Setallius' neck snap.

'No,' Ogre croaked. *He's Lyra's father . . .*

'So he is,' Naxius agreed lightly, hearing Ogre's thought as clearly as if he'd spoken the words aloud. Stepping around him, he stopped before Tarita, her Ascendant strength rendered to nothing. 'And this one . . . I've been longing to meet you, my sweetling. The little dirt-caste nothing who's turned my Ogre's head.'

'Master,' Ogre blurted, '*please –*'

'Master,' Naxius echoed, sounding pleased. 'Yes, I am *still* your Master, aren't I? I have learned a great lesson on this journey, Ogre: that humans cannot be trusted. All my Masks betrayed me, did you know that? Every single one of them. You feed humans and they try to bite your hand. Only my constructs have remained true.' He waggled a stern finger. 'Except you, Ogre. You even killed dear Semakha, who I made for you.'

That wasn't how it was, Ogre tried to say. *Semakha was evil – you made her so*. But he couldn't make his throat work.

'An eye for an eye, the *Book of Kore* says,' Naxius snickered. 'You know what: I do believe I wrote that passage, too.' Then he turned back to Tarita, his face turning savage, and balled his right fist.

'*Nooo!*' Ogre roared. He tried to move, but all he could do was drop to his knees. His axe clattered to the stone beside him. 'No Master, I beg you–'

Naxius paused. 'The punishment would be apt and deserved, Ogre: you took from me, so I take from you.'

Ogre looked up through stinging eyes to see the woman he loved was staring at him, her chin up, defiant to the end – and mouthing something . . . about *love*.

That finally gave him the strength to move, no matter the cost. His leg muscles bulged, his chest expanded and his big hands flexed as he rose, the inner beast that Naxius had bred into him roaring.

That he could still defy him clearly startled Naxius, but Ogre never got to even snatch up his axe and hurl it, for the mage's eyes turned liquid gold and blazed across the chamber . . .

As the darkness came flooding in, Lyra reached for the sun, the only thing that might be sovereign against the daemons boiling towards her like a swarm of ravenous gigantic cockroaches and with her other hand, she seized Valdyr's fingers, linking with him, and he came willingly.

The dwyma responded, but it was too slow: the daemons were already blotting out Jehana's face, even Urte itself—

– but Waqar was unleashing his own flood of mage-bolts, shouting his sister's name. Lyra could see the colour draining from his face: he was holding nothing back from the torrent of energy. Without physical bodies to house them, the naked souls of the daemons burned to ash on contact, but there were *so many* – far too many. He could buy them only a few seconds.

But in those moments, everything came together.

Light suddenly coalesced on Lyra: a bolt of brilliant radiance, bright enough to blind, but this time she knew how to channel it: she raised the hand clasped in Valdyr's and let the current flow through her – and it burst from their joined hands, searing everything in its path. She shouted aloud, exulting in the potent rush, as the solar blasts wrought devastation on the sea of darkness, the screeching of the perishing daemons tearing at their senses.

But the sense of victory was illusory, she realised, for there were so many more. Neither she nor Valdyr could drop their guard, but if someone couldn't reach Jehana and somehow stop this, they were all doomed . . .

<*JEHANA,*> Waqar shouted, raged, pleaded, <*JEHANA – STOP –*>

The agony was that he could see what to do – but he couldn't do it himself. *I should have embraced the dwyma months ago but I let other things matter more . . . I've failed everyone.*

His mind racing, he begged, 'Help me!' but Valdyr and Lyra were caught up trying to buy him time, not knowing he couldn't do anything without them.

He couldn't distract them, for the daemons would overwhelm them; already they were all but engulfed by reaching talons and snarling faces, the nightmarish forms on all sides –

– when suddenly he felt a small hand in his and looked down to see a young Yurosi girl with shining red-gold hair looking up at him.

'Aradea is with you,' she said in a small, sing-song voice.

Waqar had no idea what that meant, but if the girl was here, she was like Lyra and Valdyr. He reached out with his mind, and there she was, welcoming him.

'Help me reach her,' he begged.

The girl seemed to understand, because her face tilted up past his to the giant shape of his sister's face in the stars above, and together they shouted, <*JEHANA – PLEASE STOP –*>

Then, with a sob of utter loss, he sent a blazing mage-bolt into the stars, right between Jehana's eyes, seeking to kill his beloved sister because he couldn't think what else to do. With the girl channelling energy through him, that pallid blue bolt became a burst of concentrated light that flashed across the skies . . .

<*Jehana – please stop –*> The words reached her like a whisper, but she heard them loud as a clarion call: her name, spoken by her *brother*, wrenched her back from the precipice.

She tried to call out to him, but the daemon was riding her and she had no mouth; she was just a *tunnel*, a passage for the unearthly to tear their way through. She was helpless – then a ray of light slammed into her skull and she howled in pain, for she was half-daemon now, half of *their* world.

But the rest of her, the *not*-daemon, rallied. The pain was bad, but nowhere near the agony Lucian, bound to her dwyma form, felt when that concentrated beam of light struck like fire on parchment. He, who'd not felt direct pain in the millennia of his existence, howled and thrashed about – and lost his grip on her.

Like a mongoose caught by a cobra, poisoned and near death but still possessing teeth of her own, Jehana turned and struck and through her own intense pain, held on to that burning light and channelled it inwards, *inside her* where millions of daemons were enveloped in its radiance, then shrieked and died. Even as she did so, she reached back to the source of that light – Waqar, she suddenly realised – and drew more, then channelling gnosis and dwyma, she sent a brilliant beam through the being that rode her.

Lucian howled for mercy, but she closed her ears; and the Lord of Daemons came apart in a burst of glowing sparks, comets that quickly faded and winked out.

Gone . . .

He was gone.

And she was free . . .

Healing the Elétfa took but a thought, directing the energies into restoration, burning through the daemons still clinging to it. Then she thought of the ichor – and after she burned it from herself, she extended herself through the living tree, burning it away from there too.

Gone . . . It was gone.

She floated free, hollowed out and filled up, and suddenly, beyond all hope, at peace.

It is done.

She closed her eyes and hoped to die.

Ogre stared helplessly as Ervyn Naxius licked his lips and pointed a finger at Tarita, purple light gleaming as he prepared his spell of choice. 'Master, please,' Ogre begged, knowing it was hopeless—

– when suddenly, Naxius blazed from within as if he'd swallowed a sun. He rose into the air, arms and legs splayed, light streaming from his eye sockets and his mouth, as his beauteous youth, his radiant skin and lustrous hair crumbled to pallor and wrinkled age. He was screaming light, venting a burning agony beyond human endurance. The darkness gathered within him, the light dimmed . . .

. . . as Jehana Mubarak vanished from the image above, her face cast in serenity . . .

And the Master's face went slack, as if he were utterly unable to comprehend what was happening.

But Ogre, hearing Tarita gasping for breath, groped for his axe, rose with a snarl of utter rage and hurled it. It spun through the air and buried itself in the Master's left breast, crunching through ribs like kindling and lodging there, the silvered steel cleaving apart the chambers of whatever kind of heart Ervyn Naxius still retained.

The mage staggered, groped for balance as he fell to the floor . . .

. . . *and then sat up and wrenched out the axe.* With a fiendish grin, he rasped, 'Oh, *bad* Ogre.'

Ogre's heart almost stopped – but even as Naxius rose, his face a mask of bestial ferocity, an argenstael dagger plunged into his back and this time ichor exploded and ash came blasting out in a cloud, hurling him back.

When the dust finally settled, there wasn't enough left of Naxius to fill a bucket.

'Hmm. Definitely one of my better throws,' said a dry voice.

Ogre turned and stared as Dirklan Setallius, his face grey, clicked his neck properly back into place. 'But . . . I thought . . .' Ogre stammered.

'Dead? Me? Necromancy, my friend,' Dirklan told Ogre. 'They say a bone-dancer's harder to kill than a roach nest, although I rather think that flatters cockroaches.'

Ogre put a hand to his heart in thanks, then hurled himself at Tarita and gathered her to his chest, trying to tell her all he felt – until she put a finger to his lips.

'Ogre,' she whispered, 'shut up and kiss me.'

Epilogue I

A Western Sunset

A Dream of Better

I've been told that I'm never satisfied, always yearning for the impossible: universal peace and prosperity, equality and love, an end to war and a world without frontiers. It's better, I'm told, to seek the attainable. My answer is that one can do both: achieve that which you can, but also strive for that which is beneficial and still out of reach. It's in our striving that we grow, as a person and as a people.

ANTONIN MEIROS, 877

Rym, Rimoni
Martrois 936

The halls of Ervyn Naxius' secret citadel echoed with the sparse footfalls of those few who remained. It was a strange place to linger, but there was no sane reason not to rest on a soft mattress or to dine on food and wine fit for kings and emperors.

Or princes and empresses, Waqar supposed, looking across the huge lounge to where Valdyr Sarkany and Lyra Vereinen were sharing a divan, sitting primly enough, although their bodies were inclined towards each other in longing.

They say after wartime that people seek out love to heal the hurt.

But he feared there would be no healing for his sister. Jehana, sitting across a low table from him, was staring blankly into space. She hadn't spoken since they'd found her at the foot of Naxius' blasted dwyma tree in the aftermath of the previous night's horrors. Waqar immediately took over her care, only letting her out of his sight long enough for Lyra

623

and Tarita to bathe and clothe her. He hated her bone-white hair and the burn-marks around her face where the mask had been, but most of all he hated the emptiness in her gaze.

Valdyr said that a lot of what one saw inside the dwyma was symbolic, but it had looked horribly real to him: a true vision of Hel.

He steeled himself and tried again to reach her, 'Jehana, will you eat? Please?'

Dirklan Setallius joined him. The Volsai looked twice as ghostly as usual, although he moved with his usual economic precision. They'd shared the bare outlines of their stories and he now knew the empress was Dirklan's daughter: a deadly secret in the outside world, but it felt just that her father had exacted vengeance on Naxius, who had so assailed Lyra.

'Is she responding?' Dirklan murmured.

Waqar shook his head. 'Nothing. I don't think she even hears me.'

'Be patient,' the spymaster advised. 'She needs the very best mystic-healers – we can arrange this in Pallas.'

Can I accept such aid? he wondered. *They're the enemies of my people.* 'I must return to the Shihad,' Waqar replied. 'My people need to see me, to know I'm with them.'

'I'm sure they do,' Dirklan agreed. 'You saved us, Prince Waqar – we're in your debt.'

Waqar shook his head. 'No, for without Lyra and Valdyr, I wouldn't have been there; and without Coramore, I would have failed – and Coramore, I understand, would not have been there at all had it not been for the heroism and sacrifice of others.'

'We all played our part,' Dirklan agreed. 'Jehana saved us, because she heard you and loved you enough to fight back – or that's how I read it. In the end, I think we all saved each other.'

'You speak truly,' Waqar conceded, before indicating Lyra and Valdyr. 'I think they are drawn to each other.'

'That's Lyra's business,' Dirklan said mildly. 'I let her make her own mistakes.'

'With what result?' Waqar asked doubtfully: few Eastern fathers would do such a thing.

'A lot of mistakes,' the Volsai chuckled, his face crinkling. 'But no one grows without making mistakes. The woman she was before all her misadventures could never have done what she did today.'

Waqar thought on that. In some ways, Jehana had been on a similar journey, pursued though the wilderness with Tarita and Ogre, then caught up in the machinations of Alyssa Dulayne and Ervyn Naxius, making mistakes, but growing.

And he's right, Jehana needs help I can't give – no one in the East can, except perhaps the Ordo Costruo.

He bowed deeply. 'Thank you. I accept your offer. Please, ask your mage-healers to help her – anything she needs. I stand surety for all costs,' he said solemnly, touching hand to heart. 'But what of you and your daughter?'

The Volsai's face turned serious again. 'We must return to Pallas. A lot was left in the balance when we came here. I've been in contact with my second there and the news is good, but Lyra is the key. With her present, the new republic has a chance.'

Republic. Waqar had had the term explained and it sounded like madness. Yuros really was another world.

'And you say the safety of the Shihad is guaranteed?' he asked again. With this crisis averted, he half-expected the war to resume: Teileman still had a giant army in northern Noros and there were now far fewer foes to oppose him.

'Those in Norostein will be housed and fed and they remain armed. The rest is up to your commanders – and to you. I hope you will urge them to retreat into Verelon. The next Moontide is four years away, in 940. There is much to be resolved, but the war doesn't need to continue.'

Waqar looked away, thinking hard. The Shihad might be broken, but they still had many men, combatants and camp followers alike. However, he doubted there was much appetite for taking up the struggle again. Ali Beyrami was dead and Teileman was no warrior. He'd want to return to Kesh and claim his brother's throne. This conflict now felt like a disastrous folly, not the great and just war Rashid had declared it to be.

I'm sick of fighting, Waqar admitted to himself.

Slowly, he offered his hand, in the Yurosi way. 'Spymaster, I declare, insofar as I have the right to do so, that the Shihad is over. Evil has been vanquished and my people wish only to return to their homeland.'

They clasped hands and raised a toast to peace.

Tarita found Ogre in the chamber of the constructs, wandering from slab to slab, studying each creature: lamiae, goat-men, lizardmen, bull-headed Mantauri and others. There were several ogres, his mirror-images; like him, they would also have gnostic ability, the better to serve Naxius. For now they slept, life sustained, but not awareness.

They were divided over what to do about them. Dirklan and Waqar wanted them slain painlessly, without waking them. Lyra and Valdyr hadn't yet ventured opinions. Tarita herself was unsure, and right now she was too tired to think. None of them had slept much since the ordeal, still too wound up and with too many unknowns in this citadel of the enemy to relax.

'Ogre?' she called from the door. 'What're you up to?'

Gazing at the sleeping constructs, he said, 'They're all like me. It's like coming home.'

She joined him, squeezing his hand. 'But it was never a good home for you, was it?'

'No,' he admitted, 'but I belonged.'

He looks lost, and torn, she thought. *He thinks now this is over, I'll leave and he won't be able to follow.*

Kissing him last night had been strange – physically awkward, for he was so much bigger – but it had been the truest kiss of her life. 'Ogre, what is it *you* want?'

He looked around, then rested his hand beside a male ogre far bigger than him. 'These are living people – they can be woken: I know how. But there's no one to teach them right from wrong, to care for them, to tell them about the world . . . unless I do it.' He bit his lip miserably. 'This is what I must do, even when you all leave me behind. It's the right thing.'

You noble, beautiful man, she thought. She leaped up onto the edge of the slab so that they could talk face to face and pressed her cheek to his.

She was suddenly a little frightened, because commitments were scary, but it was time to make some.

'Ogre, if that's what you want to do, I'm with you. We'll do it together.'

Even now, he looked like he didn't quite believe her, and that hurt a little – but she supposed she wasn't known for faithfulness.

'I thought you wanted to travel – that you wanted adventures?' he asked, sounding shy.

'And I'm sure you do too. But that doesn't mean we can't put down roots as well.'

'With the war over, people are going to come here, try to take this place,' he warned. 'My Master's knowledge is valuable and dangerous.'

'All the more reason for us to take charge of it,' she told him. 'And with my Merozain and Ordo Costruo connections, I can ensure it is kept in safe hands.'

'But . . .' He hesitated, then plunged onwards, 'Tarita, you don't belong here like I do. You're so beautiful and perfect: you belong in the courts of kings and magi.'

'No, I belong with you.'

'But . . . it's impossible. You said so . . . I'm too big and . . . uh . . .'

She fixed him with a look. 'Do you really want *that* conversation, Ogre?'

'Um . . .'

'Excellent. Listen, Big Man, you're what? – about a quarter taller than an average man, similarly wider across the shoulders and hips: that sounds manageable to two people with morphic-gnosis, don't you think?' He went utterly scarlet, as she pressed on, 'No woman's going to complain about a big lover, Ogre. We'll manage just fine.'

'Ah . . .'

She put her nose to his. 'As soon as we can push the others out of the door, you and I are going to test that theory. We're going to get naked.'

She didn't wait for his reply – Ogre wasn't managing much in the way of articulate speech – but pressed her mouth to his as his arms came round her and enveloped her in a way that made her feel both safe and deliciously endangered.

Suddenly, the night couldn't come quickly enough.

*

Lyra woke suddenly, pulled from a harrowing dream of daemons and burning trees by Valdyr rolling against her. She studied his face in the half-light. In repose, freed of all his worries and bad memories, he looked his true age, which was more or less her own. This might be another romantic mistake, but so far it didn't feel like that.

We've shared so much inside the dwyma, inside each other's heads. This felt so natural, and I wanted it so much. She glowed at memories of the previous night, thinking, *So did he.*

He'd been tentative at first, but they'd eased their way past his traumas without fuss and the moment they'd joined had been truly beautiful: considerate, caring, loving, without the domineering conquering roughness of Solon or Ril's want-away eyes. *Perfect.*

'Good morning,' she whispered, rolling on her side to face him. Rosy light was glowing through a roof-dome, setting the marble walls aglow. 'Sleep well?'

'Mmm,' he murmured, tickling her face with his *ridiculous* moustaches.

They basked in the moment for a while, as the light outside grew. She wished she could just halt time and live in this feeling for ever. But life didn't work that way.

'What happens now?' he asked softly.

She'd been wondering that herself. 'I must return to Pallas – I have no choice. My "constitutional republican monarchy" needs me. Someone has to hold the threat of ice-storms over the Dukes of Argundy and Dupenium and whoever else might try to invade. And my son is there. I have to arrange some kind of life for Cordan and Coramore, too.' She met his eyes and cautiously added, 'I may well adopt them.'

He didn't flinch. 'They'll need you.'

Bless you, she thought. 'So, my life is there, right now.' Her voice faltering, she asked, 'What about you?'

He grimaced. 'My brother needs me. Mollachia has been devastated and he has two peoples to bring together as one. A failed harvest could destroy us all – I have to be there for him, help make sure that doesn't happen.'

She swallowed, even though she'd expected the answer.

'But after that . . .' he went on, earnestly, 'by the end of summer, I might be free, if things go well. If you . . .' He hesitated, then blurted, 'People say Pallas women go lightly from one bed to the next, but if you were to wait for me, I would come as soon as I may.'

Thank you, Kore, she breathed inside her mind.

She gave him a teasing smile. 'Well, I've heard that Mollach men go from bed to bed like hunters, but if you were prepared to wait on me, I will certainly wait on you.'

'There will never be anyone else for me. There is only you.'

She shifted against him, gripped his shoulders and encouraged him onto her, relishing the weight of him as he settled and the glorious feeling of wrapping herself around him. She nuzzled his neck, and whispered, 'If this is our last chance for a time, give me something to remember.'

Norostein, Noros

Ramon stirred awake, sniffed the wine-laden, stuffy air and winced.

On his right, Amiza, Calipha of Ardijah, was snoring in gusts, her smooth copper back bare and her hair tangled in sweaty knots. On his left, Vania di Aelno lay on her back, breasts uncovered and her own snoring rasping and contented.

It was impossible to sleep through it all. He yawned, grinned, and then slithered away, found a gown – one of Vania's – and headed for the balcony and some much needed fresh air. *Got to clear my head, work out what on Urte I'm doing.*

When Vania had shown up at the door, willing to fight for "her man", Amiza had stunned them both by letting her in. The widowed calipha had apparently had to forgo men to ensure she remained the ruler of Ardijah – so she'd seduced women instead. 'I like this one,' she'd declared, then the two of them had dragged him to the bed. He hadn't resisted much.

But now what?

Before he could think through his options, his senses tingled.

<*Son?*> Calan Dubrayle sent, his mental voice echoing through a relay-stave.

<*Father,*> Ramon sent back blearily. He strengthened the connection, then opened it up so they could see each other. Calan looked tired, but at ease. <*What's happening?*>

<*What's happening?*> the Treasurer mused. <*Well, Solon Takwyth has capitulated and civil war is averted. Pallas is settling into recovery and awaits her true queen.*> He paused. <*Why are you wearing a woman's gown?*>

<*It's the latest fashion,*> Ramon replied. <*Wait 'til it catches on in Pallas.*> He yawned, then went on, <*Here, all's well. The possessed are no longer so – although it wasn't our doing. Seth's been talking to Setallius. It appears the queen's mission succeeded.*>

Calan nodded. <*I've spoken to Dirklan too. Obviously we can't proclaim it, but you're right. They saved us all.*> He hesitated, then asked, <*Have you considered my proposal?*>

Ramon had, but he'd been considering Amiza's too. <*I have – but I must decline, Father. I've agreed to take my mercenaries into the East. The Calipha of Ardijah has a claim on my aid and needs me to help reclaim her throne. One of her cousins was left in charge, but it appears he's suffering from a bad case of greed.*>

Calan's face fell. <*What's her hold over you?*>

<*She's the mother of my son.*>

The look on his father's face was priceless. <*You have a son . . . ? My . . . my grandson?*>

<*His name's Rameez . . . Father, Amiza wants me to marry her, to help rule her city. I'm tempted, but it's early days. If it does work out, there's no reason I can't visit. And I promise I'll bring Rameez to meet you as soon as I can.*>

Calan looked disappointed – but Ramon hadn't finished.

<*Meantime, I'm sending our daughter to you,*> Ramon continued. <*Her guardian is Lanna Jureigh, a charming and reliable woman – and very marriageable – if you don't mind courting someone I've slept with. She's already en route to Pallas. I trust you'll make them both welcome? Julia is dying to finally meet her grandpapa.*>

Gratifyingly, Calan's jaw dropped. <*I shall, of course.*>

<*Excellent!*> Ramon stifled another yawn.<*Well, I must get on with my

day. It's been good speaking to you, Father.> He broke off the contact and squinted at the rising sun. *Too damned bright.*

So he went back to bed.

The devastation was horrific. All that Seth and Latif could see from the Copperleaf Gatehouse was destruction. No building in Lowertown remained intact, no roof unbroken, no wall complete. Water still pooled in the low-lying streets, smoke still rose and corpses remained unburied.

They'd at least made a start on the burials. He and Latif had set the example, walking out together with shovels in hands, pitching in with the labourers to clear the main roads, before assuming command, giving directions and solving problems. Now the construct-army of the Lord of Rym had dissipated, its members no longer possessed, carts were taking the dead to the mass burial pits being dug outside the walls. Wild construct-men might be a problem in the future, but that would be a matter for another day.

Rani, the last elephant of the Shihad, had been set to work hauling lumps of masonry. Sanjeep, her mahout, told anyone who stopped to watch that she was a heroine of the siege. Seth remembered Latif atop the elephant, guiding the Shihadi soldiers inside the gates, and thought Sanjeep was right.

The magi were doing whatever they could. Overworked healers from both armies laboured together. Earth-magi cleared debris, Water-magi cleared the canals and purified water and Fire-magi tended the conflagrations still springing up all over the place. Miracles were being performed and the greatest of those were the men and women of East and West working together in harmony.

'My friend, may I ask you something?' he said to Latif. For once they were alone, their retinues relaxing below. 'What will you do next?'

At first he'd thought this charade of impersonator assuming the mantle of a dead ruler was a short-term measure, something bound to unravel at any moment, but it was as if no one *wanted* to know the truth. Latif *was* Salim, returned from hiding, or captivity, or death . . . any manner of tales were circulating.

People believe what they want to believe.

Latif pulled a face. 'Here, everyone wants Salim, but in the north, Teileman is claiming the throne and at home, who knows what power-hungry caliph or emir is already pulling together an army. Kesh is not like Rondelmar, my friend: we're not an empire, more like a collection of emirates and caliphates, sometimes united, more often not. If I return, it will be to conquer or die.'

Seth considered that, then made the offer he'd been preparing. 'Then stay here, with me. I'm the Earl of Bricia, and if this *res publica* movement spreads, maybe more. I've got a manor house near Bres and a castle in the hills and so many wings and rooms I could house half your army and not notice. You'd have anything you wanted.'

'Your wife would accept this?'

'My wife would barely notice. Camilla's life is full up with our children and her soirées and projects and lady-friends. We occasionally bump into each other, but it's a big house.'

Latif went silent, looking away. 'What would I do in your big house?'

'Whatever you wished, my friend! Write, play music, charm all the locals with your wit. Live a life free of the threat of murder and the stress of pretence. Surely you deserve as much?'

Latif remained looking away, blinking big, moist eyes. 'Thank you. I will consider it.'

'Please do. Latif, I've missed you, and friends should be together, not continents apart. Believe me, with all that's happening, you won't be bored.'

They fell silent again for a long time, until Seth became convinced that Latif would tell him that the call of his homeland was too great. He could barely breathe.

Then the impersonator turned and smiled. 'I think Sultan Salim has had his time. The dead should not return. And Latif . . . well, I think he would like to see your big house.'

Seth's face almost split in two from the smile that burst across his whole being.

Hegikaro, Mollachia
Aprafor 936

The people of Mollachia were becoming used to strange sights, but half
the town still came to gawk when a giant reptile swept down from the
skies to land in the fields outside the walls. Frightened militia joined
wide-eyed Sydian riders in surrounding the beast, but when they saw
who rode it, their fear turned to cheering and they sent for their Kirol
Kyrik at once.

Kyrik and his queen grabbed horses and pelted out from the walls.
Dismounting in a rush, Kyrik snagged his foot in the stirrup and spent
three seconds hopping madly, trying not to fall flat on his face as he
unhooked himself, then hurled himself at his brother while everyone
laughed. He barely noticed, lost in the joy of reunion, pounding Valdyr's
back in pure happiness.

At last he gripped his brother's shoulders and drank in his face, noting how different Valdyr had been when they were first reunited a
year ago.

Was it just a year? He's so much calmer, so much more composed . . . even
happy.

Hajya appeared beside them, murmuring, 'Nice dismount, husband!'
before embracing his brother.

The old Valdyr would have flinched from any woman, let alone one
of darker skin, but this Valdyr swept her into a bear-hug, exclaiming,
'It's so good to see you whole.'

Hajya beamed, then cuffed his cheek gently and said, 'Tell me of your
new woman.'

Valdyr's eyebrows shot up. 'I never said–'

'You don't have to,' Hajya scoffed, her moon face lighting up. 'What's
her name?'

'Uh, Nara.'

Ah, Kyrik thought, a grin spreading across his face. 'The famous Nara
of Misencourt? Where is she?'

'She, erm . . . she has some matters to attend to in, um . . . Pallas,' Valdyr stammered, his expression caught between pride and embarrassment.

'Pallas, oh-la,' Kyrik laughed. 'Too fancy to come here, eh?'

'No, no, she's just . . . ah,' Valdyr's eyes flashing around the crowd of people watching them, hanging on every word. 'She's . . , um . . .'

Hajya came to his rescue. 'You can tell us later – we want to know *everything* about her.'

'Er, everything . . . right.'

Kyrik threw an arm round Val's shoulders. 'Kore's Blood, it's good to see you.'

Those watching took that as the right time to cheer and press in, offering their own greetings. Kyrik watched his brother being passed round, while people spoke of how he'd appeared like a sorcerer of old to slay Asiv, and his other deeds during this harrowing time. It was some time before they could respectfully back away and walk up to the castle together.

'How are you doing?' Valdyr asked Kyrik, arms draped over each other's shoulders, with Hajya holding Kyrik's other hand.

'Well enough, for now,' Kyrik told him. 'There was a storm a few nights ago in which those awake swear they saw giant monsters in the skies, but most of us were in bed . . . ?' He glanced questioningly at his brother.

'It was the Last Day,' Valdyr said wryly. 'I hope you enjoyed it?'

Kyrik glanced sideways at Hajya. 'We . . . um . . . slept through it.'

Hajya snorted.

'Anyway, we don't appear to have run out of days,' Kyrik went on. 'I won't lie – we're in for a Hel of a summer, Val. We've lost so many people, the granaries are virtually empty and we've had to ask the Vlpa to cull their herds again, just to avoid starvation.'

'Kyrik will turn my people into farmers at this rate,' Hajya noted, not entirely in jest.

'Kip's brought his people out of Freihaafen to help us rebuild, and the Mantauri are incredible, but we need the thaw to come early and a perfect summer or we'll starve.'

'Early thaw, lots of sunlight,' Valdyr repeated, like a shopping order. 'You'll have it.'

Kyrik blinked. 'You can do that?'

'I can now,' his brother said quietly. 'I'm at your service, for as long as you need me.'

'And Nara will wait?'

Valdyr coloured a little. 'Well, until autumn, I think.'

Kyrik slapped his back. 'I won't let you keep her waiting, brother.'

Valdyr threw him a grateful look as they paused before the gates of Hegikaro and looked around them. Mollachs and Sydian riders were working side by side with Schlessen Bullheads. Women of both races laboured over laundry in the lake while their menfolk hammered and sawed the timber lugged in handcarts by the Mantauri. Children of all races scampered around getting underfoot in never-ending games of chase and hide 'n' seek, singing songs with elements of Schlessen, Sydian and Mollach, and a new mishmash language seemed to be growing up around them.

We've lost so much, Kyrik thought. *But this is exactly what I hoped for, that day I left here to find allies. We've beaten them all: the Rondian tax-farmers, the Imperial Legion, even the Masks. Most of all, we've beaten hate . . . for now.*

It was going to be a hard spring and an exhausting summer; but he didn't feel daunted. Valdyr was back and anything was possible.

Pallas, Rondelmar

The promised horse was waiting at the rear of the Bastion in the hour before dawn. Unarmoured, his cowl up and no blazon showing, just another traveller with a few saddlebags and some coin, Solon limped towards it, not caring if arrows feathered his back. The mount was a mare, ageing and placid with just a hint of old fire in its eye.

A bit like me, Solon mused, automatically checking the cinch and stirrups. In reflex, he went to kindle gnostic light, but nothing happened, of course.

The Chain-rune weighed on his soul.

He looked up at the castle which, for a brief time, had been his: the fulfilment of a dream that had become a nightmare. *It was too much for me. I did atrocious things and broke under the strain.* That was so easy to see now. *How does Lyra manage it with such grace?*

They were letting him leave, the interim rulers, thanks only to his final act, his one moment of clarity and truth. The mercy had surprised him, and he knew many still disagreed, but apparently Lyra, wherever she was, had decreed it.

And my estates are going to Nita's family . . . that is apt.

In time, Basia had promised, they'd release his Chain-rune, once they were sure he wasn't going to do something stupid. And they'd woven bindings into his gnostic aura, too. 'We'll always know where to find you,' she'd told him, with cool disdain. 'Now go, and never come back. This exile is forever.'

South? West? East? North had been forbidden to him. He hung his head, trying to think, then just sighed. He'd let the horse decide. He put his foot in the stirrup and was about to mount when the postern-gate behind him opened and a woman called, 'Solon?'

He flinched as Brunelda hurried across the courtyard, her cheeks wet. 'You're really going?' His throat choked up and for a moment he couldn't speak, just nodded roughly. He tried to turn away, but she caught his sleeve. 'Where will you go?'

Reluctantly, he turned to face her. With her inch-long brunette hair wrapped in a scarf, a plain smock and a thin cloak, she looked nothing at all like Lyra. She was shivering, and not just from the cold dawn. Her hands were clasped over the small bulge in her belly, the one thing he'd left her.

'I don't know,' he admitted. 'I have a little coin, but Dubrayle's taken most of it. I don't care – I have no heirs. I'll find a small farm some-where, someone who needs a hand, and let the world forget me.'

She gazed up at him with full eyes and blurted, 'I won't forget you.'

'You should,' he croaked. 'Brunelda, I treated you *abominably*. I made you dress as another and never asked permission when I used you. And now I've left you with a child you likely don't want. I've asked Dubrayle to look after you and he swears he will. All I can say is that I'm so ter-ribly sorry – and I'll soon be out of your life.'

He turned to the horse again, but she pulled his arm. 'Take me with you,' she begged.

He looked back at her, incredulous. 'How can you—'

'You were my hero,' she said, fighting tears. 'I worshipped you as a child – and even in the darkest moments I could see a better man inside you. I want to help you find him again. And I want our child to have a father.'

A father . . . ? That was one thing he'd never been. But he still couldn't comprehend.

'I don't deserve that,' he whispered, as a vision of a kind of future opened up in his head, of a smallholding somewhere, a home, a child . . . a wife. *Peace.* He tried to speak, but somehow, tears were streaming down his cheeks.

At last he managed, 'I'm not a hero, I never was, I just hurt people—'

She glared up at him. 'Self-pity doesn't become you, Solon. I've known plenty of men and I know a good heart when I see one. You have that within you. I'm not saying marriage, not yet. We will be as brother and sister until you prove yourself to me, and you won't touch me unless I permit it. Fuck up in any way and you won't get a second chance. Power corrupts, the *Book of Kore* says – so put it aside and be the man you should be.'

Faced with such determination, he could only yield. So he dismounted and carefully helped her onto the mare, then mounted behind her and clicked the horse into motion.

Together, they rode out of history.

Confusion had reigned in Pallas for days, with rumours flying in all directions: Queen Lyra was dead – but no, it was Solon Takwyth who was dead . . . or fled, maybe, because someone had sworn they'd seen a man who looked exactly like Takwyth leaving by the western gate, with a woman riding double.

But where was the queen – and why wouldn't she speak to reassure her people?

Duke Garod's kin were advancing to claim the throne – no, they were retreating, and renouncing that claim. The Argundians were going to invade – but no, their barges had been destroyed when Lac Siberne froze for the first time in history. The republic was undone – ah, no, the republic was strong and flooded with capital, thanks to the new Bank of Rondelmar. The Corani were in revolt – no, the Duke of Coraine had re-pledged allegiance to Lyra. The Church was fragmenting – no, Grand Prelate Wurther had taken a leaf from some Eastern religion and called a Convocation, whatever that was, to renew Church unity. The Shihad was destroyed – no, a truce was now signed and the Easterners had agreed to withdraw to Verelon.

All of it was true, a mass of contradictory events happening all at once.

But sometimes a single symbolic gesture could change the mood of a nation – and that day came when Queen Lyra finally broke her silence.

She had arrived after dark and barely slept, instead spending every moment since Pearl left her in her garden closeted with her advisors, being briefed and formulating plans.

Now, at last, she walked out onto the Place d'Accord, Basia behind her, jittery as ever.

We bodyguards breathe paranoia as others do air, Basia thought, quite unable to relax as Lyra paused to shake hands and exchange greetings with the people pressed hard against the barriers. Exilium, on her other side, was just as nervous: in his mind, he was now bodyguard to two women.

Finally Lyra reached the raised dais, where the giant statue of Corineus towered over them, the gleaming dagger at his heart lit by gnostic light on this grey day. Dirklan Setallius, lurking nearby, watched the crowds, flanked by Mort, Patcheart and Brigeda, as did Basia, even though everywhere she looked, people were beaming.

The war was over and the queen was among her people.

Lyra ascended to the throne on the dais, to be joined a few moments later by Dominius Wurther. The symbolism of Church and Crown together was not lost on anyone. Lyra looked up from her notes as a mage-herald got ready to amplify her words so they would fill the vast square.

'People of Pallas,' she began, her voice clear and confident, 'I have been told that many have been speaking of the "Last Days" – but here we are, the sun is shining and the war is over. Only the bad days have ended; better ones are on the way, I promise you all.'

Basia smiled as the crowd lapped it up, cheering lustily. People loved good news.

They'll never know how close we came.

'This is the first day of our new republic,' Lyra went on. 'Today I sign the constitution.' She gestured and Ari Frankel came forward and waved, receiving a hearty cheer, especially from those of Tockburn and the docklands.

'Master Frankel's fine document encapsulates the vision he inspired in me,' Lyra went on, 'the vision he has championed fearlessly for years: that leadership must be at the *consent* of the ruled, that it must be *for* the ruled. No voice should go unheard, no person be barred from participation – and *merit* matters more than wealth or birth.'

The huge plaza fell increasingly silent as she went on, most still not quite understanding what they were seeing.

Basia glanced at Exilium, who was watching the queen in reverence.

Between his love for Kore and his adoration of Lyra, I'm going to have to fight my corner, she thought wryly. *But I'm up for it – they don't stand a chance.* The last few nights had been testament to that.

'It is to that last, the matter of *birth*, that my thoughts are increasingly drawn,' Lyra continued. 'My advisors tell me that periods of great change require continuity; that trusted institutions must remain strong so that we may all feel secure. There may come a day when a hereditary monarch is no longer needed as figurehead of this nation,' Lyra declared, 'but for now I remain in your service as Queen of Rondelmar, until the republic has set down roots.'

The cheering was muted; the people had only ever known monarchy.

'But that day will come,' Lyra went on. 'You all know I wasn't raised to rule: I fell into it, and I would be just as happy to fall out again. I have done my best, but I have made mistakes. The weight of this kingdom will always be too great for a single pair of shoulders to bear, so I happily pass it on, and I will sleep the better knowing my son need never put his heart on trial as I have had to.' She raised her voice and concluded, 'When this republic is secure, when the first Assembly gathers and passes their first laws; when no one needs to wonder what I might think, then it will be time for me to step aside.'

A hushed mutter rippled through the crowd and some, mostly women, called, 'Milady, never leave – we love you!'

Same biddies who hurled rotten fruit at her, Basia sniffed.

But Lyra sailed on, 'My closest advisor once told me that empires always fall in bloodshed and destruction, so it is my greatest pride that this one is ending gently. I have been called "Empress of the Fall" – and I embrace that name, for we are falling not into calamity but into grace. Who are one people to rule another? What gives us the right? I renounce conquest and rejoice in the newfound freedom of Argundy, of Ventia, of Estellayne and Bricia and Hollenia and Midrea and Noros. May they use it well.'

The hubbub grew until she raised her hand again. 'Thank you all, for your belief in me. Now you must learn to believe in yourselves. You, the people, are the Republic of Rondelmar. *Never forget that.* Bid farewell to kings and queens, emperors and empresses. Choose new rulers, and do so wisely: make them accountable to you, to the law and to Kore.' She smiled and added, 'And, for a while longer, to me.'

Basia could see the ambassadors of the newly independent kingdoms and the two new republics, Noros and Bricia, taking that in. They all knew she had frozen Lac Siberne, destroying the Argundian fleet. She was sure they hadn't missed the point.

Lyra rose and before most of those in the plaza had realised, she was gone.

An hour later, Lyra knelt beside her pool, communing with the dwyma, Coramore beside her like a young disciple. Cordan was watching from a few feet behind them. She withdrew reluctantly from that peace; she'd been hoping to reach Valdyr before she went to bed, but so far he was absent.

Becoming aware of another presence, she called over her shoulder, 'Father?'

Dirklan ghosted from the shadows, holding a sleeping Rildan in his arms. 'Most people don't know when I'm around,' he noted, a little ruefully.

'This is my garden – I know everything here.'

'Well, I suppose that's better than thinking I'm too old to sneak about.'

'You are.' She rose, pulling Coramore up beside her, noting the princess still looked apprehensive around Dirklan. 'It's time you retired, Father.'

'To do what?'

'Write a memoir, then blackmail everyone *not* to print it.' Lyra laughed, winking at Coramore. 'That should keep you in plenty.' She squeezed the girl's hand and sent her off with Cordan, hand in hand. She was negotiating their return to Dupenium, once she had ensured that a loyal Regency Council was in place. Cordan would be the first King of Dupenium – *if* he renounced any claim to Rondelmar. He claimed to be willing, and she believed him.

'Who says I want to retire?' Dirklan asked, a little huffily.

'I'm sure you don't, but I'd like you to be a father, not always away on some secret mission from which you mightn't return. You've earned some peace.'

He gave her a testy look, but sighed. 'I'll think about it.'

That's progress. She took Rildan, cradling him as they settled on her favourite bench overlooking the pool. A new Winter Tree sapling now grew here, like its predecessor, stubbornly out of synch with the rest of nature and withering as the summer blossomed. The dwyma was regaining strength here too, despite the damage Solon had wrought.

'I think the speech went well,' she said, breaking the companionable silence.

'The people are confused,' her father said, 'but they trust you and Frankel.'

'They'll get to grips with it when Ari's elections start.'

'I understand all manner of chancers and crooks are planning to stand for office.'

'Like Jean Benoit? I heard that too,' Lyra laughed. 'He won't win, as long as the officials are vigilant against corruption.'

'I'll make damn sure of that,' Dirklan growled. 'So do you really mean to abdicate?'

'I do, eventually. Maybe in a few years, if the republic is working properly. But I will remarry before that. I'm not getting any younger, Father.'

'You're twenty-seven. That's hardly ancient.'

'Even so.'

'To Valdyr Sarkany?' he asked rhetorically. 'He's a good man. I'm sure you'll be well-matched.'

She kissed his cheek. 'Thank you.'

She looked up at the sky. The sun was setting and the night's chill was coming on, but for now a brief, beautiful twilight held sway in Pallas – the heart of empire no more, but still a glittering jewel, the greatest city in Yuros.

She kissed her sleeping child, then handed him back to his grandfather, thinking, *It's dusk already in Mollachia – surely Valdyr's waiting for me by now.*

Once she was alone, she went back to the pool, opened her mind and found him . . .

Epilogue II

Four Years Later: An Eastern Dawn

The Leviathan Bridge

Where this Bridge stands, once there was an isthmus, joining East and West. Let me tell you this: the monuments of the Elder Races of Antiopia predate any constructions in Yuros. The West was colonised by man via that isthmus. Therefore it is as brothers that the men of the West should greet those of the East, not as enemies. Please, call off this invasion: we came here in peace, and beg that you honour that legacy.

ANTONIN MEIROS, LETTER TO EMPEROR MAGNUS DURING
FIRST CRUSADE, HEBUSALIM 904

The Dhassan Coast, Ahmedhassa
Julsep 940 (4 years after the Sunsurge's end)

It had been a long journey from Noros, through the Kedron Valley and the Brekaellen, over the mighty Silas River into Verelon. The merchant caravans travelled in the wake of the departing Shihad armies, all the way to Pontus and onto the great Bridge, past the newly repaired Midpoint Tower, while the waves lapped at the giant span. It was the Moontide, the seas were low and the weather calm and finally the end came into view: a dark wall of land lit with bonfires. The drivers and their passengers cheered, eager to reach land and begin the trading season. For the first time in many Moontides, no legions marched, set on conquer and plunder. There were only traders, hoping to make a different sort of killing.

Vann Mercer was tired and travel-worn, but incredibly proud of his son Alaron and Ramita, Alaron's wife. With the rest of the Merozain Bhaicara, wielding forces he couldn't begin to imagine, they had saved this Bridge.

Kore bless you and all who worked with you.

Once he'd been a trader himself, much of his livelihood depending on this twelve-yearly journey, but this time Vann's wagon was small and barely stocked. *I'm really just here to mark the moment in time,* he thought, smiling to himself.

He hummed an old legion marching song, remembering the First Crusade and that dreadful day he'd crossed over in an imperial windship, personal guard to Tesla Anborn, a beautiful, brittle battle-mage, with no idea what Hel they were about to encounter, but duty-bound and proud to serve.

It broke her, but it bound us as well: it culminated in a marriage and a son.

Nothing could compensate for the terrible things he and his fellow Crusaders had done, but perhaps this new peace would hold? The Queen of Rondelmar had abdicated last year and a council of representatives elected by the people now ruled Pallas, as similar councils did elsewhere, including his native Noros. Bad things were still happening, but fresh energy was sweeping Yuros. New men were arising, interested in progress, not just the preservation of the status quo. The role of the magi was subtly changing too: they no longer set the agenda but served the people.

These are good things, he thought. They pointed to a better world, where superhuman, rich and divinely appointed egotists no longer made all the decisions. So long as they all watched each other – and someone watched the watchers – perhaps a brighter future awaited all of Urte?

His small wagon was well down in the order of march and by the time he arrived at the instant market town of tents and pavilions a mile inland – and safely away from Southpoint Tower – the bartering was well under way. He nudged his horses into the clamour, seeking a berth amid the colour and clamour of East and West colliding in the long-neglected form of combat called commerce. Goods were being inspected, carpets and spices and furs and leathers and steel and jewellery and so much more. No one paid him much notice, but he soaked it up in a reverie of nostalgia.

'Vann? Vannaton Mercer?'

He looked up as a plump Lakh man with thick white moustaches and thinning grey hair came waddling towards him, arms outstretched. 'Vann, is it you?'

'Ispal Ankesharan—' Vann exclaimed, pulling his wagon from the queue and leaping down, to be swept into the embrace of his son's father-in-law. 'You came—'

'Of course I came,' Ispal hollered above the din. 'Who could stay away from *this*?'

They had to pause as horns blared, heralding an old female elephant coming though the crowds, festooned in coloured prayer ribbons. An old Lakh man in the howdah was raising his hand, acknowledging the cheers.

Ispal raised an eyebrow, but Vann just laughed. 'It's Sanjeep, with Rani the elephant,' he explained. 'They are heroes of the Siege of Norostein. There's not a tavern in the city where Sanjeep can't drink for free. I'm surprised he left.'

'I'm surprised he survived,' Ispal laughed, 'but a Lakh will always dream of home.'

Shihad soldiers were marching past and here and there someone would wail a greeting and a returning warrior would break from the ranks to be engulfed in a weeping throng. Rashid's great windfleet had been all but destroyed by the time peace broke out, stranding most of the Shihad for four years, so this Moontide was a time of long-awaited reunions.

'So, my friend,' Ispal said, 'you must show me your wares. I am in the market for anything you have – and I'm prepared to overpay extravagantly.'

'I'm really just here to see Alaron and Ramita,' Vann replied, then he grinned. 'However, I have secured from Lord Korion the sole rights to distribute his Brician Red. I have samples, and a need for local distributors.'

Ispal beamed. 'Then look no further, my friend, for I am your man.'

'I was hoping you'd say that,' Vann laughed.

This Moontide was going to be the most beneficial ever.

ACKNOWLEDGEMENTS

Another series ends, and it's a strange feeling. The characters become a big part of your inner life, so saying farewell to them appropriately, without clouding the vision of the story, is a fraught process. And the story world becomes a tangible place, one you're reluctant to leave.

I've not been alone in this maze though, and owe huge thanks to the team behind the stories. The test readers (Kerry Greig, Heather Adams, Paul Linton and Cath Mayo) have been fabulous and told me the things I needed to know about the early drafts, filtering the good from the not-so-good decisions in those drafts, and enhancing the stories immensely. Heather, with her husband Mike Bryan, is my agent and I reiterate my thanks to them for getting my work out into the world.

I'm also so grateful to Jo Fletcher and the team at JFB/Quercus (especially Molly Powell), for supporting this series and letting me build more tales in this world. It's been a wonderful journey and I feel blessed to have worked with such a talented, supportive and experienced publishing editor as Jo.

Thanks to my nearest and dearest for their support, especially my children, Brendan and Melissa, my parents Cliff and Biddy, my sister Robyn; and all my friends – you know who you are.

But most of all, thanks to my wife, love and inspiration, Kerry, who's enjoyed/endured being a writer's partner for more than a decade now, sharing the highs and helping me through the lows. We've lived in four cities in three countries during that time and had a fabulous adventure, and I look forward to more.

Hello to Jason Isaacs. Tinkety-tonk and down with the Nazis.

David Hair
Bangkok and New Zealand 2019